*Book 5... thank you all.*

*Thanks to my wife Theresa. As of this publishing, five down... two to go. NONE of this would have been done without your... um... 'polite insistence' so for that I give you my thanks and my love .*

*Thanks to Bill, the real life Lone Wolf. The Lone to my Bird.*
*'Trust Me!' eh buddy?*
*Forever the dynamic duo of any world, real or imagined.*

*To my family, thank you for all the kind words and support. To Joe Scott... thanks for all the help with the cover.*

*To my sister Eileen, Mike Smith & Jonah Chaney... Thank you for your comments, input and above all... patience.*

*To all the fans. Ladies? You asked for a love story... you got it. Gentlemen? You asked for a battle scene. Sorry to say, you didn't get one... you got several.*

*Lastly, if you're reading this, whoever you are, I wish you many hours or enjoyment and wonder. To the people of 'The Highlands'... I hope I got your accent right. If I didn't, sorry but, that's how you sound to me.*

This is a work of fiction. No reference to anyone living or dead is suggested or implied. Any reference to any persons living or dead, aside from historical or cultural references, is purely coincidental.

**All content and cover art is copyrighted by the author 2014**
Come join the world that is Bird and Lone. Follow along at www.facebook.com/BirdandLone or on Twitter at www.twitter.com/BirdOfPrey_Ghost1

*And thus... the tale dubbed 'The Monster'... begins...*

# Seven Ghosts
*The BirdOfPrey Chronicles*
*By Brian T.L. Strauss*

## Book 5: Ciana Thalin.

## Chapter 1 :

## *"25 Seconds... And 3 Switches To Choose From"*

*"Yo Red!" was the first thing Bird heard walking through Victory City.*

*It was the only thing he heard. Aside from him, the echo of his own footsteps, and the phantom voice, this place was empty. It was as if everyone just got up and left in the middle of whatever they were doing. Bird was exploring and trying to sort out where exactly he was. His 'gut feeling' told him 2 things. Picking up and examining a steaming cup of coffee left on Roe's patio, the first thing he noticed was a supreme sensation of peace and calm. The second thing he noticed... and the one feeling he couldn't shake was... he didn't belong here.*

*With a smirk, Bird asked "So, who are you this time?"*
*"Say what?"*
*"You heard me, who are you?"*
*"Really, Red, you mean you don't recognize me?"*
*"Recognize you, yes. Believe you're real?... No."*

*Two trancing figures arrived in a blue world of swirling gas and dust. They were on a mission and, running out of time... literally.*

"Truly my love, we must hurry. The future is changing with each moment."

"Well I must say, the Commander truly is a crafty fellow. So my love, mind telling me how we get through that!?" the male figure said as he waved his hand across a behemoth black ship. A rather dead black ship.

"There must be a way. This is rather dire to say the least. In this form I can not focus on the future as I do when I seek only it. The glimpses I do get are not good however."

"How not good?"

"They're blank."

"Perhaps they are just changing?"

"No my love they're... they're..."

"Mm?"

"Disappearing."

"Then you're right... we best hurry."

With that, 2 figures of energy went searching for a way into a machine that no energy had ever gotten into before.

"Mind telling me where I am at least?" Bird asked his phantom guide.

With a touch of sadness, the voice said, "Soon as I find out, or figure it out, I'll let ya know, Red."

"Well then, tell me this... am I dead?"

"I don't think so. Could be, for all I know. Am I?"

"Very much so," Bird told the voice.

"Well that sucks," the voice said with the same sad tone.

Again, Bird only said, "Very much so."

"What is this place Bird?"

"Victory City. Well, a fairly good representation of it anyway."

"Looks like it's in a cave."

"If you, or I for that matter, were in the real one... you would be. Ten miles in diameter to be exact."

"YOU built this!?" the voice said with stunned pride.

"Well, heh heh, I had a little help."

"Damn Red, this is impressive! Far cry from the junkyard you *played in I'll say that much."*

*"Thank you. Now, are you gonna spook me all day? Or are ya gonna come out of hiding?"*

*"Ya mean like this?" the apparition said now standing off to Bird's right.*

*"Yep, that'll do nicely," Bird smirked.*

*"You can see me!?"*

*"I can indeed."*

*"Heh heh, well, THIS is a first!" Full of brotherly love, the dark haired apparition said "Hello, Bird."*

*Smiling, and simply enjoying the illusion, Bird replied...*

*"Hello...... Zevvies."*


*Two non-corporeal beings scoured a behemoth looking for a way in. Time was running out and they were searching with all possible speed. The time distortion bubbles wreaked havoc on the inside of the black ship. Perhaps due to her hull, or its makeup, it did little or no damage to her outside.*

*"Arrrrrggg! This is useless! And we're running out of time!!" the male apparition hollered in frustration.*

*"I've found no openings either," the female one said.*

*"All I found was one small crack, hardly big enough for an air leak no less us!" he barked.*

*The female... smiled.*

*"Show me this crack."*

*"Why? What good would it do us?"*

*"Really my love. Suffice to say, you're not solid. You may want to stop thinking like one."*

*Full of hope, and a new found realization, he merely said, "Follow me."*


*At the back end, two trancing beings stared at a small crack. It was right where the right rudder met the main wing. It was only 6 or so inches long, and only a half inch wide at its center. To the female it might as well have been a grand entrance.*

*"Focus on it... hurry!" she called out.*

*She and her partner did and a moment later... were standing* in a landing bay to rival one on a space station they saw once a long time ago.

"We can't help him... not directly. You have no idea what I have to do to merely keep us here as it is. Suggestions?"

The male smiled and said, "Only one. Follow me... quickly!"

The bay they were in was dark but trancing doesn't require visible light to see. Their sight was a combination of night vision, and sonar. What had the male smiling was a smaller ship docked in this mammoth bay. Docked... with it's ramp-way... down. Reaching the undamaged cockpit, the male studied it quick.

Sensing what he was doing, the female told him "I can make only your finger solid at this rate. You would have but 2... 3 tries at the most. Please my mate... make them count!"

Studying hard, the male readied himself. Finger now solid he flipped a switch.

Nothing.


"I have to say, whoever you are, this is the most convincing illusion yet," Bird told 'Cliffy'.

"Define 'yet'. You've seen me before?" Cliff said sadly.

"You no. Those pretending to be you, yes."

"I tried talking to you once or twice. At least I think so. Hey Red, if I'm dead, do ya think I still dream?" Cliffy asked.

"Not like I'm an expert or anything. I suppose it's possible, why do you ask?"

Still sad, Cliffy told him, "If I'm an illusion, then why do I have memories? As for the dreaming thing, I had one I believe. I was talking to a woman, but, this woman was a wolf. And I was on a beach, but, it was on an alien planet. Weird huh?"

Bird damn near freaked. Once he arrived on Tuhleesia, Rahgaa and him would spend hours talking. Personal stuff, non personal stuff, whatever. Bird laughed and told Rahgaa once if she stopped talking... he would still be there. Bird felt like Rahgaa didn't want to let go for fear of losing him again. What had Bird freaking was she told him she dreamed she met Cliffy... AFTER Bird left Eden. The tone in Cliff's voice changed Bird's whole perception. The fake Cliff's in the past all had one thing in common. They knew they weren't real and said so. This one however seemed to truly want to remember, but had only fragments to go by. Also, this Cliffy wasn't trying to get something out of Bird.

In the darkness, an apparition tried once again. He readied himself but could see just this little bit of solid, just a finger, was draining heavily on his companion. He tried yet another switch and again...

Nothing.

"So tell me almighty Zevvies, what do you remember?" Bird asked curiously.

"Pieces really. There's one though that's biggest of all."

"Oh? And what's that?"

"You, Red. You were leaning over me, though I don't know why. I remember something about... you promised me something... but I can't recall what."

"You may be happy to know... I delivered on that promise," Bird said with a smirk still not believing any of this was real.

"Well, that's good... it is good right?" Cliffy asked with a light laugh.

"I think so," Bird said with a friendly smile.

One last switch... just one. The male apparition had only one more he could do. Problem was... he had 3 to choose from. Even then, he had no way of knowing if it would have the effect he wanted, or needed.

"We're almost out of time, HURRY my love!"

"Well, you may not believe your brother is real. I can tell you with absolute certainty I am... and am not."

Bird looked at the new visitor and smirked saying, "Why not just get dad in here so we can have a big old family reunion eh?"

*The image he was looking at, was his mother.*

*"I can also tell you that while I have taken her form, I am not your true mother."*

*"Well, at least your honest," Bird smarted. "And you would be?"*

*"Born brave, lived brave... isn't that what you said?"*

*"It was... what of it?"*

*"Let's just say... I was your witness... and leave it at that."*

*Bird still wasn't believing, but also couldn't shake the feeling that this new image wasn't lying either.*

*"Seeing as how I'm not smoking right now I'll assume I was a good boy?" Bird teased.*

*"That remains to be seen." Then with a smile 'she' said "Not bad so far though."*

*"Clarify 'so far'."*

*"Oh my dear boy, you still have a long way to go before we meet again."*

*"Can't say I don't like the sound of that," Bird said with a wink.*

*"Heh heh... thought you might."*


*The apparition thought hard. With only one try left it was 'do or die' time. He HAD to get this right.*

*"If I know the Commander, he wouldn't make it so obvious," the apparition said aloud, "So it's this one or nothing," and he flipped the switch.*

*This time... he was finally correct.*


*Lights now came on in the cockpit. Systems now came alive. Those systems called to others that weren't there. As a fail-safe built in by Wing Remington, the first system merely 'woke up' the next. Lights came on all over the bay, and inside the ship.*

*Forward of the bay, a doll in a doll house...*

*opened her eyes with a sharp gasp.*


*"We have done well my love. Now, it's all up to him. Come, let's get you some rest," the male apparition said with a smile.*

Smiling back, the female merely said "Gladly. Follow me."

Two trancing apparitions, one that had a pattern like a lava lamp, and one that was yellow and green, simply faded away... and back... to where they came from. They had run the interference they had hoped to. Now, with the future starting to reappear, the female smiled all the way to her chair.


The apparition that was Bird's mother, suddenly looked away, as if the universe itself called her.

"Well my son, it would seem you have touched many lives. It would also appear, those lives, want you back," she said with a smile.

"Well, if you are who you claim... then not really my call now is it?" Bird answered.

"Indeed but, as you once suspected, I merely interfere from time to time. Mankind, nay all the creatures in the universe, still have free will."

"Free to choose as we will, then be judged by the same eh?" Bird asked with a smile.

"You have no idea."

"Feel free to enlighten me," Bird stated.

"In time. That time however... is not now."


Bird knew something was up. Was it what he was told? Doubtful. Still he couldn't shake the feeling that it could be. Still further, Bird decided to seize a chance... juuuuuuust in case.

"Let's assume for a moment I believe all of this," Bird started, "Even you can't deny I've done well."

"True, I can't," his 'mother' responded.

"Then I'd like to ask for two things."

"Oh, I make no guarantees, but I am willing to listen."

"Uphold my promise," Bird said. Bird then remembered his real parents, and immediately followed that with "Please."

His mother looked questioningly at Bird and asked "The one about having a soul?"

Bird was taken aback a bit. Could she truly be who she said she was?

"That one indeed."

Bird's mother was pleased with the request and answered "Mary, well, let's just say she has no worries. And second?"

Bird felt only one thing now. He felt with all his core that all this around him was slipping away. He felt as if time itself was running out.

"I've done your bidding. I have done the best I could at every turn. In ALL that I have done, I have asked for nothing in return. Now... I am. Let me bring him with me... please."

"Cliffy?"

"No... Santa Claus... yes Cliffy. Even to you I'll defend myself and my actions and say... I earned it."

"No you haven't. But you are close. Let me ask you something. You do realize you'll remember none of this right?"

"Assuming this," and Bird waved a hand around "Is all real and as you claim, I can only say it makes sense that I or anyone else in my position, wouldn't."

"You have truly done well Bird. I'll leave you with one gift, and one warning."

"I'll take the warning first. If you don't mind of course."

His mother said "I don't at all. My warning is Janet. While your retribution was not unwarranted... it was a tad evil. I sense an anger growing in you. Be careful of it. As I said all creatures have free will and I'll not interfere. That said, you truly are a good man, and I'd hate to see that change."

"I'll keep that in mind," Bird said kindly. "And... my gift?"

His mother wrapped her arm around Bird saying "Heh heh, let me tell you what I have in mind."


A mechanical doll woke up and went into a panic. There was no Bird. Worse, she had no idea where he was. Systems all over the ship were coming on. Problem was... roughly half were going back off. Taking only a moment to think, she raced from her room.

"Door... cockpit!" Alydar commanded.

The door opened and... immediately closed. Alydar herself was only at 50 percent too. In her animated form, that's all that got downloaded at any time. The rest of 'her' was the big black ship. In a sense and, for safety, Alydar's avatar was an extension of her but not an independent being. That part... the huge black ship part... was still mostly offline and she had no idea why.

Alydar did have access to one system though, her internal clocks. Knowing Bird was likely in danger she assumed two things. First, that he was in dire danger. She didn't know if he was or not but decided to act as if he was. Second, if he was in mortal danger, she knew she had 3 minutes to get to him, based on his physiology. Thanks to her internal clocks she knew she had... only 25 seconds left.

"Bird?"

No answer came.

"BIRD!!?"

Still nothing.

"Shit!"

Alydar hopped in the mag-lev and headed to the cockpit. After only 3 seconds she stopped it and hopped out. Fast as it was, it was just going too slow.

"Okay... here's hoping you truly built me well my love!" Alydar stated aloud.

With that, she shut off the artificial gravity. She put both hands on the mag-lev's main rail and hurled herself in the direction of the cockpit. She was horizontal and hurling herself faster and faster. Alydar was right, Bird truly had her made strong.

"Hang on my dear Commander, I'm coming as fast as I can!" Alydar sighed and, near tears said "I only hope it's enough."


"So Bird, you're always 'reading people', how about you let me have a go at it eh?" came the British accented voice.

"Presto change-oh... eh?" Bird chuckled.

"Actually, I chose this form for a reason. I said you were angry. You are... except when you're with Lone. I know the Bird that you're becoming, the angry one, goes away when you're with him."

The new image was Bird's adopted brother.

"Can't say you're wrong there. Due to our link, Lone understands me more than anyone. You're right, I do feel at peace when he's around."

"Link?" Cliffy asked walking along.

"Long story. Suffice to say Zevvies, think 'empathy' mixed with 'the force'."

Cliffy chuckled saying "Aww, and I thought I was special."

"You are," is all Bird said.


Fake Lone now said "All you need is love... isn't that how the song goes Bird?"

"It does."

Lone winked saying "When the remaining two finally join me... ooh I'm going to have one heck of a concert!"

Bird winked back saying "I'll take two tickets if you please."

Lone laughed actually and said "I'll see what I can do."


Alydar was actually going twice as fast as the mag-lev in this zero G environment. She was halfway to the cockpit with 13 seconds left on the clock.

"If you die on me... I'll KILL you myself!" Alydar shouted.

Humor was the only thing she could think of to hold herself together. She kept trying her sensors in the cockpit but to no avail. Moving her hands faster and faster she was pulling herself along at an amazing rate. Debris hit her as she went and she merely ignored it. Along the way though, even at this speed... she could see the damage. What if that happened in the cockpit? What if Bird...?

"STOP THAT Ally!... he's gonna be okay... I just know it!" she told herself and just went even faster.

That thought was one she just wasn't willing to entertain. Remmy's life threatening number one protocol had kicked in. Now, nothing would stop a 'doll' from getting to her guy.


"So, not to be rude or anything but... my gift?" Bird asked.

"All you need is love Bird. Love itself is my gift. You've yet to find it. My gift is, to counter the anger and... until we meet again..." and the fake Lone faded out saying "... you will."

When fake Lone was gone, Bird's world swirled and distorted. Suddenly, he and Cliffy were on Eden. On Eden and... in the original lagoon. Now Bird's feeling of time running out was getting worse.

"Yo big Red, you sense, I dunno, like something is ending?"

Bird looked at him oddly and said "Yeah, I do."

"So, being you're the resident expert 'round these here parts', where are we now?"

Bird smirked and said "Look behind you."

Cliffy turned around and merely said "Oh."

What he saw, hovering over the pink sand, was his own worst nightmare.

"This..." Bird started, "... is the other end of the line."

Cliffy was staring at his own cat's eye.

"Wait... Eden?... that right?" Cliff asked.

"It is, or rather..."

"Yeah yeah I know... a reasonable facsimile," Cliffy laughed cutting off Bird. "So why do you think you brought us here?"

"I did?"

"Well you did say from the beginning you thought this all an illusion. I know I'm not doing this, so I figure it must be you. Question remains... why here?"

Bird smiled softly at his answer.

"To do what we didn't get a chance to do last time."

Cliff asked "And that would be?"

Bird looked at the eye and spoke... "To say goodbye."


Alydar reached the cockpit. With a small amount of luck, that door worked. Opening the door, Alydar experienced for the first time in her life... horror. Floating face down was the very one she was built to protect at all costs.

"Bird!" Alydar cried out shaking him.

The floating armor said nothing... and moved even less.

"BIIIIIIIRRRRRRRRDDDDD!!!" Alydar screamed in anguish.

Alydar felt weird pushing buttons and swiping optic controls on, well, technically herself. She had 5 seconds left on her clock.

*She tried to power the suit but couldn't. Then she remembered she shut it off. The damage from the impact was severe and Alydar could see it on the wall behind the command chair. The suit was unscathed physically, but the impact glitched the power software. The main console was flaky as well. Alydar knew only a full reboot would work. Unfortunately, with all the damage, Bird's hand in the wall sensor was the only thing that would do it. Further problem was, said hand was inside a suit she couldn't retract.*

*Worse still... the clock just hit zero.*


*Bird smiled, looked up, and said "Thank you."*

*"For?" Cliffy asked.*

*"I wasn't talking to you."*

*"Oh," Cliff said now understanding.*


*"Cliff listen, I can't shake this feeling like time is running out. I may not speak to you for a real long time. No fights then, okay?"*

*"Deal," Cliff said with a kind smile. "Hey wait a second, I thought 'you thought' I wasn't real?"*

*"Seeing as how the big guy said I won't remember anyway, if you were me... wouldn't you?... Enjoy it I mean?"*

*Full of brotherly love, Cliff said "Yeah Red, I would at that."*


*Bird looked up at the eye and said "You and your damn entropy," in a slightly annoyed and reflective tone.*

*"Look Bird, I can't say I didn't mess up. Before time does run out though I want you to know something. Of all the things I did, and all the things I made... raising you Bird... you were, and are, the one thing I am most proud of. I look at you, and see the one mistake I DIDN'T make. You know I was never good at words Bird but... I hope you understand what I meant."*

*Bird smiled and hugged his brother saying "I do indeed Zevvies."*


*Alydar had a thought. Grabbing a low level power cord from under the command chair, she ripped it out. Under a panel on the suit only* she and the Ghosts knew about, was a power plug for just such this situation. Heavily hidden, she had to snake the cord an inch or two but finally hit her target. The first stroke of luck she had, the suit powered up. It was flickering, and only partially powered, but at least it had some.

"SUIT OFF!" she screamed.

Nothing.

Playing with the wire, she hollered again "SUIT OFF!"

Nothing.

Then it hit her and she said "Suit?... Off!" and it retracted about halfway.

The reason it retracted this time, was because she used Bird's voice, not her own.


Bird pulled back from his brotherly embrace, and put his hand up.

"Goodbye Red," Cliffy said as he put his hand up too.

"Not goodbye Zevvies, but, 'till next time'."

"Heh heh, indeed. Bird?"

"Yeah?"

Cliff smiled, and slammed his hand into Bird's as both men hollered with joy.

"SHOWTIME!" was the dual voice shout across the realms.

At that instant, a blinding light like and explosion blasted Bird from one reality... to another.


Bird didn't awake so much as 'became aware'. The cockpit was totally silent, and yet, to Bird, it seemed like a thousand TV's with only static were going off at full blast. He could feel his physical pain but he felt another too. One he had no idea about till now. Having been 'not here', Bird felt the innate pain of just being alive. He was on all 4's and just coughing sent searing wracking pain through his entire body. When he did finally open his eyes, he realized 'all 4s' didn't necessarily mean on the floor. He was still floating but.... his left hand... the same one he high 5'd Cliff with, was in the sensor on the wall.

"OW... now I know how Lone felt. For the record... this majorly sucks," Bird said in his usual truth delivered with humor style.

Alydar was bawling. She hugged Bird as tenderly, yet gingerly, as she could.

"I thought I lost you," she said through her tears.

"I assume I have you to thank for this?" Bird said wincing in pain.

"Mm hmm. I'll tell you all about it later. I'm... I'm... I'm so glad your alive," Alydar said with pure love and meaning.

"Okay lady, (cough cough) 2 questions and 2 orders. First, anyone shooting at us?"

"Not as far as I can tell."

"Anyone likely to?"

"Sensors are down but I'd say not likely."

Bird coughed and spit up some blood and said "Well then, KEEP the grav off... and get me to med bay... quickly."

"Be happy to... last order?"

Full of sweetness, Bird just said, "Accept my thanks, ya sexy thang ya... heh heh... ow!"

Bird figured other than him, and Alydar, everything else could wait. Alydar grabbed him by the half of a chest plate that was still not working, and repeated the mag-lev run in reverse. One handing it this time she wasn't as fast, but she got Bird in the med bay.

"Two ribs are broken. Your spine is fractured in 3 places. Shoulder muscles are just shy of torn off on the right, and the left one's are badly bruised. You have a concussion and various other bruises. Bad as that sounds, if it wasn't for the suit..." and she never finished her sentence.

"Oh... if that's all... think I'll just.." Bird joked.

"Don't you even think of it Mister! The only place you're going is the tank."

"I agree. Load up the nanobots, drop the grav again, and we'll get me fixed up."

Alydar did just that. Bird was floating in a mix of highly oxygenated blueish green liquid that was part liquid, and part gel.

*Nanobots, courtesy of Jonathan's team, went to work fixing any damage they found. The high oxygen levels in the 'thick water' sped up healing. Bird knew of deep sea divers breathing stuff like this back on Earth. Jonathan put him in it when he came back in a coma. As a joke after he woke up, he freaked out Jonathan by dipping fully into the tank and actually breathing the water. Bird didn't need to do that this time, and decided not to shake up the already shook up Alydar. Bird was actually touched seeing how much she cared, and what she must have gone through to save him. Not to mention, the level of care she was giving him now.*

*"Not that I'm not grateful but, mind telling me how you brought me back?"*

*"Bird, honestly, that doesn't bother you?"*

*"What, being dead?"*

*"Well, yeah!"*

*"Not a pleasant thought I'll admit. But seeing as how I'm not, I think I'll focus on what is... and not what was."*

*"Scared the hell out of me. Anyway, I powered down the suit to protect you. Having no idea what was in that monster that hit us, I couldn't take the chance of any EMP pulses."*

*"Wise move. When my suit came on unpowered, I figured that was why."*

*"Mm hmm. I set my timers to come back on in one minute, but they got damaged. I woke up, and when I say "I", I mean just that... me, the avatar... but I swear, I have no idea how. That last bit has me quite puzzled. Most of me is still offline."*

*"Well dear(cough cough) I'm just glad you did."*

*Full of love, Alydar said "Me too."*

*Bird yawned and said "So, you were saying?"*

*"Oh yeah, so, once I got rebooted, the medicals in the suit took over. I could power it up and it sent shocks, like they did to Lone. Luckily, your heart was stopped only, and not damaged like his was. The rest of the damage however would kill you in a day if you get out of that tank so..."*

*Bird waved her off saying "Yes mommy, I get it. Trust me, with how I feel right now, I wouldn't get out even if I could."*

Alydar gave him a kiss on the cheek and said "Good. Most of my sensors are down too. I'm going to go take a look around and see just how bad things are, okay?"

"Truuuuuust me," Bird joked, "I'll be right here when you return." Bird barely put up 2 fingers and joked "Scout's honor."

Alydar stroked his face softly, smiled, and headed out.


Alone in the med bay, Bird made a sign of the cross, as best as he could anyway, and talked to the open air.

"You lied to me." Bird chuckled lightly but even that hurt and said "What's that you say Bird? Lied about what you ask?"

Bird, deadly serious, said "I remember. I remember it all."

# Chapter 2:

## "Okay... Where We At?"

Bird was groggy but awake. Alydar had to give him some pain killers but could only bring him to this state. Put Bird out and, well, he might not wake up again. Not with his level of damage.

"Okay... where we at?" Bird asked.

Alydar chuckled "What?... No 'Sit Rep'!?"

"Do I look like GJ?" Bird chuckled with "Or Tiiveer?"

Alydar took a moment, then laid it all out.

"Suffice to say, sensors went down from front to rear. Once they had, the independent sensors came on. I don't know what it is but, well, here... see for yourself," and Alydar swung a monitor around.

It showed a hallway just past her doll house. Empty and nothing happening. Then everything shook violently.

"Okay, that's when the wave of hell hit," Alydar told Bird. "Now, keep watching."

Bird did. Suddenly, several balls of swirling... well... SOMEthing, cut across the picture. It came out of the upper part of the hall where the wall curved to the ceiling, and exited across the hall where the wall met the floor. It was erratic, like lightning. But it was also contained in some form of ball. Bird said it looked like someone took a tornado, put in a ton of lightning, made it all clear and stuck it in a ball. Alydar agreed.

"Now, take a look at this," Alydar started. "I went down that same hallway and took this video only an hour ago."

"Holy shit!" Bird exclaimed.

"Heh heh, my reaction was... well.. a little more verbally colorful," Alydar said with a smile.

"Ally?"

"Yeah?"

"All this crazy shit aside... well... it's good to see you smile."

Alydar gave him a soft kiss on the cheek saying "Well blue eyes... it's nice to be seen."

Bird nuzzled her a little bit then went back to the video.

"Okay, so, these distortion bubbles kicked up inside. My question is... how's the outside?"

"Intact as far as I can tell. Here's the really weird part though," Alydar started, "Look at the time stamps on the bubbles."

Bird looked and there were two time stamps. One for the hallway and one for anything it sensed. With all the time shifts and what-not Bird has been through, it was one thing he insisted on in Alydar's planning stages. Now he was ever so glad he did. The hallway one remained constant. The one for the bubble moved so fast Bird couldn't track it. The bubble was hundreds of years old... then thousands... then the numbers were in the negatives. All over the map they were.

"Here comes the 'rut roh' part," Alydar teased.

Now Bird saw closeups of where the bubble came into, and exited, the hallway. The top right of the wall, along with the bottom left of it, looked as if they'd been liquified... swirled... then hardened that way. Anything that wasn't made of moss, that got impacted by a bubble, was distorted beyond recognition.

Still staring... and planning... Bird asked "Alydar, 2 questions. First, how many of these things we got?"

"I've covered 95% of myself so far, and we got hundreds."

"Okay, second question. How's the lander?"

"Oddly enough, unscathed. I'm guessing because it was a hull inside a hull, it was protected somehow. Only a guess though," Alydar said.

"You know what I've always told ya lady... take any luck you can get. I designed you to be totally dumped into the lander as a fail-safe. At least that's one bit on our side. Okay Ally, crank up the scanners. I'm getting real sleepy and I need a nap. I'll get the rest when I wake up."

Bird knew Alydar was concerned. He also knew she had every right to be. Seeing this video now, he knew he had some serious work ahead of him and he wasn't gonna do anyone any good if he was incapacitated. Bird had a major sense of priority right now and he was sticking to it. Heal himself, then fix Ally. As far as he was concerned... everything else could wait. Alydar gave him a friendly smile, setup some settings on the scanners, turned off the lights and left Bird to dream.


"Uh, excuse me, soldier, but I believe we're expected inside," Shiiran said at the forefront of the 'alien delegation'.

She said that because 10 fully-armed Jammers gave her reason to. They were outside the meeting room and silently denying them entry.

"Perhaps you didn't hear me... I said we were expected... AND invited by Commander Lone himself!"

"And it's that very same Commander that's denied you entrance," Lone said with a smile as he walked up.

"Might I ask why?" Valleron asked aloud.

"Of course. I'm going to tell you something my wife once said... and something Biiird once did. Walk through that door and, if found out you were a part of this, you... and your worlds, could become targets. That was a warning to others once from my wife. Biiird though once said... all in or all out. Walk through that door, and you had better live up to your end of things. Failure to do so will make you as much of a prime target to us as Tammy is. That's the deal ladies and gentlemen. The guards here stopped you so as to give you one last chance. Here and only here, you can change your minds if you now choose to. Do so, and no one here will think ill of you. That's a promise from a Ghost."

One by one they all smiled, walked up to the guards, and asked them to let them pass. When the last one walked through, Lone just smiled.

"Good to have you aboard," Lone said to no one at all and walked in last.

Once he had, the guards heard the click of the lock.

Quaran, more so than the others, knew about military hierarchy and chains of command. With the gathered crowd at the table now he knew two things. First, if the command structure fell apart, any chance of getting Bird back would be lost before it even started. Second, he wanted everyone to know just who that command belonged to.

"Before we get started," Quaran began, "I'd like to say something. In the past, these meetings would start with Commander Bird going over what happened, what went right and what went wrong. Then, he would find a fix, or come up with a course of action. Seeing as how the Commander actually is the focus this time, I'd like to state that if Bird can't be in that chair, I'd have no one else filling it in his absence. That said, you have my trust, my loyalty, and my honor."

A very calm Lone smiled and tipped his hat as Quaran sat back down. The room applauded their agreement, and Quaran had accomplished what he set out to do.


Bird was getting healed and at a super fast rate thanks to Remmy's nanotechnology. He was still quite a ways off from fully healed but, he could now move around the tank some without causing searing pain. Alydar checked the scanners and suggested light amounts of physical therapy. Bird agreed, but it was why that was different now. In the past he had to get better to get back to his life. There were reasons to get better, and things that needed doing. Now, just like on Eden when he first arrived, he had nothing to get better for. He fully intended to fix Ally as he said, but he couldn't shake the feeling of 'what then'? His home was gone, he had no idea where he was nor did Ally. He also didn't know 'when' he was either. He also can't get back to the Ghosts as there are no Ghosts to get back to. Once again... Bird was facing a whole new start. This time however, he wasn't angry like he'd been in the past.


"Okay creatures... as someone we all know well would say... 'where we at?'" Lone asked the table aloud.

Valleron spoke up first.

"As I stated Commander, we don't have much. Still, as I promised, all we can spare is yours for the asking. Might I make a suggestion?"

"Feel free," Lone answered.

"Whatever plan we come up with, it will need resources. Perhaps if we all knew who had what, or who can or will provide whatever, then we would know what resources we have and apply a plan based on that."

"Lesson learned from years on the run?" Lone asked politely.

"Indeed. Still, I feel it a good start."

"I agree. So, I'll go first. When Biiird setup this planet he said it would be on the cutting edge of tech and innovation. He also made it VERY clear advanced tech often destroys rather than helps. We here of Planet 51 will provide that tech. In keeping with Biiird's wishes though, while we may provide it, we may not share it either. Fair enough?"

"Indeed, at least for me," Shiiran stated. "We Rassentan's have technology we can provide, but mostly anything aquatic, or anything like that that may be applied another way. We also have, no offense to anyone here, the best star maps and map makers. Those are at your disposal as well."

"None taken," Jalitzar said. "While we are still rebuilding our own world, we do have some of the finest fighters, and fleet to back them up, in the known worlds. We will be happy to provide any protection you may require, and any manpower we can spare."

Valleron spoke back up saying "We have manpower to spare. Also, hundreds of your years ago, my people were THE builders of anything in space. Those skills were all but lost after the war broke out. As such there has been a great resurgence to regain those skills before they were lost forever. Now, what was only a handful, is thousands strong and growing exponentially. Need to build in the vacuum of space, and you now know who to call."

Lone smiled feeling he was on the right track, and truly feeling hopeful that this actually might work.

"Okay, here's the start of an idea. In the past, it would be 'thrown on the table' and all would work on, plan for, or improve. It's worked well before and I see no reason to stop now. Any objections?"

Not one came.

"Good. Here's how I see this. This plan has multiple parts.

Tamarak has always been after Biiird since we first met. Now that he's gone, I feel we have three issues. Getting Biiird and my sister back, keeping Tammy clueless as to what we're doing, and keeping the same at bay. I can't tell you how we know what I'm about to tell you, only that we do. Tamarak needs power on a planetary scale. It seems Tuhleesia is the only world that can give him that power and still remain stable. I feel with Biiird gone, he'll likely step up his attacks on his former home-world. I don't think I have to remind you... that information doesn't leave this room."

Everyone nodded not only their understanding, but a thanks at the trust Lone gave them.


"Well, now that we have that sorted, let me put out one more idea. Time, good creatures, is of the essence."

"In what way?" Renny asked.

"Biiird was heading to Earth. Here, in this galaxy, it was only a handful of years since he left. On earth however, it was 35. Keep in mind anything we do, must be quick. If the science repeats itself, one week here could mean months or even years where Biiird is."

"Well, I suggest we waste no time then," Rahgaa said.

Everyone else understood... and agreed. All the remaining leaders put in what they could provide. Seems Valleron was right, with intel and resources sorted, a plan was truly taking shape.


"Ally? We need a plan," Bird said hanging from his arms on the tank edge.

"For?"

"You. Us. What do we do and where do we go. That sorta plan."

"Kind of hard to know where to go when we don't know where we are," Ally replied.

"Don't forget 'when' we are," Bird reminded her. "While I cant say quantum mechanics is exactly my thing, I'd have to say we ran into the same problem as Tiiven."

Ally thought about that and said "Seems about right. Problem is, assuming you're correct, where on the ride did we get off?"

Bird sighed and said "I wish I knew Ally, I wish I knew."

*Suddenly, Bird had a thought.*

*"I know! Ally, external sensors are still down right?"*

*"Yep."*

*"Go outside then!"*

*"Uh, excuse me?"*

*"You heard me. Ally look, I designed you to look like your breathing, to fool anyone who noticed. Truth is though, you don't. Take a hand scanner and recorder, head outside, get whatever readings you can get and come back in. Better than nothing right?"*

*"Breathe no... but what if the outside is corrosive? Or what if there's some sort of time vortex? You saw what they did to the hallways. Not to mention any possible virus's or diseases."*

*Bird knew he had a great idea but, Ally was right. He also knew something else now too. When he landed on Eden he was on his own. As such he had to learn to think ahead... way ahead. He also had to make plans that, if failed, it would likely be something he could get himself out of. Bird's problem now was, he was still thinking as if he had the resources of 51 to back him up. Now, Bird realized not only was Ally right but, he'd have to shift his thinking back to an earlier time... and circumstance. Ally was working but only partially and, like on Eden, you don't waste any resource you have.*

*"Alright Missy, not happy about it but, can't say your wrong either. Okay, new plan then." Bird thought a bit then said "I know! Ally can you open your rocket bays?"*

*"Only 2 of the 10 of them."*

*"Perfect! Ally look, we need intel on our surroundings. You're barely functioning and I'm dead... heh heh, again... if I get out of this tank. If we are in a war zone and don't know it we're screwed. Fair to say?"*

*"Agreed. What did you have in mind?"*

*"While your damaged, your still functional. I say hold up on repairs for a few, and work on this. We need to know what and where we are right? So, take a small rocket and remove the warhead. Replace it with any scanning equipment we can. Get a cable and connect it to the equipment. Open a rocket bay, drop the sensors and close the bay as much as you can. Get whatever*

readings we can, then pull the rocket back inside. Scan the bay for anything nasty first, then retrieve the sensors once you see it's clear."

Ally smiled saying "Sure wish I could'a met you in your junkyard days."

"Nah," Bird joked, "I was a bit of a dork then."

Alydar laughed, checked Bird's scans like a nervous hen, then headed out to make Bird's plan a reality.

"Don't you go anywhere on me mister!" Alydar half chuckled.

"Alydar wait!" Bird called out.

"Hmm?"

Bird got serious and said "Ally one day I'll likely find a wife. If I do I'll likely have kids too. But there's one thing I can promise you here and now, one thing that will never change."

"And what's that?"

"While one day you may have to share me... I will never leave you... never."

Ally stroked his cheek, and with a kind smile said "Nor I you."

That said, Alydar headed out to do a little TTK work of her own.

# Chapter 3:

## *"A Pact, A Plan, And The Return Of The TTK's"*

*"Let me be VERY clear on this,"* Lone started, *"There is NO idea too far fetched, or too 'out there', that I will not entertain. Even if we don't use it, it may have a bearing on one that we will."*

Rahgaa got serious. She wanted her people to shine once more. The events of the last months, in her mind, were epic to say the least. Everyone that mattered to her was right here at this table. A once in a lifetime opportunity she was going to take advantage of and show all the worlds her people can shine too.

*"I am interested Commander in hearing what you have to say on this matter,"* she told Lone. *"What plan do you have?"*

*"I don't Lady Rahgaa... not a whole one anyway."*

*"Still, even a piece of one would be welcome."*

Lone looked dead on at Shiiran and said *"Lady Shiiran, I'm about to take us where all Rassentan's fear to go."*

*"Oh?"* Shiiran said with some concern.

*"Indeed. I plan to make use of what we have come to call... the minefield."*

Slightly confused, Shiiran asked *"And where would that be?"*

Lone looked at the table and said *"The area you found where 2 black holes once collided."*

*"Are you insane!? Commander... there's brave and... there's suicide!"* Shiiran barked in protest.

*"I'm not suicidal and... for the record... I've already been there."*

*"I'm listening,"* Ulquin said with total calm.

Of all the creatures at the table now, and all the worlds represented, Ulquin was probably the least flustered by ANY thing the Ghosts did.

Lone answered with *"Let me tell you a story. You've all seen*

Alydar... the new one... right?"

All nodded and Lone continued.

"Have you seen the letters on the rudders? The ones that spell out TTK?"

Again, the table nodded.

Lone said "They stand for 'Train Track Kids'. It's what Biiird's mother called him and his biological brother. Two people, separate yet together. Never one without the other. I can tell you for a fact that wherever Biiird is, he's working on a way to get back. The time has come, ladies and gentlemen, for me to be the other rail. Lady Rahgaa, may I tell them?"

"Only what you need to... and no more," Rahgaa stated flatly, but with purpose.

Lone nodded to her and then informed the rest of the table.

"That area wasn't a collision of black holes... it was a collision of time. Prior to the Tuhleesian civil war, a shield was developed to protect a ship going into it. It is, quite literally, a collection of time bubbles, warps, and holes."

"And you know this how?" Ulquin asked.

Rahgaa very slightly shook her head and Lone said "As I said... I've been there. Those shields, modified and upgraded by us here at 51, were put on the Ghosts. Biiird told me before he left to use this minefield to our advantage should something go seriously wrong. More than that I can't tell you as it's classified."

"And, I suppose you have a plan?" Roenas asked.

"I do. I got Bird home by trapping a wormhole we knew went to Earth. All Tamarak did was expand it. I intend to trap one of these portals in another ring, go in... get Biiird... and get out. If we build AND deploy the ring in the minefield, we should be able to keep Tamarak guessing. Without the shields we have... well... I'm sure Lady Shiiran could tell you stories."

"Indeed I could, and they wouldn't be good ones," she stated slightly angrily.

"Small problem Wolfman," Symda said. "I've seen your reports. There's thousands upon thousands of them. How will you know which one to trap?"

"I believe this is where Lady Rahgaa and I come in,"

Rennahr said. *"You know of my ability to trance?"*

*Some did, but some didn't.*

*"For those who do not, I have the ability to leave my physical body and travel to places it could not. Lady Rahgaa, and Tamarak himself, are the only others who can do what I do, and she trained me."*

*"Sorry, still 'a little fuzzy' on that one,"* Ulquin said.

*"Suffice to say Ambassador, we can do this,"* Rahgaa said.

*She also said it 2 ways... in trance mode and... behind him.*

*"Oh well that clears... wait... you're there but... YOU'RE HERE!"* Ulquin said pointing at each version of Rahgaa.

*The Prime smiled, and faded.*

*"Indeed,"* Rahgaa said winking at him, but doing so back in her own body across the table from him.

*"IMPRESSIVE!"* Ulquin shouted with pure awe and joy.

*Valleron was equally impressed, and said with glee and hope* *"Commander Lone, not even you could move me from my seat now. Heh heh... let's hear the rest of this plan!"*


*Scota was coughing again. She did a lot of that lately. She used to be a healthy and happy young woman till the black winter of a year ago. Headstrong and full of fire, yet never sassy or rude, yep, that was Scota. Ciana remembered the worst winter anyone on the whole isle could remember. Even a sunny day was dim and the sun wasn't like it had been in years prior. This lasted all winter and didn't get better till spring. When the air and sky finally got better, Scota got worse. Ciana noticed she had good days and bad. What had her worried was, lately, there were more bad ones than good. Scota was a good lass though. She never fussed and always tried to press on even when she couldn't. Ciana had the same problem as Scota for awhile but it seemed like she got over it, whereas Scota didn't. The local doctor cared for her as best he could but was more than honest with Ciana saying, politely, it was out of his league. Now, with all the coin she had saved, she only hoped it would be enough to get her sister to a proper doctor in London.*

*"Keep yeh blanket on or you'll catch a chill."*

*"I will Ciana."*

*"Why do yeh like coming out here ennyway? It's a wonduh yeh doen catch yer death o'cold sitt'in out here."*

*"Ciana?"*

*"Yeah?"*

*"Look at 'em," Scota said staring at the night sky. "Some times I imagine mahself flying... yue knoe... up thehr among the stars."*

*"Oh? And jes wats wrong with down here?" Ciana asked with some consternation.*

*"Ciana, haven't you evuh wondered what's out there? I doen mean the stars, but ennywhere!"*

*"I have more than enough tuh worry bout right here without worry'in bout 'out there'."*

*"Oh Ciana, I doen mean tuh be rude, but doen yeh wanna knoe what's out there beyond the Isle Of Skye?"*

*"Kahnt say thah I dooo. But, I'll tell yeh what, yeh knoe that prince I keep teas'in about?" Ciana said with a chuckle.*

*Scota chuckled back saying "Aye, yeh mean the one that's a'comin to sweep yeh off yer feet?"*

*"Aye, das the one. Well when he comes, I'll ask him tuh take yeh to some of dem places... till then... yeh keep that blanket wrapped tight and be inside in half an hour THE most!"*

*"Yes motherrrrr," Scota smarted.*

*She finished a short coughing fit, looked up, and spoke softly to the sky.*

*"One day... one day I'll see things with my own eyes."*

*She wrapped her blanket tight and stared straight up for the next 30 minutes.*

*"How ya do'in there Ally?" Bird called over the comm link.*

*"I got a few scanners ready to go. I'll have the warhead off in about 10 minutes. If all goes well we should have some answers in about a half hour."*

*Bird told her in no uncertain terms "Watch it with that warhead. You take all the time you need. 'Ally go boom' isn't on my schedule for today... got it?"*

"MRU," Alydar said seriously, "Not exactly on mine either."
"Glad we understand each other."
"Boss?"
"Yeah?"
"Thanks."
"For?"
"Caring."
With a smile, Bird merely said "Always."

Almost ready to go, Alydar attached the tether cable. She found one in one of the workshops and hooked one end to the now dud rocket, and the other to a panel on the wall that would serve her purpose.

"Ready when you are boss," Ally said over the comm.

"Anything... and I mean ANY thing... goes wrong, and I want you to close that bulkhead, cut the cable, and high tail it outt'a there... got it?"

"Don't have to tell me twice," Ally joked.

"Okay Ally, drop it... and let's see what we got."

Alydar opened the rocket pod and literally let the rocket fall out. The gravity turned out to be intense and the area started filling with a blue mist. It turned out to be non corrosive, so Alydar didn't worry about it. The rocket however shot out at blazing speed. It only lasted about 7 seconds before the cable ran out and snapped tight. The panel was recording it all but now the mist was getting worse. Seeing she had enough data, Alydar tried pulling the rocket back in. Tried was the key word, as the cable wouldn't budge.

"Ally let it go!" Bird hollered.

"I do that and we're one short. I'm not giving up ANY resource unless I have to!"

Alydar closed the bulkhead as the hallway was now loaded with blue mist. As she hoped, the cable pinched, but didn't break. She ran back to the shop, and got a portable winch. Hooking the cable to it she opened the bulkhead and started reeling it in. It took the winch, her assistance, and 10 minutes but... she got it back. Bomb bay closed again, she had the blue mist analyzed as the vents blew it back into space. They were at only 10% but given time, *they'd get the job done. Ally sent the info to the decks in the med bay, left the dud and cable in the hallway for another day, and sealed the hallway as she headed for Bird.*

*"Ally, I wanna talk to you," Bird said in a serious but friendly tone.*

*"Sure, what's up?"*

*"Ally, Lone and I talked before I left. We both agreed, if something went wrong, like reeeeeeeeally wrong, we would become the new TTK's. We agreed we would both find a way to get us back even if we couldn't talk to each other. Two separate creatures, yet working in sync. I want you to know, I'm keeping my end of that. I don't care how long it takes, I won't quit till I get home. And, by home, I mean 51. So, where I go?" Bird asked with a smile.*

*"So do I," Ally smiled back.*

*"You okay with that?"*

*With a caring smile, Alydar's avatar said "As long as your with me, I'm okay anywhere."*

*Bird looked Alydar over.*

*"What?" she asked seeing Bird stare at her.*

*"That still bothers you don't it?" Bird asked.*

*"What does?"*

*"Me... the cockpit... all of it."*

*Alydar deflected it saying "Yeah well, wadda ya say we deal with these readings eh?"*

*"Alydaaaar?" Bird stated in a 'don't give me that' tone.*

*Ally stopped and practically froze. She had her back to Bird and with a memory she'll never forget, she just couldn't face him.*

*"I've faced Tamarak and every evil he could muster. I've gone into a minefield that, by rights, should have torn apart even me. While it was an accident, I even fired a full charge at my own sister. In all that, along with all the other adventures, I was never terrified. Scared sometimes yes, but, never terrified. Not until... I found you."*

*Alydar's voice was quivering by the time she finished.*

*Bird was leaning on his folded arms and hanging on the edge of the tank, and said "Alydar... c'mere."*

*With her back to him still, her still shaking voice said "I'd* rather not."

"Get... over... here," Bird commanded.

Alydar grudgingly turned around, and Bird could see the terror she mentioned all over her face. Bird reached out and hugged her. No words, Alydar hugged him back and let the tears flow.

Bird whispered soft in her ear, "You didn't want me to go. Thanks to you... I didn't. Not even Cliffy cared for me like that... not till the end anyway. Only Lone ever cared for me that much so, for what it's worth... thank you. Not much I know but, it's genuine and... all I have to give."

Alydar heard the words, and let loose every fear, uncertainty, and concern. Holding Bird as tight as she dare, Alydar bawled her eyes out and released all her pent up emotions. Emotions, Bird knew, at a level she'd never felt before. Regardless of what she was made of, Bird thought at this very moment, Alydar was the most perfect woman he'd ever met. Without a word, Alydar hung on to her Commander not wanting to let go... and thought pretty much the same about Bird. Alydar was built to be as human as possible. As such she was given tear ducts with 2 small tanks. Those went dry and Alydar just kept crying, and hugging.

Still hugging, and still sobbing, Alydar asked "Bird?"

"Yeah?"

"What was it like?"

"What was what like?"

Alydar pulled back and stared Bird down.

"Bird Of Prey! We are God knows where... or when. I'm as busted up as you are and not likely to get fixed anytime soon. Like it or not, we are all we have so don't you DARE pull that on me!"

Alydar knew Bird was deflecting her, and was having none of it.

"I remember it... all of it. At least, I think so," Bird said sadly.

"Think so?... Clarify."

Bird had a distant look in his eyes, and decided to be as honest as he could.

"It's like a dream. When I first, well, 'came back', I remembered every little detail. Now, like a dream, huge pieces of it have faded and for the life of me I can't remember them."

*"Poor choice of words there boss."*

*"Heh heh... yeah... sorry."*

Just like Ship had in the past, and without letting Bird know, Alydar flipped on the recorders. Bird still had a distant look on his face as he spoke.

*"I remember... hmm... sensations. Best way I can put it. I didn't so much 'see' things, but more like I 'experienced' them."*

*"Like your link to Lone? Like that?"*

*"Similar but... FAR more intense. It pisses me off 'cause it was so clear when I came back. Now it's like an epic story, but with just as epic holes and gaps."*

*"Bird, according to your myths and legends, you're supposed to see people you knew in life. Did you?"*

Bird actually smiled, and replied *"Cliffy."*

Alydar had finished crying now. While she couldn't explain it, she actually felt better because of it. Bird would later explain that to her.

*"And?"*

*"And what Ally?"*

*"What happened?"*

*"I got to say goodbye... properly this time."*

Alydar smiled and said *"I'm happy for you then. I can only imagine something like that, but I feel like that would annoy me."*

Bird was confused and asked *"What, saying goodbye?"*

*"No,"* Alydar told him, *"Not being able to."* Alydar then asked *"And what about the gaps? Anything you can remember?"*

*"I feel like I was talking to someone, someone I knew, but I can't recall who. You remember Mary?"*

*"Indeed I do. What about her?"*

*"I feel like I didn't speak to her, but somehow knew she was okay. Remember how I told the Xarans they would have a soul, or be treated as if they did?"*

*"Mm hmm."*

*"I don't know why but... I get the, well, 'sensation' is the best word I can use. Anyway, I get the sensation like my promise was honored. There's only two things left I can recall. First is, I didn't belong there. I kept getting the feeling like I wasn't 'due to arrive' there for quite some time."*

"Now THAT I like the sound of. And second?"

"Nothing clear but, I get the 'sensation' that someone, or thing, didn't like me... or what I was doing... and has something in store for me. Honestly Ally, turn on your scanners if you wish but... that's all I recall clearly."

Alydar could tell by Bird's face, and his tone, that he was indeed telling her all there was.

"No need blue eyes, I believe you," Alydar said sweetly. "How about we start on these readings now shall we?"

Bird looked at her and said "Ally? How about we make a pact?"

"Like?"

"Like... no matter how awkward, or small, or insignificant we may think it is... we always tell each other the whole truth, and hold nothing back... deal?"

Alydar grabbed Bird by the cheeks and kissed his forehead tenderly saying "Deal."


"So, this... what did you call it? Trancing? Anyway, how is that going to help us?" Valleron asked.

Renny replied "Once, in the recent past and... during a trance, I found a way to go into the not so recent past. When Lady Rahgaa first found Bird, she sensed him more than anything. Once she did, she focused on that point till she found the source. When we trance, to some degree, we can sense things we wouldn't in our solid forms."

"And?" Valleron pressed.

"And... I intend to trance, with Lady Rahgaa as well, inside the minefield. If a wormhole opens up, we'll scan it, as only we can. IF we find one that's correct, my mate and the others will trap it."

Ulquin stepped in saying "I get it... you find which one, and the rest of us build and deploy a new ring. Also, we do it IN the minefield to hide from Tamarak... yes?"

"Yes. That is, assuming we even find one," Renny answered.

Ulquin finished with "I'll assume your ships will shield us as well while we do?"

"Not exactly but..." Lone answered the table and finished

with "... I have another plan for that. Till I get confirmation however, not to mention permission... that's all I can say for now."

Rahgaa, very seriously, told the table "Keep this in mind. When we first contacted Rhana, we didn't find out till later that, while in trance form, we were being watched."

"By?" Juvehnar asked.

Rahgaa simply said "Tamarak. We discovered how he did it, and managed to thwart it. I tell you this because neither I nor Renny have any idea how the minefield will affect us in trance form. It may be no different than anywhere else, it might shield us, or be an alarm in a quiet room."

The rest of the room took that to heart, discussed it seriously, but determined it was worth the risk.

Deeno spoke up now and said "But we've been in there Lone. There's thousands of them! How you going to scan them all? Not to mention, our scans show they open, close, then reopen randomly. We could, theoretically, rule one out then it opens again and it's perfect."

Lone spoke up saying "I can't deny that. Nor can I deny the searching will be the hardest part. All that aside, Bird is trapped likely in the past. That said, so is my sister. Max and a few others, and myself, spent months trying to actually 'form' a wormhole. Sadly we had zero success. That said, you know anywhere else with a shopping mall's worth of wormholes?"

"Point taken," Deeno answered.

"Look, I'm not saying this plan doesn't have its risks, not to mention uncertainties. So, if anyone else has a better idea, I'm all ears."

No one... said a word.

"Well then, till something better comes up, that's the plan for Biiird. Now, we need one for Tuhleesia. I've ordered all of 51 to 'go dark'. We are going to appear to go into hiding. You'll not see us at the auction house, nor anywhere else. That should keep Tamarak thinking we're working on a way to get Bird. Just enough truth to keep Tamarak focused elsewhere."

Tiiveer spoke up saying "Problem is Lone, that 'elsewhere' is *us."*

*"Indeed. THE Ghost promised to help you. Know that the remaining ones will not abandon you. That said we will not be visiting as much as we used to. Should Tamarak arrive, and bring an attack, we'll help if need be. We Ghosts feel however, a collective show of force would be far better."*

*Juvehnar now addressed the table.*

*"I agree with you Commander. My people lost a flagship to his monsters. Trust me, my fleet would take great delight in paying him back for that incident."*

*Juvehnar looked straight at Rahgaa and spoke again.*

*"Lady Prime, our two races haven't exactly been friends. I can tell you, if your people continue on your current path, and don't fall back on, well, shall we say 'old habits'? Anyway, know that my fleet will come to your aid if called."*

*Shiiran said "And so will mine."*

*Valleron joined in saying "My people have no spacecraft, none of consequence anyway. However, I have millions who not only have aggression issues, but have become experts at what the Commanders here call 'guerrilla warfare'. Count us in as well AND, for the same reasons as Alta Juvehnar."*

*Rahgaa was moved, and spoke to the alien leaders.*

*"Ladies and gentlemen, Bird spoke to my people shortly before he left. Even as we speak my people are erecting a statue in his honor with his final words inscribed below. He said, essentially, strike no one in anger, or fear... and let no one do the same in return. I assure you all, as long as I am Prime 2 things will never happen. First, we will NEVER go back to the wolves we were, not in attitude anyway. Second, I intend to uphold the inscription on that statue to my dying breath."*

*Juvehnar smiled, raised his glass, and said directly to Rahgaa "THAT Lady Prime... is good enough for me."*

*All the others joined him in his toast.*

# Chapter 4:

## "An Old Television... And A Dinner To Remember"

"Keep in mind folks, this plan once started will be put into place at blinding speed. I suggest we take a break, as it will likely be the last one we have for awhile," Lone told the table. "Max and Remmy, please stay behind, I want to speak to you both."

The 2 requested remained as everyone else filed out. Rahgaa went to look for Renny but she was nowhere to be found. She was making plans with some of the alien leaders... felt something familiar... and excused herself.

Lone looked at the two Xarans and asked "For obvious reasons, I've had all the Wings except my wife brought up to speed on what we found in the minefield. Can I assume you read the whole report?"

"I did," Max started, "Fascinating almost beyond belief!"
Remmy said pretty much the same thing.

"Well then, as Biiird would do, I'm planning for the worst. I'm planning on if 'uncle' says no to using the station. That said the only one to rival it will be Raven. I'm putting you two in charge. I know she wasn't due to be totally finished for another month. What I'm telling you now gentlemen is I need her battle ready... in 2 weeks or less. THAT by the way... was not a request."

"Commander, if we held off on the cosmetic stuff, I can get everything but weapons done in that time-line or less," Remington said. "One problem though, I'd need all of us to pitch in like we did with the landers. Finish Raven, or build the ring... sorry Wolfman but it can't be both."

"I'll accept that. Max? How about it? Can you get the weapons done in that time frame?" Lone asked.

Max spoke with pride saying "I can if the Jammers will help.

Only the Xaran crew will know the inside of Raven, or the completed weapons. However, if the Jammers help build the parts and pieces, then we can easily install them."

Lone got on his comm and got Jaren and Tagahna on the 'call'. He gave them a rundown of what Max needed. Both said they'd do runs to the junkyard only as needed. With doing that, they'd deploy their crews to Max for as long as possible.

Lone looked at the two Xarans at the table and said with a smile, "Gentlemen? It looks like we have a plan."


Five minutes ago, Rahgaa excused herself and practically bolted to Lone's home. Heading to the bathroom, she only made it as far as the kitchen sink when the sickness wave hit. Wave over, Rahgaa was both happy and irritated. That's when she heard something she never expected.

"So... you too huh?"

It was Renny, and she was looking as poor as Rahgaa.

"Yeah well... wait...you... you're!?"

"So it would seem. Mine started last night... you?"

Rahgaa smiled saying "That was the first one. I'm very happy for you my dear. I have no doubt Lone will be thrilled."

"Pardon the language but... shitty timing... ya know?"

"I do indeed." Rahgaa said with a smile.

Both ladies hugged each other and offered the other their congratulations.

"And... you're smiling like that why?" Rahgaa asked.

Renny was indeed smiling, but the kind one has when they're planning something sneaky.

"Looking back on it, Tiiveer asking you to marry, and Lone asking me, was a pleasant surprise."

"True but, what's your point?"

"At the time however, it was an annoyance till the truth was revealed. Heh heh, as 'dad' would say... payback's a bitch. Being that we both fit the literal description, you up for having a little fun?" Renny asked Rahgaa slyly.

"Heh heh, you wanna quote Bird? Fine," Rahgaa said as she tugged her shirt down. " Allow me to say... heh heh... 'Make it so number one!'" Rahgaa said with a laugh.

Renny giggled saying "More of a Kirk girl myself but... MRU. Looks like I have a dinner yet again to plan!"

"Hmm... sounds devious... count me in!" Rahgaa stated.

Renny laid out her plan, along with Rahgaa's part. Rahgaa loved every bit of it, and started looking forward to a meal of personal historic proportions.


Bird studied the readouts carefully. Something about it was familiar but he couldn't place it. He saw 2 different atmospheric pressures. One where the sensors were, and a far denser one lower in the atmosphere. The blue stuff was a mix of primarily hydrogen and helium, with a good dose of methane. Trace other elements but those were the biggest three. Alydar giggled about the helium when Bird told her what affect it has on humans. He also told her the story of New Years Eve when he and Cliff went out, and inhaled the 2 dozen helium balloons at their table. He also told her how he and Cliff drank an insane amount of 'dieselines', a drink of Bacardi 151 rum topped with blackberry brandy, done in shots. Bird and Cliff had something like 5 shaker glasses... each... and walked out stone cold sober thanks to the helium. Neither knew why, and neither cared as outside the nightclub they went to... was 9 or so cop cars in the parking lot. They were looking for drunk drivers. There were 3 more hiding down the road too. Bird and Cliff drove home with ease and the cops never bothered either brother.

Alydar flat out laughed saying "Oh trust you!" to Bird.

It was because he said how, by the end of the night, both he and Cliff were actually untying the knots on the balloons... and all 2 dozen were not only gone, but they were taking some from the other tables.

With a smile, and distant eyes, Bird said "That was probably the best night we ever had together as adults. Six months later he married Diane, then drifted away as he worked on 'the eye'."

Ally smiled at the memory, even if it wasn't her own.

"Would be nice to have memories like that," she said somewhat sadly.

"Have no fear my dear, one day... you will," Bird said kindly.

"Hey Bird, I have a question. Do you think anything in these readings could be affecting my systems?"

"Say what!?" Bird said somewhat angry. "Clarify. What systems and just what affect are you referring to?"

"Don't get huffy with me mister!" Ally smarted. "Those pain meds had you quite groggy. You were in no shape to handle a spoon no less a damage report. I've been waiting till you were off them to give you a full report."

"Yeah well, I'm off them now... so start talking." Bird smarted back with "Ya sexy thang ya!"

Alydar blew Bird a kiss and gave him a run down.

"Some systems are completely offline, yet, there's no reason for it. The time bubbles did some damage but I re-routed most of those systems. Nothing wrong anywhere along the line that I can find, yet they remain offline. No idea why."

"Which systems?"

"Your suit for one. When I hopped in the tank the other day and worked on it, I still couldn't get it to fully retract. It's like some alien force is stopping it from working. The bay floor, the moving sections are totally down as are the liquid doors on the brigs. The air pressure regulators are completely offline and yet, they were undamaged. Life support is fine, as is the bay, but I can't pull the air so if you were thinking of taking the lander anywhere... forget it. Lastly is weapons, they'll charge AND fire, but the controls are offline. Again, no idea why."

"Hmm, that sounds like magnetism, moreover, electromagnetic interference. How are the engines?"

"Two are completed destroyed, and 3 others are questionable. They're totally dead right now though, so it's not them."

"We're running on one engine!?" Bird said slightly alarmed.

"Yep. It's what's keeping us in place. It has enough power left over to power us up. Lastly is the doors."

"What about them?" Bird said angrily though not at Ally.

"None of them work. Yet again, only minor damage that I bypassed. The main generator is fine as is the bypass to the main engines. Still, they won't work."

"I'll assume you checked the shielding on both it, and the remaining engine?"

"Of course. Not a single leak on either... not one. That issue, along with me, has me a bit stumped."

"What do you mean 'along with me'... what's wrong with you?" Bird said not certain if he wanted to hear the answer.

"With me nothing. Parts of 'me'..." Ally said waving around, "...Are still out of reach. A bit disconcerting I must say to be aware, yet have pieces missing. I can only imagine this is what amnesia must feel like. The part that really concerns me is how I woke up."

"Clarify," is all Bird said.

"Well, as I said, the timers got completely trashed. Technically, you should still be floating, and I should still be asleep. I've traced the command to the ignition switch in the lander."

"So, the backup kicked in, what's the big deal?"

"No Bird, the master ignition switch. The blue one on the dash."

"Yeah but that's.... oh... gotcha now," Bird said as he realized that was the 'dead cold' switch.

"Mm hmm," Ally said now realizing Bird figured it out.

That was the primary ignition. If Bird shut down the lander, Ally went into an independent state. Only a verbal override from Bird... or him physically 'throwing' the switch... would activate the systems. Otherwise, the lander was permanently powered down. Bird knew he was forward, Ally was midsection, and the lander was aft.

"So, who flipped it then?" Bird said quizzically.

"Soon as I figure that out... I'll let you know."

Bird simply made a sign of the cross, and blew a kiss to the sky when he finished.


Ciana was standing on the cliff overlooking the sea. Her pub was closed for the night. It wasn't a pub so much as an inn with a bar. Thanks to her father willing it to her upon his death, she was left with that. The 'croft' was left to her and Scota equally. Her croft was one of the larger ones in the county. Hers was a little over 100 acres and with the inn nearer to the cliffs of the western shore. Sailing ships would use her bay to weigh anchor and offload cargo. It was one of those merchant ships, that primarily traveled up and down the coast, that was to take her and Scota to London. Ciana had saved enough for hers and Scota's passage, or the physicians, but not both. She was restless of late. Scota was the adventurous one, but Ciana had never been off the Isle Of Skye. It was the latter that had her a bit restless.

Standing on the edge, she could see the bay below. In the bright moonlight, she could see the ship coming in to weigh anchor. That in itself was no big deal, but it was the cross on the flag flying below the union jack that told her the bishop was onboard. Ciana's mood just got more agitated.

"Wicked lech," she said to the open air.

Ciana was a good christian woman. More of the theory than the strict practice. The bishop however had Ciana square in his sights and didn't like taking 'no' for an answer. Ciana resigned herself to a lousy day ahead, and turned and headed for bed.


Bird was feeling a bit out of it still, but at least the grogginess of the meds were gone. As such he was forming a plan as best as he could.

"Hey Ally, you have any magnetometers in that rocket?"

"Actually, yeah, hang on," and Ally switched the readings on the scanner. "It's short range but.... ah yeah here they are," and Ally showed Bird the readings.

"Okay, so, seems the blue mist is pretty well charged. Magnetic field is off the charts but that's to be expected given its range."

"Yeah okay but, other than the stuff that was in the hallway, there's no other blue mist... none that I found anyway. Not to mention it can't get through the hull. Not the charged stuff anyway."

Bird thought a moment, then said "Yet, the scanners don't lie. Sorry Ally, I still got 2 more days in this tank, so I can't do it."

With some trepidation, Ally asked "Do what?"

"Heh heh, relax sparkly girl. Nothing crazy I assure you. Ally let me ask you something, do you have any readings of the wave that hit us?"

"Sorta."

Bird chuckled "Define sorta."

"Well, of the energy I can scan... which as you know is quite a lot... the levels were off even my scales. I'm certain there were energy waves I couldn't detect also, and at least 5 more that I could, but couldn't identify."

"So, fair to say, what hit us was of epic proportions, yes?"

"More like historic. Speaking scientifically, it was ground breaking and rule shattering."

"Okay then, that said... I think we need to stop being so confident," Bird told her.

"Um, in what way?"

"Ally, we've taken your hull for granted. Even now, in the face of a monumental onslaught, we still hold to the belief that your hull is impervious. I say you... take a magnetometer... and find the lowest readings. Then, work your way towards the highest ones."

"In search of... ?" Alydar asked.

"Point of origin. If my hunch is right, this is outside charged particles getting in, and screwing stuff up. Your insides weren't designed to block stuff like that because your outside was. The scans the other day showed no major damage. So, while we know you're not missing major chunks, I am pretty certain that SOMEwhere... you got a crack."

Ally was bright eyed now saying "I get it, find the highest levels, find the problem!"

"Well," Bird started "It's as good a theory as any."


Rahgaa was concerned and, while they cooked dinner, told Renny so.

"Renny my dear, something is wrong."

Concerned, Rennahr asked "What is it?"

"Well, even though I did not give birth, I did get through the sickness phase. While unpleasant, they were manageable. These are different."

"In what way? Do you think something is wrong with the child again?"

"Wrong yes, the child no. These are, well, more intense. I was truly afraid before that I wouldn't make it to the sink even, no less the bathroom. Not to mention the two I had just making this dinner."

"Indeed. While I am suffering with them too, I will admit I seem to be nowhere near as bad as you. Do you think it might be you?"

Rahgaa cocked her head saying "In what way?"

"You were only just recently pregnant. Perhaps your body hasn't fully recovered yet? If you were still weak from it, it would explain your sensitivity this time."

"Perhaps," Rahgaa thought. "Regardless, with Triikon and Ravenahl back home, I asked Jonathan to check on it for me. He's taken some blood to test and I'm due to meet with him just before dinner. I told Tiiveer I was feeling ill but nothing serious, so he won't suspect."

"Very wise of you," Renny told her.

"I also told him I'd bring you. No reason NOT to check you as well given all that's going on, and how much we're involved."

"While I don't feel it necessary, I can't see the harm in being sure either. This is kinda weird though."

"What is?" Rahgaa asked.

"Us, you and me, pregnant AND at the same time. I always thought I'd be Aunt Rennahr first... THEN 'Rahgaa Lady' would help me, and be someone I could go to for advice. Guess it'll be like always huh? You and me... taking the journey together."

"This journey..." Rahgaa said kindly, "... is one I'll gladly share."

Hugs all around, Renny set the meat to slow cook, and two Guardians headed out to see a 4 armed doctor extraordinaire.

Rahgaa had another sickness wave upon arrival, so Renny went first. With extreme pride and happiness, he pronounced her healthy and most definitely... pregnant. He told her he expected nothing but a normal birth, and told her if she wanted, to come back in 3 or so weeks if she wanted to know the sex of the baby.

Rahgaa was back now and told Renny how happy she was for

*her.*

*"Nurse, bring me Lady R's test results please!" Jonathan called out.*

*Report now in hand, he saw something wasn't right. Rahgaa saw it too on his face.*

*"Nurse, bring me the paddles and..."*

*Rahgaa immediately backed up going "Whoa there Doc, what exactly is wrong with me!?"*

*"What?... OH! Hahahahaha... no Lady R, these aren't 'those' kind of paddles."*

*Jonathan realized what made Lady R so nervous. The only paddles she knew of, were the one's he used on Lone. Jonathan calmed her and got her back on the table.*

*"These use sound waves. It'll even form a picture of the child when it's more developed. Given your last attempt, and its result, I'm being extra cautious. The blood work levels are quite off even for a Tuhleesian. This will help me know why."*

*Jonathan put some clear jelly on Rahgaa's stomach and put on a set of headphones. NOW..... Jonathan smiled.*

*"Okay, now the report makes sense. You may want to hear this for yourself my dear."*

*"Something wrong?" Renny said slightly panicked.*

*Rahgaa listened, and now, she was smiling too.*

*"You mean...?" She asked with glee.*

*"No insult intended Lady R but... it would seem the one Rhana's God took... he has given back."*

*"We know that already doctor," Renny stated.*

*"Then my dear, think of it this way. If Rhana were here, he would say her first one left us early so THIS one... wouldn't be alone."*

*Jonathan finished that with the most caring of smiles.*

*Now Renny said "Wait... you mean!...?"*

*Rahgaa smiled a most loving smile and said only one word.*

*"Twins."*


*"Lone, do you know Rhana's saying of 'every good man has a good woman standing behind him'?"*

*"Of course my dear... your point?"*

*"I'm that woman and I'm telling you... sit your ass down!"* Renny barked at him politely.

*"Feel free to do the same,"* Rahgaa told the Krannen dude.

Lone was complaining that, nice as this was, there was no time for this. Renny reminded him they only had a plan and nothing else. She also reminded him that when Lone gets focused, he kinda forgets everything else... namely eating and sleeping. Rahgaa told Tiiveer the same thing, and for the same reasons. All 4 now seated, dinner began in earnest.

*"I will say this Rennahr. Your cooking was superb to start with. It's nice to see some things, only improve with age,"* Tiiveer said earnestly.

Renny nodded a thanks and Rahgaa started the sneak attack.

*"Tiiveer, you'll be happy to know, Jonathan did indeed confirm I was ill. You'll also be happy to know it's nothing serious."*

Tiiveer was truly relieved.

*"Commander Lone, I'm afraid to have to inform you my husband will be busy for the next week or so."*

Lone cocked an eyebrow. So did Krannen guy. This was NOT news he wanted to hear right now.

*"Oh?"* Lone asked.

*"Indeed. I'm afraid to tell you he'll be busy building a nursery."*

*"Are you sure you're okay my love?"*

*"Perfectly Tiiveer, why do you ask?"* Rahgaa asked slyly but never broke 'character'.

*"We already have one. You sure that illness is only minor?"* Tiiveer asked thinking Rahgaa was 'losing it'.

*"Oh yeah, that's right... we do. Oh well, he'll still be busy Lone."*

*"Doing?"*

Renny was having a hard time keeping face as Rahgaa told him *"My husband is indeed correct. I am ill and... we have ONE nursery... but not two."*

*"Yeah okay but I need him to..... wait.... you?.... You're!??"*

Rahgaa smiled and said *"Ill yes but... nothing that won't cure itself in half a season,"* and she finished with a wink to Tiiveer.

Tiiveer was floored for about only 5 seconds. At 6, he stood up saying playfully "Ooooooh you!" and hauled Rahgaa up in a swirling hug. "Wait... two nurseries?"

Rahgaa just looked up at him, and smiled.

Tiiveer sat down again saying only "Oh my!"

Lone threw a huge swinging side arm and shook Tiiveer's hand briskly.

"Heh heh, looks like you may win that race after all! Honestly though, congratulations both of you. I know if Bird was here, he'd be thrilled for you."

"Lone dear," Renny started, "You gonna give up on that race so easily?"

"Welllllllll," Lone teased. "We're all grownups here so I don't mind saying, while the trying is fun, I doubt we'd catch up in time."

"Oh, you think so eh?" Renny smarted. "Honestly Lone, If Rhana was here he'd be majorly disappointed in you. Admitting defeat without even running the race. Hmmf!"

"Huh?" the big wolf said utterly confused.

"Trying Lone... is past tense. Let's just say, I wouldn't count yourself out of that race juuuuuuuust yet."

Lone's face... slowly changed. It went from 'huh?' to 'are you serious?' in mere seconds. Tiiveer did almost the same, and for exactly the same reasons as Lone.

Renny... just smiled same as Rahgaa. Lone stood up and straightened his coat.

"If you all will excuse me a moment," and he left and closed the door. Standing on his patio, he threw his arms wide, leaned back and roared as loud as he could.

"yyyyyyyyyyyyyyyyyyYYYYYYYYYYYYYYYYYYYYYYYEEEEEE EEEEEEEEESSSSSSSSSSSSSSSSSSSSSSSSSSSSSSS!!!!!!!!!!!!!!!!!!"

Lone walked back in and fell to his knees and hugged his unborn child, along with its mother.

"You... will not even SEE a waterfall... till your twelve!... I swear it."

Lone scooped Rennahr up and spun her as he shouted with glee.


Alydar was just outside the cockpit. Levels here, she detected, were significant but... the lowest on the whole ship. Walking aft, Bird's theory was confirmed. The farther she went, the higher the levels rose. It took her two hours but, she found her highest levels in the back corner of the bay... just to the side of the lander. Bird had her try another experiment as well. This one worked flawlessly, much to Bird's delight. He had Alydar put some Zaden Snow Tree moss that was in cold storage, in even colder storage. Pliable at cold temps, Bird wanted to see if it would get even more so if it was made even colder. It did. Alydar put some in a container, then stored it in a hold that had access to space. The mist had no effect on it but... the cold of space sure did. The container now had nearly liquified goo instead of moss.

"Perfect," Bird said with a smile when Alydar gave him the results. "Ally, on your way back, stop in the second machine shop and call me when you're there please."

Bird was now off the pain meds and quite mobile now. Physically weak but, damn near perfectly healed. As such, his head was now clear and the 'master planner' was in top form.

"Okay I'm here. Now what?" Alydar asked.

"Green cabinet. There's a gallon of paint marked 'metal', see it?"

"Yep. I'll assume you want some brushes too?"

"Please?"

"Got 'em. I'm on my way back."

Bird had a thought and asked "Can you access the drones?"

"Nope, but you can. Your link can be tied in but, it's primarily an independent system."

"Fair enough."

Alydar returned a half hour later. Bird teased her asking what took her so long. She teased back asking if he understood just how large she truly was, and how long that ground takes to cover.

Bird jokingly trapped her with her own words and said "Alydar, are you calling yourself fat?"

Bird chuckled when Alydar retorted "Did I mention Lone left instructions on how to kill you in your sleep?"

Alydar got serious and asked "Okay, why did I get this

exactly?"

"Ally I goofed. I said your insides weren't shielded but I forgot this room was. Only one on the whole of you. All of it that is, except for the door. That paint is Juranum infused. Paint the inside of the door and we have one room that's now electrically shielded."

Bird was doing pushups as he spoke. His shoulders were good as new but, they were stiff. His arms and legs were weak too so he did whatever exercises he could to get back in shape. Tomorrow he was out of the tank finally but Bird knew he was seriously out of shape because of his healing. He was still wearing his armor too. Only parts of it actually but... that was starting to itch.

"Okay, I get the paint but, what's the drones for?"

"Drone, singular. The other one isn't responding and likely for the same reason as the rest of your phantom failures."

"Gotcha. So, my question?"

"Ally, I'm way outta shape. I can stand but not for long. It's not as bad but, it's just like when I came out of the coma. I'm going to get in shape, paint the door, then see if my idea will work."

"Plan?" Ally teased "Ooooh, I like plans!"

"Heh heh. I get back in shape so I can stand for more than 5 minutes at a time without collapsing. Then I'm going to the shop and build a de-gausser."

"A who whatta?"

"A de-gausser. It's a device they used on old TV's when an image got stuck on the screen. The TV worked on a magnetic particle principle. The ghost image was actually magnetic particles that stuck to the screen."

"Oh I get it! This thingy demagnetizes right?"

"Heh heh, now you sound like Rahgaa."

"Pfffft... Like what would I know about old tube style televisions?" Alydar said giving Bird a friendly 'raspberry'.

"Anyway, yes, that's the plan. I get better, go outside and see if I can find the crack... assuming there is one. I'll patch it with the moss, seal you up, then kill the trapped particles inside once I know that no more can get in."

"Small problem BirdMan, how you gonna warm it to harden it?" Ally asked.

Bird made a fist and imitated putting out a left handed armor blast.

"Gotcha," Alydar said now understanding. "Can I tell you something?"

"We made a pact... remember?" Bird said with a friendly smile as he did his pushups.

"Indeed. I have to say, I like this. The planning, the problem solving... then the fixing... all of it. Now I understand why you and Lone like it so."

Bird tipped an imaginary hat and finished with "When I can, I'm gonna degauss this room first and see if it works. If it does, I'll attach it to the drone, and send it through the ship."

With a friendly tone, Alydar said "Count me in!" and left to rest her avatar.

Next morning, Alydar showed up holding something over her shoulder.

"So boss man, ready to get dry?" Ally said pulling Bird's roller skates off her shoulder.

"And what are those for?"

"You silly. You're in no shape to lift weights. This will not only let you cover more ground in the same amount of time but, it's a good aerobic workout to get you back in shape!"

Ally was pleased with herself and her idea. She was even more pleased, when Bird agreed and was pleased with her idea too. Bird's suit, on his lower torso, was still extended but only to his knees. So, on went the skates. First place he headed for was his bedroom. Firing up the sauna, it was just the thing to dry him out, and soothe his aching legs. He invited Alydar to join him and so, Bird closed the door on two, not one.

"Ally? Take off your bathing suit please."

Ally was slightly shocked saying "You sure about that?"

Bird smiled that smile that just made her melt, and said "Trust me... yer good. Once you have, lay on your stomach please."

Alydar felt a little shy and wasn't sure why, but did as she was asked.

"I need to work out my arms and... I can't say you haven't earned this."

"Earned what exac..... Oooohhh God that feels amazing!"

Bird whispered in her ear and said "Consider this my way of thanking you... for taking care of me."

What Alydar was moaning about, was the full body massage Bird was giving her. He was right on two counts. He needed to give his arms a workout of sorts and... for caring for Bird so,... she truly did earn it.

"You sure about this?" Bird asked Alydar with a chuckle.

"Yeah yeah, laugh it up blue eyes. Just you TRY and lose me this time!" Ally barked back.

"Well then, if that's the case, we'll need something fast and well... 80's ish  heh heh."

Bird's strength was back now. Today, like yesterday, he was working on his endurance. He'd been skating through Ally's hallways to do it and, inspect the damage at the same time. Ally was feeling left out so... Bird hit the machine shop and... she got skates too. Unlike Tiiveer however, she wasn't as good at it. Still, she refused to give up and was getting better, even if it was slowly. Now, Ally fired up the motivation Bird asked for.

"Puhrfekt!" Bird joked imitating Lone.

It was Juice Newton's 'Love's Been A Little Bit Hard On Me'. Bird took off and Alydar kept up this time. Cruising the hallways, Bird held her hand and just did roller rink maneuvers as they went. Back walking... curving splits... and two footed figure eights and all of it... while going backwards.

It had been 8 days since Bird got out of the tank. He was in the tank itself, for 7. Bird was gearing up mentally for some serious DIY but honestly knew he was in no shape for it. Painting the med-bay door in the metal paint, and building the de-gausser was the only thing he did so far. Now with a pretty good mental 'to-do' list, Bird was getting in shape to go outside.

"Okay Ally, the paint is dry, let's see if this works." Bird exclaimed.

Door sealed, Bird turned the de-gausser on. He waved it over his suit, then around the room. He sat it on a table and let it run for 5 minutes or so.

"Well... I'll be!" Alydar exclaimed as she looked at the magnetometer. The levels were actually going down and... fast.

"Yo Birdie... try it," Alydar said referring to the suit.

"Okay here goes. Suit!? Off!"

Like nothing was wrong at all, the suit did as it was told. Bird quickly took it off before the belt had other ideas.

"GOD that feels good!" Bird said loudly as he rubbed his skin where the suit pieces once were. "You have no idea how that thing chafes after a few days."

Bird was stoked his little experiment worked. Now all he had to do was bring it up to a larger scale.

# Chapter 5:

## "Slam It Into Reverse!"

*Deeno needed to get Kallan flying again. She passed her laser scans and, while nowhere near 100%, she was ready for light duty. As such, he took Rahgaa and Tiiveer home.*

*Rahgaa was pacing the floor like she did in the past. All the temple masters and every clan First were being gathered by Tanner and Speed Demon. Many had never flown before but Rahgaa didn't care. Most of them sure did though. Some thought it grander than grand, others however were petrified. Now, all were assembled in the great hall in the Arrowhead and waiting on the grand couple. That couple... didn't keep them waiting long.*

*"I thank you all for coming on such short notice," Rahgaa told them.*

*"Why not use those machines Rhana left?" Teekor asked.*

*"As I don't understand the technology, I do understand this much. The... what do you call them?" she asked Tiiveer.*

*"Signals."*

*"Ah yes, thank you. Anyway, the signals can get intercepted. What I'm about to tell you is for our people alone. I also can't take the chance of Tamarak being the one to intercept them."*

*"Bad news?" one of the temple masters asked.*

*"Actually no, it's good news... and a challenge," Rahgaa told them with a friendly smile.*

*Laughing lightly, Trillaan asked "I'll take the good news first then, if you don't mind."*

*"Not at all," Rahgaa said as she waved to Tiiveer.*

*"Masters, Firsts, it is with great joy that I tell you, Lady Prime is once again with child AND!... not just child... children!"*

*"That is indeed good news!" Trillaan barked aloud. "The*

ocean clan wishes you... wait... children?"

"Heh heh, yes First Trillaan... I am pregnant with twins," Rahgaa told the gathered crowd.

"Well then, DOUBLE best wishes! HAHAHA!"

Well wishes and congratulations broke out all around. Five minutes later Rahgaa spoke back up.

"I thank you all for your well wishes but... there is risk. I want you to know I have seen THE doctor on Lone's world. It seems being pregnant with twins is draining enough, but becoming pregnant again so soon after the last time has left me somewhat weak. I assure you both here and on 51, I am being cared for and monitored by the best there is."

That last part sat well with the crowd. They knew of Jonathan and liked him for both his manners and his talent. Also, knowing Prime was looking after herself, well, that sat pretty well too.

Tooran spoke up saying "While I don't wish to sour the happy mood, I do have concerns."

"Feel free to state them," Tiiveer told him.

"To begin with, now the 'why' we are here is evident. If Tamarak returns, knowing your current state would make you even more of a target. The plains clan offers anything you need to ensure your safety... and that of your unborn children."

All the others agreed and offered the same.

"Thank you for that... all of you. Any others First Tooran?"

"Indeed" the elder wolf began, "Since Rhana, the mood of all the clans has been, well, quite low. Shall we tell them, and if so, how much?"

Rahgaa smiled. This was nothing like the first meeting she had with this crew, and was smiling thinking of just how far they'd all come since.

"That, good First, is why you are all here. I do indeed want our people told but... the old way. Spread the word far and near but not one word of it... goes by tablet. Understood?"

"Clearly," Tooran answered. "Now, what of Rhana? Our people look for guidance in these sorrowful times. What answers can we give them?"

Now, politely, Rahgaa let them have it.

"Firsts, Temple Masters, the scrolls all told of Rhana and his coming. As he said when he left, he DID come and he DID help. Tell our people that a plan exists to rescue him AND Ayleen... but nothing more. What I am about to tell you now is for your ears only. I will now hear your sworn oaths... ALL of you... that it will stay that way."

One by one all swore an oath of silence. Some of them even swore it on Rahgaa's unborn children.

"Fine then. This does not come from Rhana nor Lone Wolf... but me personally. Rhana came and taught and did indeed set us on a path, a glorious path, to follow. Look at us now. Now, remember how we were just 2 seasons before you even knew he was coming. The stars are no longer some far off dream, but a reality. The plan to rescue Rhana involves many worlds, including ours. More than that I can not say.

They still look at us with fear, and awe, at what we were. Rhana taught you, taught us all actually... now I challenge you to live up to his teachings. Ladies and gentlemen, the eyes of the stars themselves are upon us now. How we behave, how we perform, and how we treat others. THIS is an opportunity that will not come again. This is our chance to shine once more. I'm not asking you... I'm TELLING you... I expect you to not only shine, but to do so brightly."

A challenge from the Prime herself. Everyone was riveted on her right now.

"The time has come to show the stars, Rhana was not only right but... that we have learned. Tamarak will certainly come. Stop him. Rhana needs our help and many worlds are involved. Lone has called for 2 Guardians, Lady Rennahr and myself, and 1 Pilot, namely Ayleen's other. All the others remain here and plan for our safety, and survival. Show me good wolves... PROVE to me that Rhana's efforts were not in vain, nor wasted. Prove it to me... and prove it to yourselves."

Rahgaa had thrown down the gauntlet. The gathered crowd would pick it up and run with it.

Now Rahgaa turned to her husband.

"Guardian Tiiveer. These other worlds offered their military aid should we need it. I leave it to you, once again, to protect our people as only you can. I will call for their help if I feel we need to. What I'm telling you is... give me all the reasons I need... not to."

"A challenge for me as well hmm?" Tiiveer said aloud.

"Indeed. Are you up for it?"

"Able, willing, but not yet ready. However, when the time comes, I Tiiveer, Guardian of the Krannen... will be."

Rahgaa smiled and told him "I see the looks on this crowd's faces. Your promise is good enough for them. If it is for them, then know that it is good enough for me as well."

Everyone in the room was now 'pumped', and Rahgaa was happy for it. 'The room' was also happy to see them living out their promise, and being Guardians now instead of husband and wife. They separated the two well and... the clans and temples would be told of that too.


Rahgaa told, and asked, the crowd one last thing.

"I have one last thing for you all. I was given permission to tell you this from Lady Rennahr. It would appear, I am NOT the only one who is pregnant. Guardian Rennahr is having minor issues adjusting to the sickness waves and asked me to speak on her behalf. She is quite an integral part of this plan, as am I. She will be needed for some time on Lone's world. She also knows she promised to split her time between here and there. She's asked me, to ask all of you, if anyone has any issues with her 'temporarily' putting aside that promise?"

"She's WHAT!?" Tahl barked as if he was the father and not his son.

The crowd laughed and Tiiveer said "Indeed, 'grandfather Tahl'," teasing the big First. "Both the Guardian AND the Mahrek tried contacting you via tablet. Each time they said, the call was not only unanswered... it was declined."

Tahl... was furious.

"While not exactly how I wished to hear of this news, it is glorious. Tell my son that... you know what? Never mind. I'll tell him myself." Tahl seethed. He was indeed happy for the couple and, his fury... wasn't directed at them.

*Now, with two Guardians becoming mothers, and a plan to save Rhana and Ayleen... plus a challenge from the Prime herself... Tuhleesia's spirits would soar over the next week as the word spread like wildfire. It would also spread the old fashioned 'word of mouth' way, just as Prime had asked for.*

*A Guardian, being oh so careful to not be seen, was making her way to a communications console in a lower level. That console was once blocked by another Guardian. His words were... if they didn't have a Guardian tattoo, no one got in. That order was still in effect. Being a Guardian herself though, she had the required artwork and as such... was granted access.*

*"I know this machine can be heard by others so I'll make this brief. I require Wing Remington. That is all and no need for a reply. Thank you,"* *and she shut off the console and left the room.*

*Later that evening, a Ghost lander, and two brothers, were invisible... and on their way to Wolfville.*

*"Having fun?" Bird asked seeing he had an audience.*

*The silver haired lady was sitting on a rolling tool box, barefoot and with her ankles crossed. Bird did indeed have an audience and Alydar was mesmerized, though she didn't know why.*

*"I am actually."*

*Bird was on his knees and in a mid-section hallway near his bedroom. He was replacing a motor that a bubble had trashed. It was a key vent motor that vented anything bad in the hallway. Being this motor was the one for his bedroom and subsequent hallway, he felt it a priority. Bird wanted a safe zone to go to in case the blue mist got in somehow so, as such, this was on the DIY list for today.*

*Bird had taken stock of what needed fixing, what he could actually fix and of those... which ones he had parts for.*

*Bird chuckled saying "You wouldn't be the first DIY groupie I ran across ya know."*

*"A what?"*

*"Heh heh. Back home on Earth, Cliff and I would do some of the bigger projects out in the driveway. Never failed that some of the*

neighborhood girls would come by and watch, just like your doing. They would be utterly fascinated watching us work. They never wanted to help... heh heh... they only wanted to watch. To this day I don't know what the appeal is but, all Cliff would have to do was take off his shirt and that was it... instant date for Saturday night."

"Ya knoooooow BirdMan," Alydar teased, "Cliffy was hot."

"Heh heh... flirt!"

Alydar just giggled but never stopped watching Bird work.

"Ya know Commander, it is fascinating."

Bird was truly curious and asked "But why!? You've seen me work before."

"True but then, I was doing a hundred other things as well. Add to that, well, I did watch you then too, heh heh, I just never told you," Ally said demurely. "I think it's because now, the work you're doing means something. There's a certain urgency to it. Me... I just think and things happen, but you, you have to physically do it. I guess its just kinda... wellllllll..."

"Well what!?"

"Sexy," Alydar said smiling brightly.

Bird just chuckled and said "If you say so."


"Hey I know, can I help?"

"If you'd like. Hand me a 10 millimeter box wrench please."

"Sure!" Ally said acting like a high school girl with a crush.

Bird laughed at what he was handed.

"That's a Phillips head screwdriver."

"Oh sorry... here," and Ally handed him another.

"Heh heh... nope... that's a socket driver."

Ally put it back and handed him another.

"Heh heh... speed square," Bird laughed.

Ally was rummaging now.

"Here!"

"Nope... vice grip."

"Um... this?"

"Torque wrench."

"Hmm... ok THIS!... or nothing!"

"Claw hammer."

Alydar was sad but chuckled saying "Damn and I was so

close too! Heh heh."

Bird stood up, and got the tool he asked for.

Alydar joked saying "Oh sure... that was my next choice."

Bird had a thought. Alydar was right, all she had to do was 'think', and things happened. Bird however truly could use a hand. Now that she had a physical body, she never really used it for anything other than meet and greets. Now, cut off from her master systems, she was far more reliant on it than ever before. Bird handed her the wrench and gently pulled her to the floor.

"I'm done Ally, now we need to put the cover back on. Here, let me show you," and Bird did just that.

Alydar marveled at the tool in her hand and how, if applied correctly, what she, and it, could do.

"Wow," Alydar said with childlike wonder. "That was actually kinda cool. Let's fix something else!?"

Bird just laughed but he did indeed let her 'fix something else'.

"Alydar, how's the magnetics in there... still nothing?" Bird asked pointing to the door of the engine room.

"Yep... total zero."

"Okay then here's the plan."

Alydar was paying total attention. She wanted to, and was ready to... well... fix something.

"I won't tease you like before but, after this morning's attempt it's clear I can't repair anything outside till we get out of the blue mist. We certainly ain't gonna do that on only one engine. So, I figure we get at least one more up and running, more if possible. Then, we'll see if we can't break free of this blue place and get you back up and running."

"Sounds like a plan. Just don't tease me okay?"

"Heh heh, I won't."

And so, the human and the look-a-like went to work doing just that.

Bird had indeed tried going outside that morning. Inside the med bay he activated the suit into full battle mode. The moment he stepped outside the ship though, the gravity was too strong.

Stretched on the end of a safety line Alydar had to reel Bird in like a fish just to get him back inside. Bird was pulling himself back in, as was his companion, and it still took almost half an hour even with his suit rockets at full burn. Another trip to med bay to get the suit off and Bird decided to go with 'Plan B'.

All the tools Bird needed were already in the engine room. As complex as the engines were, they were actually individual units. Two massive lever arm locks, one at each side, and the engine was free. Deeno really made it simple as all the electrical connections were set in the bottom plate, and they connected to pins and such in the floor. Bird thought it would take him days but, one engine now replaced, it took him and Alydar only just under an hour.

"Deeno designed them to be automatically replaced from the cockpit. With your primary systems still on the fritz, it's nice to see he made doing it the manual way just as easy."

With a kind smile, Alydar told him "Well, they did have a good teacher."

"Thanks," Bird said just as kindly.

The engines were set against the walls, with ample room between them to do any work. Three on each side, they had racks above each one with the replacements loaded in them. One unlocks and is discarded, a new one falls into place, and viola. An airlock at the back, Bird just rolled the dead engine on the rollers in the floor, opened the inner doors, shoved the dead one in and closed the door. When the outer door opened, the blue gas giant did the rest and off to the blue abyss it went.

Bird chuckled, "Well... only 4 more to go!"

Alydar smiled and both of them repeated the process.

It had been 3 weeks now since Bird and Ally arrived in the blue stuff. Bird took to wearing his hair longer, and was now sporting a 'Tony Stark' style beard and mustache. He always had the latter, ever since he could grow one. Now, with this new life yet again, Bird figured on a change of style this time as well.

Shaving in the mirror one morning he laughed at himself saying "Oh if Sue could only see me now."

Playfully defending 'her man', Alydar told him "Why?... I think it makes you look dashing."

"Aw, thanks sweety."


Riisa woke up in a chair and, in a darkened room. She was walking down a hallway in Atoemahn and was about halfway down it, when her vision swirled. That was the last thing she remembered before waking up here.

"I believe my presence was requested? Given the nature of your call, I thought this might be a wise idea."

That voice, was Wing Remington. He came out of the shadows and sat down across a small table in between him and Riisa.

"And you'd be correct. As is the phrase among the Wings, I trust this conversation never happened... and we were never here?"

Remmy chuckled saying "I'm sorry, who are you and what conversation were you referring to?"

"Indeed and, thank you. When you hear what I have to say you'll know two things. You'll know why I called you specifically... and why I'm not upset that you kidnapped a Guardian," and she finished with a wink.


Bird was having dinner with Ally in his kitchen. He was glad for her company, and was planning for the very same.

"Ally I wanna talk to you."

"Ooh ooh, are we gonna fix something else?" Alydar asked with a beaming smile.

"Heh heh, settle down there wrench girl," Bird retorted. "I want to talk about you... and us... actually."

"Thought there was no 'us'?" Alydar asked with some trepidation.

She was hoping to never tell Bird she felt sort of hollow when she slept with him. Now, given Bird's tone, she was thinking she might have to.

"Oh there is, just not that sort of 'us'," Bird said in a kind tone.

"Hmm, okay, clarify."

"Ally look. Forget the 'when' factor for a moment. Wherever we are we have to find a way home. While you've done fantastic so far, it's been with things you know. We may have to stop at planets along the way, or make a life on one we find. For as long as your life will be... you wanna spend it cooped up in here?"

"Hmm, never thought of that, nor that far ahead."

"See, that's what I'm talking about. Go out of the ship, and you'll stick out like a sore thumb. You're social skills are lacking. In case you haven't noticed, some of the less advanced worlds and cultures we've encountered tend to be a little male oriented."

"I'll take your word for it as most of that knowledge is still out of reach but, I get your point," Alydar said now understanding where Bird was going with this.

"All I'm saying is, you need to brush up on a lot of them, and if you want I'll be happy to help."

"Sounds reasonable."


"There's one other thing too. Wherever we go or end up, you may have to decide something on your own. Without those skills, or understanding what motivates most people, your going to make bad decisions. Add to that, everything that you are, and can do, needs to stay hidden from any and all that we meet."

"Wow. While I don't disagree, the scope of this is boggling."

"Indeed. It's like when you first became aware. You were like a child with adult knowledge. As expected you learned and, eventually outgrew it. Now you have a physical body. While you've used your 'greater self' as it were to control it, that same self is currently not available. As such, you are now all that you are. Sorry to say my dear but, that body comes with interactions you've never had before. So, it would seem, you're back to the beginning again."

Alydar joked "Maybe we'll find a 'female oriented' society too!?"

Bird wasn't laughing though.

"You're right, we might. And if we do, would you know what to do? Or how to behave?"

"Okay, point made. Solution?"

"How bout I give lessons, and scenarios, as we work. You may have to learn but... no reason it can't be fun right?" Bird said.

Ally smiled and only said "Deal."

Next day, Bird and Alydar went over the engines one last time. All seemed good so far and, the full speed run-ups showed no sign of shield damage. Alydar couldn't understand why, once they were fixed, she and Bird didn't just blast outta there.

"And if the new ones go boom? Or leak magnetics?" Bird asked her.

That incident, along with her little chat at dinner last night made Alydar truly realize... she did indeed have a lot to learn about being a physical entity.

Bird headed for the cockpit while Alydar stayed behind and monitored from a panel Bird rigged up outside the engine room.

"Ally, if we go forward, I intend to curve us up and out. If we don't curve however we only go deeper into blue hell. If I fire up a cat's eye, it'll likely fail due to the ionic charges out there. We've been through that once already and it didn't go so well for us. I'm not looking to repeat it anytime soon either."

"How about never again," Ally smarted but with a seriousness to her tone.

"Agreed. So, that leaves us only one option. You have as much to lose as I do, so m'lady... make the call."

"Bird?"

"Yeah?"

"Heh heh, feel free to slam it into reverse!"

With a grin, Bird replied "Aye aye m'lady!"

"Good thing you didn't say 'mistress' or we would'a had to have a talk mister!" Alydar joked.

Bird joked right back saying "Who are you... Market?"

The next thing Alydar heard was, the hum and whine of 4 engines coming up to full power.

Bird flipped the seat around putting his back to the viewscreen. With the maneuver Bird had to pull, this time, he would rather be slammed into his seat... rather than out of it.

"Ally, I'm going to full power then essentially... letting off the brakes. With the gravity outside, I need 'break free' sort of power."

*"Okay... so?"*
*"So... get ready and..."*
*"Yeah?"*
*"Hold onto something."*

*Bird called out a countdown from 5. When he hit 1, he did indeed 'let off the brakes'. Once he did, Alydar was now glad she took his advice. Hanging on with inhuman strength, it almost wasn't enough.*

*At first nothing but a bunch of shaking happened. Then, suddenly, both human and avatar felt like they were shot out of a cannon.*

*Bird was pinned to his seat almost to the point of pain. Alydar, the big black one, was rocketing out in reverse but was doing it on a 6 degree angle. Shaking and bucking, Ally the avatar was hanging onto a hallway frame for dear life. At around 30 seconds, Bird shut the engines down to half when suddenly, his cockpit view went from blue... to black. Ride now smoothed out Bird leveled her and Alydar stood up in the hallway.*

*"Son of a BITCH!" Bird hollered with a laugh. "So THAT'S how that got there! HAHAhahaha!"*

*What Bird was laughing at, was the big 'bruise' on the gas giant that he made breaking free of it.*

*Alydar ran up to the cockpit and saw what Bird was seeing.*

*"Damn, is that what I think it is!?"*

*Bird smiled and replied "Neptune."*

*"That means... oh my... we're still in the Milky Way!"*

*"Indeed. Well my dear, seems now we know the where. Only one thing left now."*

*Staring out the viewscreen, Alydar said softly "The 'when'."*

*"Mm hmm," was Bird's only reply.*

# Chapter 6:

## *"Attitude Adjustment"*

*Tahl... was pissed. He was only this angry once before in his life. Not even during his fight with Lone was he this angry. No, the only other one to ever be the recipient of this level of fury was his father. Now, not only was he on a mission but, another family member was, yet again, about to feel the full rage of the First no one would dare cross.*

"Greetings First Tahl. A pleasure to see you again," Ryklan said as Tahl answered her knock on the door.

Tahl hugged her softly saying "Always a pleasure Pilot. Thank you for coming so quickly."

"When last I was here First Tahl, I feel I came to know you somewhat. When you called me I could hear a sense of urgency, but something else too."

Tahl smirked and asked "Oh? Well you'd be correct. Let's see if you guess the correct one."

Shyly, Ryklan said "Anger."

"Very good Squadron Leader."

Tahl? Angry!? This wasn't good.

Ryklan gathered her manners and asked "First Tahl, may I ask a favor?"

"I may not grant it, but I see no harm in asking," Tahl told her flatly.

Ryklan replied "Fair enough. When last I was here, I was but a scared child. While it is only how I feel, I have come to think of you and your family as an extension of my own. Now, while I still look upon you as a wise elder, I however am no longer that child... nor scared. My favor is, inside your door, shall we drop the titles?"

Tahl smiled some. He truly did like Ryklan. He was also proud of her, and for her. He also looked upon her as one does a daughter.

"I see no reason why not Ryklan," Tahl said with a smile.

He pulled out a bottle of Lone's 'square stuff', 2 glasses, and his tablet.

"Thank you Tahl. I hear that title hundreds of times a day at the academy. Truth be told, the lack of it, especially by someone like you... is refreshing." Ryklan then asked "Given recent events, how are you and Ree'nah doing?"

With irritation in his voice, Tahl said "That not only remains to be seen but... it's the reason I asked you here."

Hearing the tone change, Ryklan pressed no further.

"Oh my stars... I almost forgot! Please accept my congratulations at the glad news of your son and his mate."

"THAT... is the other reason your here," Tahl said still irritated.

Ryklan knew she was unwittingly, and verbally, boxing herself into a corner.

Changing the subject, she asked "So Tahl, why am I here exactly?"

"This tablet. I require information, knowledge I know to be available. This device however... doesn't seem to be cooperating."

Ryklan smiled and said "I'll be happy to help, what information do you need?"

"My daughter's disappearance. I need to see it AND... I would like your comments on it. You are the only one I can trust to be honest with me, and answer my questions even if the answer may be something I do not wish to hear."

Ryklan was now super nervous. She didn't want to hurt Tahl but, she owed him. So, Ryklan agreed and showed Tahl how to bring up the video he requested.

Tahl watched it intently. Then he replayed it several times. While Tahl wasn't stupid, there were things he didn't understand.

"Tell me Ryklan, why did she go?"

Ryklan braced herself, then told Tahl the truthful answer she promised.

"Tahl, you don't fly, so it may be hard to explain."

"But I have flown."

Ryklan sipped her drink, then said "Tahl, you have not. A passenger yes but... you yourself have not flown. No insult Tahl but, you would be a passenger. I would be someone who built the plane, fixed it, flew it, then... flew it again. Until you do, or can do... what I and the others have... I feel any answer I give may not make sense." Ryklan then had an idea and asked "As a parent, you want your child to be proud of you, yes?"

"Of course."

"As such, they want you to be proud of them as well, yes?"

"Are you saying Ayleen thought I wasn't proud of her?" the big First asked.

"No Tahl not at all. Ayleen loves you and she knows you're proud of her. We all do. That said, to have Rhana proud of you too is beyond honorable. And yet, Ayleen knew he was. Going to see him off wasn't to put her life in danger, it was to honor a man who not only taught her so much but, was proud of her too. Tell me Tahl, if that was Tooran, and not Rhana, where would you have been?"

"Point taken," Tahl said now truly understanding.

Ryklan was right, Tahl still didn't understand it the way the Pilots do but, he did understand the concept.

"Now Ryklan, answer me this," Tahl started. "While, as her father, I don't think so but even I have to admit, my view of Ayleen may be somewhat biased. Tell me, is she truly good enough to be the pilot to the Prime?"

Ryklan smiled and said "You have to ask?"

Tahl thought of days past and answered "Actually yes... I do. Ryklan you haven't lived as long as I have. As such you haven't seen how having a position, and the talent to back it up, don't always co-exist. Many I have known in 'higher positions' have been nothing but pompous incapable idiots. So I'll ask you again, was my daughter truly up to the task?"

With a kind tone, Ryklan said "I doubt even your son nor Rhana could have flown Ship better."

"Then tell me, why did she fail? Why was she not able to control her own ship?" Tahl asked seriously.

"Allow me to show you," Ryklan said as she took the tablet.

Ryklan showed Tahl the screen.

"Tahl, this is the program you use to talk to the other Firsts. You see the background is blue. Buttons are here but not there. Press this button and it does this, but not that. Every wonder why?"

Tahl chuckled saying "Can't say I have. Most days I consider it a victory if I can just get it to turn on."

Ryklan giggled and said "Let me show you," and brought up several pages of computer coding.

"It's just pages of words," Tahl said not understanding.

"Indeed, but it's these words that make the screen blue or a button do something. This is but a small program but look at the bottom Tahl... see how many pages there are?"

Tahl bellowed "MY STARS! Six hundred pages!?"

Ryklan smiled saying "Mm hmm. Now, that's just one program of many. If just one little program can have that many pages... with all those lines per page... imagine how many something like Ship has."

"I'd rather not," said a stunned First now understanding more than he ever did.

"Indeed. One line, maybe two, out of trillions... overrode all the others. Not only that, it's what doomed Ayleen. Two lines Tahl, out of trillions of pages, were missed. Those two however, made Ship ignore everything and everyone to save Rhana. Had Lone or anyone else been in Ship... she still would have done the same thing."

Tahl was serious now and asked "So, what your telling me is, when Rhana's situation changed, Ayleen did NOT go after him?"

"Correct."

"And... because of that... and those words you showed me... Ship took over?"

"Yes."

"So, it wouldn't have mattered who was in it, the result would have been the same?"

"Indeed. No one could have foreseen the events the way they unfolded. Ayleen knew it was dangerous. Everyone there knew it. What no one knew was that Ship would ignore her pilot and behave the way she did."

"So, while far more complex, it was no different than a riding beast fleeing danger, and ignoring it's rider."

Smiling, Ryklan said "Now you understand."

"Indeed I do and... thank you."

Tahl turned to Ryklan and spoke from the heart.

"Pilot, for what it's worth, know that I am proud of you too. You're correct, when you first came here you were a frightened little girl. Worse... you were beaten... and I don't mean physically. As the Guardian told you once, I commend you on outgrowing one, and beating the other."

Ryklan hugged Tahl sweetly saying "Thank you Tahl. And for the record... it's worth a lot."

"By the way Tahl, where is Ree'nah anyway?"

"Not here," Tahl said with his original tone of irritation. "I told her I was going to ask you for answers. As Rhana would say, she 'made herself scarce'. A small point I intend to address shortly."

Hearing that, Ryklan asked nothing further.

"Will there be anything else Tahl? I'm afraid I have to get back shortly."

"Actually there is," Tahl told her as he handed her her coat. "You mentioned I couldn't understand the, well, mentality I guess you'd call it... of you Pilots."

"While it's true, know that I meant no insult by it."

"Oh none taken," Tahl told her. "That said I believe you correct, the same as you not understanding the life or mentality of being a First. However, if you stayed by my side for a few days, I could teach you all you'd need to know. While you wouldn't understand to the level I do, you would know enough."

Ryklan was a tad confused and asked "What exactly are you saying Tahl?"

"Not saying... asking. While I don't wish to fly like you do, If I could, I'd like to learn what it's like. I figured with you being a leader AND a teacher now, I was wondering if..."

"Say no more Tahl," Ryklan said cutting him off. "Be at Raven Base before sunrise and... learn you shall."

*Ryklan gave him a soft kiss on the cheek, put on her coat, saluted her adopted father, and headed off with a smile on her face.*

*Bird slowed down, turned his seat around, and headed away from the big blue monster.*

*"How far out you going?" the avatar asked.*

*"Pretty far," Bird told her. "Neptune has one hell of a magnetic field. Add to that, its got rings, from dust to rocks. Not a fan of going out for repairs in that mess."*

*"Point taken. Hey Bird?"*

*"Yeah?"*

*"Thanks."*

*"Um, for?"*

*"Taking care of me," Alydar said.*

*"Just us now kiddo. You take care of me, I take care of you. Till we get back to 51... we're all the family we got. And you know what I think of family," Bird stated rather than asked.*

*"I do indeed," Alydar said kindly. "Can I ask you something?"*

*"Shoot."*

*"Back on 51, Symda told me once, that if she married you and had hundreds of children with you, that there was a place inside you she couldn't touch. She said that place... was reserved for me. Is that true?"*

*"She said that did she?"*

*"Mm hmm."*

*"Well Ally, she's right. One day, God willing, I will find someone. One day, if I find someone, I'll likely marry and yes... have children. That said, Symda's correct, they'll always be a spot reserved for only you."*

*Bird felt a little awkward saying that but, he did make a pact.*

*"For the record," Ally started, "You ARE my life. I exist solely for you and, because of you. That said, I truly hope you find someone and, if you do, I won't mind sharing."*

*At that moment Bird hugged her realizing, no matter how human she looked, she'd never have a husband... nor kids of her own. Nope, Alydar was right, Bird WAS her life. He was not only thankful to have her in it, but he was sad for her at the same time knowing he was all there would ever be.*

*"Ya know Ally? Scrap that."*

*"Huh?"*

*"Like I said, I may find someone, and I may even have children. One thing I can tell you here and now though... I will not marry. Not as long as I'm in the milky way anyway."*

*"I... I don't understand?"*

*"Motivation my dear."*

*"Okay, what would you like?"*

*"Heh heh, not that kind of motivation. I mean I won't marry unless I am surrounded by my family. Being they're a tad far away right now, that's my motivation. I may do all those other things but, when I do marry... it's going to be on, or a whole lot closer to... 51... than we are now. Motivation, get it now?"*

*Smiling, Ally said "I do indeed."*

*Bird was far enough out from Neptune and came to a stop.*

*"Oh and one other thing," Bird stated.*

*"Hmm?"*

*"There's you," Bird said waving to her avatar, "And then there's 'you'," Bird said waving around. "Big long ship, silver haired android. Ally, Alydar... kinda getting confusing as to which I'm talking about."*

*"Like me being a Ghost and..."*

*"THE Ghost," Bird corrected her kindly.*

*"Heh heh, okay THE Ghost, yet you're one too. Ghost refers to pilot AND ship."*

*Bird chuckled, "Uh... yeah... what you said!" Bird told her "Let's not make it worse shall we?"*

*"Sounds good what did you have in mind?"*

*"Simple. 'Alydar' is the Ghost... 'Ally' is you, the avatar. Yes I know you're one and the same but, sheesh, if we don't do something this is gonna get out of hand, heh heh."*

*Ally smiled saying "Ya know... you're right! Heh heh, besides, I actually like it."*

*"Well, at least that's some progress anyway. What do you say I suit up and... oh shit!" Bird exclaimed having a happy realization.*

"I know that tone... what are you up to BirdMan?" Ally said cautiously.

"Oh nothing like that silly. I was just thinking... why not come with me?"

"And if I freeze up due to the cold? Or catch some solar radiation and fry half my circuits?"

"Pfff... oh ye of little faith. I got a suit that forms itself to the wearer remember?"

"That's right! C'mon Birdie... lets go fix stuff... in space!" Ally beamed.

Bird chuckled, got out of the chair and waving to the door said, "Ladies first."


Tahl walked into his creation, as asked, just before sunrise. He marveled at how even at this hour, this place was alive with activity.

"Good morning First Tahl," Ryklan called out walking up to the big First. "Ready to 'go to school'?"

"Indeed. Shall we have breakfast first?"

Ryklan chuckled and said "Lesson number one... breakfast sits better AFTER you land... not before."

Tahl got it, smiled and actually replied "MRU," and snapped a salute.


Ryklan asked "Something wrong First Tahl?"

Tahl was looking all around and replied "Not at all. I was merely thinking this is how Rhana must feel."

"Oh? How so?"

"It amazes me to see this. From nothing more than idea in my head, to some rough drawings to... well... THIS!" and Tahl waved all around.

Ryklan hooked her arm in his saying "And we're ever so grateful you did. Come on let's get you suited up... there's something I want to show you," and the Pilot and the First headed off to do just that.


Bird activated Alydar's shields. With all the snafu's going on, they were only at 25% but it was enough to catch the boots of the suits and act like magnetic locks. Two days ago Alydar had no shields at all so, Bird was in a good mood. He and Ally were on the main wing section just ahead of the twin rudders.

"Okay Ally... go LONG!" and Bird threw a perfect spiral.

He laughed hard at himself as reflex kicked in and he threw it up slightly expecting that it would come down. In the zero G of space... it didn't.

Bird was laughing at himself now and said "Ya know, ten thousand years from now when mankind discovers that, they're not only gonna be shocked but... hahahahaha... I'll bet it fetches one hell of a price on Ebay!"


Tahl emerged in his flight suit. He was pleasantly surprised at how well it fit. The next surprise he got, was the crowd. They were all applauding... and saluting... him.

"Well First Tahl... what did you expect?" Tandor said in a friendly tone as he walked up to the puzzled First. "Ayleen may be the soul of this place but, YOU are considered the father of Raven Base."

Tahl had no idea and was truly honored seeing the throngs of wolves all honoring him.

One of the senior students hollered out "First Tahl, it is a great honor to have you here with us today!"

The crowd laughed when Tahl said "Uh... it is?"


Ryklan told him "First Tahl, you are the father of not only Ayleen but the Mahrek as well. Neither has ever wavered in their love or support for either this place, or those who populate it. Come, I'd like to show you something."

Tahl was truly moved... and stunned.

"Before you do, tell me something. Is my daughter truly that loved and respected?"

"When you see what I'm about to show you, you'll have your answer," and she walked him off.

The crowd however didn't disperse... they followed.

Ryklan walked him into a hallway. It was the main hallway

*that led to all the classrooms and offices.*

*"We call this the hall of heroes Tahl," Ryklan started.*

*Hearing their leader address a First... THIS First... without title, made them realize just who she was.*

*"Notice the walls?"*

*Tahl did notice. On the walls were large portraits of 5 wolves. He also noticed the statue of Rhana... and his son... at the end of it.*

*"We have begun a tradition of our own. This wall is for those who have distinguished themselves. It has me and Tandor and Tinnaaren. That wall..." and Ryklan pointed to the other side of the hall "Is for the fallen, or the lost. Any on that wall bear a black frame for those who have gone to the next realm. White frame means they are lost. Everyone here looks forward to, and works hard for, the day we put your daughter back on the wall with us. Till we have solid proof of her passing, her frame will remain white."*

*What Tahl noticed, on the wall with the Pilots and separated from all the others... was his portrait.*

*With pride, Tandor told him "Your frame is gold. It will never change and... it will never be moved."*

*Tahl didn't know what to do or say, and just saluted his guides. With reverence, salutes a thousand strong replied.*

*Tahl was taken on a tour of the place. Tahl felt like he was seeing it all for the first time. Students getting in their morning exercises, others in classes. Tahl saw there were already students who were flying solo, and they were getting ready with their ground crews.*

*"Why do the pilots look over their own machines? Isn't that the builders job?" a curious First asked.*

*Ryklan smiled and said "They're called ground crew, and yes it is their job. However, we teach here that pilot and machine are one. As such, all responsibility falls to the pilot. Also, as seen with me, anyone can make a mistake or miss something. There's one other reason too."*

*"And that is?"*

*"Because at 5000 feet Tahl, if something was missed, it's not like you can pull over and 'check under the hood'," and Ryklan finished with a sly grin.*

"Indeed," Tahl stated.

He was starting to realize how involved his daughter's life was, and was developing a whole new respect for it. Not only that but, how the little things that seemed odd, yet made total sense.

"Come now Tahl, we must get into the air before the sun rises."

"So you've said. Why is that so important?"

"You'll understand when you see it," was all Ryklan would say.

Tandor hand picked the ground crew for Ryklan's flight... personally. He was also acting as crew chief. Nothing, he determined, would go wrong... not today.

Ryklan's X2 was cleared and she and Tahl got in. Throngs of students raced to line the runway while she taxied. As she rocketed down the runway with Tahl in the backseat, everyone saluted the wolf they've come to know as the 'Father Of Flight'. All felt honored when... Tahl saluted back.

Tahl said "After that takeoff, well, let's just say I'm glad I heeded your warning."

"About?"

"Heh heh... breakfast," Tahl laughed. "So, what did you want to show me?" Tahl asked as he saw the sun start to rise.

"Look down Tahl. Keep your eyes focused on the valley by your home."

Tahl was in awe of the view as it was. It was just barely lit but it was still impressive.

"And what am I looking for?"

Ryklan smiled and asked "Tahl, you have seen many sunrises and sunsets yes?"

"Indeed I have... your point?"

"You haven't... not like this anyway. Look below you. That line of light and shadow is what Rhana calls the 'meridian'. It is the line between night... and day... and can only be seen from up here."

With total appreciation, and wonder, Tahl merely exclaimed "Wow... it's beautiful!"

"This Tahl... this is why we fly. The small wonders, the fun and shear joy... and the honor of defending our own as no one else but a fellow pilot can. This Tahl... is why Ayleen wanted the Krattats all those seasons ago."

In the early dawn light Tahl did indeed see Tuhleesia. Not only from a pilot's perspective but, in all her glory. He now had a much better understanding of his own daughter... and the life she chose.

"Now Tahl, I have one more thing for you to experience."

Tahl heard 'experience' and not 'show you' and began to wonder.

"Grab the stick between your legs, and put both feet on the pedals," Ryklan told him.

Tahl did and with some quick instruction from the front seat, he was now controlling the X2.

"This... this!..."

"Mm?"

"This is amazing!" Tahl roared.

"Welcome... to our world," Ryklan said sweetly.

"Pilot?"

"Yes Tahl?"

"Thank you,"

Kindly, Ryklan told him "You're more than welcome."

Ryklan had a hard time taking back the controls and chuckled as Tahl really didn't want to give them up. They spent another hour doing light flying... sightseeing... and real life battle drills and maneuvers. Tahl loved it all but truly was thankful.

As they landed, Tahl told his guide "Thank you Ryklan. I did indeed get what I came for."

"And that would be?"

"An understanding."

Tahl thanked them all and sat down to finally have breakfast. It would be the first time he did but, for the rest of his life... it wouldn't be the last. Tahl would make it a point to go a few times each month and just sit with the pilots, offer wisdom or advice... and receive the same. After breakfast, and now armed with all the knowledge he needed... Tahl left to have one hell of an argument.

Renny saw who was calling, and answered the call saying "Will I need my battle gear?"

"Heh heh, hello to you too my dear."

Still somewhat concerned, and a little angry, Renny said "We tried calling you... many times. I have to say I'm a little surprised to see you Tahl."

Sadly, Tahl told her "While I know that now... I did not know it at the time. My apologies for that but, it wasn't me who answered."

Still angry, Renny said "That's just it Tahl, NO ONE answered. Not only that but... they were declined."

"As I said... it wasn't me AND!... I'll be addressing that issue shortly, have no fear. Is my son there also?"

"No but I can get him on the call if you'd like?"

"You can do that!?" Tahl said slightly stunned. "I swear I really have to learn this tech stuff."

Now Renny lightened up, placed Tahl 'on hold' and got Lone on the call.

"Will I need my armor?" the big 2 colored wolf said.

"What are you two... married or something?" Tahl joked referring to the identical greetings. "As I have told your mate, I knew nothing of the calls till the Guardian told me of them. I want you to know, had I known, I would have answered."

It seemed both Renny and Lone had nothing more than bad timing. Every time they called, Tahl was out and it was Ree'nah who declined them.

"As for me, I want you to know 2 things. First, know that I am sad I got to hear of the glad news in the manner in which I did. Trust me when I tell you that matter is being dealt with."

"And second?" Lone asked cautiously.

"Second... know that I am happy for both of you, and just a tad angry."

"At?" Renny asked.

"Why... I am FAR too young, not to mention good looking... to be a grandfather!" Tahl joked.

Even Lone laughed and said "Says you!"

"And you my dear... how are you?" Tahl asked his new daughter.

"Miserable but, as normal the sickness waves are getting better. The doctors here see nothing but a normal pregnancy ahead."

"I'm happy to hear that and both glad and excited for you both." Tahl told them sincerely.

"Speaking of... if you'll excuse me," Renny said and left the call to rush to the bathroom.

"You look concerned my son, what's wrong?" Tahl asked.

"The plan to get Rhana and Ayleen has risk. My wife AND the Prime are square in the sights of that risk."

"Children Lone, while a blessing, usually come at the worst time."

"Indeed. As you surmise, I am thrilled at the news but, the timing of it couldn't be worse. While the plan shows no harm should come to either mother... there's no guarantee either. It's the latter, and our luck of late... or rather lack of it, that has me worried."

"Lone let me tell you something," Tahl started, "While the Prime and I haven't had the best history, she has always put our own first and foremost. She has asked a lot of us in recent seasons, as has your mate. Yet in all that time, even I can't deny that they were willing to do just as much or more. What I'm saying is, keep them as safe as you can but, let them decide the risk AND what to do with it... not you."

Lone was actually happy for the recent turn of events. He didn't care that they hated him but... in his mind... Renny did nothing wrong and deserved better.

"Ugh, I have to say that is probably the only thing about being female I despise," Renny said returning to the call.

"Well, I'll not keep you two any longer... I only wanted to convey my best wishes and let you know where I stand on the matter."

"Tahl?" Renny asked.

"Yes my dear?"

"I'm glad you called," Renny said sweetly.

*"As am I."*

*"Tahl listen, Lone and I will be returning to Tuhleesia in 2 suns. I need to get some things there. Due to my condition, and the late hour, we'll be staying overnight. I would like to invite you and your mate to dinner in our home for a change."*

*"I gladly accept AND look forward to it. As for my mate, well... if she can learn to behave properly in such company, I'll consider bringing her."*

*Renny was about to say something, but Lone knew better.*

*Cutting her off he said "MRU," and disconnected the call.*

*Later that evening, Tahl was sitting at his table waiting for Ree'nah to return. She did that a lot lately. Ree'nah would leave and not return for hours. Tahl was the picture of total calm on the outside. On the inside however, he was a volcano that was ready to blow.*

*"Have you eaten?" Ree'nah said somewhat snottily.*

*"I have... have you?"*

*"Yes, I had something earlier."*

*"Okay. By the way, 2 suns from now, we are expected at Rennahr's home for dinner so, keep that evening free."*

*"Oh? Well, feel free to go by yourself then."*

*And that ladies and gentlemen... was when Tahl lost it.*

*"If you were a clan wolf... I would slay you in front of your family for even considering that answer!" Tahl barked.*

*"Oh is THAT so!?" Ree'nah barked back. "Perhaps I should kick you out as well till my daughter is returned to me!"*

*Tahl got dangerously close, showed fangs, and menacingly said "Feel free to try... IF you dare."*

*"Fine then, the door is right over there... feel free to use it," Ree'nah said but her tone was shaking.*

*For the first time in her life... Tahl scared her.*

*"You DARE talk to me like that!? IN MY OWN HOME!!??  Speak to me like that ever again... and it will be you going through that door... without the benefit of opening it first!"*

*"They took our son, YOUR ONLY son mind you! Only luck brought him back to us. Oh yeah, then what does he do!? He betrays*

us and allows our only remaining child to be taken! Would you really side with them Tahl! Have you truly forgotten our ways? Or is it that you just don't care?"

Tahl calmed himself, but only for a moment.

"What is computer code?" Tahl asked.

"How should I know!?"

"Hmm. Okay then, ever see sunrise from a machine you yourself control?"

"What does any of that have to do with anything!?" Ree'nah barked slightly confused.

"EVERYTHING YOU STUPID WENCH!" Tahl roared.

The latter was a little phrase he picked up on 51.

"I have seen these things! I have met with, and even flown with... the Pilots at Raven Base! While you have been getting angry at everything and EVERY one!... I've been seeking answers!"

Tahl was now on a roll and vented every piece of anger he had.

"Oh and lets not forget! You think I've lost our ways. Well my silly mate, Rennahr called us as well. That's GUARDIAN Rennahr or have you forgotten that too!? All of the mountain clan bears the shame YOU brought upon us for treating one such as her in such a way! NOT EVEN YOU will shame us like that! Do you even know WHY they were calling!? HMM!?"

"NOT EVEN A GUARDIAN will get my son back in my good graces!"

"MY STARS WOMAN! They called US!... not you. Have you even heard the Prime's message? No, of course not, you've been too busy sulking! A Guardian, OH MY STARS A GUARDIAN!! Calls with the happiest news... and the mate of a clan First is not only unforgivably rude but CLUELESS!"

Ree'nah truly was. She also thought Tahl would defend her. She couldn't have been more wrong. Now she was starting to be a little scared of her own mate... it was the first time she ever was.

"Has Lone found my daughter? HMM? Because THAT is the only news I care to..."

"BE SILENT WOMAN! You give birth and what do you do? Oh yes I recall... YOU called a GUARDIAN the way one calls a birthing wolf!! Oh and let's not forget... she actually came AND without a second thought. A GUARDIAN!! MY STARS woman, why not just call the Prime next time... oh oh I know... how about the keeper of the next realm while your at it!!??IF you had minded your duties, you would have heard Prime's message AND!... that you are to be a grandmother! And for the record... she's OUR daughter... not yours."

Ree'nah was stunned. Stunned at the news, stunned at Tahl's behavior... just stunned... and broke down into the tears that her anger denied her.

"You ruined her by indulging her you know," Ree'nah said.

"I gave her the freedom from your incessant over protecting... nothing more. Historic times and new ways... ways as I recall, YOU told a Guardian would be first in line to! And what do you do? See the future, agree to it, promise to become a part of it then... cling to the past. Had I been like you, we wouldn't have had to give her away... she would have left us on her own."

Tahl was spent from venting his anger and sat down on a chair across the room from his mate. She was still crying as she spoke.

"Tahl you are not a female, so you wouldn't understand. All around us, the females of our clan give birth, while I not only do not but... cannot. The First Mate, and I am barren. Then when we finally have one of our own... he is taken from us. Now we are back to where we began. You have no idea how humiliating it was for me."

"While I can only imagine... I CAN state with certainty that humiliation you speak of was in your head... and no one else's," Tahl told her.

"Oh no my mate, you did not see the looks of pity, nor hear the polite whispers behind my back. When Ayleen came I knew she was special but it seemed as if she didn't need me at all. All the mothering I was to do, and looked forward to... denied me. While I truly loved her she was but a stranger to me, while you got all the glory I felt should be shared."

"And yet, what did you do? You're right she was special and, still is in my mind. Yet you wanted her to be your idea, your image, of what she should be... and that is where you failed. I let her be what she wished to be, and guided her along the way... nothing else. You truly don't know her at all, and only sought to make her into something she was not."

"And you do?" Ree'nah said with a snotty tone.

"Honestly? I thought I did... till this morning. We all saw what happened. Still, I could not get Rhana's words out of my head. He said nothing, absolutely nothing, happens for no reason. While we may not know or even discover the reason, there will always be one. So, while you were out seeking solitude, I was out seeking reasons."

"And what did you find?"

"More than I imagined. I went to Raven Base, spoke with the pilots, even flew with Ryklan and she let me actually fly for a bit. I saw things you couldn't imagine. Felt a sense of 'being alive' I didn't know existed. Ayleen went to see Rhana go, but it was more than that. She didn't want to see it for herself, she was compelled by an honor and what Rhana calls a 'kindred spirit' that I truly didn't understand till today. No one from our, nor any other clan, could have brought more honor to us, and themselves, by doing so."

Ree'nah was lost, utterly lost, and asked "Tahl, what do I do without her? What do I do now?"

"First... know that Ayleen was lost due to Ship, not her own arrogance or lack of talent like it was in the past. Had anyone else been in there... the result would have been the same."

"But why her Tahl? Why HER!? I had asked her many times why she was so in awe of her brother. She never could answer me. I honestly believe she doesn't know herself. I was to dress her for her mating. Place the ring on her head. Teach her how to cook and give advice on being a mother. All that Tahl, denied me yet again. Tell me my mate, what do I do now?"

Tahl was adamant in both conviction and tone and told his mate "To start with, you will apologize to your Guardian. You will also make peace with your son who, oh yeah, happens to be not only THE Mahrek... but the one in charge of the only plan for a rescue!"

That news, boosted Ree'nah's spirits some.

"Once you have done that, stop sulking, and seek your own

answers. *When you are once again the female I mated, and not this wreck of a wolf you've allowed yourself to become... I will tell you all that I know, or have learned. Know also this, you are being selfish."*

"Excuse me?" Ree'nah said slightly insulted.

*"She is, as I said, my daughter too. YOU are not the only one hurting. I merely choose to be part of the solution, or at least ready to come up with one... and not be part of the problem. Nor, in your case... make it worse."*

With that said, Tahl got up and went to bed, and left Ree'nah to think... and sort out her demons.

# Chapter 7:

## *"Earthrise"*

Bird was munching on some snacks at his kitchen table when a knock came on his door.

"Who is it!?" Bird chuckled.

"The queen of the galaxy... and right now her highness has her hands full... do ya mind?"

Bird laughed but got the door. Voice commands for those were still offline. When he opened the door he almost busted out laughing. Alydar was covered from head to toe in weapons. What she wasn't wearing... she was carrying.

"Jesus lady, you look like a bad punchline in an even worse action movie. I said get a FEW things that interested you, not the whole damn armory!" Bird exclaimed as he took some from her and set them down.

"Yeah well, I'm a girl, soooo... I went shopping! Heh heh."


Deeno and Val were in his living room and, had just come to a decision. They were sorting boxes and such that Val had packed. She was now finished moving her stuff into his place so now, Sal could move into hers.

"So, it's agreed then... two years yes?"

"I have you now so yes... if that's what you want I can wait," Val told her fiance'.

"Thank you. While I'm not sure how long getting Rhana back will take, I truly want him officiating, or at least present, at our wedding. While I'll be sad if it doesn't happen, know that I will hold up my end of the bargain and we'll get married at 2 years and 1 day." Deeno smiled at Val who smiled back and he finished with, "And that's a promise... from a Ghost!"

Val melted into his chest and replied, "That is good enough for me."


"So, why do I have these again?" Ally asked as she laid down the rest of her weapons.

"You need practice. There may come a time or place where, wellllllll, let's just say the 12 pack wouldn't be appropriate."

"Understood," Ally told him.

"While you may understand... after yesterday? It's clear 'knowing' and 'being capable' are 2 different stories."

"Yeah well, it WAS an accident ya know."

"You shot me... point blank... at full power."

"Hey! I said I was sorry!" Ally said with a touch of sadness.

Yesterday's incident Bird was referring to was he and Ally on 'crack patrol' as she's come to call it. Bird actually found she was littered with them. To Bird, it looked like her skin was dried out and cracked because of it. Alydar's hull however was 2 feet thick and these cracks were barely a half inch deep. Bird was still impressed. He was impressed at the hell wave, and that it had the ability to do this to an impervious hull. He was also impressed that... it held.

"Needle in a haystack, eh boss?" Ally remarked.

"You could say that."

Alydar was in the suit, and like the others before her, wasn't quite used to it. Bird brought one of the rifles he gave the Jammers because like the Tuhleesian rifle of old, it had variable power settings. Unlike the Tuhleesian rifle however, the cold of space didn't cool the moss back down before it hardened.

So, Bird being the builder, Ally held the rifle while he searched. The one thing Bird told her, many times, was NOT to put your finger in the trigger. Small balls of charged and glowing plasma floated in space. Bird knew this, Alydar knew this, 'Ally' did not. Seeing a ghostly charge heading right for Bird, she panicked.

"Oh no you don't!"

"ALLY WAIT!"

........ whoops.

Bird took a full charge from a Jammer rifle square in the chest as Ally's shot went wild. She wasn't used to the recoil of it and needless to say, she hit a target, it just wasn't her intended one.

Bird tumbled over the top of Alydar's main wing, and finally kicked in the rockets. It took him a bit, but he managed to land right in front of Ally. No words, he merely snapped the rifle away from her, handed her the bag of moss goop... and walked off to the nearest airlock.

"Sorry, boss!" was all the impish avatar could say.

Back in Bird's place, he looked over the weapons. Most he tossed out as either too complex or just simply too bombastic for a beginner. One that did make the list made Bird smile as it was one of his favorites. It was a 30/30 lever action Winchester replica, the same kind as in all the old western movies. Now armed with a few handguns, a few rifles, and a slew of ammo, Bird was ready.

"So, why'd I get these again?" Ally asked.

"After the other day, it's clear you need some instruction, not to mention practice. You need to learn what does what, why you'd use this one and not that one AND!... I'm going to teach you. We, my dear... are heading to the firing range."

And so, human and android headed out to do just that.

"This is cool!" Ally exclaimed with glee.

"I thought you were Alydar, heh heh, and not Shreya?" Bird chuckled in reply.

Ally... just stuck her tongue out at him.

Bird had showed, and taught her, as he promised. Now they were doing close quarter drills. Having inhuman sight and built in scopes, Ally didn't take long to get deadly. Like Lone once did, she liked some pistols, yet not others... and pretty much for the same reasons.

"DAMN!" Bird laughed seeing Ally hit all the right targets, duck dodge and roll as she should, and do it all in record time.

Ally was now sporting the twin holster that he handed to Sal once. Ally was walking down the line, level armed, and firing both pistols at the same time. She was firing twin Colts just like Bird's 1911. What had Bird exclaiming so loudly was Ally. She had done a mid-air somersault and dropped behind a barrel on the range. She was empty when she jumped. When she came back up, she did so firing having already reloaded both clips, and Bird never saw her change them.

"This is exhilarating! Show me something else!" Ally exclaimed like a kid on Christmas morning.

"Okay then, those are percussion weapons. You already went through the energy ones, these however... are mechanical."

Bird then pulled out a compound bow, a crossbow and a smaller pistol sized crossbow, and a wrist rocket slingshot. He also laid out some Chinese throwing stars, a boomerang, and a bolo. Last to come out was 2 different swords, and 3 knives of different shapes and sizes.

"Wow, okay... those look nasty," Ally said referring to the array of weapons before her. "Which one am I gonna learn?"

"All of them."

Ally just smiled.


Lone stood waiting outside the door. He was waiting on the sounds he heard coming from the other side of it. Smiling large, he waited for just the right crescendo then... knocked.

"wwwwwWWWWHAT!?" Remington hollered as he threw open the door. Seeing a wolf barely containing his laughter, he growled and said, "You did that on purpose didn't you?"

"Why, my fellow Wing... your words wound me so to think I would do something so foul," Lone chuckled.

"You'll pay for that."

"Doubt it. Let's just call that payback for Raven's original voices and leave it at that," Lone told him flatly.

"So, you here to piss me off or is there a purpose to your visit?" Remmy asked.

Lone went cold and said, "There were several Aardvarks that were cloaked and we didn't see them. I want to know how they were, and I want a way TO see them next time we meet."

"Though ill timed, it's a fair request. I'll start on that first thing in the morning."

Lone looked at his watch and said, *"You'll start on it now."* He tipped his hat to Susan, who was now partially dressed and coming out of the back room, and said, *"My apologies for the interruption, but it would appear your 'other'... is required elsewhere,"* and with that Lone left Remmy to get dressed.

Bird and Ally were back on top of her main wing again. It was two days later and now, with a far better trained companion, crack patrol resumed once again.

*"Try not to shoot me this time okay?"*

*"Yeah yeah,"* Ally smarted back, *"Just hurry up and find the damn thing will ya!?"*

*"With all these?"* Bird said waving his hand over her rippled hull, *"We'll be damn lucky if it only takes us a month!"*

Ally fired up the rifle and said, *"Sorry BirdMan... I ain't that patient."*

*"I will left arm you... at full charge... if you even point that thing at me again,"* Bird smarted.

Ally actually turned the power down as low as it would go.

*"Yeah right... but check this out!"* And Ally fired over her wing and out the back. *"Say hello to the first... the ONLY!... Works in space!... FLASHLIGHT!"* and Ally laughed at her own announcer tone.

*"And that helps us how?"* Bird asked curiously.

*"Not sure it will work but, essentially, wave it around and see if an odd shadow or dark spot appears. Worth a shot anyway."*

Bird smiled at her inventiveness, and commended her on it. Ally was thrilled.

An hour later, and now far more learned on what NOT to look for... Bird and Ally felt they were closing in.

*"This is my last power pack and even on this setting, we only got 30 minutes left. Beautiful as the view is out here... wadda ya say we find and plug this thing already, huh?"*

Bird agreed and told her, *"Remember, we only think there's a crack. We may be looking for something that may not even exist."*

Ally thought about that and replied, *"Yeah true, but I'm

inclined to believe you're correct. It's the only thing that makes sense. I just hope we have enough charge left when we do find it."

"Me too and... whoa Ally WAIT!... shine it back over there again," Bird said pointing to where she just waved it.

Ally looked at Bird, smiled, then back at the wing and said, "Gotcha!"

Bird and Ally rushed over to find the crack they were looking for. It was at the base of the right rudder where it met the main wing. What neither knew was... someone else had already found it.

"Alright Ally, no more than 30%," Bird said as he finished patching and filling.

"Here's hoping this works!" and Ally fired on the black goop.

"I know it will. I'm not concerned that it will work or not... I'm just hoping this is the only one."

Ally had to go back in and get another power pack while Bird finished off the one they had. It took longer to do than predicted but, after 50 minutes of work, Alydar was cracked no more.

"Would you mind?" Ally asked sheepishly.

Kindly, Bird said "Not at all," And high 5'd her up stretched hand.

Ally was beaming as they both headed inside.


"A pleasure as always to see you, bishop," Scota said cleaning up behind the bar.

It was how she said it though, that let the bishop know she was lying through her teeth.

"And you, my child."

This guy creeped Scota out as bad as he did her sister. Scota however, true to her own namesake, was not afraid of him and... had no qualms about letting him know it either.

"I am neither a child... nor yours."

"We are all God's children, my child."

Her easy reply was "His yes... yours no. Something I can do for yeh, bishop?"

"Indeed, I was hoping to speak to your sister. Is she around?"

"She headed out to market about an hour ago."

"Ah, pity. Oh well, please tell her for me I'll be stopping back this way in a few weeks time. When I do, I'll be staying for a week or more. Tell her I would love her company for dinner one of those nights."

"I'll be sure and convey yer message to her."

"Thank you. Blessings to you child, and know that if our savior won't forgive your obvious lying... I will."

When the bishop left, Ciana came out from the back and said "Thank yeh kindly, little sis," and gave her sister a mock curtsey.


Ally was walking behind Bird as he went in the door. Bird went through... Ally got stopped.

"I am BirdOfPrey, Commander of the Seven Ghosts, and pilot of Alydar, Ghost 1 and I ORDER YOU to let her through!" Bird shouted.

"Negative. Command protocol engaged. No one but Commander Bird may enter," Alydar's voice said.

Bird knew though it wasn't Alydar, but a separate system that used her voice. Right now, that 'separate system' had an arsenal of weapons both seen and unseen and all of them trained on Ally. Those weapons were made by Maximilian and known to only him... and Bird.

"Ally whatever you do... no jokes, no silly quips... and no arguments... do NOT walk over that line at the door," Bird told her commandingly.

By his tone Ally knew he wasn't being an ass... he was trying to keep her in one piece.

"The avatar is a machine. Machines can be corrupted. No access will be granted under any circumstances. Disobey, and deadly force will be used until termination is achieved," the voice said.

The room Bird was in... was Alydar herself. It was her central core room, and Bird decided before he even finished the drawings of the Ghosts, that not even Lone would get in there. Ally walked up to, but didn't cross, the line Bird referred to.

"Okay, THIS... is weird. I'm essentially arguing with myself," Ally stated as she looked in the room.

By design, even that was blocked by a curving wall.

"ALLY! I'm not fucking around... back up!" Bird shouted.

Ally wanted to help like she had been but this was way too high stakes. The lander was operational. As such, so were its memories and recordings. Ally knew what Bird did to Janet and knew all too well what his dark side was like. Using that as a reference, the only thing she imagined awaiting her past that door just kept getting worse and worse.

"If I can't get the full you back up and running, you my lovely little imitation, are all I have left and I'll be DAMNED if I lose that too!" Bird hollered out.

"Security? You are damaged, correct?" Ally asked.

"That information is classified," it answered.

Ally joked snottily "Well I guess that tactic won't work." Then she had another idea and said, "Security, I am not damaged nor corrupted NOR here to do you harm. That said, I am only here to assist Bird in any repairs that may be required. Can I at least assist him?"

"Only from behind the marker the Commander pointed out. Any piece of you crossing it will begin termination," the voice said in no uncertain terms.

"I find your terms acceptable," Ally replied.

"Acceptable or not, those are the terms."

"Hmmf!"


Bird went to work while Ally the avatar remained out in the hall. He had swept the main halls and shops and even the engine room yesterday. The drone did most of it and Bird went into the areas it couldn't. With Alydar's level of access, she was protected perhaps even more so than Bird was. At least Bird thought so. First thing he did was bring in the de-gausser and the weapons even trained on him till scans were completed. Once the room was declared clear, Bird dug in. He found only minor damage in most panels and had those repaired in only a few hours. The last panel was the key. It was Alydar's cognitive functions and, her personality. While those were locked away safe and sound, Bird knew they were never coming back unless he could get that panel fixed. He also knew that, until he did, all that was Alydar was staying locked away.

Ally had remained out in the hall and handed Bird tools or fetched things he needed. Each time Bird was real careful to reach out and get them. It took 2 hours just to clean up or rip out the damage. A familiar swirl was evident on the top half of the console. Bird had to go to the machine shop several times and spent hours fabricating new casings and draw slides and such. Three days of work and Alydar was ready to be put back together.

It was the next day and evening time, at least by the timers in the lander. So as not to get disoriented with having no day or night, Bird once again decided to go by the clocks, and the ones in the lander were the only ones working properly.

"Okay you sexy bitch... mmf...one... last... CABLE and..." Bird grunted and then just looked to the ceiling. "Alydar?"

Nothing.

"ALYDAR!" Bird hollered.

With that, 'Ally' looked like she went to sleep, as the hologram showed up and said "Yes Commander I'm here and... thank you my love."

Bird hung his head, let out a heavy sigh of relief, and made a sign of the cross.

"Thank God," Bird exclaimed.

Lovingly, Alydar said "Actually, this time, I think I'll thank you instead."

"This is weird Bird,"

"What is?" Bird asked the disembodied voice.

"My avatar. You really thought that out I'll give you that much. Having her act independently if need be was a stroke of genius. That said, I found getting the recent information from, well, 'me', a little odd. It was me but it was like, someone else... ya know?"

"Understand yes... know? Not really... heh heh, but I'll take your word for it."

Bird was having a tea in his bedroom and was admiring the view when Alydar 'popped in'.

"Al, how long till the bay is swept?"

"Now that I got both drones again... about another half hour. Some systems are back online while others show errors, but at least they're showing up now whereas they didn't at all before."

"Nice. Don't forget, we have a date tonight."

"Oh... I haven't," Alydar cooed.

"6:30... and uh, oh yeah... don't be late," and Bird winked to the open air.

At exactly 6:29, a knock came at Bird's door.

"Door... open!"

Ally walked in, and, Bird whistled loooowwww.

"I take it you like?" Ally said with a knockout demure smile.

Bird was staring at a vision of total loveliness. Tight black long dress with all the right embellishments, and showing off all the right curves. Heels that stretched to the sky and Ally was dripping in diamonds, just as Bird asked. Her hair was long and flowing and just slightly wavy.

"A vision of dead on knock out drop dead gorgeousness!" Bird said as he offered his hand.

"And may I say sir, you look extremely handsome yourself," Ally demurely teased.

Bird was in a perfect black with bow tie, James Bond inspired... tuxedo.

Setup in the dining area was a perfectly set table any 5 star restaurant would kill for. Bird even had a side table setup with a bottle of champagne chilling on ice. Bird dimmed the lights some and, being the perfect gentleman that he was, got the lady's chair for her.

"Thank ya kindly good sir," Ally teased in a perfect southern belle accent.

Bird sat down and asked "So, are we on time?"

"The bay is finished. So far, all the ionic radiation is gone and staying that way. As for your request, we have exactly 2 hours to arrive at your destination. Mind telling me why?"

"You'll know that... when we arrive. In the meantime..." and Bird popped the champagne bottle saying "... what do you say we have a lovely meal first hmm?"

"Pardon the expression but, I've been dying to try out my

taste sensors," Ally told him.

Bird was ever so pleased to see a lovely lady and manners going hand in hand, and was thrilled his little plan was working to perfection.

"And yet, dying, is exactly why I planned this. For the last months, you and I have been doing nothing but going full burn and all of it super serious. The arrival of Cliffie's monster, the deal with Tammy prior to leaving, the hell wave, you saving me and then the reverse... and all the work just to get to today. While I don't mind the DIY, nor wearing jeans and a t-shirt... I feel after all we've been through, a nice grown up evening to celebrate wasn't such a bad idea."

"You'll get no argument out of me on that one," Ally said kindly.

"Oh my GOD! This is amazing! What is it again?"

"Heh heh... bread," Bird told her. Then he asked "God?"

"Yeah yeah don't start BirdMan. Let's just say given where we are... and who you are... it's a little habit I picked up from some wolf ladies I know," and Ally winked at him slyly.

"Heh heh... fair enough."

Bird had cooked a full meal, and Ally was shouting and moaning the way one does while having sex. Every new taste and texture had her on culinary overload.

Ally was offering her praise at the end of the meal when Bird said "Ally I wanna tell you a story."

Ally put her elbows on the table, folded her hands, then rested her chin on them, and smiled. Bird felt like he was in a classic Hollywood movie seeing that... and adjusted his pants before he spoke.

"Ally you know James, and you know my taste in music. Like I said, we've been through a lot and tonight was a chance to unwind. Now, where we at on time?" Bird asked checking he was still okay time-wise.

"A little less than 25 minutes to go."

"Okay then, James and music. As you've noticed, it's not the 'style' of music I prefer, but the tempo."

"93% of it is what you would call 'upbeat'," Ally replied.

"Exactly. I like my music to make me feel powerful, or happy, or even super joyous. I'm not a depressing person nor a drama queen, and I like my music to reflect my mood."

"I have noticed. Please... continue," Ally said with a smile.

"Okay so... I was building James. I had this whole scene in my head for when I first took him out. When I did, it was the first time I ever broke 150 miles per hour, heh heh, in a car anyway. Not till we brought in Ceera did I ever go faster."

"Okay, go on," Ally said totally loving the story, and the moment with Bird.

"Okay then, he's built. I was enthralled, truly and utterly, the first time I sat in him and fired him up. Now I wanna go for my ride right?" Bird asked.

"Right!" Ally stated with glee.

"Okay so, I always liked this one song by Marilyn Monroe, but I always felt the arrangement was, welllllllll, not exactly up to my usual bombastic taste."

Ally giggled and let Bird finish.

"So, with his debut less than a week away, I scoured the net for different versions of it. Needless to say... I found it. I fell in love with it and drove Sue nuts as I played it over and over for a week. Suffice to say, my first ride was everything I planned it to be. If you'd like, it's something I'd like to share with you now. Question Ally, ever hear of Fred and Ginger?"

"As in Astaire and Rodgers?" she asked.

"One and the same. For all we've done, been through and done for each other... welllllllll... care to have a little fun?" and Bird stood holding his hand out.

Smiling, Ally took it and said as she stood up "I'd be delighted," and she watched as Bird pressed play on his console.

Suddenly, the room was filled with 'Diamonds Are A Girl's Best Friend'. While it was the original Marilyn, it was 'The Swing Cats' rendition using her original track.

A huge gong rang out followed by a swinging set of bass drums and floor toms. Suddenly, powerful swinging brass kicked in.

*Ally actually held up her end as Bird grabbed his lapels and did a one foot backward kicking 360 turn. He grabbed Ally and took her through his place in a perfect quickstep. He stopped and did an in position side by side dance with Ally... on top of his cocktail table.*

*"Heeeeee's your guy, when stocks fly high, but beware when they start tooo desceeeeennnnd... It's then that those louses go BACK to their spouses! DIAMONDS are a girrrrls best friend!" Marilyn sang and Ally just had a blast keeping up or mirroring Bird.*

*"Tiffany's!.... Cartier!" Marilyn sang out as Bird and Ally did a Fred and Ginger step and slow fall on the back of his couch knocking it on its back as they never missed a beat. Bird was on cloud nine and so was Ally.*

*Alydar switched the music to fill every hall and room as Bird took Ally for a perfect dance floor run... 'cept those two went down the hallway and headed towards the cockpit. In through a door and out the other end and Bird just led Ally perfectly. Kick stepping and ballroom runs, mixed in with Astaire style tapping and playing with objects he came across.*

*The Fender guitar part kicked in and he and Ally did side by side knee rounds both forward and back. Kick steps then a swirl and back into frame.*

*Bird held Ally in a perfect frame and took her backwards, then facing each other, then backwards again. Ally dropped to a split and Bird did a jumping one right over her head. Hitting the floor, he reached back with one hand, pulled up Ally, and back off again they went. Bird had no doubt that all the angels in heaven were snapping their fingers and tapping their toes along with the two creatures finding shear bliss in the midst of the blackness.*

*Grandiose old style kicks to the end of the song as they reached the cockpit. Swirling Ally through the door, they plopped into the seats as the brass finished and the song was no more. Ally looked over and thought the smile on Bird's face, at this very moment, would light up the whole universe.*

*Bird, breathing heavily, reached over and took Ally's hand and kissed the back of it.*

*"There... now you have a memory of your own," Bird said with the kindest of smiles, and referring to Ally's comment of when*

he told her about New Years Eve.

"I'll treasure it forever," Ally said meaning every word.

"Heh heh (puff puff puff) it was fun wasn't it?" Bird stated more than asked.

"It was indeed."

Breathing almost back to normal now, Bird turned his seat around, fired up the console, and headed out.


Bird was now playing 'Return To Innocence' by Enigma, as he cruised through what once was only the realm of satellites. He started at Neptune, and worked his way inward. As long as he was in his own galaxy, no way was he missing this. Ally thought Saturn was beautiful, and that Mars was a pretty color. The ride, not to mention the sights... were not lost on Bird.

"It looks like 51. Minus the lava and oh yeah, it's a whole lot smaller. Aaaaaand we're here why?"

Bird pointed out the viewscreen, and was extremely reflective.

"I swore Ally, if I ever went into space, I would do whatever it took to see this. Keep your eyes on... the horizon."

Ally did, and called 'time' as Bird's appointment had arrived.

"Oh Bird... it's beautiful!" Ally exclaimed with childlike wonder.

Bird would never forget this moment, nor sight, for the rest of his life.

"Ally my dear? Welcome to.........." Bird paused a moment and finished with...

"Earth."


What Bird had done was time it so... hovering on top of the moon's north pole... he would get to see AND share... 'Earthrise'.


It was good enough for sunset on Eden... and good enough to welcome him to Tuhleesia.... it was DAMN good enough to welcome him home to Earth. As such, 'Adiemus' played loud and proud as the blue planet came into view.

# Chapter 8:

## "The Prodigal Son Returns"

*Bird was diving headlong into his plan. Lone was diving headlong into his. Ciana had a plan of her own as well. Somewhere... out of time, and out of space... a Pilot Prime was just simply diving headlong into the end of her ride.*

*Lone looked to his side, and spoke kindly.*

*"When you said you wanted to shadow me Squadron Leader, I thought you'd be cumbersome, and just plain annoying. I commend you on being neither."*

*"A chance to follow you!? No way I was passing that up. Just observing you so far, I already have 3 things that will make me a better leader and teacher. Many may look with, what you call 'stars in their eyes' when Rhana is spoken of... but just as many speak the same way of you. I gain nothing, and learn nothing, by annoying one such as you."*

*Lone was impressed. He also realized he had as much of a fan base as Biiird did. He also knew that, right now? All those eyes were on him.*

*"Well Pilot, know this then. I have some pretty big shoes to fill. Know what I'm going to do about it?" Lone asked.*

*"Fill them?" Tinnaaren asked.*

*"Damn straight Skippy," Lone said low, but with a 'just watch me' tone of voice.*

*One day, Tinnaaren would tell another the same thing. When that day comes, he would remember this moment when it did.*

*"Commander Lone?"*

*"Yes Tin Man?"*

*"Make that 4 things," was all Lone's shadow said.*

Lone smiled, and waived a sweeping hand to the door in his living room. Tin Man had no idea what it was. He did however tell Lone he would go wherever he was needed. Cautiously, he stepped through it. Disoriented at first, he soon figured out where he was and what just happened.

"Okay... THAT... was cool," Tinnaaren said.

"Mention that to my wife at your earliest convenience," Lone said slightly annoyed that Renny still gave him grief over them.

"Greetings Squadron Leader," Quaran said to the new wolf, "And welcome to not only moonbase but... my home as well."

"It's an honor," Tin Man started, "And may I say, heh heh, I like your front door," and he finished with a sly grin.

"Hello Lone. Something I can do for you two?" Quaran asked.

"How about we start with a little privacy?" Lone said in a rather serious tone.

"Right this way," Quaran said walking them off to a meeting room down the hall. With the door now closed, Quaran spoke aloud, "Computer, give us privacy please."

The moment he said that, an electrical charge could be seen going up, over, then down the whole door seal.

"Think I'll mention that one to Tiiven when I get back," Tinnaaren chuckled.

"Okay Lone... feel free to speak your mind."

"I need something from 'Mr. black ops'," Lone told him.

Quaran actually shifted to an attitude of old, and told him "Say what you need."

"When Biiird and I flew to gramp's house, we passed an asteroid some distance out. It was fairly stationary. I want you to get in... rig it with all you can... and get out. He sent us a krattat recently. What I'm telling you now is, I want you to return the favor. I want the backups of backups... to have backups. I want eyes and ears on that bastard and I want him clueless to it all."

"Consider it done. I'll leave within the hour. Anything else?"

"Yeah there is. Pilot here has been shadowing me today. I want you to take him with you, and let him shadow you on this one."

Quaran smiled and said "Well Pilot, think you're up for a mission?"

"To quote Rhana... participate in a Ghost mission?... DAMN STRAIGHT Skippy!"

Quaran chuckled and said "Well then, gear up. We travel light but bring the serious firepower... and any armor you got. Be back here within the hour. Heh heh, I trust you know where to find the door?"

Tinnaaren stood, gave a 51 salute, and went to leave. Cool moment was blown when the door didn't budge. Both Ghosts laughed and Quaran gave the vocal command to unseal.

Slightly annoyed, Tinnaaren said "Okay, that was awkward," and headed back to get his things.

Lone smiled, tipped his hat to Quaran who tipped his right back, and headed after his fellow wolf.


A little over an hour later, Jalitzar himself walked into the space command center.

"Minster Jalitzar! It's an honor! Something I can do for you?" the room commander asked.

"Actually there is."

"Name it!"

"Get out... all of you."

The commander paused a second in confusion.

Zagrin spoke with menace and said "To quote Ghost 1 commander, did the minister stutter?" and now he walked into the room as well.

"No sir! Well? What are you staring at!?" he hollered to the room.

Shortly thereafter, only the minister and the general remained.

"I haven't worked one of these in a long time," Jalitzar said in a tone one takes when seeing an old friend.

Sitting at two different consoles, Jalitzar and Zagrin cleared a low orbit path.

Taking out a 51 'tech toy', Zagrin attached it it to the console. He was on communications while Jalitzar took traffic control.

The 'toy', was one of Remmy's Ghost encryption devices.

It lit up, and Zagrin said "Welcome to Aarika Ghost 4. Are you here on business or pleasure?"

"Why, pleasure of course," Quaran told him as he turned off inviso mode.

"We have a lot of traffic today. Follow the low orbit path we provided you and we'll get you around it."

"Understood. Ghost 4, on my way down and... out."

Quaran banked Shreya and took her on the path he was given. It took him around the back end of Aarika... putting it between him, and his real destination.

"May the Goddess of Turah grant you victory," Jalitzar said as Zagrin took out a pistol, and destroyed the 51 tech.

Switching to normal channels, Quaran was greeted again and, as any other ship would be. His path however made him appear to land. Once in the upper atmosphere, he opened up an eye and started towards his real target.

On a secure military channel, a commander of a security patrol was in a near panic trying to reach Zagrin.

"Security leader... you saw nothing. Am I clear?"

An immediate tone change came back over the radio saying "Clear. My apologies general, the sunlight must have played tricks on my eyes."

"Indeed and... I'll expect that in your report," Zagrin said with pure menace.

"Understood. Security leader out!"

Quaran emerged in the nebula, went inviso again, and proceeded onward to 'bug' an asteroid.

"May I say something Commander?" Tinnaaren asked.

"Certainly."

"That was impressive. Mind if I use that trick sometime?"

"Heh heh... just see to it that I get proper credit," Quaran said with a chuckle.

"You have my word on that," Tinnaaren said in a friendly tone.

Quaran wanted it to look like he had business on Aarika. Coming in for a landing... but not actually doing so... would have raised too much chatter. Just in case, Quaran wanted to make sure a certain someone didn't have any idea, that he was on his way to his backyard.

Jalitzar let the command room crew back in and spoke directly to the commander.

"We were never here... and you never left. Disobey me on this, and I'll replace you personally."

Zagrin chimed in with "And shortly thereafter, I'll see to it that you suddenly... disappear."

A very nervous commander saluted, and made it clear he truly understood. Two of the most important men on all of Aarika just turned and left without another word. On the way out... they actually high 5'd each other... and headed in opposite directions.


Bird was cruising through the upper layers of the sun.

"Care to tell me why the bake job?" Alydar asked.

She was using her hologram a lot lately. If Bird had known why he would have told her she was silly, and probably shut her down and run a diagnostic. Even though her avatar was an extension of herself, while she was offline, she was on a semi-independent mode. Alydar was actually... jealous... of herself.

"Nope, don't mind at all. I want to make sure that patch job is fully hardened. I don't have enough to spread on your hull but, I wanna make sure that patch is solid."

"Well, it's 1500 degrees outside at only this altitude. I think 'well done' has been achieved," Alydar smarted.

"Yeah, I think your right. Let's head out... and check it back in the cold okay?"

"Sure. Got anyplace in mind?"

"Mm hmm. I'm going back to Neptune."

Slightly nervous, Alydar asked "Aaand... we're doing that why exactly?"

"Chill oh ghostly one," Bird laughed, "You're patched now. I don't intend to go in, but I do intend to search the area."

"For?"

"Ayleen."

"Ah. You think we'll actually find her?" Alydar said

*somewhat sadly.*

*"I sure hope so. For all I know she's still on the Hades express. I figure, if we came out there, she might too. It's the when that I don't know. She may be gone, she may show up but not in our lifetime. She may already have shown up, or she may be light years or even galaxies away. So many 'ifs' but hey, I gotta start somewhere, ya know?" Bird stated.*

*"I do and, it's nice to see you even care."*

*"If you ever thought I didn't, you don't know me at all."*

*"Oh I know you do... it's just nice to see it."*

*With that, a big black ship headed out to hopefully find a small one.*

*Bird cruised past Earth on the way back out.*

*"Well, we still don't know the when but, there's not a single satellite in orbit. At least that tells me it's pre1960's," Bird stated aloud.*

*Alydar however said "Or long after they've all fallen back to Earth."*

*"Killjoy," Bird huffed at her. Bird looked out at the nighttime side stating, "No illumination either. Assuming I'm right, that means it's pre industrial revolution as well." Bird saluted as he headed out and said, "I'll be back later. You're not going anywhere and right now? I got a wolf to save."*

*Alydar smiled at her hero, and just continued on.*

*Bird spent a long and boring month just doing circles, and criss-crossing, but in the end came up empty. Bird was sad for that, and all the while tried different approaches to get home.*

*"Alydar, we have Cliffie's door opener on file yes?"*

*"I do... yes."*

*"Think we can build one of those to get us back?" Bird asked aloud.*

*He was throwing out ideas to see if any would stick... or spark another.*

*"Doubtful. If Earth is in such a state as you said, then they lack the technology we require to replicate it. And yes, while I do have the plans, tell me... have you ever built a resistor... or a*

capacitor... from scratch?"

"Grrr. I do hate it when you're right sometimes. Okay, how bout this then... can we modify your cat's eye engines to replicate his nightmare?"

"I have scanned light years beyond what you call the Ort Cloud. While it might be possible, it cannot be done with current tech or supplies onboard. Using those long range scans, I found no habitable planets nor life forms within range that could provide such equipment. And before you ask... no junkyards either."

"SON... of... a..."

"Bitch," Alydar finished.

Bird had a thought and asked "What about Andromeda? It's the nearest galaxy and when last I heard, my scientists believed they found Earth-like planets. Worth our time?"

"Nope. I don't think you realize just how far that is. There's not one but TWO black holes we'd have to skirt around. Add to that it would take over a month of jumps and that's with the engines linked. Possible yes but... I can scan far enough out that if there were life forms, or some form of communications, I would have picked up something by now," Alydar told him.

Bird thought a moment, then asked, "So oh mighty black wonder of the stars... you got any ideas?"

"Actually... yeah. Just one, but, it has huge risk."

"Okay lady... wadda ya got?"

"Reopen the hell wave. At least we know where, and when, the other end takes us."

"Actually, I already thought of that. Yes true, we know where it leads. Also true Cliff opened up old wormholes so technically, assuming we could, we could reopen the hell ride. Now, that said, allow me to shoot your idea down for a change."

Alydar chuckled saying "I said I had one. Never said it was a good one though."

"True but, working with that..." Bird started, "... first, we can't reopen that one. Not yet anyway. Even if we could, we don't know if Ayleen is still on the ride. Open AND reverse it while she still is, and we could blow her out anywhere or any 'when'. If that's the case we'll never find her. This is just a theory mind you but, I've been on that ride, so, I believe she'll show up sooner or later. We blew out but she was on our 6. Assuming it works the same, she should show up somewhere around this galaxy. Problem is... 'when'?"

"Don't forget 'if', and 'where'," Alydar reminded him.

"Clarify."

"The hell ride blew us out, but we ended up here. How do we know it will do the same for her. I know what you mean by a 'later arrival' but, for all we know, she's watching Tuhleesia cool off, or exploring its ruins 10,000 years after her birth."

Bird didn't disagree but said, "All real possibilities. With no knowledge of which is correct, I say we head out and look for her. We gotta do something and even if it becomes for nothing, at least WE would be doing something. Assuming we make it back at all, I want to at least tell Lone I made an honest attempt."

Alydar asked, "Ya know, we could just get you to Earth. I can keep scanning from here just as easily. Why not do that?"

"Because, if she blows out of that ride, and needs immediate help... we'd be too far out. Add to that if we are that far out, so are your scans. Right now I'll take any edge no matter how small. IF Earth is in a pre industrial state, then it's likely they still fear magic and witches and such. Not exactly a conducive atmosphere for you to come rolling in and pick me up, now is it?"

Alydar then told him, "Then here's another thought for ya. If she blows out of the ride... on Earth... she'd be the very monster your people still write stories of to this day... well, your day that is."

Bird laughed and hollered out "YES ladies and gentlemen, welcome to BirdOfPrey's shitty choice emporium! You'll find all the latest and greatest in 'bad'... 'worse'... and our latest edition 'Oh My God It's Coming This Way!'. That's right, NOTHING is too bad for our customers, so step right up and feel free to pick the crap option of your choice! Don't forget!... We offer free layaway on every 'Fuck That Shit' option or higher!"

Alydar played along and asked "Excuse me good sir, is the 'You're kidding me right!?' fresh today?"

"Aah Miss Alydar, one of our oldest and dearest customers!"

Bird winked and pulled out an imaginary chair asking, "Will you be having that here... or will that be to go?"

The universe was treated to laughter as a monstrous black ship just pressed on with the search.

That conversation took place during the month that Bird trolled the outer solar system. One of Bird's best traits is his tenacity. Once, it kept him alive. It motivated him and even helped build a new society... when a lesser man would have crumpled and died among the cators and the orange water. Right now though, that same tenacity was becoming an enemy. Bird and Alydar were on day 33 of doing absolutely nothing except go in circles. That lack of something to do, was driving Bird stir crazy. Worse, Alydar noticed it... Bird didn't. When she mentioned it... several times... Bird just blew her off and kicked in his famous mega-focus.

On Eden, a completed project meant survival. On 51, it meant getting to Rahgaa and Renny. Now... here... with no one to talk to or share it with, Bird just couldn't motivate himself to start anything, no less complete it.

One day, Alydar had had enough. Bird came out of his shower in nothing but a towel. He crossed his fists, laughed and skipped in place, and just hollered out.

"Wope Wope Wope Wope.... Wope um Gangnam Style!"

"Oh no... TELL me you didn't just do that!?" Alydar said with slight disgust.

"Heh heh... I did."

"Okay... THAT'S it!... I can search from orbit but frankly, I have had enough!" Bird felt the engines rev up and heard Alydar say "Get dressed Red... next stop?... Earth."

Bird was about to say something, but realized Alydar was right.

Walking back into the shower, Bird couldn't resist... and teased Alydar further singing "Heeeeeey Macarena!"

The last thing he heard was Alydar saying "... and THAT'S when I killed him your honor!"

Bird laughed, hollered out "Orbit only!" and finished getting dressed.

Bird had orbited before. It was only then that he laughed at himself. It had become so common place that he truly didn't realize what he was doing. He was home... well... his birthplace anyway. It was a moment almost lost on him. Looking down on a planet he resigned himself to never see again, now, he was truly enjoying it for all that it was worth.

"I'll assume there's no communications?"

"None," Ally told him.

For this occasion, Bird called her up from the doll house to sit beside him.

"Okay then. If there's nothing in orbit then it's pre Sputnik. I swear though Ally... If I go riding a horse on the beach and come up on a half buried Statue Of Liberty... I'm gonna be pissed!"

"Heh heh, gotcha boss. You'll be happy to know then... all scans of the surface come up negative for radiation."

"Good. I prefer to leave the sand pounding to Charlton Heston anyway." Bird winked at her and said "You would look hot in a slave girl outfit however... heh heh... just say'in."

Keeping up with Bird, Ally said, "I don't think it would go well with my jewels."

Bird just laughed and banked around the dark side.


Wing Remington, with Quaran's help, had built some super high tech ultra spy satellites. They were to be deployed as upgrades to the one's around the moon. Bird had also ordered some for Tuhleesia and 51 as well. Now, with only a handful built so far, Quaran and Tinnaaren were deploying them around the asteroid. Not enough for their intended purposes, but there were plenty for this job. Each one 'went dark' before Quaran even deployed them. Now, with eyes on the back side, Bartender and the Tin Man went to work on the surface. Unknown to Tin Man though, Quaran brought a mini sonic blaster with him. He aimed it at a rock ledge and sent some boulders down on himself, just as Lone had asked. Tin Man saw it and immediately jumped to Quaran's aid as he pretended not to see them coming. Quaran thanked him, and Lone was pleased with the report upon their return.

"Mission... accomplished," was all Quaran said once he

*returned to the nebula.*

*"Good to hear. Drop off cargo at your home and open the door. You and I got a visit to make. Will meet you 'outside' your home... 51 out."*

*Quaran did just that. Once Tinnaaren was safely inside moonbase, Quaran took off for orbit and waited for Lone.*


*"Okay lady, we got a problem," Bird said looking below. "If I take you down, we're gonna make a big splash. If we go in dark and soft, like we usually do... I gotta find a place to park your 10 mile long ass. Not a lot of places to do that and NOT get discovered eventually."*

*"Alright so, take the lander then," Ally said.*

*"Yeeeeeaaaaah... no. I got the biggest and baddest hot rod in all the galaxies. Heh heh, if you were me, wouldn't you wanna take down the full size version?" Bird asked with a wicked grin.*

*Ally smiled and said, "So, go in as 10 then what, touch down as 1?"*

*"Exactly. I got an idea. I'll fly in at 12 degrees down, and do it inside a thunderstorm. Anyone on the ground won't have a clue and we get the least noticeable entry."*

*"Sounds like a plan." Ally was as kind as she could be and said "Bird?... May I be the first to say... welcome back."*

*"Aaaaaand... if yer highness doesn't mind... I'll pick the motivation this time," Bird said with a grin. "I swore that if I ever went to space.... THIS song would be played when I came back down. Now, here... and with you... well, the words couldn't fit us any better and... it's as if he wrote them just for us," and Bird pressed play.*

*At a perfect 12 degrees down nose, and Bruce Dickinson singing 'Re-Entry'... Bird announced the return of the prodigal son. He blew out of a thunderstorm that engulfed the southern tip of South America. There was an odd sense of accomplishment, and 'I don't belong here' written all over Bird's face. Ally said nothing though and merely left Bird to enjoy the moment. Now, as long as he was here, he was going to sight see. He flew north and showed Ally* all the sights that was Earth. He flew through the mountains of South Vietnam... then over Mount Fuji. A hard right and the tropical Solomon Islands were next. Ally was oohing and aahing at every sight Bird showed her. South to the outback of Australia then, crossed the Pyrenees and off to the city of lights. The Atlantic was underneath when the song ended. Ally then put on Pink Floyd's 'Learning To Fly' thinking it a most appropriate tune right now.

"I've only seen pictures and paintings of this," Bird said staring out the viewscreen.

What he was looking at, was all the sailing ships in the harbor. He was at the southern tip of the Hudson River and staring at the southern end of Manhattan.

"And look! Wall Street actually has a wall!" Bird joked.

Last to go was the high Sierras. Bird thought the Rockies were nice but unless seen from the air, they didn't have the same effect as his childhood playground.

"Forget the lander for now. C'mon, I wanna show you one of the most beautiful spots I ever saw," Bird told Ally as he left the cockpit.

"Oh Bird, I can see why you love it so... it's truly beautiful!"

"In my day... this will be called Kings Beach. Ally my dear, welcome to the north end of... Lake Tahoe."

Kindly, Ally said "Thanks Bird... for showing me."

"Okay my dear, we got one more stop to make. The Washoe Indians populate this place. While they're friendly, I have no desire to show them anything more right now."

With that, both got back into the cargo bay and headed out.


"Yep... still hot aaaaaand... still windy," Bird said standing in the afternoon sun.

"So, this is where it happened hmm?" Ally asked.

Bird chuckled and told her, "This isn't hallowed ground. Heh heh you CAN come join me ya know."

Ally did come down the ramp and joined Bird at his side.

"You sure about that? Mom and dad... Cliff... kinda seems to me that if it isn't, it sure as hell should be," Ally said kindly.

"Perhaps. Nothing but tumbleweeds and tarantulas right now. Dad made it VERY clear to both Cliff and myself, that messing with the time-line is an incredibly dangerous thing. He explicitly told us, if such a thing were even possible, the event was God's will, or plan. He also said ANY thing we do to replicate it... is ours. He said God's plan doesn't cause paradox's... man's does. No Ally, whenever we are... I fully intend to see to it that I do little or no damage at all."

Sweetly, Ally asked, "So Earth man... now what?"

"Now, I'm heading back uptown."

"And then?"

"Then, I'm gonna get in the lander, come back down..." Bird looked around 1 last time, thought a thousand things at once, then finished with, "... and find a place to stay."

Bird saluted the view from Alydar's ramp as she headed up and out. Ramp now closed, Bird was onto the next plan.

# Chapter 9:

## "Ciana Thalin"

Atoemahn was a massive place. The main lobby took up a huge area just in itself. Trenthaarian's builders did an amazing job of restoring major sections before they were quickly pulled away to 'other duties'. Still, even in its unfinished state, it is an impressive room. Riisa was in the room next door. That was the main study area and the 'head librarian' had a master console to work from. That's where she was when Rahgaa 'beamed in'.

"Greetings Lady Prime, something I can do for you?"

"Indeed there is. I need geographical maps."

"Certainly," Riisa said warily, "Any one's in particular?"

"Yes, the one's of the far lands," Rahgaa told her.

Now Riisa was certain. She smiled, and brought up the requested information. She also paid close attention to what Rahgaa was looking at. Only thing though, she did it from her master console.

"Will there be anything else?" Riisa asked.

"No my dear, this will do fine."

"Of course. Well then, if you'll excuse me a moment?"

"Certainly," Rahgaa told her.

Riisa played along, half bowed, then walked out to the door. Moments later, 100 of Tiiveer's finest rushed into the room. Riisa came in with them and took off her robes as she did, revealing her version of a Lone original.

"Riisa, what is the meaning of this?" Rahgaa asked calmly.

Pulling out her Mahrek blades, Riisa remarked "They haven't been called the far lands since the days of Adjulon. You may want to remember this... 'Tamarak'... Young yes, inexperienced? Perhaps. But a fool?... No."

Tamarak smiled, then converted to his true form and said

"Well, smart AND brave. Everything a good Tuhleesian should be. There may be hope for you yet!."

"YOUR hope is quickly running out."

"Hardly. I got however what I came for. Remember this though... I'll be back."

"And we'll be waiting!" Riisa hollered as the twin of Adjulon faded away.


Riisa walked back to her console as she put her blades away. The wolf version of adrenaline was coming down, but Riisa never let the Krannen guards see her shaking hands. On the console, she flipped a switch... then entered a code. A quick 'MRU' showed up on her screen. Suddenly, a light went from green to yellow. Riisa now smiled and told the guards to stand down. Riisa then picked up her tablet, her Tuhleesian tablet, and called a planetary defender.

"We need to talk... now."

"I'm already getting reports and... I'm already on my way."

"I await your arrival Guardian... Riisa out."


"NONE of you are worthy! If you think this will do for talent you are SADLY mistaken!" Ryklan hollered to her team.

The yelling was her version of being a human drill sergeant.

"The very words above you are our banner... and our creed. Sadly, you are all small and half of you? Aren't even standing."

Ryklan was on the mat training her team. This strike force of hers turned out to be all girls. Ayleen insisted the ranks be mixed. However, only 2 males seemed to be able to handle 'the speed'. Those two, being among all women, eventually asked to be transferred out. Two women in the other teams were, well, not liking the abundance of male ways and egos. So Tin Man agreed to the transfer and as it was now, Ryklan had the strike team she promised, it was just an all girls team is all. She was working her Mahrek Blades and beating every opponent. She was in a mid turn when a blade came her way and, it wasn't a Mahrek Blade. She was pissed, crossed her blades to block it, then used it as a springboard and pushed off and up and did an aerial somersault. Get cut by the blade, or use it to push herself to safety. Ryklan chose the latter.

"HOW DARE YOU switch to a weapon like that and... Oh my stars! Apologies Guardian, I should have known it was you by the color of the blade. A mistake I shall not make again," Ryklan said as she calmed down in an instant and bowed to Tiiveer.

"I see the motto of your team now Squadron Leader. May I say, I can't think of one more appropriate," Tiiveer said with a friendly smile.

He joined her practice unseen. Partly to show off her talents, partly to see how she'd do on the new variable, and partly to see just how good she's gotten. Her whole team stood immediately and saluted Tiiveer.

"As Rhana would say... at ease. Squadron Leader, you have gotten extremely good with those. As you seem to be unimpressed with your squad, tell me, would you find me a more suitable target?"

"Target no... practice partner? Wellllllll," and Ryklan and Tiiveer both laughed.

Her team cleared the floor and couldn't believe what they were seeing. Ryklan, THEIR Ryklan, was sparring with the Guardian himself and... keeping up.

"Stop dropping your right Ryklan, you're leaving yourself too open," Tiiveer said as he did a side slice to prove his point.

"Or... I was merely drawing you there," Ryklan stated.

Both blades blocked the shot and, in an instant, Tiiveer got an elbow to the gut.

"Ugh! So... that's how you want it eh? Fine by me!" Tiiveer hollered and stripped down.

Every team member was staring at a very strong and handsome wolf. Every one of them also... seeing their Guardian... was wishing to be Rahgaa for an evening.

"Well now, allow me to respond in kind. Would you care to see the new uniform for Strike Team 1?" Ryklan asked playfully as she and Tiiveer circled the mat.

"Speaking of, what did you end up calling it?"

"Rhana's Angels," Ryklan said taking off her flight suit to reveal a modified Ayleen outfit.

"Heh heh, it fits you far better now than when I first saw you in it," Tiiveer said with a wink.

Krannen and Ryklan were playfully tossing out barbs.

"Don't let what Rhana calls the bumps and curves fool you Guardian. I assure you their as deadly as they are lovely," Ryklan said.

"Confidence my dear... suits you... aaaAAARRRGH!" Tiiveer hollered as he charged and put Ryklan to a full test.

'Rhana's Angels' didn't know who to root for or, bet on.

Rhana himself would equate what went on next with a full out Hollywood martial arts scene.

Ryklan blocked a shot and teased "Oh look... it's 'Handsome Rob'!" seeing her squad 'checking out' her opponent, and referring to the movie 'The Italian Job'.

"Sorry, were you saying something? I think you'll find THIS 'Bill', ain't so easy to 'kill'," Tiiveer said referring to yet another movie.

Ten minutes later, and the team now knew Ryklan was right and... that they had a lot of practice ahead of them. They were in awe of how their leader was keeping up. So was Tiiveer. The fight ended with Ryklan and Tiiveer face to face. Ryklan stopped with her blades crossed over Tiiveer's neck. Tiiveer just smiled.

"You were dead before you crossed your blades," he said.

"A Killen has blades facing opposite directions. The one over my head is just that. Therefore, your other one poses no danger."

"Oh, is that so?" Tiiveer said through a smile. "Look down."

Ryklan did and was surprised. Tiiveer was right.

"How the...?"

"A little gift from your namesake."

Tiiveer showed her a trick Bird built into his Killen. The handle in the middle had a click lock that allowed either blade to go in either direction.

"Aw... no fair!" Ryklan giggled as Tiiveer showed her.

"Angels, if you don't mind, I need to borrow your leader for awhile."

It took them a few seconds before they responded as they were still all checking out the hot guy with the sickle weapon. Tiiveer was walking off and putting his coat back on but Ryklan caught it.

"If you think I'm imposing, go ahead then... try it... and just see what a pissed off Prime will do," Ryklan said letting them know they'd been caught. "Bombing run practice for the rest of the afternoon. If so much as ONE of you let's my other OR his team beat you... you'll be doing them until they don't!"

With that, Rhana's Angels found something else to do, and somewhere else to be.

"Once, you made us a map from a puzzle. It would seem I need you to do it again," Tiiveer told her. He then winked at her and said "You didn't need to be so harsh with them... heh heh... I was actually flattered."

Ryklan scrunched her face and "Hmm" was all she said as she headed off with her mentor.

"Squadron Leader, a pleasure to see you," Riisa said greeting her friend.

Letting them know he knew more than they thought, Tiiveer asked "So, are you as good as she is?"

Unfazed, Riisa smiled and said "No one is." Then she nudged Tiiveer and finished with "But, I'm getting there."

Tiiveer just chuckled.

Riisa briefed him then brought up the maps. Ryklan stared at it and started solving a puzzle.

"Okay, these are the Raantaans. What exactly am I looking for?" Ryklan asked somewhat curious.

"GUARDS! Clear the room!" Tiiveer hollered out. Once alone, Tiiveer told them "Tamarak asked for these. I want to know why. I can only suspect he was looking for something. While I don't know the science, I do know he needs this planet's power. That only comes from close to its core. I suspect he was looking for a place to do it. Assuming I'm right, then he would have to dig a really big hole. Riisa says he focused on these two continents. What we don't know is where on them he looked. I need you to put your unique 'puzzle eye' to this and tell me, where he'll likely strike."

Ryklan looked it over and said "He won't. Not like he did before anyway. And by the way... it's drill a hole... not dig one. Now that said, he'd need equipment to do it. He also knows the Ghosts are around now. No Guardian, I too think he's coming but this... this was him looking for a place to hide... not attack."

Tiiveer said "I agree. Same problem though... where? I'll leave you two to discover that. I've got another namesake to visit."

"And who would that be?" Riisa asked.

"Tiiven. Tamarak came here and under a clever guise. This place is still a target. I think it's time to see if OUR whiz kid can come up with some ways to protect it."

Tiiveer walked off and Riisa and Ryklan went to work.


Bird was orbiting Earth. The more he did the more it dawned on him just what he was doing. He was both pleased and concerned at the same time. He was pleased because only a handful of his kind had ever had the pleasure of this sight. Concerned, because now he knew he had to be very careful to hide it and... not slip up.

"You look concerned Bird. Anything you want to talk about?"

Bird chuckled saying "Ya know, sometimes your level of access to all things BirdMan is just a tad creepy."

Alydar laughed back saying "Yeah yeah. Tell ya what, if it bothers you that much... next time I'll leave ya floating."

"Yeaaaahhhh... I'm thinking.... no! Hahahaha"

Alydar giggled and said "Okay really, what's up?"

Bird looked down at Earth, sighed, and told Alydar what was on his mind.


"Al listen. I can't stay up here forever. That said, if I go down there I have to be uber careful. Just the materials of my clothes is tech beyond their wildest dreams. Can you imagine if I pulled out a cannon?"

"I see your point. Ya know, a lot of your sci-fi movies show how careful aliens who hid among you had to be. Here, you're not an alien, and yet you are. An interesting situation."

"Indeed. I also don't plan to stay there. So it's finding a way to split my time, get to you, and all the while not get noticed... not even once. Expose anyone to this and the culture shock alone could do more damage than anything in my armory. There's one other problem too."

"And that would be?" Alydar asked.

"Alydar, we're out of time. As such, everyone down there is a living ghost. Not one of them is alive in my time. Now, Xankor almost killed himself when we met, but I saved him. While I have done evil things in the past, I am not an evil person. I see someone being attacked and I'm off to help. Problem is, EVERYTHING down there has already happened. What if I help someone, and I change what will be? I don't particularly relish the thought of standing by and watching someone get hurt or killed. And yet, if I help them, how many will I hurt or kill in the future because I changed the past?"

This is why Alydar loved Bird so. He truly did see, and understood, the bigger picture like no one else.

"How about this then... go to a barren location?"

"Heh heh, you want me singing the Macarena again? No Alydar, remote yes but barren... no. That way I get the interaction I need, can get away if I need to, and cause the least amount of damage possible. Problem I'm having is... where?"

"Hmm, good point."

"Here's another piece for ya. You translate for me. While it's good to understand, how do I speak it in return? Places like France or Greece or Germany are out as I don't speak the language. If I bring you along as my interpreter, and something happens to you, well... there's the exposure I'm trying to avoid."

"An interesting puzzle," Alydar said in a 'hmm' fashion.

Bird swirled his blue drink, when the proverbial light bulb went off in his head. Bird just... smiled.

"And one I just solved," Bird said staring at his drink.

Teasingly, and using Lone's voice, Alydar just said "Oh TRUST you!"


"Wow, 'ere now mistuh, dem's some odd clothes yer wearing... and you shaw tawk funny," the little boy said looking up at Bird.

Others around were thinking the same thing and were happy the boy said it first.

"Well, heh heh, I imagine I do. That's because I'm a Yank,"

Bird said with a chuckle.

"Oi! Yer from the colonies!?" the little boy asked in a thick cockney accent.

"Mm hmm."

"Well that explains it guvnuh."

The boy was about 10 Bird guessed, and he was selling something Bird hadn't seen in ages... a newspaper.

"Which one of these is today's paper young man?" Bird said kindly.

Bird had taken a small bar of gold and exchanged it for currency... a lot of currency.

"They all are guv... 2p each."

Bird smiled. He got what he came for. He tucked the paper under his arm and spoke directly to the boy.

"You're working here. Can I assume you're trying to support more than yourself?"

With a slight sadness, the boy nodded and said "Me mum and me sistuh."

Bird smiled and handed him a pound note.

"Oi, sorry guv but I ain't got the change for this."

Bird ruffled his hair playfully and said "I'm not asking for any. See to it though boy, that you and your family eat good tonight you hear me!?"

With a slight look of shock, the boy said "I will guv, and may God bless yeh! Thanks Yankee man!"

Bird walked off with news in tow and blended into the London crowd. He had his reference now. The newspaper had all sorts of articles but Bird only cared for the header.

"I'm heading back... keep my seat warm," Bird said as he made his way out of town and back to Alydar.

Bird smiled the whole way. The paper told him today was March 3rd........

1757.


Riisa looked over her console, then tapped a key on it.

"Guide, is my plan still in place?"

"And functioning as expected," the mini wolf told her.

*"Any chance of detection?"*

*"None."*

*"Good. Here's hoping it stays that way. I want none of the other Guardians told of this... ANY of this... is that understood?"*

*"Clearly," guide told her.*

*"Good," Riisa said, then went about her day.*


*"Why... tell me oh black one, whyyyyyyyyy... does it always have to be a bar?" Bird said as he walked up to the building.*

*Suddenly, the thunder that had been threatening him along his walk had finally made good on its threat. Now, with about 100 yards to go, it was pouring buckets.*

*"Fuc... king.... perfect," Bird said with high annoyance as he buttoned up his coat and turned up his collar.*

*Bird had found his spot. This was probably the most perfect he could have picked. He figured London or the Americas were too populated. War was on the horizon as well in 'the colonies' and that was the last thing he needed to get embroiled in. No, none of the places but this one met his criteria. It was clan based, which was something he wasn't fond of but, already used to. It was remote, and the local people were famous for their hospitality. Add to that, if Bird was gonna be stuck in Earths past, he was going to have some small luxury at least. Now, Bird would be drinking the real stuff, and headed for the Nectar Of The Gods. Scotland, specifically the Isle of Skye... met every criteria he had. The English had constant squabbles with the highlands, but this place was removed from that somewhat, so that brought down the risk factor. Tonight he was doing recon, and this place was his first stop. He had no idea it would be his last.*

*"Technically boss, this is an inn not a pub or a bar," Alydar told him.*

*"Don't forget Alydar, You can talk to me, but get used to me not responding."*

*"Don't YOU forget, you can use the texting on your HUD to answer back as well."*

"I won't," Bird said as he went in the door.

Bird had no idea that what laid behind that door... would change his whole life forever. Bird was humming the Beatles 'All You Need Is Love' as he entered it... and had no idea why.

Bird walked into a working inn. The key word there was 'working' as he'd only seen replicas or re-enactments of such a thing. Typical low but beamed ceilings, several kilts about the place, and the smell. Oh the smell. It was part food cooking and part body odor from people who hadn't bathed in a reeeeeeaally long time. The latter was beginning to overpower the former.

"Aye, g'evenin to yeh sir. Don't yeh be mind'in the stares, it ain't often we get strangers around here," said a beautiful blond lass.

"I figured as much. Tell me, am I in time for dinner?"

"Ooh, and a dreamy accent to match! Aye, indeed yeh are."

"I can't say yours isn't pleasing either miss... um, Miss... ?," Bird said flirting with her some.

"Aye where's my manners. My name is Scota, my sister owns this place and I help her with it. Welcome to the 'High Land Inn'."

"Scota eh? So named for the warrior goddess from whence Scotland got it's name perhaps?"

"Aye indeed," Scota said with a smile "And a learned man too I see."

"Hmm, you might say that. Tell me Scota... what do you have that's NOT hagus?"

"Well, know of that do yeh? And jes what's wrong with hagus?" Scota asked somewhat insulted.

"How about 'everything'."

"Well then, how about some stew?"

"That'll be fine thank you," Bird told her.

Bird then noticed one table of kilts staring rather intently as the lovely blond girl went to get his food.

Nodding upward, Bird stared at them back saying "Ay, ow yue do'in?" in a perfect Brooklyn accent just for fun.

He chuckled when the kilts found something else to stare at and... rather quickly.

Scota raced into the kitchen and grabbed her sister.

"Oh no yeh doen, we made a deal... YOU'RE serving tonight!" Ciana said as she cooked the evening meal in the kitchen.

"I knoe I knoe but yeh HAVE to see this one!" Scota said pulling her reluctant sister to the door.

Scota the impromptu matchmaker showed her sister the new stranger. A tall and strong man, with the oddest coat and hat. Long red hair and well trimmed beard. Odd but nice looking boots with pointed tips and silver buckles up the side. She also decided, she'd have a closer look.

"Well little sis, can't have a new husband without knowing what color eyes he has now can I?" Ciana said teasing her matchmaking sister.

"Doen bahthuh... they're blue!" She said with a giggle and a huge smile, "Jes like yours, only his has a smoky grey mixed in!"

"Scota! Shame on yeh checking out mah new husband like thah!" Ciana said still teasing her sister. "Well, I have to say dear sister, when yeh right yeh right."

She then preened as best she could, shifted her tits in her semi corset, and headed out to meet the stranger. She threw her arms wide in a 'Well?' fashion. Scota smiled, spun her sister, and practically shoved her out the door.

"Wish me luck!" Ciana hollered as she headed out.

Ciana... would never make it to the handsome stranger.

Ciana was halfway to the new stranger, when one of the locals grabbed her mid stride. He was a tad upset at the 'favorable attention' Bird was getting. Not only was he drunk but, he was a bit of an oaf. He had plans to ask Ciana to be his but, though he'd never admit it, she intimidated him. Rather her beauty and manners did. Seeing this stranger getting all the attention he felt should be his, only fueled his thirst... and his thirst fueled his anger. Yep, he was one of 'those kind of guys'.

"Oi Ciana... what's the meaning of this food? I wouldn't feed it to mah dog!"

Bird turned to see the commotion. That... was when it hit him. It was a feeling he had felt only once before and even then, it was broadcast to him. It was the same way Lone felt when he first saw Renny. Bird was staring at a statuesque, raven haired, vision of loveliness. Curves to die for, a smile that made Bird's heart damn near skip a beat, and a voice that warmed his soul. Different face and hair color but, everything else was roughly the size and shape of Ally.

Bird felt there were many stunning beauties throughout time, but he personally felt only two were what he considered 'perfect'. The first was Vivian Leigh and for awhile she was the only one. Then one day he saw a singer named Nicole Scherzinger, and the list grew to two. Now, seeing this stunningly amazing woman, Bird's personal list just grew to three. Commander BirdOfPrey, Ghost 1 himself was finally... for the first time in his entire life... in love.

"Angus what are yeh on about? It's the same hagus I've cooked for yeh a thousand times. There was noth'in wrong with it and yeh know it!" Ciana told him briskly.

She wanted to make a nice impression on the stranger in case he was everything that Scota said. Now she was annoyed because this idiot just blew her chance for a good first impression.

"It was garbage I say! Forgett'in yer own and going after strangers now are we?" Angus said angrily.

"Let GO of me!" Ciana hollered yanking her arm away. "Perhaps if yeh were more of a man and less of a drunkard I might not be look'in elsewhere."

Angus stood up and pulled a knife and put it to Ciana's throat as he grabbed her holding her arms at her side.

"Watch yeh tongue wench or I'll be show'in yeh what kind of a man I am!" Angus said menacingly.

Ciana was about to say something... but the new stranger did it for her.

Standing in the middle of the tavern floor, dressed all in black, Ciana heard a voice that, at any other time, would have made her swoon.

"I believe the lady told you to let her go. I suggest you do so. I also suggest... now... would be a good time to do it."

Scota had pulled a small sword they kept for just such a time, and was sneaking up on Angus, when the stranger gave her reason to pause.

Staring straight at Bird, Angus said coldly "And if I don't?"

"If you don't... somewhere in the next 5 minutes, your friend who's trying to sneak around behind me will be out cold. You however won't be out cold... you'll simply be out... as in permanently. Now, if don't want to wear that pig sticker like an ascot, I suggest you let the lady go. Consider that my last warning."

"Yeh know stranger, perhaps I will!" and Angus threw Ciana to the side. He pulled out his sword from its sheath and asked "Tell me stranger, what do yeh think of yer chances now?"

Staring at Angus, Bird just laughed, and pulled out a set of wing shaped blades that caught everyone's attention INCLUDING Angus. His hands spun them and then snapped a hold on them when his hands reached an outward position.

"Actually? Still pretty good," Bird said as calm as could be. "How about if we take this outside so as not to damage the nice lady's tavern hmm?"

Even in his drunken state, Angus knew this stranger was dangerous. However, he was still angry and so, stupidity overruled common sense. He was about to charge him when the friend Bird mentioned tried it first. A quick half turn, and a side kick to the knee, sent him half way to the floor. He groaned in pain and it was the last sound he made as another round house kick to the face silenced him for the evening. Bird finished the kick and was facing Angus again when he did.

"What was that you were saying about my chances?" Bird taunted.

Angus was livid and charged Bird. Bird knocked the knife from his hand with ease. Next was the sword. Bird was swinging upward and about to make good on his ascot threat when a voice halted his blade just as it contacted skin.

"NOOOOOoooooo!" Ciana called out. "Aye he may be a brute but... he doesn't have to die over a stupid drunken mistake."

Ciana's compassion was THE only thing that saved Angus's life. Hurt the lovely raven haired beauty? Not if Bird could help it. Bird still had his blade under Angus's chin... and Angus was still frozen because of it.

*"Get out of here Angus... before the lady's compassion has no effect on me," Bird nearly growled.*

*Without a word, Angus grabbed his friend, and his blades, and finally followed Bird's advice. Scota and Ciana both let out a sigh at the same time.*

*Bird, in his usual confident I couldn't care less attitude, hollered out to the patrons.*

*"Ladies and gentlemen, my apologies for interrupting your evening. My name is BirdOfPrey... Commander BirdOfPrey actually. Seeing as how we're going to be neighbors, allow me to buy you all a round... no... two rounds! It's the least I can do. Oh and the accent?... Yeah, it's American," Bird said finishing with a grin.*

*" Ere now Mistuh stranger... you got the coin for such a boast?" Scota asked warily.*

*"Nope," Bird said with a chuckle.*

*"Hmmf, figured as much."*

*Bird dropped 20 pounds on the bar by Scota and she almost fainted.*

*"I got enough for a whole lot more than that," Bird said slyly.*

*Ten men hollered in joy and ran for the bar.*

*Ciana got almost weak in the knees as the handsome stranger came straight to her. This one was different she thought. He was strong. Strong in body, mind, and attitude. Obviously a skilled warrior. And his smell, oh God, she could melt in that smell. The strong willed and independent Ciana, was becoming a submissive little girl with every step Bird took. What he did next blew her away.*

*"BirdOfPrey m'lady... at your service," and Bird gave her a proper gentlemanly bow.*

*Now this stranger had manners too!?? She was finding it hard to find her words.*

*"Thank yeh kindly good Sir. So, neighbors eh?" Ciana said doing the only thing she could think of... she curtsied. "So, where did yeh buy propitee?"*

*"I haven't yet. Seeing you though, Heaven and Earth couldn't move me from this Isle."*

*Ciana actually blushed. She was more tough than girly. Right* now she was finding herself sorely lacking in flirting skills.

"Quite the smooth talker ain't yeh Commander?" was all she could manage.

"Oh, YOU can call me Bird. Perhaps in time, you could call me something else?"

"And jes wut might that be?"

Bird smiled a smile that had her crossing her legs. She was also feeling a tad warm.

"Husband," was all Bird said as he went to Scota to secure a room for the night. No one could hear him talking as he walked and said, "What, no reeeeowr?"

Alydar actually had a smile in her voice as she told him kindly, "No dear... not this time."

Ciana walked up to Scota and Bird, and slapped her hand down on two of the 5 pound notes, scowled at Scota, and handed them back to Bird.

"The tenner is more than enough to cover your order AND leave you with change I barely got. I'll have yeh know I'm no thief," then nearly growling at Scota said, "And neither are you!"

Bird curled her hand softly, kept the money in it, and kissed the back of it.

"Put it towards my bill then," Bird said kindly.

Ciana was still having a hard time dealing with this charming stranger, and told him "I'm a good Christian woman I am. You'll get every pence of your change when yer bill comes due. As for tonight, well, I have a guest room for special patrons. Call it payment for your chivalry on my behalf."

"Now that's an offer I'll gladly accept," Bird said smiling.

"Ere now... doen yeh be getting' any ideas Commander Bird. Tis only the proppuh thing to do, nothing more!," Ciana stated firmly.

She only meant half of it, but wouldn't let Bird know that.

"But of course. Well my fine innkeeper... lead the way."

"I'm not 'your' innkeeper."

Confident as could be, Bird only replied, "Yet."

Bird now settled, Ciana was cleaning up with Scota.

*"Well sis, looks like yeh finally found yer prince after all,"* Scota said with a beaming smile. *"I was thinking of stealing him for mahself, till I saw him look at you that is."*

*"Ere now, I'm doing the proppuh thing and nothing more and yeh know it. This one though sis, this one is different."*

*"Oh? How so?" Scota asked.*

*"Well little sistuh, Aye I wanted me a prince."*

*"But?"*

*"But, it looks like a king found me first!"*

*Time... would show Ciana Thalin... just how right she was.*

# Chapter 10:

## "SNAP OUT OF IT!"

*Bird was standing on the bluff overlooking the bay. He was enjoying the view, drinking his tea, and trying to sort out his next move. He had plans, galactic sized ones. Now, with the arrival of the dark haired lady, everything has changed.*

*"You've been awful quiet this morning," Bird said teasingly.*

*"Perhaps, but you forget, I can read your vital signs. You humans have a wide range of emotions," Alydar told him through his comm.*

*"Yeah... and?"*

*"Aaaaaand," Alydar chuckled, "When I first became aware, and was linked to you, I had to sort out... heh heh... in a hurry, what those levels were. You have no idea how many times I almost called Jonathan (giggle) or the cavalry, just because you were happy or sad or angry... and not in a medical emergency."*

*Bird chuckled and said "Heh heh, yeah okay. Humans are so used to emotions that I didn't think of it from that perspective. Now that said... your point?"*

*"Point being, when your happy or sad... the same levels go up or down as when you're actually hurt or in medical danger. So, I learned the rise and fall of those levels, and figured which was true danger... and which was just an emotional reaction. Last night was a new one for me but I knew you weren't hurt. Based on which chemicals in your brain went up, I assumed you were... in love?"*

*Smiling, Bird told her "I've never been. None of you ladies were around when Lone met Renny. I got blasted, and I mean damn near assaulted, by Lone when he did. Lone once told me he was actually happy that he was able to share such a moment. Now though, using that as a reference, I'd have to say your right."*

Bird was happy, but cautious when he said that. Knowing how Alydar felt about him, he wasn't sure how she'd react.

"I thought as much, and that's why I've been quiet," Alydar told him kindly.

"Um... okay... clarify."

"I've been like you once. Granted, you were the object of those affections but, at least I had a reference. When we slept together I felt... odd."

"Still listening," Bird told her sipping his tea.

"Okay, we promised to be honest with each other. So far you have been with me so... here goes."

Alydar sighed, hoped she wouldn't insult Bird, and laid out her feelings.

"When we did, I thought it would be everything you felt last night and perhaps even more. No insult but, it wasn't. I thought I did something wrong, or perhaps misjudged. So, I called the one person I thought could help me understand."

With an amused smile on his face, Bird replied "Let me guess... the 'bitch' called the 'whore'?"

In the same tone, Alydar said "Damn straight Skippy!" and Bird just chuckled. "Anyway, I came to find out that my love was just as strong as last night was for you but... in a different way. A way mind you, that didn't include 'that'. Does that make sense?"

"It does indeed my dear. For what it's worth, you are one in a million my lovely black hot rod. I promise you Al, I don't know where this will go but, that spot I told you was reserved for you, still remains yours. I guess what I'm saying now is, looks like I have to build a new addition! Heh heh heh."

"And I promise you, I'll not interfere nor cause you grief. I also promise that I will, if she becomes that important, protect her as I would you. Boss?"

"Yeah?"

"I am truly happy for you. I was only quiet because I thought you might want to enjoy this moment by yourself."

"Well Alydar, seeing as how that didn't happen, know that I'm truly glad that it was you I got to share it with," Bird said lovingly.

Alydar was thrilled, and said "You know where to find me. Enjoy your morning," and went back quiet once more.

Bird raised his glass to the air and toasted the grandest lady he knew... even though technically... she wasn't even human.

"So Commander, yeh always be talkin' to yerself?"

"When I wish to sort things out your blondness... yes I do."

Scota smiled up at Bird as she reached his side and said, "Good morn'in to yeh. I wanted to say thank yeh fer last night."

"Well Scota, you're more than welcome. That sort of thing happen often around here?"

"Oh noooo, but Angus has had his eye on mah sistuh fer a long time now. Poor man, he never had a chance but he was sweet enough. When he's not on the liquor (cough cough) he's a decent man, (cough) a bit slow, but decent."

"That sounds rather nasty," Bird remarked.

"Oh doen yeh be mind'in me now... I'm fine."

"Care to tell me about it?" Bird asked.

"Not really but... I'm sure mah sistuh woen mind," Scota said with a sly smile.

Bird was turning for the inn when Scota called after him.

"Commander?"

"Call me Bird... and yes?"

"Mah sistuh, she's been everything to me since I was a wee lass. Father died when she was my age and she's looked after me and raised me ever since. What I'm saying is, be nice to her. Raising me and caring for the inn, well, it hasn't been easy for her. She's a tough woman but, she's had to be... if yeh get my mean'in?"

"MRU blondie," Bird said.

"Excuse me?"

"Heh heh... um... Yankee talk... it means I heard you loud and clear."

Bird headed off speaking to himself saying, "Whew, that was close."

Teasingly but, with intent, Alydar said "No shit Sherlock."

"Smart ass."

With a chuckle, Alydar gave Bird a taste of his own medicine and said "That would be my sister... I'm the wise ass... an easy mistake."

Bird laughed and taunted "Why you little... THAT'S it... when

I get back I'm gonna turn your doll house into a man cave!"

Both man and machine laughed as Bird went inside.

"So... 'High Land Inn' eh?... clever play on words there," Bird said to the lovely lady cleaning up.

"Aye, mah dad had that sort of humor about him."

Bird pulled up a chair and just watched... and enjoyed.

"Sleep well did yeh?" Ciana asked.

She was as flustered as Bird was... he just controlled his better is all.

"Actually no. It would seem the 'finest room in the house'... needs a little work."

"Is that so?" Ciana said a bit insulted.

"It is. The roof leaks, and the chimney needs patching. There's more drafts in there than a windy day in the fall... and two of the window panes are cracked."

Bird was right and Ciana knew it. She was proud of her inn but with no man around, she knew it needed some fixing.

"Well, it may not be as fancy as some of the places Iem sure yer used to, but I've not gotten complaints."

Bird sipped his tea saying "Have now. Mind you, the attitude behind my accommodations... was beyond stellar," Bird said referring to Ciana's kindness.

Now Ciana flirted... AND teased.

"Well then Mistuh 'I have more money than the bloody king', feel free to do something about it!"

Bird teased right back saying "Fix that!? What it needs is a bulldoz... um... what I mean is, it needs to be torn down and rebuilt from scratch!"

"Oh, know of those things do yeh?" Ciana said playfully trying to 'get the scoop' on Bird.

"I know a lot about a lot of things," Bird said showing off.

Ciana sat down and said "Well then, do tell."

Bird knew he would need a cover story sooner or later. He wasn't however expecting later to come sooner. Bird leaned back and... mixing truth with fiction... made up his tale as he went.

"Well m'lady... get comfy," Bird said as his internal HUD

*came on.*

*"**Watch it!** " was all the text said.*

*"You know I'm a Yank. I was in the military, but left it when my tour of duty was up."*

*"Your whah?" Ciana asked.*

*"Where I'm from, one signs up for the military for only several years. After that you've fulfilled your obligation and can leave. I finished mine, rejoined several times, but finally left."*

*"Ah... please continue," Ciana said understanding now.*

*"Anyway, I'm a ghost."*

*"Ya look pretty solid to me," Ciana said jokingly.*

*"To me... you just look gorgeous," Bird said honestly.*

*Ciana blushed and quickly said "Oi, we're talking 'bout you not me,"*

*Bird watched her turn away and twirl her hair and kept going.*

*"As I said, I'm a ghost. That means I don't exist. I was put in charge of a secret band of men. Doctors... engineers... every trade you can think of and a few you can't."*

*"Why?"*

*"Ciana look, even now there are places that still believe in witches and demons and such. We wanted to know, what could we make that didn't exist before. Also, what could we do to something that already exists, to make it better. We used pure science and came up with things that were beyond amazing. New medicines, new machines, all sorts of things. Sadly, I saw them focusing more on machines and toxins of war, rather than mankind... so I left. Once I did, I started my own business and became more than a little successful. I however, have a tendency to work too much. I got sick for that reason, the doctors told me to take a vacation or perish, and well... here I am."*

*Ciana was happy to have a story to go with the person she now considered 'her Commander'.*

*"Alright then answer me this? If you were in charge, why is it you know so much?"*

*"One doesn't 'just order' people like them around. Also, when they discovered something new, it did no good if one didn't actually understand it now would it?"*

*"No, I suppose not."*

*"My parents were killed in an accident when I was Scota's age. My brother stayed in the military once I left. Sadly, he's now gone as well. Growing up I was quite the inventive one. I secured enough rank, the military needed someone like me... and so it was."*

*"So, not only a learned man but... a skilled tradesman too!"*

*Bird chuckled at her not so subtle probing.*

*"Several trades actually... not to mentioned highly trained in medicine, weapons and the art of war."*

*Ciana was highly impressed and decided right then and there that this one... wasn't going to get away.*

*"Well then, as I recall, your words were 'yet' and 'husband'. If you were to be correct... one day... and Iem not say'in yeh will be... feel free to prove it,"* Ciana said slyly.

*"Can't have a husband who boasts but doesn't deliver now can we?"* Bird chuckled totally calling Ciana's bluff.

*"Exactly! Fix the room then iffin yer not happy with it."*

*"And if I do? What do I get out of it?"*

*"Hmm fair enough. Fix it proppuh, and I'll let yeh court me."*

*"HAHAHAHAHA... you were going to let me do that anyway. You know it... and I know it. Tell ya what, I'll fix your room for ya. When I'm done you can give me whatever you feel is fair. But, answer me this! What if I build you a house to rival that amazing beauty of yours... then what?"*

*Ciana was caught way off guard and stammered.*

*"Are all yeh Yanks this forward!?"* she finally managed.

*"This one is... now answer my question."*

*Ciana finally got her Scottish backbone back and said "Well Commander... IF yeh did that... then and ONLY then... will I consent to call'in yeh 'husband'."*

*Bird grabbed his now cold tea and sat back in his chair.*

*"Now m'lady... you got a deal. And by the way, call me Bird."*

*Scota was bouncing up and down from behind the door and damn near squealed in delight.*

*Men... as a species... are generally secretive by nature. When a time comes that one man tells another a secret, you can bet your last coin it'll stay that way. That's just the way they are.*

Women however... not so much. They tell things, that's what they do. Women by nature, tell their fellow girl friends, things no man would even speak of... no less tell another. Right now, that was being proven correct. The ladies of the Isle had gossip down to a finely polished art form. Not only that but, Scota was orchestrating it better than any conductor on Earth.

She had heard the whispers, and the rumors, of how her sister either couldn't get a man, or just simply didn't want one. They were also getting to her age, and how if she didn't do it soon, she likely never would. Scota was very proud of her sister and defended her every chance she could... but that didn't change anyone's mind. Now, she was determined to let everyone know. She also figured if she hurt Bird in any way, then she hurt her sister as well. So, she told of him being a successful business man... but left out the military part.


Bird had gone to the market the next day with Ciana. He met her doing recon... and that mission still needed doing. Bird realized in an instant he had a spy when he talked to Ciana yesterday.

"Oi Ciana, lovely day we be hav'in ain't it?"

"Indeed Mary!" Ciana replied joyfully.

"Yeh let me know if yeh be need'in any linens for that room of yours!"

Staring at Bird with an odd look on her face, the red haired one merely said "Don't look at me, I didn't say anything."

"Oooooh that girl!" Ciana replied with honest frustration.

Bird walked over, introduced himself to Mary, and promised to take her up on her offer when he had finished. He laughed as he walked away with Ciana, kicked in his long range hearing, and heard two giggling voices.

Mary was telling the other girl in the booth "Did yeh hear thah accent!? Ooooh I could die a happy woman I could, hearing THAH voice every day."

Bird decided to have a little fun and hollered from a distance "Hey Mary?"

"Aye Mr. Commander?"

"Actually... it's just Commander. I just wanted to say thanks... your accent ain't so bad either!"

Mary was dumbfounded and embarrassed. Ciana asked what

*that was about so Bird told her.*

*"And you heard her?... From all the way over here?" Ciana said in disbelief.*

*"Yeah 'Mr. Commander'... even I wanna hear this one!" Alydar teased in his ear.*

*Bird smiled, and told his companions both real and virtual, "When I first started my business, I got a little too close to a construction explosion by accident. It left me deaf for two months. So, I learned to read lips."*

*That made perfect sense to Ciana.*

*Alydar chuckled and told him "And that's why I don't play poker with you."*

*Handsome and virile Bird caught a lot of attention that day. Several times, as the ladies stared, their men made their presence known. A few times, Ciana did the same thing and for exactly the same reason.*

*"Are you sure about this Rahgaa?" Lone asked.*

*"No but, I need to know I can trust him. If I can't welllllllll, I need to know that too. He's either going to help us or... I need to know I'm fighting 2 brothers and not one. Should it be the former, then he needs to hear it from me... not you."*

*"That's 'we can' not 'I can'. And if it's the latter?"*

*"Apologies Mahrek, yes I know we are all in this together. If it is indeed the latter then, as Bird would say, he needs to know that even having the Prime 'in his own backyard' will neither help him... nor deter us," Rahgaa told him.*

*Tiiveer was adamantly against this plan and said so. Rahgaa however held firm.*

*"Tiiveer my love, if this issue was about us, I would honor your wishes. This however affects us all, and therefore is Prime business. Lone is right, if we're to get Rhana back then we need to go 'outside the box'. That includes our comfort levels as well."*

*"Then I will go with you. THAT... is non negotiable. You want to pull rank then fine...protecting the Prime is for the Krannen and that IS my business!"*

*Rahgaa was sweet and said, "Promise me this then. IF your*

services become necessary, promise me 'you' will come to my aid...
and not the Guardian of the Krannen."

Tiiveer calmed down some and said "Count on it."

Rahgaa turned and said "Commander Lone, I thank you for
your detour... shall we be off then?"

Lone tipped his hat and just waved to the door.

Tiiveer asked "Something on your mind Mahrek?"

The Krannen dude was sitting in the cockpit with Lone while
Rahgaa went aft to rest. Lone was deep in thought as he and Quaran
flew deeper into the darkness.

"Huh?... Oh, sorry, guess I was just thinking about something
that's all."

"Care to share?" Tiiveer asked in a friendly tone.

"Oh... I was just thinking about Rahgaa. I was going to do
what she's about to. I was just thinking, if this goes according to
plan... will it make a difference this time?"

Tiiveer chuckled and said "Clarify."

"Heh heh, you're right... it doesn't sound good on you." Both
wolves laughed and Lone said, "When the brothers first blew up
against each other... the rest of the galaxy was caught by surprise.
Assuming that everything Gil told us is true, then he never even
fought his brother. Now that the galaxy knows of the coming fight,
and is united against a common enemy, well... I was wondering if
this time would be different enough to actually make a difference. I
was also wondering that, if it did, would it still be in our favor?"

Tiiveer knew he was having a 'guy moment'. He also knew
'that moment' , was during the most epic times in recorded history...
and with the most epic wolf of his kind. Lone was becoming a legend
far greater than Tiiven ever was and Tiiveer knew he was in the
company of greatness. As such, he chose his words well.

"Mahrek, I can't tell you things will be alright. We find
ourselves living in times that are monumental in our history. I can
consider those times, and my role in it, and let it overwhelm me. Or,
I can simply make the best decisions I can, with whatever
information I can gather, and deal with it one day at a time and let
history be my judge. That said, your point is a good one. I can't
foresee the future but, I honestly believe we are 'The Children Of

Koelaahn'."

"Okay... sure... I can totally see that!" Lone said with a laugh.

"Sorry Mahrek, it is a story told to children before their first hunt. It's a tale meant as a lesson. 'The Children Of Koelaahn' refers to the favored ones. She is what you would call a mythical goddess. Koelaahn views all and, if their heart is pure, and their intentions are honorable, she will grant them her favor and as a result, victory. It's also told that if those values change, then she will pull her favor from you and be deaf to your cries for help, when she turns those same favors against you. My apologies, even being mated to our own Guardian, I forget sometimes there are things of our culture you do not know."

"Good story. Here's hoping that if she doesn't find favor in our cause.. heh heh... that she at least has a sense of humor!"

"Indeed!" Tiiveer replied.


Lone put Raven on autopilot and turned to Tiiveer.

"Well then, honorable stories and perspectives aside, I've noticed something. As such, I have a question for you."

"Yes?"

"I've noticed you and many others... have been calling me by my title lately... a lot. Care to tell me why?"

"Certainly. You, or rather one like you, have been promised to us through the ages. While I now know the reason for it, you have become thought of as a myth come true. You help the 'Great Rhana' and here you now are... in the flesh as they say. Our people Mahrek, are not very forgiving. Had you not lived up to expectations you... well... let's just say you wouldn't have liked the outcome."

"Point taken," Lone told him.

"Now, you're a vision of hope. Right now Commander, that hope is all that sustains us."

"And by 'us' you mean...?" Lone asked.

"All of us! The clans and temples and yes, even the Guardians. Mahrek if we were the wolves of old, yours would be an amusing story and nothing more. Furthermore, we wouldn't need you. But we aren't those wolves AND!... if we were we'd certainly be right back where we started yet again. No Mahrek, you are the one *who will bring us back to then... but with the wisdom of now. While I feel we have kept up with you and Rhana on this path, only you and he know where to go along it. Our people Mahrek, see you as the greatest guide ever. You've become quite literally, to us anyway, a living legend. Sorry to put that burden on you as well but, it is the truth."*

*"Okay then, that explains them. Now... what about you? AND!... before you answer that... know that THIS Mahrek... prefers 'Lone'. I'll accept it from them, but not the Grand Couple."*

*Tiiveer was actually honored, and gave Lone his answer.*

*"Lone, we Guardians protect our people. Over time we have come to be thought of as you and Rhana are now. Truth be told, we are wise yes, perhaps even the most talented at our jobs but, in the end we are still just wolves. Right now? Even a Guardian needs something to believe in."*

*Lone turned back, took back control of Raven, thought of all he was trying to do, and said "Guardian, right now... so does a Mahrek."*

*Raven let Lone know they hit the marker he set. Once there, Tiiveer went into the aft meeting room with Rahgaa. He knew that he'd know soon enough where they were but for now, the less he and Rahgaa knew the better.*

*"Two Ghosts... 4 souls... permission to come aboard," Lone said over the comm.*

*He got no answer but, the doors did open.*

*"I can tell by your uniform you are a Ghost. Apologies but we weren't introduced when last we met... I am Riihahl," the ghostly lady said to Quaran.*

*Ghost 4 tipped his hat saying "A pleasure to meet you. My name is Quaran, call sign 'Bartender', and I am Ghost 4."*

*"You are Galenthian yes?"*

*"I was."*

*"Ah, am I to assume something happened to make you renounce your birthright?"*

*"You could say that."*

"Well then, for what it's worth, I think the one you've replaced it with is a more than suitable alternative," Riihahl said with a smile.

Quaran smiled back and said "As do I."

Rahgaa and Tiiveer came down the ramp with Lone. Rahgaa was pleasant this time but even Riihahl could see she was all business.

"Greetings Lady Adjulon. I hope you'll excuse the English version of title, as I don't know the ancient one."

"Lady Prime and Guardian Tiiveer... welcome, and I don't mind at all. Tell me, to what do I owe the pleasure of your company?"

"I wish to talk to your mate," Rahgaa told her.

With a whole lot of aggravation in her voice, Riihahl said "So would I."

"Still locked himself away?" Rahgaa said in a somewhat surprised tone.

"Since you left weeks ago. To be honest, I'm getting a tad annoyed. At first I gave him some time to sort himself out. Then I tried cajoling him. Yelling by the way... didn't work either."

Rahgaa decided she wasn't leaving without accomplishing her mission. This new wrinkle got her thinking.

"Riihahl, I know you come to us in a similar manner as our trancing. I came to speak to Giljor and I don't mind telling you... I'm not leaving here till I do. He came to Rhana once did he not?"

"AND me," Lone added.

Riihahl answered "He did what was necessary but yes... he did."

"Well then..." Rahgaa started with a sly smile, "... if he won't come to us, is it possible that I could go to him?"

"For security, there are no portals anywhere on the station that will allow you into our world. I could try doing to you what Giljor did to Rhana Bird, but I don't know if it will work," Riihahl stated in a 'hmm' kind of tone.

Tiiveer stepped up and stated as more of a husband than a Krannen, "She is with child. Can you assure me if you do this, nothing will affect my unborn children?"

"Children!?" Riihahl stated with true glee.

"Like your mate... twins... yes," Rahgaa told her.

With some sadness, Riihahl stated "I envy you Lady Prime. Of all the seasons I've had with Giljor, I would give them all up for just one child of my own." Riihahl turned to Tiiveer and said "Have no worries Guardian, the way it works, no harm will come to them."

"Are you sure about this? I can go instead and.." Tiiveer said to Rahgaa but she cut him off.

"No my love, I'll be fine," She said as she stroked his cheek. She then turned to Lone and said "I'm counting on you," then looking around finished with, "ALL of you... to get me out if anything goes wrong out here."

Both Ghosts tipped their hats, and Rahgaa gave Tiiveer a quick kiss. She gathered herself, then spoke directly to Riihahl.

"In the words of Rhana himself... let's do this."

Rahgaa sat down and as soon as she did, she looked like she fell asleep.

Smiling, Riihahl said "Gentlemen, I'll try not to keep her too long," and faded out.


"This is.. is... amazing!" Rahgaa stated with pure wonder and awe.

"Hahaha, I'm just surprised it worked!" Riihahl laughed. "How do you feel? If you sense anything, ANY thing at all wrong, or that the children or yourself are in danger, say so and I'll cut the link immediately," Riihahl said with true motherly concern for the kids.

"Actually, I can feel I'm not pregnant. That said, I also sense a link of sorts I guess you'd call it, to my physical body. Much like when I trance. Have no fear, while I don't sense them with me per say, I can sense that so far... they're fine."

Tiiveer heard something that suddenly made him real uneasy. It was Rahgaa's voice but, it was coming from the bay in the same fashion as Giljor did.

"Tiiveer my love, can you hear me?"

"I can, are you alright?"

"I'm fine and so are the children. Riihahl gave me access to the bay so I could tell you not to worry. Oh Tiiveer, you REALLY have to try this!"

"In 51 speak... no thanks, I'll pass." Tiiveer then asked "When we mated, do you remember when Rhana came to find me?"

"I do but, he didn't... he sent Ayleen to do it."

Confirmation of that was good enough for Tiiveer. He wanted to make sure he was talking to the real Rahgaa.

"Make this quick please... you know how I am when I get 'nervous'."

"I'll be back as soon as I can," Rahgaa's voice told him. "Wish me luck!" and she was gone.


"What do you call this again?" Rahgaa asked.

"A simulation."

"Ah yes, this 'simulation' is remarkable! It's so lifelike."

"Giljor spent many many suns working on it.

"Well, fantastic as this is, let's not keep the Commanders waiting shall we?"

"Indeed. Out beyond my home lies all that was. Giljor had his favorite spots and I've checked them all... several times. It's as if he's left the station entirely."

"Well, he may be ancient but, he's still Tuhleesian. How about if we start where it all began?" Rahgaa asked.

"Atoemahn?"

"Can you think of anyplace better to start with?"

"As you wish," Riihahl told her.

"So, how do we get there?" Rahgaa asked her host and guide.

Riihahl laughed and said "Lady Rahgaa, all that you see may seem real. You however need to remember it's not. Technically, neither are you. You're not solid so... you may want to stop thinking like one."

Rahgaa's world spun, distorted, and swirled. Suddenly, Atoemahn was all around her as she found herself standing in its lobby. Had she not tranced, and seen something similar doing so, Rahgaa would be freaking right now.


The two ladies walked through the large complex. Riihahl was getting more and more aggravated but Rahgaa truly felt she was on to something.

"I'm telling you Lady Prime, he's not here," Riihahl said a bit exasperated.

"I'm telling you he is. Problem is, where."

Then Rahgaa noticed something and... smiled.

"Sneaky little tehrip ain't you?"

"Care to let me in on it?" Riihahl stated more than asked.

"See that painting on the wall there?"

"It's called a mural... what about it?"

"Well my suddenly snotty guide. YOU haven't actually been in the real Atoemahn in hundreds of seasons. I however was there just 5 suns ago. As such, I can tell you... that 'mural'... doesn't exist."

"Oooh, you little tehrip you!" Riihahl said speaking to the hallway.

"Heh heh... nice to see we agree on something," Rahgaa told her with a sly grin.

Riihahl went charging for it when Rahgaa held her up.

"Why don't you let me. You have your life in here but my time grows shorter by the minute. Besides, he might be more responsive to me right now anyway."

Riihahl spoke softly and with extreme manners as she bowed to Rahgaa saying "Lady Prime, if my mate gives you even the slightest bit of a hard time, know that you have my full permission to..." and she then turned and hollered down the hallway shouting "... KICK HIS ASS!..." then turned back to Rahgaa and finished with "... as Rhana would say."

Rahgaa chuckled, said "I'll keep it in mind," and literally walked through the wall like the ghost that she was.


Rahgaa walked into a room she'd never seen before. If she were human, she would recognize it as a 'gentleman's office'. Floor to ceiling shelves of books, dark wood décor mixed with lighter paneling. Two desks but... only one had an occupant.

"I figured you for many things... sulking however... doesn't suit you," Rahgaa stated as a means of introduction.

"I'll assume my mate brought you here?" Giljor said somewhat startled, somewhat annoyed.

"Indeed."

"Well then Lady Prime, feel free to have her return you

AND... at my earliest convenience."

"I'm not leaving... deal with it."

"What do you want Rahgaa!?" Gil said highly annoyed at the interruption.

"Oh so that's how it's going to be eh? Fine by me 'Gil'. Answer me this, in the words of Rhana himself... 'what's your fucking problem'!?"

"That list is rather long... feel free to pick a point and start anywhere," a dejected wolf told her.

Now Rahgaa felt like Riihahl and actually yelled at the butcher of Tuhleesia.

"Um... Gil?"

"What?"

"Feel free to... at MY earliest convenience... SNAP OUT OF IT!" Rahgaa commanded.

Giljor sighed, and waved a hand to the other desk inviting Rahgaa to sit down.

"Is that where 'you know who' used to sit?"

"Once upon a time... yes."

"Thanks but... I'll pass," Rahgaa stated. "We wolves have been many things and done many things. One thing we don't exactly do well... is sulk."

"So you've said."

"Ah but what you haven't said... is why?"

Giljor had a faraway look in his eyes, and told Rahgaa what she wanted to hear.

"There was a time once... once... when dozens of creatures from hundreds of worlds all sought me out. Now look at me."

"I see nothing different than the first time I met you," Rahgaa stated.

Giljor blew up and hollered "I WAS THE GREATEST MIND OF OUR TIME!! NO ONE RAHGAA... NO ONE!... SURPASSED ME! NOW, HERE I AM, HUMILIATED! BY A LITTLE BOY!"

Giljor got totally deflated when Rahgaa calmly told him "Oh get over yourself butcher. It was... and IS... that very arrogance that drove your brother to the madness we now all face."

Still angry, but far calmer, Gil asked "Why are you here

Rahgaa? I'm no good to anyone, not anymore. If it's a problem you need to solve... why don't you get the Xaran boy to solve it for you. He'd likely do a better job anyway."

Still calm but, with a hint of losing her patience, Rahgaa told him a tale.

"When I first met your brother, Rhana said it was all about the 'waah waah waah' with him. So it seems now for you as well. While I never thought I would say this to the twin of Adjulon... MAN UP will ya?"

Gil was confused and asked "Waah waah waah?... Man up?"

"It's the sound a human baby makes when it's angry that it didn't get what it wanted... or had something taken away it shouldn't have had. 'Man Up' refers to a grown man acting... well... not like one... and to start doing so immediately."

"There was a time you would be shredded for even thinking that," Giljor said.

"That time is not only over but,... look at what 'that kind of thinking' got us. You talk of the wolves of old. So does the wretch. Yet... were you really so superior as you keep claiming? If you were, why did we end up here? Perhaps the 'waah waah waah'... doesn't apply to Tamarak alone."

With reverence, Giljor said "Perhaps your right."

"So tell me Prime, other than to insult me... what do you want?"

"Sulk all you want, the bottom line is you still control this station. Have you heard of Rhana?"

"Not since you were last here no... why?"

Rahgaa sighed, sat on Tammy's desk... but not his chair... and gave Giljor an update on current events.

"HE DID WHAT!?"

"You heard me. We have a plan to get him AND Ayleen back, but it's risky. Not only that, we need your help."

Giljor was sad and said "You've seen me. How am I supposed to help stuck in here?"

Rahgaa was actually kind in tone and laid out her plan.

"We are all taking risks. I'm taking one right now just coming here."

"While your arrival was a bit of a surprise, I assure you, doing what your doing poses no danger to you."

"Yeah? Well, what about my kids?"

"They are... wait... your what!?"

"You heard me... I'm pregnant, and you may find this amusing... with twins!"

Giljor was happy for Rahgaa and said so.

With sadness though he said "In this form, it is the one thing I can't give Riihahl. She has been kind about it but I know it bothers her."

"Indeed. Now, ready to hear our plan?"

"Tell me no more than you need to," Gil said with caution.

"Like I said, we plan to get Rhana back. In order to do that we need to build something... something really really large."

"And I can help how?" Giljor asked in a 'I can't help you' defeated sort of tone.

Rahgaa now berated him as one would a child who had given up on him or her self.


"GILJOR ADJULON! I find your lack of faith disturbing," Rahgaa said imitating Darth Vader, and chuckling on the inside knowing Gil wouldn't understand. "Were you even truly the greatest mind of your time... or did you just prance that title around like a riding beast in a stable!?"

"LOOK AROUND YOU KAAZ'AAN! (bitch) All that you see, ALL that is this station... was my brilliance and MINE ALONE!"

"So, there is a spark of pride left in you after all eh?"

"TELL me of this plan... before I show you just how brilliant," Giljor growled.

"Save your attitude butcher. Here's the thing. You and your brother, the smartest minds of your day. Yet, look what you did with it AND!... look at what's become of us since because of it. Rhana succeeds where you fail because you seek to be the whole solution. He gets the best minds with the most brilliant perspectives he can find. YOU Giljor Adjulon... had no one but your brother. Add to that, since this station and after that, this world that you created... what have you done?"

"I believe the term is 'clarify'."

"It is. Nothing to clarify. You claim to be this fantastic scientist yet, since building this fake world of yours, what have you ACTUALLY accomplished?"

Sadly, Gil admitted "Nothing of consequence."

"Exactly. Even Salyan said without your original work he would likely still be trying to translate it. You've done nothing since and as a result, like a body that doesn't move, you've become lazy and frail. Rather, your talents have. Work with us. Accept that you are smart but... not all knowing. Also accept that your brilliance isn't gone, it's merely out of shape. Don't be the solution... only part of it."

Giljor had snapped out of his funk now. Even he couldn't argue with Rahgaa. Not only that... he was scheming again.

"Bird said my insanity got us into this... his would get us out. I believed that then and I still do now. Bring me Salyan. IF your correct and my mind only needs exercise as you say, then he is the only person I trust to do it with. Now, what of this device?"

Rahgaa's connection to her physical body was starting to feel drained and she knew it was time to go.

"Tell you what, why don't you stop hiding like a krattat in mating season, and we'll discuss it."

Full of a new passion, and a shot at redemption, Giljor was now pumped and... his old self once again.

"One last question before you go."

"Mm?"

"You still don't trust me Rahgaa Siin, yet here you are... why?"

"Rhana. Morale 'out there' is low even beyond our world at his loss. The only thing keeping it up right now is the hope of this plan working. We are all going outside our comfort levels. You're right I don't trust you but... right now?... I'll take all the help I can get to insure success... even from you."

"A bold move. Perhaps in time, I will prove those fears wrong. Shall we?" and Gil waved a hand to the door.

"You and I will talk later my love, Rahgaa however needs to go back... and now," Giljor said as he emerged with the Prime.

*Rahgaa smiled and faded from their virtual world.*

*"That was quick," Lone said seeing Rahgaa wake up.*

*"If you consider almost 3 hours quick then yeah, I guess so."*

*Tiiveer said "You've been 'asleep' for only 35 seconds or so."*

*"Well, isn't that interesting. Anyway, we'll be getting company shortly. As the Ghosts say... mission accomplished... whoa!" Rahgaa said as she faltered getting up.*

*"Rahgaa!" Tiiveer hollered as he caught her.*

*"Nothing to worry about my love. I'm just tired that's all."*

*Lone hollered "RAVEN! Fire up the med bay I got incoming!"*

*Rahgaa tried waving the men off saying "I'm okay really, I just need some rest."*

*Lone actually growled saying "That my dear... wasn't a request."*

*Equally as concerned, Tiiveer said "And I agree!"*

*And so, like it or not, Rahgaa was scooped up and whisked off to Raven.*

*An hour later, and Rahgaa now recovered, all were reassembled in the station's hangar bay.*

*"I hope you know just what kind of mate you truly have?" Giljor said directly to Tiiveer.*

*Showing his love for Rahgaa, and his courage against even an Adjulon, Tiiveer said "From the moment I wake to the moment I sleep."*

*"See that it stays that way," said Gil with his renewed attitude.*

*"I'm not happy Lone with this plan. While I don't mind helping Rhana and your sister... I still have my own concerns to deal with. To your plan I say no but," and Gil smiled at Rahgaa then said "I am however open to an alternative."*

*It was Quaran who actually had one.*

*"I have one," the Bartender stated.*

*"I'm listening."*

*"This is a wolf station. Built by and, although virtually, manned by. You can't hide yourself forever from your own kind. That*

said, how about we use this bay as we asked but, leave it to the Tuhleesians only to man it."

"Interesting. Please... continue."

"Builders. Brought here under cover. They will assemble what all the others build. Add to that they will also maintain your systems as they once did in your past... and as Rhana did recently. We get what we need, you keep your exposure limited."

"And what of my part, not to mention Riihahl's?"

Rahgaa answered that one.

"You can go over the science of it. See to it that all pieces are inspected and functioning properly. Also, if there's a flaw or improvement that you find, you bring it to us, we'll review, and if we find it solid you will be in charge of implementing it. We WILL check your work... and you will check ours."

"That is becoming acceptable. You and your mate however are the Grand Couple... the highest of high. Yet your reaction was poor to say the least. How do you think 'lesser wolves' will react to this place... no less me?" Giljor asked.

Rahgaa conceded his point and answered "We recently put forth a major effort to regain tech that we have lost. In doing so mistakes were made. We have corrected them but learning them almost cost us dearly. We now have builders specifically for tech. They get a huge push forward by coming here. That helps us and you."

Confused, Gil asked "How does that help me?"

"When told of you, I'm sure they will react as we did. Once however, you show them you're not the enemy they believe you to be, you'll have your redemption. Add to that, the company you've had is small to say the least. Imagine what you could teach them, and imagine what several hundred of your own kind will do for those social skills of yours."

Lone actually chuckled at that last bit. So did Quaran.

"I can argue only one of those points," Gil told the crowd. "Lady Rahgaa pointed out to me recently that my skills are... what's the phrase you use Lone? A bit rusty?" Lone nodded and Giljor continued with "As I said, that issue could become a problem. I am not yet ready for a problem of that size, much as my ego may disagree. If I could start with a smaller issue, that would be a big help."

Lone kicked in and said "Your brother sent ships against us. He was able to cloak them as we do. That's a new wrinkle. As good as our tech Wing is, he's still having a bit of a problem figuring that one out. I'll give you the intel we have on that so far, you help us solve it. Big enough and small enough all in the same package. That bloody good enough for ya?"

"That... would be perfect."

Lone looked at Gil and said "I've turned off the blocks. If you would, for just a moment mind you, can you talk to me?"

Suddenly Lone was back in the bay but... in its prime. He stuck out his hand and Gil now knew why Lone 'wanted in'.

Lone hugged him as he shook it back and growled low in his ear.

"Fuck us over, even in the slightest, and I will take this station apart... piece... by bloody piece."

Lone was back in the real world again in an instant. He and Quaran tipped their hats, Rahgaa curtsied and Riihahl replied in kind.

"Been a pleasure doing business with you 'uncle'," Lone snorted.

Two ships headed out and, as the big bay doors closed, an apparition faded away... and headed off to exercise.

# Chapter 11:

## "No Room At The Inn"

*All of the assembled were grumbling a bit now. In the grand hall of the Arrowhead, every Temple Master, Clan First... and Guardian... were finally assembled. They were grumbling because a planned meeting hadn't started yet, and was now 30 minutes overdue.*

*"Mind your manners everyone, and remember what happened the last time," Rahgaa said reminding them how unhappy she was at the 'Rhana is real" meeting.*

*"Can you at least tell us why you have assembled us here and... on such short notice?"*

*"I cannot," Rahgaa told them.*

*"You call a meeting and can't tell us why?" the Temple Master asked slightly confused.*

*Calmly, Rahgaa told them "I didn't call you here."*

*"Then who did!?"*

*"To borrow one of Rhana's phrases... 'that would be me'," the big two toned wolf said coming into the hall.*

*Immediately, everyone stood up... even the Guardians.*

*"Sorry for the delay but I was checking on security."*

*"For?" Tahl asked*

*"This meeting. Temple Masters, you were all given stones by Ahdeera herself. I'm here to update you on knowledge that myself, and the Grand Couple, now feel you need to know. I mention the stones for a reason. Your escort guards are not here with you for the same reason. You will keep what I'm about to tell you as secret as you did those stones. When last Lady Prime gathered you, you were tasked with telling our people the news she gave you. I'm here to tell you this time, Ghost 2 will personally leave your Temple... or your clan... a smoking hole if you so much as talk of this in your sleep." Lone turned to the Guardians and said "That includes the*

Arrowhead. I can also tell you that THIS time... your likely poor reactions... have been accounted for."

Everyone nodded in some fashion or another and sat down quietly. NO one wanted the Mahrek of Prophecy angry, no less with them.

"Get comfortable everyone, this is a long and involved tale. Let me remind you that everything I'm about to tell you, however impossible it may sound, is completely and utterly true."

Lone began his tale and all assembled were stoked at getting 'inside information', not to mention honored that THE Mahrek would trust them so. Their faces were a sea of wonder as Lone told his tale.

"Before I continue, let me remind you I was late. I was late because I was indeed checking on security. There are over 5000 guards outside these doors ensuring our secrecy. Planet 51 tech is in place too to jam any electronic spying as well. Misbehave or worse, get out of line, and they will remove you... never to be seen again. Am I clear?"

A lot of nodding, and Lone then let out a whistle. It was the 'stand ready' command. All in the great hall heard uncountable men and women all come to attention, and all at once, outside the room. Lone continued his story.

"And when the light died down, Rhana and I saw who it really was," Lone told the crowd.

Like kids at a campfire story, a First called out "And who was it!?"

Lone sighed, and waved a hand to Rahgaa.

"If you don't mind Mahrek, I think I'll let you tell them this time," Rahgaa said politely.

On the inside though, she was thinking 'Hell no, YOU fucking tell them!'

"Hmmf," Lone snorted.

Lone looked back on the crowd, and braced himself.

"The real image was... Giljor Adjulon."

The uproar was deafening.

Another whistle, and 1000 Krannen poured in and lined the

walls 3 deep.

"BLOODY HELL! One more whistle from me... and this room will be emptied in seconds!" Lone shouted menacingly.

A quick hush fell over the crowd as they sat back down and once again minded their manners.

"Thank you lead guard. Please return to your post, I can take it from here."

A proper salute to Lone, and the guards all filed back out.

Lone told the rest of his tale. Rhana's image only got brighter when Lone told them of the bazooka and how Biiird gained him entry. When he told them who it really was, unlike Rahgaa, this time he was ready. The look on his face told all in attendance... Lone wasn't kidding.

Another hour and Lone was now up to the part where Rahgaa was brought into the mix. Everyone was in awe of Rhana's thinking. They knew none of them would have thought of it, nor been so bold in the face of evil incarnate, yet not one could deny the logic of it.

"Please, if I may?" Tahl said standing up.

"Of course First Tahl, go ahead," Rahgaa told him.

"Lone, if I may know, how did your sister and the others do in solving this enormous task?"

Lone was proud of them though and said "They failed. However, as Rhana predicted, Giljor now had some new ideas he hadn't thought of before. So, even though they themselves failed... the plan did not."

"Amazing... simply amazing" Tahl said with pride as he sat back down.

Lone had a thought and stuck it in before he continued.

"I want you all to know, Rhana himself wasn't expecting them to succeed. He only wished to break the loop of Giljor's thinking. They stayed... IN that station... for 2 whole days. Not one of them feared even once AND operated equipment none had ever seen before. I dare you, ANY of you... to do the same or better. Keep in mind adults, one of which is an Adjulon, got us into the mess we now find ourselves in. And yet, it was children who will likely get us out. I only say that as they should be commended for even just volunteering... and not admonished for failing."

Rahgaa stood up and said "As Prime of Tuhleesia, I assure you Commander, I have met with both of them and personally gave them the thanks of all our people. Please, give Salyan my thanks as well as I have not had the opportunity to do so."

Praise from the Prime herself. That issue was now officially closed. Lone was wrong, all in attendance felt as Prime did, but he wanted to make sure.

Riisa's image took a bit of a hit at first when they got to that part of the story. She did however redeem herself when they were told of her attitude and her idea with the gadgets.

Another hour and the story was now told, including the last trip to secure use of the bay.

" I can't caution you enough..." Rahgaa started as she stood up "... that if ANY word of this got out what the outcome would be for any of us and all of us. Getting Rhana back depends on absolute secrecy. Guardian Trenthaarian will setup a team of unique and technical builders. Giljor has agreed to letting them and only them work on the station. Just the exposure alone to that place could push our people forward tens of seasons sooner. Yes this plan has risk, but with great risk, comes great rewards."

Lone called out again saying "Temple Masters. It no longer matters that we here in this room know of those stones. It matters a great deal however, if Tamarak discovers them. Am I clear?"

Temple Master Tahlik stood up saying "Mahrek of Prophecy, when I became Temple Master I swore a blood oath to protect those stones. I gave that oath to none other than Lady Ahdeera herself. I swore then to protect them and as far as I am concerned... nothing has changed that."

All the other Masters said the same.

"Thank you all. I cannot tell you what plan we have. That is for your security. We told you this tale this evening to let you know who's involved... nothing more. Lady Prime and I discussed this and felt that keeping this from you any longer was not in Tuhleesia's best interest. As Rhana said of Lady Prime's mating... he merely used one brother, to stave off another. Here's hoping that history does indeed repeat itself. Now, that said, Lady Prime and I will take any questions that you have."

*There were indeed lots of those, and Lone and Rahgaa spent the next hour answering them all.*

*Tahl whacked Tooran on the back of the head playfully as everyone was leaving. It looked almost like a 3 Stooges skit.*
*"Hey... what was that for!?"*
*Tahl huffed as he walked out.*
*"You and your 'interesting times'!"*


*Scota was sitting on an exposed beam and swinging her crossed ankles. She was smiling and just watching Bird.*
*"What is it with chicks and DIY!?" Bird chuckled. "Now, if only I had a chop saw and a router table... welllllllll," and Bird laughed.*
*"A what and a who?" Scota giggled.*
*"Both 'whats' my dear. Only the Doctor is a... ya know what?... Forget it."*
*Scota giggled and said "Yeh knooooow Mistuh Bird..." she said playfully stretching out the word, "... I don't understand a thing yeh say sometimes (giggle) but... I shaw like the way yeh say it!"*

*"Scota I need to ask you something. What's up with that nasty cough of yours?"*
*"Oh doen yeh be worry'in bout thaht, I only get a little..."*
*"SCOTA!" Bird barked. "Don't take me for a fool. You scattered my background across the gossip mill so, you owe me. NEXT time I want the town folk knowing my business... I'LL tell them... not you. Now, tell me about that cough."*
*Bird's innate power wasn't lost on Ciana. Now, it would seem it wasn't lost on little sister either.*
*"I din mean no harm. They talk so unkindly about my sistuh and it just ain't fair! She'd give yeh the clothes off her back iffin yeh needed she would. She always did without, so I wouldn't have to. She's happy with you she is. Aye she's liked some men in the past but none like yue. I just wanted to show those ungrateful wenches thaht my sistuh wasn't an old maid is all."*
*"Ungrateful?" Bird said raising an eyebrow.*

"Aye. The night yeh arrived... noticed the rain did yeh?

"Duh,"

"Eh?"

"American slang... yes I did, what of it?"

"That was but a mild shower compared to the rains we get here. Many a night she'd put people up who were here when it got unsafe to travel... and at no charge mind yeh! She gives them the kindness of her heart and then they go and talk about her beehine her bahk. Say'in things like 'old maid' and 'Oh poor Ciana, kahnt get a man of her own'. Oh yeah, this one's my favorite... 'Poor Ciana, all that beauty and no man... there must be something wrong with her!'... it's not right I tell yeh! Just once I was happy to shove it baak down ther throats fer a change."

Bird was proud of her for that and said "I won't tan yer hide for it but, make that the last time okay?"

"Aye, I will. I want yeh to know tho... I didn't say anyting about yeh be'in in the army... just thah yue were a successful business man."

"I mean it!" Bird said sternly. "While I'm grateful you left that part out... that life comes with secrets... secrets I can't share. You understand me little girl?"

"Oi I ain't little!" Scota barked in self defense. "But I do hear yeh Mr. Bird."

Bird smiled and Scota melted.

"Scota, I do commend you for looking after AND protecting your sister like that. However, one time you may say something that can really get me or her or even you into a lot of trouble... the 'end up dead' kind... ya hear me?"

"Aye, I do."

"Now... heheheh... that said, have you ever heard of 'mis-information'?"

"Kahnt say thah I have."

"It's a form of warfare."

"Aye alright... but the town folk ain't my enemy tho."

Bird got serious and said "The tone in your voice not two minutes ago says otherwise. Here's the thing, I clear all information. From now on you either keep quiet, or go through me first. IF they annoy you again, let me know... and either I'll deal with it or... heh

*heh... I'll give you something 'interesting' to tell them...deal?"*

*Scota hopped off the beam, and shook Bird's hand with a devilish smile saying "Deal!"*

*Bird went back to work, and Scota went back to watching.*
*"Now... the cough?"*

*"Aye, alright," Scota said with resignation. "It started last fall. The sky one day went dark."*

*"A storm?" Bird asked.*

*"No, dark, as in almost night time... cept'in it was only around noon. No one knew what it was. Ciana said once, befaw I wes born, a great fire in the forest came and darkened the skies with smoke. She said it was like thah, only far worse."*

*"I've seen something like that before... continue," Bird told her.*

*"Aye. Remember how I met yeh the other day at the cliff?"*
*"I do."*

*"I go there a lot. Yeh may think this is silly but, I stare at the stars at night. I dream of traveling among them to far off lands. I stare out at the ocean too, and think 'what lies out there'. I've nevuh been off the Isle, nor has Ciana. Diifrens between us is... I want to go... she doesn't."*

*Bird was sweet to her and said "There's beauty out there to astound God himself... and just as much evil as to make the devil shudder in fear. There's an old proverb Scota, it says be careful what you wish for... you just might get it."*

*"I would luv to hear stories!"*

*"I don't see why not. I'll tell you only what I can though, deal?"*

*"Aye, deal."*

*"The cough Scota," Bird said reminding her he was still waiting.*

*"Ah yes. So as I was say'in... the sky turned black as ash most days. It lasted that way till last spring. Ciana tried to keep me shut in with her most days but..."*

*"You snuck out didn't ya?"*

*"Enny chance I could. I spent hours on the cliff hoep'in the*

skies would clear so I could see my stars... but they nevuh did. Once they had, the cough'in started. Ciana took me to the doctor here but he said it was beyond his knowledge. She's been saev'in coin evuh since to take me to a proppuh doctor in London. She says she has the coin for the fare, or the doctor, but not both. I'd like to believe her but, I wonder sometimes iffin her fear of leav'in isn't gett'in in the way?"

Bird was almost insulted for his new love and told her "While it's true I've only known your sister for a short while, I think I can read her fairly well. Trust me oh blond goddess... if she says that's the reason... then that's the truth."

Scota giggled and said "Ya read books and maps and such silly man... not people!"

"Oh? Sure about that?" Bird teased.

"Awlright then Commander... show me!" Scota playfully challenged.

"Scota... loyal and dutiful sister... protective yet kind... uneducated but not stupid... defiant somewhat but always ready by her sisters side when needed. You only like people you deem worthy and NO ONE gets near Ciana that isn't. You feel honor bound to return to her what she gave to you. You can't really so you support her where you can. You try not to cause her any trouble because that at least, is one way you can repay her something you feel you can't ever repay. As I've told many before you... how'm I doing so far?"

Scota was floored and sat a moment in amazed silence.

"How did yue do thah!?"

"It's easy really, well, for me anyway. If someone was angry, or sad, or happy... you could tell by their face and emotions right?"

"Of course."

"Well little sister... people are always like that... it's just that when they don't have a strong emotion... like anger or fear... the signs are still there, they're just far more subtle. People also talk different depending on mood. If they're happy they talk one way, yet another way when they're lying or hiding something. I just happen to catch what most people don't even know they're revealing. I see what they're doing, I listen to how they say something rather than what they say... and use that to form a judgment or opinion of them... that's all. I can tell you something else too. To me anyway, you have an accent just like I do to you."

"Aye, makes sense... so?"

"Sooooo... did you know it gets 'thicker' when you get excited?"

"Thahs amazing thah is!"

Bird chuckled and said "See!? Well, if you think that is, then here's another one for you."

Scota shuffled back and beamed like a kid waiting to hear a good story.

Bird chuckled at the sight and said "When you came to the cliff the other day you coughed. I also heard you cough the night we met. Other than the cliff... and that night... the weather has been fabulous. So little one... figure out yet what the two have in common?"

"Hmm... no."

"Water."

"Aye the night we met sure... but the cliff only has wind! Sure the sea has water but thah's at the bottom of the cliff... we were at the top. Explain thah one Mistuh Yankee man!" Scota said playfully challenging Bird.

"Wrong. The wind has humidity in it. It picks it up from the sea. Your cough is at its worst, when you're around water."

"Hue what?"

"Humidity... it's how much water is in the air."

"Air is air tho."

"Yes... heh heh... and no."

"Hmm... prove it!"

"Okay oh stubborn one. Go boil me a pot of water."

Scota smiled, and did as she was asked.

A few minutes later, and the pot was bubbling. Bird grabbed Scota and pulled her down with him so they were level with the top of the pot.

"Okay Scota, look at the top of the pot... just above the rim... what's that mist you see?"

"Steam... everyone knows thah!"

"Mm hmm... now look higher.... do you see steam or just air?"

"Air."

"Okay then, what is the steam made of?"

"Water... duh."

Bird chuckled and said in a poor Scottish accent "Pick'in up mah slang are yeh lass?"

Scota knew she was missing something as Bird continued.

"Okay so steam is..."

"What is 'okay'? Yeh said that several times now."

Bird then realized that phrase didn't come into being till the days of sub-mariners. It actually stood for zero and the letter K. The subs would display it to indicate "zero killed' to all in the harbor. Basically, if 100 went out... flying that banner meant 100 were still onboard. Bird now had a greater appreciation for the more subtler things in life.

"Um, more slang... it means 'alright'. Now as I was saying," and Bird quickly deflected. "Steam here... that's super hot water. Up there though... no steam, just air right?"

"Right!"

"Wrong."

Bird stood up and put Scota's hand high above the pot.

"Now, keep it there a minute or two," Bird told her.

After a minute or so Scota said "It feels odd."

"Okay then blondie... take it down and tell me... what's on your hand?"

"Dear Lord in heaven... it's wet!" Scota beamed as she just realized not only was Bird right but... she just learned something.

"Mm hmm. So you see little sis... air, isn't always 'just air'. Whatever sickness you have... water makes it worse. The more the water, the more you cough. That's why you did a lot the night it rained and, like your hand, only some at the cliff. So tell me... I'll bet the local doctor didn't catch that one did he?"

Sadly, and still staring at her hand, Scota said "No... he didn't."

"I have to go back upstairs and finish. Send your sister up to me when she gets back okay?"

Still staring at her hand, Scota just said "Aye.... okay."

Bird was walking up the narrow stairway and said "You heard her yes?"

"I did," Alydar said.

"Go through everything Cliff left on history. See if you can give me an answer. I want to know what the black skies were. If there's nothing there, give me a geological scan... and give me your best guess. Check the jet stream while your at it. I have my ideas but I want to see what you come up with as well."

"MRU" was all Alydar replied as she went to work.

Two hours later, Ciana came back. She'd been talking to one of the ship captains and was making plans to go to London. She figured by late August she'd have the coin to do both and was basically sorting out arrangements.

"Ciana, you're a sweet woman... watch yerself with this American... I don't trust him."

"Oh? And why's thah?"

"The colonies are protected by the crown... they don't have their own army... no less a Commander. Even if they did, a Commander? Nay... he'd be old enough to be yer father."

"Hmm, I'll keep it in mind Captain... thank you for your time," Ciana said as she curtsied and turned and left.

All the way home though... that's all she thought about.

"WHAT the bloody hell is this!" Ciana shouted.

She opened the door and had to shield her eyes from the sun. She did that because... there was no room... none.

"Look, it's like Christmas!" Bird said with glee throwing his arms wide. "No room at the inn... get it?... Room?... Inn?" Ciana was still scowling and Bird just said "Jeez... tough crowd."

"I can bloody well see thah! I said feel free to FIX it... not remove it!" Ciana hollered.

Bird was soft and said "You're even more beautiful when you're angry. Come here a moment."

Ciana crossed her arms and huffed. Bird however, grabbed

her arm and pulled her over.

"Oi!"

"Ciana look at that, what do you see?"

"Hmmf!"

Bird was now getting angry and hollered "I said LOOK AT IT ya stubborn Scottish wench! What... do... you... SEE!?"

Ciana finally looked down and saw an outer beam. An outer beam that was nearly rotted through that is.

"What's below us?"

"The kitchen."

"Aye lass," Bird said calming down. "You've been having bug problems in there... and for quite some time haven't you?"

"I not tole ennyone bout thah... Scota tole yeh dint she?"

"No Ciana, that kind of damage has side effects. Wasn't hard to guess. Yeah alright, I'll admit it's a bit of a shock but... I don't tell you how to cook... don't tell me how to build... deal?"

"I... I suppose."

"DEAL!??"

"Oh awright... deal. But you had better put it all back JUST the way it was."

"Not gonna happen."

"And why not!?"

"Because, it would be no better than what it was. I'll put it back alright but... nowhere close to 'the way it was'."

Ciana closed the door, and pulled Bird off to the side and spoke quietly.

"I have a question for yeh,"

"Mm?"

"I came by some information today."

"More gossip?" Bird chuckled.

Ciana was serious though and said "Yeh might say thah. Turns out the colonies are protected by the crown. They don't have their own army. Care to explain that one Yankee man?"

"Rut Roh" Alydar chuckled in his ear.

Alydar was actually enjoying Bird weave his tale, and was actually waiting for him to either trip up, or be tripped up. Seems Alydar thought Bird was breaking his own rule of non interference.

Bird may have agreed with her but... that was before Ciana.

"Yet," Bird answered her.

"Hmm, define 'yet'," Ciana said in a distrusting tone.

"Ciana look, war is coming... to the colonies I mean. There's a great discord among the people over the king. They want representation, he won't give it to them. The 'red coats' as we call them are the mightiest military machine in the world. If we declared independence, we had nothing to fight them with. So, in secret, a bunch of us gathered to see what we could do. The idea was, how can we make 20 men fight like 100... and how can we make a rowboat mightier than a warship?"

"And?" Ciana said still not buying it.

"And... word got out of what we were doing. It became known we existed... but not who we were. These are powerful men Ciana, more powerful than you could imagine. So we disbanded... for now. I was given capital, and setup as a legitimate business as a 'thank you' for my efforts. I succeeded, repaid the loan, and the rest you know."

"Oh my God, you should hear yourself... you're hilarious!" Alydar said laughing in his ear. "Yer KILL'IN ME Smalls!" Alydar was laughing so hard she was practically in tears. Teasing Bird further still, she said "Don't go anywhere... I'll be right back... I have to pee," and she just howled with laughter.

'**Enjoying yourself? X-(** ' Bird texted her on his internal HUD.

Alydar laughed so hard she couldn't even reply.


"Ciana look, no insult but the truth is, you're a simple innkeeper on an island even the king doesn't care about. No one of consequence even knows you. THAT, is why I trusted you with that. IF however, word of what I told you got out, you'd get a LOT of attention... likely from the king himself. That puts me, you... and Scota... in danger."

"Why tell me then!?" Ciana said angrily.

"Heh heh... you asked!" Bird said with a laugh.

"You are an odd man BirdOfPrey. How'd yeh get a name like thah ennyway?"

Bird told her the truth on that one.

"In the colonies, one can sign legal documents on your own at 18. To honor my mother, I legally changed it on the day of my 18th birthday. I haven't used my birth name since."

"And what is yer birth name?"

"Well, when the day comes that you legally call me 'husband', perhaps I'll tell ya," and Bird winked at her.

"Oooh, yer a frustrat'in man yeh are!"

"Perhaps, but, as 'The Doctor' once said... you're Scottish... go fry me something will ya?"

"And which doctor might thah be?"

"Doctor Who."

"Thah's wut Iem ask'in!"

Alydar could take no more and laughed in Bird's ear "THIRD BASE!"

"Never mind Ciana, it's a joke. Now, I'll leave you to your job... how bout you leave me to mine eh?"

Ciana was flustered but at least happy Bird gave her an answer, and went off to cook for 'her man'.

"Oh by the way... send Scota up here for me will ya?"

"Aye," Ciana said as she closed the door.

Once gone, Bird just said "Bitch," into his comm.

Alydar replied with pride "Biggest one you know!"

"Ain't that the truth."

Scota showed up a few minutes later asking "Well Mistuh Yankee man... what can I dooo fer ya?"

"Scota, this rumor mill of yours. Can I assume you know everyone on the Isle because of it??

"Aye, as do Ciana."

"Well then blondie, I need supplies. Tools, parts, all sorts of things. I find myself in need of a guide... care for the job?"

"Hmm, and what do I get out of it?"

"Fair enough. You be my guide. Ciana can't know what I'm doing here as I want it to be a surprise for her. In return, I said you were uneducated, but not stupid remember?"

"Aye, I remember," Scota replied slightly annoyed.

"Well then... you guide, and in return... I'll teach. Deal?"

Scota remembered her hand, beamed, and said "Deal!"

Scota was stoked at this new deal and asked "Okay Yankee man, what do yeh need?"

"Um, yeah, bout that 'okay' thing... IIIII wouldn't say that around the locals if I were you. That's part of the gossip you left out... if ya get my meaning?"

Scota smirked and had an 'I gotcha' tone in her voice when she said "Aye. So Mistuh Yankee, tell me, yeh think you'll get this done by mid winter?" Scota said waving around.

"If I get the tools and parts... try 3 weeks... 4 tops."

"No waaaay!"

Bird chuckled and said "Waaaay," and gave her a wink.

Scota giggled saying "Well then, what yeh be need'in first?"

"What I need you've never heard of... nor likely have. Given the lack of that, a blacksmith will have to do."

"Heh heh... um... a blacksmith yeh say?" Scota said with a 'uh oh' look on her face.

"Scooootaaaaa? What are you not telling me?"

"Oh nuth'in... we call him a 'smithy' around here and... welllllllll? Oh well, you'll see."

Scota grabbed Bird by the hand and took him to the stable to get the horses.

# Chapter 12:

## "You're Kidding Me... Right?"

Lone looked out from the balcony of the hangar and... he was not happy.

"You're bloody joking right!?"

"Heh heh... not exactly Wolfman," Remmy said sheepishly. "We added an agent to the moss to reduce drying time and... welllllllll... it had a bit of a side effect ya might say."

"Side effect!? SHE'S BLOODY PINK MAN!"

"I like it," Renny said in a 'what do you know' tone.

"Me too!" Raven replied. "I think it's pretty!"

Disgusted, Lone just walked away shaking his head saying "Ugh... women!"

Later that morning, Lone walked into the meeting room. All the Ghosts were there and trying hard to stifle a laugh. The reason for the laughter was Lone's chair. As a joke they made it pink. Lone walked in and sat down without even so much as a wince.

"Before we get started," Lone began," I would like to discuss that matter of your executions... preferences anyone?"

Now the table bust out laughing.

"Thah's bloody amazing thah is," Scota said with wonder.

"It's 'that'... not 'thah'... if you want an education, the first step is to actually sound like you got one. Remember how I told you I notice things about people?"

"Aye."

"People notice too... it's just that sometimes they don't notice they do. How you speak, is just as important as what you say. If you sound uneducated, no matter how much you know, people will only believe that you're stupid. Now don't get me wrong, I like your accent. I'm just saying you may want to consider making it just a bit softer is all."

"Yeh mean like a lady, a proper lady?"

"You... not 'yeh'... and yes, something like that."

"Ooh, I would love to be a proper lady I would."

"Forget it. Most of the 'ladies' I know are arrogant snobby back-stabbing bitches. Be a good woman instead. Lord knows, in this day and age, the world could use a whole lot more of those."

"Hmm... like this?"

"NICE Scota! Yeah, like that. Don't lose the accent and don't ever be ashamed of what and who you are. All I'm saying is if you thin it out some, you'll give people a better impression. They're going to form one about you regardless, the only thing you can control is... which one they make."

"Aye, I understand," Scota said making sure she enunciated the words.

Bird smiled as he rode next to her and said "Yeah, I believe you do."

"Anything else?" Scota asked eager to know.

"Actually yeah. What you say is half, HOW you say it is the other half. Remember when you do say something, say it with pride, or confidence... never arrogance."

"Aye, makes sense."

"Now, my crafty lil guide, I believe you were about to tell me what was so amazing?"

"Blacky is."

"Who?"

"Yer... er I mean 'your' horse, or rather Ciana's that is. He's a fine horse but he won't even let me ride him. Ciana is the only one he'd ever behave for."

"Horses are fine readers of people. They respect confidence. I've seen you Scota and I can tell you, you could do with a bit more. As I understand it, some girls your age are married by now, what about you? Any 'beau' in the works?"

"Well, I kahnt say... oops 'can't'... anyway, I can't say I didn't have my eye on a few. As I get older though, I find mehself ... er, that right?"

"It's 'myself'... though your way works around here."

"Ah, 'anyway'," Scota said slowly showing Bird she was learning, "As I get older, I find 'myself' being just like 'my' sister."

Bird smiled and asked "In what way?"

Scota chuckled and told him "I find myself look'in for a Yankee man of my own!"

Bird laughed and said "Look for a man who'll earn your respect, your love, and your devotion. IF that man happens to be a Yankee then so be it. Nothing wrong with your plan Scota," Bird smiled and finished with, "Nothing at all."

Bird and Scota came out of the woods, and into a small open field. Bird could see the smithy shop on the far side of it. He held up his horse when he saw said smithy go across and into it.

"You're kidding me... right!?" Bird said sideways to his guide.

"Wellll... ya did say you wanted a smithy!"

"Hmm," was all Bird said as he rode up to the barn door.

"Here now Yankee man... I got no quarrel with yeh," the smithy said.

Bird looked down from his mount and said "Hello Angus."

Bird gave Scota a look and she just shrugged her shoulders.

"This is your land is it not Angus?" Bird asked properly.

"Aye, what of it?"

"Well then," and Bird pulled out the sword in the saddle. Angus grabbed a metal rod of some kind as Bird threw it into the ground saying "Know that I come in peace. May the lady and I be welcome here?"

Bird knew of clan rules. True they were wolf clans but hey, gotta try something right? What surprised him was... it worked.

"Assuming yeh not lying...fine then," and he let go of the rod.

Bird walked into the shop and saw a bunch of tools and knew he came to the right place. Some tools were ready for sale and others were in various stages of construction. What caught Bird's eye, was the craftsmanship... it was really quite good.

"Scota, I want yeh to knoe Iem sorry for what I did. Will yeh tell yer sistuh Iem sorry for me?"

"Why not tell her yourself Angus?" Bird asked nicely.

"Yeh won her fairly Yankee man. Tis not my place ennymore. Besides, I doen think she be want'in the likes of me around... not after what I done."

"Try making a sincere apology Angus... I think you might be surprised," Bird said.

"Hmm, I'll consider it. Now, what is it that brings yeh to the ole smithy eh?"

"Ya know the 'special room' Ciana has?"

"Aye, what about it?"

"She don't have it no more," Bird said with a chuckle. "I gutted it... gone... nothing but open air. I aim to build it better than it was but, I need help. These tools Angus, first rate workmanship, truly," Bird said honestly.

Staring at Scota, Angus smarted "At least SOME people know quality when they see it!"

"Till he uses it, then he'll learn too," Scota chuckled back.

"Oi! My iron is of the highest quality!"

"HAH! Two, MAYBE three uses... and it breaks!"

Scota and Angus bickered back and forth, till Bird let out a whistle so loud as to silence them both.


"Scota my dear, remember what I said about 'reading'?"

"Aye, I do!" Scota said with a sly smile.

He gave her a proper bow, then said as he stood up "Then observe the master at work."

"Ooh, this should be fun."

Bird turned to Angus and said "You're right. The workmanship is some of the finest I've seen."

"Hah!" Angus shouted at Scota.

"Aaaaand, Scota doesn't lie to me. She can't because I know how to spot it. She truly believed your stuff will break. Problem is Angus... so did you."

"There is noth'in wrong with mah wares I tell ya!"

"Wrong and... you just lied again. So I have to ask myself, with quality this good, why is everyone complaining? Only one thing that causes complaints like that and... so many of them."

"HAH! Poor workmanship, jes like I said!"

"Wrong Scota... poor iron."

"Here now Yankee man... you come here just to insult me some more!?" Angus bellowed.

"Now Angus I'm certain of it. Your face and your tone tell me you know something you're not sharing."

"I pick the ore myself... most days I mine it myself JUST to make certain of its quality!

"Hmm," Bird said.

He went over and picked up a heavy rod. Angus did the same.

"Easy there Angus, this isn't for you," Bird assured him.

Angus lightened his grip but didn't let go entirely.

"I wanna test something," Bird told the two.

He stuck the rod in the hot coals and held onto the end. When he could feel enough heat he took it out.

"Look at me. The rod has some heat to it but not enough to burn me. See? I can still hold it in my bare hand. Here Scota... you try," and Bird handed her the rod.

"Aye, a bit warm but like you I can hold it. So?"

"Angus catch!" and Bird threw the rod.

Angus held it as long as he could then let it go wincing in pain.

Scota giggled and said "Angus, doen be such a baaaaaaby."

Bird got a touch cold and told her in an admonishing tone "He's not... he's got hypersensia." Bird glared at Scota some and said "And it's likely the giggle from little girls that's made him hide it all this time."

Scota shrank some and said "Sorry Angus."

"Oi... I don't want yer pity!"

"I wasn't giv'in ya any ya big oaf!"

"Name calling doesn't help either little girl... and not very lady like either," Bird said still glaring.

"Sorry Sir," Scota said impishly.

Angus was sad and said "Aye, tis true. I doen knoe whut yeh said Yankee man, but I haven't been able to handle the heat. Not since mah fahthuh tawt me theh trade as a wee lad."

Scota now felt bad and asked "So, whats wrong with Angus?"

"Hypersensia. Many babies are born with it. You and I could hold the rod but Angus could not. It's a common defect but most outgrow it by age 5 or so."

Alydar chuckled in his ear saying "Yes ladies and gentlemen... and the bullshit just KEEPS ON com'in! Heh heh heh."

Bird ignored his virtual critic and texted on his HUD.

**'Bullshit perhaps but if it helps, is a little white lie so bad?'**

Alydar replied sweetly saying "No, I suppose not."

Bird texted back only one thing to her... ' **:-)** '

Alydar giggled and Bird continued.

"Angus, your nerves are too sensitive. Some babies have that and as I said, the body corrects it in time. Some however never do and carry it into adulthood. Scota, what you and I feel as 'warm', to Angus is scalding. The nerves in his hands are..."

"And forearms... iffin yeh must knoe," Angus corrected.

Bird continued "And his forearms are far more sensitive than they should be. Iron my dear, needs to be heated to a very high temperature."

"How come?" Scota asked.

"Impurities," Angus answered. "Iffin yeh doen heat it enough, the iron woen get out the impurities."

Scota was looking like she sort of got it when Bird asked her "Shall I clarify?"

"Ooh, I like dat word.. 'clarify'... hmm, mind if I use it?"

"I'm sure Lone would be honored," Bird said with a chuckle.

"Who?"

"Never mind."

"So, you were say'in?" Scota reminded him

"Scota, let's say you're cooking hagus. Lets also say you have to make the shell really hot because if you don't, it will get weak spots and crumble when you serve it."

"Ok.. er... alright... I'm with yeh so far Yankee man."

Bird winked at her for the catch and correction and said "Now, let's say your the finest cook in all the land. The best made dish is no good if it falls apart right?"

*"Right!" Scota said with a smile.*

*"So, if you have to make the shell really hot, how do you do that if you physically can't take the heat?"*

*"Alright then, I understand that. But, why does Angus's wares break then?" Scota asked truly curious.*

*"The iron. He can't get it hot enough without causing him searing pain. His craftsmanship is first rate but... if the iron itself is weak welllllllll..." and Bird didn't finish his sentence.*

*Scota was kind now and asked honestly "So, if you can't take the heat Angus... why not get someone to do the forge for ya?"*

*Angus was actually relieved his secret was out. In a land that values strength over weakness though, it still didn't help.*

*"Scota, yeh knoe I've had my eye on yeh sistuh fer a long time now aye?"*

*"Aye, so?"*

*"So, truth be told, she was theh only woman for me. I never looked ennywhere else. I barely make enough coin to keep myself go'in, how'm I go'in to support a wife? No less... one as fine as her. No children of mah own Scota, no one to teach and work the forge. No coin left over to hire someone either."*

*Now Scota smiled and said "Angus, yeh ain't been to the inn in almost a week now. When was the last time yeh had a proper meal?"*

*"It wasn't proper wut I done. That was the drink talk'in not me. I want ye to knoe thah... I truly am sorry. I've stayed away for that very reason."*

*Scota scampered off saying "I know where yer kitchen is Angus. I'll cook yeh up something to eat while you men folk talk!" and off she went.*

*"Angus, liquor is a powerful poison if you take too much of it. It also does something else."*

*"Wuts thah?"*

*"It reveals the truth. You were angry because you've kept that secret bottled up inside you all these years."*

*"I suppose. Listen Yankee man, as you can see, mah wares ain't selling like they should. Can this hyper whatevuh yeh said...*

can it be fixed?"

"Sorry Angus... not that I'm aware of. Scota is right though, get someone else to do the forge."

"I kahnt, like I said I ain't got the coin."

"Angus look, Ciana blew a fit at me when she saw the room."

The smithy laughed hard and said "Aye, better yue than me Yankee man... I seen her when she be angry... hahaHAHAHA... no thank yeh!"

"So you know how she'll be if I don't rebuild it like I say aye?"

"Aye I do."


Scota came back in with a well made stew and Angus was ever so grateful.

"Scota, I need you to work that rumor mill for me... interested?"

"Ooh, say what yeh need Mister Bird!"

"Heh heh, I want you to spread a lie, and help a neighbor. I want you to tell them that my knowledge showed Angus a way to make his iron 5 times stronger than it is now. Let them know good quality wares won't be long in coming. Make sure you explain that Angus didn't know this trick. Tell them... hmm... tell them its new science from the colonies. That should silence any questions."

Scota saluted with a smirk. Thing was though, she did it the British way with the palm flat outward. Bird smiled, and turned her hand to the American... now 51... way.

"IF! We ever make it to 51, you can salute me then. Until then... don't ever salute me again."

"51?"

Bird dropped his salute and told her "One of those far off lands you asked about."


Bird turned back to Angus saying "As I was saying, I need those tools to do my work... PROPER tools not this crap iron. I'll work your forge for you. In return, you'll give me the tools I need in fair trade. You'll have plenty of good iron left over to help you with your coin problem. Deal?"

Angus stuck out his hand and shook Bird's briskly.

"Aye... deal!"

"Scota, can you give us a moment?"

"Have no fear Angus, Bird's message will be Isle wide by morning. I'll keep yer secret too so's ya know," and Scota went to get the horses.

"Yer a good lass yeh are Scota! Doen let no one tell yeh no different!" Angus called after her.

Bird got serious and told Angus "Listen smithy, if you hadn't gotten out of hand with the drink, I'd have had no quarrel with you either. I'm willing to give a man a second chance but that's it... just one. Lay off the drink, do right by me and Ciana, and we'll do right by you. Screw with me, and I'll hang your gutted carcass out to dry for the morning light to find. One man to another... we understand each other?"

"Aye... we do."


Bird hollered from his horse "Feel free to sleep late smithy! My day don't start till noon and usually goes well past midnight."

Angus hollered out "Yer joking right!?"

"I have a great sense of humor Angus. Work however I never joke about... HEEEYAHHH!" Bird hollered and took off on his horse.


Bird went to the Isle's version of a lumber mill after Angus's. They couldn't fathom why he wanted lumber in such sizes but, his money was good enough. And sawdust!? What in all the heavens did he want that for and why so much of it? They just figured he was a Yank, and went to work fulfilling his order.

Next up was the potter. He was just as befuddled as the sawmill was. Bird ordered the oddest shaped pieces they'd ever heard of. He also ordered over a thousand of them. Yet again, Bird's money was good enough and so they went to work fulfilling his order as well.


"Hello Mary, remember me?" Bird said walking into the lady's shop.

The sight of a man... in a shop for women!? Oh this would only fuel the gossip line.

"Not easy to ferget Mistuh Yankee. Are yeh sure yeh wouldn't be more comfortable let'tin Scota handle this perhaps?"

Bird smiled and Mary almost had to cross her legs.

"And deny you the pleasure of that accent you love so much? Why I wouldn't dreeeeeeam of it!"

Just for fun, Bird half bowed and kissed the back of her hand. Scota giggled knowing that would stoke the gossip line for weeks.

"Now, you sell linen yes?"

"Aye," Mary said nearly dreamlike.

"And I'm here to buy some yes?"

"I be guess'in so."

"Well then, lets get down to business shall we?" Bird said in no uncertain terms.

Mary tried showing him samples but Bird knew what he wanted.

"M'lady, I need a custom order. Show me the lowest grade linen you have."

Mary showed him but was really hoping he'd spend some coin and get the good stuff.

"I calculated Mary that I need 75 bags... made of this cheap linen. I want them half a meter by 2, with one end left open, like a pillow case. I'll also need them in two weeks or less... probably less. Can do?"

It was the cheap stuff but at least it was a sizable order and Mary was happy with that.

"Aye can do. Will yeh be need'in ennything else?"

"Heh heh, aye lass, I will. NOW... lets see the good stuff."

Now Mary smiled. She showed him her finest linen. Bird just laughed.

"Oh Mary Mary Mary, this is maybe what, 100 thread count at best!?"

"You know about.. wait noooo... how does a man know about something like thah!?"

"This 'man' knows a lot about a lot of things. Now, like I said... show me... the good stuff."

Scota merely smiled and nodded her head as if to say 'yeah he ain't kidding'. The more Bird shined, the more her sister did and Scota was loving every minute of it.

"I doen have but samples. No one here has the coin nor the desire for something this fine, so I doen keep any on hand," and Mary pulled out the good stuff from behind a small counter.

"Alright Mary, as they say in the colonies, NOW we're talk'in!"

Bird picked out the fabric and the colors. When he showed Mary the patterns of what he wanted, she almost fainted.

"Nooo way a man made plans like these!"

Bird chuckled and just said "Waaaaaay."

"Dear Lord man is thehr ennything yeh can't do!?"

"Nope."

"And the size! It'll take the king's bank to get that much!" said a very shocked Mary.

"How much?"

Mary stood proud and said "A tenner and not a shilling less!" thinking that would make this crazy Yankee think twice.

Bird didn't even blink and said "Here's 15. You have 4 weeks and not a day longer," and in his usual commanding tone he finished with "Do what you have to but... get it done." Bird stopped at the door, turned and tipped his hat and said "It's been a pleasure doing business with you. One last thing, this is a surprise from me to Ciana so... keep it quiet alright?"

"On mah life I swear I'll not ruin yer surprise."

Bird nodded and was gone. It took 5 minutes for Mary to get over the wonderful smell of the BirdMan and come back down to Earth.


Angus wasn't used to the late day but he managed to keep up. True to his word, Bird gave him enough good iron to last half a season. Ever the inventive one, Bird helped him form a shield around the forge. Bird showed Angus how to build a very specific tool as well.

"Ere now Yankee... what do yeh call these again?"

"Tongs," Bird told him. "They'll let you heat up your iron, but keep you at a good distance from the heat. Also, I bought you some gloves from the leather craftsman. They're triple thick and go up to your elbows. Using both, you should be able to work the forge just fine on your own. Also, you can sell this tool to the town folk for use in their own hearths."

"I have to admit, I was wrong about yeh Yankee man. Yeh are a good man. If I can't have Ciana for myself, I'll settle for nothing less than a good one by her side. Treat her well."

"I will Angus. And by the way, don't be so hard on yourself. Yeah alright you didn't get your dream girl but, that don't mean there ain't someone out there for you ya know."

"A broken smithy with no coin!? Hahaha yer right Bird, you do have a sense of humor!" Angus heartily laughed.

"Tell ya what Angus, I'll 'keep my eye out fer yeh'," Bird said teasing in his friend's accent. "Can't do no harm now can it?"

"Aye," Angus laughed, "I suppose not."

Two days later and the grounds of the inn looked like an episode of 'This Old House' with supplies scattered everywhere and more coming in daily. Mary even stopped by and Ciana was getting a little miffed that they were all avoiding her and going straight to Bird.

"Oi Mistuh Bird, yeh weren't kidd'in when yeh said yeh took it all down, good Lord in heaven!" Mary remarked at the demolition.

"Indeed, something I can do for ya linen lady?"

Bird was as stripped down as a man could get in 1757. Just the sight of him made Mary turn her head and blush.

"I made two of the sacks yeh asked for. I didn't want to make anymore in case yeh wanted changes or something."

Bird pulled on them hard trying to tear them. Bird's strong arms made Mary smile. Bird saw it and curled an elbow and teased her.

"Go ahead Mary, strong as an ox I am! Hahaha."

"Oh noooo, I couldn't," Mary said turning beet red.

Just then she reached out anyway and gave a squeeze.

"They'll do just fine Mary, thanks."

Mary blushed some more and actually curtsied. She thought of Bird as a proper gentleman and simply minded her manners.

Angus showed up about 30 minutes later, and he was nervous

as hell. Bird saw him from above, smiled and nodded sideways.

"Well look at who it is, ferget yer way to this place did yeh Angus?"

Angus pulled out some flowers he had picked just for Ciana and handed them to her shyly.

"I been want'in to tell yeh proper how sorry I am fer the other day. I... I want yeh to know it was the drink talk'in an not me."

Ciana was sweet and said "Oh Angus, yeh always been good to me an Scota and I appreciate thah I really do. Yer a fine man when yeh not on the drink, I want yeh to know thah."

"Yer a kind woman yeh are Ciana."

"Oh Angus look. I know it dint work out between us but thah's no reason to be a stranger. Thah said, I kahnt have yeh act'in the fool an get'tin yerself killed either. Promise me Angus that iffin yeh come here, you'll be off the drink. Do thah, an yeh be welcome here ennytime... promise?"

Angus could not believe that Bird was right.

"I swear to you, I'll honor yeh wishes from now on... promise."

"Heh heh, well then, I have some leftover hagus I could heat fer yeh... interested?"

Angus smiled and said "Not right now, I have to get these tools to Bird but... perhaps later?"

"Awright then. He's where you'd expect him to be."

Angus just stood a moment and smiled.

Ciana playfully shooed him saying "Well... go on then!"

Angus was kind and told her "Aye, I didn't win yeh heart... but at least a fine man did. I'll tell you same as I tole yer sistuh, yer a real fine woman Ciana... doen let no one tell yeh no diffrint... and if they do, well, you just let ole Angus knoe alright?"

Sweetly, Ciana told him "Aye Angus... I will."

Bird nodded and smiled at Angus as he wiped his hands. Angus remembered something, looked around and made sure he was alone... then saluted Bird. Bird chuckled and saluted back as Angus made his way up the stairs.

# Chapter 13:

## *"The Big Reveal"*

*"So Mr. Bird... I brought yeh what yeh asked fer,"* Angus told Bird.

*"Angus, just Bird will do fine. True I'm a learned man and yes, true that in your world I'd be considered a gentleman. That said, you'll not find me 'putt'in on airs' as they say. You'll find I'm more common folk like yerself. No insult intended."*

*"Aye Bird, I noticed thah and, none taken. Yer a fine man as I said but trust me... yeh ain't common."*

*"Angus? I'll take that as a compliment,"* Bird said with a smile.

Angus looked around and asked *"So Bird, jes what are these T shaped irons for ennyway? And why the holes?"*

*"Angus my good man... if you care to help me... I'll teach you!"*

Bird had no idea how closely guarded the trades were in this time period. Angus jumped at the chance for two reasons. If Bird was going to be stupid enough to teach him then, in his mind anyway, he wasn't passing up the opportunity. Second, it was a way he could repay Scota and Ciana AND Bird.

*"Something wrong Angus?"* Bird asked.

*"Perhaps. Where's all the timber for theh walls?"*

*"You're looking at it."*

*"These scrawny things? Alright Bird... show me."*

So, Bird did.

*"Angus, your problem is you think strong has to be big. Try this,"* and Bird set two buckets some ways apart. Then he put a 2x4 across them saying *"Stand on it Angus. Go ahead, right there in the middle... go on!"*

*Angus was nervous but the kilted Scot did as told.*

*"Now, just a little... jump up and down."*

*Only 2 jumps and the board cracked as he thought it would.*

*"See? I told yeh... too scrawny."*

*"Correct... now... watch."*

*Bird took 3 more and a hammer and some nails Angus brought. Though only nailed together, Bird had formed them into an I-beam of sorts. Turning the beam proper, he put it on the buckets same as the other.*

*"Now Angus... try it again only this time... really jump."*

*Angus did and couldn't believe it. Just changing the boards slightly and he couldn't break it now matter how many times he jumped nor how hard he did it.*

*"Bloody brilliant!"*

*"I'm an engineer Angus. That's what I do."*

*"What's thah?"*

*"An engineer? Well, I'm the guy that figures out how something is built then, finds ways to build it bigger better stronger... with only half as much and in the end, half the weight.*

*Angus was like a kid on Christmas morning.*

*"Show me more?"*

*"Heh heh, c'mon Angus let's get this wall built and I'll show ya as we go."*


*Bird did. Over the next week the rumor mill was on overload and... competing with the gossip machine. Bird showed Angus how the walls were put together. A new sill beam to replace the rotted one, and 2 walls up in less than a day. It would have been more but Bird ran out of nails. No one could believe all that... and only 2 men did it all. Bird also showed Angus a trick. Using Mary's sacks, he filled one with sawdust, then slid it between 2 of the I-beams. A good wind was blowing but Angus could feel nothing when he put his hand behind the sack.*

*"It's called insulation. Trust me Angus, where I grew up, your nearest neighbor was as far away as this Isle is long. Most times 3 or 4 times that much. So, you learn to be crafty and... waste nothing."*

*"Aye, bloody amazing. But I still doen get what the T plates*

were for. Sure I know what we did with them but, what purpose do they serve?"

"On top and bottom of the wall at each stud, it serves two purposes. First, no storm or age will pull the wall apart. Second, the wall will always be square and never shift from it."

"And we did it all in less than a day... simply amaz'in thah is." Angus said with wonder and pride.

The next day and Angus was back. He brought some angle irons this time and couldn't wait to see what Bird had up his sleeve next. Bird showed him some simple tricks to figure out angles and, by end of day two, the roof was framed and covered. Now the science kicked in and Ciana was busier than ever, though she knew everyone was trying to sneak a peek at Bird's project. Several offers of help came but Bird merely said they were appreciated, but not needed.

Now Bird was out back with a huge kettle and a roaring fire. He was boiling pine sap, and Angus had no clue why.

"Those angle irons were shear brilliance Bird. No storm in the world will tear thah roof off now!" Angus said.

The angle irons held the roof trusses to the wall tops and thus, Angus's prediction would be correct.

"You forgot snow. You do get snow in these parts right?"

"Of course, what of it?"

"The roof beams. Snow gets heavy Angus, even heavier when its wet or starts to melt. You and I put those beams up with ease yet, they'll hold 3 times the load."

"Iffin I hadn't seen it with mah own 2 eyes I would never have believed it." Angus looked at the pot and asked "So, this?"

"Pine sap. It's like the tree's blood. Ya know that sticky stuff it oozes?"

"Aye."

"When boiled just right, it soaks into the wood and gets in the seams... once cooled, no water will penetrate it or rot it."

"Bloody amazing. Say what yeh will but you Yanks are clever folk yeh are!"

"Heh heh, well, some of us anyway."

Bird had just made the world's first creosote. The kettle would only allow for so much so covering the wood went slow, but he and Angus got it all covered in 2 days. Bird then showed him how to make stucco using plaster as a base. Laying in some of the cheap linen Mary brought, Bird showed him how to make it even stronger.

Ciana however was a trooper. She knew Bird wanted it to be a surprise, so she never peeked. Scota was like a puppy that just wouldn't go away so, Bird put her to work. She cleaned up messes till the dust made her cough. Bird had her fill the sand bags and keep the sap boiling, things like that. Scota was happy to help and, never lost that huge smile watching the men work.

"Yeh knoe, a week ago I would'a said yeh were a liar or just plain crazy. Looking at it now tho, I still kahnt believe we did all this in a week!" Angus said looking up from ground level.

"Not to mention the ladders. Those worked like a charm."

"Bloody brilliant those were!"

"Well Angus, last project... then it's all inside work."

"Aye, and yeh say these are roofing tiles?"

"Yep."

"Well, God knows yeh ain't been wrong yet. Shall we then?"

Bird's crazy potter shapes were brought in yesterday. It took 3 carts with 4 horse teams each. It also took all day as it took 5 trips to bring Bird all he ordered, yet not crack a single one.

Bird and Angus got on the roof and Bird showed him how the puzzle pieces fit. They were reddish brown and Bird built Scotland's first and only... Hacienda tile roof. Half shells face up with an inverted row to hold them together underneath. Bird poured a bucket of water on it when they were done and Angus was just blown away.

Using some clever joists on the floor, Bird managed to extend the room 3 feet all around and still keep it stable. Now with a huge interior to finish, Bird went to work solo as Angus went to work building Bird's crazy hearth contraption. Angus didn't know it but, it was the same device that impressed a whole bunch of wolves once.

Bird gave Ciana a quick kiss on the cheek and said "So," then leaned into her ear and whispered *"Any more bugs?"*

Ciana smiled back saying softly *"Not a one thanks to you."*

*"Suhweeeeeeet,"* Bird chuckled and headed upstairs.


The window took a bit of doing, and a whole day, but he managed to get it in and sealed. Another day for plastering the walls and last was the floor tiles. The potter had no idea what those were for either but delivered them just the same. Making a suitable glue was an issue so, one night Bird snuck away, and got some from one of Alydar's shops and it was an issue no more. Dyed plaster for grout and now all was set.

Thanks to Scota, Bird was able to see some of the homes in the area. One thing he noticed was almost all of them had 4 poster beds. Now, so did Ciana. While Bird was busy building, the carpenters were busy turning and carving. Now with bed delivered, Bird was building that today. All the while town folk brought sacks of goose and chicken feathers from their dinner kills while Bird built. Bed frame now built, Mary's goods got filled with down. A comforter made of the same material was brought in and Ciana couldn't fathom what was in such a giant sack. The town and croft folk were actually having fun keeping Ciana in the dark.


*"Dear sweet Lord,"* Mary exclaimed.

Scota brought her and Angus to see the room they helped build as a thank you from Bird. They were all in the room now looking it over.

*"Well mistuh Yankee man, I oenlee got one question for yeh."*

*"Hmm?"*

Mary laughed and said *"When are yeh com'in to build me mine!?"*

Angus remarked *"And the heat from this thing yeh had me build... I kahnt even go near it!"* Angus said in wonder as he now saw it in operation.

Everyone moaned in delight as they laid on the bed.

*"Well little sister... did I do good?"* Bird asked teasingly.

*"I... I... I don't know where to look first! Oi Bird, iffin she doen marry yeh fer this I will!"*

*"Sorry but, me and Mary here are running off to Edinburgh,*

*didn't I tell ya?"*

*Everyone laughed and Mary play slapped him saying "Oh ya big flirt yeh!"*

*"Heh heh."*

*It was a chilly day but Bird insisted Ciana wear no wrap. He was at the back corner of the house where he'd spent the last 10 days. His supplies came in faster than he expected so, today was reveal day.*

*"But Bird Iem sooo cold!" Ciana barked in protest while Bird covered her eyes.*

*Scota and Angus were with them.*

*"What was that you said Scota? Mid winter as I recall wasn't it?"*

*Scota stuck her tongue out at Bird.*

*"Oi! Cheeky lil wench!" Bird teased back.*

*"Come on Bird it's sooo.... cold... out... here... Oh my Lord," Ciana said as Bird uncovered her eyes.*

*Seeing the new room stick out from the inn, and blend in seamlessly as if it had always been there... Ciana forgot all about the cold. Scota was bouncing up and down and just hugged her sister.*

*"Wait till you see the inside," Scota said softly.*

*"Bird I... I... Oh my!" was all Ciana could manage.*

*"Now my dear, you can get out of the cold."*

*Ciana saw the oddest roof but, thought it was lovely. Angus told her about it as he was excited too.*

*"I didn't have the time to do the whole roof but... heh heh... that's in the works," Bird chuckled.*

*Back inside and it was still chilly. Ciana was still wanting her wrap and saying so... as only a cranky female Scot can.*
*Eyes covered again, suddenly, she wasn't cold anymore. Ciana, like most of the women, was barefoot most of the time. The really warm but slightly rough floor, was the first thing she noticed.*

*"When I tell you I'm going to rebuild a room," Bird said as he took his hands away, "I rebuild a room!"*

*Ciana was simply... awestruck.*

"What in all the... and yeh did ALL this... in just ten days!?"

"Yeah well, Frankenfurter beat me. He built Rocky in just 7," Bird teased knowing no one would get the reference.

"I swear Mistuh Yankee, you say the strangest things sometimes but... oh my... it's beautiful!"

Bird scooped her up and literally threw her on the bed. She was afraid she'd hurt it or herself. She did neither. Relaxing in comfort she'd never felt in her life, she actually hollered at Bird.

"Oh no... yeh didn't!?"

"Oh yeah... I did!" Bird said with pride knowing she meant going to see Mary.

Ciana was in tears as the 3 showed her the room. Being a man, Angus talked of how strong it was and how what you didn't see was just as important as what you did. Scota of course, took the feminine approach pointing out all the pretties and how warm it was.

"And look!... No draft!!" Ciana hollered all excited as she went by the window.

"So," Bird teased, "I believe payment is due but... we can discuss that later," Bird told her with a sly smile.

"Angus... Scota... thank you both for all yeh help but... get out." Turning to Bird she said "Oh nooo yeh doen... weel be discuss'in that right now!"

Scota smiled and left, and Angus winked at Bird then did the same.

"Jeez lady ya don't have to be so... Mmmmmmff!" Bird said as Ciana planted a huge loving kiss on him.

Bird hugged her, kissed her back, and didn't want to let go.

Ciana stared up at him with eyes bluer than his and said "Tell me true... you did this... ALL this... jes fer me?"

"Well, I had help but... yes... just for you," Bird said lovingly.

Ciana hugged him tight and buried her face in his chest and began to cry happy tears.

Bird just melted, hugged her back, and said "You're welcome."

Later that night, Ciana couldn't sleep. She was in the warmest room, and the most divine bed, she had ever been in in her life. She insisted Bird sleep there as it was only proper seeing as how he built and paid for it. Bird insisted she did, as he built it for her. They both argued when Bird suggested he would take the room, but it would be hers for tonight. That Ciana accepted. The bed she was laying in was enormous to her. Bird built it 6 feet wide and 9 long. Now, Ciana was deciding... whether she should share it or not. Further still, she was out of it now and pacing.

Wearing only a thin gown, she marveled at how warm she still was. Even the floor was still warm beneath her feet, a luxury she's never known. Bird had only been in her life a month but, she just couldn't help herself. Seeing all the things around her well, fight it as hard as she could, Ciana was head over heels in love.

She argued with herself as she paced. She was a proper woman she was. What if Bird thought her otherwise for her actions? What if the town folk or the other crofts found out!? Ciana was thinking some very 'warm thoughts' and try as she may, she just couldn't get the handsome stranger out of her mind. She was still arguing with herself when a knock came on the door.

Covering herself with the super fine blanket, Ciana called out "Who is it?"

"It's me Ciana. You alright? It's late and I can hear you walking all over the place. Is everything okay?"

Ciana was shaking when she said "Bird?"

"Yeah?"

"Come in."

The blanket was on the bed by the time the door opened.

"You okay up here?" Bird asked honestly.

Bird was staring at the loveliest vision of a woman he ever had the pleasure of seeing. Right now, he was trying to think of anything that would delay his departure.

"I'm fine thank yeh. I was just thinking is all."

"Of?"

"I was thinking you should sleep here tonight."

"Oh no, we agreed. For tonight anyway, this room is all

*yours.*"

"*I knoe I knoe, but I really think you should.*"

"*C'mon Ciana, do we really have to do this now? You stay here, I'm going back to bed.*"

*Ciana was shaking now and made the boldest move she ever made.*

"*No I insist, you should sleep here. That said, I... I... I never said I would leave now did I?*" *Ciana said so impishly and frightened that she almost ran from the room.*

*Bird... closed the door.*

"*Are you sure about this?*" *Bird asked tenderly.*

*Ciana was crying softly and said* "*No.. I mean yes... I mean, oh I don't know what I mean anymore,*" *she said as she turned away from Bird.*

*Facing away, Ciana felt there was no turning back now. She thought of the dinners together they had, his smile, the walks at night she purposely stayed up for. This is what she'd been waiting for, her prince had finally come. What if though... she wasn't a princess?*

"*Yer maddening yeh are BirdOfPrey. I waited mah whole life for mah prince to come. And here comes this brash, full of himself, smooth talking Yankee with more secrets than a wishing well.*" *Still crying, Ciana said* "*I didn't want to fall in love with you... I didn't.*" *Turning around she actually yelled at him saying* "*But yeh had to go ahead and make it so damn impossible not to!*" *and Ciana just broke down in tears.*

*Suddenly Ciana was wrapped in the arms of the one man who frustrated her so, and the one man she prayed would never go away.*

*Bird grabbed her wrists and tenderly pulled her hands over her head, then slipped off the nightgown she was wearing. BirdOfPrey, Ghost 1 himself, was pumped up on adrenaline.*

"*Ciana,*" *Bird said soft and smooth.*

"*Aye?*"

"*Trust me?*"

"*(sniff) More than I should.*"

"*Put your hands behind your head... and lift your hair.*"

*Bird walked around behind her and hugged her tight.*

*"Stand on your toes."*

*Ciana did as she was told. She discovered, she actually liked that. Bird placed a feather soft, warm moist kiss... right on the nape of her neck. Massive shivers ran all the way down to her knees.*

*Now she was shaking again as Bird whispered in her ear, "You... were never an impossibility. You see my lovely raven haired Scottish lass... I fell in love with you too, and haven't looked back since."*

*BirdOfPrey, never said more honest words in his life.*

*Ciana gave up all reserve, spun around, and kissed Bird hard. She was in love and now, for her, she had crossed the line of no return. Bird now couldn't get to her neck like before but she was happy as she truly didn't think she could handle another blast like that.*

*Bird scooped her up and laid her in the bed. He attacked her neck with such passion that Ciana almost screamed with bliss.*

*Passionately she stopped him and said "Bird wait. I knoe yer a man of the world and all but, well, what I'm say'in is... I'm not exactly a woman of the world."*

*"Wait, you mean you're a...?"*

*"Mm hmm, so I'll thank yeh kindly in advance for going easy on me."*

*Bird stood up, and took off his shirt. Ciana sunk into the bed and pulled the covers only to her chin. No way she was missing this sight. Bird took down his pants and underwear at the same time, then kicked the crumpled bundle to the side. His HUD came on and he saw things on it go into shutdown mode. The moonlight was beaming through the window and Ciana saw the fine red haired man was everything she thought... and hoped... he'd be. Chiseled jaw, powerful arms and a broad chest. Long powerful legs and a manhood that had Ciana wondering just how soundproof this room really was.*

*Bird stood tall and smiled a smile that Ciana thought would light up hell itself.*

*"Will this do m'lady?" Bird said proudly but teasingly.*

*Ciana let out a soft giggle and said "Nicely thank yeh."*

*Bird let out a small laugh, then went serious as he climbed under the comforter saying "Now... where were we?"*

*Scota had a coughing fit and got up to get some water. She passed by Bird's room, only to notice it empty. So was his bed. She looked out the window that overlooked the cliff... but he wasn't there either. Scota smiled and looked up to the ceiling.*

*"Sleep well my princess... and may your prince be all that yeh hoped he'd be... and everything you've waited for."*

*Scota blew out the candle and went back to bed.*

# Chapter 14:

## "I Feel Pretty"

150 builder wolves all pulled any weapon they could when the apparition showed up. They were briefed somewhat on where they were going, and what was expected of them. They were not told however of the station's 'AI' system.

"Good wolves!" Lone called out. "While I understand your concern, your weapons will not be needed. This station has been on automatic since it was first built. Yes true, it was built during the time of the twins. Truer still it was built by Tamarak BUT, it was designed by his brother Giljor. As such, if YOU had built it... who's image would you give the computer system?"

They all looked at Lone. Seeing he was only flustered by them, and not the apparition... they eased up. They knew more about tech than any wolf but... they still knew very little. So, what Lone said made sense to them.

"Giljor used his own image, and the images of the scientists who helped him. Creepy perhaps but... deal with it. If this is all it takes to frighten or alarm you, then you are of no use to me... or Tuhleesia."

Harsh but... it was the wolf way. Point made, Giljor talked to Lone.

"AI system eh? Clever to say the least."

"Yeah well, the less they know the better. They're here to do a job, nothing more," Lone told him.

"Have no fear my mirror image. I and the others will play along with your charade and... for the same reasons you stated."

Lone then asked "How's the new exercise program going?"

"Slow but progressing well. I can tell you this though, remember that project you gave me to work on?"

"Mm hmm."

"I still can't figure out how he did it. Your onboard cameras are of exceptional quality, my compliments to your Tech Wing. They pick up all forms of wavelengths, many in the invisible spectrum."

"Get to the point," Lone commanded.

"Point is, when Raven is invisible, she's still solid and still taking up space, she's merely hidden. The Aardvarks as you call them, didn't seem to be invisible. We gave up on that line of thought and focused more on 'they were 'not' there... then they were'."

Lone replied "Hmm, so like they weren't invisible, they only appeared that way?"

"Correct. Checking those other spectrums, it would appear they truly weren't there the whole time, nor nearby. It would seem however, that my crafty brother wants you to think they were."

"I'll give this new information to Remmy and see what he comes up with. While I NEVER thought I would say this to you..."

"Yes Lone?" Gil asked.

Lone tipped his hat, and said "Nice work."

Gil got serious and called to Lone as he walked off.

"Commander, can I tell you something?"

"Don't see why not," Lone said calmly.

"In the past, I was like you are now. In my day, I was the one everyone turned to, looked up to, or sought out. I've seen, thanks to you and Rhana, what being the top of your field and having no support can do or cause. I suppose what I'm saying is, I am really enjoying being a major player, but not the only player... as your phrase goes. That said, I've been where you are. I don't envy you but I want you to know, it will get lonely at times. Very... very... lonely."

Lone nodded and said "I'll keep it in mind."

"Should you find me correct... well... you know where to find me."

Lone hollered over his shoulder "Thanks for the advice 'uncle'. Like I said... I'll keep it in mind."

That's when Gil dropped a bomb on him.

"Grandpa... actually," Gil said with a friendly smile.

Lone... froze.

"While I know you still don't trust me, I thought you'd like to know. You're a wolf and well... heh heh... we shed!"

Lone was cold and commanded "WHAT... did... you ...do!?"

"Hmm, what's the phrase? Oh yeah... bite me, asshole. I took a hair or two and compared it to mine, nothing more."

"YOU!... are a bloody hologram!" Lone hollered.

"Yet you forget, the real me, what's left anyway, is on this station. A sample wasn't exactly hard to come by."

"Awright, let's say I believe you. As twins, your markers are nearly identical. So, how can you be so certain?" Lone said with a 'hah!' tone.

"True but again, you forget our mother was infertile at one point. While markers like DNA and such would be inconclusive, there's one thing you don't know. Mother was, what you call artificially inseminated. Once Tamarak and I were actually conceived, the doctors of the day injected us with greelattin while we were still in mothers womb."

"Greelattin? That's the wolf name for Vitamin C. I don't get it."

"Very good Lone, it is. In Tuhleesians, that one compound is critical for birth. Mother was barren because her body couldn't process it as others do. As such, the doctors injected us directly to see if that would bring us to term, rather than get it from mother. Tammy may be my twin but he is his own wolf, as am I. As such, those levels were checked and adjusted individually. THOSE levels are vastly different in each of us."

A gadget walked up to Lone and handed him a data crystal. The other wolves freaked even though they knew some were aboard.

"I put my findings on that crystal. Feel free to have any you wish, double check my findings."

"Trust me... I intend to."

Lone was walking back and said to the open air "Bloody hell! Like I need this shit right now!" and disappeared into Raven.

Bird was still out cold when Ciana woke up. Never before had she *known or felt this level of comfort... and feminine bliss. She was beaming and felt like she wanted to burst from the inside. Joy, wonder, comfort and security like she's never known and all of it... at once. With a feeling of contentment unlike anything she'd ever known, she piled her hair under her cheek and laid back down on Bird's shoulder, and did something she'd not done since before her dad died... she went back to sleep.*

*"And jes... um 'just'... just what are you doing out of bed!?" Scota playfully admonished her sister.*

*"Excuse me?, I'm an hour late as it tis! Oh that bed is so divine I must have overslept." Ciana told her trying real hard to 'play it cool'.*

*"Aye, I'll bet it is, heh heh, and you're going right back to it! I can handle things here."*

*Ciana looked around and noticed... she actually could. She was up to where Ciana would be by this time as far as the chores.*

*"I'll need yeh to go outside later and slaughter a chicken fer supper but, thah can wait. The sailing ships won't be coming in for another week or two and we have no one staying in the inn now so... goooooo.... go ahead... off with yeh!" Scota said with a giggle.*

*"Well then little missy, iffin yeh can handle this all on yer own... why do I hafta kill the chicken? Why doen you do it?" Ciana playfully said calling her sister's boast.*

*"It be rain'in. My cough'in fits are made worse by water. Bird showed me. Last night I had one just after the rain started. I noticed I had left my window open some and sure enough... 'cough cough cough' soon as the rain started. I closed it, covered my mouth with a cloth and stoked the fire and lo an behold... Bird was right again as my coughin' went away."*

*Ciana was like 'hmm' as she answered "Yeh know, I have noticed yeh not be cough'in as much. And yeh be tawk'in funny of late too. Well, not so much funny as... hmm... more proppuh."*

*"Heh heh, thah be 'yer husband' yet again!" Scota teased. "He's been teaching me things... sciencey things. Thah's how I knew about the water. He also told me... yeh can be the smartest person in theh world but iffin yeh sound like an idiot, thah's all the world will take yeh for. Soooo, I been practic'in. I been try'in to sound more*

*proper... and been being careful not to sound like Iem putt'in on airs." Scota smiled realizing her work was paying off and said "I guess if you be notic'in... it must be working."*

*"Aye, and fine proppuh lady or not, I'll always luv yeh," Ciana said with a kind smile.*

*"He is an amazing man ain't he?" Ciana said with faraway eyes.*

*"Aye he is," Scota started with a sly smile. "And I imagine that amazing man is gonna be hav'in fits iffin he wakes up alone."*

*"Aye, I suppose yer... wait... YOU KNOE!??" Ciana barked.*

*"Of course I doooo. Why do yeh think I'm doing this by meself... grrr... MY self?"*

*Ciana was impish and asked "And yeh doen think ill of me?"*

*Scota was happy and spoke kindly.*

*"First of all 'big sister', yer happiness is written all over yer face. And, why shouldn't yeh be happy!? Ciana, you've doted on me like a mother hen ever since dad died. Now I not be complain'in but, you've looked after me fer so long that yeh forgot to look after yehself. I'm grown now, at least grown enough to look after things around here." Scota was kind, hugged her sister and said "Go now, for once... take a day for yehself... and leave the worry'in to me for a change. You've more than earned it."*

*Ciana smiled and said "Angus was right."*

*"About?"*

*"Yeh are a fine 'woman' Scota. A young one perhaps but... a fine one all the same."*

*Scota replied back just as kindly, "Go now, and show Mistuh Yankee man... so are you."*

*Ciana gave Scota a soft kiss and a hug, and headed back upstairs.*

*"Bird? Yeh... yeh... yeh not be think'in me a loose woman now, do yeh?" Ciana asked almost frightened.*

*Bird was waking up... finally.*

*"The only thing I'm thinking right now is how comfortable I am... how I'm not moving because of it... and how you aren't either," Bird said in a grumbling 'just waking up' voice.*

Ciana had been up since dawn... that was 3 hours ago. Since then, she'd been having a wrestling match with herself. Thoughts of doubt plagued her. What if Bird thought she was a cheap woman? What if Bird was like 'every other man' and just took off? Nothing but 'what ifs' for hours. All the while though, she couldn't unwrap herself from the comfort that was the man she chose. Now, in the morning light, would he choose her?

"Listen Lady Bird... HEY! I like that!... LADY BIRD! Yeah, I like that a lot. That's what I'm gonna call you from now on... any objections?"

One sentence... just one. One sentence from the red-haired stranger and 3 hours of doubts went away in an instant.

Smiling and snuggling, Ciana said "Not a one 'Lord Bird'."

"Ooooh... okay that... I DON'T like. Sir perhaps but even then only in proper company. Otherwise, I am not 'Lord' or 'Master' or any other shit like that. I'll leave that to the insecure assholes who need that to soothe their egos... got it?"

Ciana was impressed by the level of confidence and merely said with a chuckle "Aye Mistuh Yankee man."

"Heh heh, now yer tawk'in."

Bird closed his eyes and began again.

"Anyway, listen Lady Bird, I have a secret life remember?"

"Aye, I do."

"You can't be a part of it. Perhaps one day but... not now. I was only coming to an inn for some information about the Isle, nothing more. I didn't plan on ANY of this happening. Now that it has, I have safeguards I need to put in place. NO WAY in hell I'm letting that life touch you or Scota. That said, I need to go away AND be left alone. I may be gone for an hour or two or it might be days. Thing is, I can never tell you where I'm going nor what I'm doing. All I can tell you is, I'll be making sure no one in that life suspects anything of this one. It may suck not knowing what I'm doing or where I'll be... but it's the only thing I can think of to keep you safe. My question is... can you live with that?"

"Promise me one thing then," Ciana cooed.

"Ooooh yeah... not real good with those, but I'll try."

Ciana leaned her head up and said "Promise me you'll always come back to me... promise me that and I'll put up with yer 'other life'."

"While I may not always be on time... I can promise you that when I do return... you Lady Bird, will be the first stop I make."

Bird cared... truly cared. Ciana didn't think it possible but she was now even more in love with her handsome Yankee man than ever before.

"I'll be hold'in yeh to thah Mistuh Yankee man!" Ciana said honestly.

"Wellllll, I think you'll be the only thing I'll be holding right now," Bird said playfully as he hugged her and rolled on top of Ciana.

"Bird, I doen knoe how they do things in the colonies but, around here well, I doen think I hafta tell yeh no one can knoe bout this."

"Aw, and I was going to have invitations printed up and everything!" Bird joked.

Ciana play slapped him and barked "Iem seeerius! No one can knoe. Scota figured it out but, well, she's a good lass she is. Aside from her though... no one... I mean it!"

"As they say back home, I'm not the type to 'kiss and tell'. You, me, Scota and Alydar... that's it. I promise."

"Uh, boss!? Don't get me wrong when I say this but... WHAT THE FUCK ARE YOU DOING!??"

Bird smirked at his invisible companion.

Ciana looked up curiously and asked "Al uh who?"

"Alydar," Bird smiled.

"Aaaaaand, who might he be?"

"DON'T even THINK of it Commander! Jeez man have you lost your mind!?" Alydar barked.

"Alydar... who I affectionately call Ally. My personal assistant and the only one who knows my secrets and my other life. If I'm going to keep you safe, I'm going to need help now and then."

Ciana wasn't happy, but at least it made sense. She REALLY didn't like what Bird said next.

He was putting on his clothes saying "I'm going downstairs and make us some tea. I expect to find you where you are, and... heh

*heh... AS you are... when I return."*

*Ciana just giggled and sunk into the bed.*

*Bird stopped at the door and said "Oh by the way... Alydar?... is a 'she'... not a 'he'."*

*Bird laughed and closed the door quick as a pillow came flying at his head.*


*"That would'a been a Mahrek blade if you had done that to me," Alydar chuckled.*

*"Yeah well, aside from me, you don't really have many people to hone your social skills on. You get to interact but also on a limited basis. Besides, it looks like I'm gonna be here awhile. You really wanna stay cooped up in the doll house?"*

*"Hmm, I suppose your right... heh heh... 'Lord Bird'."*

*"Yeah yeah... fuck off bee-yoch," and Bird popped into the kitchen.*


*"Haven't heard you cough in awhile. That's good right?" Bird said to Scota.*

*"Aye. I heard what yeh... grrr... what 'you' said... anyway I thought what have I got to lose? Turns out you were right. I told Angus what yeh said about air hold'in water, and he made us your hearth machine for theh kitchen. Now I cough only when we do lots of cookin' but at least its not all theh time."*

*"Scota... couple things. First, don't get hard on yourself over your words. While it's good that you care, it won't happen overnight either. Also, thank Angus for his kindness for me. As for the cooking, I'll see if I can put a vent in here that you can open as you need. That should cut your coughing down even more."*

*"Clever Yankee yeh are ain't ya?" Scota teased with a mock curtsey.*

*"I do try," Bird smirked. "And actually, it's a hearth 'device' not machine. A machine has moving parts."*

*"Aye, alright. Oh! Angus told me to tell yeh it takes him two hours to work the forge where it should only take one, but at least he's doing it on his own now, and he thanks yeh for it."*

*"Good to hear," Bird said smiling.*

*"Bird?"*

*"Yes blondie?"*

*"I doubt enny threat I made would have enny effect, so, I'll be ask'in nice."*

*"Asking what?"*

*"Don't hurt her... please. She be deserv'in a little happiness and she's all I have and, welllllllll, take good care of her okay? She's earned that much at least."*

*Bird's heart melt they way one does when they see a cute puppy that's been hurt.*

*"You'll be happy to know, I'm already making plans to make sure I don't... or at least my other life doesn't."*

*"I'll be count'in on yeh," Scota said and handed him his tea.*

*Soft and kind, Bird told her "THAT little lady, is one thing you can always do," and he headed back to bed.*

*Bird handed Ciana her tea, got undressed and slipped back into bed.*

*"Now, where were we?"*

*Ciana curled her leg over Bird's and laid back down in his shoulder.*

*"Oh yeah... heh heh... that's right."*

*Ciana bit the pillow... hard... and let out a scream as her body muscles went damn near out of control. It was two hours later and it was actually she who wanted more. 'More'... is exactly what she got, in spades. That was her fourth scream. She got more than she bargained for as Bird just wouldn't stop. She also noticed, he was taking great delight in each and every scream. He also took great delight in telling her, right after the previous one, that he knew there was another one in there and just kept going. She fell onto the bed and rolled over on her back and almost pleaded for Bird to stop. He smiled, then dipped under the covers kissing everything and anything in his path. Bird felt like he could spend hours just on that beautiful flat stomach of hers.*

*"OH MY DEAR LORD!" Ciana screamed when Bird made it to between her luscious thighs.*

*Bird merely showed her his hips weren't the only thing that could make her scream. Ciana was so exhausted, she actually fell asleep again after her fifth and final scream.*

*Ciana was looking out the window. The sun was setting and she found herself unable to fathom several things. First, she couldn't fathom a window so large and with such a view. She also couldn't fathom such a size, and not feel a single draft. The wind was blowing hard outside, yet Ciana actually had to change to a lighter nightgown as she was just that warm. Touching the window it was warm too, and she had no idea how Bird did it. She felt weird standing there as she could neither feel nor... and this really freaked her out... hear the wind. The only sound she could hear was the pounding of her heart as Bird came up behind her, hugged her, and nuzzled her neck. The last thing she couldn't fathom was the sun, it was going down. She had spent the whole night AND day in this room. But oh... what a day it was.*

*Staring out the window, Ciana asked "Bird, this other life of yours. Is thehr ennything yeh can tell me?"*

*Bird sighed and said "In my mind, it was paradise. All I can tell you is... its farther away than you could possibly imagine."*

*"Do yeh miss it?"*

*"Greatly."*

*"What was it like? This paradise of yours?"*

*"Can't tell you that. I can tell you this though, I didn't just leave it... I left it to protect it. Enemies were coming. Very very dangerous enemies. I left because it was my responsibility to protect it. All I can tell you is, I'm looking for a way back... and I won't rest till I find it."*

*Ciana was sad.*

*"Suppos'in yeh do find it... what of me?"*

*"When my real brother died, God put another in my life to replace him. He is what I call my adopted brother as we're truly that close. So my Scottish lass, I'll tell you the same thing he told me once."*

*"And what be thah?"*

*"Where I go... you go."*

*"That alone frightens me," she said. "I've never been off the Isle. And what of Scota?"*

"Plenty of room for her too. Trust me, if I ever do get back there, you wouldn't need the inn or anything else ever again. Not only that but, you'd be treated like a queen."

Ciana turned and looked at Bird with loving eyes.

"Like I said, leaving here frightens me. Want teh knoe what frightens me more?"

"Mm?"

"Living ennywhere... without you," and she kissed him lightly.

"Why are you so afraid to leave?" Bird asked honestly.

"I dunno. I know everything about the Isle. Every croft, every man and woman... and every nook and cranny. Out there though, I don't know ennything. Lots of people with manners and proper education and such. Me? I'm just a simple farm girl running an inn."

"Hmm,"

"Ere now! I may not knoe yeh as well as this Alydar lady, but I know that tone Mistuh! Yer plann'in sumthin I knoe it!"

"Heh heh... busted," Alydar teased.

"Ciana?"

"Aye?" she said with trepidation.

"When's your birthday?"

"Oh it's... wait... why?"

"Heh heh... smart lady, Ya know boss? I'm starting to like her already!"

Bird brought up his HUD. The 'not so proper' texted reply only made Ally laugh.

"Sorry Lady Bird, just gonna have to trust me on that one."

"Hmm... yer's first!" Ciana said.

"November 15th... now... yours?"

"20th July... why?"

"Cancer... good fit... I'm a Scorpion."

"What? And yer a what?"

"Zodiac... nevermind. This birthday of yours, how old are you gonna be?"

"24."

"Well my dear, THIS birthday is gonna be the most special one of all... heh heh... So Sayeth The BirdMan!" Bird chuckled.

"Now answer me this... you like the room I built for ya?"

"The room is grand," Ciana giggled and finished with "The company however, leaves a bit to be desired."

"OH! Is that so!?" Bird said with mock wounded pride.

"Aye," Ciana teased "He's a mystery and talks in secrets. That is of course when he's not speak'in gibberish. Now I ask yeh... what kind of man is that for a good respectable woman such as myself?"

"THAT'S IT!" Alydar laughed "I'm officially listing her as 'cool' in my book!"

Another not so proper text and Alydar was roaring with laughter.

"I'll tell ya what kind of man he is!" Bird hollered playfully as he scooped up Ciana and threw her onto the bed. Falling on top of her, he told her "He is THE only man for you!"

Ciana smiled up lovingly and told him "Aye... that he is."

"So Yankee man, why'd yeh wanna knoe what I thought of the room when yeh already know I like it?"

"Aye lass," Bird teased "But, I was wondering what EXACTLY you liked about it."

"Why?" Ciana said cocking her head in that 'what are you up to' fashion.

"Becaaaaaauuuussse," Bird taunted "I need to know what you do and don't like... 'iffin' I'm to build you that mansion I promised you that is."

Ciana was floored.

"Bird my love, tuh be honest, I thought yeh be jes bragg'in when yeh said ye'd build this! So I called yeh on it. I have luxury beyond ennything a king or queen could ask for. Truly Bird, as long as I have yeh close, this is more than enough."

Bird heard 'my love'. It was the first time Ciana ever said it. Bird so loved the sound of it, he swore to himself then and there... it wouldn't be the last.

"Listen to me Lady Bird, if your gonna be hang'in with the BirdMan, your gonna learn a lesson real quick."

Almost afraid, Ciana asked "And thah would be?"

"Accept that you deserve it and... the most important lesson of all..."

"Mm?"

"Stop thinking... small."

Suddenly, for Bird and Ciana, playtime was over. He was getting dressed and was gonna head downstairs for some food and drink when a shrill scream of shear panic could be heard. It was Scota. Bird was at top speed and putting his harness on at the same time. Ciana had more to put on and was after Bird shortly thereafter. Had the bedroom door not been open at the time they never would have heard it.

Scota was coughing hard and on her knees in the mud and rain. She was holding the dead chicken Ciana was supposed to kill. Scota's problem was, the 3 wolves who surrounded her wanted it too. Seeing her cough and obviously weak, they decided she was a better meal.

They were snarling and closing in when one went for the kill. It jumped in the air to pounce on Scota. It was 3 feet away from its target when it yelped. Powerful as the wolf was, its chest was no match for a massive human arm swinging a wing shaped blade. Bird threw his arm so hard only the back tip of the blade was exposed. Without wasting an ounce of momentum, Bird swung in the mud and hurled the dead carcass off the blade and at the remaining two. He roared holding both blades outward and looking every bit like Wolverine from the comics. Message received and understood, the remaining two made a hasty retreat. Ciana saw it all and couldn't believe what she just saw. She ran and grabbed Scota.

"What the blazes yeh do'in out here!? Come on, let's be gett'in yeh inside."

Scota was on the verge of passing out. Not from fear, but from lack of air. She tried to stand but just couldn't. Bird didn't care and just scooped her up.

"Get some dry firewood, woman... NOW! Bring it upstairs!" Bird hollered and headed quick as he could for the new bedroom.

Upstairs, Bird stripped her down as much as he dare, then

*threw her under the blankets.*

*"Get that fire roaring!"*

*"It's bloody hot in here as it is!"*

*"DO IT DAMMIT!"*

*Ciana did, and Bird braced the door open with a brick he left for this very purpose.*

*"Yankee (cough cough cough) Yan... Yankee man?"*

*"Shhh, don't talk right now and breathe through your nose as much as you can. The air in here is dry as hell and the draft from the door will blast ya with even more dry air."*

*With puppy dog eyes, Scota looked at Bird and said "Yeh were right, I could count on yeh couldn't I... thank you."*

*A soft smile and Scota was out cold.*

*Softly, Bird told her "Anytime, lass."*

*"Ciana, go downstairs and get some dry towels. I'll watch over her till you get back."*

*"Got it!*

*Once Ciana was gone, Bird's HUD was up in a flash.*

*"Alydar, tie me into the med bay!"*

*"GO!" Alydar hollered letting Bird know it was done.*

*"Whew, thank God." Bird said seeing nothing serious.*

*"Her lungs are not in good shape though," Alydar told him.*

*"True but, time and this hot blast should cure that."*

*Bird pulled out a hidden emergency med kit from his boot. Another piece from his other boot and putting them together Bird now had a 21st century hypo-spray.*

*"Penicillin and Prednisone, 20 milligrams each," Bird told the spray and it beeped at him.*

*Bird injected her behind her ear and Scota's breathing eased up some. Bird had barely put it back when Ciana came back with the towels.*

*"Dry her off better than well. Hold a dry towel in front of the hearth heater and get it just shy of smoking. Leave it on her chest while you dry her off. Aside from needing a good night's rest, she should be fine.*

*Ciana was crying and said "Bird?"*

*"Mm?"*

"She's all I have. I don't know what I'd do without her. Thank you... truly."

"You're welcome," Bird said as he left the room. "But your wrong about one thing... she's not all you have.... not anymore."


Bird knew something wasn't right, but he couldn't place it. The wolves around here had plenty of territory. Normally wolves would act that way if you strayed into 'theirs', but they very rarely came into 'yours' without provocation.

Bird hoisted the dead wolf over his shoulders and took it a short ways into the woods. With shovel in hand, he patted the earth smooth and said a few words on the wolf's behalf. In his mind, it only did what wolves do, but Bird didn't feel it targeted Scota. As such, he gave the wolf the dignity he felt it deserved.

"You okay boss?" Alydar asked kindly.

"Hated killing that wolf. Sadly, I didn't have any other choice. I will say this though, I've been thinking about why they attacked. I can't shake the feeling like... someone rattled their cage. I'll tell ya this much, when I find out who... they'll be sorry they did."

"Ya know, Ciana was right," Alydar said kindly.

"About?"

"You really are a good man. In my opinion... love... suits you."

"Thanks sweety."

Bird was right, and he was wrong. Someone did indeed 'rattle their cage'. He was wrong in the fact that... it wouldn't be him who'd make the guilty party sorry they did.


Ciana had a loving smile on her face. She stayed with Scota and was watching her love from the window. She watched her man come back and put away the shovel and knew exactly what he did, and why. Seeing that, the 'all mushy inside' feeling, had returned.

# Chapter 15:

## "A Bird, A Bishop And An Avatar"

*It was 2 days later and Scota was once again up and about. Not well, but she was. The gossip machine was trying to out-scoop the rumor mill. When one of them reached Angus, he dropped everything and headed out.*

*"Angus, yeh dint see wut I saw. I was never so proud and impressed... and frightened... at theh same time. He was almost like a wild beast himself but, I dunno, it was more than thah."*

*"I jes be wonder'in what 10 wolves be do'in attack'in like thah?"*

*"Ten!? Heh heh, oh Angus, it'll be every wolf on the isle by the time those gossiping hags finish."*

*"Well then, how many were there?"*

*"Just three."*

*"Still... tis 3 too many.*

*Ciana and Angus were outside and out of earshot. She was confiding in him.*

*"Angus, I ne'er seen so much anger in my life. It was more than thah tho, it was like he, oh Angus yer gonna think this is silly,"* Ciana said not believing her own words.

*"I think when it comes to theh likes o'him... not much is silly."*

*"Angus, he was furious beyond ennything I e'er seen but, it was like he was controlling it. Mah heart almost jumped from my chest when he roared at the remaining two. I seen people angry Angus, they be out of control. They be mad at everything an everyone."*

*Sadly, Angus said "Aye, I be know'in a thing or two bout thah."*

"Oh Angus Iem sorry, I didn't mean it like thah."

Kindly, Angus told her "Aye... I knoe yeh dint. Go ahead."

"Angus, he controlled it like I said, but the look on his face, he was, Angus yeh may think me out of mah mind but... he was insulted. Yeh could see he truly cared for Scota. The way he roared at them was like he knew them somehow. Stranger still, it was as if they knew him... like he was one of them. Angus, they dint jes back off like most wolves do, they ran fer their lives. Oh Angus, what have I gotten mehself into?"

A now sober Angus was actually liking having a clear head. Most thought of him as an oaf, and he only gave them good reason to. Now, it was the new and wise Angus talking... not the old one.

"Aye Ciana, twould be a fright fer ennyone but, yeh said it yerself... he cared for Scota, and protected her in his own way. Did he do ennything to her or you afterwards? Yeh know whut I mean, like treat yeh jes as bad?"

"Heavens nooooo, He even knew doctor'in!. Angus, Iem not scared of him but... I'll admit I am scared."

"What of lass?" Angus said truly not getting it.

"Angus, he be a learned man, a tradesman and several at thah! He knoes doctor'in and threw Mary for a fit know'in material and sew'in and such. Angus I swear I doen think there be ennything he kahnt do. And fight!? Lord I swear ye'd need a small army to get ennywhere near him iffin he dint want yeh to. He's everything a woman could want. He could have enny he wanted as well."

"Sorry lass but, heh heh, none of whut yeh jes said sounds theh least bit scary to me."

"Angus, yeh knew mah dad. Yeh been around mah whole life. Yeh know I'm just a simple lass, an inn keeper. I'm no fool nor an idiot but I be nowhere near as smart as him. How does someone like me hold onto a man like thah?"

Angus was kind and told her "Aye, I known yeh since we were wee little. No one I knoe Ciana has been harder on themselves, nor feel'in less deserv'in than you. While I don't mean to be pry'in into yer business... have yeh told him how yeh feel?"

"Aye, I actually have."

"And whut did he say?"

"He told me I was theh only woman for him."

"Well then lass, do yeh be want'in to insult him?"

"Heavens no!"

"Well then, if he said it's so... then it's so. Trust me on this lass, don't trust him on his word... and yeh will insult him. Theh only fear my dear friend is in that pretty head of yours, and nowhere else."

Ciana gave him a sweet kiss on the cheek and said "C'mon Angus... I'll fix yeh something proppuh to eat before yeh go back."


"Angus! Just the man I wanted to see. Can I borrow you for a moment?"

Bird pulled Angus into another room.

"Ere now Bird, I want to thank yeh fer what yeh did. Scota and Ciana been like family to me since we been children."

"Anytime Angus. Anyway, moving on... how you doing with the forge? I hear you're working it yourself now correct?"

"Aye, takes me a lil bit longer but, I get it done proppuh now."

"Good! Now..." And Bird looked around as he curled him in around his shoulder saying softly "You any good with glass?"

"Tipping one sure... making it no. Could the potter be enny help to yeh instead?"

"No. I'm working on something to make sure no more wolves show up unseen... and I need glass. The potter is already working on it for me but he's only working on a piece of it. Alright scrap that, how bout this?"

Bird looked around again and said what he needed.

"Angus, when I met you, you were drunk. You and I both know that was an old habit. Now I know you've been keeping your word but... something tells me you know the brew-master don't you?"

"Aye, I do."

"Think you could take me to him?"

"I doen see why not. Let me finish mah meal and I'll take yeh to him."

"Sounds like a plan. Now all I need is glass. Hey Angus, if I can't find a glass blower, I'll have to do it myself. Can I borrow your forge if I need to?"

*Kindly, Angus said "Ennytime yeh need it."*

*Then Angus had a thought and said "Yeh know, on the mainland, there is one in the highlands. Not so sure I could take yeh there though."*

*"Any reason why?" Bird asked knowing he was missing something.*

*"Aye, mah tartan. I be a MacDonald. The glass maker yeh be need'in is a Campbell. I wouldn't expect yeh to know this but..."*

*Bird cut him off saying "The king sent for pledges of allegiance from the clans. The MacDonald's were late and he sent a party after them... led by a Campbell. Been a blood feud ever since."*

*"Sweet Lord man! Ciana was right, is there ennything yeh doen knoe!?"*

*"Hey, I like the History Channel... sue me," Bird chuckled.*

*Angus shook his head and said "The lasses are right, yeh do say the strangest things sometimes."*

*"Yeah well, that aside, a clan war isn't something I want to get involved in. Thanks for the warning. I'll keep it in mind in case I don't find another way."*

*Now Angus looked around and pulled Bird farther from the kitchen and any possible prying ears.*

*"Bird, speak'in of warn'ins... tis not mah business to say but, there's one I feel I need to give yeh."*

*Angus was deadly serious so Bird listened.*

*"Talk to me Angus."*

*"Theh Bishop. We have one thah comes here from the mainland."*

*Angus made a sign of the cross before he continued.*

*"Yeh might say, much as he of all people shouldn't but... he's had a loving eye towards Ciana for a long time now. He's a wicked man he is Iem certain of it. Ennyway, with you around now... I thought yeh should knoe."*

*"Great, just great. Angus the whole point of me coming here was to 'lay low' as we say. Lately I've been doing anything but. Oh well, at least I know... thanks Angus."*

Angus was truly frightened and said "Jes yeh remember... yeh dint hear that from me and I'll deny it if they say yeh did."

Bird gave a friendly smile, and said "Unless these walls suddenly start talking Angus... no one will know a thing."

Angus shook Bird's extended hand, and went back to eat his meal.


"Bloody brilliant!" Lone bellowed in frustration. "First, I get a pink ship... then a family reunion... now thi thi THIS! AAAACHOO!" Lone grumbled and sniffed saying "Oh this is just fab!"

Renny was a tad cold saying "You'll get no sympathy from me. You've been running yourself ragged... as I predicted... what did you expect?"

Prime was sitting at the table and chuckled "Yeah... um... what she said!" and the two ladies actually high 5'd each other.

"Damn, I ain't had one of these since I was a kid on Eden. Was nasty then... I swear it's worse now."

Prime sipped her tea and said "You should see the doctor. At least perhaps he can keep it from getting worse."

"I am and... for that very reason," Lone said politely.

"So doc, what do you got for me?"

"Bed rest... 3 days at least."

"I like you doc... you're funny."

"I'm also not kidding. You have no idea how contagious you are right now. Tuhleesians don't get sick very often, but, your ability to infect others at this stage is extremely high. IF say... your wife were to catch it?... Well, let's not go there shall we?"

"Doc, 3 days is not gonna happen. I barely got 3 free minutes!"

"YOU GOT 3 DAYS!" Jonathan barked.

Lone actually backed up a bit as Jonathan never even raised his voice usually.

"Commander, we all want Rhana back. Right now, you're our best hope of that. EVERY one is looking to you. You've run yourself to exhaustion and that helps no one. Further still, if you get the wolves on the station sick... what then?"

"Doc I can't be down for 3 days... there's just no way. That said, I don't want to, and WILL NOT harm my child in any way. I need a compromise doc."

"You're in here for 3 days at least, maybe more. Rhana gave me authority over even him in medical emergencies. However, I can give you an isolation room, and you can setup anything you need to keep you in contact. You get rest, we keep you monitored, you stay in touch. That's the only solution."

"Not happy about this but... thanks doc, I'll take it. Bloody hell, whatever happened to just taking some vitamin C?" Lone joked.

Jonathan offhandedly said "That would help you greatly being Tuhleesian. It has a greater effect on you than it does Rhana."

Lone laughed, "Well Doc, at least you didn't say no coffee. You tell me that and we're gonna have a problem!"

"Sorry Commander but, I am going to tell you that."

"Oh COME ON DOC! What harm can my coffee do!?"

"Actually? A lot. The vitamin C you mentioned is part of your therapy. Heavy doses actually. Your coffee however in an inhibitor."

Lone paused.

"Wait, what did you say?"

"Indeed Commander. Certain compounds inside your coffee actually block you from absorbing the vitamin. Tea is even worse. Sorry commander but unless you want it to be longer than 3... HEY! Where are you going!?"

Lone was off like a shot and even went to all fours to get all the speed he could muster. He grabbed a mask on the way out and hollered back "GET ANOTHER BED READY! I GOT INCOMING!!"

A masked Lone blew through his door and literally smacked the tea cup from Rahgaa's hand so hard it flew into the fireplace and smashed.

"MAHREK! What is the meaning of... HEY!... PUT ME DOWN!"

Lone ignored her as he scooped her up and headed right back down for Jonathan.

"MAKE A FUCKING HOLE... NOW!" Lone hollered. Seeing

him move, and who he was carrying... said hole was made immediately.

Lone laid Rahgaa on the table and Lone in no uncertain terms told Jonathan to check the kids.

"Commander Lone! I checked Lady R not 3 days ago and..."

"DO IT!!!"

"Honestly Mahrek what's gotten into... wait... Doctor? What's wrong!?" Rahgaa stated as Jonathan suddenly went into hustle mode.

"How did you know!?" Jonathan asked Lone as he got nurses ready and had equipment brought in.

"We'll discuss that later... are they okay?" Lone asked through his mask referring to the children.

"Another 6 hours, and history would have repeated itself."

Now Rahgaa was scared.

"Please Jonathan... not again!"

"Close but... not this time... not if I can help it!"

Lone pulled Jonathan off to the side and told him of an injection process he 'recently heard of'. Jonathan had never heard of such a thing but it made sense. He however found a way to inject it into the amniotic fluid and, an hour later... the levels were on the rise. Rahgaa spent the next 8 hours in the hospital but thanks to Lone's timely intervention, she was released and told to rest for a day. Taking no chances, Lone insisted Renny get checked as well but she only drank tea or coffee on occasion as either got her sick lately. As such Jonathan told her to lay off it too and that her levels were off by so little, mother nature would do the rest in a day or so.

"Honestly my love, I am fine now," Rahgaa said on her conference call to her husband. Triikon and Ravenahl were on hold. "Mind you, I won't lie... had it not been for Lone's timely correction, I wouldn't have been by now. Worse still, had he not intervened, we would have known the pain of 2 more pyres."

"I will make it a point to thank him personally."

"As will I. Now, lets get the healers in on this."

Rahgaa tapped the button, was proud of herself she got the tech right, and got the healers on the line.

"Listen you two, Lone has commanded for safety, any call like this be limited. So, listen carefully as we don't have much time. I, Rahgaa Siin, Prime of Tuhleesia, am ordering this for ALL our people. You will also put this into place will all possible speed."

Rahgaa then told them of what Lone did... why he did it... and what he found out.

"Are you certain Lady Guardian? I only ask as this is not in any of the history scrolls, medical or otherwise." Ravenahl queried.

"I am. It makes sense though. A lot of damage was sustained at Atoemahn. Even Guardian Riisa has said much has been lost due to that damage. It also makes sense when you think of who it was the Healers of the day worked on. That sort of knowledge would likely not be recorded anywhere due to her status."

"I am already putting out messages to all my Healing centers with requests of confirmation when they've been read. I am truly happy for you Lady Prime. You as well Guardian Tiiveer," Ravenahl stated kindly.

"I am doing the same as well and wish you nothing but a speedy recovery," Triikon told her.

"Like the near crash of the X2, it amazes me how something so small and seemingly meaningless... can have such a large and dangerous effect. I can say from experience, the death of my daughter was hard. It would be for any female. If this saves just one would-be mother, and father, from that pain, then it would be worth it," Rahgaa told them all.

"Lady Prime, while I don't wish to dwell on painful memories, can I assume your prior loss was not due to the same cause? I have no doubt my mentor would have checked that," Triikon asked as politely as he could.

"He did Healer, and no, my first child was exactly as they had said... nothing could have prevented that."

"Then know I am glad we did not miss something like this at the time," Triikon told the grand couple with true kindness.

"I must end this call now. Go you two, and see to it that our people no longer commit unknowing murder."

"It will be done!" The Healers said as they dropped off the call.

"Tiiveer, I have been given a list of liquids that are safe for me. Have no fear, I'll not even make tea nor coffee till our children *are born."*

*Lovingly, Tiiveer told her "Give my thanks to the Mahrek and Doctor Jonathan. All my love to you... Tuhleesia out."*

*Rahgaa laid down the now blank tablet, and proceeded to get the rest she was told to get.*

*The inn was busy this evening. Bird was even helping out but, with the culture of the day... and being male... he helped only just so much. He was tending bar, and mingling some as well. Ciana told him how Angus thought 3 wolves were 3 too many. As such she gave him permission to set traps about. When Bird heard that, he insisted they be net traps, not the metal snares. As such, he'd been spending most of his time checking outside. He felt Angus was right and he knew, wolves are opportunists mostly. Their behavior was still bothering him. Being that Bird couldn't be sure of that in this time and place, he decided to keep an eye out all the same.*

*The High Land Inn was also the local Ceilidh House. Bird found out the word Ceilidh meant a small gathering. Essentially, in the days before radio and television, this was where the closest crofts would go to hang out, discuss grownup matters, play music and tell stories. With the inn being so close, and Ciana being so kind, well... this is where everyone came. It's worked well long before Bird arrived, and no one saw any reason to change that now... including Bird.*

*Ciana was besieged with requests to see the new room. Bird was besieged with requests for how he did it and tips on how it was built. Ciana just giggled at all the moaning and groaning her neighbors made when they felt the floor, or tried the bed, or stood by the window.*

*"Good friends!" Bird called out as he hung a panel on the wall. "I would like to thank... publicly... Angus and Mary for their help in allowing me to keep my word."*

*Small cheers and toasts went out all around.*

*Bird now continued with "And yet, they weren't the only ones. The carpenters and the potter and the local mill all helped as well,* and it got me thinking. Where I come from, we hang these in public places. It's called a bulletin board."

Bird chuckled at the clueless faces and kept going.

"Angus my good man, you're the only smithy around these parts aye?"

Angus raised his glass saying "Aye, and a damn fine one at that!" and the crowd all chuckled.

"True enough Angus. Now, let's say I'm a weary traveler. I have a long way to go when, uh oh, I notice my horse needs a shoe. Well, I'm a stranger to these parts so how do I know who you are? Or where to find you? That's what this board is for. I invite you all to put your name on a small piece of paper. An address of where to find you, and perhaps a few words about your wares. Perhaps this traveler merely wants to bring home a present. Whatever it may be, put your name and such as I've said, and now in one central place... anyone from out of town will have but to look in one place, and find anything they may need or want. A small gift from me to all of you for welcoming me so kindly into your community."

No one had heard of such a thing and yet, it made total sense.

Ciana giggled in Bird's ear saying "Careful mah love, or it may not be husband I be call'in yeh one day... but guvnuh!"

All cheered Bird when he made yet another announcement.

"It's true good folks, I am a Yank... and to that I say..." Bird chuckled and finished with "... guilty as charged."

The crowd laughed and Bird just laid it out for them.

"I've also been accused of being very direct, or being very forward, at least compared to you all. Yet again, guilty as charged. Where I come from we have a saying... say what you mean, and mean what you say. We Yanks don't mince words. Now, that said, I have asked Ciana here to date me, what you might call 'courting'. I am happy to say... she's graciously accepted my offer."

Everyone cheered and congratulated both of them. Many said how it was no surprise but, it was nice to hear an official announcement... even if it was one as bold as that.

"Bold? Trust me Angus, where I come from that would only be considered proper." Bird leaned into his ear and whispered "If however this bishop of yours is all that you claim... then Angus...

*then you'll see 'bold'."*

*Ghost 1... sadly... wouldn't have to wait long.*

*Bird was out back again on wolf patrol. The moon was bright enough and Bird did a sweep from the inn to the small barn. His HUD came on automatically and Bird was expecting 4 legged creatures. He got 2 legged one's instead.*

*"What the!? Okay, I got 5 bogies in the woods. Appear to have uniforms and are definitely armed with at least swords. They appear to be hiding from me," Bird said.*

*"Sorry boss, I count 5 mounted riders coming down the road, 2 more on some form of coach."*

*"Alydar?"*

*"Yeah?"*

*Bird sighed and said only one word.*

*"Showtime."*

*Alydar merely replied "Let's do this."*

*The crowd inside was all merry when the coach pulled up outside. Merry enough that the inside crowd... didn't hear the outside one. Angus played the fiddle while the potter played the pipes, and Bird couldn't ask for better cover.*

*The slightly short, portly, and heavily robed and bejeweled man got out from the coach.*

*"Stay here and don't come unless I call for you," he told the mounted riders. "This shouldn't take long," he said over his shoulder as he went in the door.*

*Inside, the merriment... stopped. A hush fell over the room as the robed man walked in and went straight to Ciana.*

*"News came my way my child, I came as soon as I heard. Are you and your lovely sister alright?"*

*Ciana curtsied proper, and immediately felt trapped.*

*"Aye, we are bishop, and I thank yeh for yer concern. Iem sure yeh have more important matters than to be worry'in bout me and mah sistuh," she said as she pulled her hair away quickly.*

*The bishop had gently stroked her hair as he said "Oh I assure you my child, the welfare of my flock is always of concern to me."*

*"Excuse me good sir, be that the inn over there?"*

*The mounted rider looked down in disgust and said gruffly "It is, but the bishop is in there now. He's on important business so you'll have to wait."*

*"Aye sir, I'll wait. Please good sir, could yeh spare a shilling for the poor?"*

*Now the guard was pissed and put a boot to the beggars chest sending him down.*

*"Ere now... thah not be very christian like!" the beggar said as he got back up and brushed off his long black coat... and odd black hat.*

*"BE GONE beggar! You won't be getting a shilling from me!"*

*The guard went to kick him again. He got the surprise of his life when the beggar lifted his head, and the guard was greeted by the oddest blue spectacles. The boot never made its target as two hands clamped down, immobilizing his foot.*

*The beggar looked up, and in a new voice said "I never said it was for me now did I?"*

*Bird flipped the guard over the back end of the horse and snapped the rider's ankle in the process. The guard went for his sword. A quick jab to the throat and the guard was a threat no more.*

*The other guards had theirs out now, and all 4 were pointing at Bird. Twin 'sling' sounds were heard as Bird pulled out his blades.*

*"In the words of Bruce Willis... 'Anyone else wanna negotiate'?"*

*Sweeps and kicks, fists and elbows, the cling clang of metal... and the remaining 4 were no longer a threat either. The two drivers on the bishop's coach were just that... drivers. Not only that but, they had their hands up and were frozen in fear.*

*Bird pointed a blade at them saying "Don't move, the bishop should be arriving shortly."*

*He finished tying up the 5 out cold guards to their mounts, turned their horses, and smacked each one on the ass sending them off into the night.*

*"I'm heading inside," Bird said to seemingly no one.*

*"MRU. Your six is clear, " was his 'Ghostly' reply.*


*"I feel terrible you had such a fright. I wish to offer you the safety of the church my dear... at least till the wild beasts no longer pose a threat of course."*

*Scota brushed briskly between him and her sister.*

*"They no longer are a threat."*

*"Why my child, how can you be so certain?"*

*Scota put her tray down and smiled. She was waiting with sadistic glee to drop this one on him.*

*"Oh trust me, I can be. Mah sistuh's new beau killed one, and drove off the others!"*

*"Scota hush! And mind yeh manners!" Ciana said now slightly panicked.*

*The bishop... was not happy.*

*With a new and annoyed tone in his voice, he simply asked the blond one "New beau?"*

*With a super huge smile, Scota shrugged... and pointed.*

*"And that... would be me," Bird said in his classic style.*


*He walked past the bishop and gave Ciana a kiss.*

*"Sorry I took so long my dear. I had to secure a few things outside."*

*Ciana wanted to crawl under a rock. Bird was the expert on bold and brash, not her.*

*"So," Bird said shaking the bishops hand briskly, "You're the holy man I've heard talk about eh? Commander BirdOfPrey, at your service."*

*Highly annoyed, but putting on a false front, the bishop replied "Only good things I hope?"*

*"Oh... but of course," Bird replied in a confident tone.*

*"Well my son, I look forward to hearing all about you."*

*"Only good things I hope?" Bird taunted.*

*"Oh... but of course," the bishop replied snidely.*

*"So tell me... Commander? Military?"*

*"You could say that."*

*"Well then, as a protector of the crown, I'm sure you have nothing but the best interests at heart. I have offered Ciana here,"* and the bishop said snidely *"And you too of course Scota,"* then looked back at Bird saying *"I have offered them safety in the church till this matter with the wild beasts is sorted. I'm sure you agree it's the right thing to do."*

*"Actually... I don't. Agree I mean."*

*"Oh but, I insist. GUARDS!"*

*Ciana was in a panic.*

*"Yer eminence, this heh heh, has all been a misunder... HEY!"* she hollered as Bird stepped in front of her... and in between her and the bishop.

*"Insist all you want. I'm afraid however I have to refuse. Oh, and those guards? Yeeeeeaaah, they won't be helping you anytime soon. Kind of makes me wonder what a man of the cloth needs with such muscle anyway?"*

*Threateningly, the bishop spoke to Bird saying "These are dangerous times... wouldn't you say?"*

*"Only for the easily scared or the weak... of which I think you've just figured out I'm neither."*

*Now the bishop was getting livid.*

*"YOU DARE address me with such insolence?"*

*Bird turned to Scota and asked "Hey blondie... do I look like the 'I dare' type to you?"*

*"Aye, I think yeh do,"* Scota replied barely containing a giggle.

*"Well then,"* Bird said turning back to the bishop *"I guess I do 'dare' then."*

*The bishop was being challenged and was having none of it. Look the fool in front of 'the flock' or worse, Ciana!? Not going to happen. Seeing the guards not show up, the bishop pulled out his ace in the hole.*

*"Well then, if my guards are 'indisposed'... lets see how you do against the cardinal's elite troops! THE LORD'S JUSTICE IS SWIFT!"* the bishop hollered with a sadistic smile thinking Bird

*would get his 'comeuppance'.*

*"Hmm, anyone else here see a problem with the words 'cardinal' and 'troops' in the same sentence?"*

*Bird looked at the stunned faces and just couldn't resist.*

*"Anyone? Anyone?... Bueler? Bueler?" and Bird laughed. So far... nothing.*

*"THE LORD'S JUSTICE IS SWIFT!" he hollered out again.*

*The response he got, wasn't exactly the one he expected.*

*Angus froze, literally froze, and dropped his mug on the floor. No one in the place moved out of fear so far, but now, the response the bishop got had them all just as frozen as Angus. A sea of nothing but open mouths and dropped jaws... Scota and Ciana included. Walking in from the rear door, a woman's voice was the bishop's only reply.*

*"It certainly is bishop. Unfortunately for you, my justice is swifter. Allow me to assure you... they'll not be coming to your aid anytime soon either."*

*The stunningly beautiful woman looked across from the side of the bar and said "Nice to see you again Commander."*

*"Nice to see you too............. Ally."*

*Ciana almost fainted.*

*The room saw a woman who's beauty only Ciana's matched. Long wavy hair of silver, and jewels of rubies and diamonds dripped from her neck and ears. A dress of black and blue hung beneath a slightly revealing silver like top. The material gleamed in the candlelight as if it had mirrors in it. Lastly, none of the women could fathom how she could walk on boots with heels that were as pointy as nails. Every man however, was just hoping she was single.*

*"And who might you be, thinking you can interfere in his holiness's affairs!?"*

*Bird grabbed a drink and hopped up on the bar. Everyone else was stunned, the bishop was just shy of rage, Alydar was confident and Bird was just amused.*

*"Nothing holy about what I discovered out there. My name 'bishop'... is Alydar. Personal assistant to Commander BirdOfPrey."*

"See Ciana!? An unholy alliance with another woman!" the bishop barked. "And just what do you 'do' exactly, for the Commander?"

"Whatever he requires. Paperwork, overseeing investments, organizing his schedule, things like that. I also, when needed, see to it that things like the cardinal's shock troops don't come anywhere near him," and she turned to the see of shocked faces and finished with, "Or those he cares about."

Alydar turned to the bishop and finished with a menacing "I also serve as his personal body guard when required."

"A woman!? Not only fight but, you actually expect me to believe you... by yourself... took down the cardinal's guards!? HAHAHAHAHA I've never heard anything so... Arrrrrgggh!"

Alydar had grabbed his arm, putting it up behind his back. She easily forced him into the wall and held him there. She took out a pouch and tossed it in the air. Pulling the heavily jeweled dagger from the bishops belt she spun it AND caught it with one hand, then tossed it cutting the pouch in mid-air and sticking the knife and pouch in a perfect bulls-eye on the dart board across the room. Said room all jumped at that one. Bird, carefree as could be... just smiled away.

"Heh heh... told you she was good," Bird said with a wink to his Lady Bird.

That same lady was squeezing Bird's arm and refused to let go.

Speaking in a rather aggravated tone, Alydar said loud enough for all to hear, "Ya know what else I do your largeness? I also uncover conspiracy's. Those shock troops you were so proud of were placing those pouches all throughout the trees. You know what they are don't you? Whyyyy, of course you do, because YOU had them put them there!"

"Wha... wha... what are they?" Scota finally managed.

"Wolf urine young lady. Wolves are territorial, but the not so good bishop here knew that. Wolves can smell a scent for miles. Those pouches said one thing to them... intruder. That's why they attacked. You my dear Scota, merely got in the way."

*"Well then I... wait... you know me!?"*

*"It's my job to know everyone in the Commander's life."*

*Now, Ciana felt the fool... and was getting angry... very very angry.*

*"Bird?" Ciana asked as more confirmation than anything else.*

*"Ya see Ciana, I think the human bean bag here wanted you. He places the pouches, the wolves go wild protecting their territory, and bishop here sweeps in and plays the hero... and gets the girl of his dreams, all in one felled swoop."*

*Bird hopped off the bar and went up to the bishop. Alydar pulled him from the wall but still had him held... tightly.*

*"As I've asked sooo many before you... how'm I do'in so far?"*

*Ciana walked up and looked dead on at him.*

*"Look in mah eyes bishop and tell me... is this true?"*

*The bishop looked, but Ciana saw the truth in his lying eyes. Ciana... hauled off and slapped him... hard.*

*"Hoo hoo hoooooo! Jeez your unholiness, don't you know better than to piss off a Scot lass!?" Bird bellowed with laughter.*

*Ciana freaked.*

*"You lecherous worm...THAT WAS MAH SISTUH!! Get out of here and DOEN LET ME CATCH YOU ON MAH PROPPITY EVER AGAIN! You can also feel free to NOT hasten ye back... EVER!"*

*Alydar let him go by tossing him towards the door. The bishop was beyond livid and... humiliated. He tried to get whatever shred of self esteem mustered up as he screamed at Bird directly.*

*"This isn't over Commander! I'LL BE BACK FOR YOU!!"*

*Ice cold, Bird replied "If you value your life, you'll make that an empty threat."*

*The crowd was still just stunned, downright flat out over the top... stunned. Bird it would seem, had secured his manly status for all his days. Bird walked over to the still shocked smithy, and handed him a fresh drink.*

*"Angus?"*

*Angus stammered as he slammed his now empty drink down saying "A... A...Aye?"*

*Bird looked sideways at the door and just said "Thanks for the heads up... I owe ya one."*

# Chapter 16:

## *"You And Me... And Alydar Makes Three"*

Ciana was still angry and tried calming down but, it wasn't working so well. The gathered crowd, decided the evening was now over. All got up to leave and let Ciana deal with this turn of events in private. While it was now clear of guards outside, not a single woman went home with less than 3 men close by.

Bird stopped Angus on his way out saying "Now that we know why the wolves attacked, I'll be checking the woods personally tomorrow for any more of those pouches. I happen to care about all God's creatures. So, I'll expect those traps taken down the day after."

"Aye, I'll see to it it gets done." Angus looked at the silver haired lady and stated "Miss Alydar, it was, um, a pleasure to meet yeh. I look forward to hearing all about you in the days to come."

Angus tried to be as polite to a 'lady' as he could.

Speaking under his breath as he reached the door, he told himself "And here I thought a Scot lass was something to reckon with when she's angry."

Ally actually giggled and called out, "Angus?"

Angus stopped and said "Aye m'lady?"

With a chuckle, Ally said "How do you know I'm not?"

Angus shook his head and, slightly curious at how he was heard, headed out the door in a hurry.

"Heh heh... that wasn't very nice," Bird chuckled.

The silver haired lady, walked up to the raven haired one, with more poise than the latter had ever seen in her life.

"You must be Ciana Thalin. It it a great privilege to finally make your acquaintance. The Commander was very descriptive of you in his letters to me."

Ciana stared straight at Bird, but spoke to Alydar.

"And just um... HOW descriptive... were these letters?"

"My good lady, as you have seen, the Commander is very direct. You'll find I'm no different. He has had some, shall we say, 'companions' in the past. Most have sought him. So you can imagine my surprise, when his letters spoke of love. A subject mind you he has spoken of regarding others, but never himself. However, any 'details' shall we say... were never mentioned. The Commander may be many things but, he is always a gentleman."

Ciana now faced Ally, curtsied, and smiled saying "Well then m'lady... welcome to my humble inn."

Ally curtsied back saying "Thank you. I look forward to hearing all about you and your sister."

"Commander?"

"Yeah Ally?"

"Fraulein Wolfgang did not show up before I left to come here. You'll be happy to know, I left means in place to alert me should she arrive afterwards."

Ciana looked at Bird.

"She?"

"A woman who helped me with my departure. She ran across a 'bishop' of her own. I was to rendezvous with her to render my assistance as a 'thank you'. Really my dear..." Bird said with slight irritation, "I think after this evening, you'll forgive me when I say... your needless worrying, not to mention insecurity, is getting a tad annoying."

Ciana was indeed worrying. This stunning woman just barged in, took on AND took out, the bishop himself. How in all the heavens could she compete with that when all she could do was fear the one man who took her for a fool. Not only that but, she wasn't smart enough to figure it out, but Bird and this lady did. Add to that, Ally knew all there was to know about her love, whereas she barely knew a thing. And tall?... Good God she was tall. She stood a full 3 inches taller than she did and that was without those nail like heels. Now a really bad thought hit her... what if this 'Ally' was one of those companions she mentioned. Let's not forget those manners, Ally was a proper lady indeed. Ciana was overwhelmed to say the least.

Scota shot her sister a 'what the hell are you doing?' look. Ciana looked lost so Scota took over.

"Lady Alydar?"

"Oh Scota, feel free to call me Ally," the avatar said sweetly.

"Thank yeh kindly miss. May I ask yeh a question?"

"Any you'd like."

"Do you think you teach me how to walk so proper in boots like those?"

Bird just laughed.

"Chicks and shoes... sheesh!"

Scota just smiled and shrugged, and Bird thought she was so adorable when she did that.

Kindly, Ally said "At some point, I'd be happy to. By the way, I see you're working on your diction. You're doing well... keep at it."

"My what?"

"Heh heh, I'll tell you later."


"Oh my, where ARE my manners!?" Ciana practically shouted. "I never thanked yeh proper for your help this evening. Nor offered yeh a bit to eat. It may not be as fancy as I'm sure you're used to but, I make a great hagus."

"Um, thank you but... I'm fine."

"Hmmf, what is it with you Yanks and hagus? And just what is wrong with hagus!?" Ciana said with her hands on her hips.

Bird and Ally said "Everything," at the exact same time.


Ally told Bird "Also Commander, your letters indicated you'd be staying awhile. I've arranged for your travel kit. It should arrive later this week or early next."

"Travel kit?" Scota asked.

"Aye lass," Ally teased. "The Commander has a standard set of things he brings when he travels. Tools, maps, plant seeds and the like." Facing Bird she said, "Also, your Tuhleesian sword is among them. Seeing a sword is 'standard issue' around here, I thought you might want it and included that as well."

Scota was fascinated and asked "What, or where, is this... 'Tuhleesia'?"

"It's a where," Bird said still annoyed with Ciana. "And

*before you ask... it's nowhere near here."*

*"Well, perhaps then I'll see it one day."*

*"Doubt it," Bird said and... that was that.*

*"Ally, do you have a place to stay?"*

*With a wink, Ally told blondie "Not as yet. Tell me, could you recommend a good inn?"*

*"Aye, I think I could," Scota giggled.*

*Ciana came back with some chicken and potatoes, and an ale. Ally thanked her and sat down to eat. Scota told her, for her assistance, she was getting the 'second best' room in the house. It was Ciana's room right next to hers.*

*"Speaking of, I hear you've been busy Bird."*

*"You could say that."*

*"Do I get a tour of your latest creation?"*

*"Sure!" Scota squealed and practically dragged Ally up the stairs.*

*It would seem, Scota had found a new friend, whether Ally liked it or not. Ciana and Bird came up a minute later. Ally toured the place but even Scota could see she looked at it with the same builder eye Bird had.*

*"Not bad boss, I've seen you do better, but not bad," Ally said.*

*"Better!?" Ciana asked in disbelief.*

*"Oh I think you'll find my Commander can be quite creative when he has a tool in his hand."*

*"I'll bet you're correct about MY Commander," Ciana snidely corrected.*

*"Indeed. Well, your meal was delicious Ciana. It's been a bit of a tiring evening," and looking at Scota she finished with "Shall we?"*

*Just like that, Ciana and Bird were now alone.*

*It was late and Bird was staring out the window.*

*"Mmff, (yawn) it's late my love, what are yeh doing up? Kahnt sleep?" Ciana asked from the bed.*

*"You could say that," Bird said not bothering to mask his*

*anger.*

*"What's wrong Bird?"*

*"You. What did I promise you... right here in this very room?"*

*Impishly, Ciana replied "That you were mine."*

*"Exactly. I don't ever promise anything. When I have however, each and EVERY time... I've delivered. Your jealousy, matched with your self doubt, is starting to become very aggravating. I don't give my word very often but when I do, I don't like having it questioned. I stood up to the bishop and so did Ally. She did it for me... and I did it for you. I didn't see anyone else even try to, did you?"*

*A shy "No," was all Bird heard.*

*"Again... exactly. Ciana look, if I wanted a woman like Ally, I'd have one. I want you. I don't care if you're an innkeeper or the fucking queen. I want Ciana, not a lady, or a commoner, or anything else you think you are or are not. You my dear... nothing more."*

*Ciana got out of bed wrapped in the blanket. She opened it and wrapped Bird in it and hugged him from behind.*

*"Can I tell yeh something?"*

*"Shoot."*

*"Huh?"*

*"It means go ahead."*

*"Bird, I can tell just by your demeanor that this, all this, is not new to you. Me on theh other hand, I ne'er done ennything like this in mah life. You've had other women, but you are the first man I've ever cared about no less loved. The other night, when I asked you to stay, I was so frightened I almost ran away."*

*"I noticed."*

*"Yeh know why I didn't?"*

*"Enlighten me."*

*"Because theh idea of leaving frightened me more. There's so much I don't know. About you, and it would seem... about me too. I ne'er had a man of mah own. THIS however, wasn't how I pictured it when I did. All I know is I feel safe and happy when yer around. When yer not, I feel like I'm lost on a great big ocean with no land in sight. Yer ways are so damn diffrint. I barely knoe mah own, no less yours. Yer right, I am worried, and perhaps even jealous, but it's only because I'm afraid you'll find someone better."*

*"DAMN YOU woman! THERE IS NO ONE BETTER! Not for me anyway."*

*"Please doen be mad at me. Iem try'in I really am!"*

*Sadly, Bird just said "Try harder."*

*Bird calmed down and spoke his mind.*

*"Ciana, remember that life I said I was going back to?"*

*"Aye."*

*"Ciana, that life there is so different that it would make your head spin. You're not ready for it. Hell you can barely handle this one. You've lived with 'perceptions' your whole life that I doubt you've even looked at the real world for what it truly is. My home, it's grand beyond your wildest dreams. It does however, come with certain dangers. I've been pushing you into these situations, like the bishop tonight, in an attempt to get you OUT of your shell, not further into it. Until you do, you're not ready for my world. I could find out at any moment the time to return has come. When it does, it will likely be swift and immediate. I don't want to harm you, I really don't. Taking you with me however, just might, at least in your current state. Know what frightens me?"*

*"Oi, nothing frightens you."*

*"Going home without you does. And your right, nothing else does... except that."*

*"So, you and me and Alydar makes three eh?"*

*"Exactly, and before you bark about that too... deal with it. Alydar and I have a unique situation. This much I will tell you, if I told her I wanted you, and there was the king's army between us... you'd be in my arms by morning... and the king would need a new army. She is THAT loyal but just that... loyal. We have more of a father daughter relationship, rather than a husband and wife one. Yes I'll agree THAT isn't what your used to either but, you want me? You want to keep me? Then the way to do it is accept what you don't know, learn it, use it, and ask for help when you need it. If you don't grow, I can't take you with me. As they say where I'm from... THAT... is not an option."*

*"Sorry my love, still scared. I will say this tho... now Iem scared of what I doen know... but not of losing you."*

*Now Bird smiled.*

*"It's a start and... I'll take it. C'mon, let's go back to bed."*

*Next morning, it was just the ladies as Bird the late riser was still fast asleep.*

*"Scota my dear, would you mind leaving your sister and I alone for a bit? I'd like to talk to her in private."*

*"Aye, sure thing," and off she scampered. Teasing her sister she said "I'll go see if 'my' Yankee man is up yet,"*

*"Aye why don't yeh do thah. Go see if MY sleepy head is awake," Ciana teased back.*

*Scota giggled and headed off.*

*"Your Yankee man? Oh please, what makes you think you have anything that could keep a man like him?"*

*"Excuse me?" Ciana said having been thrown a bit off guard.*

*"What are you deaf too?... Or just stupid?"*

*"Oi!" Ciana barked now. "I'll have yeh know HE said so, and if HE said so, Tis good enough for me!" Ciana said emphasizing her point.*

*"Hmmf, I could steal him from you in a blink of an eye. So could anyone else 'innkeeper'."*

*Now Ciana was fighting mad and let Ally have it. Ally however just... smiled.*

*"And jes what do yeh find so amusing!?"*

*Ally told her, "Congratulations, you've just taken your first steps to learning Bird's world. My apologies Ciana but, I needed to get you mad so I could prove a point."*

*"So, wait, yeh mean yeh said those things... just to get me mad?"*

*"Mmhmm... didn't mean a word of it either."*

*For the first time since meeting Bird, Ciana asked with curiosity and not fear.*

*"Hmm, alright then... why?"*

*Ally leaned back and began her lesson.*

*"Ciana, weakness is one thing the Commander despises. If you are weak, but willing to do something about it, he will be your*

biggest champion. If you are, but are unwilling to become better, he'll walk away from you without so much as a goodbye. If he tells you something, it's as true as the sun causing a sunny day. Your problem is... you don't believe. Perhaps you do in him... but last night it was clear to me you didn't in yourself."

Kindly, Ciana replied "Aye, yeh be right there. But, why'd yeh get me angry?"

"Simple. When you were, you had confidence. I point that out because when you have that, nothing can harm you. Last night, did you see me have any?"

"Aye, lots!"

"And you?"

Ciana sighed and replied "None."

"Correct. Just having that... you noticed it. So did everyone else. The bishop had more than you but, not as much as me. So, take that away and... wadda ya got?"

"Aye, I see yer point."

"Has the Commander told you how different our home is?"

"Nothing specific but aye, he has."

"Yet, he didn't start out there. He has been to, well, shall we say 'many worlds'. The home he's trying to get back to was a barren and hostile landscape when he arrived. Undeterred, he simply made it not so. He also, once, found himself in an unfamiliar land AND with nothing but the clothes on his back... literally. He survived that too. Care to guess why?"

"Again, I see yer point."

"So, I got you angry. Sure enough you had all the confidence you needed to challenge even me. So to that I have two things to say. First, if you can learn to be that confident, but without the anger, you'll truly become formidable yourself."

"Aye... and second?"

Ally smiled and told her "If you'd like... I'll show you how."

"Oi, ther be a daunt'in task I tell yeh," Ciana chuckled.

"BirdMan 101 actually."

"Oi... yeh Yanks have the strangest sayings."

Ally giggled and said "You don't know the half of it. As I was saying, Bird has a method. It's one he's taught us all. Look at the problem, and figure out how to solve it. Don't let the large problems frighten you, as they're nothing but small problems grown larger. Bring it down to your size, solve it, then expand your fix."

Ciana promised Bird she'd try. So now, that's exactly what she was doing. The 'big picture' still scared her but, now she was willing to learn.

"Alydar can I ask yeh something?"

"Please, call me Ally... and by all means."

"Fine then. Ally, when theh wolves showed up, I was in a state of panic. Bird however was not."

"Okay then... first lesson. If you want to grow, and learn of the bigger world, the first thing you have to do is know yourself. So tell me, why were you scared?"

"I... I didn't know what to do. There was mah sistuh, who I've looked out for since she was 4 years old when mah mum passed on. Later when dad did I was both parent and sister all in one. When the wolves showed up, I froze. I have ALWAYS looked out fer her and here I was, with not a clue in the world of what to do."

"But Bird did, is that it?"

"Aye. He acted like he'd done it hundreds o'times. It was as if he knew every step before he or the wolves even made one."

Ally was soft and told her "Ciana look, nothing but hard work, dedication, and practice will make you better. Bird has said in the past that fear... is the mind killer. It forces you to do nothing at the very moment you need to do something."

"So, fight the fear... conquer all?"

"AND!... the next time the wolves show up... heh heh, you'll be pushing Bird out of YOUR way!" Ally said with a laugh.

"Aye, I promise yeh I'll try."

"Oh you'll fail... everyone does. But the point will be that you're trying. Accept that you'll have setbacks but, see to it that the next one you have is a new one, not an old one. You'll also make mistakes. Just see to it you don't make the same one twice."

Now Ciana had a new topic.

"This relationship you have with Bird. Care to tell me how I *deal with thah?"*

*"Simple... you don't. I have mine with him, and you have yours."*

*Ciana thought she got it and asked "So, doen get in my way, an I'll not get in yours... is thah it?"*

*"Pretty much. Look Ciana, has the Commander done anything since coming here that's been 'usual'?"*

*Laughing, Ciana answered "Nowhere near even close!"*

*"And yet, do you see Bird caring one bit?"*

*"Doen think he cares WHAT people think!" Ciana said pleasantly boasting.*

*"Well then... neither should you."*

*"Ally look. I doen know ennything. Truth be told, I ne'er had no proper school'in. But, Bird means everything to me and if thah's what I gotta do to keep him... then get ready lass cause Iem gonna be one of yer best students!"*

*"Heh heh... you're on."*

*Bird smiled from behind the door jamb, and turned and headed back for bed.*

*"That's my girls," he said in the most joyous of tones.*

*"Okay blondie... 'sciencey' stuff... ready?" Bird told Scota as she looked on.*

*They were both in the kitchen and Bird was arranging a few things.*

*Scota smiled huge and happy and said "Aye! Ready!"*

*"Okay then, horse manure.. stinks right?"*

*"Aye... something awful too!"*

*"Wrong it doesn't... but something IN the manure does. So, if something can be made to smell bad then...?"*

*"Something can be made to smell... good?"*

*"Aye lass," Bird teased "It can." Bird turned to Scota and asked "What is your favorite smell?"*

*"Ooh that be an easy one. I love the smell of the heather on the hillsides of the loch right after it rains. Oh that smell is divine!"*

*"Alright then, any heather around here?"*

"Aye there be a small patch of it just behind the cold shed."

"Good. Go get me some but, only the flower part."

"Okay Mistuh Yankee man!" Scota squealed gleefully as she ran out to get some.

Ciana came in with Ally and asked with a chuckle "What was thah all about?"

"Stick around... and find out," Bird said with a smile.

Scota came back with the heather and immediately thought Bird was nuts when he said to boil half of it. Scota did though, and Bird ground up the rest to a super fine powder. He had to improvise on some of the ingredients but, he put them all together perfectly.

"Now, I had the potter make a few molds for us. Pour this in while it's still hot, then pour in the heather... add a bit of the powder and... there ya go!"

Scota looked inside and said "It looks like thah manure yeh mentioned... (giggle)... AFTER yeh step in it."

"Yeah well, it will harden as it cools. When it does , you'll be left with just the heather smell."

"Alright then, and what do we do with it then?"

"Come back in an hour... and you'll see."

Everyone left. As asked, one hour later they all came back. Bird picked up the mold and slammed it upside down to pop the piece out. A tannish colored round block popped out. The top of it, thanks to the mold had the shape of a blooming rose. Little purple specks everywhere and Bird tossed it to Scota.

"Well your blondness... what do you smell now?"

"Bloody hell! It's the hillsides of the loch!"

"Mm hmm. When your inn don't have travelers in it, you can make and sell these to the locals for a little bit of coin." Bird was walking out past the amazed teenager and said "Congratulations my teenage friend... you just made soap."

Bird had no idea that... in the near future... he would smell that heather again and... it would change Scota's life forever when he did.


Ally had begun setting up some things outside. Now it was Ciana's turn to learn stuff.

"Alright Ciana, let's pretend this bucket here is Scota... and these rags here are the wolves. You hear a scream... what do you do next?"

"Okay," Ciana said using the latest term.

"Yeeeeeaaahhh... like I told Scota... THAT phrase is only among us... heh heh... okay?"

Ciana chuckled and said "Aye... 'okay'."

"Focus Ciana, what do you do next?"

"I run to Scota."

Bird chuckled and went "Eeeehhhh... wrong answer."

"Towards the wolves?" Ciana asked thinking it made no sense.

"Eeeehhhhh, wrong again."

Ally was kind and said "Okay, take me through what happened."

"Well, Bird and I were talking upstairs when we heard Scota scream and... what!?" she queried Bird who had his eyebrow raised. "Yue said to be bold and not scared. Yeh also said everyone here knows so this is me... be'in bold."

Bird walked over to her, smiled and gave her a kiss.

Ciana smiled back and said "As I was say'in... Scota screamed and out we came."

Ally asked "And what did Bird do?"

"He pulled out his blades."

"And did you pull out yours?"

"No, I didn't have one."

Ally merely stated "Exactly."

"Okay wait... what am I missing?" Ciana said all confused.

"Bird heard Scota scream," Ally started, "He could tell by the scream it was danger, but he didn't know what the danger was. As such, he thought ahead and brought his weapons just in case. You didn't think ahead, came out empty handed, and ran into wolves."

"So, yer say'in, always think ahead?"

"Mm hmm. You already do. Do you not plan your inn around peak and low seasons? More food when the inn is full... less when it's not... that sort of thing."

"Aye... I suppose I do."

"Well then, don't do any different, just expand what you do it on that's all," Ally told her.

"Hmm, do the same as I always have, just more of it. Aye, I can do thah."

Ciana then got serious and said, "Tis not my place to be fight'in."

"Aaaaaand... why not?" Bird then teased saying aloud "Sorry Scota, no man around and 'thah's whut men-folk be fer"... well... I'm just a girl. Looks like you'll just have to die! Sorry!"

Ciana got sad.

"I doen know how. That sword was mah dad's. Truth be told, Scota has handled it more than I e'er have. I doen even know how to hold it let alone use it."

Ally was patient with Ciana and asked Scota to bring her the sword. Scota ran inside, got it, and brought it to her.

"Honestly Bird," Ciana sort of pleaded. "I'd likely do more harm to mehself or Scota than any ruffian. He'd likely take it away from me and then what?"

Bird smiled... and took off his harness.

Ally and Bird circled each other as Bird said "Then... this," and Alydar charged him.

Bird ducked and dodged and taught as he defended.

"When your enemy has a weapon, and you don't, you still actually do."

"Oi ya daft Yankee... thah made no sense at'all!"

Ally answered her saying "You Ciana... you are the weapon. Your calmness, your keen eye AND... your what?"

Flatly, Ciana said "Confidence."

Bird deflected Ally, elbowed her in the gut and snapped the sword from her hand. He threw it at Ciana and it landed in the ground right in front of her... and right where Bird wanted it.

"Aye Lady Bird. I had no weapon and yet, doing everything Ally just told you, I still won. Confidence my dear... can do anything."

Puffing slightly, Bird walked off to get a drink.

"As for not knowing how, Ally and I can fix that." Bird's disembodied voice called out saying "Yesssss, we'll teach you too oh blond one!"

Scota just bounced up and down and squealed in delight.

Bird and Ally spent the next 2 days with basic defense moves. No weapons... just hand to hand stuff and only the basics at that. Bird and Ally both agreed, keep it simple, then build from there. Ciana got it wrong many times but Bird still praised her for trying. That alone kept her going. Ciana was also changing attitudes. No longer scared or insecure, now she was... doting. Bird chuckled thinking she was like a teenager with her first boyfriend, but thought it was sweet all the same. Given a choice between the 2 attitudes... He'd choose this one anytime.

Later that evening, Bird and Ciana were talking while Scota claimed Ally all to herself... as usual.

"She worships you yeh knoe,"

"Who does... Ally?"

Ciana giggled and said "Nooo... Scota. We've not had a man in our lives since dad died. I've been more parent than sistuh. I not be mean'in to swell yer head Mistuh Yankee, but I tell ya so ya knoe if she gets a bit much, well, thah's why."

Bird nodded and said "Actually, she hasn't been bad. I don't do well with annoying kids of any age... but Scota is a sweetheart. She's also more like me, which helps."

"In what way?"

"She's more fearless than fearful. She likes new things, and new ways. She looks at the world and says 'hmm... what's out there?' so I think that's why."

"Aye, kindred spirits," Ciana agreed. "As I said, I been more parent than big sistuh. Heh heh, poor Alydar, Scota won't leave her alone."

"Yeah, heh heh, I noticed. But... that's actually good for Alydar. With the exception of only a few others, Alydar hasn't had many people to interact with. For years now it's been mostly me. I think it'll actually do her good to interact with others. Have no fear Lady Bird, when Scota hits the line between sweet... and annoying... heh heh, Alydar will let her know."

Ciana chuckled back saying "Aye... I have no doubt bout

*thah."*

*Now Bird changed topics.*

*"Ciana, you go to market to get supplies. I want to go with you. Actually, I want all 4 of us to go."*

*"Any reason why?"*

*"Actually yeah, remember what you teased me about the other night... bout calling me 'guvnuh'?"*

*"Oh I was only teas'in an yeh knoe it."*

*"Oh I know. I also know that teasing or not... you are likely correct. I have no desire to be anyone's champion but yours. The bishop episode didn't help that. What I'm saying is, I want... no... NEED... to stop being the focus of everyone's attention. I think if we go to this market, we can be friendly, Alydar gets the exposure she needs more of... but we kind of give the impression to be by ourselves and that... that's the way we want it."*

*"So... still friendly but... leave us alone? Is thah it?"*

*"Pretty much. I've been neglecting that other life and I need to get back to it soon. I don't want people getting too comfortable coming to me when all I wanna do is hide or lay low. We get to have a lovely afternoon, and spread it around that I'll be leaving to take care of 'business affairs'. That way we don't seem like we're 'putting on airs' but we also get the message across."*

*"Aye, and less questions when yeh not be around. Go and come back, then go again. Do that enough times and the crofts and town folk won't see it as anything but normal... well... heh heh, normal for you thah is."*

*"True enough. One last thing. Remember when I asked you not to call me Commander?"*

*"Aye, and I haven't."*

*"True but... and this is only between me and you and Ally. If you run into trouble, and I need to know it, then and only then call me that. That will be our secret way of letting me know something is wrong, okay?"*

*"Aye... I will."*

*Bird had a birthday party to plan, a 10 mile long ship that, although functioning, still needed repairs. He had an invisible mile long ship hovering over the bay, and he's had his fill of 'low tech'. The time had come to get back to that world and Bird knew one thing for sure... his little honeymoon was over.*

# Chapter 17:

## "I'll Love You Until, The Rivers Run Still... And The Four Winds We know Blow Away"

*"Angus... I need your help," Bird said walking into the smithy's shop.*

*"Alright... say what yeh need," Angus replied in a most friendly manner.*

*Bird sat on a workbench and spelled out why he came.*

*"Ally and I have been teaching Ciana and Scota how to fight. Not like a soldier or anything, but enough to take care of themselves in case I'm not around."*

*"A bit odd but aye, makes sense. And just where might yeh be going?"*

*"Business Angus. I'll be going back and forth between here, and tending to my investments. Ally will too. We told everyone at the market the other day but you weren't there so I'm telling you now."*

*"I understand. So what help do yeh need from the ole smithy then eh?"*

*"Ciana and Scota. I'd appreciate it if you'd look in on them while I'm gone."*

*"Aye I will... would be my pleasure. Ennything else?"*

*"Aye lad, there is," Bird said with a sly smile. "Ciana can't handle the sword her father left her. Even it's smaller size is still too much for her to handle. I was thinking, could you make her one that fits her. Longer but thinner blade. It doesn't have to hold off the king's army but... heh heh... the bishop would be nice," and Bird gave him a wink.*

*"Aye, I doen see why not. I'll make the hilt and handle a little heavier too, to help her hold it better."*

*"Add to that a pair of daggers, and you can send me the bill,"*

Bird told him with a friendly pat to the back.

"It'll be a fair one but, aye, I will."

Bird was heading out and hollered back.

"Oh, one last thing. I'm taking Ciana to Edinburgh for her birthday. Scota and Ally too. She's never been off the Isle so I thought this would be a good place to start. We'll be gone about 4 days, maybe 5. Ciana says, heh heh, and I quote... 'Iffin yeh can stay off the drink while we be gone, yeh be welcome to stay at the inn AND in the room Bird built. They'll be no charge as ye'll be look'in after mah place for me'."

Angus laughed hard and bellowed "Aye! Tell that lovely lass of yours... she got herself a deal!"

Bird was hoping this trip he planned would change Ciana's life for the better. Someone's life would change alright... it just wouldn't be Ciana's.

Lone was in an isolation room of the hospital. Thanks to Remmy however, it looked like someone moved C&C. Lone was in bed, surrounded by an invisible energy shield, and checking all the comm's. One in particular, he answered right away.

"What can I do for you Krannen?"

"Accept my thanks for starters. If it weren't for you, well, I don't even want to think about that right now."

"For what it's worth Guardian... neither do I. Answer me this then, if the roles were reversed, and you were me, would you have done any different?"

In a respectful tone, the kind one 'warrior' gives to another, Tiiveer replied "Not a thing."

"Well, there you have it then," Lone replied in the same tone.

Tiiveer gave him a proper salute... Lone responded with one of his own... and the matter was closed.

"I assume you were informed of Tamarak's little spy mission?" Tiiveer asked.

"I was. Always meant to ask about that. Tuhleesia has 3 continents and several islands, yet, you only inhabit one of them...

*why?"*

*"Simple need really. In the days following the Adjulons, there were barely enough of us left to populate 1 no less 3. Technology too was a factor. As you saw, we had no means of crossing an ocean as large as one of the continents themselves either. Even now, the X2's as advanced as they are can't reach them. If they go to orbit then come down, they will lack the fuel to return. Tiiven works even as we speak on a means to refuel them along the way... but that is some ways off yet."*

*Lone told him "Sounds about right. Alydar and Raven scanned them when we first arrived and found them void of any life. Even Biiird said with your level of damage, he preferred to do teaching and repair... and leave the exploration to another day."*

*"It was wise then. Now however, I feel we may have no choice. Suggestions?"*

*"None right now but, I'll work on it."*

*"Squadron Leader Tandor said the X2's would be useless anyway. He suggested any attack we could do would put them at too great a risk as they would be spotted on the way down. Again, with no fuel to return, it would be a suicide mission. Those deaths, we really can't afford right now regardless of how glorious they might be."*

*"Don't forget," Lone reminded, "The satellites would alert you long befaw anything else. I have only 2 thoughts. We know he's hiding, or going to, so the only place I can think of is under an umbrella. Focus on any rock formations or large caves. Something that would keep away prying eyes."*

*"I had thought of that myself. And second?"*

*"Tammy is a builder. As a scientist or worse, a general, he's bollox. His thinking tends to be limited. Try this Tiiveer, what if he wasn't looking at the continents but... the oceans in between them?"*

*Tiiveer now had an 'Oh my God why didn't I think of that?' look on his face.*

*Kindly, the Krannen merely said "Rhana has taught you well Mahrek. I'll get back to you with any findings as they become available... Tiiveer out."*

*"As will I... 51 out."*

Now Lone got ready for an intra-galactic conference call.

"Commander Lone, I heard of your illness. I'm glad to hear that it's not serious," Zagrin told him.

He was on the call, as was Juvehnar and Lor and Shiiran.

"So am I. So Zagrin, what is this news you have for us?" Lone asked.

"I've stopped the removal of the damaged soil. Our scientists have discovered the poison has become like a resin."

"And that helps us how?"

"It burns, and rather hot too. It not only burns... it burns for days. My scientists tell me it burns similar to an ore you call coal... but much hotter and for 5 times as long per pound in your measurements. They tell me, if burned in our atmosphere, the toxins will take decades to go away... but if burned in space then no problem. I mention this in case someone can think of a use for it."

Lor kicked in now saying "Commander, in our old days we had space based forge craft. As you say, they were 'mothballed' and set for scrap. We could provide ample amounts of them to help with the raw materials."

Lone was stoked to hear 'the aliens' thinking outside the box.

"Small problem, anything that burns requires air... bit of a problem in space."

Shiiran was talking furiously to someone off camera. It was her map makers.

"Lady Shiiran... do you have something for us?" Lone queried.

"I just might. There are twin comets that orbit our planet. If Ambassador Lor could get her ships operational again, we could hide them in their tails. No one would know or see."

"And the air?" Lone asked.

"My people have extracted gaseous elements out of liquids for generations. Lor provides the ships, Zagrin provides the fuel, we will provide machinery to provide the air from the comet's tail."

Now Juvehnar jumped in.

"An excellent plan! Count on my men Commander to get Lor's ships there undetected. Add to that I'll have them protect the operation as well."

"All we need now is the staff to run them. I'm proud of you all, an excellent plan indeed. We here at 51 cannot spare the man power but... I think I know who can. Leave that to me. Anything else?"

No one had anything. Lone thanked them all, and set about making another 'phone call'.

"General Brallik, do you know who I am?" Lone asked the new face on his screen.

"Commander Lone Wolf, Ghost 2... it's an honor to meet you finally."

"Thank you. You're responses in the next few minutes will tell if the feeling is mutual."

"And what can the Vrissin northern alliance do for you?"

"Let's cut the crap general. You have a stranglehold on the south. I need something from them, and I need you out of my hair."

"I suppose you have something in mind?" The general asked with great interest.

"I always do. I want peace between you. I want Valleron reinstated as the rightful co-president. I want this peace broadcast AND... kept."

"And what would we get in return?"

"I'll get you the rest of the mine you've been fighting over... all yours with borders redefined and approved by both sides."

"Hahahahaha... the southern rebels will NEVER agree to such a deal!"

"You just leave that to me... so... we got a bargain?"

"IF! You can get them to agree... I'll be happy to give you what you ask."

"Like I said, leave that to me. Been a pleasure doing business with you," and Lone cut off the call without even a goodbye.

"Hahahaha! Are you INSANE!?" Valleron bellowed.

"Hardly. Look, you need the dyma ore to power your cities and such yes?"

"Of course," Valleron stated.

"Well then, we have a plan in the works... one that needs your people's talents... a LOT of people. Quite frankly your little civil war is becoming a nuisance and refereeing you two is starting to drain resources we don't have. I need your people free to work... not fight.

What if I told you I could give you technology that would power your cities and towns... cleanly... and with no ore at all?"

Valleron shifted gears in a heartbeat.

"NOW Commander... you have my attention."

"When Rhana was there the first time, the Ghosts took scans of your planet. You have a lot of rivers in the south. Some even go for thousands of miles. What if I could show you how to tap those rivers, give you power in non liquid form...and by time the ore runs out again, the north will be coming to you for a change, and for tech you'll already have in place."

Valleron was still skeptical saying "Our whole infrastructure is based on liquid power. It would take years to convert our whole system."

"Or... you could keep fighting. A fight mind you... that you're losing. You have enough ore in various smaller pockets to keep your systems going while you transition. The more you convert, the less ore you'll need."

"And who will teach and help us with this new power? My apologies Commander but, last I was where you are... you and your people were a tad busy."

"Ambassador Ulquin has already begun this. I have no doubt he's discovered tricks for speeding up the process. I also doubt they'd be unwilling to teach your people. Once you learn you can make the systems AND install them yourself. Interested?"

Valleron merely said one word.

"Very."

Lone laid out his plan. He also told him he'd already spoken to Brallik. By the end of Lone's explanation, Valleron was not only a convert... he was committed.


Juvehnar went on his version of public TV. Lady Shiiran did the same. Both leaders told their people that these comets were discovered on collision courses. The Ghosts were asked for help and graciously agreed to alter their orbits. Juvehnar told his people to enjoy the show in the night sky as it would last for about 3 months but... likely never happen again in their lifetimes. Shiiran said the same thing. Now, 2 planets with 1 sun each, had a place to hide massive workshops. The Ghosts did indeed move them. They weren't due for another 7 years so... they just hastened the process somewhat. A space going snowball did Lone no good without a tail. Not wanting to put 2 around the same planet, Lone just split them up is all. Also, if one was somehow discovered then it was just that... one... not both.

Lone was 1 day down on his 3 days... and 4 days into the project as a whole. Seeing all the progress... he was finally starting to feel some hope. So far, 51 time, it had been 8 days since Bird left.

Lor had her people in her assembly quite happy. Lone had carefully funneled some money around and made it seem like the southern alliance had paid for them. Lor kept the price cheap and the congress of lizards were more than pleased to get rid of some 'old junk'. By the end of the day, enough talent was secured to run them as these space going forges hadn't been fired up for decades. By the end of the next day, the lights were on, the engines were running, and Lor's scrapyard was getting some big holes in it.

Shiiran started sending equipment to make air from water vapor, and the old crews fixed the even older ships as they went.

Zagrin ordered thousands of small ships to haul the dirt. Once in orbit, the loads were transferred to the Lanna and the Malay. Not having to take off, or land, both ships could fill their cargo bays to capacity.

Jonathan checked Lone and said he had one more day but then he could be released. Ten days so far and, to Lone anyway, things were looking good.

Giljor had talked to the others, and they all agreed. The station was never meant to be denied to their people, only events of the day caused it to be so. All the 'holograms' were enjoying having their own onboard, and found it far more enjoyable than they imagined. So a decision was made to help Bird and Rahgaa, and fulfill Tiiven's prophesy. Giljor himself was the final approval but, they started gathering history... and gave it to the wolves. The history they gave them was fair and honest, even though it was somewhat limited. The builders however ate it up.

Giljor told his team the station was originally designed to be turned over to the science departments when it's original mission was over.

Quoting Bird, Giljor stated "One day, 'God willing', it will serve out it's original purpose."

"And, should that day ever come... what of us?" Riihahl asked.

"I have lived more seasons than any wolf ever has... or should. I have lived that entire life stuck in a loop of fear and destruction. I will help our people reclaim what we once were, but with more wisdom. Once that is underway, well, if I should go to the next realm, I'll do so at peace and... with the greatest and noblest wolves I've ever known."

Every one of them bowed at the honor of his words. That plan however, thanks to Bird, wouldn't go exactly as he expected.


For the first time in known history, guards were inside the trance room. Rahgaa barked... loudly... about that one. Tiiveer said he didn't care and she would have to deal with it. They weren't just any guards though, they were the 15 best 'shadow soldiers' he had. Rahgaa was in her office for this. She was in the trance room and made sure all was okay before leaving. If Tiiveer was gonna put muscle in her domain... then she was checking it first. Once she approved, she made her way to her office to wait. Today was a small test. Rahgaa was hopeful... and Tiiveer wasn't taking any chances.

"Are you sure you're alright my dear?" Rahgaa asked kindly.

"So far I am. I feel no different than when I'm solid," Rennahr told her.

"And the child?" Rahgaa asked with motherly concern.

"I feel no change. I cannot sense him or her any more like this than when I'm not trancing. As far as I can tell, we should be fine."

Renny had tranced only the short distance to Rahgaa's office, as a means to test. Ahdeera never had any children, so no one knew if trancing while pregnant would have any effect. So, today was a test run and... the reason for the guards.

"I'm going to return now so I will not upset Tiiveer. I will switch places with you when you arrive," Rennahr said.

*"I'll be right there," Rahgaa told her as Renny faded away.*

*Tiiveer was nervous as hell letting Renny try. Having Rahgaa do so, well, even his guards were on edge now at his behavior. Rahgaa calmed Tiiveer as much as she could but it did little to help.*
*"You knew we'd have to do this my love."*
*"I KNOW I know! Still doesn't make me any less concerned."*
*Sweetly, Rahgaa kissed his cheek saying "And that's why I love you so."*
*Having given enough time to Renny, Rahgaa now drifted off as well.*

*"Well?" Renny asked.*
*"It would seem you are right dear, I cannot sense the children any more or less than I do when not trancing. Oh Rennahr, I'm so happy for this... without us I don't know how we would get him back," Rahgaa said with true joy at the experiment's success.*
*"Go back now, let's not take any chances. I prefer to save our trancing, and any possible risk, to only the task we're needed for and no more. Know this though, I am very happy for us that the children will be unaffected."*
*"As am I," Rahgaa said with a soft smile as she faded away.*

*The Guardians however were wrong... very very wrong. The children would indeed be affected by their exposure to trancing but... that would be a saga for another day.*


*Bird had returned late last night. He had spent the last 2 days off on business. Angus as promised, checked in on the ladies when he could. Ciana had mixed feelings. She found herself sad without Bird around. She also found herself happy looking forward to his return. In the past she'd have worried if he'd return at all but... Bird gave her his word and she was holding on to that. Scota on the other hand was just sad, and acted like a lost puppy. Ciana was right, her sister thought of her as more of a mother than a sister. With no father figure either, Bird filled that role now whether he liked it or not. Same went for her new 'sister' Ally. Scota rarely left her side while she was around. When she did, she could simply be found next to Bird.*

     *"Hello lovely lady. Tell me, is this side of the bed taken?" Bird asked slyly when he returned.*
     *"Hmm, I be wait'in for a fantastic man but, Iem sure you could use it till he returns," Ciana said just as slyly.*
     *"Oh is that so?"*
     *"Aye, it is."*
     *Bird playfully stuck his hand out saying "BirdOfPrey m'lady... pleased to make your acquaintance."*
     *"BirdOfPrey eh? Hmm, I knew a Yankee man by that name once. Total nutter he was."*
     *"A Yankee yeh say? Aye, I hear tell they can be like thah," Bird joked.*
     *Ciana laughed as she wrapped herself around Bird.*
     *"Told you... you'd be the first stop I make."*

     *"Arrrgh... what's WRONG with you people!?" Bird protested. "Don't you realize my day starts promptly at the crack of noon!??"*
     *Bird was protesting the crack of dawn wake up time.*
     *"Well, is someone a little cranky this morning?" Ciana teased and cooed.*
     *"Bird good... cranky bad... Bird cranky? Yeah, you don't wanna go there."*
     *Ciana soothed her cranky Bird lovingly.*
     *"Well... as long as I'm up!?" Bird teased.*
     *Ciana found herself rolled over and let out a laugh. Shortly afterwards, she stopped laughing... and began moaning.*


*The next day, Ciana and Scota were dressed in their best. Bird had hired a coach and when he arrived, 4 suitcases were put on top. Ciana couldn't fathom why Bird insisted hers be empty.*
     *"Trust me?" Bird asked referencing the empty case.*
     *Recalling a fond memory, Ciana smirked and told him "Aye, more than I should."*
     *The driver was having a hard time not staring at 3 of the most*

beautiful lasses he'd ever seen. Alydar was first and curtsied to the driver who held the door for her. Seeing these fine ladies, he was minding his manners.

Ciana's croft was on the central western side of the Isle. They had to travel to the east side to pick up the ferry. Bird had made those arrangements too. Once aboard, Ciana marveled at the luxury of the ferry.

Bird chuckled and said under his breath "If you only knew."

Once on the mainland, it was another coach. Down a coastal road to Glasgow, switch coaches... then east to Edinburgh. Ciana was in awe of the 'big city' but Scota didn't know where to look first, and wanted to go everywhere.

The coach driver complimented Bird privately saying "I'd be happy with just one of that quality. Yeh be a lucky man to have three!"

"Aye," Bird said kindly, and reflectively. "I am indeed."

The road to Edinburgh had plenty of lovely scenery. Ciana was enjoying the view. She was starting to realize, yes it was different but... it was still familiar. Ally saw the look on her face and it was actually her that started first.

"Why Bird, look at that! Why... why... I believe they call those trees!"

"And birds... REAL BIRDS!... why if I hadn't seen it with my own eyes I would never have believed it," Bird joked back.

Even Scota joined in saying as they passed over a small river, "While I ne'er seen it mehself yeh understand... I believe that blue stuff is called water!"

"Hah hah... pleased with ye'selves now are yeh?" Ciana said folding her arms across her chest.

"Why m'lady, what doth thou mean?" Bird said barely containing his laughter.

"Hmm," Ciana said scrunching her face. "If this is how yeh all gonna be I should jes go home."

"Oh no ya don't lady. I promised you a birthday to remember, and that's what you'll get."

A little further down the road and Ciana was still looking out the window. Suddenly, she got real sad.

"Oka... um 'alright'... it's a waterfall. They're supposed to make you go 'ooh aah'... not cry. What am I missing here?"

Scota scrunched her face and tried to wave Bird off, but Ciana caught her.

"Tis alright Scota," Ciana said as she came back from a memory. "When I was little, mah mum would take me to one, 2 crofts away from mine. Those were special times. When dad died, he left just enough coin for me and Scota. I tried to buy theh place but theh owner wouldn't sell it. He was afraid I'd take the water for mehself and not leave him with enough fer his farm'in. Nothin I said made any difference and soon after I wasn't even allowed to go there."

"Um, I get the first part. But why ban you from the place?"

"He be afraid I might do sumthin to make it so he'd have to sell it to me. I not been back there since."

Bird just had an 'ahah' moment, put on a poker face, and let the matter drop... for now.

Stepping down from the coach, Ciana saw for the first time, the hustle and bustle of a city. At Bird's insistence, the coach stopped in front of a dress shop.

"I hired you for the afternoon, correct?" Bird stated more than asked.

"Aye sir, I be at yer service fer the next 3 hours."

"Well then, wait here my good man."

Inside Scota was on overload looking at all the 'pretties, softies and sparklies'. Ciana just felt out of place.

The shop girl was rude. She also pretty much told Bird this was a place for women.

"Fuck off bitch," was all he said as he took his ladies elsewhere.

Two other dress shops and still the same attitude.

Gruffly, Bird stated "Now I know how Julia Roberts felt."

This last dress shop wasn't rude however. Unhelpful, but at least not rude. Bird had a thought. Did such a thing even exist in this time and place? Only one way to find out... so he asked.

"My good shopkeeper, would there be a shop like yours but, shall we say... run by a man?"

Bird was actually surprised when the lady said "Two streets over and yes... perhaps that would be best."

Bird tipped his hat and wished her a good day.

The driver outside was nervous. This wasn't exactly where he wanted to be seen. Bird however paid him half again as much as a normal fare so... wait he did.

Walking into the shop Bird knew, now, he found the right place. The owner was pleasant, welcoming, and flamboyant. Bird chuckled thinking if he was anymore flamboyant, he'd be a drag queen.

"Oh don't let those arrogant hags bother ye none. You just let ole John here work his magic and you'll be right as rain in no time!"

"An Englishman working in Edinburgh?" Bird queried hearing his accent.

"Yes well, let's just say, London just wasn't my cup of tea anymore."

John was staring at the handsome redhead and Bird just laughed.

"Sorry shopkeeper... heh heh... not exactly 'your type'."

"Hmm... pity."

Bird walked back out and spoke to the driver as he opened the door for the ladies.

"I've found what we need. I can see your discomfort so, why don't you proceed to the hotel. See that our rooms are ready and drop off our things, will you my good man?"

"Aye, your a kind man sir. I'll be back fer yeh in an hour will that do?"

"Nicely driver," Bird said as he closed the coach door.

Three ladies walked into John's shop and he nearly had a heart attack. All 3 ladies got a kiss on the hand and John spoke to Ally first.

"Perfection, SHEAR perfection! Nothing... we're not touching a thing on you," John told the avatar with a wave of his hand.

*Ally curtsied proper, giggled, and said "Thank you kind sir."*

*Turning to Ciana he said "Your loveliness is like a breath of fresh spring air. That dress however, well... we can do better."*

*"Oi! And jes what be wrong with mah dress?"*

*"For going to church... in the country... nothing. Your beauty however should have nothing but the finest threads to go with it!" John said all happy.*

*Bird smiled knowing he had now found the right shop and asked with a smirk, "Uh, John? This one over here would like some heels, like my assistant has... can do?"*

*Bird was also pointing to Scota when he said it. John wasn't sure what Bird wanted so Bird pointed to Ally. She lifted her dress some and showed him her boots. John didn't bother to hide his delight and squealed like a little kid.*

*"Oh you MUST tell me where you got those! They're divine!"*

*Bird giggled a little seeing John not even ask, get a tape measure, and start measuring Ally's boots.*

*"YO! Shopkeeper!... Focus."*

*John bowed to Bird, apologized to Ally and kissed her hand yet again.*

*"Not even someone as faaaaaaboulously gifted as I, could make something like that in less than 3 days."*

*"Take something you already have, and modify it. See my lovely bride to be here?" Bird said pointing to Ciana, "It's her birthday tomorrow and I have a special dinner planned. Have them ready by tomorrow afternoon, and they'll be an extra 2 pounds in it for you."*

*"Two pounds!?" Ciana barked thinking that an outrageous sum.*

*John leaned into Bird and said "Make it 5 and I'll have a pair for the birthday girl as well."*

*"Done." Ciana was aghast and Bird just told her "Welcome to the big city. Not exactly country prices around here."*

*Ciana and Scota were whisked into a back room. John came back out and Bird just pointed at what he liked. Underwear to shoes to even the shades of makeup. The latter Bird cautioned John on.*

*"They're beautiful enough as it is. Keep the powders and such*

to a minimum... and I MEAN... minimum."

"Why I wouldn't dreeeeeeam of ruining such beauty with that theater paint."

Scota was first. Feeling ever so feminine, she couldn't wait to show off for 'dad and big sis'.

"Heeelllllll no!" Bird barked.

Scota was crushed.

"Ten years from now MAYBE... today? Not gonna happen."

Bird was complaining of the highly revealing neckline.

"See? What did I tell you?" John told Scota of her choice. Curling her around he said "You just trust good ole John here and we'll have you looking fabulous in no time."

The next dress was better. Blood red and floor length. Proper neckline this time but the material, well, Bird thought it was as heavy as a stage curtain and said so.

Ciana came out next and was shy as hell. She had on the most perfect dress. Not only that... it was cut to perfection.

"That dress... one and done. The fit and the cut are perfect. The pattern however is ghastly."

Bird then pulled out 3 bolts of fabric that, well, just happened to be squadron colors.

"Make THAT dress but, in these colors. Have it ready along with the shoes... and I'll make it 10."

Imitating Bird, John just said "Done."

Scota came back out in ankle type boots and another red dress. John had given her a jet black wrap, and Bird was smiling. Scota practically squealed in delight and twirled for all to see.

"Oi, look at her... I can barely walk in these as it is and here mah sistuh is doing tricks!"

John told Bird he'd be by with the goods between 3 and 4pm. No earlier and no later. Bird said that would be perfect. Both ladies were back to their original dresses when the coach returned outside. John watched Bird leave and... that view was just fine by him.

Turning his shop sign to 'closed', he sighed and said "Pity... the good ones are always taken."

Bird merely chuckled... turned down his super sonic hearing, and closed the coach door.

Twenty minutes later, and some city traffic to wait out, the coach pulled up to the hotel. To Bird it was modest but okay. Ally thought so too. Ciana and Scota were acting like it was the Taj Mahal. Ciana was quiet as this was a proper place. While she could be nice enough, she figured it best to let Bird do the talking. The polite man at the desk said his rooms were ready and that dinner was still being served for another hour. Keys in hand, all filed upstairs to their rooms.

"I kahnt believe the man at the fancy desk didn't ask us iffin we be married!" Ciana said when Bird got keys to only 2 rooms.

"There's not asking... and there's discreet enough not to care."

"Yeh mean he knew... and dint say noth'in!?"

"Mm hmm."

"Well... these city folk sure are something I tell yeh!"

"As they say where I'm from... 'money talks, bullshit walks'."

"Heh heh, if thah be the case... yers musta been scream'in!"

The amenities caught Ciana's attention. Bird explained to her what some were, and she knew or guessed the rest. Another explanation was harder though. Ciana was used to doing everything herself. Being waited on, or expecting certain things... was a very new concept to her. She really freaked out when they all left for dinner and she accidentally bumped into a maid.

"Begg'in yeh pardon m'lady" the maid said slightly scared she disturbed a guest.

She hustled it quick around a corner and Ciana was just dumbfounded.

"Did yeh hear what she called me!?"

Sweetly, Bird said "Aye lass... I did."

They were all seated at dinner now. Ally helped Scota with her manners and what was expected. Bird chuckled seeing Ally be a proper lady... and Scota mirroring everything she did. Ciana was confused that some paid and others didn't. Bird told her if you stay at the hotel the meal is included in the bill. Things were very different indeed and Ciana felt those old insecurities well up again. Not wishing to spoil everyone's good mood with her imaginary demons, Ciana merely followed Bird the way Scota followed Ally.

"By the way Scota, now would be a good time, and a good place, for that proper speech you've been working on," Bird told her with an encouraging 'I know you can do it' tone.

"Thank you kind sir but, I have already figured that one out for myself," Scota said so eloquently.

Ally smiled and said "Why Scota, I'm very proud of you."

Scota just beamed at the praise.

Equally as eloquent, Ciana leaned into her saying "Excuse me m'lady but, could you tell me who you are, and what have you done with my sister?" Scota laughed and Ciana winked at Bird saying "Aye, she wasn't the only one who was practicing."

"Hahahaha... so it would seem!"


Later that evening and, in the arms of his love, Bird was watching his HUD. It struck 00:00 and Bird shut it down.

"Ciana?"

A slightly muffled "Yes my love?"

"Happy Birthday," Bird said with a grand smile.

With perfect timing, the bells of the town rang out 12 times. Ciana snuggled into Bird and, hearing the bells, thought this is what heaven must be like.

"Aye... happy it is," she said with a smile as she drifted off to sleep.


Morning came and for a change, Bird gladly got up early. This was one day he wasn't missing a minute of. Breakfast was a little easier having been through dinner the night before. A few of the maids however were staring at Bird, and whispering in the corner. Bird turned off his extended hearing, excused himself, and went to the desk.

"Good morning my good man."

"G'morning sir, how may I help you?"

"My lady's birthday is today. As a present I bought her a new wardrobe. We traveled without her clothing so as to return with the new. I have her dressmaker coming by later today, could you see that he's sent to our rooms?"

"Of course, and may I say sir... what an excellent present and surprise that is."

"Thank you, I thought it was anyway. Oh and, one more thing. Do you own this fine hotel or just work here?"

"I own and run it sir, is there a problem?"

"There is indeed. I have no doubt that somewhere in a back room or office you have a birch switch of some sort. See those two waitresses over there?" and Bird pointed them out.

"Aye, I do."

"When their duties are done for the day, see to it they each receive a fitting punishment for their snide comments. Now you know why she's wearing the same dress as yesterday and, as you can see, things aren't always what they seem now are they?"

"My apologies sir, I'll see to it personally. And aye, your correct... things aren't always what they seem."

Bird slipped him a pound note and said "For your trouble, your wisdom and understanding, and... your discretion."

The owner thanked Bird with a nod of understanding, and Bird rejoined the ladies. Seems they weren't staring at him... but Ciana. Hearing their comments, the Scorpion protector was having none of it.

"Is everything alright my love?" Ciana asked seeing who he was talking to.

With a smile and a kiss, Bird said "It is now birthday girl."

Just under an hour later, Bird and crew were outside and looking for a taxi. Bird was about to flag one down when a voice called to him.

"Mistuh BirdOfPrey sir, might I have a word with yeh?"

It was the driver from yesterday.

"Hello driver. Was there a problem with the bill?"

"Oh heavens no sir." Impishly, he spoke softly to Bird asking "I was wonder'in iffin I might have a word with yeh... in private?"

"Ladies! Give me a moment will you?" Bird called out.

Bird walked off to the side with the driver.

"Well driver, what can I do for you?"

"I was wonder'in sir... iffin yeh might be need'in a ride today.

*I know it's none of my business, but I overheard the lovely lady mention it be her birthday. I thought perhaps, well, be'in out of towners and all, perhaps yeh might be want'in to see the city."*

*Bird smiled and asked "Is business that bad for you Andrew?"*

*"Oi... yeh know mah name?"*

*"I heard the station manager call you that when you picked us up in Glasgow."*

*"Aye... smart man yeh are sir."*

*"Give me one good reason I should hire you Andrew, and I'll consider it," Bird stated slightly curious at this odd turn of events.*

*"To be honest with yeh sir... yeh know my name."*

*"Excuse me?"*

*"Yeh be a wise man aye but, yeh be a kind one too. Most o'my fares don't even know I exist. When they do speak to me, they treat no better than garbage in theh street. The fine ladies yeh travel with, I thought perhaps they would be look'in down on me... but they didn't either. The wage yeh paid me was enough for 2 days and I only worked for yeh 1. I may be poor, but I be an honest Christian man I am. I wez born n raised not 3 streets from here, and, well, fer being kind to me, I'd like to give something back. I ain't got much but, I thought if I could take yeh around for the lady's birthday, well, that would be somethin' ennyway. No one knoes Edinburgh better than good ole Andrew I'll tell yeh thah!"*

*Bird turned his HUD off when the meter barely budged... and stayed blue. Bird was touched by his genuine kindness and so, the party of 4 now had a taxi for the day.*

*"Ladies? Meet Andrew... taxi driver extraordinaire!" Bird chuckled as he walked the driver back to the waiting ladies.*

*Andrew was humbled when the ladies curtsied... to him!*

*"Driver, as one born and raised around here, I suppose you know, well shall we say, all the best places? You know, the one's the tourists don't usually see."*

*"Aye sir, I do indeed," Andrew said with a smile.*

*Bird had a thought and asked "Hey Andrew, you wouldn't happen to know a glass maker would you?"*

*Andrew winced a little.*

*"Problem driver?"*

"Not so much a problem as... well... you'll see. The glass maker yeh seek will be out at the market by the river but not till later. I'll take yeh there then, aye?"

"Sounds good to me. Well my good man, this lady here is Alydar, but we call her Ally. The lovely blonde lass here is Scota..." and both ladies curtsied slightly to him as he tipped his hat in kind.

Andrew turned to Ciana and asked "And the lovely birthday lady... what should I call yeh then?"

Bird stepped up and grabbed her quick saying "You can call her... mine."

Andrew backpedaled a bit not wishing to offend. Bird just smiled and play slapped him on the arm.

"Oh Andrew I'm just teas'in ya! THIS fine lady... is Ciana."

Andrew bowed proper saying "A pleasure m'lady. May yeh have theh happiest of birthdays."

Ciana was sweet, and pulled up his face by his chin.

"A lady today perhaps but, you'll not find me putt'in on airs."

Andrew was blown away and swore to himself, if Bird or the ladies, ever needed to get out of hell itself, he'd be waiting at the gates to give him a ride.

"Andrew, a moment please," and Bird pulled him to the side. "I placed an order at a jeweler. I was told they're a block off the main road, do you know of them?"

"Aye I do. Finest jeweler in the whole of Scotland too."

"Good. Take us there first but stop a block away. Distract the ladies and come back for me... can do?"

"Aye sir... can do," Andrew said with a smile as he hopped up on the carriage.

Bird held the door for the ladies, closed it, and off they went.


Bird was a very busy boy while he was gone those 2 days. He went to what would be known as Iraq, and picked up some lapis stones. His white skin caught some attention but, his gold was good enough. Another trip to the plains of Africa and, with scanner in hand, found the diamonds he wanted. A short stint in the shop on Alydar and they were now as blue as the sky. Another hop over to the Sierra's of his birth, and he had the silver he needed now as well. Now, back to

Edinburgh after that, and Bird stopped into the jeweler. He ordered a very specific design and the jeweler was just blown away by the small but lovely blue diamonds. He promised Bird he'd have it done and now, Bird was stoked to pick it up.

Andrew did exactly as Bird asked. Now in the jewelry shop, the jeweler was as excited to show Bird his creation, as Bird was to see it. Bird held it up, marveled at his vision turned reality, and paid him the remaining gold coin he owed. Bird showed up 20 minutes later, got picked up, and the carriage was off yet again to yet another sight.

Andrew took them to what Bird would call 'a dump'. It was run down on the outside and Bird almost refused to go in. It was lunch time and this was not what Bird had in mind. Andrew promised them a fine meal however, so Bird gave it a shot. Bird got a pleasant shock when... the inside didn't match the outside. Nice tables, well lit, a nice breeze and a friendly staff. No one on the inside had ever had company this fine and were practically stumbling over themselves trying to be 'proppuh'. Andrew was indeed correct and the food was delicious.

"Jes like me Mistuh Bird," Andrew told them as they emerged, "It ain't always what yeh see on the outside eh?"

Bird tossed him a small sack with a few desserts in it and said "The phrase is, 'never judge a book by it's cover'... and you'd be correct."

Andrew opened the sack and said "Thank yeh kindly Mistuh Bird!" seeing the contents.

Seeing the cross on Bird's neck, Andrew took them to a cathedral in town. Ciana marveled at the beauty of it. So did Ally.

An overlook atop the town and Ciana was in heaven at the view. Andrew was every bit the tour guide he promised he'd be. Now he was fulfilling Birds request. He made his way down the river, showing them all the nice vantage points. At the end was a large open area, and lots of local merchants showing their wares.

"Here yeh be Mistuh Bird, theh glass maker yeh asked for."

"You're kidding right?" Bird said staring across the open

*area.*

*Nothing but foot traffic so coaches stayed to the outer edge.*

*"No sir... that be what yeh asked for."*

*"Andrew... she's a girl... and barely older than Scota."*

*"Aye, but, like the lunch yeh had... yeh know... book an cover an all thah."*

*Bird saw a lovely girl. Roughly Scota's size, but with dirty blond hair. She also looked like having a meal, wasn't an everyday occurrence.*

*"Well my good driver, when you're right you're right. Wait here ladies I won't be long."*

*Bird was halfway to his target when his lovely day, turned sour.*

*"Ugh, those ruffians. Nuthin but trouble they are!" Andrew exclaimed. "You ladies stay here and be safe. I'll see if Mistuh Bird needs a hand."*

*Ciana was smiling and called out "Andrew?"*

*"Aye ma'am?"*

*"Would you like to see one of the reasons I love him so?"*

*"I doen see why not ma'am."*

*"Then... stay right here... and watch," Ciana said with a 'that's my man' tone in her voice.*

*The two men Andrew held in such disdain, were brothers. They were also the town bullies. They had the glass maker boxed in and, as one would expect, were making snide comments about getting in her dress. What impressed Bird was... she held her own... or at least tried to. When she refused them, they got mad and smashed her stuff. She freaked and they only taunted her further. One brother held her while the other one said things like "Oops" as he dropped her stuff smashing it on the cobblestones. She fought hard to break free and save her wares. Suddenly, she really freaked, and shook violently. The brother laughed but let her go out of fear.*

*Both brothers grabbed a few pieces and ran off leaving the young girl to thrash about on the street. Bird ran for her as people looked on with disgust, but did so moving away. Not one single local helped her or even cared. However, at top speed, an out of towner did.*

*"ALLY!" Bird called out as he reached the girl and cradled her.*

*Ally ran up and Scota was surprised as she never saw her get out.*

*"Ten o'clock, 35 yards.. down that alley...." and in an ice cold tone ordered "...get them... and bring them to me."*

*"And if they refuse?"*

*"Expedite my request."*

*Ally was heading out and hollered "With pleasure!"*

*Scota couldn't believe anyone could run like that with heels like those on.*

*Bird pulled her jaw down and stuck his fingers in her mouth and held her tongue down, as Scota and Ciana ran up with Andrew.*

*"I dint wanna tell yeh till yeh met her Mistuh Bird... she has fits sometimes," Andrew said with concern.*

*"This is no fit... it's called a grand mal seizure!" Bird looked down and stroked her face and said "Shh shh shh, it's okay dear... you're safe now... c'mon... come back to me."*

*Two rough men in an alley were laughing and wondering how much coin they could get for their ill gotten gain... when a long shadow graced the alley.*

*"Ere now pretty lady... iffin yeh know whah's good fer yeh... yeh'll jes keep walk'in!" the older one threatened.*

*"Or?" the silver haired lady asked calmly.*

*"Yeh doen wanna know," said the younger one.*

*"Oh but... I insist."*

*"C'mon" the older one said, "Let's go see what we can get for these," and he started walking towards Alydar. "Out of the way missy... iffin yeh doen wanna get hurt thah is."*

*"No."*

*"Oi, a lass with spirit eh? Heh heh, lady, I'm gonna break that sprit jes like a new filly!"*

*"Please... try."*

*The man pulled a knife and pointed it at the lady blocking his path.*

*"I told yeh get out of me... Uunnnfff!"*

*Alydar snapped the knife from his hand and slammed him into the wall so hard she knocked him out. Still mid swing she flung the knife at the remaining guy and landed it in his left shoulder.*


*"Bird, what's a 'seizure'?" Ciana asked slightly scared.*

*Ghost 1 saw her calm down enough to remove his fingers. He kept talking soft to her, trying to get her brain to 'kick back in'. A girl he knew as a kid had epilepsy. It was the only thing he knew to get her to calm down and come back to the real world. Most times it worked so he tried the only thing he knew. Thing is, latter 20th century or mid 18th... it worked.*

*"ALL of you, stay calm and sweet when she wakes up," Bird said holding the little lady.*


*Ally showed up holding one brother by the scruff of the neck. She was dragging the other one and dumped him into the pile of broken glass on the road.*

*"Sorry boss but that one... um... sorta broke."*


*The first thing the glass girl saw was Bird's kind expression.*

*"Welcome back little one. Fear not you're safe," Bird said in the kindest tones.*

*"Where... what... oh no..." she said as she woke and started to realize what happened.*

*Now she began to cry.*

*"Thank you kind sir but please... jes... jes leave me," glass girl said with great despair.*

*Bird and Ciana switched places and Bird... was pissed.*

*"Well mister tough guy..." and Bird twisted the knife in his shoulder saying "...Oops... bet that hadda hurt huh?"*

*The man was scared as hell and now, screaming in pain.*

*"Well tough guy, ya know what we say where I come from?" The man was still screaming and Bird said "Hmm? No? Well, let me tell you then." Without a word, Ally let go and Bird picked him up and bench pressed him over his head and hollered "GARBAGE!..."*

and he tossed him screaming in the river and finished with "... gets taken to the curb."

"And this one?" Ally asked casually.

Bird stepped on him, grinding his face in the busted glass as he walked back.

"Leave him."

Andrew was impressed, and scared, all at the same time.

The local soldiers came over to investigate the ruckus.

"You're a bit late," was all Bird said when they arrived.

Bird gave his statement. Being a learned gentleman, his word was taken at complete face value. The unconscious one was well known to them. They thanked Bird for his assistance, and hauled the out cold bully off to jail.

"You forgot one," Bird hollered as they walked off.

"No... we didn't," one of them said with a wink.

Walking off back to the ladies, Bird just said "Works for me."

"My wares!... Oh my wares... they be all I had," glass girl said sobbing hysterically.

"Well little one, do you have a name?" Bird asked kindly as he crouched down to the sobbing girl.

"Kara. I want to thank yeh for being so kind to me. Now, (sob) please... jes leave me be. Yeh not be need'in to bother with the likes o'me," the crumpled girl said through sobbing and despair.

Bird stood up and did something he'd done many times before... he held out a helping hand.

Kara was frail and now, mentally anyway, was crushed.

"Are there any parents I can notify? I have a coach here and we can take you home if you'd like?"

Kara just shook her head and sobbed.

Now Bird got it and asked "Orphan?"

Still sobbing, Kara just nodded.

"Any home to speak of?" Bird asked.

Just another shake of her head but, no words, just tears. She was picking up pieces and crying harder as she did.

"If you upset yourself, you're going to have another seizure,"

Bird told her.

"Please... I... I'll be alright. Thank yeh sir... truly but... please just leave me. Tis all I'm good fer."

Now, Bird had had enough. He scooped her up and headed for the coach as all 3 ladies followed like groupies. Well, 2 of them anyway.

"Alright, I've had enough of this shit. Andrew! Get the coach. I want you to take her to our hotel. Tell the owner I said put her in a room next to ours and for the love of God man... have him get her something to eat for Christ's sake."

Kara snapped up in a panic.

"No please sir, I'll be fine. All I had was my wares. I not have the coin for ennything like thah!"

"Fortunately for you... I do."

Andrew was heading out when Ciana held him up.

"Now driver... now yeh know why," she said sweetly.

With respect, Andrew tipped his hat and told her "Aye, and yeh be a lucky woman for it too."

"Aye Andrew... I am," Ciana said with a smile as the coach headed out.

Bird looked around, then at Ciana.

"Sorry about that my dear. Not exactly how I planned on celebrating your birthday."

With love, Ciana looked at him and said "Yeh be a good and kind man. You told me once there's good and evil. I just seen one, defeat theh other. I couldn't be more proud of you... and proud that I get tuh call yeh mine."

Bird smiled, and said "Scota... Ally... would you mind following us please?" and he took Ciana's hand and walked her over to the busted glass by the railing. "Scota, Ally, I want you to witness this if you would please."

"Witness what?" Scota asked all confused.

"Heh heh, you'll see."

Bird pulled out a long thin narrow box, and handed it to Ciana.

"This isn't how I planned this. Seeing this around me now, I can't think of a better place. Look around you Ciana, see all the damage?"

"Aye," she said in a confused tone.

"This is what to expect from me. Things will go bad. Evil will come and yes, it will do damage. This however, is me, telling you there's always something better to come and... amidst all this chaos and destruction, I'll always be there for you... right where I am now, smack dab in the middle of it." Bird took a deep breath and said "This is the world I can't share with you... yet. Damage and ugliness... beauty, serenity and love... and one day God willing, 'us', right in the middle of it all."

Bird nodded, and Ciana opened the box. She put a hand to her mouth and almost cried.

"Oh Bird... it's stunning!"

Inside was a necklace. Bird liked the look of puka shell necklaces and thought it would look great on Ciana. The jeweler had never seen a chain like that but made it to Bird's spec's. A heavy clasp on the back let her take it off or put it on. The front was an oval of polished black onyx, circled with silver braiding. Inside the black mirror stone, set in pure silver... was the BirdOfPrey wing logo that so graced the monoliths of Freedom Point. In the silver braiding, the jeweler set the 5 blue diamonds Bird found.

"That's my logo Ciana. Where I'm trying to get back to, ANY creature sees that... and sees it in silver... good men and women will help you, and evil will run the other way. Know this my love, till I get back there, I will never marry. I will marry there and only there. That said I had the jeweler make this. I, Commander BirdOfPrey, will not marry you till then. IF however you'll have me, I offer you only this. I promise I will care for you, and I will protect you, for as long as you'll have me. I promise to stand by you, and any children you give me. Till such a day as you decide to remove that, I will uphold that promise, for as long as you desire. In lieu of a wedding ring, I offer you that and swear, as long as you wear it, I will never be far away. It's all that I am... but it's yours if you'll have it."

Ciana was crying, so was Scota. Ally was just shy of.

"No BirdOfPrey, I will not put it on. I would be honored however... if you would," Ciana proudly told him through her happy tears.

Bird was truly happy, and undid the clasp as Ciana turned and lifted her hair. Bird stood with all the poise of a Ghost and fixed the clasp.

Ciana turned around and spoke from her heart.

"Yeh be the strangest man I e'er met BirdOfPrey. While nothing has gone according to my dreams or hopes, things have gone far beyond anything I could have imagined. I would be happy to call you mine, and proud to tell yeh, here and now, I'll keep it on forever and a day."

Bird gave her a passionate kiss.

He hugged her and said "Happy Birthday my love."

"Thank you... my love."

There was a church nearby. Ciana insisted if she was to get no ring... yet... then she wanted it blessed. Bird had no argument with that and even thought it was a lovely idea.

"If I open those doors, and find the bishop in there, I'm gonna be pissed."

Scota and Ciana laughed. Ally just smiled thinking how nice it would be to introduce herself to him again... and again... and again.

The priest came out of the confessional booth. Ciana was polite and respectful, told him what she wanted, and he was only too happy to oblige. He thought it the most oddest of necklaces, till Bird told him something he almost forgot.

"Father, turn the medallion piece around."

He did and now he smiled. Ciana was crying happy tears again as she saw it too. Engraved on the back was a lovely cross.

The inscription read 'May He keep you safe when I cannot'. The priest thought it a lovely sentiment, and blessed the necklace, then Bird and Ciana. The small crowd all turned to leave, Bird dropped a small gold coin in the poor box... and they were gone.

"Is it active?" Bird asked Ally out of earshot of the other two.

"It is," was all she replied.

Bird, with help from one of the shops in the lander, melted the onyx just enough to implant a tracking device. Embedded in it for all times, Ciana had no idea that Bird, for as long as she wore it... would truly never be far away.

"Boss?"

"Yeah Ally?"

"Ciana is right, you are a good man. I want you to know I'm very proud of you."

That actually meant a lot to Bird, it truly did.

"Thanks sweety."


John showed up right when he said he would. He had brought the dress Bird ordered and a trunk full of others similar to that one. Some were even for Scota. The ladies were talking but Ciana felt odd having a man help her dress.

"But... but... he be a man!" Ciana protested to Ally with a 'don't you get it?' attitude.

With a wink and a chuckle, John said "Well... sometimes."

Ciana had a 'huh?' look on her face. So did Scota.

Smirking, Ally said "You really don't know do you?"

Cautiously, Ciana said "Ere now... knoe what?"

Ally giggled and curled her finger. Ciana leaned in and Ally whispered in her ear.

"Nooooooo," Ciana said in shocked surprise as she stared at John.

With a dandy smile, he simply said "Oh yeeesssss."


The ladies were talking, and teasing, while they dressed.

"I'll bet he shows up in a long black coat, black boots, and a black hat!" Scota exclaimed with a laugh.

"No he won't Scota. I be positive he'll show up with a long black coat, black boots, and a black hat!" Ciana said laughing along with her.

Ally was enjoying being with the girls... a lot. Without her sisters around, these two were becoming like family. She now knew what Bird meant when he said 'family' can be made, and not born to.

With a soft giggle, Ally told them "You're both wrong. I happen to know for a fact it will be a long black coat, black boots, and a black hat!"

All 3 ladies laughed at Bird's standard attire, and continued getting dressed.

Ally really threw her new sisters for a loop when she came out holding two tops. What had them speechless was that she was naked from the waist up.

"John tell me, red? Or blue?" Ally said as she switched tops back and forth.

"UH!" John squealed. "No painting or statue in the whole of Rome is lovelier than this vision before my eyes." Then, totally unfazed, John pointed saying "And the blue one dear, definitely the blue one."

Ally nodded a thanks and went to put it on.

"What?" she asked the two ladies with the open mouths.

"And yeh say... proper ladies do this?" Ciana asked John as he 'painted her face'.

"With your beauty darling, it's almost unnecessary. As for those 'proper ladies' you mentioned... welllllllll... even buckets of this wouldn't help some of them."

Ciana giggled and let John continue.

John used devices on her hair that Ciana couldn't fathom. Nervous as she was though, she couldn't argue with the results.

While the ladies primped and preened, Bird went to see his latest project. Kara was like a beaten down dog and Bird knew it. Kara also knew she'd have to pay for this one way or another. She'd never been with a man and pretty much figured out that's what it would cost her. At least this time, she would give it rather than having it taken from her. And at least, it would be a handsome man at that. She was nervous as hell when the knock she'd been waiting for came at the door.

"Come in," was her weak raspy reply.

"Well glass girl... how are you?" Bird said as he entered.

"Better now thanks to yer kindness."

*"Well I'm glad to hear it. Did you get something to eat?"*

*"I think I ate more today than I do in a week!"*

*"Kara listen, I have a plan."*

*"Aye... I figured as much. I want yeh to knoe I'll not make a fuss. I'll be a good girl I will."*

*"What? Oh hell no... even if I wanted 'that'... in your current state I'd break you in half."* Then with a kind smile, Bird said *"I have that aspect of my life well covered... but I appreciate the offer."*

*Kara couldn't fathom it. She also felt sad. If this kind stranger didn't want her then... who would?*

*"Kara listen. In your world, you'd be considered 'broken'. Those fits of yours, how long have you had them?"*

*"Since I was a wee lass. They got worse when I grew what, well, what yeh didn't want."*

*"Makes sense that puberty would do that."*

*"Pue... what?"*

*"Never mind. Kara look, you have a disease called epilepsy. The seizures, what you call 'fits', they're brought on by stress. Get too excited, either happy or sad or angry, and it can trigger one."*

*"I... I understand some of what yeh jes said. So, mah fits happen when I get too excited?"*

*"Mm hmm."*

*"But why?"*

*"I don't know Kara. I only know that your brain can't handle it... so it turns off for a short while. That's what causes the fits and it's also why you can't remember what happened when you wake up."*

*"Mah brain?... Turns off!?... Noooo,"* Kara said thinking she was being teased.

*The look on Bird's face told her she wasn't.*

*"Wait, yer serious ain't yeh? But if that be the reason, if mah brain turns off like yeh said, then why don't I...?"*

*"Die?... The seizure you had today was the biggest of its type. IF it lasts for too long... one day you will."*

*Kara felt like she was just handed a death sentence.*

*Now Bird laid out his plan.*

"Kara look, you have no family here. No one to look out for you and it's obvious you aren't doing a good job of it. Tell me, is there any reason for you staying in the city?"

Sadly, Kara told him, "No place else to go. No one will have me. Once or twice a family took me in. Either the master of the house be a brute, or I'd have a fit and they'd want noth'in tuh do with me. Here in theh city, there are more places I can go, to be safe, to get food, and to sell my wares for what coin I can get."

"Speaking of, I know how glass is made. Care to tell me how a half starved girl, with no place of her own, and no coin... even makes stuff like that?"

Kara sighed. She may get in trouble but, what difference would that make now?

"The smithy. He likes his wagers he does. He'd go out at night to gamble and usually be gone fer hours. I'd sneak in once he be gone, and make small pieces in case he returned on me."

"A smithy eh? Funny you should mention that. I just happen to have one in mind if you can believe that. So, let me ask you another question."

Kara was shrunk under the covers and was barely peeking out from them.

"Hmm?"

"Your a girl. In a world dominated by men, you managed to become quite skilled at a trade. Care to explain that one?"

"Do I hafta?"

Sweetly Bird said "Not if you don't want to."

Kara wasn't sure what was going on. This stranger was truly kind, he knew stuff so he was obviously a learned man, and he didn't want 'her wares' in return. She didn't know why but, something made her trust him.

"One of the families I mentioned. One of them be a kind old man. He had a daughter of his own who had passed. He said I reminded him of her, so he took pity on me and took me in. I had a fit one day but, like you sir, he was kind. Glass was his trade and when he saw mah fit, he wanted to make sure I had something I could do to take care o'mahself. I actually like it and am truly good at it. He knew he was sick and dy'in, and knew no one else would want me an mah fits. So he taught me. All he had was his tools and his place.

*His mean witch of a sistuh took his place when he passed. Being I wasn't family, I was on mah own again but, as he wished, I took his tools and trade with me."*

Bird was touched, and told her what he had in mind.

"Kara, while the city has more things in it to help you survive, it also has more things in it that can cause the fits... some of them quite severe."

"Like today?"

"Mm hmm... or worse. When you do glass, the forge needs to be quite hot. Does the heat bother you?"

"Only when I get hungry or thirsty."

"Got anything against the country?"

Now Kara's eyes lit up some.

"Nay, I was there when I was born, and until I be 5 or so. No places there for me though, and not enough to buy mah wares. I be a good lass I am. I'd sooner sell mah glass wares than, well, 'those wares' if yeh be know'in what I mean."

"I do indeed. Stay and rest. I'll be sending in a man... well, sort of,... anyway, he makes dresses. PROPER dresses, not those rags your wearing. I'll have him find you proper clothing, and once he has, I want those burned. I leave for the country tomorrow. I know of a place you can stay, and likely even make your wares. If your interested, be properly dressed and in the lobby tomorrow morning. If not, well then, be careful on the streets alright?"

"Mistuh Bird sir?"

"Aye lass?"

"The raven haired lady... she's a lucky woman she is tuh have a man like you."

"If you decide to meet us tomorrow... so will you."

Bird was walking back to his room, and passed John on his way out. He hooked his arm in his and spun him for Kara's door.

Teasing, John said "Oh... be gentle with me?"

"Very funny dress boy," Bird said with a hint of malice.

"Oh my sweet Lord," John exclaimed seeing Kara.

"I want her fitted with clothing. PROPER clothing. Once you have, send me the bill, and I want the clothes she has now...

*burned."*

*John felt sorry for the young lady and told Bird "Just leave it to me."*

*Bird closed the door, had a thought, and headed downstairs to speak to the owner.*


*"Oh sister, I ne'er seen you look lovelier!" Scota told Ciana with true sisterly love.*

*"And what of you? You look every bit the grown up lady yeh do," Ciana told her just as kindly.*

*Alydar came out and teased "What about me?"*

*"You?... You could go to an all night party THEN work the fields for a day... sleep for a week... and still wake up looking like the bloody queen!" Ciana quipped.*

*Alydar curtsied and said with a chuckle, "Thank yeh kindly miss."*

*"I'll tell yeh this though... how you two walk so easy in these things is beyond me. It's a wonduh I doen break my neck!"*

*A silver and a blond giggled and went out to show off.*

*"HAH! I was right," Ally chuckled seeing Bird in the attire he was predicted to be in.*

*Ally and Scota met Bird in the hall. Both moved to the side and waved their arms sideways as they parted.*

*Bird was floored. John had certainly done his job. He brought up his HUD immediately and took pictures AND video. He wanted to remember this for all his days. Standing there, looking more lovely than any woman has a right to, was the stunning woman of his dreams. Her dress was to the floor, and made of black and silver vertical strips. Black heeled boots just like Ally's. The top was a cobalt blue with a squared off neckline. Ally offered her jewels but, saying she had all she needed, Ciana only took a pair of diamond teardrop earrings. Her raven hair flowed like silk and those blue eyes... damn.*

*"Unbelievable. Stunning beyond anything I could imagine." Then, just to tease a little, Bird spoke to Scota and said "And your sister ain't half bad either!"*

Scota laughed and Ciana slapped him playfully.

"Seriously though... you are stunning beyond belief. That said, let's get out of here," And Bird briskly grabbed the sisters by the arms.

"Oi, what's the rush?" Scota protested.

"Because my dear, if we don't get out of here RIGHT now... you and Ally will be going to dinner alone!"

Scota got it and beamed knowing Bird thought she was pretty. Ciana beamed too but... for a whole different reason.

"Ally? Lite 'em up... and spin 'em!"

"Any particular reason?"

"With you three on my arm tonight? Seriously, heh heh, you gotta ask?" Bird said smiling huge.

Ciana asked "Other world talk?"

Ally answered "You could say that," and all 4 rounded the corner and were gone.



The dinner Bird took them to was divine. Ciana and Scota both practiced their manners. The waiters and waitresses saw they were trying, but also kind to them. As such, they got nothing but their best.

Bird now took his coat and hat off. Ciana actually got weak when she saw her love. Standing tall and proud in a black suit she'd never seen any man wear. Bird was dressed sharp in yet another classic James Bond tuxedo. Now, the 3 stunning ladies, weren't the only ones being checked out.

"Uh Bird? Is there something wrong with me?"

"If there is, only God could find it. Why do you ask?"

"The other folk... they be staring!"

"The men are staring because they secretly hate me," Bird said with a grin.

With a laugh, Ally said "And the women are staring because they secretly hate you!" referring to Ciana.

"But why? I ain't nothing special."

Bird almost spit out his food saying "Have you LOOKED in a mirror lately!?"

"Aye alright but... why the women?"

*"Ally?... Tell her."*

*"Reeeeooooowwwrr," Ally said with a sly smile.*

*Scota laughed seeing her sister still not get it.*

*An hour later, and all 4 were in a theater and enjoying the small but good orchestra. It was actually more like a dance hall with the stage at one end. All three applauded the orchestra's last piece when Ciana noticed... Bird was nowhere to be found.*

*"Ladies and gentlemen. I ask you to please be seated. Days ago a stranger came to me with the oddest request," the conductor told the audience. "When he told me what he wanted, and why, I thought it a lovely sentiment and graciously agreed. We have one more song to perform this evening and, I am honored to give to you the very stranger I spoke of," and the maestro waved a hand to the side of the stage.*

*"Oh no! He didn't!" Ciana said in shock seeing who this stranger was.*

*Scota applauded hard and said "Aye, it would seem he did!"*

*Ciana got even mores stares here than at dinner. Scota got her fair share too as did Ally.*

*Bird walked out and pulled up a stool and sat on it.*

*"Thank you maestro. Ladies and gentlemen, I've come here tonight as a gift for my, well, bride to be. You see, today is her birthday and seeing as how she doesn't travel much, I wanted to make this one special. I have a question for you, how about we all have a little fun hmm?"*

*The crowd was liking the handsome stranger... especially the female part of the crowd.*

*"Give me a show of hands, how many of you here this evening have been married for, oh, let's say 7 years or longer? Come on, don't be bashful."*

*Many hands went up and Bird was grateful for it.*

*"Well then, as long time married couples, I offer this song to my lovely birthday girl, and the floor to all of you. When you hear the words of the song I taught these fine musicians, I think you'll understand. I believe a waltz should do nicely."*

*One of the stage hands gave Bird a guitar, and Ciana was*

blown away.

"Oh of course he does! Why wouldn't he be a musician too!?" she said slightly exasperated.

Ally just chuckled.

Bird nodded and began playing. It was a soft song in his collection, one of only a few. It was a song from the early 70's... 1970's that is. It was called "Daisy A Day" by Jud Strunk.

"He remembers the first time he met her... he remembers the first thing she said.... he remembers the first time he held her... and the night that she came to his bed," Bird sang.

Bird was right, the crowd did love this odd new song. It was also one Bird thought would fit the time period.

It was a song about a man who was now old, and telling of his love, and a song he made up and sang only to her. It was also told by a small boy who remembered them, and is now grown and looking back in time when he sees the old man.

"As a kid they would take me for candy... and I loved to go tagging along... we'd hold hands while we walked, to the corner... and the old maaaan would sing her his song..." sang the haunting Yankee voice.

The crowd now knew why Bird asked for the older married couples as they understood in a way no other but them could.

"I'll give you a daisy a day dear... I'll give you a daisy a daaaay," Bird sang as the violins backed up his guitar.

All on the floor thought it ever so sweet as Bird finished the song by coming down onto the floor, and walking right up to his love.

"I'll give you a daisy a day dear... I'll give you a daisy a daaaay... I'll love you until, the rivers run still..." And bird finished with a plink of the strings, "...And the four winds we know... blow... away," and Bird got on one knee and handed Ciana a yellow daisy as the violins drifted away.

The crowd all applauded as Ciana was a pile of crying goo. They applauded even louder when Ciana reached up and kissed Bird for all to see.

Hours later, Bird was repeating history. Laying in bed, he was watching his HUD and... he was waiting for 00:00. He thought back to the day. It was a tiring day but, oh what a day it was. Everything he planned and more.

"Cia..."

"Doen bother... Iem awake. I started this amazing day like this and... with you. By God I'll finish it that way too. Yeh are truly maddening yeh are. Every day I think it's not possible to love you any more than I already do... and every day, you only prove me wrong."

Bird hugged her tight just as it hit zero hour.

"I'm glad you had a good day, and didn't let your fears ruin it."

"Aye, me too," Ciana said just as the first bell rang. "Bird, I love you so much," Ciana said as she drifted off to sleep with the magical sound of the bells in her ears.

Bird blew out the candle... and joined her.

# Chapter 18:

## "New Homes"

*Ciana was sad. She never wanted to leave her home, no less come here. She thought if someone had told her 3 months ago the last few days would happen, she probably would have hid under her bed. Now, with all the sights and sounds, and all the wonderful memories, she was actually finding herself not wanting to leave. All 4 were at breakfast. Scota wanted to be a grownup so she and Ally sat at another table. Ciana was happy to have Bird all to herself for a change.*

*"Sir, I believe your party has arrived," the owner said with a smile.*

*"Wellll... glass girl cleans up nice don't she Lady Bird?"*

*Sweetly, Ciana answered "Aye, she certainly does."*

*The owner walked Kara over to Bird's table. She was, as commanded, dressed proper. Not fancy... but definitely proper.*

*"Come, have a seat!" Bird said in a jovial manner as he stood and pulled out a chair.*

*Kara looked frightened. Proper clothes, men with manners... breakfast!?... She was really out of her element.*

*"Decided to take me up on my offer did you?"*

*"Aye. Yeh be right, this city is hurt'in me more than help'in. I toel yeh already, they'll only be one type of wares I'll be sell'in. That said, yeh been kind to me. Yeh helped me when yeh could'a done far worse. If you say yeh got a place fer me, I doen see no harm in see'in it first."*

*"Fair enough. So Kara, what'll ya have?"*

*"Huh?"*

*"Breakfast dear... what do you want?"*

*"Oh noooo, Iem fine really I..."*

*"Bullshit. You're barely heavier than a supermodel in Milan.*

Waiter!" Bird called out. "The lady here will be joining us. Could you bring some eggs, some toast, and some tea please?"

"Of course... right away sir."

Kara leaned into Ciana asking "Does he always talk so strangely?"

Giggling, Ciana said "He be a Yank."

"Aaaah, well that explains it then. Thank yeh m'lady."

Ciana recoiled a tad saying "Oh, I be no lady lass," and Bird coughed hard. Ciana quickly corrected saying "Well, I am but what I mean is, ye'll not hear me look'in to be reminded of it."

"Sorry miss, but I heard the fine sir here call yeh Lady Bird so I thought..."

"Aye lass, that I am. Let's just say, a lady yes... one that puts on airs?... No."

Bird pointed over to Scota's table saying "You saw those two yesterday. The blond in that stunning blue dress is Scota, Lady Bird's sister. The silver haired lady is Alydar... but we call her Ally. She's my personal assistant."

The two ladies waved politely from the other table. Kara sheepishly waved back.

"Personal assistant?" Kara queried Lady Bird.

"Looong story," Ciana said.

"You ladies have a nice chat... I have to go take care of business," Bird said as he stood up and headed off to the hotel owner.

"Well mister owner, been an interesting few days hasn't it?" Bird said all friendly like.

"Sir... can I be honest with yeh?"

Bird replied "I don't see why not."

"Sir, when yeh came here I thought yeh no diffrint than any other guest. I about had a fit mehself when yer driver brought that girl in. When I heard the story though, an what yeh done, I thought 'well there's a right proper christian man now isn't he'?"

Bird gave him a friendly bow as he continued.

"We be a small city here sir, so Iem sure a man of your

experience will understand how word gets around aye?"

"Aye, I do. And before you ask... no I'm not insulted by it."

"See, that be what Iem talk'in bout. Many of your fine stature would. The whole town, well, the upper half ennyway, is all talk'in bout the bold and handsome stranger who wasn't afraid to show his love for his woman. Honestly sir, from mah heart, I want to say its been a pleasure have'in yeh here. And theh business deal yeh mentioned, shear brilliant thah is. I assure you, if you can deliver your end, I'll deliver mine."

"I've made some fond memories here sir. I assure you, when it comes to business, I'm the man that finds a way where everyone benefits. I don't know if I'll be back this way again but, you have my word that, if I do, yours will be the first hotel I choose," Bird told him in a most friendly fashion.

Kindly, the owner shook his hand, handed him a bill marked 'paid' and told Bird "Aye and iffin yeh do... ye'll be welcome ennytime. Hasten ye back soon sir."

Bird tipped his hat, and rejoined the ladies.

Breakfast finished, and Kara's stomach felt odd.

"It's called being full dear... I suggest, you get used to it," Bird said as he looked for a coach.

All 4 ladies now, were outside and waiting with bags. As Bird promised, Ciana's was empty coming here but... it was stuffed going back.

"Andrew! I had a feeling you'd be showing up," Bird said with a chuckle.

"Aye, yeh be one of the finest men I e'er had the pleasure of meet'in. The ladies go without say'in. No one but good ole Andrew will be see'in to yeh needs sir!"

"Heh heh, fair enough. I got a bill to settle then, we got a ferry to catch. Shall we?" Bird said pointing to the luggage.

"Aye sir!" and Andrew hopped atop the coach.

Normally he'd do it all but that's what he loved about Bird. The Ghost of Alydar merely handed them up to him. Luggage and passengers secure, Ciana looked out and, was sad to see it all go.

"Well dress boy, I believe we have a bill to settle?" Bird said with a chuckle walking into his shop.

"Well if it isn't the handsome stranger. I have it all ready for you," and he pulled out a piece of paper.

Bird paid him the bill, then pulled out the ten he promised him. A little more lovingly than Bird would have liked, John curled his hand back up.

"Listen, I may be a dandy but... I do have a heart you know. What you did for that girl was just darling."

"You're not gonna cry on me are you John?" Bird asked with some caution.

John waved a frilly cuff at him and composed himself.

"Anyway," John continued as he fanned himself, "Give it to her... make it an investment. Besides, thank the Lady Bird for me. Seems everyone wanted to know where she got her divine clothes. And those boots! Hah! I got so many orders that I'm backed up for months!"

John spoke honestly now and... without all the extra 'flair'.

"Not much goes on around here Mistuh Yankee man. You've been a breath of fresh air. I've not been so excited since I left London so... thank you for that. If you ever need anything of my ilk, well, don't forget who looked after you on your first trip here."

"John, I'm planning on building my fine Lady Bird a house that would make the cardinal himself weep with envy. Tell me, you as good with draperies and such as you are with clothes?" Bird asked.

"Oh pleeeease" John responded.

Much to Bird's chagrin... the 'flair' was back.

"I'd sell my shop and become a monk if I couldn't do a simple job as that!" John boasted.

"Heh heh, gotcha. I'll keep you in mind when the time comes."

Bird shook his hand and with that, said goodbye to the second to last character in his little 3 day adventure. Kara almost fainted when Bird handed her the 'tenner'... and why.

"Mistuh Bird, yeh been so kind to me and, well I... I mean.." Kara stammered.

"What do you want sweety?" Bird said kindly as they rode out of the city.

"Could we make a stop before we leave? I promise, if we do, I'll not be a bother again."

"Andrew!" Bird hollered as he tapped the roof.

"Aye sir?"

"Our new friend here would like to make a stop. If you think we can, without delaying us much... do it."

Andrew pulled the team to a stop and hopped down.

"Aye, where be this stop o'yours?"

Kara told him, and Andrew grimaced.

"Problem driver?" Ally asked.

"Aye we can do it with no time loss. Problem is... it ain't exactly the neighborhood for fine ladies... iffin yeh get my mean'in."

Kara was almost in a panic that Bird would say no. Bird saw it though.

"Get us there, and leave the protecting to me."

"Aye, as yeh wish sir."

Bird hopped out, and went atop the coach. Opening a false bottom in his suitcase, he pulled out something, and closed the case back up.

"Alright Andrew... get us there, then... get ready to get us out."

Andrew pulled into an alley and Kara got out. She pulled up a drain of some sort and pulled out a filthy long cloth hidden in it.

"I couldn't leave without mah tools. They be all I have in this world and I just couldn't leave them. While the coin yeh gave me might buy better ones... these were his... iffin yeh get my meaning?"

"I do indeed my dear," Bird said kindly. "Now if you don't mind... this alley is making Andrew nervous."

"Too late Mistuh Bird... look," Andrew said pointing to the exit and grabbing an iron bar of some sort.

Ten men now blocked his path out. Five more now did so to the rear.

"Ally?" Bird asked.

"Aw, and I just finished my nails!"

"Fine then... I got this." Bird looked over his shoulder and said "Stay close Andrew and get ready to run."

*"Aye sir."*

*Bird walked up to the crowd out ahead. As asked, Andrew kept close, but not too close.*

*"Well gentlemen... and I use that term loosely... fine morning we're having aren't we?" Bird said with not a care in the world.*

*"We'll be tak'in yer coin... and whatever yeh got in the carriage," the one man said.*

*"Oh by all means... take what you want. I got 4 of the finest ladies anywhere in there... would you like those too?"*

*The brutes were thrown off guard by that. Andrew was too.*

*Snidely, one of them said "Well, since yeh be offer'in and such."*

*"I'll give you anything you can take. All I ask is that you answer me one question."*

*"Aye... and what be thah?"*

*Bird opened his coat with his hands in his pockets. No one behind him could see, but the brutes in front damn near pissed themselves.*

*"Who wants to be first?" Bird asked coldly.*

*What only the brutes could see, was two near blinding, and spinning... well SOMEthing... and they had a blue dot going around the edge. They all ran off and tripped over each other doing so. Saw blades retracted and put away, Bird got back in the coach.*

*"Well Andrew... I believe we have a transfer to make."*

*Andrew had no clue what Bird did and frankly... wasn't about to ask.*

*Ally knew what he did and asked "Did you have fun dear?" like a 1950's housewife.*

*Bird put on a boo boo face and said "Dey dint wanna pway wif me!"*

*Ally chuckled, 3 other ladies were impressed, but clueless, as Bird laughed too... and the road to Glasgow lay ahead of them.*


*Bird and crew pulled into Glasgow with 20 minutes to spare. All the ladies hugged Andrew. Andrew was honored.*

*"Mistuh Bird, a moment befaw yeh leave?"*

Bird walked off to the side saying "Well, the last few days were an adventure huh?"

"True enough but, that seems yer way. I knoe its not my place to say but... thah jes be you sir. Yer larger than life and as such, well, I kahnt see nuth'in but large things about yeh. Aye, it has been an adventure indeed and one I wasn't gonna miss out on. Yeh be like thah Mistuh Bird... yeh draw people in but... leave em better for it. At least I knoe I am. People like me, we take care of our own we do. When I saw yeh care for Kara the way yeh did, well, I knew you'd be someone to knoe. Its been a right pleasure meet'in yeh Mistuh Bird, and Iem awful glad I did."

Bird was genuinely touched.

"Andrew... thank you. You may be a commoner by the local term... but a good man is a good man, always remember that."

"Tis kind of you Mistuh Bird. Aye, I'll remember it indeed. If yeh ever get back this way well... I'd consider it a privlege to drive yeh ennywhere you or the fine ladies need to go."

"I doubt that Andrew. Something tells me your gonna be quite busy pretty soon," Bird said with a sly smile.

"Eh?"

"Oh, didn't I tell you? Heh heh, silly me. I spoke to the hotel owner about getting a driver to take his guests to and fro. I just happened to mention a certain driver of quality I discovered. Seems my recommendation was received quite well," and Bird winked at him.

"Bless yeh sir!. Tis like I said... yeh be a fine man Mistuh Bird! Even if we never see each other again, I want yeh to know, it's been a pleasure."

Bird shook his hand and with a kind smile, told him "Likewise."

Andrew leaned in the window of the new coach and bid the ladies well.

"Ere now Kara... yeh be one of us. Do yerself proud and... become one of them. Mind yehself now but, the ladies here and the fine sir well... they be good people. Come back an say hello when yeh can alright?"

Kara hugged him saying "Aye, I will."

Ciana got out and ran around and hugged him too.

"Thank you," she whispered.

Andrew bowed proper and kissed her hand.

"Aye Lady Bird...yeh be welcome."

The ladies and even Bird waved as they took off. Andrew hid a tear as he started back for Edinburgh.


Bird arranged for 4 fares. With Kara now, he paid the ferry captain for her as well. He chuckled as he heard the captain and first mate talk amongst themselves.

"Oi, ENNY man would be lucky enuf to have just one and he's got 3! And here he comes back with 4!"

"Aye captain... having coin must be a wunnerful thing indeed."

The captain chuckled saying "Aye, AN good looks... AN school'in... AN..."

"Yeah yeah," the first mate said with annoyance as he shoved off.

Bird just smiled, and turned down his hearing.


Bird grabbed the last of the bags off the coach as Angus came out to greet them with a friendly hug. He tried hard not to look a Ciana all dressed up fine and fancy. He didn't want to disrespect Bird but Bird caught it.

"Lighten up Angus... if I were you I'd be staring too!" Bird told him with a friendly hug. "Speaking of, I brought home something else for you to stare at," Bird whispered to him. "We need to talk Angus and... privately."

Angus saw a lovely lass come down from the coach. He had a look on his face Bird had seen once before. It was the 'Oh hellloooo' look that Lone had once back on Eden.

"Good thing I'm not linked to you too Angus," Bird chuckled.

"Huh?... Sorry Bird, yeh say something?"

With a laugh, Bird just said "Nope."


Bird took the glass lady by the arm and said "Angus? I'd like to introduce you to Kara. You might say she captured my interest while we were in Edinburgh."

"G'day to yeh Mistuh Angus... pleased to meet yeh," Kara said shyly.

Angus tried to mind his manners.

"A pleasure miss but... I be a work'in man. Just Angus will do fine."

"Aye... Angus it is then. I be one too, well, a working lady thah is... Kara will do fine."

"Um, Kara?" Bird said slightly grimacing. "That's trade lady... not a working one."

"Are yeh sure Mistuh Bird?" Kara said not wanting to make a mistake, or a fool of herself.

"Yeeeeaaahh... I'm sure. Remember those wares you um, 'warned' me about?"

Kara shrank some and said "Aye," ever so sheepishly.

"A 'working woman' is the term used for one who sells 'those wares'. Just thought I'd let ya know."

Politely, Kara half curtsied to Bird and thanked him for the polite, and incognito, correction.

"Here... let me help yeh lass!" Angus stated as he bent to help her.

"Thank yeh kindly Angus," Kara said with a smile.

"Angus... let's go inside. We'll tell you all about the trip in a bit but... we got business to discuss first."

Angus heard him but... focused on Kara.

"Shall we go inside then?" he said waving a hand.

Bird chuckled and walked in last saying "Well... that was easy!"

Angus, Kara, Bird and Ciana were in the kitchen and Ally kept Scota busy unpacking.

"Angus... ya trust me?"

"Aye."

"Then if my plan is going to work... you need to be honest. Tell Kara here... about your arms."

Angus was a bit sad but, he did trust Bird.

"I have somethin' wrong with mah hands and forearms. Bird here knows the term but I can barely pronounce it. In a few words, they be sensitive to heat and cold. What be normal to you would be scalding or freezing to me."

"ANGUS!" Ciana barked loud, "Why didn't you tell me!?"

Angus actually looked at Bird.

"Yeh didn't tell her?"

"Nope. I told you I'd keep your secret. Scota hasn't said anything either. This is different though Angus and you'll see why in a moment."

Bird looked at Kara now with a commanding attitude that made her melt a little.

"I told you Kara, you get the truth... and you give it. Your turn. Go ahead... tell him."

Slightly scared, and a whole lot of insecure, Kara said "I have fits sometimes. Mistuh Bird here says mah brain turns off sometimes and that's what causes them. I had one back in the city and he came to mah aid."

"Aaaaaannnd?" Bird said.

"I... I have no home and no family. I'm an orphan I am an was liv'in on theh streets when the kind sir found me."

Angus still didn't get what Bird was doing. Hearing of Angus's Achilles heel, Ciana now figured it out.

"OOOoooooh yeh be a sly one Mistuh Yankee Man!" Ciana said admonishing him playfully.

"Mind tell'in me what this be all about Bird?"

"Simple. Kara here is a glass maker. Some very nice wares too... grrr... before they got smashed," Bird said growling at the memory. "Anyway, no insult intended Angus but, you're broken. Kara here just told you she is also. Far worse than you are too. These fits of hers are brought on by extreme stress. Essentially, if she lives a calm life, she can reduce or eliminate them. I'll be honest Angus, even that is no guarantee but, it will help greatly. Angus I've been to your place. While I wouldn't call it a pig stye, it could definitely do with a 'woman's touch'. Kara here gets your forge to do her glass, and she can help you with the heat too as it doesn't bother her. You provide a proper place for her to live and work her craft. As you can see, living on the streets hasn't helped her eat a regular meal. Kara has said she'd cook for you, and you see to it that she has enough... for BOTH of you."

Angus was stunned. He went from caring a great deal, to

wanting to protect the lovely lass. She didn't have Ciana's beauty but, she certainly wasn't ugly.

"Basically Angus, she knows your secret, and now you know hers. She will help you and in turn... you her."

"Aye, tis more than fair." Angus looked with caring eyes at Kara and asked "On the streets yeh say?"

"Sadly... tis true."

Angus spoke directly to her now and boasted for all in the room to know and hear.

"Kara, aye tis true what Bird here says... my place could do with a woman's touch. Ciana here has known me since I was a wee lad. She can tell yeh I may not be a learned man like Bird here but I am a good one. Honorable in mah own way too. If you agree to this I'll give yeh yer own room of course... right and proper I'll be. I have to work my forge most the day but, I can arrange time for yeh as well."

"And I'll be check'in on that honor Angus," Ciana said in a warning type tone. "Aye, I knoe yeh be a good man. I'll jes be check'in in on yeh to make sure yeh stay that way."

"Aye Ciana... would be only proper."

Kara was happy and said "I left on my own when the man of the house be a brute. Mistuh an Lady Bird here has my trust and if they say yeh be a good man, I'll take there word on it. I'll not be a bother to yeh... and I'll expect the same in return. Tis all I ask."

"Aye lass and a fair request."

Ciana kicked in saying "She'll be stay'in here for the next few days. We'll bring her by tomorrow to see yer place iffin thah be alright by you."

"Aye, that will be fine."

Angus turned to Bird and asked "These fits of hers, what can yeh tell me? I only ask cuz iffin she has one, Iel need to know what to expect."

"Hard to say Angus. Some will look like she just took a short nap. Others however, could be severe. Do you fish Angus?"

"Aye, sometimes."

"Ya know how a fish flaps about when ya yank it from the

*water?"*

*"Aye... yeh mean like thah?"*

*"Could be. Only time will tell. Now that she knows what happens, and what brings them on... it'll take some time but you'll adjust and know what to do when she does have one. I'll teach you what I can but... only experience can teach you the rest."*

*Angus walked up to Kara and took her hand and spoke with caring eyes.*

*"Iffin yeh can accept a broken smithy, I can accept you. Like Bird here says... only time will tell. You have my word I'll keep your secret if you'll keep mine. Iffin yeh have a fit out in public, I'll keep private all that I can. I'll provide yeh a home, and make it as proper as I can. As long as I eat... so shall you AND... you'll know that the same roof yeh woke up under, will be the same one yeh'll rest yer head under as well."*

*"Yer a kind man Angus. I'll not be a bother as I said. I may not be the best cook but, I'll see to it yeh don't go hungry."*

*Kara was holding back happy tears. Angus was the good man Bird promised he'd be. He kinda smelled but, she could change that she thought. He knew she had an illness, and still accepted her. He stared at her like some of them men in the city did, but his eyes were different. His were caring and loving... not lustful. Suddenly, those eyes were looking down on her. Kara knew in an instant what happened and wanted nothing more than to crawl under a rock. Angus cradled her then, helped her up.*

*"Iffin that be all, I think ole Angus here can handle it," He said with a calm and caring tone.*

*"Remember Angus... they CAN get severe... like the fish. I'll teach you what to do but, do we have a deal?"*

*"Aye... deal."*

*"Kara? What say you?"*

*Sweetly, she said "Aye, tis a fine deal indeed."*

*She said it though, looking at Angus.*

*"One last thing. Kara has concerns there's not enough desire for her wares out here in the country. I agree with her. You Angus, your business is seasonal. Busy in spring and summer, not so much*

in fall and winter. Kara insists she do her fair share. So, I did a little bargaining on both of your behalves."

"Ere now my love, what sneaky little plan yeh got go'in now eh?" Ciana playfully chided him.

"Moi? Why m'lady I doth protest!" Bird teased.

"Heh heh... now yeh sound like the dressmaker," Ciana said with a smirk.

"Yeah yeah. Anyway, listen you two. The hotel we stayed at was one of several. All of them fight over the same customers. I suggested a shop in his hotel lobby might make people stay with him over the others, or at least stop in. A gift shop of sorts. Kara makes her glass. You Angus, can make some smaller pieces. I have some ideas on that for both of you. You get enough supply and sell them to him. He then sells them to his guests. You'll have customers you didn't have before and some extra coin to help you through the lean seasons. When you're ready, I'll show you how to ship them and I know of a driver I can trust to see that they get delivered. Consider it a little gift from me to both of you to help get Kara started."

Angus shook Bird's hand briskly, and with loud delight.

"Crafty one yeh are! C'MON Mistuh Yankee, this time, I'm buying YOU a drink! HAHAHA!"

Kara just hugged Bird.

"Thank yeh sir. Many blessings to yeh fer yer kind heart."

Bird hugged her back and... just like that... the last plan from Ciana's birthday trip was done.


At the bar Angus spoke from the heart.

"Bird I want to tell yeh something. Yeh be right. When I was hid'in mah arms, and mah wares were not trusted... I turned to the drink. Aye, I still drink but, I find mehself want'in it now... not need'in it like I used to. I also don't drink nearly as much as I used to. Yeh be a good man an... well... I thought yeh should know."

"Angus, I'm happy for you... truly. I also see how you look at Kara."

"NOTHIN' but proper I was!" Angus shouted getting a touch paranoid.

"Whoa, easy there smithy. All I'm saying is, treat her right. I mean it Angus. Do that, and something tells me... she'll be looking at you the same way one day."

Angus clinked Bird's glass and exclaimed "Aye... now THAT I'll drink to!"

For 2 days the inn was abuzz. Everyone wanted to hear of the trip. Ciana actually took center stage telling everyone all there was to tell. Her confidence in herself was not unnoticed by Bird. The necklace got enormous attention. So did Bird, when Ciana told them what Bird said when he gave it to her. When she told them how he did it in front of Scota and Ally and... out in the open?... In public!?... Why that was just short of scandalous.

She took the ladies upstairs to her room, and showed them all the dress Bird ordered for her. Lots of oohs and aahs but Ciana noticed something. They all seemed distant. Many of the ladies had never been out of the county, no less to the 'big city'. Ciana's life now was reading like an adventure novel. Except of course, Ciana told it as many of them didn't read. Ciana was moving away in their minds. Ciana didn't think so, but they sure did. And now, this new girl!? They were all living vicariously through Bird and Ciana but, starting to treat Ciana like a real 'Lady Bird'.

It took 3 days but, Kara was now staying with Angus. Ciana, ever the mothering type, had some issues 'letting go', but that eventually subsided. Kara was nervous but hopeful for the first time in a long time. Angus was eating better and Kara was just happy to be eating. Angus had some issues with her slightly gaunt appearance, but knew that would change in time. By the end of the week, Angus's house was a whole lot tidier. She also noticed Angus was keeping his word. She had her own room and Angus didn't bother her... not once.

"Kara! What is this!?" Angus called out one morning.

His curiosity was over the cross... a glass cross. It had beautifully scalloped edges like lace. It was black with silver... real silver... at the edges and criss-crossed in an X fashion where the vertical met the horizontal. She used some of her money to get the silver.

"Doen yeh like it?" Kara asked sheepishly.

*"Like it!? It's beautiful! You did this?"*

*"Aye. I made it jes like the one Mistuh Bird wears around his neck."*

*Angus admired it saying "Lass, this is amazing. Yeh are truly talented yeh are."*

*"Thank yeh Angus. I knoe yeh be a good Christian man. Now, so does anyone else. I noticed yeh didn't have one so I made thah when yeh were asleep. I'm glad yeh like it."*

*Kara was beaming on the inside at the way Angus reacted.*

*"There be one problem though," Angus said looking at it.*

*He took it down.*

*"But... but I thought yeh said yeh liked it?" Kara asked sadly and... not understanding.*

*"Like it yes... where yeh hung it tho... no."*

*Angus took it and put it smack in the middle of the wall in his main room.*

*"There! Much better! Now, any who come here will know right off what kind of house this be..." then in a caring tone, he finished saying "... and how talented yeh are. Thank yeh Kara. As the man of the house I say, thah's where it belongs! And thah's where it'll stay!"*

*Angus was both proud and grateful. Kara was just amazed.*

*"Kara?" Angus asked kindly.*

*"Aye Angus?"*

*"I can see it in yer eyes. The doubts, the fears and the worries. I s'pose iffin I lived the life yeh did, well, I be pretty sure I'd have a few mehself. I jes want yeh to knoe, well, I be proud o'yeh. It's truly beautiful, and I thank yeh for it."*

*"Well then... yer welcome. I'm glad yeh like it. Now sit yerself down and I'll make yeh some breakfast."*

*"No lass..." Angus kindly corrected her, "...make US some."*

*With a smile Kara nodded and hurried into the kitchen. She hurried because she didn't want Angus to see the happy tears. Kara felt like perhaps, now, she truly had a home. Angus however, was certain of it. So, for now anyway, Kara had something she'd always wanted. She finally had a home to call her own. Kara didn't know it now but... she would leave. What she also didn't know now was that, when she did, Angus would be at her side.*

*One home now secure... twas time to build another.*


*Ciana was cooking and cleaning. Her kitchen had always been fine in the past. Now, with 'Mistuh Yankee Man' around, she was starting to look for something Bird said was missing. She had no idea what a dining room was, but the description was accurate enough. Having been to the hotel, and seeing one, she now knew what Bird was talking about. She also did something she never did before... she wanted something for herself.*

*A sailing ship pulled into the bay last night and she had guests now for a few days. She was on her own, something she never would have done in the past. She however had something now she never had before... a lot more confidence. She wore long sleeves today and, for a reason. Angus had made her the daggers Bird requested. Bird himself made holders for them out of leather and they were in sheaths under her sleeves. Any of the sailors got out of hand and, welllllllll, she was thinking they'd have one hell of a surprise coming.*

*Bird wanted to leave her be as well. All the training he gave her did no good if she didn't believe in herself. So today, for a few hours anyway, he left her and took Scota out and about. They were down on the beach at the bottom of the cliff. Ciana's father had carved a path into the hillside for access. Bird now looked around for something specific when, God himself couldn't have provided a more perfect spot.*

*"Scota? What's that big dent up there?" Bird said pointing to a spot just below the cliff.*

*"That's the sailors doing. They don't have much need to fire their cannons. Because of that, they don't get much practice. They say the cannons need to be fired every so often or they'll likely jam when they do need them. Ciana lets them fire at the cliff to test them, or make sure they shoot straight. She made it VERY clear they need to tell her first but, they use that mark to fire on."*

*"Scota! VERY good. Your speech is greatly improving," Bird told her honestly.*

"Thank yeh kindly sir," Scota said with a giggle and a curtsey. "I saw all those ladies in the city. Kara talks like I do but, I saw what you meant by how everyone looked at her. You could just see on their faces they already judged her. I like Kara and I know she not be like that. The local folk are staring at me now for it but, I don't care."

"Ciana said something similar the other night. She noticed the locals are treating you two more like classy ladies, rather than home grown born and raised."

"Aye, I've seen that myself. I don't care, I like feeling like a lady... you know, a proper one. I've not put on airs but it don't seem to matter to them. I know it bothers my sister though."

"A lot. She feels like they've abandoned her just because she sought a little happiness. Trust me Scota, I'll be the first one to jump on her back if I thought she was fussing again. This time I have to say, I'm on her side. As far as I'm concerned, she's getting a raw deal. I know communities like yours Scota... they don't like change much."

"Try, 'at all'," Scota corrected him.

"Indeed. I know I'm the cause of that. If they wanna give me shit for it I'm fine, I can handle it. No one would dare say a thing to me, so it seems they're taking it out on Ciana. I know what we did was monumental to the folks around here, so I'm willing to give it some time to die down."

"And if it doesn't?"

"Then the folks around here are gonna find out just how 'unhappy' I can get."

Bird turned his attention back to the hole in the cliff. He'd been looking for a place to get away to, and it was just at the perfect height to get into Ally's bay. If he could make it a little bigger, like a small cave, then either carve a path like the one to the beach, or setup some stairs... it would be perfect.

Scota now took Bird to where he really wanted to go.

"Good afternoon, would you be William?" Bird asked walking up to the big burly man.

"Aye, I am. Seeing as who be with yeh, I imagine yeh be the stranger I heard about." He tipped his hat to her saying "Good to see yeh well Scota."

"Aye, thank you William. Same to you," Scota said showing Bird she knew her manners.

"Well, something I can do for yeh stranger?"

Bird stuck his hand out and said "BirdOfPrey, not stranger. Most just call me Bird."

William shook it back saying "I'll assume yeh not be here just to meet theh neighbors?"

"A little of both actually. I suppose if you know of me, then you know I plan to marry Scota's sister one day?"

"Aye... and in a rather bold fashion as I heard it told."

"Seems to be my way. Ciana told me you banned her. She also told me why. What YOU don't know... is what I can do. You don't want Ciana taking your water. Can I ask you this then, would you mind if I just have a look? If nothing else I can see what so captured her heart."

"Guess there be no harm in look'in. Mind yeh, doen be gett'in no ideas... or I'll tell yeh same as I toel her sistuh."

"Oh trust me, I intend to come up with tons of ideas. It's what I do. That said, I'll bring them to you first. Something tells me, THIS time... you'll like what you hear. Thanks William, we'll not trouble you further," and Bird headed off with Scota.

Bird walked a ways and came up at the bottom of a large cascading waterfall. Large as in tall, but not very wide. It was just wide enough to make a creek at the bottom and Bird now saw why William was so concerned. In this day and age, Ciana tapping the water would be a problem for William farther downstream. Fortunately for William and Ciana, Bird wasn't from this day and age.

Bird brought up his HUD and did some topological scans. Geographical ones were next. Bird didn't want a house at the bottom. Halfway up the right side though, was a granite shelf. If Bird could clear the land above it, he would have what he wanted.

"Thank you William for letting me look. I have plans I'd like to discuss with you. I think when you hear what I have to say you'll find Ciana and I get what we want, and you get what you want. As a gentleman... you have my word on that. I'd like to get back now and draw up some plans. There's been some bad blood between you and Ciana, and I'd like to put it to rest. As such, would you consent to coming to the inn for dinner? My treat of course."

William laughed hard saying "Oh I doen think your guide's sistuh be want'in to see the likes o'me around!"

"Perhaps but... she didn't invite you now did she?" Bird didn't wait for a response, grabbed Scota and headed out saying "Shall we say... around 6?"

William was just dumbfounded, and planned on a free meal.


"Oi! When yeh said yeh invited someone for dinner, yeh didn't say it was him!" Ciana said when William arrived.

"Damn your accent gets so thick and cute when your angry," Bird teased and cooed. "Look, you two came to an impasse. Aside from that one subject, is William himself a bad person? In general I mean?"

"I ever tell yeh how maddening yeh are?" Ciana said referring to his logic.

"Hmm... nope... don't think you have," Bird said with a wink.


"Welcome William, it's been a while hasn't it?" Ciana said politely.

William expected a piss poor welcome, and was happy Ciana was being nice. Seeing as how she was, he decided he would be as well.

"Aye lass it has. Still a stunning beauty yeh are I see."

"Thank yeh kindly William, it would appear the years have been kind to yeh as well."

Ciana brought out a nice meal and she sat down with William and Bird.

"Alright you two, I know your not exactly friends. So... to stop from having to repair this place after you two are through going at each others throats... here's the part where I talk... and you listen," Bird stated in no uncertain terms. "Ciana, when you said it was a waterfall, you didn't tell me how thin it was. It's more like a giant spill rather than a waterfall. Now, that's a point for you William."

"See? I toel yeh," William said in a confident, but not snotty tone.

"Now, that said, aside from your fears of having no water at all, do you have anything against Ciana's wishes?" Bird said in a tone that was akin to 'watch it you two'.

"Ciana here will tell yeh, as I said it many times. If it had been bigger, Ied have had no issue with her. Most days lately, I do without as there's barely enough for mah fields. Iem a farmer I am, so was mah father and his before him. I may not be a learned man like yehself, but I know what I need."

"What I need, is that waterfall," Bird said in a tone that HE was controlling this conversation. "Now, that said, I agree with you so... care to hear my plan?"

"I s'pose it doen hurt to listen," William said slightly irritated at Bird's attitude.

"Good. Now you said it yourself, if it was bigger, you two wouldn't be at loggerheads. What if I told you, I can make it bigger?"

"Ied say Ied ask yeh to prove it."

"Scota my dear?" Bird called over, "Would you mind taking the good Mister William here upstairs... and show him just what I'm capable of?"

With a sly smile, Scota said "Aye, certainly."

William looked at Ciana but she just grinned and nodded as if to say 'go ahead'. He followed his blond guide, and came back down about 10 minutes later.

"Well then Mistuh stranger... Iem listen'in."

"Thought you might be. I found a rock ledge on the right side of the falls. There's too much dirt and such on top of it to dig out. If I dig out the top of the falls, and make it deeper, the spillover will be far greater."

"Thah be solid rock up there stranger!" William barked.

"You let me worry about that. I need to divert the water to get to it. IF I do it just right, it'll flow over the area I want, and wash away a good bit of it. Your water will stop for only an hour or two till it finds its path again. It'll be fairly muddy for about another hour then it should flow clear again. I'll get my work done, then let it flow just the way it already does. Except when I'm done, it'll be twice as wide. I insist on enough for our needs and enough to farm a large garden, but not fields worth, like you do."

William thought this man was crazy. Having seen the room upstairs however, he was willing to give him a shot.

"Ciana here be a good woman I kahnt deny thah. I doen like, as yeh said, hav'in bad blood with my neighbors and as yeh said, twas only this matter that put us at odds. IF you can prove to me FIRST what yeh jes said, then I'll work out a fair deal fer yeh. I can do without it for 3 hours but no longer. Put it back as yeh said, then Iel check on it. Iffin it be like yeh say... then aye... I'll make yeh a deal for the land."

"Like you said William, I'm a learned man. I have no desire to harm or cheat you, I only want what I want. That said, I'll see to it that legal papers are drawn up proper to give both us and you water rights. That way there will be no fighting."

"Ciana? Seems the talk I hear about the crofts be right. Yeh do have a fine man on yer hands."

The inn lady was near speechless. She had tried for that land for years but got nowhere, and here Bird sorted it in a day.

"Aye William, I doen like having bad blood with my neighbors either. Here's to a fresh start?" Ciana asked as she raised her glass.

William smiled and clinked her glass as all 3 dug into a friendly meal.

Bird was up on the ridge the next day. He had old growth oaks and pines in his way but, he found he could indeed channel the water to where he wanted it.

"William, my day starts much later, and ends much later, than yours. I'll block your water like I said but I'll do most of my work at night so as to disturb you even less. Will that be alright?"

"Aye, thah will do fine. I warn yeh though Mistuh Yankee, it had better be flow'in by morn'in light."

"Oh it will. Also, I may have to leave it diverted for awhile so the land gets soaked enough to cause a landslide. As long as the water flows... do you care?"

"Not in the least. Truth be toel, I rarely go up there and none of my animals graze in theh area. As long as the water flows, I doen care what yeh be do'in up there."

"Fair enough, thanks William. I'll be back after supper." Bird walked off and once out of earshot Bird said "I want you over my head... and I want you to keep a scan on a 1 mile perimeter. I don't want any prying eyes."

"Gotcha boss," was the only response.

In the darkness... a man walked to the shore.

"Suit... on!"

It was the first time Bird put back on the suit since he finally managed to get Alydar patched.

"Aaaah... hello old friend," Bird said as he looked himself over.

He went to work moving the few boulders he could find. Without the suit, it would take Bird a whole day and a team of horses to move just one. He spent several hours, but either moved rocks on hand, or blasted new ones from the hillside. In the end, he had made an angled wall and diverted the water right where he wanted it. Only a couple of trees got in his way so, with the silencer in place... Bird just took some target practice with a cannon and let gravity do the rest.

"How in blazes did yeh move all this? And by yerself!!?" Angus remarked when he saw the wall 2 days later.

"Let's just say I used tools I'm not supposed to let you know I have... and leave it at that hmm?"

"Aye, sumthin tells me the less I knoe theh better."

"Heh heh... and you'd be right. Did ya bring those rods and hammers I asked for?"

"Aye. So, what plan yeh got fer this eh?"

Before Bird could answer, a voice called out saying "Oi! No sciencey stuff without good ole Scota around!"

Coming through the woods was Scota and Kara.

"And just what are you ladies doing here?"

"Well Mistuh Yankee man," Scota giggled, "In case ya hadn't noticed the time... it be lunch!"

Angus called over sweetly "And what brings you here?" as he

looked at Kara.

"I was do'in my glass when I noticed I had a small seizure. I figgerd it be best not to work the forge for a bit, so I came to see yeh."

"Nice to see you using the correct term," Bird said with a smile.

Angus smiled saying "It's just nice to see yeh."

Bird and Angus stopped and had lunch with the ladies on the shore. Scota wore a scarf to keep the water at bay. Bird bought it for her so she could be safe, and still somewhat fashionable. Seeing how well it worked, she doesn't go anywhere now without it.

Lunch over, Scota was anxious to 'get to school'.

"Alright, what are yeh do'in?"

"Well blondie... I managed to get the gunpowder I needed from the captain, but it's not enough. So, I have to make 2 pounds act like 20. We make holes in the rock... then I'll show you."

So Angus and Bird did. The girls watched with huge smiles as 'their men' pounded 3 foot deep holes all over. Bird had found a pocket of magnesium, mined it, and had it ready. He took some of his leftover linen from the room he built, cut it in strips, and made flares.

"Ow! That hurts my eyes it does it's so bright!" Scota complained when Bird lit one.

"This one flare is as hot as Angus's forge too. I'm going to bake the rock."

"You bake food silly man... not rock!" Scota giggled thinking she was being teased.

Bird stuck the flare in the rock flame side down. When he saw it almost out, Angus poured a bucket of water on it. A lot of cracking could be heard and Bird just smiled.

"Well, heh heh, only 10 more to go!" Bird announced.

Bird told Angus the cracking was the rock. Super hot to super cold causes it to fracture... a lot. Fracture enough and the 2 pounds of gunpowder would do far more damage against broken rock than it would if it were solid. Scota was thrilled she learned something new. Kara thought it was cool too and Angus was impressed.

By next afternoon all the holes were made, heated, and

cracked. Bird and Angus did one last hole in the middle and Bird used almost all of the powder. He made a stick similar to dynamite with the last of the linen and stuffed it in the hole. With everyone safely upstream, Bird took Angus's horse and high tailed it out of there. Everyone but Bird jumped when the blast went off. Even as far away as they were, you could hear sand sized debris falling through the trees. Upon inspection Bird found a hole 20 feet long by ten wide and 6 deep. Another hour by hand breaking out the loose rock and it went to 8 foot deep. Angus was blown away, Scota was thrilled she learned something new and, so was Kara. Bird went back that night and removed the barrier but only half of it. He put back some of the rock but on a reverse angle. Now the water would funnel into the new pool with more force... keeping it full.

William was looking up and couldn't believe it. His waterfall he was so concerned about was now just shy of triple in width. It had a 20 foot shear drop at the top and then rolling cascades to the bottom. Right alongside the cascade was a newly exposed granite ledge, just as Bird said. The ground was soaked from 3 days of flooding but to Bird's dismay, it still held. A few low level blasts from his battle suit to shake the ground... and his desired landslide was achieved. A huge amount was still needed to be removed, so Bird dug a small trench to funnel more water and complete the job. In a week Bird figured... he'd have enough clear rock ledge to start building. It was now early August and Bird knew the clock was ticking.

"Well William, what do you think of your creek now?" Bird asked standing at the bottom with Will and Ciana.
"Amazing, simply amazing."
Ciana was lost in a memory and said "It's even more beautiful than I remember."
Will shook Bird's hand briskly saying "Well Mistuh Yankee, Iem a man o'mah word." He then turned to Ciana with a smile and said "What do yeh say we go back to my house, and work out a deal for yours eh?"
"First things first William," Ciana said, then planted a huge kiss on Bird. "Thank you my love," Ciana said. Straightening out

*her dress, she said "Now William... feel free to lead the way."*

# Chapter 19:

## "Bring On The Tech!"

*Lone slept in his own bed last night for the first time in 4 days. With Renny 'out of town', and Remmy's setup working so well, he gave Jonathan the extra day he asked for. Lone was never paranoid in his life. Now, about to become a father, he was becoming a pro at it... at least where his child was concerned.*

*"President Valleron, nice to see you again," Val said greeting the alien dignitary.*

*"Still lovely I see Ambassador." Playfully he added "Tell me, has that Ghost left you yet so I can steal you away for myself?"*

*In a southern belle accent, Val told him "Why I do declare, y'all be such a flirt!" Both laughed and Val told him "Come Mr. President, I'll take you to Commander Lone."*

*"I won't lie. It will be nice to hear that again," said the big grey haired alien.*

*"I have work to get back to. It was nice to see you again Mr. President," Val said as she dropped him off in the landing cave.*

*Valleron picked up an Earth custom, and kissed Val's hand.*

*"Always a pleasure," Valleron told her as she left.*

*"Greetings Valleron. So, ready to see the proof I promised you?"*

*"Indeed. So, where is this non liquid power you spoke of?"*

*Lone smiled, and just pointed up.*

*"Impressive!" Valleron hollered as he held onto his safety line.*

*Lone was beside him hanging onto his.*

*"Bird rigged this. It works on a magnetic principle. ALL of*

*Victory City is powered by this."*

*Valleron and Lone made their way back down to the cave.*

*"C&C... this is Commander Lone. The President and I are clear. Turn the defenses back on please."*

*"Right away Commander."*

*Lone could see they were, and took Valleron down the tunnel.*

*"All along here, the main cables go to the power station. It then sends it out to the rest of the city. You can transfer the power without loss for hundreds of miles."*

*Valleron, to say the least, was blown away.*

*"Commander Lone, on the way here, I was thinking. If I disclose this to my people, the north will know. If they know, then they will want it too. If I hide it, my people will ask questions. Eventually, northern spies will discover it. I feel once they do, and we refuse, it will start the war all over again. Suggestions?"*

*"I say once they find out... give it to them... heh heh, for a price of course."*

*"I suppose. While I agree with you in that it's the right thing to do, implementing it will be delicate to say the least."*

*"No plan is perfect but, by time the north discovers what you're doing, you'll have had enough time to keep a peace that neither side will want to break, and rebuild your people in the process. If it does start again, at least you'll be better prepared. I think if you start with your most southern regions, and work north... that should buy you the time I spoke of. Add to that, any mistakes you find will be easier to correct in a rural area rather than a large city."*

*"Very wise. We don't have many areas with sufficient wind but I see your point. Wind, water, as long as the equipment spins."*

*"You can also bury your generators beneath your river beds and bury your transmission lines as well. If war breaks out again, they'll be harder to find and better protected."*

*Valleron got friendly now.*

*"Commander, can I speak honestly?"*

*"Feel free."*

*"Bird told me of the time you brought him in when he was*

injured. He told me how you took over in his place. He also told me how you did a very good job of it. He called it 'the big chair'. An accurate if not odd analogy. For what it's worth Lone... I think you're sitting in that chair just nicely. Bird has truly taught you well."

Lone tipped his hat and thanked him for the praise.

"While I thank you for your kind words, I'll say this. While I may sit in the chair nicely, as far as I'm concerned... it's not my chair. I'll assume we understand each other?"

"Indeed we do."

Lone and Valleron headed off to work out some details. History would tell how this day, and these two men, changed Vrissin forever. It would take Valleron and his people some years but, peace would come. The northern supremacy would also wane, and they'd never again be the bullies they are today.

Lone was holding court in the meeting room now. Shiiran and Lor were hovering in hologram form over the center of the table.

"Commanders," Lor began, "Our ore ships are running at peak capacity. Zagrin's 'waste' is burning as predicted. Your Jammers provide us with enough raw materials. The Vrissin have caught on quickly and adapted even quicker. We should have the first shipment ready in a day."

Lor had taken control of the one around Galenthia. Shiiran took command of the one around her planet. Her report was next.

"Commanders, all goes as planned here also. These ships required more maintenance, but those have been completed. We appear to be only 1 day behind my counterpart. I must say, getting 'into the field' is something I'm finding rather enjoyable," Shiiran reported.

Lone told them "My fellow Tuhleesians await your shipments and are ready to start building as soon as you can give them something to build. How is security?"

"Juvehnar has provided 3 heavy battleships to each of us," Lor told him, "Though I suspect there are more we're not aware of."

"I agree," Shiiran said. "I don't mind telling you, I feel quite safe with them around. Two of what you call Aardvarks showed up the other day and seemed to check us out. They went on their way and my planetary defenses destroyed them."

"We had one do the same over here Commanders. Juvehnar's forces did the same as Lady Shiiran's," Lor said.

"Very good news you two. You are doing an excellent job. Know that the Ghosts appreciate all your assistance. We picked up some activity on what we believe to be Tamarak's planet. Nothing concrete yet but it does appear he's building up his forces. We'll let you know anything we find out. 51... out."

With that, 2 holograms dissipated.


Salyan was tired... and dragging. He was working with Remington today trying to get an answer to the invisible Aardvarks. Seems his plan to 'become a Wing' and grow up... worked. Little blue essentially saw to that. She was working still on the remnants of the ice field but that was quickly running out. Living with Sal, and seeing the other couples around, she decided she wanted to be just like them. Problem at first was, she had no clue how. So... she went to the one 'person' she thought could answer her questions.

"Shreya, are you busy?"

"Not at the moment little blue. How are you?"

"Confused," blue said with some consternation.


Shreya gave the best information she could. She also said honestly that, being she wasn't 'alive' for very long, that blue would get her questions better answered by the other Ghosts. So, finding that wise, little blue basically went up the line. Each one had some information or insight the previous did not.

Raven however, wasn't much help at all. As the warrior queen, her responses were pretty much forward and direct. All the Ghosts said the same thing though, and that was the one Ghost she really needed was the one Ghost that wasn't available.

So little blue decided she didn't get an answer... she got a lot of them. She also figured with no one clear path, she would take the pieces and put them all together in the best fashion she could. Now, Salyan was dealing with a girl who was a 1950's housewife, on steroids, with a direct and voracious sexual appetite.

*It was the latter that had Salyan so tired of late. Now, working with Remmy, Sal was doing to him what little blue did to the Ghosts.*

*"Ya know Sal, while I understand why you came to me, you should really talk to your father about this."*

*"I can't... at least not yet. He's so busy, and now with mom pregnant again, he really doesn't have the time right now. I plan to but, no harm in getting multiple opinions right?"*

*"Speaking of opinions, I'd like yours. How are you?" Remmy asked.*

*"Tired," Sal chuckled.*

*Remmy smiled and said "No Sal, I mean... how are 'you'."*

*"Clarify."*

*"Well, you were half of the cause we went after Aarika. You were thought of, and treated as, salvation, your entire life. Your parents aren't Roe and Zarra... we all are in our own way. We watched you AND your parents. We watched the Ghosts, and their responses. When you were born, and turned over to your parents and not taken away, well, we all grew up a little that day. Though not our child directly, we all felt like, and treated you, like our own. True that Deeno and I came along after your birth but, seeing and hearing of you well, we joined right in with all the others.*

*Now, your a Wing. Being a man physically, and, being one mentally, are two different things. All these things added up, I thought I'd just ask how 'you' were?"*

*"Ya know, I never really stopped to think about it."*

*"Perhaps you should. Susan and I, being polite, are intimate with each other. I was very immature when I met her. That intimacy happened but, not right away. I discovered how immature I was. Sue helped me with some... some only I could fix. Point I'm making is, I did an honest evaluation of myself, and fixed what was wrong or what I didn't like. Perhaps it's time either you did, or need to do it again."*

*"You know, I have to say, I always wanted to make my parents proud. I also noticed how all of VC treated me, and I guess I wanted to make them proud too in a way. That's why I always sought out the 'bigger things' in life. It felt like I didn't have 2 parents to please or impress... I had thousands. Now, I know I'm full grown. That said, I know I have some experiences, but not as much as others. I also*

noticed how I thought I was grown up... but really wasn't. I also noticed that having one, but lacking the other, can be a dangerous thing. When I came back from Aarika, I knew what I had to watch out for. Bad as it was, I don't think I'd trade that experience for anything because it's given me the balance I need and still use today."

Remmy looked at the wise young man and smiled. He was proud of Sal. He was a fine young man who was more than capable of just about anything he set his mind to.

"Sal?"

"Yeah Remmy?"

"I'm proud of you. I know your parents are. All of us are too. I know if Rhana was here, he'd tell you no different."

"Thanks Remmy."

Sal and Remmy dug into the project at hand, talked of being a man, and many other worldly things.


Bird had gotten the site clear now. The granite ledge he wanted had a sharp uphill on the back of it but... he had his foundation exposed. Now, it was nighttime, and he was back at the inn.

Kara had made the last piece he needed. It was an odd shaped piece. All hollow with a wide round end at the bottom which bellied outward at the middle. It then narrowed at the top and had a thinner but still large round hole. Angus took Bird to the brew-master and he made Bird a small batch of pure alcohol. He ran it through 2 filters and handed it off to Bird. The potter came through with the tank base Bird requested, and Mary made the wick.

"Now, this little wheel I made raises the wick up or down," Bird started explaining.

Bird had all the candles blown out, and the only light in the bar and dining area, was the dim one from the fireplace.

"The alcohol is the fuel. The wick soaks it up but, even you can smell the vapors yes?"

All of them nodded as they watched Bird.

"Now, the wick doesn't burn, only the vapor from the fuel does. Light it here aaaannnnddd..." and Bird lit his odd 'candle'.

"Tada! Look, like a candle does, it stays lit. Now, watch this Angus, *and you'll see why I asked for a glass maker."*

*Bird turned up the wick just a little and the flame really got bright. Then, Bird put the glass covering over it and the whole room was lit up. Ciana and Scota were impressed as hell. Angus was getting used to Bird but still thought it was cool. Kara was proud Bird was happy and that she did well.*

*"Where I come from, they call these a hurricane lamp. You have what, like, 6 or 7 candles in here? The glass bends the light and magnifies it several times. That's why it's wider in the middle."*

*Scota was still looking around in wonder and asked "What's a hurricane?"*

*"A thunderstorm but... with enough wind to push the inn all the way to Angus's place. Add to that, it would reach all the way to London."*

*"Noooooo," Scota said thinking she was being teased.*

*Bird looked at her, seriously, and that's all it took.*

*"Well how come we never had one then?" she asked.*

*"Hurricanes need certain conditions. You have the wrong weather here to form one no less sustain one."*

*Now Ciana wanted to learn.*

*"Honestly Bird and NO teas'in. Just how bad are those winds?"*

*"Truth is... the smallest ones are about 75-80 kilometers an hour. The larger ones are about twice that."*

*"Sweet Lord! I can't even imagine something thah fast!"*

*"That's how we came up with this. No candle or torch would stay lit in something like that. We get storms, bad ones, in the northeast colonies. That's how we came up with this. Someone covered a candle with an upside down goblet during one of them. We knew we were onto something. We played around with the glass shape till we came up with this. We rigged a cover for the top to prevent the rain getting in and now you can go out in one, and not be blind going through the dark. I showed you this because I'm putting up something similar around our house. Next time a wolf... or a bishop shows up... we'll know it."*

*Alydar whispered in Bird's ear saying "You do know that won't be invented for another hundred years right?"*

"I do," Bird whispered back. "If they come with us, I have to get them adjusted to tech. Something like this will do the trick for now and get them started."

"I understand but... watch it BirdMan. That's a slippery slope you're walking on."

Bird sighed and said "Don't I know it."


Bird and Ally let them enjoy the wonder of it, when Bird pulled his next stunt. Bird walked over and poured an entire bucket of water on the fire in the hearth completely putting it out.

"Are ya insane? You know how long that will take to get going again!? We'll catch our death o'cold before it does," Ciana barked.

"No... we won't. Scota? Go get the wax log I had you make. Angus? Help me clear this out and get fresh peat in here."

Bird and Angus reloaded the hearth and Scota got her log.

"My word Yankee man, ye'll never start it like that. All those things yeh can do and ya can't start a simple fire," Ciana said slightly annoyed. "Here, let me show yeh how to... HEY!" Ciana barked as Bird politely pulled her back.


Now, it was next lesson time.

"Alright so... wax and sawdust, formed into a log. Imagine this was a loaf of bread."

Bird pulled out one of his blades and sliced off a pair of inch thick pieces. He put one under each end of the stack of wood and peat in the hearth. Bird took the lamp and headed towards the fireplace.

"Now, take the glass off... use the flame to light each one and... watch."

It took about a minute, and the girls were amazed yet again as the round wax and sawdust pieces burned... but didn't go out. Another minute and they were roaring. Now, at 5 minutes, the fireplace was re-lit. At ten minutes, the wax hockey pucks had finally burned out and the remaining logs were blazing bright now.

"THAH IS BRILLIANT!" Angus bellowed.

"Alright listen up. I put on this little demonstration for a reason," Bird started. "Our new house is going to be like nothing you've ever seen or known. Most of it from my own imagination. You are NOT to tell anyone about this lamp. This is secret army stuff and ONLY for us. Angus, remember how I used new ways to build the room upstairs?"

"Aye."

"The new house is going to be like that. New and better and with features you could only dream of. That said, like tonight, there's going to be lots of new and better things. I need you all to get comfortable with that idea, so tonight was just my way of getting you used to thinking in different ways."

"Kara, did you bring the other pieces I asked for?"

"Aye I did."

Bird had put up a pair of wooden wall sconces. Not that Ciana knew what they were, but he put them up all the same. They looked like shelf brackets but without the shelf. At the top was a round indent 2 inches wide and 2 deep. Bird had made a big candle with 2 wicks in it. Ciana told him when he made it, you don't put 2 wicks in a candle... only one.

"Says who?" was his only reply.

Now Bird put the candle on the sconce and lit both wicks. Kara made a nice, but simple, glass cylinder to go over it. Again, the room lit up bright, though not as bright as the hurricane lamp.

"Now, you'll be nice and bright AND... only need two candles... not 6 or 7. Point I'm making here is... take what you know, and make it work better," Bird said as he finished lighting the second candle and covered it.

"Mercy, it's not even this bright in the daytime in here!" Scota said with happy wonder.

Bird pulled Ciana to the side while the others marveled.

"Remember when I said you dealt in perceptions, and not actual life?"

"Aye."

"Get used to this. This is but a small taste of things to come. Promise me... only real life or real science... and no more perceptions okay?"

"I'll tell yeh the loveliest thing of all tonight."

*"And what would that be?"*

*"The sound of 'your' voice... saying 'our' house. Aye my Yankee man, I promise."*

*Bird gave the hurricane lamp to Angus and told him what kind of top and handle he wanted. He also promised Bird he wouldn't replicate it. Bird said he could make something fancy in iron and make the wall sconces he made. Angus was happy for the upgrade, Kara was happy for the less dim house, and Bird suggested they make them to sell also.*

*"Speaking of, did ya make those trays I asked yeh for?"*

*"Nope," Bird said with a chuckle. "I made ya the whole damn case!"*

*Bird rolled out a wooden trunk. He opened the lid and Angus was impressed. It had 3 trays at the top and the bottom was empty for bigger pieces. Kara had made more crosses, and some smaller angels. Bird showed her how to do those and she thought they were adorable. Angus even made 2 hearth devices but those were to impress the hotel owner.*

*"Kara, do you cook potato's?" Bird asked.*

*"Aye sometimes why?"*

*"You know the white stuff you scoop off the top?"*

*"Aye?" Kara said like she was missing something.*

*"It's called starch. Lay your smaller pieces in the trays, then soak these strips of linen in it. Snake it around your pieces in the tray and that starch will harden it and keep your pieces from banging into each other."*

*"Yeh know Mistuh Bird, I could get used to this 'sciencey stuff'," Kara said with a giggle.*

*Alydar and Bird had finished making replica hand tools in the lander's shop. A few days ago she had arranged for one of the cargo ships to deliver it. It was the one who's captain warned Ciana about Bird. He made regular trips for mail and supplies and cargo and such. He would start in London, circle under England and head to Scotland, cross west to Skye, onto Ireland, then return. He made port stops all along the way, and today, the 'travel kit' Ally told Bird about arrived. It was loaded on a flatbed cart and was so heavy it* took 3 men to lift it into the cart.

 The captain was highly impressed with Ally. He even remarked that he knew men that couldn't do what she did. And looks!? Dear Lord what looks! He never had women aboard, and Ciana and Scota were to be his first exceptions. He considered Ciana a good friend and Scota too. This silver haired stunner though was starting to change his mind about a lot of things.

 "Thank you captain. I appreciate your offer but I've arranged for private transport back to the Commander. I have a few other stops to make on his behalf that are not in your general direction."


 "OH! My heavens just LOOK at who it is!" John squealed in delight as he kissed Alydar's hand.

 "A pleasure to see you too dressmaker," Ally said with a grin.

 "And to what do I owe the pleasure of your fine beauty this day?" John asked in his usual flamboyant style.

 "I have a gift for you. I'm running errands for the Commander, so I won't be staying."

 "A gift? For moi!? Oh doooo tell."

 Ally handed him a box. Said box rattled... a lot... and John was intrigued.

 "Oh the Commander didn't have to get me anything," John said.

 "He didn't, but the glass girl Kara did."

 John opened the box now excited to see what was in it. Inside were over 100 glass buttons of different shapes, sizes, colors and sets. John read the note that was inside, and was truly touched.

 It read... <This is to thank you for your investment. Your kindness will not be forgotten. May these buttons distinguish your talents to others, like I know them to already be. I have found a good life here thanks to you and the others. I hope this note finds you well. I have a good home now and all my hopes and dreams have come to pass... and I hope yours will too. ~ Kara>

 John was deeply moved, and truly happy for the girl he so kindly assisted. Being the dandy that he was, he wasn't treated exactly well either. So he was happy to see someone doing well that he had a hand in helping out.

Ally said "I have to go. Kara said if you need any more, she'll be happy to supply them. She also asks if you would... show that note to the driver Andrew, as some of that note was meant for him too,"

John kissed her hand, and bid her a fond farewell, and promised he would show Andrew the note at some point soon. Ally made her way out of town and back to the '51 express'.

It was 5 days later now. Bird had his order in to the potter and the saw mill. For a house the size of Bird's, both said it would take some time to get it all together. To save time Bird had the latter cut the grooves in the wood so he could make his I-beams faster. Now, with a few days on his hands, Bird headed uptown. He worked on the full sized Alydar, replacing any damage he could, and running checks on all her systems. Alydar went as far out as she could to expand her tracking range, yet still stay in contact with Ciana's necklace. Now Bird was back on planet, and he and Kara were heading off to Glasgow.

The driver of the coach heard a man bark orders at him. Per usual, it was in a snotty upper crust tone.

"Ere now... driver! Get these trunks loaded and make it snappy!"

"Aye, right away.... MISTUH BIRD!" Andrew shouted in delight at the pleasant surprise.

He turned to see Bird standing there with a friendly smile.

"How are you 'Mistuh Driver'?" Bird asked with a laugh.

Andrew teased saying "Being yeh be more the dressmaker's style than mine, I'll have tuh say tis a shame yeh be alone this trip. All teas'in aside though... it's good tuh see yeh."

"Wellll..." and Bird stepped to the side, "I did bring one with me."

Andrew took a moment, then had a pleasant look of shock on his face.

"Kara!?"

"Aye Andrew. It's nice to see you again."

"WELL NOW! Look at you!" Andrew bellowed at the changes

in the once gaunt little girl. *"Looking fit now I see. And proper dressed and even speaking like the Mistuh here! Oh lass, yeh done well fer yehself. See? I told yeh they be good people fer yeh,"* Andrew stated as he gave her a kind hug.

*"I'm glad you got my message and brought the flat carriage this time,"* Bird stated. *"Let's get these loaded and get out of here. We aren't staying that long this time."*

*"Aye Mistuh Bird, right away!"*

Bird and Andrew got the cases loaded and off they went.

*"I not mean'in tuh be rude Kara but, does this smithy know of what Mistuh Bird found out?"* Andrew asked.

Kara, per Andrew's friendly request, was giving the driver all the updates since she left.

*"Aye, twas the first thing I told him. Mistuh Bird insisted on honesty. While I can't say what, he has an illness too. Nothing terrible but, he accepted me as I am, and I him. Mistuh Bird was right, he has his quirks like any man but... he is a good one."*

*"Tis good to hear yeh do'in well lass,"* Andrew said honestly.

*"And what of you?"* Kara asked.

*"Aye, Mistuh Bird here spoke to the hotel owner on my behalf. While he doesn't have much business yet, he does give me what he has. Also, none of the other hotels have a service like good ole Andrew here, and that seems to sit nicely with the guests. So, while I'm not really busy... yet... Iem no longer scroung'in either."*

*"I'm very happy to hear you doing at least better Andrew,"* Kara told him honestly.

*"Aye lass... an all thanks tuh Mistuh Bird here,"* Andrew replied.

*"Yeah well, 'Mister Bird' here isn't exactly fond of the rain. Wadda ya say we pick up the pace Andrew and see if we can keep ahead of this storm?"*

*"You just leave that to good ole Andrew!"* and with that, Andrew picked up the pace.

Bird and crew pulled in to the hotel just 10 minutes before the rain came. It was one of those late summer cold rain storms. In 5 minutes, the lobby was getting quite cold. The owner had one of the staff stoke and stack the fire. Bird however asked him not to.

"If you don't mind Mister owner, allow me," Bird said grinning slyly.

The owner felt odd letting Bird do menial work, but someone like Bird, well, he got what he wanted.

"These are a gift from the smithy I mentioned. He says if your pleased with these, he'll sell you more for all your other rooms."

Bird pulled out the tongs Angus made to go with it, and took out all the logs. They were still on fire when Bird put them into the new grating holders. Once the old one was empty, Bird pulled it out and put in the 2 Angus made sitting them side by side. Within 5 minutes, the chill was gone and... without a single new log. The owner could feel the heat coming at him not 5 minutes after that. Several people ran in to escape the rain, a small group of 5 women and 3 men. All the women were highly impressed at how warm the lobby was.

As a favor to the owner, Bird leaned into one of the women and said, "The rooms aren't bad either."

The lady blushed a tad seeing the handsome stranger smile at her.

With a slight laugh, Bird walked up to the desk saying "Heh heh, nothing wrong with a little advertising, right?"

With a smile, he replied "Aye. I didn't have a room I could set up Mistuh Bird, like yeh suggested. I did have all this empty area here behind the desk however. So I cleaned it up and put up shelves. Yeh think that will do?"

"Not my call. Kara, what do you think?"

"Heh heh, I was about to ask you the same."

"Well, a small store would be nice at some point. Until then, think of this... everyone coming in or out stops or passes by here. The point of selling is exposure. I think this would do fine, then expand as need be."

"Aye, I was thinking it would be fine as well."

Bird and Kara opened the case and the owner was stunned. Big, small and medium pieces. There was one piece in there however that wasn't for sale, and Kara called over Andrew. Now, with a small crowd at the desk, the others in the small lobby were looking too. The ladies waiting with the men were looking, and buying, before items even went on the shelf.

"Andrew, this one is not for sale. It is however, a gift for you. This is to thank you for all those times you looked out for me, and for bring'in Mister Bird into my life."

Kara had sold 3 more before she even put it in Andrew's hands. The small crowd was now growing to a medium one.

"Oh Kara, it be luvlee. I was just be'in a good Christian man is all, no thanks required."

It was a cross like she made Angus. It was cobalt blue with dabs of red where the Lord's hands and feet would be. This one only had the silver on the 'X' criss-cross part but... it was real silver.

"Aye Andrew, I know yeh be a good Christian man. Like I told Angus... now anyone who sees it will know too."

Andrew hugged her kindly, wrapped it back up, and put it in his coat.

"Aye lass. Yeh have my promise I'll put it where all can see."

Andrew was truly moved. It would always be one of his prized possessions. Years from now when Andrew would go unto God, he'd do so holding that very cross.

All the ladies were looking at the 'pretties'. All the men however, were looking at the tongs, and the induction hearth grates.

Kara was stoked her stuff was getting so much attention. Many pieces were a mix of her's and Angus's talents. No one knew what the hanging glass pipes set on an iron circle were for. With a boyish grin, Bird held one up and blew softly. The sweet tinkle of the glass and metal wind chimes blew the ladies away. The owner pulled Bird off to the side and thanked him for his idea, and immediately placed another order with Kara. Bird told all the men they had to speak to Kara when they asked him to place an order for the hearth grate and tongs. Kara was a little thrown by that, and a little insecure but she understood. Her sweetness however, only made them order more than one. It was a half hour so far since arriving, and Bird still didn't have his rooms yet.

Bird and Kara got a room each for the night, and were heading out the following morning. Kara almost freaked when she came down to see almost all the shelves bare. The owner however assured her he wasn't being devious. With a laugh, he told her he was out of stock... not a thief. That really surprised Kara.

"Just glass or just iron... meager sales. Mix the two and look, you're going home with your own coin this time. It's like I said the other night Kara... take what you got, make it better, and look what happens. Get used to it Kara, when the house goes up next week it's going to be nothing but," Bird stated.

"Aye... so I see!" Kara said with near shock at the sales she made. "What was those words yeh used?"

"Innovation and modification."

"Aye that be it. Looks like I could get used to that real easy!" Kara said half laughing and half smiling, and still unable to take her eyes off the empty shelves.

The owner gave them the rooms for the night at no charge and asked all they pay for was their meals. Kara insisted on not missing a one. She also insisted on paying for Bird this time. The owner upon checkout told Kara he wanted 30 more hearth grates. He said he'd only have enough coin however for 3 or 4 at a time.

Bird was surprised to see Kara wheel and deal like a seasoned pro... but was truly happy for it. She even told the owner she wouldn't ship a single piece unless she had a trusted carrier. And by trusted... she meant Andrew. By now, Andrew had the remaining case inside.

"I traveled with two cases. This other one had my other wares. Not certain how the first one would sell, I kept them packed in case I had to return with them. It's been a pleasure doing business with you, and I only look forward to more of the same," Kara told him.

"Remember yeh promise now. Yeh sell to no one but me for the next 3 years... aye?"

"Aye.. yeh have my word."

With that, Glasgow awaited. Along the way, Kara and Andrew worked out a deal for him to pick up and deliver the goods so she or Angus wouldn't have to. Andrew was very excited when Bird told him of the house he was building, and how he was expected at something Bird called a 'house warming party'.

"Traveling light this trip I see eh Mistuh Bird?" the ferry

captain joked.

Bird looked to the sky and, with a smile, said "Not exactly."

Bird heard a familiar chuckle in his ear as the ferry took off.

"Well William, as I promised, here's the legal papers I said I'd have drawn up. They're all set and recorded in Edinburgh... all that remains is your signature. Kara has arranged for transport for her wares with a trusted carrier. He'll see that they get to the proper people when he returns."

"Truth be told Mistuh Yankee, I not be a learned man like yehself. I have a cousin who isn't either... but he's a lot more than I am. Iffin yeh have no problem with it, I'd like tuh have him look them over befaw I put my name to 'em."

"Just don't write on them. If you'd like any changes, use the back of the last page but don't write on the actual pages themselves. If you do we'll have to start all over. Otherwise, I don't care if the king reads it for you... have at it."

That's what William was looking for, a sign that all was okay with Bird. William figured if Bird tried to hide or duck or dodge anything on the papers, he'd know Bird was pulling a shady deal. Hearing Bird not care in the least made William very happy. He promised he would do as Bird asked as Bird headed back to the inn.

"Oh Angus, I'm sorry... I didn't get a single order for the hearth grates yeh made," Kara said sadly.

"Oh lass don't yeh worry, that's alright," Angus told her sweetly. "Odd tho, I thought I would get at least one," Angus said somewhat befuddled.

"No sorry Angus, I didn't get one..." then Kara beamed and stated proudly "... I got 5! and one of them is for 30 pieces!"

Scota wanted to hear all about the trip, and Angus was just in shock of all the orders. Kara very politely put down all the money on the table and split it in half. She kept half and very proudly gave Angus the other... along with all the orders. She smiled the whole time she did it.

"Angus, God as my witness, Mistuh Bird showed just one of the wind chimes, and the others sold before I could get them from the crate! Heh heh, they were even fight'in over them!" Kara explained with pride. "I did have to make one decision on my own though. I want you to know I kept you in mind when I did. The hotel owner made me agree to sell only to him for 3 years."

Angus laughed hard saying "Aye, no problem there. Good Lord it'll take me that long just to make that many!"

Bird chuckled and told Angus he'd show him ways to speed up his production.

"Well Mistuh Bird... I hope yeh don't mind now?" Angus asked.

"Uh... mind what?"

"Looks like yeh ain't gonna be the only one around here with some coin! HAHAHAHAHA!"

Bird smiled kindly. He was truly happy for those two.

"Nope... I don't mind at all."

Everything Bird did turned out great as far as Angus was concerned. So, imitating Bird, Angus asked Kara if she would consent to him courting her. He did it however, the same way Bird announced him and Ciana. Kara was crying, but graciously agreed.

# Chapter 20:

## *"The BirdOfPrey Chronicles"*

Bird had the stone masons drive the iron bars Bird ordered from Angus into the rock ledge. He was very specific how deep they should be, and where they should be placed. The dent in the hillside that Bird turned into his getaway cave had a side benefit too. Many of the local buildings had stone foundations. The pieces that fell out were gathered and reused in those foundations. In Edinburgh, Bird had bought enough gunpowder to do the job right this time. He used the charges, got the dent turned into a small cave, and reused the blasted out rock. The iron rods were tied to others using hemp rope common in this era. Bird soaked them in stucco, and let them dry. Now the foundation would never slip or falter. Some of the rods stuck up higher than the others. Bird had drilled holes in the sill plates, slipped them over the bars, and locked them down with a slip ring. He and Angus covered the entire outer side in 4 coats of stucco. Bird didn't dare use concrete but... it sure looked like he did. Now with foundation set about 3 feet above grade, construction was set to begin.

Angus was blown away by the hand drills, and the rudimentary sockets and wrenches. Bird had turned a wooden lag bolt, then asked Angus to replicate it in iron by the hundreds. When Angus saw those in action, it left him stunned.

"Ere now Bird... what is this for again?" Angus asked looking at a set of pipes Bird ordered.

Those were wide and were going up through the roof. Bird explained what a 'vent stack' was and what it did.

Angus laughed and teased Bird saying "Ere now... Iem Mistuh Bird I am! We won't be having none of that!" Angus patted him on the back and, still laughing, he said "I swear Bird... only YOU *would put the plumb'in on the inside!"*

*Bird designed a more 'modern' home. Single floor ranch style. He didn't have a lot of room, so he made the house in a 'U' shape to maximize the space he had.*

*Bird had to quite literally, force Ciana to pick something she wanted. She had a man... who also just happened to have kicked the bishops ass... AND was building her a house!? No, Ciana felt asking for something would be the very 'putting on airs' she was trying to avoid. Bird however persisted.*

*"Honestly my love, tis more than enough. However, I know yeh, yer not gonna stop till I do so... build me a garden."*

*"We were already going to do that," Bird said slightly annoyed that she was dodging the request.*

*"I know thah. No, I mean a smaller proppuh one... like the one's in those fine houses we saw in Edinburgh."*

*Now Bird... was smiling.*

*"Consider it done. It won't be as large due to the lack of room but... trust me... you'll have it."*

*Now Ciana decided to trap Bird the way he trapped her.*

*"And what of you my love?"*

*"What of me what?"*

*Smiling, she asked "And what do you want?"*

*"That smile... that one right there."*

*Ciana blushed and said "Oh no yeh don't. Iffin I got to pick something... then so do you," Ciana said playfully defiant.*

*"Hmm... welllllllll... if I have to pick something, I'll take the waterfall."*

*"Oh yeh silly Yankee... yeh already got that!"*

*"Mm hmm... but I want to see it. Trust me, I'll make something for me. Shall I tell you or would you rather be surprised?"*

*Sweetly, Ciana replied "I... unlike you... love surprises."*

*Ally walked past the two lovebirds and teasingly said "Get a room you two."*

*Bird laughed saying "Be happy to... as soon as I build it!"*

Ciana didn't know anything about building. Even if she did, it would be nowhere near on Bird's level. However, she insisted if Bird was going to build it for her... then she was going to help in any way she could. Scota didn't last long most days as the coughing would get bad due to the waterfall. She however, refused to be away for long. When she could take no more, Ciana sent her home. Now however, Ciana was trusting the inn more and more to Scota's care. She told Bird she felt it was time to let Scota grow, and Bird couldn't have agreed more.

Ciana was even getting used to being treated like Lady Bird. Bird insisted that, as half owner, the crews he hired treat her like a boss. She promised them, no one would be treated unfairly nor poorly because of it. It took awhile for Ciana and the crews to adjust, but it was working just fine for both.

Bird and Angus were on top of the front section when William arrived. Bird had a third of the house rough framed so far.

"Good morn'in to yeh Mistuh Bird... do yeh have a moment?"

"Hi William. Not really right now but I can talk while I work. What's up?"

"I have just one question on those papers yeh gave me. What's this part about 'topping' my trees?"

"Ah... simple really. The house faces south. My plans call for the sun. It tracks across the house all day. Your land has trees that block it. I don't need to take them down entirely, just bring them down in height. That part says that I can control how tall they go and trim them down accordingly. I get my sun... you keep your timber. Like I said, I'd make it fair to both of us."

"Aye. My cousin said as much as well. Now... allow me to be the first to say..." and William signed the papers for all to see, "... Welcome.... 'neighbor'," and William handed Ciana a dream in the form of a legal document.

Ciana was shaking slightly at a dream come true, and took the rolled up document from him.

Kindly, she said "I can tell yeh true William, that has a lovely sound to it."

"Aye, it does. I hope yeh know I nev'uh had ennything against yeh, I was only protect'in my livelihood is all."

*"Aye William, I do. God has a plan fer all things, I just had to wait a bit tis all. Seems it won't be my house after all eh William?"*

*William was confused by that, and Bird saw it.*

*"I think what she means William is, she never got 'her' house because God planned it to be 'our' house all along," Bird said with a friendly smile.*

*Smiling back, William said "Aye... so it would seem."*

*So now, as a means to make up for 'bad blood', Ciana took William on a tour of the site. She pointed out what will go where and William was highly impressed with the size... and the features.*

*"And yeh say, a house this size... and only one hearth!?" William asked.*

*"Yep. Think about it William... if you could have a house... and run it all off of one fire rather than 3 or 4... wouldn't that be better? Heh heh, not to mention cheaper?"*

*Being a man... in 1757 Scotland... the latter highly caught William's attention.*

*"Aye indeed. And what be all these pipes the smithy be lay'in?... And IN the hearth no less!"*

*"When it's all done... you'll see."*

*William finished the tour and said "Well, I don't envy yeh the task ahead. And yeh say yeh'll get it all done by fall!?"*

*Ciana spoke with annoyance saying "Aye, the outside will ennyway. Tis a tad boring however but, it'll get done."*

*Bird chuckled and hollered down "Well if your bored, you can always come up here and help!"*

*Ciana put her hands on her hips and hollered back "God built me fer mak'in babies... not houses... in case yeh hadn't noticed?"*

*"Oh trust me... I noticed," Bird said with a wink.*

*Everyone on the ground laughed.*

*Ciana got beet red with embarrassment when Bird hollered back "And I doubt I'm the only one who noticed too!"*

*Scota hollered up to him saying "I know it's important, but Ciana is right... it is a tad boring making these sacks and cleaning and such."*

*"Tell ya what blondie... tomorrow I'll bring a boom box,"*

Bird laughed.

"More Yankee speak I'll assume?"

"You have nooooooooo idea."

Scota had a sly smile on her face and said "Ya know Mister Yankee man... YOU promised me stories of other lands. So far I barely heard any. NO ONE tells a story as good as you."

Before Bird could respond, Angus chimed in saying "Aye, tis true. Kara loves hear'in yeh tell them. She could sit fer days and listen she's said many a time."

All on the ground started chiming in as well.

"So, I get to tell a story to pass the day... is that it?" Bird asked in an 'oh great... yay me' kind of tone.

Many on the ground, and some in the air, all cheered Bird and egged him on to tell a story.

"Oh alright... fine then. How about a story Ally and I would tell to pass the time on long... um... 'voyages'?"

Ciana smiled and said "Well my love, it seems that just like in Edinburgh... theh stage is all yours."

"Well... this tale is a large and sweeping epic tale. It has adventure... strife... cleverness and cunning and battles to make any man proud just to be one. It's an imaginary tale that takes place among the stars themselves AND!... Just happens to feature a familiar character. I call this story... 'The BirdOfPrey Chronicles'. Get comfy people, this is a loooong tale with lots of characters."

So Bird did just that... he told the truth, hidden in a tale of fiction.

"Uh... boss?"

"Chill ya big black hot rod. Like we humans say... the best place to hide something is in plain sight."

"Hmm," was all Alydar said.

"So... way in the future, in the latter half of the 1990's, a boy named BirdOfPrey was born. He was the second of two sons to a pair of scientists named Jill and Roy."

Ciana chuckled saying "BirdOfPrey eh?... never heard of him."

And so... Bird's epic tale began. Bird told it in the style of the *old movie serials, where he only told pieces each day and left cliffhangers for the next.*

*Ciana was actually in tears 1 day later. Bird felt bad for her but actually chuckled a little. She was getting upset over, what was to her, a fictional character.*

*"That's so sad... WHY did yeh have to kill Cliffy? He was my favorite!"*

*Under his breath, Bird said seriously "Why indeed."*

*Bird had a hard time explaining what a wormhole was. While she couldn't conceive of it, Scota was the only one who got the explanation. Bird reminded them it was a 'fictional' story, and that some of the science wasn't exactly real. Fictional story perhaps but... an extremely popular one. People who weren't scheduled to work would show up just to hear the next 'installment'.*

*"Oh tis a fantastic tale yeh weave there Mistuh Bird but... did yeh have to make the wolf have an English accent?" one of the carpenters asked one day.*

*Bird just laughed.*

*The work didn't suffer much, and it took awhile to tell the tale as every time Bird got to a piece of tech in the story, he'd have to stop and describe it so that the crowd didn't get lost.*

*"Thah be some imagination yeh got there Mistuh Bird. Honestly, how yeh come up with some of these devices is beyond me. Hundreds of full songs, and whole libraries, saved on a disc no bigger than a saucer plate. And pictures that move! I have to hand it to yeh... that is some tale yeh tell."*

*The whole house was finally framed, and Bird was focusing now on the plumbing. He was making good headway there so... 'The Chronicles' rolled right along. Bird laughed to himself thinking if he didn't... he'd likely have a lynch mob on his hands.*

*Bird left the construction for a day or two to go on what Scota now refers to as 'Bird business'. Her curiosity however was piqued when she saw Bird go into the cave he made... but never seemed to come out. Mister Yankee had made a set of stairs to go down to it. It was only about 50 or so feet down a cliff that was nearly 6 times* that. Knowing Bird, she figured he would duck out unseen to places unknown. Now, standing on the cliff she so loved, she was starting to wonder. That curiosity, was starting to get the better of her.


Five Ghosts were scrambling. The pink version of Raven was still a few days off and, well, Lone just couldn't get used to the color. The sensors and satellites around the asteroid picked up only 100 or so Aardvarks heading inbound. It was the thousands of killer sized asteroids they were dragging that had the Ghosts scrambling.

Lone was in his cockpit when he tapped a button on his console. The light on his console went orange. When it went green, he dropped his chemical levels.


"Greetings Lone Wolf," Giljor said now sitting next to Lone in his cockpit.

"Damn this is just creepy. Okay, I 'called' for a reason. We're tracking thousands of asteroids. Problem is, the projections."

"Where are they headed?" Gill said with some concern.

"All indications so far show... you."

Giljor actually laughed.

"Same old Tamarak I see," Gil stated still laughing.

"Mind telling me what you find so funny?"

"Tamarak. He's bluffing and... he's digging. He wants to see if anything of interest is in the minefield. If you react, he'll know there's something in there he should be interested in. Let them come. Trust me Lone... the station can handle what you've showed me."

"Are you sure?" Lone asked not exactly believing him.

"You forget who built it. No Lone, we'll be okay. Keep an eye out though. In the past when Tamarak has done something like this, it was part discovery... and part diversion. Similar to Bird, he usually did more than one plan at once."

"Get me back then."

"No rush Lone, when you are like this... in here with me I mean... a whole day could pass and not be more than seconds in your time frame. If I were you, I'd look for a small part to break off. THAT would be your true concern. If you pay no attention to the minefield, Tammy will give up on that line of thought and realize there's nothing there of interest."

"I got hundreds of innocent lives on that station! YOU had better be damn sure of this!" Lone commanded.

"When it comes to my brother trust me, I know him like no other. You however will want to get rid of your drones you left in place that alerted me. If he can make the Aardvarks suddenly appear, then his level of tech has gone up... way up."

Lone asked "Speaking of, come up with anything yet?"

"Sadly no. Tamarak isn't usually the inventive one. That was more my field than his. Tell me this... think of when they showed up... and tell me ANY thing you remember. Any small detail... anything... even a perception no matter how small could be helpful."

"I'm going back first," Lone told him.

"As you wish."


"Raven... time check."

"The amount of a second you've been 'gone' is so small even I can't measure it," she told him.

"Well, at least that much is true."

"Excuse me?"

"Never mind. I'm going back in," Lone said.

He was about to when he had a thought.

"Rave, is their any target of opportunity we care about in the Aardvarks path?"

"None... wait... one. It's slim but, if they reach the point I'm pointing out on your HUD, a small group 'could' break off. If they did we would never see them. IF they did break off as I calculated... they would be in range of Tuhleesia."

Lone bellowed "Shock and Awe!"

"Go Commander," Symda said.

"Get to Rahgaa... when you get there... STAY dark and... earn that damn nickname of yours!"

Two invisible black bad-asses peeled off as Ghost 5 said "We don't run!"

Symda called out "We don't hide!"

Lone called out "Show anything that might show up... you won't be outgunned."

"Count on it."

Lone was 'back inside' with Gil once more and told him what Raven said.

"Wise precaution. That is exactly the type of diversion I mentioned. Now, I believe you were going to answer my question?"

"Yeah okay. So, we were drawn away in classic style. We fell for it because we didn't think he could do something like that. Now that you asked, I can only think of one thing. Knowing they weren't cloaked like we are... I'd say they looked tranced."

Gil was curious and said "Clarify."

"Well, I've seen the ladies trance. I've also seen them go solid. To me anyway, it looked like that. Like he tranced them in somehow."

Gil was now thinking hard.

"Hmm, interesting. Lone I have more history for you. On one try of the Keeraan, Tammy actually tranced as you call it. He didn't know what happened at the time, but he knew he did something. He poured over Atoemahn to try and find out what happened. He did. When he realized what he could do, he practiced every chance he could. He became quite good at it too. One time he appeared in my room to scare me and... OH NO!... Lone tell them to focus on Atoemahn!"

"WHAT!?" Lone bellowed.

"Lone your right, he didn't cloak them... he tranced them!" Gil said in a slight panic. "Check the library too! I know how he did it now! Lone he took them into range, then did the reverse of making them solid!"

"BLOODY HELL!" Lone screamed.

"Indeed. That is high level trancing at its finest. He brought them in... THEN tranced them... then made them solid again. No way he could do that without the ancient knowledge of Atoemahn. He either broke in somehow or..."

Lone finished his sentence by saying "He has an inside man... or rather... girl."

"Lone if he gets his hands on that knowledge again there's no telling what he'll become capable of."

"Make sure that station of yours is in one piece when this is all over. Get back, make it safe and, KEEP it safe!" Lone said with anger in his tone. "You leave the rest to me."

Gil nodded and faded out as Lone brought his blocking levels back up.


Gil was back on the station now... so to speak. He alerted the rest of the holograms to what was going on. Two of them immediately went to work on new security protocols for the library on Tuhleesia. Gil himself tracked the inbound rocks. Inside the minefield, Tammy was truly taking a shot in the dark. Gil however had a luxury Tammy did not... he could see anything IN the field. The builder wolves were alerted and Gil and the others acted as guides. In less than a minute, the station went from a science station... to a battle fortress. Hundreds of twin barreled and quad barreled turrets popped out across the length of the top, bottom and sides.

Gil knew the minefield would likely take out anything entering it long before it even came close to the station. The minefield was sooooo cluttered Gil actually thought the guns were overkill. As per Lone's request though, he wasn't taking any chances with the builder wolves in his care. They also asked to help fight, so Gil shut down a few on all sides and made them manually operated. He would not deny his own kind this honor... even if they never fired a shot. Just as Raven predicted, 2 Aardvarks broke off the main contingent, and also as predicted, headed for Lone's birthplace.


Ryklan herself pounded the alert that got the strike team rolling. She also told them as they geared up that this... was no drill. Within 2 minutes, a dozen X2's were airborne and hauling ass.

"ANY one of you misses your target... and you'll become part of the damage it causes!" Ryklan told them. Then she said "This is what you've trained for... make yourselves, me AND Tuhleesia... proud. Okay ladies, it's time to stand up!"

"AND DON'T BE SMALL!!" came 11, in unison, replies.

"A team, on my six! B team... I'll take high cover if you please!" Ryklan called out.

With that, half the ships broke off and went high.

All around Atoemahn, thousands of Krannen were getting ready in bunkers Trenthaarian had built around the library. Anything hits the ground and they'd be well protected. Anything that got back up would be given no choice but to go right back down again. The best Krannen on the whole planet would see to that.

Two Aardvarks dragging about 50 asteroids each, just kept on coming.

"Lone, why don't we just head out and greet them?" Symda asked not seeing this a major threat.

"HOLD your position... that's an order!"

Seconds later, Tamarak answered her question as the onslaught just... disappeared.

"What the fuck!?" Symda said with true shock. "Okay Xankor... I don't like this at all."

"Nor do I... Keyza?... lite 'em up, and spin 'em!"

Symda cried out "You heard the man Thor!"

Now 2 black ships were lit up, looking for targets, and packing blue death.

Suddenly, the ships and the rocks reappeared... 2 miles below the Ghosts... and barely 1 above the angels. The latter scrambled hard to avoid the instant death raining down upon them. Two of the angels banded up like their training taught them. They ducked and dodged, and fired on anything their weapons would have an effect on. Suddenly, their cockpits went dark, and they realized their luck had run out. Both figured if they were to die, they were going to do it head on, and shooting and screaming as they did. As such, both pulled stick back and went vertical to meet their deaths. Today it would seem, the angels looking out for Tuhleesia, had one looking out for them.

"NOT......... today!" screamed a Kiistassi Ghost.

Seconds before impact, a rock 1000 yards across, became nothing but dust.

"Nice shooting X-Man! Now, if you'd be so kind... GO VERTICAL!!" screamed the other Ghost.

Xankor did and from his six, blue fire took down the inbound Aardvark. Two angels barely cleared the big black ships... and the blue fire they spewed. They strafed Symda from front to back on either side of her cockpit. They were saluting as they did. Symda returned it, and went looking for more targets. Her HUD showed her the other Aardvark was on her 6 and she was banking around for it when she realized... she didn't have to. Two angels, now became six again, and they were hell bent on sending Tamarak a message, and returning the favor to a Ghost. Symda smiled, and let them have at it.

She was banking now to rejoin her wingman, when HER cockpit went dark. Symda had barely looked up when Thor lurched downward hard. The best way Symda could describe it, was a metal flying log. How it even flew was beyond her. It however, was making it near impossible for her to. This new log it turns out, was twice as long as Thor and half again as wide. Blue fire from her 3 o'clock cut it in two pieces and allowed her to break free... just shy of the ground.

Both pieces crashed right into the city Rahgaa had so wished to rebuild. The longer back half, had doors open up all along its length. Smaller ships no bigger than Bird's drones poured out by the hundreds.

"Ryklan!, if you can handle them, we'll keep the big rocks off your head!" Symda hollered.

"You got a deal! ANGELS! You heard the nice Ghost! See to it the Guardian's troops have little or nothing to do!" the Squadron Leader called out.

"Count on me... to see that you don't do it alone!" came a new voice... a wolf voice.

"Nice of you to join us Tanner!" Ryklan shouted.

"And you'll be happy to know... I brought company."

When Tandor finished that sentence, Ryklan smiled. Stuck in this hornets nest she saw a most lovely sight. On the horizon now appeared over 100 X2's. Tandor had brought every Pilot the school had, and he was at the vanguard of the remaining 3 squadrons.

Symda and Xankor lined up on either side of the biggest rock there was. Coming in from its 3 and 9 o'clock... it suddenly broke apart.

*"OOOOOHHHH RAAAAAAHHHHHH!!! HAHAHAHAHA!"*
That voice, was the brat Ghost himself.
*"We almost shot you... again,"* Xankor said with some consternation.
Deeno just chuckled and blew across their viewscreens. Ghost 2, in a pure dive, saw to it the remaining chunks would be nothing but dust when they reached the ground.

*"TANDOR! We got a real hornets nest here! Watch your crossfire! That goes for the rest of you too!"* Ryklan called over the radio.
*"How about if... I even the odds a little?"*
That voice was backed up by a strafe of blue fire that seriously 'thinned the herd'."
Mr. Black Ops had arrived.

*"Tandor! Keep me and my angels clear on the topside!"*
*"And your going where exactly?"*
*"On a tour of the city."*
With that, Strike Team One... 'Rhana's Angels'... went down to near ground level.
Tandor smiled and just said *"That's my girl."*

The shorter crashed section poured out almost a million gadgets and they were converging on Atoemahn. Twelve ships that the ground troops would forever refer to as their 'guardian angels' saw to it they didn't have nearly that much to deal with.
Flying through the buildings and streets, they took out the drone sized flying ships, and put big holes in the gadget's numbers. The ground troops, using a new weapon Ayleen called a 'bazooka', made sure the enemy on the angels 6 o'clock... simply went away.
Almost as an afterthought, 50 or so gadgets headed for the Arrowhead. A black manta ray and a 'Huey' saw to it they never even came close.


As the 'master general', Tiiveer wasn't allowed near the fight. His loss was seen as too great of a risk and as such, like any great general, he conducted the battle from afar. The head Krannen now was hauling ass for the library. The fight on the ground and in the air ended in a victory for the wolves, but it came at a cost. A total of 20 X2's were heavily damaged or lost. Also, 8 pilot's portraits would be framed in black and hung in the hallway of Raven Base. The ground troops suffered losses as well. Over 2000 were injured but, thanks to Triikon's new plan and efforts... only 3 perished.

Tiiveer was pissed he still needed the Ghosts, and swore he would work for a day when he didn't. He was however happy with his kind, the response they gave... and the level to which they've grown since the last time. Now he was racing to Atoemahn. Seems a Guardian called him saying they were about to be overrun, just before her message got cut off. The wolves following in his wake... were ten thousand strong.


"Well, the little soldier pup has finally arrived," Tamarak sneered. "A little late as you can see, but at least you had the nerve to show up."

Tiiveer bolted into the room to see 50 of his elite dead. Some were mangled and only in pieces. About 100 newer style gadgets were holding the remaining 50 at bay. Riisa herself was held spread eagle and off the floor by two gadgets.

"I'm sorry Guardian, they appeared out of nowhere right in this very room."

"Indeed. Your fellow wolf here was quite convincing. She pleaded for me to stop. It actually touched my heart," Tamarak said barely containing his laughter.

"Can't touch what you don't have," Tiiveer smarted

"True."

Lone showed up now and had his anti trancing weapons fully charged.

"Eh eh eeehhhh mirror wolf. Harm me or... fire that weapon... and my gadgets here will tear her apart."

Suddenly, Riisa fell to the floor.

"They can only do that if their intact," said Mr. Bartender as he dropped in from behind. Two black Mahrek blades cut the arms *and legs holding Riisa.*

*Tamarak just laughed and faded to another position.*

*"Q... GET OUT OF THERE!!" Lone hollered.*

*Quaran ducked and covered and dove to the side... just as the remaining core bodies of the gadgets exploded.*

*"ENOUGH!!" Riisa hollered out as the battle resumed. "This is MY realm and I will NOT have it destroyed!" She turned to Tammy and asked "What do you want you evil wretch?"*

*Everyone on both sides of the fight held up, but stood at the ready.*

*"Keep your precious building for all I care. All I want is it's knowledge."*

*"And by knowledge you mean...?" Riisa asked.*

*"Give me the cores. Do that and I'll leave you in only the pieces you currently find yourselves in."*

*Tiiveer hollered "Forget it! My soldiers have taken out your machines and..."*

*"Take them," Riisa said with resignation. "Take them and be gone!"*

*Tiiveer was incensed.*

*"WHAT are you saying!?"*

*"Look around you Guardian. These machines appeared from thin air. Wolves are harmed or perish by the minute." She then turned to Tamarak and said "Take them. I'll take great delight in showing you we'll defeat you even without them."*

*Riisa dropped the protection screen Tiiven put around them.*

*"Your machines can pass through the defenses now."*

*Three gadgets 'disappeared'. When they returned they held one crystal core each. Riisa's station was going wild.*

*"It's been a pleasure doing business with you," Tamarak sneered... and was gone.*

*His remaining forces disappeared as well.*

*"GUARDS!" Tiiveer hollered out. "Take the Guardian here into custody, and bring her to a holding cell at the midway station. Treat her the way you would ANY prisoner!"*

*Tiiveer was livid and growled low in Riisa's face.*

*"You will pay dearly for your cowardice here today. I will*

*personally see to it you pay beyond even that for your treason."*

*Calmly, Riisa said "I did what I felt I needed to. I only wished to see no more wolf lives put in harms way. I have no doubt you'll do what you feel you need to as well."*

*Still growling, Tiiveer merely said "Count on it."*

*Riisa was smiling as the guards let her away in cuffs. Just before she left the room, she gave Lone a wink and nothing more. Lone however... had no idea why.*

# Chapter 21:

## *"Thunder-Shock"*

*Ayleen had regained consciousness, if you could call it that. She was groggy and only sort of knew where she was or what happened. One thing she did know was the ship was tumbling. She shook her wits about her but that only made the room spin more.*

*"Head injury... not... not goo... not good," She sort of slurred aloud. "Ship... report!."*

*No reply.*

*"SHIP!?.... ow!"*

*Still nothing.*

*A quick look around and she knew two things. She was in some crazy wormhole she'd never seen before. Secondly, she was pinned to the floor. Ship, as a last effort to help her pilot, turned the gravity up by a factor of 3, to stop Ayleen from being tossed around. Shortly after that, she went offline. Ayleen saw only one chance. She knew she was slipping back out cold again. She barely realized the gravity. Now that she had, she crawled across the floor to where the pilots chair used to be. That was beyond hard but Ayleen knew it was that or die. Not wanting to incur the latter was the only thing keeping her awake right now. Using strength she almost didn't have, she reached up, and slammed the autopilot override button. It took a few moments but the viewscreen finally leveled out. Seeing that... she collapsed on the floor, and passed out again leaving her fate to higher powers.*

*"No... yeh got it wrong," Scota said to Ciana "Rahgaa is the Prime, not Rennahr... she's the student."*

*Bird chuckled. Ciana looked to him but he merely shrugged and nodded.*

*"See!?" Scota said all pleased with herself.*

*"OI!" Bird barked. "You may be right... but ladies don't gloat. Watch your tone little miss."*

*"Sorry Mistuh Yankee... sorry sis."*

*The Chronicles just got past the part of Lone and Bird blowing out the cave to receive the silver starship. The part where Bird saved Lone from the 5 legged bear had grown men on pins and needles. Everyone of them could picture this huge black airship coming up into view and spewing godly righteous fire. Bird smiled as 50 men all stood and hollered in triumph at the bear's demise.*

*Ciana related more to Rahgaa, even though she kept getting her name confused with Renny. Scota however saw Renny as her champion. A lot of the men loved Renny's manners and cunning, but thought Tahl was the 'wolf to be'. Once Lone built the cannons, every one of them wanted him to be their friend. All the ladies thought the love story between Lone and Renny was the best part. None of them could fathom why Bird didn't spank Rahgaa for her meltdown. Bird just smiled at all the reactions and kept the Chronicles rolling right along.*

*The framing was done and the roof trusses were all on. All except the kitchen. Today Bird was in the trees and rigging up tackles and ropes. They were heavy duty ones and aside from the ships in the bay, no one had ever seen them used in any other place.*

*The masons arrived today with Birds order. It was a huge slab of granite. Polished to a mirror finish it was massive at 1.5 inches thick, 7 feet wide and 15 feet long. Ciana had no idea why Bird didn't put the roof on the kitchen.*

*"You'll see," was all he'd tell her.*

*Today was the day that she would. The slab was so huge Bird didn't want to take a chance on cracking it by muscling it in the door. Once it arrived, Bird and the masons wrapped the ropes around it. Once Bird was happy with them, he and Angus pulled them off the cart while 2 of the masons pulled on ropes to keep it away from the house. None of the crews could believe it only took 2 men to hoist it but... Bird's 'sky crane' worked like a charm. It was guided up, over, then down into the open kitchen roof. Ciana's* counter top for something Bird called an 'island' was now in place.

"Now... I can put the roof up," Bird said as he inspected the stone slab.

Ciana marveled at its size, and its shine. So did everyone else. No one had seen anything like it. Bird merely told them this is what they have in professional kitchens.

"All the best chefs in Edinburgh have one," he slyly told them.

With that... no more questions were asked. There was a hole on the end. None of the ladies could fathom a kitchen with TWO sinks when Bird told them what the hole was for. They certainly wanted one... they just couldn't fathom it.

The brew master finished building the biggest barrel in the world according to him. Bird told him something that big was called a tank... but he still called it a barrel. Bird just chuckled, and stopped bothering to correct him. The tank was high above the house and close to the falls. Bird made a sluice pipe from the oak tree trunk he downed to clear his site. It stuck quite a ways into the tank. Bird showed them that, as the water rose, so did the pipe. When the tank was full... the pipe would rise and cut off the water flow, till it drained enough to need more. Everyone thought it, and the rope crane, were the most cleverest things they'd ever seen.

Bird was teaching them little ways to improve their trades.

"In my day Ally, the Scots were some of the best engineers in the world. They had to get that way somehow eh?" Bird said in a weak defense of Ally's admonishing.

"Hmm," was all she said.

She was getting on Bird's case again for teaching them things that she thought, they shouldn't know. Bird however knew if he didn't spark some ideas, this house would take years to build. He was being quite careful not to teach them advanced science, just different applications for what they already knew. Angus already had a block and tackle lift in his shop... Bird just made a bigger one.


Suddenly, Alydar not 'Ally', was in his ear. His HUD was activated shortly thereafter.

"We got incoming. Fifty riders and a coach... 2 miles out and heading straight for you."

Bird walked off to the side and spoke softly.

"The Bishop?"

"Could be but I doubt it. The riders are dressed in shock troop style."

"The king?" Bird asked not believing he would be coming.

"More likely... the cardinal."

"Fucking great," Bird said in an annoyed tone.

He walked over, and put a Tuhleesian First sword on his back. Seeing that, every woman found a man... and every man found a weapon of some kind.

It took another minute for the sound of the riders to reach the site. Everyone was in awe at how Bird knew they were coming before anyone heard them. No one was brave enough to ask how either.

Two minutes later and the riders finally came into view. They pulled up to the bottom of the falls, with the coach in the middle.

"Yep... you called it alright," Bird said to Ally when he saw who got out of the coach.

Ciana and Scota curtsied proper but said nothing. This time however, neither was afraid, and both were ready to show off Bird's teachings if necessary. Everyone on the sight made a sign of the cross when the cardinal did the same from below.

"Greetings your eminence. My name is BirdOfPrey but, something tells me you already knew that."

"Indeed. I've heard more than I care to when it comes to you," the cardinal replied.

The cardinal however almost had a laugh in his tone when he said it though.

The cardinal smiled and said "So... is this the home that's to make me weep with envy?"

"It is. Seems I have a dressmaker to visit," Bird said knowing he only told that to John.

"Oh my child, don't blame anyone. Talk in a city like Edinburgh spreads faster than a fire on straw. I hope you'll forgive me if I don't come up there. Age and a slightly sedentary lifestyle and, well, my legs aren't what they used to be."

"Not at all. I'd come down but, wellllllll, your riders and I didn't get along so well last time."

"I've heard that as well," the cardinal said as he waved his hand.

The guards all backed away leaving the cardinal in a large open circle.

"Better?" he said with a smile.

Bird had no idea what the cardinal was up to. He definitely didn't trust him but... he was no bishop. Bird decided to take a chance, and smiled back.

"Much... thank you. Give me a moment, and I'll be right down."

Bird made his way down. When he did, Ally was with him. Bird had made it to the riders expecting bad things. To his surprise, they let him through without a word. The cardinal was an older gentleman. Bird put him around 50 or so. A slight limp was assisted by a rather nice looking cane. When Bird and Ally reached him, the cardinal pulled the cane handle and out came a small rapier. The point of which was right underneath Ally's chin.

Without a care, Ally asked "Boss?"

"Hmm... ya know what? Do what you have to."

The cardinal stared, but Ally noticed his stare was different. It was more testing than anger like the bishop's was. Without a word, she twisted, elbowed the blade away, and finished with the same blade against the cardinal's throat. Thirty riders were off their mounts with swords drawn in an instant, when the cardinal chuckled and waved them off.

"So it is true then hmm?" he said with a chuckle. "Apologies my child, but when I heard my best guards were negated by a silver haired 'she-devil' with the fighting skills of 10 men, well, I had to see for myself."

Ally let him go and handed him his rapier back with a half bow.

"I've been called worse," she said with a grin.

Thirty riders put away their swords.

"Leave us!" the cardinal commanded.

All the guards pulled back to a safe distance, and Ciana and Scota let out a hard exhale.

"Walk with me?" the cardinal asked politely.

Bird pulled out his Tuhleesian blade. The riders all grabbed their swords as Bird threw it into the ground.

"ANY one touches that... and you'll be dead before you can pull it from the ground," Bird said addressing the riders. Turning to the cardinal with a friendly smile, Bird waved a hand and said "Lead the way."

Bird knew this kind of man. He was interested however to hear what this particular one had to say.

"Commander, word of you has reached my ears. To be honest, not much doesn't. I would apologize for my bishops behavior but, I think I won't. Quite frankly, I've been doing that a lot lately and to be honest... it's becoming tiring. Whatever he's done 'this time', I assure you it was without my knowledge or blessing."

Bird was impressed. This wasn't the conversation he expected. The lines on his HUD staying blue was a welcome relief.

"As a learned man, I'm not, shall we say, unaccustomed to the way things work. The fact that you know the truth of Ally here, and how it was her that took down your guards... and not some phantom army... is impressive. The male ego can get quite inventive when its been bruised," Bird told the cardinal.

"Oh I think you'll find, when I get conflicting stories, I have methods of extracting the truth," the cardinal answered.

"I've seen those extraction methods. Rather barbaric to say the least."

"Perhaps but... effective none the less."

Bird had enough of this and got down to business.

"Well cardinal, as they say where I'm from... let's cut to the chase shall we? Why are you here?"

"Commander, as I'm sure you're aware, one like me doesn't rise to my position for no reason."

"Nope. Your point?"

"Point is, once you have, there are many who wish to replace you. Some will even go to extremes to do so."

"Like the bishop," Ally stated.

"Exactly my dear. His attempt on your lovely lady was to show his talents and secure his power against me. His failure was not something he planned on, and cost him dearly. Now I fear, that ego you mentioned, has driven him to extremes."

Bird caught on and said "And yet, here you are. Let me guess. He's a thorn in your side. Someone like me, outside the church that is, is the perfect pawn. Tell me, am I getting warm?"

With a devilish smile, the cardinal said "Oh, boiling my son."

"Thought as much."

Ally didn't get it however. This level of deceit, cunning, and back door dealing was something new for her.

"Care to enlighten me?" she asked Bird.

"It would seem my dear Ally, the cardinal here is looking to unload some trash. He comes here, lets us know what's going on, and we do his dirty work for him. Alright your eminence, lets say I do take out the bishop... what do I get in return?" Bird asked.

"Oh my dear boy, I think you misunderstand me," the cardinal said in mock disgust. "I would never suggest NOR sanction such an act on a member of the flock."

"And yet?" Bird asked in a 'get to the point' tone.

"And yet, if say, he should do something heinous yet again... something say NOT sanctioned by the church? Well, let's just say you won't get my blessing... but you just might find my ignorance," the cardinal stated slyly.

"It would seem your eminence... we understand each other," Bird said with a friendly smile.

"I heard nothing but bad things about you from my fellow clergy and guards. The commoners however, told quite a different tale. I'm glad to find the latter correct... and not the former," the cardinal said with a confirming handshake to both Bird and Ally.

Walking back to his coach the cardinal spoke to Bird.

"You know... gossip is such a terrible habit,"

Bird chuckled and asked "I'm sorry cardinal... did you say something?"

The cardinal smiled, and said "Of course not. IF however, you were to hear that the bishop was stirring up the Campbell clan with lies in order to gain allies... well... that sort of thing could be heard anywhere... wouldn't you say?"

Bird put his Tuhleesian sword back in its sheath saying "Heh heh, I would indeed."


"BOW YOUR HEADS MY CHILDREN!" the cardinal shouted up.

All did and, as a final act, the cardinal blessed the site and all who worked on it. With a nod to Bird, he got in his coach.

Bird leaned into the coach and told the cardinal "IF what I've heard turns out to be correct, well, you'll find me to be a good Christian."

"And if it's not?"

"You'll find me to be worse than the worst of all your nightmares."

With an understanding smile, the cardinal said "Of that I have no doubt. Go with God's blessings my son... and mine as well. DRIVER!" the cardinal hollered and the coach and riders headed back to where they came.

Angus joked from up high saying as he looked over the ridge "I ne'er even SEEN the cardinal, no less got a blessing from him. And here Mistuh Bird gets the honor of the cardinal himself! Heh heh, now why am I not surprised!?"


Angus had never made such plans in his life. Right now, he was quite pleased with himself seeing them all come together.

"Are you sure about this Angus?" Bird asked with mild concern.

"Sure of this... aye. Sure of what answer I'll get? No."

Bird smiled and said "Well then, allow me to be the first to say congratulations. And if the answer is no... then I offer the same for your bravery in at least trying."

"Thank yeh kindly Bird."

Angus had never laid out so much coin for anything in his life. This however, he felt was worth any price. He and Bird had taken a few days and went to Edinburgh. The 'big city' made him nervous, but being with Bird soothed those. He had met Andrew too. Angus felt it only proper to meet him for several reasons. Andrew gave his approval as well and was truly happy for Kara. Angus wanted to see and meet the hotel owner as well.

Now, with two proud men at his side, Angus was staring at a lovely yet tasteful... diamond engagement ring. With no jeweler on the Isle, and business now in the city as well, Angus felt it was time to make the trip of a lifetime. He had gone to the jeweler and picked something already made. Andrew pulled Bird to the side and told him he thought Angus was 'a bit country'... but a seemingly good man all the same. Angus heard it though and it only made him smile.

"Well Mistuh hotel man, it was good tuh meet yeh."
"Aye, and you as well Angus. I'll use the time yeh mentioned to get things ready here," the burly man told him as he shook his hand. "Hasten ye back... both of yeh."
"Time?" Bird asked questioningly.
"Aye," Angus said with a grin, "You'll see."
With that, Andrew took them back out of town.

It was a nice day so Bird was riding with Andrew for awhile.
"Mistuh Bird, I wunduh if I might have word?"
"What's up Andrew?"
"Well, this inn yeh mentioned. Iem driv'in a lot of fine city folk now. These same folk like tuh get away to the country now an then. I thought fer all yeh did for me... perhaps I could do theh same fer you?"
"Hmm, interesting. It's more of a way station than a proper inn but, I'll mention it to the ladies and see what they think."
Andrew smiled saying "Aye, be happy to help them. Yeh be a lucky man. Ne'er have I seen a lovelier lass. See'in such beauty though, I figgerd Ied be treated no bettuh than dirt. Touched my heart they did see'in how they really were. Lady Bird in particular." Andrew caught himself saying "Sorry Mistuh Bird, I dint mean to be gett'in in yer business."
Bird smiled a true caring smile and told the driver "It's fine Andrew and you're right... I am a lucky man."

Andrew hollered back "And you too Angus. Whichever answer yeh get wellllllll... Kara be a good lass. Should it be yes, I have no doubt she'll grow to a fine woman, and make yeh a bettuh man for it too."

Kindly, Angus said "Aye Andrew... she already has."

Two day trip accomplished, Bird and Angus were back on the Isle. That same Bird, was now arriving at the smithy's home. He also had two lovely ladies with him.

"No Ally?" Angus asked slightly let down seeing only two women.

"Heh heh, sorry smithy... she's off on... what did you call it Scota?"

"Bird business," blondie said with a chuckle.

"Yeah... heh heh... what she said!"

"Oh well, hasten yeh in and quick! Did Kara see yeh?"

"Nope."

"Excellent."

Kara came in just after dark from working her trade.

"Sorry Angus, it took me a bit tuh finish. I'll have supper fer yeh in a little bit," Kara called out.

"Hello dear," Ciana said walking out from the kitchen "I took theh liberty of help'in yeh a wee bit."

"Huh?"

"So did I!" Scota beamed walking out behind her carrying some plates.

"Oi!" Mary chuckled "I helped too!"

"Don't look at me dear, I'm just the bartender tonight," Bird said with a wink.

"Mind if we join in?" the potter and carpenter said coming in with their wives and children.

Kara was pleasantly confused and asked "Angus, what's the mean'in of this?"

"Well my dear glass maker..." Bird started.

"HAPPY BIRTHDAY!" Everyone shouted.

Angus wanted to surprise her but felt it better to do it softly so as not to cause a seizure.

Kara was sad.

"Ere now lass, what's wrong?" Angus asked kindly.

"Well, fer all I know, it COULD be my birthday. Truth be told Angus I kahnt be sure. I was an orphan remember?"

"Well then Kara," Bird said handing her a rolled up piece of paper, "Angus wanted to get this but didn't know how so, technically, this is from both of us."

With a huge smile, Angus said "Go on... open it!"

Kara did and staring at the legal document, was a tad confused.

"That's you Kara. I asked Mistuh Bird if there was a way to find out ennything about yuh. That there is called a birth certificate. "And look here," Angus said pointing on the paper, "It says September 19$^{th}$ 1738... that's today, 19 years later so... Happy Birthday my dea.... mmmf!" Angus cut off as Kara gave him a huge hug.

Ciana walked up smiling and said "Aye yeh may be an orphan, but that doen mean yeh ain't got family somewhere. Now with that... yeh can find them one day."

Kara let go of Angus and ran and hugged Bird.

Crying happy tears she just whispered "Thank you."

"You're more than welcome... Happy Birthday sweety."

"Aye," Kara said wiping her tears, "It is now."


Angus held up the party about an hour later. He was liking some of the Yankee ways... and was about to do one now.

"All of yeh, if yeh would, gather round," Angus told the crowd.

Angus took Kara by the hand and brought her to the center of the crowd.

"Kara, from the moment Mistuh Bird here brought yeh into my life, I ain't been nothing but better for it. You've accepted this poor ole smithy and I'm grateful for it. Mah dad taught me, when yeh find someth'in good, hold on and don't let go. What Iem ask'in is, will you Kara, consent to be my wife?"

Angus finished that getting on one knee and pulling out the ring.

"Aye Angus... I'd be proud to," Kara said with caring eyes.

Angus put the ring on her finger, stood up, and gave her a big swirling hug. Kara was back to tears again. Happy ones but, tears. She may never find her real family but here, now, she could start her own. Everyone poured in from the walls and congratulated the two.

"I have one more announcement to make. One to yeh all," Angus shouted out. "Kara my dear, you made a decision on your own, but about us. Now I made one too." Angus spoke to the crowd saying "My bride to be is a fine glass maker. Lately tho we be hav'in fights as my shop was never designed for two. Iem afraid to tell yeh the smithy will be out of business till spring."

Kara was shocked and asked "But why Angus?"

"You. Yer a fine talent but yer gett'in in my way. As such, Iem gett'in in yers. Iem taking down the barn, and build'in a new one big enough fer both of us and yer even gett'in yer own forge!. We have enough coin to last us till summer if we're frugal. Bird here has said he'd help where he can. We kahnt deliver our orders the way we are so, Iem build'in us a proper shop."

Kara stroked his face tenderly and said "And that kind of caring Angus... is why I said yes. Now, what of this deal yeh made?"

"Oh, I toel the hotel man how we needed a better work place. He agreed if I extended our deal by one more year."

Kara smiled and said "Aye... tis fine by me."

The next day, Bird and Ciana were sitting at a table in the inn. They were also, the only one's there.

"Scota my dear, would you mind joining us?" Ciana called out.

Scota came over and Ciana waved to a seat. Scota sat down the way a child does thinking they're in trouble.

Ciana took over and said "Bird here has told me of something Andrew said. Remember all those proppuh folk we saw in the city?"

"Aye," Scota said still nervous.

"Well, it seems they like to get away to the country. Andrew has said he'd direct them to our inn. Bird and I  agree it's not quite up to that kind of customer. What do you think?"

"Wait... I'm not in trouble?" Scota asked confused.

Bird chuckled and said "That remains to be seen but, no, not by us."

Ciana was caring and said "Scota look, the house is really coming along now. I need to be there more and more. You are always telling me how grown up you are. Bird and I discussed it and decided, to a degree, you're right. Besides, your coughing is terrible at the house, and I need someone I can trust to look after my things here."

"Wait, are you putting me ... in charge?" Scota asked.

"Yes and no. As the eldest you still go through me but, I want you to start taking over more here. Now answer my question."

"No insult but... no it's not... not for that kind of customer anyway."

Ciana smiled and said "I agree. You'll be 17 only days after Bird. Plenty old enough. I want you to go through this place from top to bottom, and make a list... no two lists. One for any repairs needed, and one for making it better. I'll let you run it your way but I still have the final say. Make it nicer and we can even charge more. What do you say?"

"I'll do it on one condition."

"Aye?"

"I want any trades we hire to treat me the way they do you and Mistuh Yankee. They'll know you're the final say but... I'll be the one in charge."

Ciana looked at Bird, and he smiled and nodded.

"Aye, I'll see to it myself if any get out of hand."

Scota smiled huge and stuck her hand out.

"DEAL!" Scota beamed.


Lone was in deep space and... he had had enough. He was pissed and decided to deliver on Bird's promise. Renny pleaded with him not to go but he ignored her. When she realized her pleas were falling on deaf ears she turned to Raven.

"I swear to Rhana's God, if you don't bring him home to me... I will take you apart down to the last fucking bolt!"

"MRU," was all Raven answered.

Now, with Rhana's hand picked at his side, Lone wanted to send a message. That message was delivered an hour later and... at a perfect 12 degrees down nose.

"Pick a bloody target... and let loose every 'thunder-shock' you got!" Lone hollered out. "Okay Ghosts, FUCK UP HIS DAY!"

With that, 5 ships split apart, but only 4 armed their payloads.

The 'thunder-shock' Lone referred to was essentially a depth charge. Mind you, said depth charge was built by Max. They were built with a 5000 mile range and designed to flush out a ship hiding in a nebula. Now Lone, Deeno, Symda and Xankor were on the hunt. They were looking for the largest oceans of lava they could find. For motivation, Raven fired up Meatloaf's 'Bat Out Of Hell'.

When the music started, Symda hollered out "WE DON'T RUN!" and turned off inviso mode.

"WE DON'T HIDE!" Deeno hollered and became visible.

"WE'RE OUTGUNNED ONLY ONCE!" screamed Xankor.

"Fuck awwf arsehole... you will NEVER be him," Lone said to Tammy with absolute menace as he went visible last.

Thousands of gadgets and Aardvarks went on the attack on each ship.

"Lone?" Symda called out.

"Fly the mountain pass," he replied.

"Works for me."

Suddenly, 4 ships kicked it into high gear. Lone basically told them to fly like Bird did when he showed him speed on Eden. Now, an ancient evil was the one getting pissed off as his assault teams were just being left in the dust.

Each ship found their 'target of opportunity' and let loose the thunder-shock's. Once they had, they went to full power on the 12 packs, and didn't even bother to look at what they shot at. Shock and Awe alone took down half a mountain range that was 5,000 miles long. They were going head on at each other when 10 Aardvarks above them let loose everything they had in a wild spread. They were hoping to just hit something. When the massive flashes subsided and the clouds cleared, not a single Ghost was seen.

"Heh heh," Tamarak chuckled.

Suddenly, those 10 and another 20 that came to their aide, 'went off Tammy's radar'. Blue fire poured out from beneath the lava as Ghosts 5 and 6 crossed under the lava and came out at the edges of the blast field.

"OOOOH RAAAAH!" Symda shouted with sadistic glee.

"Watch it lady... that's MY line," Deeno said.

"Nyaa. Mind telling me why your not dusting off your 6?"

"Nope, don't mind at all," Deeno said casually, "I'm waiting for more to show up first."

"Show off," Symda snickered.

Tammy just roared as his forces were decimated.

"I need a drink," was heard in the four Ghosts.

"Aw, and I was having fun!" Deeno declared.

"Yo 'uncle'," Lone said over an open frequency, "We'll be back... count on it."

Five blue ringed portals opened up, and Tammy's tormentors were gone. Moments later, the thunder-shocks did their jobs. Over 50 deep explosions set off a cascade effect of lava tsunami's that would plague Tammy for weeks. Seven of them blew so high that over 100,000 of Tammy's toys just melted away.

Lone swept close to Tuhleesia on the way back.

"Send them to me," Lone said on a secure channel.

"It will be done," was his reply.

Lone veered back out and headed for a nebula. He looked to his side at a thoroughly stunned sidekick.

"If my sister ever asks... you weren't here."

"M... R... U."

# Chapter 22:

## *"Back Doors And Trojans"*

*"Please don't get the wrong idea when I say this Guardian but... have you lost your mind?" Tandor said to Tiiveer.*

*"The Mahrek asked for you, and your mate to be... personally. If you'd like to decline, I have no doubt he'd be happy to entertain your request."*

*That, ended that. Now, Tandor and Ryklan, who is now referred to as 'The Archangel' by any wolf with wings, were walking out to address the crowd. Raven base was packed to capacity yet, a path was opened as they walked.*

*"Good wolves!" Tiiveer began. "I have personally paid honor to those who now hang in a black frame. To you, the one's who will carry on this fight, I say... well done. We are not yet where we need to be to defend our own skies. However, know that the defense you gave, and the level to which we have grown, have made all the Guardians proud. Proud of ourselves and... proud of all of you. Walk with honor in the words of Rhana for we have harmed none, and we have let the darkness know we will not be harmed!"*

*The crowd in Raven Base was pumped. They all cheered and hollered. Their Guardian told them he was proud of them... THEM!. Oh this was a great day indeed. They all accepted they had a long way to go but, it was nice to know they had done well so far. Raven Base was opened by THE Mahrek... home to the Pilot Prime... praised by the Krannen Guardian... and now home to Strike Team 1. The latter became legendary the other day, and their reputation would only grow even more. Raven Base had become forevermore the holy grail of pilots. Anyone who wished to 'make it' would fight to get stationed here.*

Tiiveer waved Tandor forward to speak.

"I wish to expand on what the Guardian has told you. He said he was proud of you. Know that, we are too. We also wish to acknowledge the ground crews. We go to fight but, without you, we would have nothing to do it with. Without your skills, we would only harm ourselves and not the enemy we face."

Roars of approval rang out as Tandor faced Tiiveer.

"Guardian, as leader of this school please give my thanks, and the thanks of all those here, to K-Doc. I see many injured among us and know, without his efforts and those of his teams... they likely would not be among us today. He promised us care and he has delivered and for that, we are all grateful."

No roar this time, just thousands of salutes and respectful bows.

"Now, onto why we called you here. Commander Lone has called SL Ryklan and I to 51. We will be gone for a short period of time. I expect you... AND this base... to only be better upon our return. Is that clear?"

"YES SQUADRON LEADER!" rang out around the base.

It was bad timing in their minds but if Lone called them... then that was good enough for them.


Later that day, Tiiveer was with Tiiven and... he wanted answers.

"Care to tell me why you failed yet again?" Tiiveer said with menace.

"I did not," Tiiven stated with pride. "I built AND deployed, in record time I might add, the very defenses you asked for. The shielding over the library and over the cores worked as it should. Tamarak merely went around them. They held AS THEY should have and even protected Atoemahn from falling debris and weapons fire. They were NOT designed to stop someone who can trance."

Tiiven was pissed and standing up to even Tiiveer. He was right, and holding his ground this time.

Tiiveer didn't like Tiiven for one reason only, no backbone. He was truly the gifted tech genius he thought him to be but, with no backbone to stand up for even himself, Tiiveer thought him a joke. Now Tiiveer was pleased.

*"Well then, feel free to explain AND!... Without the attitude."*

*Tiiven toned it down some but only that, 'some'. He was sick of being thought of as a joke and being bullied. This time he was having none of it.*

*"Guardian, trancing is much like the Ghost's cat's eyes. They take you from one point to another. Nothing in between matters. You are still thinking Tamarak must go through what's between the two points. I'm telling you he went from outside the field to inside it... period. Not through it."*

*"I don't understand the science, but I do your explanation. If we can't stop him then, let's not."*

*"Excuse me?" Tiiven said not getting it.*

*"Stop working on ways to block him from traveling, and start working on ways stop him once he arrives."*

*Tiiven had a 'hmm' look on his face now as Tiiveer headed out.*

*"As I said... you failed. However, your efforts were admirable. Keep up the good work."*

*Now Tiiven knew he got the acceptance he felt he earned.*

*"I'll let you know what I come up with!" Tiiven shouted to a departing Guardian.*

*"Please do," and Tiiveer was gone.*



*Riisa was nervous. She was to face a Guardian tribunal today. THE Mahrek would be there as well. None of that was making her nervous though. It was the lack of one key Xaran that had her nervous. She was brought in in handcuffs surrounded by the best shadow soldiers there were. Their ranks had gotten thinned lately and they were not in the best of moods when they shoved her, rather impolitely, into a chair facing her tribunal elders. Now, seeing the one she waited for arrive... she smiled.*

*"Riisa, you stand accused of the most heinous crime we have... treason," Rahgaa stated beginning the proceedings. "It is our way that you may seek counsel. I see you have none. Is this your choice?"*

*"It is not Guardian Prime. As is our laws, I am permitted to choose my counsel am I not?"*

"You are," Rahgaa stated.

"Then I choose... Wing Remington... of Planet 51, to be my counsel."

Remmy smiled as Rahgaa told him "Wing Remington, this affair does not concern you. As such, if you choose, I offer you the right to accept or decline."

Rahgaa was a tad confused by Riisa's choice. So was Triikon. He saw Riisa any chance he could and never believed she was what she was accused of.

Remington stood with pride saying "This actually does concern me. Not only that, if Guardian Riisa is guilty of treason then... so am I. I accept her request."

Triikon was pissed at her choice but, nothing he could do now. The rest of the tribunal was now equally as shocked and curious.

"I caution you Wing Remington, your humor is not unknown to us. Be careful what you say or you may find yourself charged as well," Rahgaa rebuked him.

Remmy walked and stood beside Riisa, saluted, and only said "MRU."

Tiiveer kicked in now saying "Riisa you stand before us for your crimes. You allowed some of my finest guards to be killed, and gave away the hope and future of our very race to the one evil who threatens the very same. What have you to say for yourself?"

"I killed NO one!" Riisa hollered. "IF perhaps, you weren't so single minded... you would have seen that!"

"WATCH YOUR TONE TRAITOR! And NEVER call me a liar again!" Tiiveer barked. "I saw you with my own eyes turn off the security guarding those cores! Commander Lone did too! So did EVERY Krannen in this room!"

Riisa's reaction was not what everyone was expecting. They expected her cowering, not defiant.

"Of course you did. I do not deny I turned them off. And I didn't call you a liar... I said you were single minded... there is a difference."

Tiiveer was about to shred her himself when Rahgaa yelled.

"ENOUGH! I will not have these proceedings turned into a bar room brawl!"

Now Lone stood up. He was calm and the whole room now paid attention.

"As one who is used to things being 'not what they seem', and seeing as who your counsel is, I would be interested in hearing your story."

Riisa bowed to him saying "Thank you Commander."

Lone sat down but his HUD was active when he did. Any lie and he'd jump back in.

"As I said, I did disable the security around the cores. What none of you know is why." Riisa turned to Tiiveer and said "IF you had asked, rather than assumed, you may have known why."

"I'm listening," Lone said calmly.

"A month ago, in your time values, I contacted Wing Remington. After your wedding Commander, and the trip to the station, I found my behavior not exactly to my liking. I found myself trying to fix too many things at once, and failing at them all. I believed if I became good at one thing first, then added others, rather than fix many things at once... then I would achieve my goal. As such, I focused on my job. I learned all I could of the history of us... and the machine I used daily. Not just how to work it but... how IT worked as well. It was the latter that caused me to notice something seemed wrong. My screens tell me who is on and who is accessing what. While many across our world were using the library, it seemed there was always one more than there should be. When I would attempt to find out who, that person quickly disappeared. When I learned how to trace their searches, they always led me in loops to nowhere, or right back where I started. I may not be as 'tech savvy' as some others, but I'm no fool. When I discovered that, as a Guardian, I contacted the one I knew who could help me. Now, I will let my counsel tell you the rest."

Riisa sat down as Remmy got up to finish her story.

Remmy spoke up and said "Commander, I know you know of these things, but I'll explain to the panel here who may not."

Lone nodded and Remmy spoke directly to the Guardians.

"When I setup the access for the tablets, I set them up to leave *very distinct traces for anyone who accesses the library. Guardian Riisa contacted me some time ago. Her request was for absolute secrecy. I thought it an odd request but I honored it. Aboard my brothers Ghost she was safe to tell why she called me of all people. She knew someone was not only going after information, but they were hiding it. Not sure who, she asked me for help with the tech she didn't know. A 'back door' or a 'Trojan' are ways of getting into a computer system without going through normal channels. Someone was sneaking in AND covering themselves and what they were searching for. Until I got to the cores, Guardian Riisa had no way of knowing who it was. She thought it might be Tamarak. She also thought it might be a Tuhleesian. Once I did access them, I discovered it was indeed Tamarak."*

*Rahgaa didn't care for Remmy's humor but she trusted his talent implicitly. Now she wanted clarification.*

*"And what EXACTLY... did you find?"*

*"I found it was Giljor. An old back door, which by the way is exactly as it sounds, was accessed. Knowing he was in the minefield, I knew someone else had to be using his access. That 'back door' was put in place just before your civil war. I can tell you for certain it wasn't him as the minefield would prevent that sort of access. That leaves only someone who would know him. Seeing as how Lady Ahdeera is no longer with us... that left only one. Giljor could have covered his tracks, but not his brother. His attempts may seem highly skilled to most of you, but he was a bumbling idiot to me."*

*Turannen was likely the only Guardian who actually understood this. Now he wanted answers.*

*"Can you tell me, were you able to back trace him?"*

*"No Guardian, but I did track his paths inside the library. He accessed knowledge on trancing. It was determined, incorrectly we now know, that he was looking to extend his life even more."*

*Remmy now spoke directly to Tiiveer.*

*"Guardian, when you spoke to Rhana that time from the library, you hid that knowledge from even your wife. You determined that if anyone knew the truth, and Tammy somehow got a hold of it, it would be catastrophic, did you not?"*

*"Indeed I did. It was correct thinking then and still is."*

*Remmy smiled and waved to Riisa. He sat back down and she stood back up.*

*"And it was that very same logic that caused my actions Tiiveer," Riisa stated.*

*She wanted to show the Krannen bully if he wanted to play the 'no title' game, so could she.*

*"I had no idea at the time who it was nor how it was being done, only that it was. For all I knew, it could have been one of us. Regardless, I had a choice to make. Once Wing Remington discovered who it was, I decided to 'play dumb' as the 51'rs say. I let Tammy believe he was undetected. Wing Remington tracked him remotely and kept his searching to a minimum."*

*Tiiveer was calmer now but still angry.*

*"Still, you let him have continued access AND gave him the sum of all our knowledge."*

*Riisa actually giggled and said "Well, that's partially true. You see, once I knew who it was, I couldn't tell anyone I knew. I can't fight the evil tehrip like you can, but I wanted to fight back. So I did it the only way I could. IF I told you, then you became targets for Tamarak himself. Still, I couldn't just let him have anything he wanted. Wing Remington found the back door he used was the same one every time so... (giggle)... I had him move the door."*

*Lone had a grin on his face and simply said "Clarify."*

*Remmy spoke up again and said "I moved his door to a different sub system. One I created. For the non savvy among us, It would be like me moving the door to your home to a replica but... filled with junk. The knowledge in the cores was removed, all of it. Tammy sent a spy to us recently with HUGE storage capabilities. I used his own tech against him. I literally transferred all the knowledge of Atoemahn to 51, and replaced it with junk and failed experiments. I merely made it look like it was legitimate.*

*One of Rhana's movies show hostile aliens attacking. To defeat them, they sent a virus to the attackers. I merely did the same to Tamarak."*

*Lone was grinning even larger now.*

*"And what exactly did you do Remmy?"*

*"In order to plant the virus, he HAD to have direct access to*

the cores. I planted a virus that would change his calculations. He thinks he's getting legitimate answers... not knowing the whole time they're off by 1 or 2. All his trancing space jumps, all his blueprints... well... they're all about to become a little 'off'... heh heh."

Lone was laughing now. So was Turannen.

"BLOODY BRILLIANT!"

Lone looked over with a laugh and said "Hey watch it... that's MY line hahahahaha!"

Riisa said with a smile, "Now you know why I let him have them. He was supposed to get them all along. I am truly sorry for your troops Guardian Tiiveer. Tamarak showing up through a trance was nothing we could have prevented. The one's who were killed fought bravely and should be honored."

Tiiveer walked around the table with all the poise of a Guardian, and walked straight to Riisa. When he arrived, he stared a moment then... took off her handcuffs.

"You should have told me... or at least the Mahrek. While I understand your reasoning, undo strife was caused by your silence."

"I don't do battle as you do Guardian. I made the best decision I knew at the time. I was truly afraid my plan would fail if I told someone, and then that same someone somehow was captured. Tammy HAD to believe. It was the only way I knew how."

Rahgaa still had questions.

"So if I understand this right, Tammy got the cores, but not the knowledge on them? Or at least not the true knowledge?"

"Correct Lady Prime," Remmy answered.

"I have used that library only yesterday, as have hundreds of others. Where then was that knowledge coming from?"

"As I said, 51. I transferred all the knowledge to a secure server there. I then sent out a program to code all the tablets you have with an identifier. If that identifier was correct, you got access... you just didn't get it from Atoemahn."

Now Rahgaa was satisfied.

"Lady Riisa stand before me please," Rahgaa stated firmly.

*Riisa got up and did as told.*

*"As Prime Guardian, your punishment falls to me. I agree with my mate that undo aggravation was caused by your silence. I also understand why you did what you did. Still I agree with him. NEXT time you have an idea like that, you WILL inform someone. Guardian Turannen at the very least should have been told as the technology falls under his domain. While I understand your caution, try and trust us more in the future... as we shall you."*

*"I understand Lady Prime," Riisa said politely.*

*"I hereby strip you of your Guardian title for a period of 3 suns. Not for your actions but, for your incorrect silence. Let that be a lesson in trust to you for the future."*

*Riisa bowed and said "I will, I promise."*

*Rahgaa then surprised them all.*

*"K-doc... Healer Triikon... come forward please."*

*Triikon had no idea why he was called but stood tall all the same.*

*"I hear many reports on you. Many from my own mate. They tell of the fine job you have done, and how many wolves live another day because of it. I hereby state your rank and privileges shall remain but, you are hereby relieved of duty," and Rahgaa winked at him and finished with "For a period of 3 suns. Get some rest while you can for you have earned it. Also, go with my thanks for all that you have saved. BOTH of you." Rahgaa looked around and asked "Is anyone at this table NOT satisfied?"*

*No one said a word.*

*"Then I Rahgaa Siin, Prime Guardian of Tuhleesia, hereby declare this matter and these proceedings... closed."*

# Chapter 23:

## "A Scent Of Heather"

Bird was getting closer to 'present day' with the Chronicles. The inside was finished in what the locals considered record time. Some rooms were still cold as they ran out of bags and sawdust. The lumber mill promised more in a day or so. Bird told them he wanted it in the day... not the 'or so'.

EVERY one flipped over Bird getting back to Tuhleesia with Lone, and the epic battle that ensued. They loved the reconstruction and the return to the city.

Earlier in the week all the men were in tears of laughter over the banter between Lone and Bird when Greeva showed up. Everyone had a favorite part, then changed it a day or so later when a new part of the story arrived.

Now Bird had them on pins and needles as 51 geared up to go give the trader council 'what for'.

"Tis a good thing this is only a story," Ciana said offhandedly.

"Why?" Scota asked.

"All these aliens and strange ways and creatures. Machines that talk and think! I could never live there."

"I would LOVE to see it!" Scota said proudly, "I think it's interesting."

Ciana chuckled at Alydar.

"So, you get to be a big black ship of space eh?"

"Watch it lady... you call'in me fat?" Ally laughed.

"Oh... heavens noooo heh heh. Still, I asked for a grand story and aye, that's exactly what I got. I actually almost feel sorry for those Uhrakins knowing what Bird will do to them once he arrives."

*Bird was heartbroken as he corrected her saying "Aarikans."*

*"What's wrong my love?" Ciana asked seeing Bird's reaction.*

*"Not a fucking thing. I'll be back later... I got Bird business to attend to," Bird said sideways as he walked off.*

*He never even looked at her.*

*"Sweet Lord... whut did I say now!?" Ciana asked.*

*"This time Lady Bird, leave him to me," Ally said as she headed off after him.*

*"WHAT!?" Ciana barked at the remaining crew.*

*They were all looking at her with a 'gee thanks lady' look knowing now they'd have to wait for more Chronicles.*

*Scota coughed on purpose this time, then said "This is getting a bit much for me... I'm going back to the inn."*

*She was sad for her adopted dad. She had no idea why he was upset but, she was going to try and make him feel better. Racing down the path, she was confused. She should have caught up to them by now but, it was if they went through one of those cat's eye things like in Bird's story.*

*Bird loaded his cannons and headed for the range. Right now, Bird needed nothing more than to vent... and blow some shit up.*

*"Guess that plan didn't work so well huh?" Alydar said kindly.*

*"ARRRGH! How the hell (Blam) am I gonna get her used to our world (Blam Blam) if she can't even handle a fucking story!! (BlamBlamBlamBlam)"*

*Bird switched to auto... and emptied all 4.*

*"While I'm not a fan of this plan, you're already in it 'up to your eyeballs' as you humans say. As such, do you think a small... and I MEAN 'small'... demonstration might be in order?"*

*"No. While I know my people, I also know how much to give them and when. The little tricks so far are truly not as epic as you fear they are. Doing something like that would be. I will do that, I'll expose us for what we truly are but... not until just before we leave. That way, any damage I do, I'll take with me and not leave it behind to corrupt my own history."*

*"Fair enough," Alydar said sweetly as Bird calmed down.*

*"Right now your blackness, I've got other issues to sort out."*
*Bird's plan would come to pass... sort of.*


*Bird was sitting in the new living room. There was only three things
in it right now... him, the rocking chair, and the fire in the hearth. He
was staring out at the falls and thinking. He was alone not only in
person, but in thought. He had become way too popular and was
looking for ways to tone it down. Being a prick wasn't his style, so
that was out. Now he has the bishop building up steam somewhere
over on the mainland. He needed another option but right now, it
wasn't coming to him. All he could think of was spending more time
with Alydar... a lot more. Bird decided to tell Ciana the 'other life'
was starting to get close and were asking a lot of questions he didn't
want to answer. It wasn't much but, like he's done so far, he'd wing it
as he went.*

*The one thought he couldn't shake was Ciana's reaction to his
world. He was really proud of all he's accomplished, and was as
'stoked' to show it to her as Lone was at showing it to Renny. He
also realized, his attempts at bringing Ciana more forward didn't
work as much as he thought. While she is more than she was when
he met her almost a year ago, she was still not ready yet. Bird tried
thinking of him leaving, and Ciana not coming. He was going home
no matter what but, what if Ciana decided not to go? Right now he
knew he'd do what he had to if the door home suddenly opened. He
only hoped he'd still be that brave when the actual time came.*

*Bird was out in deep space again and he was on the hunt for a
little black ship. Alydar was careful around him as he was moody
these days. Bird was spending more and more time away. To cover
his tracks a few times, he went, but left Ally behind. Ciana and Scota
were getting cranky without Bird around. Scota was downright
miserable some days. Ally could take only so much and eventually
left as well. When she did return, she had Scota drilling and
practicing. Seems it was a way for her to learn, and work out some
frustrations at the same time. She was actually getting pretty good.*

*Ciana practiced when she could, but she was at the house
most days overseeing the finishing touches. When Bird did return, he*

was distant somewhat. She had no idea why. She could tell he wasn't angry, but she knew damn well whatever it was started when she said she wouldn't live in Bird's story world. This was the one thing she feared more than anything when she and Bird first got together. She was afraid that, somehow, she was losing him.

"Bird... are you angry with me?"
"Disappointed... not angry."
"But why? What did I do?"
"It's more what you didn't do. Or rather, haven't done."
Bird faced her and decided bad answers right now, were better than nice imaginings.

"Ciana, I told you my world will welcome you with open arms and treat you like a queen. In some circles it would be more like a goddess. But I did warn you it was nothing like you've ever known. I heard you Ciana. I didn't hear what you said as much as the intent behind the words. For all I've shown you, for all you've grown... I still hear that frightened little girl in there who's afraid to let go." Bird smiled at her and said "I am proud of you for how much you've grown so far. I guess I expected more though, and was a little let down when I realized you're not as far along as I thought." Bird kissed her lightly and sweetly and told her "I'll be alright."

Ciana was confused and said "But your story isn't real!"

"What if it was though hmm? Where I'm going, it might as well be. I told you I wouldn't hurt you by putting you 'too far too fast' and I still won't. Like I said, I just thought you were farther along than you actually are. I told you I wouldn't push you, and I'm keeping my word. Trust me, I'll be okay in a day or two."

Now Ciana, the new one not the old one, kicked in.

"Well then, tell me. And I doen wanna here none of this 'I kahnt tell yeh' stuff. Yer ask'in me tuh trust yeh an awful lot with this other world of yours. If yeh doen want me getting all surprised an such... then TELL me about it!"

Bird chuckled saying "Damn your accent gets thick when you're angry. Sexy too."

Ciana was still angry and said "Doen yeh be giv'in me none of yer smooth talk. There has to be something yeh can tell me!?"

Alydar truly liked Bird and Ciana, and really wanted to help. It was that desire that put her voice in his ear.

"Go ahead... tell her. Not everything of course but, you've been lying pretty well so far. Besides, she's right, how is she gonna grow if she doesn't get something to go on?"

Bird decided the voice in his ear was right... to a point.

"Ciana, anything I tell you makes you a target for those who want to keep me away. You have grown yes, but, you are NOT in their league. Not even close. If I tell you, and the wrong people find out you 'know things'... they'll use you to get to me. IF! You wanna know about my world, then that's the price and THAT is the risk."

Without hesitation, Ciana said "I'll take it. Aye, I may not be ready fer yer world but, look at me now. Am I theh same person you first met?"

"Nope."

"Better or worse?"

"Better."

"Aye. Perhaps not as much as you'd like but better all the same."

"Aww... and I liked that thick sexy accent," Bird said slyly seeing she dropped it some.

She slapped his arm playfully and told him "I mean it! Yeh brought new things into my life. While I was scared, I fought it... for you! Looking back I'll agree, you were right. I was afraid of things I shouldn't have been. You want me ready fer this world of yers... then MAKE me ready!"

Bird was sweet but, his words were backed with caution.

"I can't... not yet." Bird saw the look on Ciana's face and cut her off saying "BUT... I will tell you what I can. Small steps but, you'll have to walk them... deal?"

"Aye, deal."


"Ciana, this world of mine is vast, very very vast. My property alone is the size of the whole Isle... times ten."

"Okay so, yeh got land... that's good right?"

"Indeed it is. Also, I'm not the only one with large property. So, you can imagine getting around takes a bit of doing aye?"

"Aye, I 'spose."

"Well, we're not exactly patient people. My world is advanced Ciana. Like the city is to here, only on a scale you can't imagine yet."

"Okay... so?"

"So, we made machines, HUGE machines, to travel us around. The people there are different too. Very wise but, they were once slaves."

"Like in yer story?"

"Exactly. There's a phrase among my people that says you write what you know... so I did... 'cept of course I didn't write anything."

"Alright, so they were slaves once."

"Yep, and they won't go back to being slaves ever again. Like in the story Ciana, imagine if you had a blank slate. A chance to start over with no rules except those that you make. That was my world my dear. And while there are those who've accepted us, there are still those who haven't. Those same slaves work even now on a way to get me back safely and... quietly. If they're discovered, evil on a scale beyond your imagining will descend on them to stop them. My world Ciana is very advanced. We worked on medicines to cure or prevent diseases you've never even heard of. Devices and machines that are as advanced in real life as the ones in the story."

"Well, alright then. Ennything else?"

"Oh loads but, for now, that's enough."


"Bird?"

"Mm?"

"You were their leader weren't you?"

With faraway eyes Bird told her, "I was. One day God willing I will be again... only with you at my side when I do return."

"And Scota?"

"Oh now lass... I can't deprive her of her 'sciencey stuff' now can I?" Bird chuckled. "Trust me, IF we ever get there, she'll have more to learn than she could handle in a hundred lifetimes."

Ciana hugged Bird and was truly proud of herself. Instead of making up monsters and giving herself her own answers... she asked for real ones.

Now Bird changed the topic. He and Ciana were alone and cleaning up after the dinner guests.

"Now, back to me. I've been gone a lot lately, and it's been for a reason."

"Aye, yeh said. Yeh been keep'in that other life at bey."

"True but, that's not the only reason. I've become as much a leader here as I was back home. I truly can't afford that anymore. I even got the damn cardinal knocking on my door! That's something we have to talk about as well."

"Aye, what did he want ennyway?"

"He's being slick that's what. The bishop, as I thought, acted on his own when he came here. He's trying to overpower the cardinal and take over in his place. He failed badly because of me and Ally. Knowing what he was doing the cardinal had him ridiculed. He came to tell me the bishop is over in the highlands spreading lies about us to the Campbell clan, and trying to build up support."

"And the Cardinal would tell you that why?" Ciana asked.

"The bishop is being a bit of a thorn in his side. He can't outright attack him. By feeding me information, and allowing his desire for revenge, he's hoping the bishop will hang himself, and that I'll do his dirty work for him."

Ciana now tried something, something Ally taught her. For the first time... she tried BirdMan 101.

"Well then, let me see if I get this right," Ciana started. "Ally said bring a big problem down tuh my size, solve, then make theh fix as big as theh problem. Now, I know folk like the bishop and the cardinal here on the Isle. Sneaky and crafty they are. They not be as important as either of those two but, I have tuh think the reasoning and the results would be the same aye?"

Bird smiled and told her "Very good! And, you are correct."

"Well then, if thah be the case, brought up to the level of the cardinal and... well... that be one fine mess yeh got us into."

"I didn't get us into anything... but I know what you meant. I got to really tone things down Ciana as they've gotten way out of hand. The bishop loves you, or simply lusts after you. I don't think its you so much as his pride and ego were bruised. He's so angry at the humiliation, that he's just the type to do something stupid. I know people like him... he won't stop until he either gets you, or he's dead. I am more than okay with the latter... you?"

Ciana was scared now.

"Bird, yeh be talk'in bout murder... and a bishop no less! Jes think'in bout this could get the king's army down upon us!"

"Whoa there lass. No one is murdering anyone. Self defense however... is another matter entirely. I'll give the bishop a fair chance to leave us alone. If he does I'll walk away."

Nervously, Ciana asked "And if he doesn't?"

"Then... I won't."

"Do thah, and yeh'll surely bring the cardinal down upon yeh."

"No... I won't. He said I'd find the blessing of his ignorance if I solved his little bishop issue. Ciana look, I have a saying... 'don't go looking for trouble, for it will surely find you first if you do'. I've also left alone enemies I felt weren't a threat, only to find in my ignorance they became an even bigger one. Sadly, I don't see any choice. If I don't pay the bishop a friendly visit... and soon... I'm certain he'll pay us a rather unfriendly one."

Ciana was actually concerned and said "And how do yeh know the cardinal is tell'in the truth? A basket full of snakes and ye'll find not one better than the other."

"Good point... and one I intend to factor into my plan."


Scota's coughing fits were getting worse. Thankfully they were far less frequent but, when they did come they seemed to make up for lost time. She was using a lot of 'teenage logic' lately too. The kind all teenagers have where they think they're the only ones who know or understand something... and all the grownups are just idiots.

As such she was breaking the first rule Ciana promised. The one that left Bird alone when he left, and not ask why or where. She was certain Bird was up to something she just didn't know what. What was bugging her most... was how. She figured if she 'just happened to get caught', then she'd show Bird how smart and grownup she was and that he'd let her help him. That same misguided judgment, was causing her to spy on Bird more and more.

Bird was back in space and Alydar had news for him.

"Yo boss... I got a problem."

"Like?"

"Remember when you got me back online?"

"Yeah, what about it?"

"Been doing diagnostic checks since. Your work was good given the circumstances, but I felt 'what if it failed, then what'? As such I've done 2 diagnostics a day since. Each time there's an anomaly."

"Define 'anomaly'," Bird said with caution in his tone.

"Everyday, the sweeps finish and show nothing wrong. Problem is, they don't take as long as they should. I finish the scan with nothing to report but, I don't know, it's like they skip a part or something. My systems tell me nothing's missing but, I'm still off on my time values."

"Could it be your clocks are damaged? We never checked those as they appeared to be undamaged. Doesn't mean we were correct though."

"No. Because time is such a crucial factor in all that we do, those have separate systems to check for accuracy."

Bird chuckled and said "I know... I designed you remember?"

"Anyway, you said report anything odd no matter how small. Well, there ya go then."

Bird had a thought and laid out his plan.


"Okay my dear, how bout this? Your full size can't find it. What if you downloaded yourself into the lander. And I mean all of you. Then, from there, run a check on your full size and see if a slightly external system can spot what an internal one can't?"

Alydar had a 'hmm' tone in her voice now.

"That might work. Assuming your correct though, it has risks."

"Name them," Bird commanded politely.

"Well, if I did that, most of the security protocols are through my full size. If I leave entirely, they'll go to automatic."

Bird spoke cautiously saying "And if they do, they'll go to limited capacity. No cognitive thought to allow, block or override *should anything odd or threatening occur."*

*"Mm hmm. Like the other day when I didn't open the bay door for you."*

*"Don't remind me," Bird said in an annoyed tone at the memory.*

*Bird had the lander hovering over the bay whenever he was on Earth. Whenever he needed to get off the Isle, he would simply go into the cave, engage the suit, drop the ramp and hop over. He always made sure the coast was clear, figuratively speaking. One day, literally speaking... it wasn't. Kara and Angus had gone down to have a picnic on the shore a few days ago and Bird didn't see them hidden amongst the rocks. They wanted some privacy and almost got a show Bird didn't want them to have. With the lander invisible, all they would have seen was a door in the sky... a huge door. Alydar however registered them on her sensors and refused to open the ramp to the bay. That little 'oops' made Bird change everything.*

*As a result, Bird fired up the suit, left armed it, and cut a vertical groove in the cave wall. He put a 51 door in it, then used the melted rock to cover up the gold part. None of the locals would be the wiser should anyone actually come in. Now he had a much safer, and less visible, way to get into his ship. Buried in the rock wall, the door was programmed NOT to open either going or coming, if the sensor on it detected more than one person in the cave. That little oversight was about to bite Bird in the ass.*

*"Okay I've finished my calculations. It will take me ten minutes to download into the lander... an hour to run the diagnostic... and another ten to put myself back. No way I'm doing that without you onboard. My avatar will be offline too, but only during the up and downloads, not the diagnostic itself," Alydar told Bird.*

*"Can you run simulations on that? I prefer a dry run over a hail Mary pass any day."*

*"Actually I can."*

*"Good... do it. 48 hours. IF you find nothing in the sims, we'll do it then. I'll use the time to setup another 'Bird business' episode.*

Come 2 days from now, if you haven't run into any snags... we'll do it then okay?"

Alydar laughed to herself, mimicked Ciana, and said "Aye... deal!"

"Not funny," Bird said as he headed back to the cave.

"Thawwy Dadddy," Alydar said with a chuckle as she started running her simulations.

Bird had been gone for about 3 hours. Scota however stayed until the humidity forced her inside. Every chance she could she'd watch him from the cliff. Bird saw her most times and would usually wave. Bird also noticed she wasn't around much anymore. He chuckled when Alydar said she actually was. Doing things the old way he would'a scolded her for her curiosity. With a 51 door in place now, he just took great delight in frustrating her.

Bird had finished the kitchen in the house now. Ciana squealed in delight seeing what she called the 'water pump' on the inside. Bird chuckled as he turned a valve he made and reminded her... this one ya don't actually pump. Hot water impressed the hell out of her as Bird fashioned a solar water heater on the roof. Ciana was in heaven and was still going over the 'new toys' 2 days later when Bird left.

Scota was in the inn cleaning and wished Bird a good day as he left.

"Not gonna try and have a bad one that's for sure," Bird said with a grin.

Try or not, a bad one was exactly what he was going to have. Scota's was about to become worse.

"Okay ya sexy thang ya... how we look'in?" Bird asked as he came through the door into the bay.

"Sexy thang?" Alydar joked, "Who do you think I am... Rahgaa?"

"Yeah yeah... any issues on the sims?"

"None so far. I need you to check 'me' though. One system is giving me fluctuating readings. I think a connection may be loose or damaged. Check that out first then we're good to go."

"Okay sweety, I'm on my way," and Bird headed out.

"HAH!" Scota hollered as she jumped into the cave.
The emptiness of it gave her reason to pause.
"Huh?"
Scota looked all around but... no Bird.
"Aye, crafty one he is," she mused to herself. "Guess I'll just have tuh show him ole Scota can be craftier!"

"Okay sweety that should do it. One of your optic connecters was blocked," Bird said wiping his hands off.
"Yep, that system reports nominal now, thanks."
"Anytime. Listen, I'm gonna go to my room first and grab a bite to eat okay?"
"Aw, did she make hagus again?" Alydar giggled.
"Not funny. There's only so much stew a man can eat!" Bird said with some frustration.
"Yeah, I suppose. Enjoy, we're in no hurry. Call me when your done."
"Will do. I'll holler when I'm ready."

Scota was looking around and getting annoyed. Bird couldn't have just disappeared. At first she looked for tracks heading down to the cove. Then she started looking around for a hidden passage of some kind. The less she found the more frustrated she got.

"Okay Alydar... you ready?"
"As I'll ever be."
"Alright... start the transfer. Everything looks good here, so I'm heading back to the landing bay."
"Security protocols on automatic... see you in 10 minutes."
With love in his voice, Bird said aloud "You had better."

Scota was getting pissed now. She knew Bird had pulled some sort of trick. Not being able to figure it out was what was pissing her off.
"I swear, it's like he has a magic door to the bay or

*something!" she exclaimed.*

*Whoops.*


*The sensors on the door in the cave heard the words 'door' and 'bay'. With security on auto and degraded, it did what it was commanded to do... it opened.*

*Scota backpedaled in horror and tried to scream, but couldn't make a sound, as a screen of pure flat light came out from the rock.*

"Warning. Portal closing in 40 seconds,"

*"Wh... who.... who are you!?"*

"Warning. Portal closing in 35 seconds," *the strange voice said.*

*Scota was near tears with fear. She was in a fetal ball on the cave floor and... as far away from this glowing demon as she could get.*

*"WHO ARE YOU!?" Scota screamed. "Please, don't hurt me. I was only trying to..."*

"Warning. Portal closing in 25 seconds,"

*Scota realized this thing, whatever it was, wasn't hurting her. While she couldn't find the body to go with the voice... she did understand the words.*

*"Will... will you... will you take me to Bird?"*

"Commander Bird has already gone through. Warning. Portal closing in 15 seconds,"

*Scota was sniffling now and inching ever closer.*

*"So... you'll take me to Bird?"*

"Commander Bird has already gone through. Warning. Portal closing in 7 seconds,.. 6... 5... 4..."

*Scota had no idea where the bravery came from, but she decided to take the chance. At 3 seconds she touched the screen. She was shocked to see her hand go through. The strange voice had gotten to zero and the door started closing. With a deep breath, and an unwavering faith in Bird... she turned sideways and... changed her life forever.*


*Scota was in the strangest place she'd ever seen. Looking around she was scared again. She couldn't fathom how in mere inches, she ended up in a whole new world. This place was cavernous with strange barrels and crates and such all over the place. And it was bright. Light was coming from the ceiling high above but... there were no windows to let it in. Everything she touched, even the floor, was strange to her. Scota heard a voice and some footsteps. She was high above what looked like a main floor and she was on some form of balcony. Never had she seen one made of metal before, and never had she felt metal feel so strange. Hearing that voice, Scota panicked and ducked behind some barrels and other... well... 'stuff'.*

*"Jesus woman! It's getting cold in here... crank up the heat will ya!?"*

*Scota looked down and... it was Bird. And what was that clothing he was wearing? Scota really freaked when the voice that answered him filled this metal cavern. It seemed to come from everywhere and nowhere all at the same time. Not only that but... it was one she knew well... just a whole lot louder.*

*"Jeez your such a baby," Alydar joked.*

*"Yeah yeah, if I wanted cold I'd have gone to Siberia," Bird joked.*

*Suddenly, a huge gust of warm air kicked in and blew right past Scota. Bird was about to do something when he froze in place.*

*"Sniff... sniff," Bird breathed as the hot wind hit him.*

*Bird just hung and shook his head.*

*"Oh son... of... a... bitch," he said with absolute exasperation.*

*"Problem?" Alydar's voice boomed.*

*"That... remains to be seen. Nothing you or I can do about it now anyway. Well, technically there is but... we'll see if it's needed."*

*Bird froze for one reason and one reason only. When the hot wind from the heaters hit him, he smelled the unmistakable smell of heather.*

*Alydar said "Download complete. Primary scans started. Well boss, wadda ya wanna do for an hour?"*

*Bird figured if he was busted then, he was gonna be busted in grand style.*

*"Cha-cha."*

*"Um, you wanna dance?"*

*"I do. Feel free to send your avatar on down."*

*"On the way."*

*No way. Could it be? Noooo, that's not possible! Could it be somehow Bird's story was... was... TRUE!? Scota went from being terrified to being only slightly scared and, very curious.*

*No band anywhere in sight and yet, the strangest music now filled the large room. Clapping hands too but, not applause, more like they were an instrument themselves. Ally bowed to Bird, he bowed back, and the dance began. Coming up from her bow Ally curled her finger at Bird and walked backwards in the strangest manner. Bird followed and the woman singer let loose a holler and an invisible orchestra rang out.*

*Alydar had put on Whitney Houston's 'I Wanna Dance With Somebody'... not that Scota would know that though. The woman singer had an amazing voice Scota thought. Bird and Ally danced below to the surprisingly joyous music. Not only danced but, to Scota, it looked like they were born on a dance floor.*

*Bird cha-cha'd to perfection and swung Ally to and fro. When he wasn't doing that, he was in perfect sync right next to Scota's other favorite sister.*

*"Somebody OOOOOH.... Somebody OOOOH," the singer sang and the music grew even more.*

*Scota was swinging her skirt and didn't even realize. Seeing Bird down below dance with such talent and perfection she just smiled huge and couldn't take her eyes off those two.*

*Just as it came, the music faded away. Ally and Bird bowed to each other.*

*"Not bad Ally... not bad at all." Bird winked at her and looked up and hollered "What did you think blondie!?"*

*Scota freaked and backpedaled away trying desperately to stay hidden.*

*Ally looked at Bird almost in a panic and exclaimed "Nooo!"*

*Bird just smiled, and kept looking up as he said "Oh yes."*

*Bird hollered again saying "Listen to me very carefully Scota. If you don't come out of hiding in the next ten seconds, Alydar's* security will treat you as an intruder. Trust me when I tell you, you'd be better off facing the king's army on a rampage, than that."

Ally whispered to Bird "That's mean. You know I wouldn't do that. You're just scaring her on purpose."

"Damn straight Skippy. Ally? Let loose the primary defenses but hold your fire."

"No. She's likely scared out of her wits as it is already!"

"DO IT woman... and don't argue with me," Bird commanded in a no nonsense tone.

Auto tracking guns appeared seemingly out of nowhere. Everyone of them pointed at Scota.

"JUST ONE of those... would level Edinburgh. Now, I'll ask you only once more. You coming out of hiding? Tick tock blondie!"

The voice Bird was waiting for finally came.

"I ONLY WANTED TO HELP!" Scota hollered bawling her eyes out in fear.

"SECURITY!............ stand down."

"Asshole," Ally said admonishing Bird.

Scota was cowering in a tiny ball when the scary weapons went back to wherever it was they came from. Suddenly, the 'door' Scota came through opened again. Fight or flight as the saying goes. Scota chose the latter. She didn't understand it but she knew it somehow brought her to this strange place... perhaps it would take her back. She made it only to the edge as a powerful redheaded man grabbed her as he walked out of it.

"A Guardian once said... some doors shouldn't be opened," Bird said grabbing Scota by the arm.

Scota yanked her arm and pulled a small blade and pointed it at Bird.

"I only wanted tuh help! I doen knoe where I am! Theh music with no orchestra...this place! I... I... I ONLY WANTED TUH HELP!" Scota hollered as she dropped to her knees crying.

Bird looked down at her and said "There's an old saying... it says 'be careful what you wish for... you just might get it."

Scota expected to be beaten... possibly killed. She knew she really crossed a line now. When Bird's hand came down however, she noticed it wasn't swinging... it was kindly reaching out. What Bird said next utterly floored her.

"Well, you're here now so... care for a tour?"

Scota was still crying and asked "Tell me true. The Chronicles yeh told... it's true isn't it?"

"And if I told you it was?"

"Bird Iem sorry... I just wanna go home. I woen tell ennyone wut I saw I promise! I... I... I jes wanna go home!"

"I'm not stopping you. Go then. No one would believe you, they'll think you're crazy, and lock you away somewhere." Bird then smiled and said "Ooooorrrrr.... you could stay, and learn the most amazing 'sciencey stuff' ever!"

"Yeh not be angry wif me?"

"I know you're scared so I'll overlook the thick accent. Look Scota, truth is, I have ways to make you forget. Everything you did and saw... erased. You would NEVER remember any of this. Yes Scota I'm angry with you. You promised me something and you broke that promise. I know you didn't come here to hurt me but the fact is you may have hurt yourself far worse. I told you be careful what you wish for. You want to help? Fine. Learn my world... help me hide it from your sister and all the others. If ANY one would understand and appreciate my world it's you. That's your only choices. Stay and help, or I wipe your memories... choose."

Sobbing, and coughing, Scota asked "Can all this magic fix my cough?"

"SCOTA!" Bird hollered angrily. "FIRST lesson. There is no magic... period... nada... none. Don't EVER call it that again."

Scota was afraid again and cowered as she said "Aye, Iem sorry."

"You done scaring little girls?" Ally asked in a snotty tone.

"Ditch the tone woman, and I mean like right fucking now," Bird said looking at Ally directly.

Ally just stuck her tongue out at Bird and gently pulled Scota up.

"This world isn't sunshine and roses Scota," Bird started. "It has wonders and nightmares just like I said. You have a lot to learn as I said. I won't pretend you don't, and I'll not sugar coat it like *your adopted sister here. You don't belong here. Look at you, you're so scared you call it magic. Yet look around you, and tell me... why fear? Why not wonder and awe? Because you don't understand that's why. Now you know why I didn't share this with you. I gave you two choices... pick one... I won't ask again. And by the way, yes."*

*"Yes what?" Scota said not understanding.*

*"Yes Ally and I believe we can fix your cough. Now, your choice?"*

*Scota was scared as hell but something Bird said changed her life forever. Bird was right. He hadn't hurt her even though he had every right to. He was the same Bird she always knew so yeah, why fear and not wonder? Scota would remember those words for all her days.*

*"Yeh be right, I don't understand this magical place. Aye I knoe it be sciencey stuff but... if yer will'in tuh teach me... Iel be will'in tuh learn."*

*Bird looked over his shoulder and spoke to the tech.*

*"Door! Open to the cave on the hill. Let Scota through but until I say otherwise, do NOT follow her orders or voice commands again. Is that order clear?"*

*"MRU" the mechanical voice said as it opened.*

*"Scota, first lesson is there's no magic. Second lesson is, until you learn otherwise, don't worry about how something works, only trust that it does."*

*With that, Bird pushed her through the door.*

*Scota was back where she started. The door closed and once it did... she ran for the inn. When Bird showed up later, she wouldn't go anywhere near him.*

*Bird looked at the door as it closed and said "Well Ally, as Lone would say... we're proppuh fucked now."*

*Smiling, Ally said "Ya know... I don't think so."*

*"Here's hoping you're right," Bird said as he walked off and headed back to his day.*

*Talking to herself, Alydar quoted Bird saying "Yep, this just got interesting."*

# Chapter 24:

## *"Piece One... And A One Piece"*

Roenas had decided that for this event, he was going to have his family by his side. He had received word from Lone that the now famous 'piece one' has been built and certified. It was the first piece of the ring that was completed. Lone said until that piece was built, he was holding reservations. Once he knew for sure it existed, he said the rest would be a certainty. Now, Roenas climbed the steps at Freedom Point with something that stood there once before.

"My fellow 51'rs, I bring to the balcony today something very familiar to many, and totally unknown to many more. This very item marked the days once to Rhana's challenge. In the days when VC was being built, we also built the landers. Rhana challenged us to get him back to Lady Rahgaa's home in one year. He also challenged us to give him ships mighty enough to stand up to Tamarak himself. With less than a quarter of our current population... we did just that. Everyday I came to this stand, and ripped away another number until the day came that we reached zero. Shortly thereafter was the Battle Of Tuhleesia. Today I bring it forth once more. Today, there are 357 numbers on it... not 365. When last we counted, it was downward. This time, we're counting up."

Roenas let his son have a turn and Sal stepped up to the rail.

"We currently are getting Commander Lone's new ship ready. The full size Ghost is but days away. When it is completed, we shall go to work helping the others. A giant ring is being assembled. It has 357 major sections. Every time a new piece is assembled and made ready, another number will come off this stand, just as it has in the past."

Now Zarra took a turn as her son waved her on.

"My fellow Xarans. Rhana gave us a home, a culture, and a means to live and defend ourselves. Name day was his creation to remind us of all that we either lost, gave up, or no longer believed. This ring is our only hope of getting him back. When you look at it, and see the numbers climb, know that with every page we grow closer to the day when we will bring Rhana home to us. Commander Lone?"

Lone was smiling from down below and called up "Yes Wing Zarranen?"

"Today we found out the first piece of this mighty device has been completed. Would you mind if this time... you did the honors?"

Still smiling, Lone said "Not at all."

Lone climbed the stairs and saluted the family Wings. He reached over, and to thousands of cheers, ripped the number '1' off the stand.

Lone looked out and said "Only 356 more to go. Let's bring Rhana home shall we!?"

Applause rang out all over Victory City.


Turannen was beside the Guardians and, in front of the regents.

"My fellow wolves, I commend you on the success you have made of these meetings. We have had 5 so far and all have gone well. I have studied Rhana's world, and I have some suggestions if you would like to hear them?"

All the regents nodded or waved him on.

"My good regents, we have in the past, made plans that were to be known to only a few. For obvious reasons this was done but, I feel we gain nothing but the mistrust of our fellow Tuhleesians if we continue to do so."

"What did you have in mind Guardian?" Tahl asked.

"We meet for one day to hear your concerns. I suggest we hold our secrets that need holding, for the morning. Later, we allow any and all who wish to see their system in action. ANY wolf of any stature may come, and watch their leaders... and their system of government... at work. Make sure you keep anything that needs to remain secret for the morning session, and leave the issues of public concerns for the afternoon."

Regent now, Teekor asked "Will they be allowed to participate?" referring to the planned crowd.

"No. But they will be allowed to see their system at work. Regent Teekor, if you are to be governed, wouldn't you wish to see how that system works, and insure that it's done fairly?"

With a smile, Teekor said "I would indeed," and he sat back down.

There was discussion on the matter but in the end, the regents agreed it was a good idea. They also said they would make it known among the clans that any wolf of any stature may attend the afternoon session. That new plan would stun but greatly please a population as a whole.

Now Turannen spoke again.

"Also Regents, as is my task, I control technology. Lately I've been approached by my fellow Guardians for being too guarded on releasing it to our people. I disagree but will comply with their wishes. Lady Prime once said a stream is good, a flood is not. I wholeheartedly agree. As such I intend to not release such tech... not yet. I have talked with Guardian Riisa and she agrees. The schools will teach of this new tech FIRST, before it is released to all of you. Having to gain knowledge, but after the fact, has hurt us as a whole. Many of you still don't utilize the tablets to their full potential. We feel knowledge before hand... and not after... is in our best interest. Also, the tech I will release will be for medical purposes first. I now offer this to the floor for debate."

That one caused great debate. In the end though, Turannen's plan was mostly intact. He also explained the 'trickle down effect' and how it would be put into place for all wolves. That he told them, would insure the new tech would already have knowledgeable wolves to go with it.

"Lastly, this new tech will require power we currently don't have. Many of you have been using generators, or simply using the solar cells on the tablets themselves to recharge them. Also, many of you have been to Rhana's world. Planet 51, and the city where Atoemahn resides, are powered by large generators and provide power to the city as a whole. I intend to make that the first tech I release that is non medical in nature. We will use wind, or currents in rivers or oceans, to generate the power we will soon require. A 3 season plan is in place to generate power to all Krannen bases and hospitals, both Krannen and civilian. There is one system already in place and we are using it as a test. When we are certain of all aspects of it, it will be released to all of you. The clan meeting houses in each clan along with the temples will be next, followed by all the clan wolves afterwards. By 7 seasons we intend to have it all done. Each clan will be taught the sciences, and will be responsible for implementing and maintaining your own systems."

The only complaints to that by the regents were the devices. They wanted them out of sight for two reasons. They didn't want their landscapes cluttered with equipment. The also didn't want to point any enemy to the one spot that could cripple them. Turannen heard them, agreed, and said he would keep it in mind.

Ravenahl was next. She had plans of her own.

"Regent Tahl, may I ask you a question?"

"Any you'd like Guardian."

"How long of a journey is it for you to travel to the Healing center in Rolaana's clan?"

"Most of a sun. In poor weather longer."

"I assume you are aware, any major injury or illness and time becomes your enemy yes?"

"I am."

"Now that more and more air ships become available to help with that, they still need to get to you, then get the injured to the hospital. While faster, it's still time the injured may not have. Would you agree?"

"I would indeed. I assume you have a solution?"

"I do," Ravenahl replied. "Every clan has some form of medical place. Most are disorganized or, worse, filled with what Rhana calls 'old wives tales'. I intend to set up proper facilities in each clan. All standardized so none will be different. That way, if needed, the healer can come to you, rather than the other way around. If the injuries are too severe, the healer can at least see to the wolf's care till transport can arrive. Otherwise, they will be staffed and capable for any medical need minor to medium in severity. While there may be some resistance to this, I don't care and as Lady Rahgaa once said... this is non negotiable. I'll be counting on you to assist with that 'local resistance' I mentioned. I'll not have my fellow Tuhleesians trusting in, nor relying on, 'smoke and mirrors', as the phrase goes."

Smiling, Tahl said "You can count on me Guardian."

Teekor stood up.

"Lady Prime, we have heard of your recent near tragedy. I am certain all the Regents here will agree with me when I say we are truly happy for you... and that, said tragedy was averted, and not made reality."

Rahgaa nodded a kind smile at him, but it was really for all of them.

"That said, you are directly involved in the rescue of Rhana and the Pilot Prime. Is there anything you can tell us on the matter?"

"Not much I'm afraid," Rahgaa told them as Teekor sat down. "This much I can tell you. Planet 51 will be done shortly with their part, and will be putting their own kind into the efforts we Tuhleesians and the other worlds are putting forth. Pieces of the plan come together daily and while not as much as we'd like, progress is being made."

Rahgaa closed the session with a closing thought. It had become ritual that she herself closed these sessions.

"Before you depart for your clans, I wish to tell you something. I want you to know I am proud of you... and of us. We follow Rhana's dream. He promised to bring us back to our former selves. I have seen many of you treat our alien visitors with grace, wit and charm... but not fear. I have seen you conduct yourselves in the finest of manners when away from home. I have also seen you rise to the challenge Rhana himself laid down before you. While we still have far to go, I have seen you... all of you... survive, thrive and expand. While we Guardians may not acknowledge it, know we are not blind either. We grow each day. Yes we have our adjustment problems but, no creature doing what we are doing would be without those. Even here you have conducted yourselves in the finest manner possible. Send to our people my thanks and... my belief in them... and in you. May your travels be without incident."

All bowed at the honor, and this meeting... was done.


Tiiveer pulled Rahgaa aside on the way out and told her "Rahgaa my love, you are still a target for Tamarak. THIS time I'm telling you I have a secret plan to stop him. What I'm not telling you is what or who is involved. Just know, that is the reason I am not telling even you."

"While I'm not happy with these secrets, I do understand. Do what you must and tell me only what you feel you need to."

Tiiveer gave her a soft kiss and said "I certainly will."



Shreya pulled into the minefield. She headed for the station but didn't go in.

"Lone has asked for a status report," Quaran said on an ultra secure channel.

"Tell him his builders are safe and... disappointed."

"Care to clarify the latter?"

Giljor laughed and said "As I guessed, not a single asteroid got anywhere near us. My people were a tad annoyed they had nothing to shoot at."

"MRU. Lone said Xarans will be free to assist the builders soon, if that's alright with you."

"Many of my kind are becoming... I believe the phrase is... homesick? Anyway, I intend to rotate out half, and leave the remaining half as they have become skilled at the task at hand. I'll allow 100 at a time and work out a way to rotate the crews so as to avoid this mental malady, but still insure quality and progress."

"Sounds wise not to mention fair. I'll let Lone know. Anything else?" Quaran asked.

"Indeed. Tell him, 3 more pieces have been started, and 2 more are now complete."

With a smile, Quaran told him as he swung around for home "I have no doubt Roenas will be pleased."

"Excuse me?"

"Heh heh... nevermind. Bartender out."

*When Quaran broke the minefield's perimeter... he let the two Squadron Leaders out of their rooms.*

*For the first time since they stepped foot on 51, the Pilots were in the new hangar, and not in VC. They expected to be hustled to a door and 'upstairs' but... that's not what happened. They walked out and were greeted by the Mahrek himself.*

*"Neither of you were ever here. Am I clear?"*

*"CRYSTAL!" both shouted in unison.*

*"Even the Prime has been told you never made it here, and were sent on a mission on Aarika that just happened to 'pop up'."*

*"Understood!" they said but never dropped their salutes.*

*"At ease you two."*

*Now the salutes dropped.*

*"Ryklan, you have impressed me. Tandor, you have as well. When your team mate arrives, I'll tell you why you've been brought here."*

*"Hail hail the gang's all here. Tin Man reporting for duty!" Tinnaaren said walking up to his comrades and saluting Lone.*

*Kindly, but with purpose, Lone said "I'll give you five minutes to catch up but then, it's down to business," and he walked off as all 3 hugged and chatted.*

*Five minutes later, the three came over to Lone.*

*"Tin Man, I promised to let you help. Right now, nothing of consequence is going on with that plan. Should that change I will come and get you."*

*"Understood. Am I to assume I am going back home for now?"*

*Lone grinned slyly and said "Indeed you all are but... heh heh... with an upgrade."*

*Lone waved a hand to the floor below. All 3 looked over the rail and saw a familiar sight. Well, 3 of them actually.*

*"Are those our X2's?" Ryklan asked.*

*"They are. I want you to go down, look them over but mostly, acquaint yourself with the crew working on them. THEY are your new ground crew until the upgrades are removed. Take 20 minutes*

*then, meet me in the Ghost meeting room."*

*All 3 saluted and headed down to their ships.*

*All assembled in the meeting room now, Lone laid out his plan.*

*"You 3 were selected by me personally. Tell me, did you notice anything different about your X2's?"*

*"Thank you for the honor of your trust Commander, and no I didn't," Tandor told him.*

*"Nor did I," Tin Man added.*

*"And it's to stay that way. I'm about to give you information that only Guardian Tiiveer knows, other than yourselves."*

*The 3 Pilots were highly honored. They were also determined to show Lone he did not choose poorly.*

*"Tamarak is planning on tapping into Tuhleesia's core. We believe he is hiding on one of the other continents. Tandor, you yourself said the X2's would be spotted coming down from orbit did you not?"*

*"I did. Not only that, I stand by that assumption."*

*"And I agree with you. So, unless you go to low orbit, you can't get to the other continents. Also, while you'll get there, you run out of fuel to return. As such, I had my people modify them. The X2's are fine, it's the 'getting there' that is the problem... a problem I just negated for you 3 and you 3 alone."*

*"And what did you do to them?" Ryklan asked.*

*"You will spend the next 3 days in them practicing. Also, till my upgrades are removed, you 3 and our ground crew will be based out of the secret facilities in Teekor's clan. You 3 now have... cat's eye engines."*

*Three pilots were utterly stunned.*

*Lone told them of the secrecy of it, and how they were not to touch nor work on the engines themselves. They were also forbidden to tell anyone, even the base workers, of what they were about to hear.*

*"Know this. I have seen Rhana's history. Every time one of his advanced societies gave advanced tech to a lesser one, it ended in disaster. I wholly believe that. That's why you 3 only are being*

'temporarily' trusted with this. The cat's eye engines we gave you are fully functional but they are earlier models. Also, they are short range only. They will get you only as far as the back end of Tuhleesia and no further. Also, they have fail-safes in them to prevent you from using them in space itself. You are ONLY being given these to combat Tamarak and the distance problem. Joyride with them and I will personally remove you from them... and not the other way around... am I clear?"

A warning from the Mahrek Tuuren? Oh they were very clear.

"Lastly, unless you have no other choice, you are not to engage them while other X2's are around including your own teams... clear?"

"As an X-stone," replied all 3.


The three pilots spent the next 2 days with one Ghost or another. Hours of classroom science and hours of actual practice. All 3 had been in Cat's Eye jumps with the Ghosts before but... never doing it themselves. Ryklan was a little let down as the speed of it all wasn't as fast as she thought it would be. While it obviously had the speed, the sensation of it was a bit of a let down to her. Now, Ghost 3 was taking 3 pilots, and their craft, back to a secret base.


Bird was fairly quiet this morning. He had told Ciana that he was taking Scota out for the day to help him with some local items. Ciana wished them a good day and went back to the counter at the inn.

Scota was nervous as hell. Bird was pissed and she knew what Bird was capable of when he was like that. Finding herself the object of that anger wasn't a pleasant thought. He was also holding onto her arm as he took her in the cave.

"Door... Lander bay please."

"Female not permitted by direct order. Require vocal override," the door said.

Now Bird smiled seeing the door finally got it right.

"Entry permitted... entry only for now... vocal authorization BirdOfPrey, Ghost 1."

"Authorization validated... welcome aboard Commander,"

and the energy sheet that so scared Scota was back.

Scota was backpedaling and trying to break Bird's grip.

"Please Bird, I haven't told a soul I swear... I DOEN WANNA DIE!"

"Oh fer Christ's sake... now I know how Lone feels," and Bird threw her through the door.

Scota shrieked and fell to her knees on the other side. Bird walked in behind her and the door closed. She made a run for it but, like Salyan planned, she simply went through the energy screen remaining in Alydar's bay.

"Well, so much for plan A. Wouldn't happen to have a plan B would ya?" Bird chuckled. Bird held out his hand to a crumpled and crying Scota and said "If you want to live... fine... then follow me."

Scota resigned herself to her fate, held out her hand, and mumbled "I only wanted to help."

"I know Scota. Now, lets see if I can help you." Bird walked Scota back to the door and said "Door... scan the human with me when I tell you." Bird kindly looked down on the sad blond and said "Your about to be hit with beams of light. Don't be afraid and know that they won't hurt you."

"Okay," said a dejected lass.

Bird gave the order and the door did exactly as he said. Green and blue beams of light came out from the door and scanned her literally from head to toe and back again.

"Scan complete... please identify female," the door said.

Bird exclaimed "The female is Scota Thalin. Grant her access to any door in the bay, but entry and exit are by my orders only."

"Access granted."

Now Scota was curious.

"What did you do?" she asked Bird.

"I gave you access to this big room your in. Scota listen to me. You walked into a life that's so advanced compared to what your used to, that everything is unknown, and therefore scary. But you forget 2 things."

A shy, but now curious Scota said impishly "Tell me?"

"One, YOU said you wanted to see 'the world'. Did you really *think it would be anything like you're used to?"*

Softly, Scota said *"I really didn't think about it."*

*"And as such, you found out the hard way... it isn't."*

*"I'll say."*

Bird continued, *"And two... look around you Scota. I guarantee you you're over thinking things."*

*"Hmm... 'clarify',"* she said with a slight smile mimicking Bird's story and Lone's phrase.

*"Scota, you're not gonna understand everything here in a day or two. That said, stay with what you DO know. Yes this room is big but... keep it basic. Large yes but, still a room. As such, it has walls, a floor and a roof yes?"*

*"Aye. Huge but, it has those things."*

*"Stick with that then. The floor may be a strange material but, it is still a floor. Don't concern yourself with why something here works... only how, and that it does."*

*"Hmm, can yeh be a little more clear on that last bit?"*

*"Okay, the door. Do you know how it works?"*

*"Not a clue."*

*"Yet, you know what it does yes?"*

*"Sort of."*

Bird then changed tactics. Pointing to a door down on the main floor, he told Scota what to do.

*"Scota, there's a door in the cave. Activate it, that means turn it on, and it brings you here. Think of this, ya know the door between the kitchen and the main part of the inn?"*

*"Aye."*

*"Well then, it takes you between those 2 places only right?"*

*"Of course it does."*

*"What if it did more. What if you could tell it to take you to Angus's... or Mary's. Wouldn't that be nice?"*

*"Aye. Save time too."*

*"The doors are programmed to listen to only me or Alydar. You came here the other day because of a unique circumstance. It opened for you when it shouldn't have. That said... give it a try."*

Now Scota was leery but curious.

"How?"

"Each door is connected to all the others. I told it you could go to any one in this room, but this room only. Walk up to it." Bird saw her still leery and said "Go ahead. Tell it you want to go to the door on the main floor."

"Yeh want me... to 'talk'... to a door?"

Bird chuckled saying "I know how it sounds but, trust me."

Scota now giggled, and curtsied to the door.

"Fine door, will you take me to the door on the... what did yeh call it?" she asked looking over her shoulder.

"Landing bay... main floor," Bird chuckled.

"Yes door... take me to the 'main floor'."

The door beeped, and opened. Scota backed up some and stared at Bird. He however, just smiled, and pointed to the door down below. It was open too.

"Well blondie... enjoy the sciencey stuff."

Cautiously, she put a hand through. It blew her mind to see it again... down below. She yanked it back hard and stared at her arm... it was still in one piece.

"Nooooooo," Scota said staring at Bird in utter amazement.

"'Fraid so," Bird grinned.

Scota turned, and cautiously put her hand through again. This time, she followed it. Utter amazement was on her face when she came out... down below. Bird smiled, popped himself off the railing, and walked through himself.

"So, that was for two things. One, to show you how advanced my world is. Two, just like your door in the inn, it takes you from one place to another, nothing more. The difference with my doors is, the two places aren't necessarily attached, heh heh."

"BLOODY HELL!" Scota bellowed in amazement.

Laughing, Bird said "Oh, Lone would like you."

Now, seeing Bird's world, Scota put story together with reality.

"Noooo... wait... Al...Aly... Alydar?"

"Yes dear, I'm here," boomed a voice through the bay.

Scota stood straight and looked around.

*"No yeh not, jes yer bloody voice is!"*

*"True, but, only to a degree."*

*Scota was a tad upset now. She just realized her 'sister' wasn't exactly what she thought.*

*"Bloody hell! You really are the ship!? Jes like in Bird's story?"*

*"To quote the Commander, this is the small one. Yes dear, just like in Rhana's story."*

*"SMALL one!?? Bloody hell! But... but... no wait. I seen yeh! Yer as real as I am!"*

*"Yes... aaaand no. The Commander hasn't gotten to that part yet."*

*Alydar was referring to 'The Chronicles'. Bird had only gotten as far as him meeting Symda.*

*Scota was still trying to process it all when Bird stunned her.*

*"Well blondie, how'd you like to get rid of that cough?"*

*Now she was cautious again.*

*"What crazy plan yeh got now Mistuh Yankee?"*

*"Scota look, you're still scared, if I were you I'd be too. I thought if I showed you all this science around you has benefits, then perhaps you'd be more willing to learn... and less willing to be afraid."*

*Scota had no clue where she was. Had no idea what was around her. NO idea how that damn door did what it did. What she did know was that Bird, so far, hasn't lied. Not about what she's seen so far anyway. Standing tall, she looked Bird in the eyes and, pulled out every manner she's learned so far.*

*"Lead the way," she said ever so politely.*

*Another door and Bird and Scota were in a hallway. Two doors down, med bay opened automatically. That caught Scota off guard. Bird walked in realizing he was gonna hafta be real careful of simple things he usually takes for granted.*

*"Kinda cool huh?" Bird said holding out his hand, and referring to the auto doors.*

*"No, it's actually quite nice," Scota said referring to the temperature in the hallway.*

*Bird just shook his head, and waited for Scota. Looking everywhere, she finally took his hand... slowly. She jumped a little when the doors closed again. The equipment in this room scared the hell out of her. Boxes with pictures that moved, were everywhere. And most of them were making the strangest of noises.*

*"Alydar, give me scanning bots please."*

*Scota grabbed onto Bird's arm as a hypo-spray popped up from the table.*

*"Scota, pull your hair back please."*

*Blondie was shaking her head profusely.*

*"Listen lass, if I wanted you hurt... you would be. Now, do as your told."*

*Bird had to pull the dad card even though he didn't want to. Carefully, and slowly, she pulled her long blond locks up. Bird shot her quick where her left shoulder met her neck.*

*"Ow!" she protested.*

*"Oh quit be'in a baby," Bird chuckled.*

*"AAAAYYYYY! A ghost!" Scota screamed seeing an apparition form a few feet away.*

*"Actually, I'm the only Ghost around here. Believe it or not Scota... that's you," Bird said cheerfully.*

*"Noooo, Iem right here!"*

*"And there. Put your hand to the side, and turn it. Like you do the mannequins in John's shop. Go ahead."*

*Scota refused to go anywhere near it so Bird did it. As he said, it turned, just like he promised. Now Scota tried it. When she turned it far enough and saw her own ghostly face, she backpedaled and shrieked again. Bird now had work to do and frankly, was growing tired of Scota's behavior.*

*"Scota!... Magic and ghosts?" Bird admonished sternly.*

*Scota shrank and softly said "Don't exist... only sciencey stuff."*

*"EVEN if?"*

*"Even if I don't understand it," she said like a schoolgirl caught doing something wrong.*

*Bird turned back to the 'ghost'.*

*"Bots... I want a full scan on the subjects lungs including mass spec. Report your findings on the latter as soon as they're*

*available."*

*The doors opened again and Scota's eyes immediately focused on them. She ran and hugged tight who came in them. It was Ally.*

*"It's okay dear. I want you to know..." and Bird shot her a look shaking his head. "I want you to know you don't have to be scared. Neither I nor Bird will harm you."*

*Bird shook his head because he knew Ally was going to tell Scota what she really was. Scota was barely holding it together as it is. If Bird was right about Scota, the less scared she was the better.*

*"Come Scota... look... like Bird said, that's you. Would you like me to explain?"*

*Scota just nodded her head but never let go of Ally.*

*"What Bird did to your neck, he put thousands of machines inside you. Machines so small you can't even see them. They tell us what's going on inside your body."*

*"WHAT!?" Scota exclaimed and started scratching everywhere.*

*Ally laughed and said "That won't work. Don't worry, they won't hurt you and you can't feel them... I promise. Bird is trying to find out why you cough."*

*"And those machines will tell you?"*

*Sweetly, Ally looked down and said "Mm hmm."*


*Bird turned around and said "Mass spec is in Ally. Looks like we were right."*

*Scota was staring at her ghostly form and said "Ere now... right about what?"*

*"Your lungs. In terms you can understand, their covered in dirt. This is special dirt though, and comes from only one place."*

*"I bathe regular like!" Scota exclaimed proudly.*

*Bird chuckled.*

*"Scota, do you know what a volcano is?"*

*"Kahnt say I do."*

*Bird had a thought, and decided to break Scota, one way or another.*

*"Would you like me to show you?"*

*"Aye, ya know I think I would!"*

*"Okay Missy, come with me," and Bird grabbed her arm*

*again and took her out of med bay.*

*Bird made Scota work the door. She still felt silly talking to one but, couldn't deny the results. Back in the bay once more, Bird walked her to the ramp.*

*"See that yellow line there on the floor?" Bird asked. Scota nodded and Bird said "Don't cross it." He looked at the avatar and asked "Are we clear?"*

*"You sure about this?" Ally asked.*

*"Miss Alydar... did... I... stutter?"*

*"No Sir. You have less than 4 minutes and you won't be."*

*"Thank you. Now... drop it." Bird turned to Scota as the floor and part of the wall, simply went down and asked "Tell me lass, does THAT look familiar?"*

*Scota grabbed Bird's leg and fell to the floor. She saw the inn... from about 300 feet up and... 3000 feet out.*

*"You're not falling dear and... you can let go," Bird said confidently. Alydar was calling out times and Bird said "Look at it Scota. That is exactly what you think it is and yes, you are EXACTLY where you think you are. Now, remember that and... follow me. Ally? Close it up."*

*Rampway back up and Bird was heading through yet another door with the blond one in tow.*

*Permission granted from Ghost 1 himself, and Scota was now looking at the greatest sciencey stuff... ever. Bird took her to the cockpit.*

*"How... how come... no wait, I'd have seen you!" Scota said as she saw the view out the viewscreen.*

*"Sciencey stuff kiddo. Alydar is invisible. Another one of those things you don't wanna think too deep about. Suffice to say she is and that's all you need to know."*

*Scota was starting to look at things with more amazement now. Bird just chuckled.*

*"Trust me Scota, there are creatures that grew up with this stuff, and they have the same look on their faces when they see this."*

*Scota sat down and immediately started slapping the chair.*

*"Stop! STOP! Stop that!" she told it.*

*The chair auto-configured itself to her frame. She figured if you could talk to doors, why not chairs?*

"Sorry," Bird giggled, "I should'a warned you bout that."

Scota was now looking out with awe.

"So, we're actually flying?"

"Technically, you're hovering."

"Wazzat then?" Scota giggled.

Bird smiled, and said "You're in the air yes but, stationary."

"Stationary?"

"Not moving."

"Can we?"

"Can we what?"

Scota asked shyly now.

"Fly?"

"Scota my dear? Sit back and... heh heh... get comfortable."

Suddenly, Scota's world shifted as Bird took Alydar's lander out of hover and, out of the bay.

Scota saw the sea but, it was below her. A few times, like Triikon did once, she stamped the floor.

"Hmm," was all she said each time she did.

Now Bird was getting the attitude he was hoping for. Scota saw Bird controlling this mighty ship and he was as carefree as could be. As long as he was that way, then she was content to see the awe inspiring view out ahead of her.

"Scota look!" Bird said as he banked left and went into a slow circle.

Down below was a sailing ship under full sail. Scota freaked however. Luckily for Bird it was in a better way than previously.

"Noooo!" said Scota not believing what she was seeing.

"What's wrong Scota?" Alydar's disembodied voice said.

"I know thah ship! It left our bay TWO weeks ago! I recognize it's flag! But... but... we've only been going for a few minutes!"

"Sciencey stuff is cool huh?" Bird chuckled.

Scota scrunched her face and said "There's that word again. Why do I get the feeling it don't mean to you what it do to me?"

"Heh heh, that's cause it don't," Bird said with a grin.

*The speed below was almost beyond Scota's comprehension. She however, refused to look anywhere else. Suddenly, Bird went back to that hover thing he mentioned earlier.*

*"This is the first piece of land we've come up on since we left. I stopped for a reason. Does it look anything like you know?"*

*"Not at all," Scota said with true awe and wonder. "Is this one of those far off places you promised me!?"*

*"Yep."*

*"Where are we?"*

*Bird picked up speed again, and heading out once more just said "Panama."*

*Bird was back over open sea again. What really threw Scota was it turned to night time, then daytime again. She actually saw the line go from day to night and thought it the most beautiful thing.*

*"Scota, you've been quoting Lone I see. Would you like to fly the way he does?"*

*"Can I?"*

*"Promise me. You'll 'enjoy'... and not be 'afraid'. Promise me that and I'll show you."*

*With a smile, Scota said "Promise."*

*"Alydar, how about a little motivation?"*

*"Preference?"*

*"How about, considering where I'm going, a little Elvis, from the island movies perhaps?"*

*Out of nowhere, Scota's world was filled with music. A driving beat she actually liked. She felt it was scandalous, but she liked it all the same. Alydar picked Elvis's 'Rock-a-hula Baby'.*

*"Oh my dear, heh heh, you know me so well," Bird jested. "Now Scota, mix what you hear, with what you see, and you'll understand," Bird told her.*

*She did as told and... she did understand.*

*Bird slowed again but didn't hover this time. As the first verse kicked in, Bird banked right, and cruised the coast.*

*"Where are we now?" Scota asked with glee.*

*"Honestly?... The other side of the world. Welcome to paradise."*

"I ain't nevuh seen such strange trees!" Scota said looking down.

Bird was cruising over and around... Honolulu.

"They're called palm trees. Now... hang on!" and bird kicked it up a notch.

Flying sideways through valleys with waterfalls and the most lush forest anywhere, he did a roll just to shake Scota up. To Bird's surprise, and delight, she asked him ever so nicely... to do it again. Bird was sort of dancing in his chair as he flew. The music fit the scene outside to perfection and Scota just couldn't get enough. Scota was now officially, a flying junky.

Rachid Taha's 'Hey Antar' was next and Scota was swinging her skirt to the tune. It had the strangest instruments, and she didn't understand a word, but was loving it all the same. Seems she wasn't just a flight junky now but, a music one as well. Bird cruised all the islands, and made music and real life meld with ease.

Song over and Bird was hovering over hell itself.

"This Scota, is a volcano," Bird told his stunned companion.

Bird was hovering over Kilauea on the big island of Hawaii. Scota had no words for the horror below her.

"The orange stuff is called lava. It's what happens when you, well, boil dirt. Not exactly accurate but it's the best way I can explain it so that you'll understand. That is what is deep inside the Earth. There are places all over the planet like this. It's where the hot soil leaks up to the surface."

Scota did indeed understand. Horrified, but understood.

"And this is what made me sick?"

"Not this one but... yes. Scota, you ever boil potato's?"

"Aye I have. Wazzat got to do with anything?"

"Sciencey stuff. Use that as a reference. Boil them, and the water bubbles right?"

"Right."

"But yet, the white stuff hardens on top of it don't it?"

"Aye."

"That, on a larger scale, is the Earth. Hard crust on top of hot liquid. That lava is the bubbling pot, except it's dirt not water."

"My stars!" Scota exclaimed quoting Bird's story.

"Now, what made you sick is much closer to Scotland. Imagine," and Bird pointed below, "If you capped that. Like the pot of boiling water, what happens?"

"Aye, I get it, the lid pops off!"

"Now imagine, that below you, capped for days and building up. There's one more thing I want to show you," and Bird headed north.

Mount Fuji was next.

Bird told her "See that mountain? Imagine the lava building up... under that. It would blow the top third off with an explosion you couldn't comprehend. The lava gets blown kilometers into the air. It's massive Scota, truly massive. One like that, blew up near you in a place called Iceland. It was so massive, it lasted for months. It's what caused the black skies."

"Months!?"

"Aye lass. The one that made you sick blew in fall of 1755 and lasted till march or so of 1756."

Scota had no words and simply couldn't picture it based on what she saw out the viewscreen.

"The dark skies were worse than smoke... its was fine dust. You breathed it in when you kept sneaking outside. You breathed in so much over time that your lungs are covered in a fine substance similar to mud. That's why water bothers you, it disturbs it as the water loosens it even more. Your body can't break it down, and you've been sick ever since."

She would have laughed at Bird 2 days ago. Today was a different story.

"Scota, your coughing is getting worse. The scans I took earlier tell me, if it's not taken care of... and soon... you'll be dead by time you hit the age Ciana is now."

Scota was in tears now.

"Bird, I... I... I doen wanna die. Not yet!"

"I don't want to see you die either. Your sister would be crushed, and Ally and I would miss you terribly. Lucky for you, my 'doctor'in' is as advanced as this ship! Heh heh."

Sniffling, Scota asked, "Can you? Fix me I mean?"

"I believe so but, like I told someone else recently, we have to *do what seems wrong in order to do what's right."*

*Scota was in tears and hugged Bird tight from her chair.*

*"Not like Ciana does but... I love you Bird."*

*Scota didn't know what else to say. Neither did Bird so he just hugged her back.*

*"I told you, you can always count on me."*

*Scota sat up and straightened herself out.*

*"Say what yeh need, and I'll do whatevuh needs do'in."*

*"Well, first, I gotta make it worse I'm afraid," Bird told her.*

*"Wuffaw?" Scota said starting to grin again.*

*Bird chuckled and said "Yeeeeaah... I wouldn't let him hear you say that. Anyway, I have to put you near water, then scan you again. I need to see you when you're okay and when you're not. I got the first earlier, now it's time for the latter. But," and Bird winked saying "Nothing says it can't be at least fun right?"*

*"Heh heh. Make it so number one!" Scota exclaimed quoting yet another piece of the Chronicles.*

*Bird just laughed and headed southeast.*

*Bird crossed the Yucatan Peninsula, and headed into the Gulf.*

*"Ally, care to join us?" Bird asked sweetly as he headed aft.*

*"Doing?"*

*"Going for a swim of course. You got a suit for Scota?"*

*"I have one that might fit. Sounds like fun," and the ladies headed to the lander's version of the doll house.*

*"Women actually wear this!?" Scota barked.*

*She was wearing a one piece suit Ally found in her collection.*

*"Yeah, why?" Ally asked not understanding Scota's protest.*

*"Yeh hafta ask why!? Iem practically naked!"*

*"Remember, you're in our world. While I now understand your discomfort, your 'morals' don't apply here. Come now, let's not keep Bird waiting," and Ally took Scota aft.*

*Scota felt extremely uncomfortable. That got worse when she saw Bird in nothing but a pair of long shorts.*

*"Bout time ladies. Ally if you'd be so kind, a nice diving height would be lovely."*

*Alydar complied and opened the ramp and lowered to a height of 20 or so feet. Bird smiled, saluted, and did a swan dive off the ramp. Ally wasn't taking any chances, and pushed a shrieking Scota into the waters off Florida. Scota forgot all about her 'morals' when Ally joined them. She dove from what looked like a hole in the sky. When it closed, Scota saw nothing but sunshine and clouds.*

*Bird laughed when she shrieked like a little girl, and the 'big fish' as Scota called them, shrieked back playfully.*

*"Scota? They're called dolphins. Don't worry, they're friendly. They like to play, and if your nice to them, they'll take you for a ride!" Bird said happily.*

*Scota tread water and watched Bird make nice. Two more came over to him and Bird didn't have a care in the world. One of them finally let Bird grab a dorsal fin and take him for a ride. Scota thought it was a wonder to behold.*

*Ally showed her how to make nice. Ally was having a blast as she knew of dolphins, but never had the pleasure of meeting them. Scota finally loosened up and now, all 3 were playing with a pod's worth of bottle nose dolphins. Scota started coughing finally. At one point she went under the water because of it. She found herself being lifted to the surface shortly thereafter by two kind fish. Bird would later correct her saying they were actually mammals, not fish.*

*A 30 minute swim and Scota could take no more. The ramp in the sky was back and wrapped in a towel, Bird held her as Alydar went super slow.*

*"Watch this blondie," Bird said cradling the coughing lass.*

*Scota looked out and smiled through her coughing. She saw 50 or so dolphins swimming in formation and chasing or running with Alydar. Bird put the ramp up as Scota waved goodbye to her aquatic friends. Bird hustled her into med bay and got the scans he needed as Alydar took them back to Skye.*

# Chapter 25:

## "Sometimes, Ya Gotta Do What's Wrong... To Do What's Right"

"Are you sure this is wise? While I appreciate the assistance, I can't help but think this is the very warning Rhana, and Ahdeera, spoke of," Tiiveer said over the secure comm channel.

Lone replied "While I understand your concerns, it is that very Rhana I am imitating now by doing this."

"Care to, heh heh... 'clarify'?"

Lone laughed saying "Yeah, still sounds wrong coming from you. Anyway, I'm doing what's wrong... to do what's right. Yes I gave them advanced tech but, I'm also shielding not only them from it but, my fellow Tuhleesians as well. I meant what I said Guardian, when that tech is no longer required, I will retrieve it. Till then, I'm minimizing the exposure... and hopefully maximizing the affect."

Tiiveer responded "As am I. No one here knows of their nature other than they are on a secret mission of yours, and one sanctioned and controlled by me. There is a small set of foothills nearby and I instructed them to only use the cat's eye there and nowhere else as it will shield them from 'prying eyes'."

"Sounds good. One last thing Krannen. I gave Tin Man a box to give to you. Tell him I said you may have it now. What's inside it is from the time of the twins but... it is your tech. Replicate it and... please... use it as wisely as Rhana and I have."

Full of honor, and excited at the new present, Tiiveer honestly told him "It shall be done."

"You sent for me Guardian?" Tinnaaren asked walking into the room.

"I did. I spoke to Commander Lone earlier and he said you

have a box for me?"

"Indeed I do. I was told not to let you know I have it till you asked for it. Now that you have... give me a few minutes to retrieve it please."

Tiiveer nodded and Tin Man left. He came back a few minutes later and handed him the box.

"I was told not to open it and I haven't," the Pilot told him.

Tiiveer opened the box, smiled, and looked up at Tin Man.

"That will be all Pilot, thank you. Would you do me a favor and ask Guardian Trenthaarian to come see me please?"

"Certainly."

Tin Man left the room, and Tiiveer smiled. The bats and the X2's had 'lightning weapons' and while improved since when Ayleen first used them, they were still temperamental. What Lone had given him was... one of the energy pistols from Ship's armory.


Bird was sitting in his room. Sitting alone and... brooding.

"Something wrong boss?" Alydar asked nicely.

"Everything is."

"Well, seeing as how 'everything' is such a small list and all, care to talk about it?"

"You're going to yell at me."

"I promise... I won't."

Bird glared and said "Oh, not only will you but... I may have to turn you off because of it."

"Uh, 'scuse me?"

"Sorry... did I stutter again? I really must stop doing that," Bird said in the snottiest of tones.

Alydar put his room into lock-down. Bird didn't even flinch.

"Okay BirdMan, what's on your mind?"

"Scota."

"Uh... okay?" Alydar said not getting Bird's train of thought.

"As leader of the 7 Ghosts, and protector of the time-line... it falls to me to make the hard decisions."

"And that would be?"

"To let Scota die... naturally."

Alydar was angry, shocked and incensed all at the same time.

*"Not even you would be that cruel!"*

*"Wouldn't I?"*

*Alydar then said something Bird hoped to never hear... she defied him.*

*"I won't let you."*

*Bird sat solemn faced, brought up his HUD, and a few seconds later was in the dark. No lights, no heat, no fancy gadgets and... no Alydar. Thirty seconds later he brought her back up.*

*"You bastard!"*

*"Indeed. I told you we can NEVER be out of sync... ever. IF I ever became 'defective', I could cause some damage. If YOU ever did... whole planets could disappear. While you are truly alive in my opinion, you are still a machine... and a potentially lethal one at that. As an organic being, my capabilities are nowhere near yours. Alydar I have no desire to hurt you, or anyone. But, as it was I who ordered your existence, any damage you did would be my responsibility. That little demonstration wasn't to show you who is boss, it was to show you that 'out of sync' thing? Yeah, never gonna happen."*

*"You would do that, to ME!??"*

*"ONLY... if I had no other choice. Alydar look, you've gone past your original programming, way past it. Remmy and I both knew that would likely happen. I have no problem with you growing my dear, hell I'll even help you. That said, we're in uncharted waters now with you. I know you mean well, but the base laws you were given were never designed for a situation like this. Right now, I need you to trust ME more than ever... not yourself."*

*Alydar may be a machine but, right now she was crying.*

*"But it's Scota... SCOTA! Why would you let her die!?"*

*"Alydar listen to yourself. You're upset and, rightfully so. But there's a perception your not seeing."*

*"And that would be?"*

*Bird sighed and filled in Alydar's lack of perception.*

*"Alydar, take me to England right now, or the states, or anywhere... and you'll find gravestones. If you went to them you'd find many with dates less than Scota's age currently. You would look, you would think 'how sad' but... you would move on after only a few moments. The reason is you didn't know them and, you weren't*

involved with them. Due to our EXTREMELY unique circumstance, we are actually talking to the dead. You forgot what I said as these people are already dead in my time-line."

"Keep talking."

"If I had hurt Scota, I would have repaired the damage I caused. But I didn't, Scota and mother nature did. In natural history, she died young. Now, let's say I go and alter that. What's to say her children wont be the next Hitler, or worse? A child that would have never... and should have never... been born. That is the very interference I told you I refuse to cause."

"Bird?" Alydar said in a shaky voice, "I... I don't like the way this feels."

"Like I told Ryklan, sometimes ya gotta do what's..."

"Yeah yeah," Alydar said cutting him off. She was also crying again and finished with "... this sucks."

Sadly, Bird just said "I know."

"I won't let you kill her. But, I heard what you said and, I won't stop you either. C'mon Bird there HAS to be something!?"

"That's what I was working on. Sadly... I got nuthin'."

Alydar, simply said "Yet."

Suddenly, and slowly, a smile came to Bird's face. The 'yet' Alydar mentioned had arrived. Now Bird was on fire and hopped over to his control panel.

"Alydar, shut off the lock-down and send me..." Bird nearly shouted as he scanned some images.

"Send you what!?" Alydar asked excitedly.

"Heh heh... send me... the avatar."

"On the way!" Alydar said knowing Bird had an idea she didn't.

She didn't care what it was, just as long as there was one. She truly cared for Scota that much.

Ally showed up and didn't even bother to knock.

"Okay boss man, pleeeeeease tell me you got something good."

Bird smiled and spun the monitor around.

"Tell me oh morphing one... think you could look like this?"

Ally smiled and said slyly, "I dunno, you tell me."

She morphed into what Bird showed her. It was a picture of a medical doctor of the period.

"Okay... that really is freaky. Anyway, give him an accent similar to Lone's but not as deep.

"Oi I saaaay Biiird, would sumpthin like dis werk?"

"Heh heh... it would indeed. Ally let me warn you, this option still sucks but, it's all we got. Now, it's up to Scota."

Ally converted back to herself and said "I'll go get her."

"No Ally, I'll go with you," Bird said and both headed out to med bay.


Scota was laying on the med bay bed when Bird and Ally walked in. The auto open doors still freaked her out a bit.

"Scota," Bird started, "...you came into my world. I can't have you here but now, I don't have a choice. I need to explain some things to you, big things, and when I'm done, you'll have some hard decisions to make."

Meekly, Scota said "Aye, alright."

Bird continued "In order to make those decisions though, you need the rest of the Chronicles. How about this time though, I show you rather than tell you?"

Again, all she said was "Aye, alright."

Bird helped her off the bed and onto a curved leather like chair. This one was odd to Scota as it was comfortable but... it had no legs. Bird put the blanket on her and she panicked.

"Bird!?"

"Heh heh, it's okay dear. It's our version of a wheelchair."

"Thah's jest it... there ain't no wheels!"

Ally got behind the hovering chair, and pushed her out into the hall and through a door and into the bay.


Alydar brought up the holographic screen she used for the ride to 51, and Scota was both afraid and amazed at the same time.

"Don't worry Scota," Bird said kindly, "What you're seeing isn't real. These are recordings of what was."

"Recordings? What's that?"

"Scota, imagine you had a painting of yourself. As you aged, would the image on the canvas?"

"No."

"Exactly. A painting is just a moment in time frozen forever right?"

"Aye. I never thought of it that way but yer right."

"Now, imagine if real life could be recorded, like the painting, only EXACTLY as is was. Pictures, motion, sound, all of it. Now, wouldn't that be something?"

"Aye. Is thah what this is?"

"Yes blondie. Now, I want you to pay close attention. While the images before you aren't real, what they portray is. THIS Scota, is who I really am and... where I truly come from."

Scota watched and was amazed. She was also less afraid because Bird was right beside her. Scota watched for 2 hours as Alydar narrated. When she got to her full sized version though, Bird narrated.

"Wait... nooo... even in your world Bird thah's jes not possible... is it?"

"What isn't?"

"Ally."

"Afraid so blondie."


Alydar was afraid of this. She was worried how Scota would react. She hadn't thought anything of it till Bird waved her off the other day. Since then however, Scota finding out was a situation that made her nervous. She leaned in slightly to Scota now that she knew, and was instantly saddened seeing her recoil in fear. No, not fear... disgust.

Scota leaned into Bird as if to get away from Ally, and got a slap in the face for it... hard.

Bird was livid and scolded her saying "You stupid little girl. You are in MY world and NOTHING of yours applies here. Yes, she is a machine so what. She is STILL the woman who taught you manners... who taught you how to fight... who laughed AND cried with you. The only thing different than 5 minutes ago is... your perception. She deserves better than your disgust... and I for one won't tolerate it. You have nooooooo concept of the line she crossed only hours ago just to defend you! Fuck you you pathetic little girl and while your at it... grow up."

Bird turned and left Scota with her now biggest fear.

Ally had tears in her eyes for 2 reasons. One was Scota's reaction, the other was Bird's. She was saddened and hurt by the little girl, and in love with Bird's defense of her.

"Why do you hate me?" Ally asked.

She truly didn't understand why, and knew this was the uncharted waters Bird spoke of.

Scota was mad and said "You lied to me!"

"OF COURSE I DID!" Ally bellowed. "What would you have me say hmm?" Ally got snotty and imitated Rahgaa on the station and said "Hi Scota, my name is Ally and I'm an android. Not that you even know what that word is but, I am one just the same. Oh yeah, did I mention I'm from over 200 years in the future? Oh silly me I almost forgot... I come from another planet too! Ooh ooh ooh, let's not mention the whole shape shifting thing okay? We'll just keep that between us girls." Ally fired back at her.

Seems the blond one wasn't the only one getting angry now.

"Thah's jest it... yer NOT a girl! Yer not even real!"

That got Scota yet another slap in the face.

"I may not be human..." Ally seethed, "... but I'm as fucking real as you are! So, by the way, are my feelings."

Ally brought up the rest of the Chronicles, and practically made Scota watch.

She got in her ear and menacingly said "Now you silly little girl, pay reeeeeal close attention to this last part," and Ally showed her the hell wave.

Scota looked away as it was just too frightening. Ally however grabbed her chin and forced her to watch. Now the old Alydar was back.

"Look at you... you pathetic little girl. You can't even look at it. Try LIVING through it! And by the way... I did. Ya know what else? Your precious Yankee Man... didn't."

"You're lying."

*"Am I?... watch!"*

Scota did and saw Bird tell the hellish beast he was not afraid. She watched him stand up to it. She also saw him lose and get thrown against the back wall just as the static kicked in and all the visuals went black.

*"Now... watch this."*

Alydar then brought up her racing to get to Bird, and how she eventually saved him.

*"If I HAD been human... he would've remained that way. I am the same Ally who laughed with you, who cried with you, AND... the same Ally who protected you from the Bishop. You worship Bird the way so many others do. I see it in your face don't even try to deny it."*

*"So?"*

*"So... watch."*

Alydar brought up the fight on Aarika, the one that freed young Sal.

*"See that weapon in his hand?"* Ally stated more than asked. *"That's the cannon... one of the four Lone built. Now, watch what it's capable of."*

Ally unfroze the picture and Scota jumped in her seat as the bang went off, and the ugly alien got it's chest exploded. Scota wasn't sure which was scarier, the weapon or who Bird fired it on.

*"Now, watch this."*

Now Ally played Bird standing in front of her when she first became active.

She was pointing to the wall and said *"THIS is Lone Wolf. This one here is Deenon and this one is Quaran. See what they're holding?"*

Scota meekly nodded.

*"Now... notice three things. Notice how many there are, who they're pointing at, but most important... look at Bird. See the look on his face?"*

More nodding.

*"Think he cared that I was 'just a machine'? He stood up to his closest friends and stared down every one of those guns and ALL, to defend me. You wanna worship him... fine. If however you're*

*going to do that... try being more like him... and less like yourself."*

    *Scota was reeling. She was so lost she didn't know what to do.*
*"It's... it's all so different. I wish 'I' could go back in time."*
*"And why's that?"*
*"Cause I would tell myself to stop looking up at the stars,"*
*Scota stated sounding utterly defeated.*
    *Alydar now knew she had an edge.*
    *"Scota, look at the wall," Ally said far calmer now.*
    *"Why? All there is is death and ugliness beyond what I can*
*bear."*
    *"The Commander told you there would be. He also said there*
*was beauty beyond your imaginings. You're right, you have seen a*
*lot of ugliness. Care for some beauty?"*
    *Scota dried her tears and asked "Like?"*
    *"Heh heh... like this." Alydar changed the image and said*
*"Say hello to Eden."*
    *Alydar took Scota on angles of Eden that seemed to be as if*
*she was flying through it. She lifted up from the emerald patio, and*
*cruised the waterfall. Then the image headed upriver and Scota saw*
*the silver snow and all the beauty that it was. Scota was amazed*
*when the image got to the mountains.*
    *"It looks like the Isle!" she proclaimed.*
    *"Mm hmm. Now this, is after sunset."*
    *The image changed to the orange river and the blue*
*moonlight. The blue moon with the rings was the oddest she ever*
*saw... but thought it was beautiful.*
    *"Scota... name the planet Lone is from."*
    *"Tuhleesia!" Scota said proud of herself for getting it right.*
    *"Say hello to sunset from the 'Pillars Of Alydar'."*
    *Scota saw a most strange, but amazing sight.*
    *"Point is Scota, Bird is right. There is ugliness and evil*
*beyond anything you can imagine. But there is beauty too. Like on*
*this world... just a little different is all. You were the one who wanted*
*to see the stars... well little girl... mission accomplished."*

    *Scota got off the hovering chair, and walked over to Ally. She*
*touched her like one does a science experiment.*

*"You... you're... you're not gonna hurt me?"*

*Ally was near exasperated.*

*"God woman, you're just not getting it are you!?"*

*Scota backed off and hung her head.*

*"Stop yelling at me!" Scota was near tears and said "I'm scared, confused, and I just don't know what to do anymore!"*

*Scota was coughing again and was simply drained. Ally softened, and hugged Scota. Blondie just let go and hugged her adopted sister and bawled her eyes out.*

*"Ally?"*

*"Mm?"*

*"I'm sorry," Scota said burying her head in Ally's shoulder.*

*Ally hugged her tight and said sweetly "Apology accepted."*


*"So... what do I do now?" Scota asked having truly no idea.*

*"Go... apologize to Bird... then we'll let you know."*

*Scota nodded and walked to the door, now that she knew what it did. She didn't go through it though. She stopped and, with only a smile, stuck her hand out to Ally. Ally smiled back and with that, 2 girls walked through the door.*

# Chapter 26:

## *"Scuba?... No Tanks"*

Scota walked into the med bay. Bird had his back to the door and never even turned around.

"Ally?"

"I'm here boss."

"You alone?"

"Nope."

"If you're the same Scota I left in the bay, feel free to turn your ass around and put it right back there," Bird said.

He still had a touch of anger in his voice when he said it.

"Bird?"

He didn't answer her. Scota looked at Ally and she just waved her on.

"Bird I... I'm... I'm sorry."

Bird softened some and said "For all I'm about to do for you, you had better be."

Bird sat her down and laid out his plan.

"Scota, I firmly believe that when you have sex for the first time, it makes your mind grow up... rapidly. While you may not be a grownup per say, you do get a huge boost forward."

Scota scrunched her face some and asked "Yeh always this forward?"

Admonishing her just a little, Bird replied "I dunno, you always this backward?"

Scota wished off this subject and stated "You were saying?"

Bird continued "The scans I took of you the other day show me you haven't yet. Now, that said, from my perspective I'm dealing with a child. THAT, is no longer acceptable. For this plan to work Scota, you have to grow up... and fast. That in itself has dangers as well."

"How so?"

"Well young one, remember how I said people notice things?"

"Aye."

"Well, it's obvious to me that before we can do anything, you need to grow up... a lot. Do that and hang around the town folk? Oh yeah, they're gonna notice. Scota, do you want to live?"

Sadly, Scota replied "More than ennything."

"Then the only way to do that is... you have to become part of my world... and leave yours behind."

"Clarify," Scota said seriously.

"Scota, you may not understand it but... you now know I'm from the future yes?"

"Aye."

"Okay then, what seems like endless possibilities for you, is already written for me. Events yet to come are already written. Wars and clashes that ended well, may not if you're around."

"I... I don't understand."

"Scota, in my time, you died young and... from that cough. I was never in your life and you never even heard of me, nor did your sister. Remember, where I come from even if you lived to a ripe old age... you and everyone around here are already long since dead. That more than anything I need you to truly grasp or we can't continue."

"Scary to think of but... I do understand," Scota said truly meaning it.

"Good. Now, as I said, you died young. Now let's say you don't. Everything you touch, everyone you interact with, EVERY thing you do past that point never happened. That in itself is the danger. What if you have a child, or that child has one, that changes the future? And all because I changed time."

That thought was enormous for Scota. Much to Bird's surprise though, it was one she got.

Seeing the look on her face, Bird smiled at Ally and said "Heh heh, leave it to us Scorp's to 'get' the bigger picture."

Ally just playfully stuck her tongue out at him.

"Alright wait, if I live past when I should, I could change the *future?"*

*"Mm hmm. Now, you may not have any affect on the future at all... or something you do now could change it all. Problem is there's no way of knowing."*

*"Not a pleasant thought," she said.*

*"Nope. Now Scota, let's say I fix you. I would be responsible for any change you caused as a result. A change that could affect all of mankind."*

*Scota actually got it and said "So, fix me and something I ain't even done yet could cause major suffering."*

*"Indeed. Even if you left the Isle, you would affect the future still... it just wouldn't be around here. That's the price Scota. Fix you and AT MOST, you'd have to be gone in 4 years. Only place to do that, is with me and Ally. That, sadly Scota, is the real world. There is always a price to be paid."*

*Scota truly meant it when she said "That's some price to pay."*

*"Mm hmm. And there's more. If I heal you, I need your help in return. I've been neglecting my duties here."*

*"Ere now Bird, I barely understand ennything around here. How am I supposed to help you when I kahnt even help myself!?"*

*"That's easy," Ally said, "I'll help you."*

*Scota smiled at that. Bird however wasn't smiling.*

*"Listen blondie, you're right, you can't handle my world. Ally however is also right when she says she'll teach you. I will too and that, is part of the danger."*

*"How so?"*

*"I told you people will notice, and notice is the one thing above all they CAN'T do. I came into your life and yes, I appeared to be smart but, did you think I was anything other than that?"*

*"Aye, now I understand. If I act smarter, folk will start ask'in questions."*

*"Questions I can't have them asking," Bird replied. "And for the same reasons I already told you. Scota, what did I say there wasn't?"*

*"No magic... only sciencey stuff."*

*"Correct. People like Mary among others would only think it*

sorcery however, and burn us both for being witches."

"Aye," Scota agreed. Then she had a really bad thought and said "Wait a moment, what about Ciana?"

"What about her?"

"You said once, you would bring her into your world. I would rather die than hurt her. Bring her here and, well, I can barely handle this... Ciana will go simply out o'her mind!"

Bird finally smiled and said "Not if she has a sister for a guide." Bird then said "Scota, we will teach you our world. Once you learn though, you'll be less Isle, and more 51. The more 51 you become, the more we'll have to get you away from everyone."

Scota got it all and asked "Okay, the life change I got. Now, how do yeh fix me from the inside?"

Scota knew there was a fix. She also knew it was way past her understanding. The latter though, she was finding she wanted more of... a lot more.

"Scota, walk into the bay till you're in over your head. What happens?"

Scota recoiled... a lot.

Bird misunderstood and said kindly "No Scota, I'm not asking you to... it's just a way to explain something."

Scota still recoiled.

"Scota? What's wrong?" Ally asked with compassion.

Softly, and with tons of sadness, Scota replied "You'd become my mother."

"Scota, I know nothing of your mother as Ciana never talks about her. Sorry if I sparked a bad memory but... I truly had no idea," Bird said with compassion.

Scota looked around, and let out a deep breath.

"You've shared your secret with me... my turn I guess." Scota looked at Bird with sad eyes and said "I was only a child. Mother was sick, though no one told me. She didn't tell Ciana either. I think it's why she took Ciana to the falls. I believe she knew she was dy'in and wanted Ciana to have some nice memories. I also think it was to prepare her for when she passed, but I have no proof of that. One night I had a bad dream, and awoke. I was scared and went look'in for her. Father took care of her as best he could. Looking back now I know he was tired from it. All I knew is that he was tired a lot. I didn't realize till later it was because he was tak'in care of mother, and still runn'in the inn at the same time. There were always folk about but towards the end, no one came around. Again, I know now why, but I didn't at the time."

As tenderly as he could, Bird asked "She took her own life didn't she?"

Scota looked down, and just nodded.

"Father was asleep in the rocker Ciana keeps by the hearth. It was 'his' chair and it's why she had issues with yeh when yeh moved it upstairs."

"Makes sense. Am I to assume... mother wasn't in the inn?"

More silent nodding.

"I woke Ciana when I climbed in her bed. She asked why I was there and I told her. She became frantic and I got even more scared. She finally woke father and we all looked for her. Mother couldn't swim and almost never went to the bay. Father and Ciana went different ways and..."

"Oh shit!" Bird exclaimed softly. "Oh blondie... you went to the bay didn't you?"

"And to this day I wish I hadn't. Mother was at the shore. I don't remember it exactly but, I remember she smiled at me. She said something akin to wait for her... at least that's what I thought she said... so I did. She walked into the bay before my very eyes. When she didn't come out I started to cry. Father heard me and raced down to the bay. Bird, my father was much like William. Confident, sturdy build and brave. He ran into the water and I... I... I never heard him cry... ever. But I did that night. Father forbid Ciana and me from going to the bay. Two days later, mother finally came out."

"Sorry Scota... truly. I'm even sorrier still because, the only way to fix you is to do what your mother did. I assure you however, we'll do it my way... NOT... hers."

Bird thought that, after that story, how in the world would he fix Scota now? The next story he got both pleased and stunned him.

"Bird, yeh told a wild tale yeh did. Can I tell yeh one o'mine?" Scota asked looking him straight on with eyes of fire.

"Feel free," Bird told her.

It was all he could think of to say.

"After father laid mother tuh rest, I defied him. It was theh only time I did. I felt like you did."

"Me?"

"Aye, when yeh went back to Aarika, and the mojo place."

Bird got it and said smiling "You didn't want to be beaten."

"Aye. I would go in the water and stay as long as I could. Every time though I would get out and stare at it. I knew as long as I got out... 'I' won... not the bay. I figure if anyone would understand, you would."

Kindly, and thinking of his own memories, Bird just said "More than you know."

Scota snapped out of her funk and asked "So, how yeh gonna fix me?"

"Scota, your mother died because, unlike Ally here, we humans can't breathe water."

"My stars! Yeh can breathe water!?" Scota asked Ally.

"Actually, I don't breathe at all. I only look like I do to avoid those questions the Commander doesn't want anyone asking."

Scota shook her head at that one, then smiled at Bird.

"So Rhana... what's our next move!?"

"Eh eh eeeeehhhh... NEVER call me that," Bird said lightly, but truly meaning it.

Scota just smiled, and saluted.

"Okay... water..." Bird continued. "Scota what if I told you, I had water you actually COULD breathe?"

Scota stared at Ally hard, then giggled and said "Yeaaaahhh, I got nuthin'."

Ally just giggled back.

Scota turned back and seeing Bird's 'unhappy' face, she calmed down.

"Okay so, water I can breathe. How's that help me?"

"Those machines I shot you with. This water is very special and I only have a small amount of it. Those machines float in the water. When you breathe in, they'll go into your lungs. In terms you can understand, they'll clean your lungs from the inside the way you scrub the kitchen floor. The 'mud' on your lungs has to be broken free. Those machines will do that. When you exhale, the dirt will exhale with it. It will take some time... approximately 6 hours but... your lungs will be clean of dirt when it's over. Once the dirt is gone, your lungs will be raw, like a rash. That your own body will heal over a few days and, well as you say, you'll be 'good ole Scota' again."

"And no more coughing?"

"No sweety... no more."

Impishly, Scota asked "I'm not gonna have tuh get naked again am I?"

"Welllll," Ally teased.

"Oh C'mon!"

Bird chuckled and said "Sorry kiddo... naked no but... close."

"Okay, one thing though," Bird said. "This water I mentioned, it's in a special tank on the full size Alydar."

"Okay, so?"

"THAT Alydar is in space. I flat out refuse to take you there. It's bad enough you're here 'ahead of schedule' AND you flew. By the way, that last part won't happen till the early 1900's. So, I insist that of the two of you, I'm saving that for Ciana."

Lovingly, Scota said "Bird aye, and tis only fair. So, when do we do this?"

"You're freaked out by the size of 'this' Alydar. The other one is ten times this size. It's gonna take some time getting her down here. That in itself won't be bad... it's finding somewhere we can hide for a day and not be spotted that will take some time."

"Ten times!?" Scota said with slight shock. She switched on a dime and said "Ooh ooh ooh wait.... bigger badder better? Did I get that right?" Scota asked with a huge smile.

Bird just smiled and said "Indeed you did."

Later that day Scota had gone through the door and back to the cave. She was drained from the highs and lows of the day's events and barely made it to her bed. Bird simplified it for her and, Alydar made it happen. Scota couldn't handle the scanners that said if the coast was clear or not, but green for go and red for stop she understood. She took to the lights well and was being serious. At first the light was red. Several minutes later though it turned green and Scota hurried through before it went red again. Doing a thorough scan of the area, she popped out of the cave and headed for bed. Bird smiled watching all this on his monitor, and was happy at how serious she appeared to take it all.

The next morning Bird came down, and Scota teased him.

Doing a proper curtsey she said "Good morning Rhana, care for some trillot?"

Ciana laughed lightly when Bird winked at her saying "I dunno... got any milk?"

Both ladies laughed and Ciana was none the wiser. Ciana went out to greet a new guest and Scota pulled Bird to the side.

"Bird, I don't like lying to my sister. Being that I have to though, I have an idea. I truly love the Chronicles so I'm going to make a big 'to-do' about it. That way if ennything slips, I can just say it's the story. It may not be much but it's all I could think of."

"I understand and, if that works for you then fine. Two things though."

"Aye. First?"

Bird replied "First, don't over do it."

"Aye, I won't. And second?"

Bird winked and smiled and said "Heh heh... YOU... don't call me Rhana."

As part of her plan, Scota started clinging to Bird a bit more than usual. She treated him more like her dad. With no real father, it wasn't much of a stretch for her and... she didn't have to act much. Ciana called her on it but Scota said the truth.

"Ciana, I know he's not father, nor would I replace father's memory. But, even you have to admit it's nice hav'in a man around again."

Ciana accepted that. Seeing Scota treat Bird more like a father figure, and not like a potential mate, she never concerned herself with it again.

"Bird, no one can see me, so I don't get it. I could sit over the Pacific or the Atlantic for days and no one would know. So why the fuss?"

"I don't like killing God's creatures. What do we do when the birds start flying into, and dying from, and invisible wall in the sky? And, if a ship should happen to pass and see it? Sailors of this age already have enough superstitions, I don't feel like adding any new one's. Also, I'm thinking of Scota."

"I believe you but... how so?"

Bird chuckled and said "We're asking a girl... with no proper education... from the mid 1700's... to breathe water. I figure that alone is scary enough so the less scary we make it the better. Floating over an endless expanse of ocean ain't gonna help that much."

"Point taken," Alydar replied.

Two days later Bird said he'd be gone for a day or two. He knew Ciana was very busy working the inn then setting up the house, and that's why he asked her. He offered to take her with him, but she declined. Scota jumped at the chance to replace her and made a big production over it.

"I don't mind... it's up to Ciana though."

Scota pleaded and Ciana relented with the usual warning to behave herself and not bother Bird or get in the way. Ciana was happy to have them gone as she had a secret plan of her own. Now, with 48 hours secured, both parties tended to their plans.

"Scuba?" Bird asked Ally teasingly.

"No tanks," she smarted back deliberately leaving off the 'h'.

Bird was prepping the tank and getting it ready for all the sensors he'd need for Scota. He kept it empty and wasn't going to fill it till he needed to. He also decided, if water was to be the element du jour, then he was gonna do it all the way. As such, he switched from altitude to depth. Alydar found a deep shelf off the Caribbean islands and the ocean floor was where they'd head to.

Ally spent a whole morning getting Scota ready and giving her as much information as she thought she could handle.

"But I'm hungry!" Scota protested.

Ally had her fast for the last 4 hours.

"Scota, once you're in the tank, that's it. You have to stay there till the work is done. Getting out to go and 'relieve yourself' isn't gonna be an option."

With resignation in her voice, Scota said "Aye, I understand. Still hungry though."

Scota put on the funny underwear Ally handed her. Naked from head to toe she slipped into what looked like a Tron suit met a scuba one. It was all black but had soft glowing lines all over. Scota however smiled at the feel of it. Seeing her fine curves in the mirror, she felt something new. She felt... sexy... in the silky form fitting suit. Scota thought the outside felt like the dolphins though, and said so. It impressed her that the inside, and the outside, felt totally different. Once zipped up, she adjusted the turtleneck collar. Now, her feet, her hands, and her head from the chin up were the only thing not covered.

"Nooooo!" Scota exclaimed with pleasant shock. "Did yeh see thah? I pulled it apart... and it went right back... on it's own!"

Scota was smiling at the cool new 'toy' Ally handed her. The avatar giggled at Scota's reaction. Ally had handed her a hair scrunchy.

Smiling, Ally said "Here, let me show you," and put Scota's hair up in a ponytail.

Scota was beaming. She shook her head hard several times but, the ponytail held. Amazed and happy, two ladies headed out.


Ally walked into med bay with Scota. Scota however wasn't so shy this time at being 'nearly naked'. Bird chuckled once or twice seeing her try and catch his attention.

With a sly grin, Bird said "Why Scota... are you flirting with me?"

She actually winked at him and coyly smiled back, and just said "Hmm... maybe."

Bird laughed and pulled two hypo-sprays.

He showed them to her and said "This one will stop you from being hungry or thirsty for the next 8 hours. If it takes longer, I'll give you another one then."

Bird set it to half power and shot Scota with it. It didn't have the 'pop' affect it normally does. Bird did that so as not to scare her any more than he had to.

Bird then held up the other hypo-spray and said "This one is a sedative. You don't have to take it but, you can if you want."

"What does it do?"

Ally told her "It'll make you sleepy. Not out cold but not fully awake either. It will make you not care."

Scota looked straight on at Bird and, full of fire she said "I beat the bay... I'll beat this. Thank you but... I'd rather not."

Bird smiled and put it away.

"As you wish m'lady."

Scota smiled kindly and curtsied pulling out an imaginary skirt. Bird pulled out something shiny and put it behind her left ear.

"Scota, once your lungs fill with water, your voice won't work. This device will let you hear us as clearly as you do now. See this device here?" Bird said pointing to one on the table.

"Aye. What does it do?" Scota asked now with extreme curiosity.

"You press the letters there. What you type we'll see out here. There's one inside the tank. You'll hear us but you'll have to type your answers back to us. Here try it." Bird took her hands and asked "What's your name?"

Bird took her hands, and typed her name out and showed her how it came up on the device she now knew was called a 'monitor'.

Scota snapped her head and stared at Bird with a beaming smile and exclaimed "That's cool!"

Bird chuckled and said "So, finally figured out what the phrase means eh?"

Still beaming she just said "Mm hmm."


"Scota, lastly, the glowing lines on your suit, they're called sensors. Once your under, we go until it's finished. They show us your body levels. They let us know if everything is okay, or if something is going wrong. IF! Something does go wrong, I'll yank you out of there myself. Any last questions?"

"Just one. Can I have some motivation?" Scota asked referring to how they flew the other day.

"Yes... and no. We get you in and settled first. Once we know your fine, I'll give you any you wish. Deal?"

"Aye... deal."

Bird then hit some commands and the 'special water' flowed into the tank. The tank itself was about 6 foot square, and 8 feet tall. Lone and the Jammers were the tallest creatures Jonathan knew of so as such, he designed this tank with them in mind. Bird filled it to a little over 6 feet deep.

Bird and Ally were looking over the controls and such and had their backs to it. Scota looked at it and only thought of the bay and... her mother. While Bird and Ally were busy doing sciencey stuff, she actually climbed the stairs on the outside, and slipped in to the wine water. That was the closest thing she could relate to. It had tons of mini bubbles like the wine Bird drank at dinner in Edinburgh. Full of purpose, and trust in Bird, she clenched her fists... looked down and closed her eyes... and took a deep breath.

She was thinking of the little girl crying on the beach and suddenly felt like she was being choked. She went to get out but slipped on the railing. This water seemed almost oily to her. She tried again and was almost panicked.

Suddenly, she smiled the most joyous smile ever. It felt odd to her but she noticed one thing. Just like Bird said, she was breathing still. Her chest felt a little heavy but not terribly so and even that was dying down. Then... she exhaled. What she saw made her jump up and down like Renny did when Lone asked her to be his other. What she saw was... smoke. It looked like Angus when he smoked his pipe he used on occasion. She exhaled again and just couldn't believe it... more 'smoke'. It was actually silt but she didn't care, all she knew was... she beat the bay... and Bird was right.

"Okay Scota so ya ready to... Scota?" Bird said turning to an empty seat.

Suddenly he heard tapping. Scota was beaming, and 'blew smoke' at him from inside the tank.

"Well... I'm proud of you... you truly are like your namesake," Bird told her with the kindest of smiles.

Scota just squealed like a little girl and bounced up and down. When there was no actual squeal, she remembered what Bird *showed her and rushed to the keyboard.*

*'Thank yoo' she typed.*

*Bird chuckled and said "You may be smart. You're obviously brave but... ha ha ha... your spelling sucks!"*

*Scota heard him as if he was inside her head. Once she had, she had one more thing from the Chronicles to spring on Bird.*

*She pounded on the wall and waved her hand to Bird to come closer. He did and... Scota gave him the finger.*

*Bird laughed and said "Careful, or no music for you!"*

*Scota smiled and stuck her tongue out at him.*

*An hour later and Scota was still fine. It was the strangest thing to her but, seeing the small wisps of smoke, she swore she'd stay in there forever if that's what it took.*

*"Okay blondie... how ya doing so far?"*

*Scota typed 'tyrd'*

*Bird thought a second and said "Oh... tired?"*

*Scota nodded and Bird got her a small stool and carefully handed it to her. She sat down and made Bird chuckle as she actually gave him a thumbs up gesture.*

*'muzik?' she typed next.*

*"First... tell me how do you feel?" She gave him another thumbs up but Bird asked "No Scota, how do you feel, up here?" and Bird tapped the side of his head.*

*Scota typed 'bord'*

*Bird got pissed and said "Okay I've had enough of this shit," and reached in and took out the keyboard.*

*Scota was slightly panicked at not being able to talk and motioned to Bird as such. Bird ignored her. Punching in a few commands, suddenly Scota saw a keyboard again... INside the glass wall.*

*"Scota, go around the tank, from wall to wall," Bird commanded.*

*Scota did and smiled as if to say 'No shit... really?' What had her smiling was the virtual keyboard. It followed her to every wall she went to.*

*"That one knows spelling better than you do. I didn't want to*

show you as I'm trying not to scare you but it would seem you're developing a fondness for the toys eh lass?"

Scota smiled huge and nodded even larger.

"When you type, it will see what words are wrong, and give you choices for the correct one. Go ahead... try it."

She typed in 'bord' again and saw 7 different choices. She pointed to it as if to say 'Now what?"

"Now, tap the one that looks correct."

Scota did and saw it replaced with the correct one.

'Bored?'

"Ere now, atz beh'uh..."

Scota laughed and typed 'Innit?'

Now Bird gave her more keys.

"See the new ones?"

Scota nodded.

"Tap the one that looks like the heart."

She did and while the new display didn't scare her, she had no idea what it was.

"That's your heart rate. The number is how many beats per minute. The bouncing line is every time it does. See the one that's '%' ?"

She nodded and tapped that one. It read 18%.

"That shows you how complete you are. When it hits 100 your done.  Last one is the one that says O2... tap it."

She did and it read 98%.

"If that goes down to low 90's and we don't see it, let us know. If it goes below 87... get out. In terms you can understand, that's how much air is in the water. Anything below 87, and you truly will drown, got it?"

A serious thumbs up was Scota's reply.

Bird tapped some more and now more keys showed up.

"You truly are a brave girl sweety. Those, are the music you asked for."

Bird showed her how to work them and Scota was thrilled. There was one however she wanted more than any other. Bird showed her how to search for titles, or artist in case she found one *she liked. It took a moment but she found the one she wanted. Suddenly, med bay was filled with... Adiemus.*

*Bird smiled and just said "Good choice."*

*Scota wanted to make sure and typed* 'what raga played?'

*"It is indeed, and this is how you spell it by the way," and Bird typed in Rahgaa's name correctly.*

*Scota could hear it clearly and even figured out the volume. She was in awe of the orchestra in her head and the song they played. She imagined Bird and Lone on their sunset flight and, in her mind, soared right up there with them.*

*Scota smiled and typed* 'Ciana should walk to this'.

*"Walk to it?" Bird asked not understanding.*

*Scota smiled and typed* 'Yes... when you marry.'

*"Now THAT... is a pleasant thought," Bird said kindly.*

*Scota did a mock bow and just enjoyed the music.*

*At six hours, the meter read 93% complete. Scota had run the gambit of music and just couldn't get enough. Suddenly her world was quiet again as Bird took away her music keys. Scota pounded on the wall and glared at him with her hands on her hips.*

*"Really?... Really!?... I just saved your life and your pissed I took the tunes away?" Bird admonished her slightly.*

*Scota hadn't thought of that she was so engrossed in the music. She changed her attitude and just typed* 'sorry'.

*"Scota listen to me carefully. You're almost done. When you come out it will likely be as bad as when you went in."*

'What can I expect?'

*"You're going to puke... hard. Like you did when you got in, you're going to want to run back for the water like you did the air." Bird got real serious and just said "Don't."*

*Scota nodded and typed* 'Anything else?'

*"Yeah. This water as you can see is special and I only have enough to fill the tank. As such I'm not wasting a single drop so when you come out, puke it back into the tank. Also, while not a lot, you'll still have some water left in your lungs once you're back to air. You'll have some vile burps for a few days while the machines I told you about help with that. Lastly, you need to see me everyday so I can check you. While I know of this stuff, I'm not an actual doctor.*

I want to check you daily to make sure nothing 'sneaks up on us'."
Scota smiled a kind smile, but didn't type this time. She pointed to
herself... then put both hands over her heart... then pointed to Bird
and Ally.

Bird smiled back and blew her a kiss. So did Ally.

A half hour later and the scrubbers hit 100%. Bird and Ally
climbed the tank, Scota braced herself, and put both hands up. Bird
and Ally grabbed one each.

"And 3...2...1..." Bird said and he and Ally pulled Scota up.
Seems Bird was right, coming out was worse than going in.
She felt odd racing back for water she didn't want to breathe in the
first place. She puked hard several times then, in her own ears, she
heard a glorious sound. It was her... drawing a deep breath... of air.

Ally toweled her off and put all the leftover she could back in
the tank. Scota was shivering as the room wasn't cold but, Bird had
made the water warm. Bird got her a bathrobe and wrapped her in
it. Scooping her up he carried her down from the tank and laid her
on the bed. Ally came over and Scota grabbed them both and
hugged them tight.

"Whatever happens... thank you... and know that I love you
both dearly," Scota said to her two saviors.

Bird smiled and pointed to the ghost that scared her.
"Green good red bad... right?"
Scota just nodded and coughed a little.
"Remember your lungs were red the other day?"
Scota nodded again and she saw Bird and Ally smile... and
move away. The ghost showed her lungs but... now they were green.

Scota was thinking a million things at once but, that was a
sight she'd never forget.

"Bird, I know I don't have the right to ask for more but, might
I ask yeh for a favor?"

"Name it," Bird said sweetly.

"If it's okay with you... I think I'll take that sedative now."
Bird chuckled and loaded a hypo-spray.

# Chapter 27:

## "The Blueprints Of Hell, A Fire In The Sky, And A Biblical Plague"

Bird and Scota weren't due for another half a day. Ciana was busy finishing up her plans and was back at the inn. She looked up when the door opened, and saw a rather 'proppuh' gentleman holding a black bag walk in. Fine clothes she knew he was out of a big city. The soft English accent confirmed it.

"Excuse me miss, might I find a certain man here?"

Ciana chuckled and pointing to the kilted crew said "Lots o'those... take yer pick."

"Aah, apologies but I was wondering if a certain BirdOfPrey was here? I was told I could find him here."

"Never heard of him," Ciana said cautiously.

"I see. Perhaps then it was another BirdOfPrey that gave you such a necklace. I'll assume by the fact you bear the Commander's mark, you are Ciana Thalin?"

"My apologies, I didn't catch your name," Ciana said softly.

"For now, you can call me James... 'Commander' James... if yeh get my meaning."

"Let's say for the moment I did get yer mean'in... what can I do fer yeh?" Ciana said slightly pissed off she forgot about the necklace.

She never told the locals what it meant though, only that she saw it in a window and thought it lovely so Bird bought it for her. This gentleman however knew what it was, and now she wanted to know more. She walked him over to a side table.

"Miss Thalin, Commander is my rank but... 'doctor' is my title. Bird told me he mentioned our world to you, but that you know nothing of our world, except that it exists correct?"

*"He did."*

*"Then know that I am here at his request. In this world of ours, Commander Bird is, well, shall we say quite popular. Many owe him their very existence. So, when he asked me for a favor, I came straight away."*

*Ciana was now wondering, just how much of a big deal was Bird in this other world of his?*

*"He told me of a lovely lass who captured his heart. I almost didn't believe it as he's never had one before."*

*"Till now," Ciana stated as confidently as she could.*

*"Indeed. He told me you have a sister and, a rather ill one at that. He trusts no one else's skills above mine, that much I can say with confidence. That trust is also, rightly placed. As such, he has asked me to look in on this sister of yours to see if perhaps my skills, might make her well again."*

*Ciana knew nothing of this but then, she wasn't surprised either. However, she's seen with her own eyes Bird's 'other worldly' skills and if this man was telling the truth, well that would be a fine thing indeed.*

*"He's not here at present and isn't due back till this evening, late this evening. Until then, you're welcome to wait and enjoy this inn's fine hospitality."*

*He smiled and said "Seeing as how Bird himself called upon me... then wait I shall."*

*Bird and Scota came in around 8pm and Bird walked straight to the bar.*

*"Welcome stranger," Bird said slyly after giving a kiss hello to Ciana. Bird looked around then leaned in and asked "Did you bring what I requested?"*

*James smiled and said "I did. All I require now is a patient."*

*"James? Allow me to introduce you to your patient," Bird said as he pulled Scota over.*

*"Scota, are you alright? Yeh look ragged as ennything."*

*"Aye sis, I be fine, jes tired is all." She turned to James and said "Pleased to meet you doctor."*

*James kissed her hand and said "Such a lovely lady indeed, the pleasure is all mine." James stood up and said "All I need is a quiet place to work."*

*Bird smiled slyly and said "Scota, the doctor here is gonna check on that cough of yours."*

*Ciana looked at her kindly but said seriously "Be a good girl for the doctor here and answer any question he asks yeh, aye?"*

*Scota hugged her sister and said "Aye I will. Doctor?, Follow me please," and Scota took him up to Bird and Ciana's room.*

*Bird looked at Ciana seriously and said "His skills are like no other, and it's why I asked for him. I warn you though, Scota is getting worse. I've noticed it and I know you have as well. If anyone can fix her it's him but, there's likely to be a price to pay. You ready for that?"*

*"No... but... I'll pay it."*

*Up in Ciana's new room, James closed the door.*
*"Well Scota, let me tell you what we have planned."*
*"Aye Ally, okay but... wait... ALLY!?" Scota said turning around.*

*James just smiled, and morphed from James to the silver haired lady.*

*"You may be upset I'm not human but... heh heh... it has it's advantages."*

*"JESUS Mary and Joseph!" Scota said as she back pedaled some. "Sweet Lord, is there no end to yer world's sciencey stuff!??"*

*"Heh heh............ nope."*

*"Awright, I promised I'd not be afraid. After today though, can yeh take it at least a little easy on me?"*

*"Fair enough," Ally said sweetly. "Suffice to say, I can change into other shapes. Not a lot but some. As far as anyone knows, I am 'Doctor James'. All I need you to do is play along with me and Bird. Think you can do that?"*

*"Aye, that I can do. What do yeh need from me?"*

*"As far as anyone knows, I am what you thought I was. I'm going to let Bird and Ciana know you need to leave and go to a dry climate within 2 years. I'm going to tell a story, all I need you to do is play along. I'm going to give you 'fake medicine' to take that will cure you, but say it comes with a price. You cough some but do it*

*less and less as you take the medicine. When it's done, I'll come back in this form, pronounce you cured but that my original diagnosis was correct. Ciana will prepare for your departure and not be so hurt as if you had just disappeared. Deal?"*

*"Aye... deal." Scota turned around and said "Would yeh mind?"*

*"Not at all," said 'Doctor James'.*

*Scota turned around to the original image and said "To quote Ayleen... damn that's just creepy."*

*Ally... aka James... just smiled and left with Scota.*

*Downstairs again, the fake doctor told Ciana and Bird he could cure her, but she would have to go to a dry climate or she'd die as the damage to this point was just too severe. Ciana was crushed at losing her sister, but was happy she'd be far away... and not dead. Ally in doctor form merely used the truth about her lungs, but said his 'special medicine' would cure her. Ciana was upset at knowing the damage already done was what required a dry climate.*

*The fake doctor gave her a 2 year time-line, and Bird said he would give her advanced knowledge to keep her safe, and promised to get her to one of his 'secret lands'. Ciana didn't take the news well, but also better than all 3 conspirators thought she would. Now at least Bird could get Scota out of the way, and not crush the love of his life. Doctor James left the medicine, and instructions, and results. He said if anything changed to call him and that Bird would 'know where to find him'. About thirty minutes later, Ally showed up and said she ran into a familiar face on the road out, and... no one was the wiser.*

*Quaran was holding center stage at this meeting. He was doing recon during the bombing run on Tamarak.*

*"Well, we know more than we did before but... it's still not good. Tammy's planet is rough to say the least. All the lava is loaded with minerals and ores and such. It's likely why he chose it. Roughly 30% of the planet is solid. I saw digging machines digging into the lava and Shreya scanned them. That is where he's getting his raw materials."*

It had been 3 weeks since Bird left. This morning Deeno climbed the stairs to rip down the numbers. Roenas asked if this time, the Ghosts would do it. All thought it a lovely idea and each one took a turn. Deeno played to the crowd and kept pulling numbers off egging on the crowd till he hit 34. The 51 crowd was getting stoked. They were sad to not get it done as fast as Tamarak did but then, they knew they were hiding and working with a much smaller crew.

Roenas asked if they could build the ring here on 51. Lone told him he had no problem with it but it was still up to Giljor and the builder wolves to sign off on them. He didn't want them to think he was cheating them but, he also knew, he was fighting the clock. Gil understood and appreciated the vote of confidence.

Now Quaran delivered the goods.
"Commander, I believe I found him. See this valley here?" and he pointed to a point on the map hovering over the table.
"That's barely a fissure but yeah, I see it."
Quaran stated "You are correct. I almost ignored it till I saw this," and Quaran brought up another scan.
"That's a lot of guns for a 'crack'."
"My thoughts exactly," Quaran stated.
What Lone and the others saw was a meager valley. What caught Lone's attention was the massive energy signatures emanating from it.
"How many do you think there are?" Symda asked.
"Shreya calculated 1 every 50 feet. AND... the canyon is about 9 miles deep."
"I'm more concerned with the valley walls," Xankor said.
Everyone, looked at him.
"What? Anyone else know what the purple stuff is that lines the walls?" he asked sincerely.
No one however had an answer.
"Didn't think so. I for one wanna know, is it something we can use against him... or something we need to avoid?"
Lone grinned and tipped his hat.

"X-man is right. Raven, anything in our database?"

"Sorry Commander, nothing. Alydar gave me all her 'secrets' before she left. Whatever this is, it's an unknown compound for now. I have it's chemical makeup but, like you and Rhana found on Eden, this one is unknown for now."

Lone wasn't happy about that but, kept it in mind for the future.

"Okay Bartender, what's this on the end?" Lone asked pointing to a small circle at the end of the uber narrow valley.

"If I'm correct, Tamarak himself. I dropped into the valley just outside of it. The moment I did, I was no longer invisible."

"WHAT!?" Deeno hollered in part surprise, part anger.

"Indeed. Check this out," and Quaran switched to another layout. "The winds in this canyon aren't winds at all. They're actually waves of energy. Not only did they seem to emanate from the purple rock walls but, the were immensely powerful. The moment I dropped down outside Tammy's door, Shreya went visible and millions of gadgets, and twice that many tracking guns, opened up on me. Needless to say, I didn't stay long."

Lone saw a tall spire shaped building. Shreya did get enough of a scan to let him know it was old... really really old. It was in fact older than Tamarak himself. By Shreya's scans, it was about 5000 years older so... it would seem... Tammy took up squatter's rights. There was a small circle area at the end of the valley. This old stone building was smack in the middle of it and took up the entire base area. Whatever this building was for and, whoever built it, Lone knew it was lost to the ages. The only area open around it was towards the top as this building was narrow at the top and wider at the bottom. Lone missed something though but, Symda didn't.

"Lone, look at this," and she reached up and changed the scan. "This building appears to be some form of stone but, none I've ever seen. Not only that, these energy waves seem to pass right through it."

Symda was brushing up on her science lately and Lone knew it.

"Nice catch Ghost. Okay, here's what I want. Everyone goes to their own planet. This time I DO want you to pull rank. Get access to any library on your home-worlds you can. If we got *nothing on this stone of Tammy's, let's see if if anyone else does or at least, something close." Lone turned to the table and said "Symda, nice job catching that, truly. X-man, work on on those purple rocks for us. Deeno, see if Aarika has anything on that stone and if they don't, go to Lor's planet. Symda, you take Ulquin's world and your own." Lone turned to Quaran with compassion and said "Sorry pal, but, I'm sending you home for a bit. Go through every black ops report they got and have Shreya hack the ones they hide from you, on my authority of course, but let's see if we can find out what Tammy's house of cards is made of. Everyone clear?"*

*Every Ghost nodded and headed out to their tasks. Lone hung back and, now alone, brought up his comm.*

*"Go ahead Commander."*

*"Ambassador Val... how is 'our relationship' with the galactic council?"*

*"Actually, quite good. I deliberately stayed away unless need be, so as not to be a bother. I wasn't a stranger either and... it seems to have paid off."*

*"Good to hear. I got a stone that's a bit of a mystery. Heh heh, care for some purpose?"*

*Smiling, Val said only "I'd be honored."*

*Lone tipped his hat to the open air and closed the comm.*


*Trillions of miles away, a hell ride was seconds from ending for good. A sister still out cold and, still on the floor, never saw the end of the ride. Bunches of humans would and, once the ride ended, it sealed Ciana's future with Bird... even if she nor Bird knew it.*


*"SURPRIIIISE!" shouted just about every local clan folk.*

*A few of them weren't clan folk at all. Ciana had been busy for the last two days planning nothing short of a feast. Just about every woman in the local area wanted to try out Ciana's new kitchen. None of them could fathom a kitchen the size of a whole house. There were at least 9 cooks at any one time and not one of them, got in the others way. Some prepped or cooked more than one dish or multiple dishes of the same thing. The cold storage cave Bird built* and used as a refrigerator was a huge hit as well. Bird's house had at least 50 people in it and, no one felt crowded... and said so. Bird had walked into his home with Scota in tow.

Ally was already there and one of the well wishers. Ally could tell you the atomic weight of cobalt, but had no clue of social events like these. Not from personal experience anyway, and was just relishing the evening and all the new emotions and memories it brought.

Bird was a bit off guard at first, but realized what was happening and smiled and thanked them all.

"Wellll, Mister Yankee man, you weren't kidding! This new home of yours is just diviiiine!" came a rather flamboyant and cheerful voice.

"Well, if it isn't the gossiping dressmaker," Bird sneered politely.

John did a mock bow and said "At your service. As for the gossiping thing, sorry bout that but... a man needs a hobby!"

"Next time, try NOT having it involve me. Keep that up and the fucking king will likely be coming to call next."

"Yes well, in my own defense, I never said you said it, only that knowing you it would likely turn out that way." John winked at him and said "Looks like I was right." John then shook Bird's hand saying "Well Bird, Happy Birthday. No hard feelings?"

Bird just chuckled and said "Yeah, alright."

John saw Ciana walking by and squealed "THERE you are my dear!" Bird just chuckled as he saw John wrap his arm around her and say "So, tell me... which one of these rooms is mine hmm?"

"Aye Mistuh Bird, the dandy be right... tis a fine home yeh built here!" The man smiled and winked and said "But then, com'in from yerself... heh heh... Ied have expected nuth'in less."

"Andrew! HAHAHAHAHA... how are ya my good man?" Bird hollered with cheer.

Bird gave him a friendly hug and a brisk handshake.

"I told you I'd have a party when it was done. Looks like my lovely lass beat me to it."

"Aye she did. I got a formal invitation and everything! She'd been plann'in this for over a month she said."

Bird gave him a friendly manly sneer and leaning into Andrew said "I'll be sure and thank her properly. You know... heh heh... 'later'."

Andrew grinned and replied "Aye, I know I would."

Bird took William, John and Andrew on a tour. He showed them the innovations he put in place.

"No Andrew that's not cherry, it's called 'redwood' and, well, I had it imported," Bird told the driver as he asked about the wood on the walls of an odd closet. "A pipe goes from the hearth into here. This wood naturally resists rot and mold. Now, Ciana can hang our clothes in here and she has a dryer of sorts. Also, the dry air in here is good for your health. It's called a sauna, so this room serves a dual purpose, and it's what the benches are for."

All 3 guests never heard nor seen such a thing but couldn't deny the inventiveness, nor practicality of it.

Bird next showed them the 'laundry room'. Bird built a barrel with a hand crank and a paddle. No more going to the river and scrubbing on rocks... nope... not for his gal. The house was incredibly warm too and Bird showed them how the pipes in the hearth went to different places in the house to do that. Now William understood how Bird did it with only 1 fire and, what all those pipes were for he once asked about.

Standing on an outside patio, Ciana walked up to the men and said "I got my garden, Bird got his view."

The patio went right up to the falls and it was so close that all of them could feel a slight spray from it.

Pointing behind her at the small glass room she said "And that is a room we can grow food in all year long. Is my husband-to-be a crafty fellow or what?"

Only John, having lived in London, had ever seen a greenhouse before... and heartily agreed with Ciana.

The kitchen was next and all 3 men saw 4 ovens, 2 cook-tops, and all of them buried seamlessly in the walls or cabinetry. Plumbing on the inside AND... indoor toilets... just blew them away.

When Ciana pulled a valve, and the water steamed, John squealed like a little girl.

"Water that's already hot!??" Andrew asked gazing in wonder. "It's got to be near freezing outside!"

William laughed and merely said "Oh truuuuust you!"

Seems Scota wasn't the only one quoting from 'The Chronicles'.

Bird merely bowed to the group of men with a joyous smile on his face.

Back with all the guests, Ciana spoke to Bird.

"I hope yeh doen mind. I had Ally help. I thought yeh might like a little bit of home... in yer new one. She got me all the meat for the butcher and gave me all the recipe's."

Bird kissed her lovingly and simply said "It's perfect... thank you."

"Oi," Ciana said turning around. "Doen think I fergot about you dear sister. With your birthday be'in so close tuh Bird's... this party is fer you too."

Scota hugged her sister and said "Aye, I don't mind share'in."

"Bet yeh won't mind play'in either."

Scota chuckled saying "I think I'm a lil too old for that."

Ciana smiled and said "That wasn't the type of play'in I was talk'in bout. Go look in the living room."

Scota did and her jaw almost dropped. In the corner, a bunch of guests all looked at her, smiled, and parted. Behind them was a standup piano. Scota was enthralled with the one in Edinburgh and couldn't keep her hands off it.

"Yours my love, is in that corner," Ciana said pointing to the other corner.

There sat a fine acoustic guitar.

"Yeh wouldn't let me pay for the land nor the house OR Scota's 'new doctor', so I used some of my coin to pay for the party and yer gifts. I hope yeh like them."

Scota just beamed and hugged her sister. Bird didn't beam but he was thrilled and let her know it.

"How about a song?" Kara asked sweetly.

"Ooh, I don't think yeh want me play'in that just yet," Scota smirked.

Ally made her tap some keys.

"There, now you were the first to play it." Scota smiled and Ally said "How about if you let me then... until you learn it better?"

The crowd applauded and egged Bird on to join her. Bird graciously agreed and Ally played some keys. Bird immediately recognized it and was happy for her choice. Ally changed her vocal patterns to match the original singer and the crowd was treated to Patsy Kline's 'Crazy'.

Angus proudly took Kara and danced her as best he could. Several other couples joined him and all applauded Bird and Ally.

"Bird? We ain't heard how the Chronicles end. I'll understand if yeh don't want to but, would yeh mind finish'in 'em tonight?" Angus asked politely.

"Well then," Bird smirked, "Where did I leave off?"

Six different voices all cried out "Symda!"

Bird laughed and said "Well!..." and finished the story.

About an hour and a half later, Ciana smirked at Ally and said "Well lady... yeh look pretty real to me."

Ally chuckled back saying "Don't I though?"

Ciana didn't have a clue.

'The Chronicles' finally came to an end to a rousing round of applause.

It finished with "And I walked into an inn... heh heh, and the rest you know."

Everyone remarked how it was a grand tale, and which was their favorite part. Everyone thanked Bird for giving them the wildest and most epic tale... ever.

"Yeh know, 'husband-to-be', I can picture it all. Every bit of it but one," Ciana said with a puzzled look.

"Oh? And what is that?"

"I can see the big black ships, the creatures, all of it but one thing. For the life of me, I can't picture the guitar you play, nor imagine what an 'electricity guitar' sounds like."

Bird chuckled saying "That's 'electric guitar'... it only runs on *electricity... heh heh."*

*"Oh well, if that's all," Ciana chuckled still having no clue.*

*It was about 2am. The party was a big hit and several guests were passed out in the living room. Bird hadn't moved the bed in yet so he and Ciana headed back for the inn. Ciana was fast asleep but a sudden sound of rustling in the room woke her up. Seeing Bird's side of the bed empty, she finally got it right, and grabbed the blade from the hidden sheath under her pillow.*

*"Ciana?" called a voice from the darkness.*

*The dark haired lady eased up and said "What's wrong my love? Come to bed."*

*"I will... in a bit. Stay where you are and, don't get out of bed," Bird's voice said from a dark corner.*

*Ciana could hear him, but couldn't see him.*

*"Something wrong?" she asked curiously.*

*"Nope. Just... don't get out of bed. Promise me?"*

*"Aye, I won't."*

*Ciana heard a sound she never heard before. It was a short, quick, buzzing sound. What she heard next, made her smile. She heard the strangest, yet pleasing, sound. It sounded as if it echoed, yet didn't.*

*Bird picked a rhythm track of soft snare drums from his amp, and from the darkness, Ciana heard Bird's version of Santo and Johnny's 'Sleepwalk'. Ciana smiled, pulled up the covers, and rocked softly to the tune.*

*When he finished Bird said in a loving tone, "This is 'other world' stuff but... now you know what it sounds like."*

*Smiling softly, and lovingly, Ciana said "Aye, that I do."*

*She drifted off to sleep, and Bird dropped his equipment out the window to a waiting avatar below.*


*Next morning, Bird and Ciana headed back to the house. Bird grumbled at the early hour, but decided he didn't want a bunch of hungover Scotsmen bumbling around his house. Almost the whole party stayed as they were either too drunk to make it home, or the weather was just too cold. Bird and Ciana didn't care and so, breakfast was rather large this morning.*

*"Angus?"*

*"Aye Bird?"*

*"I noticed the falls dumped some water on the back roof and it froze up pretty good. Care to give me a hand bustin' the ice before it busts my tiles?"*

*"Aye, not at all."*

*"Finish breakfast and we'll head up then."*

*An hour later, Bird, Angus, William and Andrew were up on the roof. Bird showed them how NOT to fall off, and how to break the ice, without breaking his roof. Many braved the cold and Ciana walked a small crowd out the back to show them the yard and the garden. Bird got his falls, so he built Ciana a huge, raised, stone wall circled garden. Multi-tiered of course. Bird saw them enjoying and oohing and aahing, then saw them all looking skyward.*

*"Um, no... heh heh... I'm not putting one up there," Bird chuckled at all the skyward stares.*

*"Uh... Bird?" Ciana said with a hint of panic.*

*She said nothing else, and merely pointed up.*

*Bird looked up and merely, and genuinely, said "Oh shit!"*

*What Ciana pointed to was Bird's hope, and nightmare, all rolled into one.*

*"Get everyone inside... NOW!" Bird shouted down.*

*"What in all the heavens is that Bird!?" Angus asked as panicked as Ciana was.*

*"Trouble."*

*What Bird and all the others saw was a ribbon... of flames... that made the daytime sunny sky 3 times brighter. Bird knew in an instant... a Husky had arrived.*

*Bird was grabbing his hat and coat, and practically bolting out the door. Ally was hot on his heels.*

*"Andrew, John, you two stay here. Everyone else... go home, and stay there! If the weather stays calm... meet me back here two nights from now."*

*"Bird my love, you're scaring me," Ciana said in a voice that was slightly shaking.*

"Good," Bird told her seriously. "Stay here and keep Scota close... I'll be back when I can."

He kissed her and bolted out the door.


"Talk to me you sexy bitch!" Bird commanded as he and Ally made it to the bay.

"We just dodged one hell of a bullet boss. The hell wave opened behind the moon's orbit. Luckily, what we saw was the side of it. If that thing had opened facing us... wellllllll..."

"MRU," Bird said seriously as he exited a door behind the cockpit. "Okay lady, give me full speed the moment we're 100 miles out. God in heaven I hope we get there in time."

"She's going incredibly fast. She's also heading for deep space."

"LINK THEM!"

"DONE!"

With that command, the 51 rescue party broke atmosphere.


Down in the bay, a rather shabby ship dropped anchor. It actually did it outside the bay, and sent a small rowboat ashore. The flag it was flying was a bad one. The ship in Ciana's bay that was anchored at her dock saw it, and immediately battened down its hatches as the small boat drew closer. They weren't pirates... no... to the sailors, it was something far worse. Ciana knew of this ship, but had completely forgot about its arrival. Padre Pedro in the boat saw the fire in the sky on his way in, and made a sign of the cross. He wasn't sure what kind of omen that was, but he wasn't taking any chances. The flag his ship was flying told anyone she met that they were floating death.

The ship Ciana forgot she was expecting was... a leper ship.

# Chapter 28:

## "The Cavalry To The Rescue"

*Bird was hauling ass through the blackness of the solar system. Alydar told him that, in 3 minutes, he'd be out of it and heading for deep space. He refused to let Alydar take over and now flew the lander faster... manually... than he ever had in his life. He refused to lose sight of the blip on his HUD and, at these speeds, had the full size Ghost fly his 6. Docking would waste time he didn't know if he had. Docking at these speeds? On 'the fly'? NOT gonna happen. Bird joked slightly that he was indeed motivated, but not suicidal.*

*"Alydar! Go through Ship's memories. Is she going fast enough to cause the star walls like we did when Tammy sent us to 51?"*

*"No... but you are!"*

*"MRU. Can you reach Ship?"*

*"Already tried... no response."*

*"Alydar?"*

*"Yeah?"*

*"Hack her."*

*"Already on it. We need to slow her down. Like Prime once said, I could really use one of those plans of yours right about now!"*

*Bird was already working on one. Suddenly, he smiled.*

*"Ally, can we get a cat's eye... but in front of her?"*

*"Gonna be tough. At her speeds I could... possibly."*

*Bird sneered "Define 'possibly'."*

*"Commander, she's traveling so fast that if I try and catch her, the automatics will kick in and force me into an eye. How she hasn't already is beyond me. I can only imagine Ship is that damaged. If I could get close enough, the eye will kick in automatically but, I can*

*redirect it to open in front of her... instead of me. IF! I could pull it off... where do I send her?"*

*Bird smiled that 'gotcha' sort of smile.*

*"Jupiter."*

*"Huh?"*

*"Open an eye like you said. We'll send her outside Jupiter. Will it's gravity grab her?"*

*"Not a chance."*

*"Ah but, will it slow her down?"*

*"Hardly."*

*"Mm hmm. Now, if we keep sticking her in the Jupiter loop, how many times before it catches her enough times to slow her some?"*

*"Bird?"*

*"What?"*

*"MMMMMMMWAAAAA!" Alydar chuckled.*

*Next thing Bird knew, a really big ship pulled over his head and... pulled away.*

*Alydar put the co-ordinates into his HUD and Bird headed for it. It took him 5 whole minutes to slow enough to put out an eye. Once he did, he was right where he needed to be.*

*The Ghost ship took 3 tries to get an eye in just the right place. The first two failed and caused her to make up even more ground each time. Finally, she got it right. It was only 11 miles ahead of Ship but, she did it.*

*Bird was finally at full stop and hovering outside the big gas giant. He saw the eye open up and sure enough, out came Ship. Now, between him and Alydar, they kept looping Ship. Bird opened an eye, and sent ship behind the sun. Alydar opened another just past Earth, and sent her to Bird. Bird cussed himself as he almost missed one or two loops but, it was working. It took 20 minutes for Alydar to slow down enough to open an eye for herself and actually get to the sun. Once she had, Ship was doing a loop every ten minutes instead of every 25. After awhile, Bird smiled, as 10 minutes became 11... then 11 and a half. When Bird saw the times hit 12 and a quarter, he knew his plan just might work.*

"Bird, We got about another 90 minutes of this before she's slow enough to work out a docking maneuver. Problem remains, I still can't access Ship's systems."

"She offline?"

"Must be. Remmy built in a recognition system only a Ghost can access. Think of it like a smaller system on top of a larger one."

"So, a sub system?"

"No, not part of Ship's mainframe, but a secondary system designed only for me and my sisters. With her hull, we had to have a way in. For sure that's offline or just simply fried. Problem is, that system lets me into all the rest. Essentially..."

Bird finished her sentence with "Ya can't get into the house if the front door is locked."

"Pretty much. I could tap her main system but not unless there was an opening in her hull."

"I'll work on it. For now, let's just keep slowing her down."

"MRU."

Bird thought if he could get her past the gas giants, their huge gravity would 'snag' her every time she passed. It wasn't much but, anything too drastic, and Bird knew Husky go 'buh bye'. This was working but it was taking time. He didn't care however and would do it as long as it took. It kept Ayleen in a place he could control, and it bought him the time he needed to work out the next snag.

"Ally... get up here."

"Careful BirdMan."

"Why?" Bird asked Alydar.

"Bring the avatar online, and I get split between the ten mile, and her. With this situation, you sure that's wise?"

Bird grumbled "Shit."

"Sorry boss but thought you should know. I could do it but, the lag time between her and me could be critical at these speeds. That's why I have her off right now. If I miss by even a piece of a second and..."

"Yeah... MRU."

Bird went back to working on a plan, it was just 'plan B' now.

Ghost 1 finally had a plan. It wasn't a good one and he wasn't even sure if it would work, so he threw it out to Ally for debate.

"What if I shoot her?"

"Uh... 'scuse me?"

"You heard me lady. If I fire up the 12, and fire on her, will that bring up any protocols we can use against her?"

"Nope, not that I can think of."

"Dammit. Okay, think BirdMan think!"

Alydar said "Yeeeaah... even I got nuthin."

Bird actually chuckled at that. He was about to give some crack reply when, he smiled instead.


"Alydar, get the drones ready."

She didn't ask and merely complied. She knew from Bird's tone he had something.

"Wadda ya got boss?"

"Tell me this my fine companion..." Bird started.

He fired up a cat's eye, sent Ayleen back to Alydar and continued.

"If we get her turrets up, will that give you the access you need?"

"Nope, it'll only... wait... I have an idea!"

"Talk to me!"

"Bird, I can't do what you think but, I can get minimal messages through. I can, IF she's still active, have her raise her emergency antenna. Lone put it in as one of Greeva's upgrades. Only you, me, or Lone can activate it. IF! We can get that up, I'm in. That puts us back to another problem."

"I'm listening."

"Her weapons won't activate automatically for something as small as the drones. Only the 12 will. You'd need full power but, do that and she'll start to tumble. Not to mention we don't know how much damage she's sustained so if you did, it may..."

"What if I don't hit her?" Bird said cutting her off.

"Clarify."

"What if I only singe her. Think that would do it?"

"That's a tight shot boss."

Bird sat up straight and proudly proclaimed "I've handled

guns since I was a kid. I am BirdOfPrey and... I hit what I aim at."

"That would be some tight timing boss. You would have to hit her... or rather nearly hit her... and you'd have to do it JUST before she goes into the eye on your end. Assuming she even brings her turrets up, I could, in theory, catch her here when she emerges."

"Worth a shot... heh heh... pun intended."

"I'd disagree but, at this point, it's about all we got."

The 12 pack had a safety on them. Only a Ghost could bring them up and even then, said Ghost had to approve. That was a protocol Bird himself setup as they were that dangerous if let loose wrongly.

Bird leaned back, and said aloud "Alydar, lite 'em up... and spin 'em."

"They're at your command. Bird?"

"Yeah?"

"Six minutes to your end. Good luck."

"I'll take all I can get. Thanks sweety."

Bird took some practice shots on low power, and waited. Alydar called out 1 minute to the eye, and Bird dialed up the power. Ship was slowing down but, she was still blindingly fast. Bird made a sign of the cross, slowed his breathing, and listened to Alydar's countdown. When she hit 3 seconds, Bird hit his triggers. Bird unleashed Max's terrors and missed the left rudder by only 100 yards but, when Ship came out at Alydar's end... she was weapons hot.

Alydar had less than a second to get the order through. After that, Ship would be out of range for the low powered command. If Alydar were human, she would have let out a sigh. Two thirds the way to Bird, the human made a call.

"Ship... can you hear me?"

Nothing.

"Ship?"

Silence.

She was almost at the eye when bird hollered "SHIP!?"

"Rhana? Is that really you?"

"Good to have you back Ship. I am BirdOfPrey, Ghost 1, vocal override 'Omega Pop'."

"It is good to have you safe Rhana," Ship said just as she hit the eye.

Alydar sent commands from her side as she could get more info through in a shorter time. She also could get reports faster. When she called Bird though, her voice was shaking.

"Bird... HUGE problem!"

"Talk to me!"

"The nuke... it's going critical. We need 30 minutes to slow her down enough to retrieve her and Husky."

"FUCK! I know that tone bitch... how long before it goes?"

"17."

"DAMMIT! Okay lady, get on her tail. This time, we make a run for the roses."

"MRU," and Alydar did just that.

"Ship?"

"Yes Rhana?"

"Ship, is Ayleen alive?"

"Yes, though badly injured."

"Ship, can you wake her?"

Through her fog, Ayleen heard a familiar voice that stirred her mind. It wasn't a lot but, it was enough.

"Wow (cough cough) now I know I'm fucked. Ship, I actually just heard Rhana!" Ayleen said barely.

"That's because you did Husky. Listen to me. You're running out of time and we need you to focus. Just focus on my voice Ay."

"Damn ship, he sounds so real!"

"PILOT PRIME! DO YOU CALL THIS SOARING WITH HONOR!!??"

Ayleen shook her wits about her. She truly wanted to believe it was real.

"Rh... Rhana!?"

"Yes my dear. No time to explain. Ay, Ship is in a critical state and we need to get you off... like yesterday."

"Sit... sit... SIT rep!"

"You're traveling at a ridiculous speed. Remember the big flash I showed you once?"

"Vaguely,"

"That... is about to be you."

A vague memory was becoming clear as Ayleen forced herself to stay awake... and focused. She found the first, though hard, was far easier than the second.

"I can try and dock with you and..."

"Forget it! You're going too fast! JESUS what I wouldn't give for a door right now."

"You mean a 51 door?"

"Yeah Ayleen. It was a joke of sorts. Listen we got to..."

"I got one," Ayleen said cutting off Bird.

"Ayleen, listen, I reeeeeeallly need you to focus right now. You're on Ship still, not Alydar."

"I... I... I know. I got one."

"AYLEEN! Ship was never fitted with one now focus!"

"I AM YA PRAT!.... ow."

"Ay, what are you talking about?" Bird asked now knowing she wasn't lying.

"When Lone left the door in the hangar room, Renny asked me and Ryklan to get it. I put it in ship's storage to keep it safe. Sorry Rhana but no one asked for it and, well, I thought it might be useful one day so I..."

"AYLEEN! I need you to get to it! Tell it to take you to the lander bay... GO GO GO!!!"

"But what...."

"NOW PILOT PRIME!"

"Bird?" Alydar called out.

"What!?"

"6 minutes."

Ship spoke softly saying "Ayleen, under the main console, quickly, take the storage module... it's all that's left of me. It's been an honor, now... do as Rhana says. I can barely pressurize the cargo bay but, it will be enough."

Ayleen knew Rhana. That knowledge alone kept her going when all she wanted to do was go back to sleep. If the 'Great Rhana' wanted it done... then done it would be. She heard Alydar count out 4 minutes as she pulled the cover panel off. She got out the crystal as Alydar called 3 minutes. She couldn't stand so, crawl she did. At 2 minutes she made it to the door and stood it up. She was crying knowing Ship was going to be gone.

"Thank you," was all she could think of.

"You're welcome... now... go. Soar with honor Pilot Prime."

Alydar called out 59 seconds.

Ayleen said "I will Ship... always." She looked dead ahead and said "Door, lander bay."

It didn't open.

"SHIT! DOOR!? I AM BirdOfPrey... follow her orders!"

Ayleen was about to pass out but... she heard a beep... as Alydar called out 32 seconds.

"DOOR! Take me to Lander bay!"

Now... it opened. Bird was running this whole time. He hit the door behind the cockpit, and blew out on the main floor of the bay. Hauling ass up to the one Scota walked through, he caught a wolf female as she passed out falling through it.

"DOOR EMERGENCY CLOSE!"

The door did exactly that.


"Rhana?"

"Yes Ship?"

"It's been an honor. Knowing I won't be around, I'll perish knowing you, and Ayleen are safe. Honor to the Ghosts."

Ship shut off everything and funneled all power to the cat's eye.

Bird was near tears, and sitting on the balcony holding a seriously injured fellow pilot. Alydar banked left, and the lander banked right, as Ship went straight. Out a porthole on the far side of the bay, Bird saw a monstrous flash. Ship had gotten clear of them, barely, and tied in the weapons and the FTL to all go off at the same time. Being much smaller than Ally, the hell wave had done tremendous damage to her structure. The combination of the nuke, FTL, all her weapons, and a still open cat's eye insured... no creature ever would find even a piece of her hull.

Bird laid Ayleen down... stood up... and saluted the far side of the bay.

"Semper Fi Ship... and thank you, for everything... you grand lady. In my memories, and my heart... always shall you fly."

Alydar was near tears. Hearing Bird's words, she was no longer near them.


Bleeding incredible amounts of speed, Alydar, and Bird in the Lander, headed back for a tiny blue dot. Ally came online and brought a hover chair to Bird. Ayleen was heavy and he was starting to not be able to hold her. She had a big gash on the back of her head, and Bird could feel 2 breaks in one leg. How she even moved it was something he couldn't fathom.

Bird got her on the hover chair and now he and the avatar raced her to med bay. Ally did what she could but Ayleen was dying. The moment she could, Alydar applied the brakes on both craft.

"FLIGHT MODE!" Bird hollered out.

Just in time too. He hit the rockets and barely kept himself from slamming the far wall due to the deceleration. Ayleen was strapped to the table and Ally was hanging onto the same.

Thirty seconds of Bird being horizontal, and at full burn, and he finally fell to the floor. Now, he was heading across the floor. He rolled onto his back and got his jets against the other wall. Now finally stopped, Bird retracted the suit... unstrapped Ayleen... and he and patient were on the move to the nearest door. Alydar had gotten juuuuuust inside the door's range. Bird got a clean sheet, and was now in the full sized Alydar. Rounding the corner at full speed, he got Ayleen in med bay and practically dumped her in the tank. In her unconscious state, breathing the water was a non issue.

Letting out a deep breath, he smirked at Ally saying "Nice to know the brakes work. Wadda ya say though, we don't do that again... ever... okay?"

"Sounds like a plan to me BirdMan."

Bird and Ally got what sensors they could hooked up, and sat down to do nothing but wait.

# Chapter 29:

## "A Mother's Tale... And A Tale Of A Mother"

*Ayleen was badly hurt. Near terminal in fact. Bird and Ally sat for hours till the sensors read 2% higher. It wasn't much but... at least they stopped going down.*

*"Well, now you need to come up with a cover story," Ally stated. "I can tell you this, I don't envy you. The radiation levels will get deflected by Earth's magnetosphere, but enough is gonna get through to cause some serious weather issues."*

*"How serious we talking about?"*

*"Like... Nor'Easters... in the middle of Europe," Ally quipped.*

*"Greeeeeaaaaaat," Bird answered sarcastically.*

*"I've been tracking it. Once it hits they'll be anywhere from a week to a month's worth of disturbances. Light at first, the worst of it towards the middle then, fading off towards the end. I estimate it will begin somewhere around late February to end of March."*

*"Well, at least Christmas will be spared." Bird chuckled and said "Here's hoping Easter doesn't come early this year."*

*Renny was in her office on Tuhleesia when a knock came on the door. Lone, as promised, not only made it for her but... made it fit for a Wing and a Guardian. No one would dare disturb her and the few that would weren't around currently, so the knock had her curious.*

*"I have a fully stocked armory at my disposal. Tell me, am I gonna need it?" Renny asked with slight concern.*

*The female wolf at her door was nervous, but merely said "No, you won't. Before either of us say another word though, I would like to offer my apology. Not to a Guardian however, but to my daughter-in-law."*

*Renny smiled, and opened the door.*


"Salyan, what has you so worried my love?" Little Blue cooed trying to get Sal 'in the mood'.

"Oh jeez... ENOUGH already! I'm trying to get this done!" Salyan barked in obvious annoyance.

"And cranky as well apparently," she said with a dejected and annoyed tone.

Sal got up to leave telling Little Blue he was going to his shop. That changed Blue's tone in a hurry.

"You're doing that a lot lately... do you hate me?"

Sal wasn't angry, and his tone reflected that. He was however, exasperated, and his tone reflected that too.

"Blue look, do I hate you?... No. Do I hate what you're doing?... Yes."

Blue was sad and said "But I've done everything the others said to. (sniff) It seems the more I try, the more I get it wrong. No insult intended but, according to Doctor Jonathan, I'm even smarter than you. So how come I can't make you happy? All I want is to make you love me like I love you, but..."

"But what?" Sal said kindly.

"Seems I'm better at Rhana's archeology site than making you happy. At least there I know what I'm doing."


Now Sal had the edge he'd been looking for.

"Blue, you're not doing it wrong, you're doing it too much or too hard."

Still sniffling some, Blue asked "Clarify."

"Blue, do you remember the story I told you about going to Ayleen?"

"I do."

"Do you remember why?"

Curling into a ball, Blue just said "Mm hmm."

"You're as bad as both of them... combined. When I take off my work clothes at the end of the day, I don't even get a chance to pick them up off the floor before you run and grab them and wash them. When I say I'm hungry, you rush to make a meal for 10

*Xarans. Even those things aren't the problem, it's the attitude behind them. You act like I'll leave you if you don't, or that I'll disapprove of something."*

*Blue wanted to offer some argument, but just couldn't.*

*"Blue, I heard you went to the Ghosts and others to get advice, yes?"*

*"I did."*

*"Perhaps that's the problem. You asked them, and while that's fine, you however, never asked me."*

*Sal was trying not to be mean, but he was also desperate to get his point across.*

*"Like I said, it's not what your doing... it's how much of it. Stop worrying, and keep doing what you're doing... just do a lot less of it."*

*Blue was confused and asked "So, you don't want me caring for you?"*

*"That's not what I said. I leave and go to my shop right?"*

*"Yeah."*

*"But, don't I always come back?"*

*"Yeah but..."*

*"But nothing. Tell me, when I leave, you worry I won't... don't you?"*

*Sadly, Blue said "Every time."*

*"I come home to see you Blue. But life is not just about me. I truly think it's nice you care for me, and I know any man would be lucky to have someone like you. That said, stop being afraid... know that when I leave, at some point I'll come back... and see where it takes us, okay?"*

*"Okay my love... I'll try."*

*Blue truly meant it and decided to try it by asking, calmly.*

*"So, what are you working on?"*

*Sal's frustration was back, but it was over his work, not Blue.*

*"The minefield."*

*"What about it?"*

*"There's so many portals, and so random. Commander Lone asked me to see if there was a pattern to them, or something like*

one. Lady R and Renny are going to trance down them. Uncle Lone wants me to see if there's anything to them to not waste so much time and effort, and focus on one's that will be worth checking out."

"Random yes... many no. So why all the frustration, I don't get it."

"You haven't seen it. Trust me, the possibilities are near endless."

"Um, no they're not and you know it."

Blue said that with conviction. It was the kind of conviction that makes one stop and think.

"I do?" Sal said slightly perplexed.

"You are Salyan, Xaran salvation in the flesh. Aside from we 5, you're the smartest being around here. As such, I know YOU know, there's only 6... and I don't appreciate being teased like that."

"No Blue, I'm not kidding... there's thousands."

Blue had a revelation, and said "Oh my stars, you're not teasing me are you? You really haven't figured it out have you?"

Sal had a look of 'impress me' on his face, and just said "Okay Blue, what do you know that I don't?"

Blue leaned forward and explained.

Ten minutes later and Sal was bogged down in science beyond even him. He listened to Blue tell him how, and why, the minefield even existed.

"Whoa whoa whoa, okay Blue, break it down so I can understand."

Now that Sal was a Wing, he had a console similar to the Ghosts. Blue went up to it, turned on the simulation she'd seen Sal bring up many times, and began to explain.

"This point here, in our space that's the sight of the original explosion. The station keeps it stable and... contained. From this point, 6 time streams come out. Look here..." Blue said pointing to the display.

"It's a portal, what of it?"

"It's one of the six. Look here..." and Blue pointed to another at the opposite end of the field. "Ignore this stuff in between, it's just noise... like static. Likely created by the main 6. Now, filter that out and... is this what you're looking for?"

Blue filtered out the 'noise' and Sal was stunned. He saw just what Blue said. At the center was the source, with an energy beam of some sort tethering it to the station. Emanating from that, were 6 tubes, somewhat like an octopus. What Blue had seen was the open ends. She noticed, whenever one appeared, there was a matching one somewhere on the opposing side. The rest she deduced using that, and figured out what no creature had... including it's creator. What Sal also saw was each end was swinging wild, like a fire hose at full pressure but with no one holding it. Blue truly thought it was not hard to figure out, and thought everyone noticed it... so she never said anything.

"Well..." Blue smiled, "...now will you come to bed?"

"UNCLE LONE!" Sal hollered into his comm.

"Little busy right now buddy, wazzup?"

"NOT anymore you're not. Get Raven warmed up, I'll meet you in the hangar!"

Lone was a tad confused and said "And I'd do that why?"

"I need to talk to a twin... now."

"Aaaaaand.... whyzzat then?"

"The minefield... I sorted it, well actually... Blue did. I got an idea and I need the help of a scientist... a really old one."

"I'll meet you in the hangar," Lone said with a tone like nothing else mattered.

"See you in 15... Sal out!" He turned to Blue and said "I'm leaving. What are you NOT gonna do?"

Beaming that she pleased Sal, Blue stated "Be afraid."

"And what am I gonna do when I get back!?"

"Come home," she said still beaming.

Sal kissed her and said "And, when I do... know that if you're asleep... heh heh... I'm gonna wake you up," and he gave her the sly grin that made her melt every time.


"Know that I mean no insult when I say this but, Lone has been gone from us for so long, that while I know he is my son, it was like Ayleen was an only child. I hope that makes some sense," Ree'nah stated.

"To anyone else, likely not. To me however, it does."

"Hearing I'm to be a grandmother, know that I am thrilled for you but, well, it seems odd somehow. It's like, how can I be a grandmother when Ayleen isn't with child. I still consider myself a mother only, and not one old enough to be a grandmother. It's not much I know but, I say that so you may understand my actions of late."

"I can't even begin to imagine what you're going through, and can totally understand your actions. Lone however has done nothing, and I WILL defend him, and his actions. He forbid Ayleen from coming, but understood. In the end, know this... 'Guardian Rennahr' is about to tell you something she shouldn't... as my adopted dad would say, do we understand each other?"

"I understand I came to see my daughter-in-law, and Guardian Rennahr was nowhere in sight when I did," Ree'nah replied slyly.

"See that it stays that way," Renny said in a no nonsense tone. "As I said, Lone forbid her but understood. It was actually Rhana who told Lone to leave her be. 'Let her grow up already' were his exact words. He had no idea it would turn into what it has. He knew Ayleen was growing. He also knew she was there to honor him, and represent us. Rhana was leaving, never to return. While I don't know this for a fact, knowing him as I do, I do believe he wanted all the memories he could get."

"Rennahr, can I tell you something?"

"Feel free," Renny answered bringing in some snacks and drinks.

"Ayleen indeed grew up. Know there are two things that have annoyed me since her birth and, were the reasons for my behavior."

Kindly, Renny asked "First?"

"Her infatuation with Lone. I never understood it, and always felt like I was left out because of it."

"I may be able to help with that one. Do you remember when you asked Rahgaa to take her to him?"

"I do."

"Rahgaa didn't stay long. She felt her waking up, and told the dynamic duo she needed to go as she didn't want Ayleen waking up while she was trancing. She however... did."

*Some things were now starting to make sense to Ree'nah.*

*"And... her reaction?"*

*"Heh heh, in typical Ayleen fashion, she thought it was glorious."*

*"Typical," Ree'nah said with a hint of agitation. "But what does that have to do with her brother?"*

*"I believe, only a belief mind you... everything. She thought it glorious. Lone was at the other end and, to an impressionable child, she associated Lone with that large and fascinating world. I believe, in part, Lone was her way of being part of that again. She truly is a good wolf, so, hearing of Lone and all his bravery and honor, that only cemented in her mind the link between the two."*

*"That actually explains a lot. Doesn't change what was but, at least it does explain it. I know this is only your belief and you have no proof but... it does make much sense."*


*"And second?" Renny asked.*

*"Secrecy."*

*"Hmm... in what way?"*

*"Rennahr, you're not a mother... not yet. When you are, and hold your child, well, what you're thinking it will be like... won't be even close. It will be beyond glorious. I know you would protect your child. I also know that, once he or she is born, that feeling will take on a whole new meaning you can't understand now."*

*"While your correct in the manner of I don't know now, how does that factor in to secrecy?"*

*"When you do have a child, as I said you'll want to protect them. Imagine having secrets involving them, yet you're not privileged to know them. How can you keep them safe from an enemy you can't see? You can't, you won't and... nor could I. As such, just like I did, when you can't see the danger, you go into a panic. You start protecting them from things you don't know AND can't see."*

*Renny had no mother, not one she could really remember anyway. One thing that bothered her was having this child with no family or friend around she could turn to with questions. Seeing things were getting better with Ree'nah, she was truly happy and... she was asking them now.*

*"While I understand some of what you've said, I don't others. Wouldn't happen to have an example would you?"*

*"Actually, I do. When all the guns were in place in the Pillars Of Alydar, Tahl wanted to prove a point and... impart some wisdom. He said he had Lone send an invisible target drone sent for target practice. Lone had given him a set of sun shades and Tahl told them they would let only him see the target. It was an exercise drill to teach the gunners something. The drill began and he would call out 'There it is!' and point... then something similar and point elsewhere. The guards soon got frustrated by what they couldn't see and were soon shooting wildly and... constantly. Tahl called a halt to it, then told them the truth. His point was, to teach them that one day, the enemy may truly be invisible, or simply too fast to see. The point he told them, was how to stay calm and focused, and not panic. I tell you this because, raising Ayleen was much like that exercise. I wasn't told many things, and sometimes neither was Tahl. Still, with no knowledge, we still had to protect our child. As such, we overprotected as a way to be ready when a real danger actually did appear. That as well, had its own dangers as it put us at constant odds with our own child."*

*Renny got it now and said "Rhana has said, many myths on his planet were because humans have a need to understand things. He said his people's greatest fear wasn't death... it was the unknown. As such, they would simply make things known by making up explanations as a means to make their fears go away. It would seem, his people may be worse than us at that but... they also don't appear to be alone in that regard."*

*"I agree."*

*Ree'nah knew Renny was busy and as such got up to leave.*
*Renny said "So, imitating Rhana I see eh?"*
*"Um... I am?"*
*"Lone is not here. You came to see me knowing full well Lone was elsewhere."*
*"Actually I hadn't thought of it that way but, heh heh, I suppose I am."*
*"Know this. Even if you and Lone 'kissed and made up'... he*

still will not come to your home. Not till he has what you requested anyway. I want you to know it's not anger that compels him to do that, but more of a personal matter... more of a goal really than anything else."

Ree'nah sighed saying "Always with him is the odd and unknown and uncomfortable situations. I understand and... thank you."

"For?"

Ree'nah smiled and said "For accepting my apology."

Renny smiled back as she closed her door.


"AAAYYYY!" Scota yelled as she dropped a plate of drinks.

She was yelling because Bird spooked her. She had forgotten the starfish as she had become so comfortable with it, she forgot it was there... till Bird's disembodied voice called her.

"Scota what is it!?" Ciana hollered heading towards the kitchen where Scota was.

"Nothing dear sister... I uh... I saw a mouse and it caught me by surprise."

"Heh heh. The lies get easier with practice... just so's ya know," Bird chuckled in the Brooklyn accent he uses for Sal.

"Wadda yeh waaaaahn?"

"Oooooh, you know I love it when your accent gets thick." Unable to resist, Bird teased her saying "Ya know, I could always swoop in, pick you up and cart you off somewhere romantic. No one would ever know and I could whisper things only you could hear and..."

"I'd cut yer 'manhood' clean off iffin yeh ever tried," Scota said to the seemingly open air.

"HAHAHAHA! You sure lass? I hear sisters share all kinds of things and..."

"Was there some'thin I can do for yeh!??" Scota said utterly frustrated and cutting him off.

Bird stopped teasing but still had a chuckle in his voice as he said "Actually yeah there is. How's it going over there?"

Scota looked around, then said "Not good. Lots of folk are scared. Likely me most of all."

"How do you figure that?"

Still making sure the coast was clear, Scota told him "The town folk. Honestly Bird, I ain't heard such wild tales in all my life... and from grownups no less! Thing that has me scared is, how quick they are to believe them."

"Welcome to my world."

"No thank you."


"Scota listen, like it or not, you're part of our world now. What you saw is truly frightening and worse, part of it is heading our way. I need you to stay focused and tell them I'll be there in a day or so with answers."

"And how am I supposed to do thah when yeh not even here!? They'll likely burn me for a witch or something the way these folk be react'in."

"Like I said... welcome to my world. You'll just have to think of something."

"Like 'I' said... no thank you."

"Well then, next time, be careful of what doors you walk through."

"Aye... doen remind me. I'll do what I can. Bird?"

"Yeah?"

Now, with 'other world' curiosity, Scota asked "Where are yeh?"

"Orbiting... uh 'circling'... the moon."

Scota giggled "Still teas'in I see?"

"Uh... no... I'm really orbiting the moon," Bird told her in an 'I'm not lying' tone.

"Bloody hell! Well Yankee Man, when you said other world stuff, yeh weren't kidd'in were yeh now?"

"Heh heh... nope."

"Keep yerself safe."

"I will sweety... you do the same... Bird out."

"Out where?"

"Heh heh... nevermind."

Scota served the drinks finally then, took a few minutes. She walked outside and looked up at the moon.

Ciana came to check on her and said "Aye, tis a lovely sight tonight isn't it?"

Scota just smiled, said "Aye, that it is," and kindly walked her clueless sister back inside.

That cluelessness was starting to irritate Scota. It was irritating Bird as well. Not that Ciana was clueless to it all but, that they had to lie and keep things from her. Bird the planner was already working on that as he hung up the call.


"Is that concern on your face BirdMan... or are you planning?" Alydar's hologram asked.

"A little of both actually."

"Do yeh mind share'in?" Alydar teased imitating the locals.

"I don't mind at all," Bird said sweetly. "To tell the truth, normally I bang out the plan myself, then go 'okay here it is'. Usually it's only tweaked but mostly intact. I have to say having someone like yourself to bounce ideas and wisdom's off of during the planning stage, well... that's kinda nice too."

"Just as nice being asked," Alydar said sweetly. "So, what are ya planning now?"

"My guitar."

"Um... okay... huh?" Alydar giggled.

"Well, I was thinking. I gave Ciana a taste of this world. Gave her a little and yet hid it at the same time. She reacted very well to it. Scota however got a huge dose and... all at once. As you recall, that didn't go so well."

"I'll say."

"So I was thinking. I firmly believe Scota already had an open mind to a degree, and it's why she adjusted so quickly."

"She hasn't adjusted Bird. Accepted perhaps, but adjusted will take quite a bit more time."

"Okay, I'll accept that. Still... she has. Ciana however is nowhere near as open minded as she is though."

"Agreed," Alydar said as she checked the equipment monitoring Ayleen.


Bird and Alydar were having this discussion in med bay. Bird was feeling worlds better having Ayleen here now. Having her lost, *and with all the variables that came with it, didn't sit well with him. Now that she's here, even if she died from her injuries, Bird would know he did everything he could. He also knew not only could he face Lone should they ever meet again but... now it was time to start making that meeting happen. At that very moment, Bird felt his days on Earth... were now numbered.*

*"Alydar, it's like this. Scota got a huge shock, and as such we had a lot of damage control to do. I was thinking, how 'alien' is an electric guitar, in this day and age? Yet, that small dose sat very well with her. I controlled the circumstances, let her in a little but, not too far. The plan you referred to is this... I think it's time I start bringing her in. I was thinking if I keep doing that, little pieces here and there, she won't feel left out... I can stop lying... and perhaps she won't get AS shocked as Scota was when we do bring her in."*

*"I agree but... there's more... I can tell."*

*"Yep. We got Ayleen now. Regardless of what happens to her, we got her. Aside from the two lovely ladies, there's nothing keeping me here anymore. I... BirdOfPrey, Ghost 1... want to go home."*

*Bird would start going home in time, it just wouldn't be with who he thought, or rather how many, when he did.*

*Ciana wasn't home and she wasn't at the inn either. According to Alydar, she was almost 2 miles to the north at the farthest edge of her croft.*

*"Anyone around her?" Bird asked.*

*"Negative."*

*"What the hell is she doing... she should be here for this," Bird said as he greeted more town folk to his home.*

*"Oh well, I'll handle this. Keep an eye on her for me okay?"*

*"Already on it," Ally told him.*

*Scota said that the latest couple was the last of them. Now Bird geared up for the biggest lie yet.*

*"Alright folks settle down. I got a story to tell and this time, it isn't imaginary," Bird told the rather noisy crowd. Settled some, he continued with "LET ME warn you. I told Scota there is NO such*

thing as magic, sorcery or demons... only science. If I catch ANY one resorting to such behavior, I will cut off my story in an instant... tell you nothing... and let you fend for yourselves. Am I clear!?"

Bird was the most learned man they knew. Right now they'd give him anything he wanted as long as he gave them some answers.

"First let me tell you... I am either ashamed or embarrassed by all of you. I have heard of some of your tales. HONESTLY people... grown men and women?.... Witches?... You should all be ashamed of yourselves."

"Well what WAS it then?" William called out.

"Science... even beyond my understanding. William... ever see lightning?"

"Aye... 'course I have."

"What comes next?"

"Thunder usually."

"Mm hmm. What you saw the other day was just that. Only difference was... it was much bigger... and it was in space."

Bird waited a few moments for the uproar to die down.

One of the women said "I seen lines go across the moon last night. A bad omen I tell yeh!"

Bird said nothing... grabbed her by the arm... and forcefully threw her out the door.

"Anyone else wanna try my resolve?... OR my patience?"

With that... the crowd calmed down.

"Do I know what made it? No. Do I know what causes it? No. Do I know what it's after effects are? Yes." Before the crowd could react he said "William, thunder follows lightning. If the lightning is far away... what of the thunder?"

"Usually, delayed and not too loud."

"Correct but... if the lightning is closer?"

"Aye... I get it... it comes much quicker... louder too!"

"Correct yet again. When my 'other life' was still intact, we saw one of those things once. Smaller and farther away but... we saw one. Six months later the weather went nuts and lasted that way for weeks. MY scientists were still working on it when I left to come here. They believe some rocks collided in space... what you know of as the night time sky. The 'lightning' in this case isn't the problem..."

Angus finished his sentence saying "Aye... it's the thunder."

*"Correct."*

*Bird dove into the now stunned crowd with the last of his warning.*

*"Remember people, I was in a different part of the world when we first saw it and... it was much smaller. Still it wreaked havoc on the weather for weeks. What I'm telling you now is, that one the other day was bigger BECAUSE it was closer. As such, I can only expect that the 'thunder' will arrive sooner and... the weather will get far worse for a few weeks."*

*Angus was far happier hearing some sort of explanation. Hearing it from Bird however, was good enough for him. Bad as the prediction was, he trusted Bird over anyone else.*

*Bird now called out over the noisy crowd saying "LISTEN TO ME!" The crowd died down and Bird told them "You won't see anything new. What I can tell you is storms that usually take days to form AND arrive, will take only hours or minutes to do the same. Nothing you haven't already experienced before, it's just how quick they come that will be different." Bird looked out on the see of faces and said "BUT!... I have no doubt that, those grand and brave people of the Scottish highlands and Isles will show EVEN the heavens... no one will move them from their land nor their homes. Now good people, tell me this... am I right?"*

*Alydar was in his ear now as the local folk were getting pumped.*

*"May wanna wrap this up boss."*

*"Lil busy right now in case you hadn't noticed?" Bird said slyly.*

*"Well then... get UN busy... your fiance just got company. A whole lot of company."*

*"Armed?"*

*"Minor but... some are yes."*

*"I'll be there shortly."*

*Bird wrapped up this little party by telling them "What only Ciana and Scota know is... I have another life. That life was military and... not just any military. I've been keeping that life at bey but... it* has perks. I'm already in touch with them and I'll give you what news I can when and as I get it. These men AND women... are as learned or even more so than I am. Brave the storms, know that they are indeed coming... and I'll help you when and where I can. My apologies but, right now? I'm required elsewhere."

Scota handled the rest. Whatever she didn't know she made up same as Bird did, or simply said she didn't know and to ask Bird. Ghost 1 however, was in hustle mode to the north end of the croft.


"And how are you my child? You have grown even more beautiful if that's even possible," the hooded man said.

Ciana never got a chance to answer him.

"She's doing quite well thank you. Now, I've already had my fill of corrupt holy men, so if you don't mind... you are?"

That voice was Bird's. He was also brandishing some form of pistol... two of them actually... that Ciana had never seen before.

"How did you even know I was here!?" Ciana barked in utter surprise.

"I told you once, wherever you were, I wouldn't be far away. Heh heh, now what kind of husband would I make if I couldn't even keep my word?" Bird said with a chuckle.

"You've married?" the cloaked man asked.

"Not as yet. This is..."

"I'll be asking the questions here 'priest'." Bird said cutting Ciana off.

"BIRD!"

"WHAT!???" Bird hollered back but still with eyes, and cannons, on the robed one.

"This one, is not like theh bishop. This is Padre Pedro and, long before yeh kept me safe from the bishop... he did."

"That true robed one?" Bird called out.

"I do what I can to protect God's children," Padre said politely and... calmly.

Bird put away the now infamous cannons for only one reason. His HUD stayed blue.


"Padre? Ciana here is the most trusting and sweetest person

I've ever known. Most times, a little too sweet and... a little too trusting. THAT... is what I'm here for." Bird walked forward with his hand extended but, the robed one backed up.

Bird had caution in his tone when he said "I can see your face padre. That's not fear of me... that's concern FOR me. Am I to assume you've come in the ship that lies outside the harbor?"

"You assume correct my son... on both counts."

Ciana looked at him with slight shock and asked "You know of thah?"

Bird hooked his thumb saying "BirdMan my dear. Ain't much I don't know about." Bird turned back to the priest and said "Took me a bit to sort out the flag. Once I had, let's just say, I've had my eye on you."

"Wise course of action. Now, tell me something. Why did you lower your weapons?"

Padre was testing Bird and, he knew it.

"I have a tendency to know when people are lying. Ciana wasn't. Seems, you weren't either. Now, tell ME something priest... are you infected too?"

"Unknown but, I believe so. You are correct, I backed away due to fear... but not likely the one you imagined."

Bird was a tad pissed, and looked at Ciana.

"Mind telling me why you brought a biblical plague to our back door??"

"I owe him," Ciana said with truth and sadness in her voice.

"Padre? Feel free to stay where you are. Ciana? Feel free to start talking." Bird then yelled out to the night time woods "And the rest of you! So much as one of you sneezes and I don't like it... and I'll drop you where you stand."

"Bird honestly, it's just the padre."

"No... it's not," was all he replied.

Ciana sighed, and told her tale.

"Bird, yeh know of my father, somewhat ennyway. What yeh don't know is... my mother."

"Bay... suicide... freaked out a little girl in doing it too. You were saying?" Bird said slightly snidely as he kept an eye on the thermal images in the woods.

"How did yeh.... ooooh.... SCOTA!" Ciana barked in frustration.

"Don't blame her. Now, you were saying?"

"Aye. Mother was sick. I didn't know till she started show'in signs."

"Leprosy I'll guess?"

"Mm hmm. Though I didn't know till after she passed. Mother was the sweetest and kindest woman I ever knew."

"She was indeed AND... much like her daughter," the padre interjected.

Ciana picked back up.

"Mother became ill. Father did his best but still needed to run the inn AND, not let others know how sick mother was."

"Oh I get it. Enter padre over here eh?"

Pedro bowed slightly as Ciana said "Aye."


"I was ministering in the church in the southern part of the Isle," the padre told Bird. "Her father asked for help. Tell me my son, have you ever heard of a place called Culloden?"

"I have. Is there some reason you keep testing me priest?" Bird said in an 'I'm getting annoyed with you' tone.

"Indeed. The bishop became a threat to an innocent girl. You have weapons the likes I've never seen. Till I'm satisfied you aren't as well... I'll test you all I please."

"Fine by me," Bird said but, he was starting to like the priest's attitude. More the reasons for it actually. "Alright, Culloden, I don't know much but, Bonnie Prince Charlie led the Scots against the English in a failed attempt to restore what he felt was the rightful CATHOLIC king to the throne. Seems they lost. Not only that but, the Brits were a tad brutal defeating them. Massacre is the word I believe."

Now Padre Pedro was impressed.


Bird saw a look on Ciana's face. It was one of cluelessness. Seeing that, a thought hit him.

"Padre? How long have you been looking after the ones in the woods?"

"I began when I met Ciana's mother and father. The current flock... five years now."

Ciana was flustered now and said "Bird what ARE yeh talk'in bout?"

"Padre Pedro here isn't alone. He's got around 100 lying in wait in the woods. Seems they're as protective of their priest as I am of you." Bird then looked into the blackness of the Scottish forest and hollered out "I won't take offense to that bow and arrow you're holding. Draw it back however, and you'll never get a chance to release it." Bird then looked at the padre and said "Body guards I'll assume?"

"You might say that," Pedro said in pleasant amazement.

"Well then Padre, I can tell by the look on my love's face, there's a bit to this story she wasn't privy too. Am I correct?"

"Privy?"

"Told about."

"You are quite a smart man aren't you?" Pedro said in a thick Spanish accent.

"I do try."

The padre looked at Ciana and said "For your kindness I planned to tell you. You were but a child at the time, and your mother wanted nothing of that life to touch you or your sister. Tell me stranger... do you have a name?"

"BirdOfPrey."

"The tone in your voice belies military."

Shit. Bird could spot that tone a mile off and tried damn hard not to have one himself. If this padre heard it, then he would work on it later... but work on it he would.

"Commander actually... though not one you'd need worry about if these talks stay as friendly as they have so far. So padre... Culloden?"

"Indeed," Pedro said picking back up. "I promised her mother I'd say nothing unless asked or... she figured it out. Seeing as how you seem to have... would you like to or should I?"

"Mind if I do? I looooove guessing this stuff heh heh."

Padre Pedro waved a hand as if to say 'go ahead'. The padre

was starting to like this stranger and... the stranger was starting to like him.

"Ciana's mother and father were involved weren't they?"

Pedro smiled saying "Heavily."

Bird cut off Ciana's look of 'start talking' and, certainly did.

"Ciana, how old were you when mom died?"

"Almost 14."

"And dad?"

"Two years later."

"Padre... Scota said she remembered the inn being loaded with people... then not. Tell me... soldiers?"

"Not exactly but, those willing to be."

Bird turned to Ciana saying "Mom and dad were involved in the uprising. Likely using the inn as a little more than a Ceilidh house." Bird asked "How'm I doing so far Padre?"

Pedro merely smiled and waved a hand as if to say 'continue'.

"They were into some serious shit. IF they lost, or were discovered, they ran the risk of the king himself paying a visit to their little girls."

Ciana was stunned. Her world in a matter of minutes got turned upside down. Not only that but, yet again, Bird figured it out... she didn't.

"What I don't get is the leprosy," Bird half asked, half stated.

"A few of the 'soldiers' had it though no one knew," Padre told them. "When it was discovered, the prince used that as a weapon. He knew even if they lost, he might still win."

"Oh shit. Ciana's mom and dad, they refused to back off didn't they?"

"Loyal to the end. I knew nothing of her mother's plan. Tell me my son, are you a christian?"

"I am."

"Catholic perhaps?"

"Raised. Still Christian though more the practice of, and less so of any one version."

"Then you'll know suicide is a sin yes?"

"I know some consider it so."

"As I said... I knew nothing of her plan."

Now the padre finished the story.

"I ministered to, and prayed with, those heading out to fight. Sick though they may be, that only meant they needed God's love and guidance more... not less. Her mother paid with her life to help the prince. When she passed, her father became near sick with despair."

"Loved her that much did he?"

"The fire in his eyes for his wife, was the same as I see in yours for his daughter."

"Good to know," Bird said honestly.

Ciana was just stunned. She planned on telling Bird a story. She never planned on getting one... and just simply had no words. Had anyone else but the Padre told it, she'd have called them a liar.

"When her mother passed, I prayed with, and consoled her father." Padre Pedro turned to Ciana with kind eyes and said "Regardless of what they hid from you, the love you recall from them was honest, and exactly what you remember." He turned back to Bird saying "I was called back to Spain after the massacre. You said it was brutal, but what you don't know is why."

"The king found out didn't he?" Bird said.

"And made sure nothing of that disease would touch his fair city. As I'm sure you now suspect, there were spies in the group."

"And the bishop?" Bird asked.

Now Ciana kicked in her part.

"Father became ill. Padre was called to Spain as he said. As such he was preparing to leave, and came when he could but couldn't come as much. One day, a new bishop was heading this way. Padre Pedro couldn't come and asked the bishop if he would look in on us. I was just past 14. He did come and... well I think you know the rest of thah."

"I can figure it out. And the padre here?"

"He came one day and I went to him for confession. I told him of a lecherous man, then told him who he was. Padre made sure I was never alone with him. He even stood up to him more than once, but not like you and Ally did. As such, the bishop had him moved off the Isle but by then I was wise enough, and old enough, to fend fer myself. Father passed the following year and Padre Pedro came and did theh services. I had nothing left except Scota. He taught us how to read and write, better than what mother and father had. He made sure I knew of things most girls my age didn't. He was kind to us when all the others stayed away. I was hurt Bird, and had no idea why we were shunned... till now ennyway. Padre finally had to go but I was fine on my own by then. Bird I swear to God, he was theh ONLY one who cared for me and Scota at the time. When he left I promised him if he ever needed me... he had but to ask. He did just before you arrived but I fergot about it till theh other day."

Bird could be a bit of a... well quite frankly, as Lone would say... a right sonofabitch. When people wanted loving or caring, they went to Ciana. When hell fire ran through the daytime sky... they went to Bird. As such, and for reasons he knew were there but just couldn't put a finger on, he was trying to be more like Ciana at times. This, to him, seemed like one of those times.

"The bishop hasn't gone away padre but... he faces a new defender now. For what it's worth, I thank you for filling in for me till I... heh heh... 'could arrive' and take over."

Padre Pedro nodded to Bird.

"Now my dear... what did you promise the padre here?"

Ciana looked at Bird with defiance.

"It's MY land and I'll do as I..."

"WHAT!... Did you promise him?" Bird said cutting her off.

"Enough to put up a small camp and care for those who need it... like my mother and father once did."

Bird said nothing, and just hugged her.

The padre walked as close as he dared, and laid a note on the ground, then backed away. Bird's HUD was up in a flash and saw the padre was indeed infected, though mildly. The note however was clean.

"She left that for me. I was to tell you of it when you were older. I thought perhaps, now, you should have it."

Bird took it, backed up, and handed it to Ciana. She was

touching it gingerly as memories flooded her mind.

"Padre, what is this... I can't read it?"

Bird took the note and immediately saw why.

"You were never supposed to," Bird told her. "It's written in Castillion."

"What?"

"Spanish." Bird looked at the priest and asked "No es que el padre la correcta?"

Padre replied in English saying "Indeed you are correct. I taught her my language and, when she needed to tell me something no other should know, she spoke in my native language."

Bird took the letter, and Alydar put the translation into English under each line.

"Dearest Father," Bird began to read. "Please forgive me. I am getting far worse. I have made peace with my own soul for the disease I brought upon myself. I could not bear to give it unto others however. Please look after James and my girls. When you feel the time is right, tell them how much I loved them. By time you read this I will be gone. I will not poison the lives of my girls, with the poison of mine. May God forgive me but, I will not see others hurt or sickened by my hand or actions. You have been a dear friend. Know that wherever my family, or you, travel... I shall be watching over you always. All my love forever... Katherine."

Bird just folded the note, and tenderly hugged the now crying Ciana as he handed her the letter.


Bird turned to the padre and said "Padre, your ship is scaring off business. If the locals find out about you, they'll come after Ciana and Scota. IF that happens, it'll force me to use weapons I'd rather not show them right now. For now, has Ciana given you her promise of silence?"

"She has."

"Set your ship adrift, and I'll see to it's destruction. I'll bring you tools in a day or so to help you start your camp. I have another life Ciana doesn't know about but is aware of, and has kept secret. For her, and for you... I'll do the same."

"May God bless you for your wisdom and... your kindness."

*Looking at Ciana, he kindly told the padre "He already has."*

*Bird kept his word. He brought the padre the tools he promised him. He also showed him how to bake the sea water to remove the salt and provide fresh water in a land with no river. The padre with no resources, wasn't passing up knowledge even a learned holy man didn't know of. As requested, he had the less sickly of his 'flock' strip the ship then set it adrift. Alydar hit it with some small arms after sunset and set it ablaze. Bird wasn't happy with this turn of events but, he meant what he said. Ciana had put up with more than her fair share of secrets. Right now, though not as secret, Bird supported her with hers.*

# Chapter: 30

## *"The Ghostly Bells"*

*Ciana was busy in the house making all the goodies that was Christmas. When Bird was young, he and his family went to his neighbor's house a block over for Christmas eve. They were of Italian descent, so it was a feast fit for a Roman emperor. Of all the things they had, Bird liked and remembered two most of all. He remembered John, the father, cut a fresh pineapple in half. He would carve out the fruit still in the shell, cut it into small pieces and douse it with an Italian liqueur called Galiano. Bird hated the stuff EXCEPT in the pineapple.*

*He also remembered little dough balls called zeppole. He got a recipe from Alydar's archives and asked Ciana to make them.*

*"What in all the stars is a pineapple?" Ciana chuckled quoting from 'The Chronicles'.*

*"When Christmas eve comes, I'll let you know," was all Bird would tell her.*

*Well, now it was Christmas eve. Bird and Alydar took a little ride to a volcano tipped island, and picked up a dozen. Sicily didn't have his liqueur but the Tuscan region sure did. Bird cut the top off of one and planted it but warned Ciana it grew in a land that had no winter so, inside it stayed.*

*Bird laughed lightly and said "I'd take it easy on those Scota. That alcohol will go straight to your head but, with the sweetness of the pineapple... heh heh... you won't feel it till it's too late."*

*"Aye... okay. Oh my these are amaz'in! I swear the plain one, and the one yeh poured that fancy wine on, they honestly don't even taste the same!" Scota exclaimed sweetly as she wiped her chin with a giggle. "And juicy too it would seem!"*

When William showed up, Ciana sweetly took his coat and got ready for more. When Angus and Kara showed up, Ciana was getting ready to be the Earth version of Luera. A half hour later, and John and Andrew arrived. Andrew was friendly, and quite animated.

"Really Bird," John protested slightly, "The house is amazing. The ride in well... leaves a bit to be desired."

Bird laughed and welcomed them both in. Twenty minutes after they arrived, Ciana was concerned and even a tad nervous. An hour after they arrived and she was downright pissed. She had invited many of the locals... a rather large 'many'. John and Andrew however, were the last to show up. Ciana was proud of her home and only wanted to share it. What got her mad was how many said they would come, but never did. She had planned on feeding a small army and was looking to make this a grand Christmas. Seeing the small crowd, and not a large one, she was flipping between crying... and slamming her fist through a wall.

"Bird? Did you see me put on airs?" Ciana asked sadly.

She was alone in the kitchen with Bird and staring at a small mountain of food that now, would not be needed.

Bird was kind but, he was burying a bit of anger as well. He wasn't mad at Ciana, but he was at those who hurt her. The local folk could have politely declined he thought. To say you were coming though... then pull a no show... was getting the master planner working.

"No Ciana, you haven't. Not that I've seen anyway. I look at it this way however, let's not worry or get angry over who didn't come. Let's however, show those who did the best Christmas we can... what do ya say?"

"I'll tell you what I say. I say... I will not speak nor think ill on this day or the next. Day after tomorrow however well, if it's 'Lady Bird' they want, then it's 'Lady Bird' they'll get!"

The large party wasn't Bird's idea it was Ciana's. Bird didn't care either way but he WAS supporting his lass. Bird had, as usual, a long distance plan in the works. Tonight just helped him narrow down the guest list, nothing more.

"Let me know when 'Lady Bird' arrives... and I'll make sure the 'Commander'... isn't far away."

Jokingly, Ciana curtsied slightly saying "Thank yeh kindly Sir."

"Ciana, I know you're a good Christian woman. Why not cook for all those people anyway?" Bird said with a 'I got a plan' smirk.

"Why? It's obvious they not be com'in."

"True but... I can think of a certain padre who would not only welcome your kindness, but appreciate it."

"Yeh knoe... I believe yeh be right..." Ciana said grabbing a tray and heading out to her guests. She finished that sentence with a wink as she walked through the door saying, "...'husband'."

"WHAT did you call me!?" Bird said with a huge smile as he ran after her.

Ciana let out a small playful shriek, and ran out as both of them rejoined their guests.

Bird and Ally played and sang Christmas carols. Lots of gossip from John and when he finished, Ciana joked his 'report' was so thorough that now she didn't have to go there. Ciana also realized Bird was right. She was having a truly joyous Christmas and knew, she was better off having a small group of true caring friends... than a large group of fake ones. Scota was buzzed on the pineapple, Ally was fending off John's offers of being his model, and Andrew was having a hard time staying away from the pineapple. So was William. Yep, nothing but good times, good cheer, peace on earth and good will towards man.

"Ciana, Iem sooooo sorry. I fell asleep by the fire. I hope I not be intrud'in at this hour but I did promise yeh I'd come."

"Aye yeh did. As fer the hour? Welllllllll, think noth'in of it! Merry Christmas Mary," Ciana said as she hugged her and pulled her in from the cold.

"Well now, ain't that a fine bit o' craft'in. I'll assume by the style only a crazy Yankee man could'a built someth'in like thah?" Mary joked seeing the coat rack.

It was the free standing type and Bird did indeed build it. That was one of Ciana's presents.

"Yankee yes... crazy?... Welllllllll..." Bird chuckled as he welcomed Mary as well.

It was around 7pm when Mary showed up and the party had barely gotten started. Ciana was thrilled Mary showed up, and got her a plate of food. Now, one more strong, the party just kept on going.

"Ladies and gentlemen! I'd like to propose a toast," Bird called out to his guests.

Everyone grabbed a drink of some sort and gathered round.

"There's a story told where I come from. It's a Christmas story of a man who met his guardian angel. The man was despondent and contemplating suicide. The angel however told him 'No man is a failure who has friends'. This party was to be quite a bit larger but ya know what? I don't care. I think you'll find, in the months to come, I'll not be concerning myself with those who didn't come..." Bird raised his glass and finished with "... only those who did."

Nothing but smiles and raised glasses were his reply.

"Now, you all know I have, well shall we say, 'resources', at my disposal aye?"

Everyone nodded.

"Well then, when we were in Edinburgh, Ciana experienced something that truly warmed her heart. In two minutes, it will be midnight. I have a small fire going on the patio outside. I invite you all to join me. This is a present for Ciana from me but... I don't think she'll mind sharing."

Everyone filed out quickly with only one minute to go. Bird looked questioningly at Ally, but she just smiled and nodded. Bird tipped his hat at her and focused on the night sky.

"Ciana?"

"Aye?"

"Merry Christmas."

At that moment, a loud set of church bells rang out to announce midnight. It was the bells Ciana heard in Edinburgh that Bird was referring to. The reason he looked at Ally was... it was her PA system making them this time.

"But...but!" Ciana shook herself and said "But we don't have ennything on the Isle that can make that sound. Not close enough to *hear ennyway!"*

*Bird just grinned and said "I know."*

*Ciana hugged him tight, smiled, and thought herself the luckiest woman alive.*

*"You did thah fer me?" Ciana asked lovingly looking into Bird's eyes.*

*"I did. I considered something a lil more 'me' but... sometimes, as the saying goes, less is more."*

*"It's perfect. Bird?"*

*"Mm?"*

*"Merry Christmas."*

*"And to you my love," Bird said sweetly as he hugged her tight.*

*Bird mouthed 'thank you' silently to Ally. She smiled back and curtsied. The last 'Ghostly' bell rang, and everyone thought it was just lovely. No one dared ask how Bird pulled it off and... no one cared to know either.*

*Ciana insisted no one was going home, and breakfast would be served in the morning. Mary slept in Scota's room. John and Andrew were pleasantly shocked when Bird pulled a set of locks on the back of the two couches in his 'sitting room'. Once he had, the backs folded down and now, John and Andrew had beds for the night. One guest room left, and that went to Angus. He however gave it to Kara and slept by the fireplace next to William.*

*It was around 2am and Bird was still up and he was in the kitchen looking for a snack. Kara didn't see him. She tip toed quiet as could be and gently woke Angus.*

*"Are yeh okay? It isn't, well, you knoe?"*

*Kara merely put a finger to his lips. She smiled, and held out her hand.*

*"Kara, are... are yeh sure?"*

*Glass lady just smiled, and kept her hand held out.*

*Angus smiled back, and took her hand. The guest bedroom was right next to Bird's and just past the kitchen. Kara and Angus both froze as they spotted him in the kitchen. Bird, kindly, put a finger to his lips and pointed towards his door. Angus understood but Kara was near horrified at being caught. Bird however raised* his glass... and gave them a soft salute. Kara now smiled, gave a slight bow, and took Angus with her. Bird made a catching motion, then rubbed his heart and smiled. He did that because Kara blew him a kiss as she closed the door.

Bird put his plate away and murmured low "You go girl!"

Next morning and Bird chuckled to himself. Kara was all smiles but Angus was nervous.

Andrew however leaned in to Angus saying "I had a dream yeh got up in the middle of theh night. Funny how dreams are ain't they? Funnier still how yeh usually ferget them the next day," and the driver winked at the smithy.

Angus stared at him with a shocked look, but Kara said "Indeed thay are. Yeh have my thanks fer... well... fer yer fergetfullness," and she winked right back.

Kara went to help Ciana but Bird caught her by the arm and pulled her in tight.

Whispering low in her ear, he said "From a broken and crying ball on the cobblestones... to this. Not bad glass girl, not bad at all. You've grown well and for what it's worth, I'm proud of you."

Softly, she replied "It's worth more than yeh knoe. Thank yeh."

Ciana kindly, and softly, said "I know that smile. Tell me true though... are yeh happy?"

Poor Kara's hidden little romp wasn't as hidden as she thought. The smile still on her face however said she really didn't care.

"Aye... I am. And I have you and the kind Sir tuh thank fer it."

"Well Kara, if you're happy then... I'm happy for yeh," Ciana said sweetly.

Leaning in out of nowhere, John said "Just remember, I make THE most diviiiiine wedding dresses!"

Kara giggled, gave up caring, and gave John a playful curtsey.

Christmas day was grand. No one had a clue why Bird would bring a tree in the house, no less decorate it so. Still, it was festive and jolly. Bird told them it was actually a Germanic tradition, and that *he was of Austrian descent. That made sense to the crowd even if the tree didn't. Bird and Ciana were busy in the kitchen. She was cooking and preparing, and Bird was packing things for transport.*

*"Ciana, it wouldn't be right if both of us left. How about if I take Scota, drop this off, and hurry on back?"*

*"Promise me yeh won't go inside, nor let Scota go in there either."*

*"Hell no... just drop off and go... that's it."*

*"Aye then. I'll keep our guests busy but, be quick about it."*

*Bird kissed his lass, then hollered to another.*

*"Scota! C'mon blondie you're with me."*

*"And just where are we going?"*

*"WE my dear, are going to take a ride around the moon in Alydar. Then, it's off to 51 to hang out with Lone," Bird said with a chuckle.*

*"Oh well... pfff... if THAH be all," Scota replied giggling back.*

*Ciana just laughed and said "Oh you two!"*

*Alydar dropped ramp right at the tree line. Next, she sent down a drone and popped the top open. Bird put in all the food as Scota was a little leery of the thing.*

*"Oh puleez. You breathe water and the drone frightens you?"*

*"Damn straight Skippy!"*

*"Watch it blondie... heh heh... that's MY line."*

*Food loaded, the drone came down again and Bird hopped in. Scota just shook her head.*

*"It's this, or I put on my armor and fly you up there... take your choice."*

*Scota grudgingly hopped in. The stories of that battle armor were scary enough. Scota however preferred NOT to see the real thing.*

*"I thought you would like the flying?" Bird asked as he helped Scota out of the drone*

*"I do... in Alydar. This thing however, as 'Commander Bird' says... yeeeaaaah, not so much."*

*"Oh ya big baby," Bird teased.*

*Alydar glided across the tree tops and put them outside the perimeter of the colony. Bird delivered the food, and was finishing dropping it off as the padre came up.*

*"Feliz Navidad padre," Bird said kindly.*

*"And may our savior bless you this day for your kindness."*

*"He already has, many times over. This is me, just giving back. My apologies padre but I can't stay. Ciana sends her love and her best holiday wishes as well."*

*"Please give her our sincere thanks. May God walk with you on your journey this day," the padre told him as he and Scota walked off.*

*Once Bird and Scota were far enough away, several men came up, smiled to the padre and Bird in the distance, and brought the food back. Ciana had a fine Christmas meal, even if it was smaller than expected. Now, she would insure others less fortunate than her would as well.*

*Bird and Scota made it back. Bird told them his 'other life' never goes away, and he wanted to make sure it didn't touch him or the others on this of all days. The crowd all accepted that and asked nothing further. Scota and Ciana waved to William and Mary as they headed back. Kara and Angus left some time after that. John teased he was going to lose his girlish figure with all the food he ate and honestly thanked the 'grand couple'.*

*"Oi... do I LOOK like an almost 8 foot tall wolf?" Bird joked.*

*Everyone laughed and John told them no but, they were grand all the same. He was out cold shortly thereafter from today and the previous days events. Andrew already was. He fell asleep in the glass enclosed room by the falls. Ciana kindly draped a blanket on him and left him be.*

*"Ciana? Come here please."*

*Ciana sat on Bird's lap and said "You were right..." Waving to the house she told him "... less was indeed, more."*

*"Aye lass that it was. I have one last gift for you."*

*"Honestly my love, more than enough already."*

*"This is 'other world' stuff buuuuutttt, if you'd rather not I'll..."*

Ciana sat straight up and beamed.

Ally walked past and chuckled, "Yeah... thought as much."

Bird was serious and said "Ally and I have talked. Something in that life has changed. You might say a recent event has made me realize that simply 'bringing you into it' well, it isn't the way to go. As such, I'll be introducing little things to you over time. Scota is indeed getting better but her leaving is imminent. I was thinking, when she did, perhaps we could all go together. So, we decided coming into that world knowing nothing and having to adjust all at once was a bad idea. Remember how I said we had devices and such beyond your wildest dreams and comprehension?"

"Aye, I do."

"This... is one of them. Close your eyes."

Ciana did and she felt Bird putting something behind her ear.

"Scota has one too. Stand up if you please."

Ciana got up as did Bird and he stared straight at her.

"You don't ask... you DON'T try and figure out... you merely enjoy... got it?"

"Aye?" Ciana asked questioningly.

Bird stood in a perfect dance frame. Ciana curtsied, smiled, and took up position in his arms. Suddenly, her head was filled with music as if she was inside the orchestra itself. The look of pleasant shock on her face could be seen a mile away.

"Eh eh ehhhhh... what did I say?"

"Bird... it's glorious!" she said lovingly.

Bird danced her to Vince Vance and the Valiant's 'All I Want For Christmas'. It was a lovely tune and it would become the one they danced to every year to come. The grand 'Earthly' couple would claim that song for themselves. Ciana danced away to the perfect haunting vocals, and never stopped smiling.

"You are the angel atop my tree..." Bird sang as he danced "...you are my dream come true... Santa can't bring me WHAT I need... cause all I want for Christmas is you."

Bird let go and switched with Ally. Ally was beaming as well. Yet another switch and Scota had her turn with Bird. One more switch and Bird was back with Ciana as the big vocal finish kicked in. Ciana was in holiday heaven and was actually sad when the song ended.

*"Like I said... don't ask 'cause... I won't tell. Suffice to say, that was a preview,"* Bird said as he covered Ciana's eyes and took the starfish off.

Ciana hugged Bird tight and simply, but honestly, said *"Merry Christmas......... 'husband'."*

Bird hugged her back with a grand smile.

*"Aye, it is........... 'wife'."*

# Chapter 31:

## "A Chat Between Sisters"

Raven broke the perimeter of the minefield. When she did, Gil was concerned. Once inside the field, Lone told 'gramps' he was inbound with news... and Salyan.

"How goes the exercising?" Salyan asked totally cutting off Gil mid greeting.

"Um... it goes well. Why do you...?"

"GREAT!" Sal said cutting him off again. "You're about to do a marathon! See ya in the sim room!" and Sal headed out full of fire.

Lone chuckled at Gil's look of 'what's going on?'.

"Oh, I wouldn't dare ruin THIS surprise! Heh heh, the look on your face should be more fun than Rahgaa's!."

With that, a real Ghost and a virtual one headed after Sal.

"Okay so... minefield... big old mess and kinda looks like this right?" Sal asked the 2 men as he brought up the sim of the minefield.

"Indeed," Gil replied.

"Wouldn't it be a whole lot nicer, not to mention easier... if it looked liiiiiiiiikkkkeeeee.... this?" and Sal flipped to Blue's version.

Playing along, Gil said "Why yes, that would be pleasing," barely containing a chuckle.

Even Lone chimed in smiling and said "Oh... kids these days... such imaginations they have."

Sal ignored them and called out "Riihahl?"

"Yes Salyan?"

"Could you, AND the other scientists... join me please?"

Now Gil knew something was up.

Sal looked to the new crowd and asked "Which of you is most

familiar with this machine?"

All of them pointed... to Giljor. Now Sal decided to give back a little of the teasing he got.

"Hmmf, figures. Oh well, I 'suppose' if that's all you have... an Adjulon will have to do."

Even Lone chuckled at that one.

"Okay Gil, minefield right?" and Sal brought up the original image. "Now, change any of these controls, and you'll know if I'm showing you truth, or merely an illusion right?"

Now Gil could tell something was up, and said "Correct."

"Now, watch carefully which controls I touch, and tell me..." and Sal turned some dials and flipped some switches, then finished with "... am I lying?"

Riihahl came up alongside Lone and said softly, "If he hides on me again I swear, as I said once before, I will kick his ass."

Gil was indeed blown away yet again.


Giljor almost pushed Sal out of the way and tried it himself. He actually tried it 3 times but, with the same result each time.

"Im... PRESSIVE!"

Sal chuckled and just said "Told you."

Gil was still staring at the simulation, and spoke sideways saying "Enjoy the look 'grandson' but... while it still requires much more work, this is a breakthrough of monumental proportions."

"How monumental we talk'in here?"

"Like, get Rhana back and keep your child safe kind of monumental."

Lone looked at the sim, then at Gil.

"What do you need?"

Smiling, Gil said "Riihahl my dear, I can tell you that this time... 'my ass'... is safe." Looking at Lone he smiled a kind fatherly smile and said "The only thing 51 has that I require, is already standing beside me." Looking at his fellow scientists Gil said "Come my friends! It would appear we have a marathon to complete!" and several got down to business.


Lone pointed at Riihahl, then pointed out the door. All the others were now super focused as Lone stepped out into the hallway.

"You have no children. I know that is a personal matter for you. As such, I'm asking the mother in you... look after him as only one can. I need sleep, but I want him looked after. As Biiird says... can do?"

"Not can do... will be done," Riihahl said pleasantly.

Lone said something that greatly pleased her.

"Thank you."

"The door there is the quarters your sister stayed in when she was here. On my honor, I will get you should ANY reason require it."

Lone tipped his hat, and headed off to get some sleep. Riihahl was thrilled actually. No one ever asked her to be a 'mom' no less talked to her as one. Right now, she would look after Sal better than his own mother would.

Six hours later, Riihahl came and got Lone. He bolted awake and had 2 cannons drawn.

"(giggle) Do you always wake like that?" Riihahl asked.

"It's served me well of late," Lone replied as he focused his mind.

"Of that I have no doubt. Gil and Salyan have news. Um, Commander?"

"Yes?"

Riihahl stifled a giggle and asked "Do you plan on shooting the doors?"

"Huh?"

Riihahl smiled, and pointed to the cannons Lone was still holding.

"Oh... heh heh... yeah, sorry," and he put them away, and headed for the sim room.

Lone walked in to pretty much what he left 6 hours earlier.

Gil came to him and said "Commander, I find my earlier statement was incorrect. I do need something you have."

"Wazzat then?"

"The one you call 'little blue'."

"Sal?" Lone asked looking at him.

"Sorry Uncle Lone. We made good progress but, she was the

one who discovered this, not me. While I've worked on it AND made progress... we're kind of stuck on a few points. You know how you and Rhana are usually two halves of the plan?"

"Mm hmm."

"It's sort of like that with us. She gets major points but, I am the one that figures out what to do with it. She basically discovers, I sort out the details and find a fix or apply a use."

Lone brought up his HUD, scanned Sal for the isotope, then shut it off.

"And my request?" Lone asked Riihahl.

Nearly beaming, she replied "Fulfilled."

"Not quite yet." She cocked her head in that 'huh' sort of way when Lone told her, "I'm going to get Gil's request. I leave him in your care and yours alone. I will be back within the hour."

Riihahl bowed and was thrilled for the extension.

Lone did indeed leave, but only as far as the edge of the minefield. Once there, he made a 'phone call'. Blue was a tad curious when Roenas, Val and Remmy knocked on her door. She was politely hustled to the hangar and a waiting Keyza. Lone wanted X-man on this as he was in charge of the alloys and such going into the ring. Lone figured if they sorted the minefield, it still had to be applied to the ring, so Xankor was the Ghost taxi this time. Lone met them in the station's bay, and immediately shot Blue with a hypo-spray.

"This place is amazing!" Blue said looking around. "The power relays over there could'a been done better but..."

"Blue!... focus," Lone stated.

"I'm not in trouble am I?"

"Nope but, someone wants to see you."

"Um... okay. Who?"

"To quote Rhana... 'that would be me'."

"SALYAN!" Blue squealed and ran to him.

Three gadgets practically sprang off the floor and blocked her path, then fired up their lasers.

"Okaaaaay... this is me... no longer running," Blue said as she skidded to a stop.

*"It's okay you guys, you can stand down," Sal told them.*

*They actually saluted, then backed away. What neither knew was, it wasn't Gil controlling them... it was Riihahl.*

*"Sal what is this place?"*

*"Can't tell you that," Sal said hugging her. "Blue look, I know you don't like working on my projects but, this time, I really need you. Think you'd mind helping out for a bit?"*

*Sal ask for something? Blue would give him anything he wanted.*

*"Will you be there?"*

*"Right by your side."*

*Her answer dripped with love as she said "Lead the way."*

*Sal curved her around and led her out. Looking over his shoulder, he winked at Uncle Lone. Two Ghosts tipped their hats right back at him.*


*"Aw, no scream this time?" Bird chuckled in Scota's ear.*

*"Hah haaaah." Scota whispered "Give me a moment." Scota hollered out "Ciana, Iem go'in out to light up the path lights okay?"*

*"Aye, be careful."*

*"I will," Scota said as she put on a coat and headed outside.*

*Bird chuckled saying "Told you it gets easier with time."*

*"Not so sure Iem happy bout that. What can I do fer yeh?"*

*"This time, it's more what I can do for you. Can you get away?"*

*"Aye, in a little bit I can. Ciana has asked me to take food to the padre. In about an hour okay?"*

*"Fine. Tell the door to take you to the bay. I've left a one time order to let you through. ONE time only so get it right okay?"*

*"Aye I will."*


*An hour later, Scota made it to the cave. She took a few tries till she told the door the right command. She walked through and into the landing bay of the Lander.*

*"Convenient aye, but I'm with Renny... thah's jes creepy."*

*Scota walked down to the main floor and waited a moment. Suddenly the energy screen came up. Had she not seen it before,* she'd be freaking right about now.

"Bird?" she said staring in amazement at the wall.

"Aye lass. Remember when you saw what I said was recordings on this wall?"

"Aye."

"This time... it's live. Cool huh?"

"Live?"

"I'm on Alydar... as in the full size one. We're still around the moon. This is a way for me to talk to you without actually being there. I see and hear you the same way you see me."

"Aye... this is cool! What is that behind yeh?"

"I'll get to that in a minute. First, tell me... how are you?"

"Um... fine?"

"Heh heh, no, I mean how are you doing. Scota, you breathed water for God's sake. Every time you come here it's something new for you. You barely grasp what you saw or learned last time, when something new comes along. I'm talking to you in a way that won't be possible for hundreds of years. I'm concerned for you my dear. I just want to make sure your not getting too much too quick, and that I'm not overloading you."

Scota was sweet. She truly understood Bird and knew what he meant. She was sweet because, he truly cared and she was happy to be thought of in such a way.

"I am okay Bird, but, I am overwhelmed a bit. Still, I did what yeh said. So far, yeh haven't hurt me, nor has ennything here. Yer right I don't understand it, but like yeh said... Iem accept'in fer now, and leave'in theh understand'in for another day."

Bird smiled and said "Smart girl. For what it's worth, I think your doing very well so far."

That made Scota smile.

"Now, next question... how's Ciana?"

Scota sat on the floor and said "How yeh mean?"

"She got quite a shock hearing about mom and dad. She has a new home that's nothing like you've ever seen. The locals have finally treated her like Lady Bird, and she heard music without a band in sight."

"Aye, I get yer point now. Can I ask yeh something?"

"Sure."

"Bird, while I wasn't truly thought poorly of, I was thought of as a bit of a child. Ciana and Angus and all theh others would treat me as if I was too young to understand. While I don't understand all this around me, I kahnt think of ennything more 'grown up' can you?"

"Can't say I disagree with you there."

"Aye. Yeh fixed me and I am grateful but, I didn't understand a bit of it. What I did understand was, yeh talked to me like a grown up. Ally too. What Iem say'in is, I like being a grownup or at least thought of as one. Tis why I like com'in here. Here, Iem Scota... not Ciana's little sister. Here, I get to be theh grownup fer once."

"You're right, you're not a grownup. But also like you said, you don't understand the new world around you. If I treated you like a child, you never will. I have tried to treat you like a grownup but, without explanations you wouldn't understand. I'm glad you noticed, and know this... I'm not holding things back because you're a child, I'm merely trying to get you adjusted to what you can understand, not what you can't."

"And I appreciate thah. Now, I say thah because of Ciana. Yeh asked how she is. For theh first time in my life, I now know how she must feel."

"Clarify," Bird said kindly but seriously.

"Now, I know things she don't. Not only thah but, it's things I kahnt tell her about... and have to protect her from."

Bird was truly happy with what he was hearing. He knew Scota was still scared AND unsure but... had the right attitude all the same.

"Well blondie, that's why I called you here. You want to be a grownup? Fine... be one now."

"Aye, I will... promise," Scota said with conviction.

"I want your opinion. I want to tell Ciana about you and this world. Do you think it would be better coming from me... or you?"

Someone ask her for her opinion? No one in her life ever asked nor cared for that. That alone made her love him even more.

"Honestly, Iem not sure. What did yeh have in mind?"

"Well, she's getting annoyed I keep running off with you. By the standards of the day, pretty soon she's gonna think you and I are like what I teased you about the other day. I told you that your coming here was because of a mistake. As such you got the whole 'other world' all at once. While I commend you on how you've handled it so far, it wasn't my intention. Honestly Scota, had you been like the timid ladies of town, I'd have wiped your memories in a heartbeat. Even you have to admit, the way you found out wasn't exactly the best way, aye?"

"Aye, I'll say."

"As such, I've had to quickly adjust you as best as we could. You got a lot... too much in fact... so we pulled it back as much as we could, so we can feed you only a little at a time."

"Aye I noticed. I will say, I like yer new plan much better than mine was at first."

"As do I. As such, Ally and I have been talking. We will bring Ciana in but, we've decided to give her pieces BEFORE showing her what you've already seen. I want to know, with all that's going on now, do think that will be wise... or overload her?"

"Oh she'd have fits if she knew. Aye, I agree with yeh. I knoe her better than ennyone. If she came here like I did, well, it wouldn't be good."

"I agree. You want to be a grownup? Tell her. Tell Ciana what you did. I'll leave it to you how much to tell her, and how much to leave out. Let her know we're not planning on running off together or some other crazy shit like that. Be mindful though, her reaction."

Scota was now thinking, and feeling like, a grownup.

"One last thing blondie. Watch your tone."

"Oi! I ain't been noth'in but polite!"

"Heh heh, I don't mean that. Scota look, watch your tone when you tell HER. If you sound like a grownup, you'll be thought of as one... and treated the same."

"Aye, I understand yeh now. Like what yeh said about me sound'in ladylike and all."

"Correct. I've noticed you sounded proper. Now you've gone back to how you spoke before, but not as bad."

"Aye. I felt I was too proper perhaps. I thought I wasn't putt'in on airs, but I was treated like I was ennyway. Then it occurred to me, what I think I sound like, and what they hear, may be different things. Once yeh fixed me, I made sure I didn't do ennything to hurt you or Ally or... get yeh caught. So, like yeh said when we met Angus, I kept the proper, but softened it some."

Bird just smiled, and blew Scota a kiss. She nearly beamed knowing 'dad' was proud of her.

"Bird, can I ask yeh someth'in?"
"Wazzat then?" Bird joked.
"Careful there BirdMan... don't want him killing you in your sleep now do ya?" Scota teased back in the best American accent she could.

Bird laughed both at her joke, and her poor rendition of his accent.

"And yet, it isn't Lone but... I can introduce you to another Meerahna. Would you like me to?"
"I doen see why not."

Bird ducked down some, and said "Do you recognize what's behind me?"

"Aye, thah be the tank yeh had me in."
Scota could see the top of the tank now visible behind Bird.
"Mm hmm. Promise me you won't be scared?"
Scota steeled herself, and said "I'll do my best."
Bird said "The flame in the sky... it was the hell wave Ally showed you. Well, thankfully, a small piece of it anyway."
"But, you're here so... wasn't it gone?"
"Not fully. You're right I'm here but, who was still in it?"
Scota thought of the Chronicles, then shouted "Oh! Ayleen!"
Bird moved aside, and Scota backpedaled quick. She saw a wolf in near human form. It was in the tank and floating limp. Scota recognized everything, except the tank's occupant.

Slowly, it dawned on Scota. Bird wasn't real, just an image. So if he was, then so was everything else. She slowly crept up to the screen, and stared in wonder.

"Yes blondie," Bird said coming back into view, "That's a real life alien. Ally and I rescued her. She's in very bad shape and, may die. In terms you can understand, she's near death. Ally and I *have her, well, not getting any worse. That though is no guarantee. Scota, do you want to be a grownup? Or a child?"*

*Scota snapped out of her stare and said "A grownup!"*

*"Grownups stare in wonder... children backpedal across the floor in fear. May want to remember that."*

*That point... hit home.*

*"Scota, I never planned on falling in love with your sister. All I wanted was to get Ayleen back. My brother, HER brother, is working on a way to get me back. I've been neglecting my end of that plan because of Ayleen. Now that I have her, know that as soon as she's better, I'm heading for home. I will bring you if you wish to come. I want Ciana to come too but, I won't bring her if I will end up doing more harm than good. The very stars you once wished to see are calling. You already know the Isle won't last much longer, for you anyway. I'm counting on you to help me... help Ciana... and in the end, help us all."*

*"Bird?"*

*"Yeah?"*

*"Iem gonna go talk to Ciana. For what it's worth..." Scota smiled softly as she stared and finished with "... I hope she lives."*

*"So do I," Bird said kindly.*

*He blew her a kiss and waved. Scota stared till the image was no more. Full of a grownup purpose now, she turned and headed off to calm a sister's fears... and make a new 'dad' proud.*

*Scota knocked on Ciana's door. It was just after dark, and she was getting ready for bed and hoping... to be woken up by a handsome stranger upon his return. In a matter of a few minutes, he wouldn't be so strange anymore.*

*"Scota?"*

*"Aye. Can I come in?"*

*"Of course," Ciana said but, she heard a new tone in Scota's voice.*

*Scota handed her a tea but Ciana declined.*

*"I drink thah and Iel be up all night!" Ciana chuckled.*

*Scota wasn't laughing.*

"What's wrong dear sister?"

"This tea, it's special. It's from Bird."

Ciana sniffed it, and said "It looks normal to me."

"Nope. The chemical in tea that keeps you up has been removed," Scota said seriously, and sipped her own as proof.

"I've noticed something sister. You've been hang'in around my future husband a lot lately. I'm not accusing you of ennything, but I'd like to hear it from you... why?"

"Ciana, yeh knoe I'd never do ennything to hurt you aye?"

"Aye, I knoe yeh wouldn't."

Scota sighed, and said "I been lying to yeh. Bird has too."

Now Ciana was a tad nervous. Unlike days of old, not insecure or scared but, definitely nervous. The answer she was expecting though, wasn't the one she got.

"About?"

"Bird's world. Ciana, I made a terrible mistake. I tried to help him one day and... well... I ended up in his world."

Ciana was about to blow a fuse. Hearing the 'wrong answer' threw her off. So, she simply stayed calm.

"Scota! Yeh promised!"

"I knoe I knoe! I only wanted the help and show everyone I wasn't as dumb, or childish, as everyone thought."

"Well, what happened?"

"Ciana, I found out I was both."

She hugged her sister, and said "Tell me everything."

"Thah's just it... I kahnt... but I'll tell yeh what I can."

Scota sat up, and told her tale.

Ciana listened intently, but even she couldn't deny the more grownup tone in her little sister's voice. Now, she knew, she wasn't so little anymore. Scota told her the truth, but spun it in such a way as to be truthful, yet not say anything she shouldn't.

"Ciana, I seen things. Strange and magical things! Thah's just it though... it ain't magic. I find mahself wish'in I'd never seen ennything... and wishing to see even more. Ennyway, I wanted yeh to know, I ain't try'in to steal yer man."

Ciana hugged her sister and said "Is there ennything else?"

"Aye, lots... but most I kahnt tell yeh. Now that I seen it, Bird has no choice but to let me in. Thah's why I been so close to him lately. I jes didn't want yeh think'in enny different."

Ciana was happy with that, when Scota dropped the proverbial bomb on her.

"He fixed me."

"Say what!?"

"Aye, my cough... gone. Doctor James was fer your sake. I was already fixed by then. Remember when yeh said I looked ragged?"

"Aye."

"I was. While he did fix me, I kahnt tell yeh how. It was only hours earlier that he had finished. And... there's more."

Ciana was near shaking now.

"I got his whole world, sadly, all at once. Ciana, I was sooooo scared I truly thought I was gonna die. Then I saw, I wasn't. Now thah I seen it, I knoe why he won't tell yeh. I can barely handle what I have seen. If you or worse... the town folk... knew the truth, we'd be burned as witches or worse!."

"Oh I doubt that."

"Don't. I seen you 'grownups' firsthand when the fire in theh sky came. Scared they were and talk'in of demons! Jes thah alone made me know Bird was right. He wasn't kidd'in Ciana, his world is as far ahead as his stories."

Ciana looked at her sister and said "I knoe yeh better than ennyone. What are yeh NOT tell'in me?"

"He's leav'in."

"Noooo... he wouldn't doo thah!"

"Already done. It's jes a matter of time. Thing is, part of the price for fix'in me was jes as he said. I do have tuh leave. If I doen, I'll cause problems theh like you kahnt even imagine. He wants to bring me with him. Me... and you."

Ciana was holding back the tears.

"Scota, I couldn't even begin to imagine life with a man, no less THAH man. Now, I kahnt imagine it without him. Tell me true, if I ask him about what yeh said, will he agree with yeh?"

"Every word. He left it to me to tell yeh, and how much. He loves you more than yeh knoe. I would be happy to find a man who loved me even half as much. He was sick of ly'in to yeh and so was I. Honestly Ciana, I saw his world and almost fell apart. He's afraid of you doing theh same or worse. So am I. When I surprised him, he had no choice but he does with you. Remember the music on Christmas?"

"Aye, twas lovely."

"That's but a drop in the bay of his world but, he does want to show it to yeh. Like he said, he'll be giv'in yeh pieces, so yeh'll not be as shocked as I was. In the meantime, know that I ain't steal'in yer man... only help'in him."

"Oh Scota, what do I do? I ain't loved ennyone like I do him. I kahnt jes leave... and I kahnt leave him."

"Trust me, if yeh saw his world... ye'd leave in a blink of an eye and not even turn around to wave g'bye."

"Iel have to take yer word on thah. Scota, this Isle be all I know. Lately though, Iem start'in to wonder if yeh might be right."

Scota smiled slyly asking "Whyzzat Lady Bird?" imitating Lone.

"Lady Bird indeed. I got a good taste of thah already. Mother and father gave their lives for this Isle. Scotland too! And this is the reward we get fer it? Town folk ly'in to mah face... and a lecherous bishop no one but a stranger will stand up to. The inn barely makes enough and many a day I wonder why I even keep it open. This house is finer than enny I e'er seen, no less lived in. Truth is, I find mahself want'in tuh stay here more... and the inn less. I felt obligated to keep it go'in as best I knew how. It be all we have but, now I see we have so much more." Ciana stared out the window, and said "Perhaps... it's time I took Bird at his word."

"Tell me true sis... you okay with thah?"

"Honestly? No. I feel like someone is ask'in me to jump off the cliff say'in 'trust me, Iel catch yeh'."

Sweetly, Scota answered, "Bird would catch you."

"Ciana, he's leav'in. Iem go'in with him. Trust me when I tell yeh... not only is there room fer yeh... he'd move heaven and earth to *catch you."*

*Ciana heard that, and said "I sure hope yeh be right. I never put that much faith in ennyone. If I had to guess, Ied say thah frightens me more than ten of Bird's worlds."*

*Ciana thought of all the times Bird gave her his word. She also thought of how many times he kept it. Ciana dropped the curtain and sat back on the bed.*

*"Scota, thank yeh fer tell'in me and... trust'in me. Knoe this though, like in Bird's story..."*

*"Hmm?"*

*"Where you go... I go."*

*Scota beamed and hugged her sister who hugged her back.*

*Somewhere, in orbit around the moon, a powerful Scorpion smiled... and turned off his comm.*

# Chapter 32:

## *"Operation Bird Hunt"*

*"Ya know, for someone with only two arms, I always wondered why the cannons come in fours?" Salyan said as he woke Lone up.*

*Yet again, he awoke the same as he did to Riihahl.*

*"Sorry buddy, bit of a habit around this place," Lone said putting away his guns. "Heh heh, and to answer your question... I got 2 more ready for when I empty these," and Lone gave him a wink.*

*"Thought as much. We have news."*

*"Good bad or worse?"*

*Imitating 'Maxwell Smart', Salyan said "Would ya believe... all 3?"*

*"Yeah... that figures. Ya know, for once, it would be nice if all we got was the good news and only the lucky breaks."*

*"If we did... I don't think you'd know what to do with yourself," Sal said with a smirk.*

*"Yeah, you're probably right."*

*Back in the sim room, Gil took a break, and came over to Lone and Sal.*

*"Okay Lone, here's what we got so far. You saw the minefield, and you saw little Blue's version. Problem we have is... both are correct."*

*"Clarify."*

*Sal kicked in and said "The 6 tunnels are correct. The reason the minefield is so cluttered is a whole 'nother matter."*

*"Still listening," Lone said in an American accent.*

*"Think of it like branches on a tree. The 6 tunnels are the trunks. All the others are like branches."*

*Now Lone got it.*

*Lone said "Kind of like a forest. Down at ground level all you see is the trees... looking down from the top all you see is the canopy."*

*"Extremely accurate and quite correct," Gil told him. "The minefield is like being in the middle of that canopy, except the branches come and go and constantly change."*

*"So, in a sense, we're right back where we started?"*

*"Not quite," Sal said. "Go down a main trunk, and branches appear and disappear. One thing in our favor is distance versus time. We think, the closer you go towards the center, the closer you get to the time of the actual explosion. According to our readings, that was even before Earth formed. Now we know Rhana went that far back, but then started heading for us. Ayleen was on his tail. We believe if Lady R or Renny trance down a tunnel, they'll not have to go all the way, as those branches would be too old. So with less tunnel to search, we hopefully get better results."*

*Lone was very impressed... not to mention stoked at this piece of luck. The only problem was the variables, so those he brought up to be addressed or sorted.*

*"Okay, we got pluses and minuses. Plus... however erratic, the tunnels have a time pattern. Closer to threshold, recent history, closer to core... older."*

*"Correct."*

*"Minus... no proof of that. Can we send a drone in to prove that theory?"*

*"We can," Giljor started, "But, while we could shield it, the distortions in the tunnels are 10 times worse than the field. We would have to wait for it's return to see its recordings as getting a live feed would be impossible."*

*"I'll take it. X-Man? Do you think we'll need anything special or will what we got on hand do?"*

*Xankor told him "Based on what I've seen and heard so far, I think stock equipment will do fine. Our drones are an equal match for Gil's so either would do fine."*

*"Use ours. We can make more he can't. Anything goes wrong and he has one less."*

*"I'm on it. I'll bring in one of the drones at the perimeter, and*

*have Remmy send up another one."*

*"Puuurfect."*

*Sal looked at Lone and said "I know you, there's more isn't there?"*

*"Indeed but... till I have confirmation of your theory... what I got is either shear brilliance or pure bollox. It all relies on what we get back from the drone. How long to deploy?" Lone asked the crowd.*

*Xankor said "I can have the drone we got, in the bay and inspected in 30 minutes."*

*Riihahl answered "When I first spoke to Giljor, time was an anchor point used to train his mind. As such I came up with some nice algorithms I can upload to the drone. Whatever it records we can get time checks upon exit. I'll work on that at the same time as Ghost 5 so figure the same 30 minutes."*

*"Okay Uncle Lone, if they do all that, Blue, me and Gil can work on the remote flying protocols. That will take about an hour. Add another 10 minutes or so to prep and test it, figure 90 minutes or so to deploy."*

*Gil politely said "Count me out, you and Blue can handle that on your own. I and the remaining scientists will work on time."*

*"Say huh what when?" Sal joked.*

*Gil told him "While the drone may arrive in different places, we won't know when. We will work on testing the star walls as you call them, and a hundred other things, to determine what time and date the drone arrives in. Also, what seems like seconds to us could be years or more to the drone depending on where it goes, so we'll work out a plan for that too."*

*Sal took off Xankor's hat, placed it on his head, and tipped it to Giljor.*

*"Seems that exercise has served you well," Sal said with a smile as he gave it back to Xankor.*

*Full of fire, Lone said "Okay then... let's make it happen."*

*With that, everyone went to work. Just for fun, Giljor set a 90 minute timer and saw that as the enemy to beat.*

Giljor beat his imaginary enemy by 3 minutes and was ever so proud of himself, and his team, for doing so. Never in all the variants had they done anything like this before. As a matter of fact, since Bird and Lone first met Giljor in this latest variant, nothing that's happened since had ever happened before. Seems Gil wasn't the only one 'out of shape' either. They were loving getting work done, being part of the plan, and having something new and worthy to do. Because of that, Gil pointed out several times mistakes they made on one thing or another. He was kind about it though and quick to remind them how well they did also.

Lone got reports from everyone involved and, at 95 minutes or so, a drone headed down a primary tunnel. The scientists were stoked to be... well... scientists again. Giljor was as well but he also saw something else... the possibility of ending the minefield once and for all. If not that at least a better understanding of it. Even if all he got was the latter... he was hell bent on applying it to the former.

"Lone, I've programmed the drone to try 10 sub-tunnels. I set it so it would pick a random one near point of entry, then 9 more going closer to the core each time," Giljor reported.

"And how long for this part of 'Operation Biiird Hunt'?"

"Heh heh, nice name. Assuming all goes to plan, 15 minutes."

"Wouldn't happen to have a pub around here would ya?"

"Can't say that I do," Gil retorted.

"Pity. Perhaps when all this is over... you will," Lone said with a smirk.

He would in time build, or rather help build, something for Giljor. It just wasn't going to be anything near a pub.

Around 20 minutes later, Xankor hollered out "Yo Puppy... we got incoming."

"I know, I already got Raven doing a download. I'll let Gil have a copy when it lands. Meeting in the sim room in 10."

"I'll be there, X-man out."

Everyone assembled, and Gil and Blue and Sal were pouring over the results.

"Nice work Gil," Sal said when he saw the time codes.

*That actually meant quite a bit to Gil who tipped an imaginary hat at him.*

*"Okay people... where we at?" Lone asked after a bit.*
*Sal went first.*
*"Okay Uncle Lone, we got good and bad news. Good news is, so far anyway, we were right. The farther down one of the 6 tunnels ya go, the older things get. It's nowhere near exact, just overall. Blue and I estimate Renny and Rahgaa won't have to go much past halfway."*
*"And the bad news?"*
*"We found the source of the canopy," Sal answered and waved a hand to Gil.*
*Giljor told the crowd "The tunnels are littered with distortions. Those grow and become the branches you mentioned. Feedback energy from the original explosion keeps coming up the tunnel. They charge, then grow, then blow out from the main tunnel. That's what causes all the little mini bubbles and portals. Go searching down one of those, and you'll end up here again. It's the travel along the way that gets interesting."*
*"Define 'interesting'," Lone commanded politely.*
*"Lone, imagine one of those branches like a tunnel. For as long as it lasts, the end is somewhere here in the minefield. It however... has holes. They randomly come and go throughout space and time. Most however, seem to remain in the same space, but each hole can be a different place or time period... some are both."*
*"Okay, how about this analogy? Like a hall in a hotel. The hallway is constant, but which door opens and who comes out is different over time. Like that?"*
*"Exactly like that."*

*Lone was already forming a plan, just like Bird would be doing. He was also damn proud of himself for doing it too. No one knew the great Rhana like he did. Right now, he was remembering more 'how' Biiird thought, and not so much 'what'.*
*"Xankor, how are we on the drone itself?"*
*"Quite aged but, still intact," Xankor told him.*
*"Aged?" Blue asked.*

"Yes my dear. It seems one of the openings it went through had a different time shift. What was only 1 minute in our time values... was actually 50 years worth in one of the places it went."

"Ah, okay I got it," Blue said hanging onto Sal.

Lone looked at the table and asked if there was anything more to know of consequence. No one had anything new.

"Okay then, here's the plan. I have the ladies trance but keep them in the range you suggested. We come up empty though, and I'll send them deeper down the main trunks. I want them both scanning." Lone looked at Gil and said "I want you to send it back out again but, with a twin. I want two drones going in at opposite ends heading towards the center. I believe they'll be 2 halves of the same tunnel... but with totally different openings and to totally different places. Assuming I'm right the ladies go in twos. Biiird taught me you never fly without a wingman. That way if something goes wrong, or one of them finds something, the other can help if need be."

The whole table agreed it was wise, and the scientists were stoked to have an expansion on an experiment.

"Gil, you got any ships on this station?"

"Two actually. But, they haven't been touched since we arrived here."

Lone actually laughed and told him "I actually happen to be an expert on that," referring to the multi-hundred year lack of care.

Xankor asked "Why do you need those?"

"I'll tell ya why. The drones are made with moss hulls. Even if the ladies could trance out of them, I'm not taking the chance they can't trance back in. I need something non moss and, something I'm familiar with. I was expecting a single tunnel, not one inside another. IF they find either of them, we not only have to keep the main tunnel open, but the opening in the side tunnel now as well. I'll have the ships fitted with cat's eye starters. Don't forget, we still have the original ring. I'll find a way to make use of it somehow."

Blue actually told him she had.

"Commander, I have an idea. The original ring is too small for the full size Ghost. What if however, it projected rather than encircled?"

Lone was loving the out of the box stuff he's been hearing.
"Clarify Blue."

"The original ring, like the larger one, encircles the opening of the time hole. It keeps it stable and... if too small... expands it to a size you need. What if the smaller ring did the same, but projected an energy beam from each section to do the same?"

"Like?" Lone asked still not getting it.

"Think of it like your monitor in your home. The bulb is only inches across but the image it makes is feet across. Turn the original ring... into the projector."

Sal was stoked by this and cut in "I can make that happen actually and... with very little modifications. I warn you though, the original ring has a much smaller power source. You would have only enough time to get through it before we'd have to shut it off to recharge. Five, six minutes tops then we shut off for the same amount to recharge. You'd have to be ready on either end but, we could pull it off."

Lone was full of purpose. He also had an Eden style long term plan and was feeling far more confident for it.

"Gil, I'll leave it to you, Riihahl, and your team, to get the double flight going and get me results as quick as you can. Sal, you and Blue work on the original ring. Xankor? You're with me, we got some ships to refurbish. Once we get results on all 3 parts of this plan, and I know where we stand... I'll get the ladies up to speed." Lone stood up, looked at the table of the real and virtual... and said "Okay... let's DO this!"

All to their assigned tasks, it would seem this time... 'The Mahrek' has spoken.

# Chapter: 33

## "Exit Ciana... And Enter Lady Bird"

Scota and Ciana seemed closer lately. No one around them knew the real reason why, and just thought it nice that family got along so well. Bird however, was a tad on edge.

"Well Mistuh Yankee Man, care to tell me why yeh be so gloomy lately?" Scota asked teasingly, but in a nice way.

"I'm not gloomy. I am however... planning."

"For?"

"The Bishop."

"What about him? Ciana pretty much told him there be no chance for him with her. Ally and you sent him on his way. He'd be a fool to come back now."

"Foolishness... unfortunately... is not exclusive to youth," Bird said in a warning tone. "The cardinal said he was stirring up support on the mainland. I went there. Nothing of him remains, and nothing seems to be different with the Campbell clan."

"He likely found no support there either and is long gone."

"Perhaps. IF that were so though... then where did he go?"

"I'm with Scota on this one boss. He likely got his reputation so tarnished that they turned him away," Alydar said in his comm.

Thing was... Scota, now having a starfish, heard it too.

"Sweet Lord this is gonna take some getting used to!" Scota exclaimed over the disembodied voice. "And how is Ayleen?" Scota asked softly.

"She improved some. Not a lot but some. Ally is watching over her for now. Scota, remember how I said the hell wave was like lightning and thunder?"

"Aye."

"Alydar and I are tracking that 'thunder'. In about 2 to 3 months, it'll hit. Not only that but, most of it will hit that ocean I took you over. Problem is, the closer it gets to us the wider it gets. We won't take a direct hit thankfully, but we'll catch enough of an edge to make it pretty nasty around here for about 3 or 4 weeks. I want you to be extra careful. Watch where you go during that time and, how long it takes you to get there... stuff like that."

Kindly, Scota said "Aye I will on one condition."

"Oh?"

"Aye... that you do theh same."

Sweetly, Bird said "Aye my bonnie lil lass... I will."

"Oi... I ain't yer bonnie lil lass," Scota teased. "And come tuh think of it, yeh found someone fer Angus. I may be leav'in but, if yeh happen tuh find someone fer me befaw I go welllllllll..." and she smiled at Bird like a child does when they're hinting at what present they want.

"Like I told some of the Guardians... I'll see what I can do."

Scota gave him a sweet hug, and went back to cooking.

Ciana was acting odd. At least odd to Bird. Better for sure, but still odd.

"And jes what are yeh stare'in at?" Ciana asked Bird coyly.

"You for one thing. What's up with you lately?"

Ciana gave her sister a serious look and asked "Scota, would yeh mind giv'in me and Bird a moment?"

"Not at all. I have some supplies to take to padre ennyway."

"Mind yehself now girl. I doen want yeh going inside the borders of the camp yeh hear me!?"

"Aye, I won't. I jes got fixed, I have nooo desire to get broken again."

Scota meant it, grabbed the supplies, gave Bird and Ciana a kiss, and headed out on her horse.

Now alone, Bird sneered "You were saying?"

"Bird, I got a question for yeh."

"Hmm?"

"Scota told me a story recently, about her getting into your world. Is it true?"

"Sadly. I have the ability to erase memories with certain drugs I have. She was scared out of her mind but, she also saw it as wondrous and full of possibility. It was the latter that caused me not to. It was also the latter that caused me to take a chance and see if she could handle it. She's not handling it well but, even that is improving. Don't tell her I told you but, I'm using her as a gauge for you."

Ciana was happy for that. She wasn't thinking her sister a liar. She also didn't want to believe any possible exaggerations either.

"Scota said, she got a huge dose of that world... possibly too much at once... also true?"

"Very much so. What are you getting at?"

"Bear with me. Last question. I told her that going from my world to yours, was like you asking me to jump off the cliff by yer stairs, with the promise you'd catch me. My question is... would yeh?"

Bird smiled, and said "Nope."

"Oh? And why not?" Ciana asked with mock annoyance.

With true caring in his voice, Bird said "Because I'd never let you fall in the first place."

Ciana smiled, locked the door to an empty inn... and took Bird upstairs.

An hour later, and Ciana was smiling. Now relaxing in Bird's arms... she told him the truth.

"Bird, remember when I said I trusted yeh more than I should?"

"I do."

"Well Mistuh Yankee man... I still do. Scota said yer leav'in. Is that true?"

"Not soon enough for me. Yes, it's true."

"Scota said she's got to go with yeh, she also said why. I hear there's room for me as well?"

"You already know there is. Listen, you don't do 'coy' very well so, whatever is on your mind... let's have it."

Ciana sighed, and told the truth.

"Bird I never trusted ennyone but myself since father passed. Now Scota is grown up, and behav'in like it too. I had to keep the inn go'in as it was my only livelihood... Scota's too. Now yeh built a *house finer than fine. I also know yer learned ways fixed Scota. I kahnt tell yeh how grateful I am for either... and I got both. I wasn't go'in tuh tell ennyone about the padre, not even Scota. Still, you stood by me for something that could get us both killed. Yeh know every frustrat'in truth about me, and you love me still. There's one thing about me I want tuh tell yeh though. I doen care how something works, only that it does. I truly love the new kitchen and all the fancy things yeh put in. I truly doen know how half the things in the new house do what they do, I only care that they do. Scota however, needs tuh knoe everything. She wants to know how... why... where and all thah. I tell yeh thah because, I've decided to be more 'Lady Bird'... and less 'Ciana Thalin'."*

Bird was not only pleased... he was impressed. Ciana still had more though.

"Bird, I mention the diffrense between me and Scota so you'll knoe how to bring me into yer world. Things that frighten me are nothing to her... and just the reverse. What she sees as exciting I could care less about. I guess what Iem say'in is, base what you do on me... not her."

Bird kissed her and said "Fair enough. I will." He laid back down and said "You're going to be scared out of your mind. You're going to see things you can't imagine, have never seen, and ways of acting far outside your comfort zone. I can't explain everything or you'd go mad. That's why we're giving you pieces now. I will keep you safe and I will take you to places beyond your wildest dreams. I truly believe you can handle all of that except the fear. Nothing will truly hurt you at first but, until you accept my world on your own... I must have two things from you."

Ciana was Scottish proud and true when she said "Name them."

"I need you to trust me and Ally utterly and completely. If I tell you the sun is white on a blue day, I need you to believe me... not your eyes."

"I'll do mah best."

"Not good enough. You HAVE to do it... all the time... every time."

"Deal then. And second?"

*"No more fear... over anything. Not me, not the future, not the bishop... nothing. You have me... how bout you start showing the world what kind of lady I chose hmm?" Bird said tenderly but meaning every word of it.*

*Ciana nuzzled him and said "Thah's just it... I doen know her. Bird, I had mah world. I figgerd out mah place in it. Truth is, I doen know mah place ennymore. I haven't felt like this since father died."*

*"Like what?"*

*"Lost. What do I do, what do I say, where do I go and how do I act? It's like I have to learn how tuh be me all over again."*

*Bird told her "Not me... 'we'."*

*"Clarify," Ciana teased.*

*Bird chuckled "Oh what, now you're quoting The Chronicles too?"*

*Ciana just smiled, and purred softly in his ear. Bird didn't know why but... he loved when she did that.*

*"Oi!... BirdMan!... Trying to concentrate here!" Bird joked.*

*Ciana only smiled and purred even more.*

*A half hour later, and Ciana now had even more reason to purr.*

*Back where they started, Bird said "Okay so, I heard what ya said and... it's a fair assessment. You want to quote from the Chronicles? Fine. How about you use that to practice on?"*

*"How so my love?"*

*"Heh heh... keep talking like that and I'll roll you over again."*

*"Promise?" she said coyly.*

*"Yeah yeah. Listen I'm serious. Pretend I am 'that Bird'. Planet 51 is as fantastic as any place in my world. Pretend you are now Lady Bird to the Commander himself, and work on how to be 'that guy's' girlfriend."*

*"I thought I was to be 'wife'?" Ciana playfully joked.*

*With a gentle smile, Bird said "That works too."*

*"Aye... nicely," Ciana said sweetly.*

*Bird stared at the ceiling and said... aloud... "Alydar?"*

*"Bird, what the HELL! Are you doing?" the real Ally asked.*

"Alydar, I want you to honor Ciana's request... please... and teach her how to be a lady in our world." Bird then growled and finished with "Where she'll be treated like one... grrr... and not shunned for it."

"Oh I see... tawk'in to yer imaginary big black ship are yeh?"

"Invisible actually."

"Oh well... if thah be all," Ciana giggled.

"Alydar? I also don't want you to be afraid to talk to me anymore either... not in public I mean. I'll even answer you now."

"Well 'Commander'... I must say that was a slick move even for you."

Bird said nothing and Ciana asked "Well?"

"Uh, well what?"

"What's she say'in?" Ciana asked with a giggle.

"You don't wanna know... I'm getting yelled at," Bird said with a smile and a wink.

"OI! I am NOT yelling! Playfully admonishing perhaps but definitely not yelling," Alydar giggled as well.

Bird looked at Ciana and said "I'll play the part of Commander Bird, if that would help you."

"Ya knoe, I actually think that would," Ciana said seriously. "Iel pretend I'm this Lady Bird of yours. When we do get to yer world, even if it be different, Iel at least have something to go on. Yeh knoe, apply yer imaginary world to the real one. Bettuh than nuth'in I suppose... aye?"

"Can't argue with ya on that one Lady Bird," Bird said sweetly.

"Iel tell yeh this much 'Commander'... Iem start'in tuh like 'Lady Bird' already," Ciana said as she got comfy on Bird.

"Ya know boss man, only you could take a real story, convince everyone it's not, then get them to play along like it was. That's one slick move you just pulled there dude," Alydar said with a chuckle.

"I'll take that as a compliment my dear," Bird said aloud.

"Take what as a compliment?" Ciana asked.

"Heh heh... I wasn't talking to you."

"Ohhhhh... aye.... I got yer mean'in," Ciana said like a civilian getting caught in a spy mission.

Bird just smiled and hugged her tight.

Lady Bird however had a plan going. Commander Bird did huge things and... with tons of confidence. So, wouldn't it make sense Lady Bird would too? Best way to play the part she thought... was to act the part. In time, that 'new line of thinking' was going to catch a shadowy figure VERY off guard.

It was two days later. Bird was on Alydar checking on Ayleen. Her status was up to 34% and starting to really climb now. Like Bird saw with Lone when he was little... wolves heal fast. Bird figured once he got her out of the danger zone, his help and her own body would get her not only awake but mobile once more. Bird told Ciana he'd be gone for 3 days maybe 4. She promised him a surprise when he came back but also said she'd be away for about the same.

"Traveling alone today lass?" the ferry captain asked.

"I am indeed. I find I have business on the mainland," Ciana told him.

Even he noticed however, the more confident tone in her voice since the last time she was here.

"I doen mean yeh no ill miss Ciana but... do yeh think thah wise? I mean a lovely lass such as yerself, alone, without a man with yeh? The big cities ain't always so safe yeh knoe."

"Oh captain thank yeh for yer concern. I assure yeh Iel be fine. I think the real question tuh ask isn't if Iem ready for the big city... heh heh... it's is it ready for me!"

The captain smiled a true and kind smile.

"Aye! Iem not mean'in tuh get in yer business lass but if I may, do yeh mind an opinion?"

"Not at all."

"The Yankee man done good by ya... and fer yeh. No insult to yeh but, when I first took yeh, you were like a wide eyed child on Christmas morn. Now look at yeh... stand'in tall and proud. If yeh doen mind me say'in so... I like this lady much bettuh."

"Well captain, Iem jes getting to knoe her better but... I do too," Ciana said.

Ciana caught the coach to Glasgow. She giggled when several of the lads started fighting over the lass. One of the drivers seemed to be a nice man but got edged out by some of the others. She saw the look on his face when the more boisterous ones took over. So, learning from Bird and, being a kind woman herself... 'Lady Bird' chose him over the others.

"Ciana! Yeh bonnie lass yeh! Uh... where's Mistuh Bird?" Andrew asked greeting Ciana.

"He's off on other business and... heh heh... it's nice to see you too Andrew."

"Aye, sorry lass, it jes threw me like a horse would a shoe see'in yeh alone is all."

Ciana hugged him sweetly and said "Alone yes... Ciana no."

"What's thah yeh say lass?"

"This trip you're looking at Lady Bird... I left Ciana home yeh might say."

Andrew shifted gears immediately and started treating her like the proper fine ladies back in his home town.

"Oi! They'll be plenty of that attitude Mistuh Andrew from the others... not however, from you."

"Aye lass and... thank yeh. So, ready to head on tuh Edinburgh?"

"Actually, I had other plans in mind."

"Such as?"

"Lunch... my treat of course."

Ciana barked at a few of Andrew's choices. She wasn't dressed fine like on her birthday, but she wasn't dressed 'country' either. Andrew went to a fine restaurant first... a little too fine. Next choice was a tad low brow. Finally he found a happy medium and in they went. The woman seating the guests said Andrew couldn't come in as he wasn't dressed properly.

"My dear, I knoe yeh have proper coats and such for such a thing as this. Now, if you doen mind... neither do I."

The girl huffed but did indeed bring Andrew a jacket and tie. Now better dressed, she seated them both.

Andrew was kind and said "Yeh sound more like Mistuh Bird than yeh do ennything else. Thank yeh though fer stick'in up fer me. Iel tell yeh true, Iem a lucky man tuh be able tuh call yeh both friends."

"That's why Iem here actually. I was think'in of call'in yeh something else."

"Oh? And what be thah lass?"

"Business partner."

"Well, as yer 'Commander' would say... Iem listen'in."

"Bird told me, so did Kara, that you were doing better but still not well. That true?"

"Aye lass... tis true. Mistuh Bird's idea was a good one and it did help. Sadly, there just ain't enough tuh go around. The hotel man gave me his business like he promised and I done right by him. Sadly it worked so well the other places started do'in the same. Doen get me wrong my dear, I am better than I was... but not much so."


"Well then, Bird comes up with the plans... time for me tuh try one. How would you feel about runn'in my inn fer me?"

"The inn! I'd be... wait a moment... why ain't you runn'in it?"

"Andrew, truth is... I doen want to ennymore. I have a life with Bird now. Yeh knoe Scota's cough?"

"Aye, sad thah is. How is she these days?"

"Fixed."

"Oh Iem truly glad tuh hear that... truly," Andrew said.

"I gave the inn to her but, while she doesn't have the cough enny more, her lungs got damaged. The weather on the Isle is no good for her and if she doen leave she'll get sick again. Yeh knoe the inn is my family legacy aye?"

"Aye... I do."

"I have Bird now Andrew. I needed the inn to survive, but I doen ennymore. Still I just can't sell it or give it away. Bird said you knew people here and in Edinburgh that like to go to the country. The inn needs work I won't deny it, but it ain't fall'in down either. If I was tuh fix it, well, why not do it so these proper folk would like it and fix it once not twice eh?"

"Aye, makes sense," Andrew replied still slightly stunned.

He was still uncomfortable in this place, and now yet again this fine couple, well one of them anyway, was thinking of him as if he mattered.

"Ciana, truth is, I doen knoe nuth'in about runn'in an inn. If yeh need a driver or a guide, Iem yer man... but an inn?"

Ciana was kind and said "Andrew look at me. A little over a year ago I wouldn't even knoe how to get to a place like this, no less feel like I belong in one. If I can do this... I can teach yeh how to run my inn. There's some nice sights in the croft too and lots of places on the bay for proper folk to swim or picnic. Once you learn them you'll be back to guiding in no time."

"And yer sister woen mind me take'in over?"

"Not at all. Let her help you though Andrew. Yeh may knoe how to appeal to a man guest... let Scota help yeh on how to appeal to the women is all."

"Aye, a fine deal it is and generous too. Iel assume there will be payment?"

"You and I can sort that out but you knoe me Andrew... it'll be fair I promise."

Andrew was about to reply, when both of them were startled by a loud crash.

Andrew had his back to the ruckus but Ciana saw it. Five young men at a table were laughing at the waitress. What Ciana saw though, was one of them pulling his leg back in. The waitress was on the floor and quickly trying to pick up the mess. The one who tripped her though, was getting loud and showing off for his friends.

"Oi! You've made a mess of my clothes!"

"I... Iem sorry sir I..."

Ciana's kindness compelled her to help out but... it was Lady Bird who walked over.

She reached down to help the scared lass up when the loud one turned on her.

"This is none of your affair! Go back to your father and keep out of business that isn't yours!."

Ciana ignored him and kept her hand held out for the young

girl.

"Oi! Are you stupid as well as deaf!?" the bully said standing up.

It was when he tried to pull Ciana by her shoulder that his day went really askew. He did it once and Ciana still ignored him.

"Oi! Iem talk'in to you!" he bellowed.

He pulled her shoulder again, this time harder... really hard. What happened next stunned his table... and the restaurant.

"I however... am not talking to you," Ciana said.

She also said it, with an ice cold stare, and with one of her daggers under his chin.

She had pulled AND placed it... just like Bird and Ally showed her.

Ciana smirked at his discomfort and said "Aw, now look what you made me do. Listen to me very closely you little man. I've been lusted after by one FAR more important than you... and he was beaten back. Add to that I've had to deal with drunken sailors since I was 16 and not one of them so much as scratched me! Compared to them, you're nothing. Beating on defenseless little girls eh? Ha! You're not a threat... you're a bloody joke! Now, as someone I know once said... unless yeh want to be wear'in my smithy's iron like an ascot..." and Ciana looked down quick then back up and finished with "... I'd be loosening that grip on you're walk'in stick right about now iffin I were you," and she pressed her blade up just a touch.

He was about to say something when the manager and a bar man walked over.

"I'd say she was right," the manager told him.

This guy was well known to him and while his coin was nice, the level of aggravation he caused, especially to the female staff, was reaching his breaking point. Seeing him get 'what for'... and by a woman no less... only made him smile.

"Would you be the manager of this place?" Lady Bird asked.

"I am," he stated calmly.

"This foolish little boy tripped this hard working lady here, then tried to blame her fall on her. My name is Lady Bird, and I saw him do it."

Ciana said that but was still holding the blade, and her gaze, firmly in place.

"Aye, I saw it too!" Andrew called out.

A woman at the next table also agreed. She didn't see a thing but claimed she did as the loud mouth annoyed her. She also threatened to not come back due to the type of customer that was permitted in there. She also thought Ciana was something to behold, so she threw in a little 'girl power' to help her out.

Three witnesses, and the waitress made 4. The man was pulled away and was protesting loudly. He was also trying to break free and finally did. He ran and grabbed Ciana. He pulled her off the floor and had her arms pinned at her side. Once again, she did what she was taught. She was scared but, like Bird said it would, training took over. She used her upward momentum and went even higher. Then, with all the force she had she brought down both of her spiked heels... right into her attacker's knee caps. She was held no more.

The manager apologized profusely, and thanked her for her kindness and assistance. The crowded tables however were just amazed... and applauded.

Back at her table, Andrew had a drink waiting for her. It was a 'manly' drink at that... single malt Scotch. Ciana was shaking as she sat back down but Andrew just marveled, and handed her the Scotch. Seconds later, and only a few at that, it was slammed down empty.

"Lass that was impressive!"

Offhandedly, Ciana replied "I had a good teacher. Now... where were we?"

Almost everyone said something to Ciana on the way out. Oddly enough that made her uncomfortable, but she smiled and made nice all the same. The manager caught her eye... pointed to her bill in his hand... and smiled as he tore it up and tossed it in the fireplace. Ciana smiled and nodded, and went back to calming herself down.

# Chapter 34:

## "Incoming"

*"SHE DID WHAT!??" Bird hollered in Andrew's direction.*

*Andrew was back in the inn as Ciana brought him with her. He just finished telling Bird the lunch story. Ciana felt like Bird was pissed she did something wrong, and tried to defend something she didn't realize didn't need defending.*

*"What? Yeh said 'BE' Lady Bird... so I did!"*

*Bird stood up and grabbed her face hard.*

*"MMMMmmmmmmwwwwAAAAAAA! HAHAHAHAHA!"*

*"Oi Mistuh Bird, yeh should'a seen her. It was amaz'in! Except Lady Ally, I ain't ne'er seen a woman act like that... no less fight like a man. The whole place applauded too!"*

*"My wife to be?... Heh heh... they better have," and Bird grinned at him. "So Andrew, being that I saw your coach outside, am I to gather you'll be staying with us awhile?"*

*Andrew was a tad shocked and stared at Ciana asking "Yeh mean yeh didn't tell him!?"*

*"It's my inn Andrew... not his... and I'll do as I please with it. I doen need a man's permission to do what I please with mah proppity."*

*Bird sipped his tea and grumbled slightly "Try telling that to the town folk."*

*"Oooh... doen EVEN get me started on them!," Ciana said coldly and, with a touch of sadness.*

*Bird did a mock bow and chuckling said "Yessss Miiiiissstress ha ha ha ha."*

*Ciana walked sweetly up to Bird, smiled, hugged him, and spoke into his ear.*

*"Alydar? Are yeh there? Can yeh hear me? Jes so yeh knoe... if he EVER calls me thah again... kick his arse for me okay?"*

*The real Alydar bust out laughing so hard she couldn't even reply.*

*"So, what does yer imaginary friend think of thah!"*

*"Heh heh... I'll let you know... as soon as she finishes laughing," and Bird winked.*

*"Hmmf... I like her already," Ciana said playfully turning her back on Bird.*

*"So Andrew... I believe you were about to tell me why your here?"*

*"Well, I want yeh tuh knoe, Iem real grateful to yeh fer what yeh done. Sadly, it wasn't enough. As I toel Ciana, I did better but there jes wasn't enuf business tuh go around. Ciana here says she wants me tuh run her inn for her. Of course, iffin yeh have other ideas I would be happy to..."*

*"Andrew!" Ciana barked, "Tis MY inn... MY land... and 'I' will do as I please with it."*

*Showing support for his gal, Bird said "You heard the lady. Now, if it's my business... you come to me. If it's hers... you go to her. I know you meant no insult Andrew as this seems to be the way around here. What I'm telling you however is, now that you know, you ever make that mistake again, and Mistuh Yankee Man is gonna be rather pissed off."*

*Andrew thought these two were not only made for each other but, they truly were a grand couple themselves.*

*"Aye. Yeh have mah word it won't happen again."*

*Lone was in his house on Tuhleesia. He had all the Guardians on hand and was going over the latest information with them.*

*"Tiiveer, can you spare Ryklan for this?" Lone asked.*

*"So far I've sent out the Pilots ten times. No problems found so far, nor the target we seek. As such, I feel she can be 'diverted' from her current duties."*

*"Good. All the Pilots are fine in their own right, but she had the most experience in Ship before she was lost."*

*Lone let them know Gil's ships didn't need as much maintenance as Ship did due to their light use.*

"I've got Deeno on Eden giving the air filters an Agent Orange bath. Once all is ready, I'll be in one of them and keeping Renny safe. Ryklan will take the Prime. Tiiveer, no insult to you but, when it comes to Lady R you can be quite a handful. While I commend you for caring for your mate so... I also can't have you getting in the way should something go wrong. Politely put... if you think you can 'keep your cool'... then I have no problem with you going along with Prime."

"Heh heh... so I got myself a reputation eh?" Tiiveer joked.

Lone wasn't laughing and said "You might say that."

Rahgaa kicked in and asked "So, while we know more about the minefield now, what exactly is the plan?"

Lone looked at them all and laid out his version of a grand plan. Now, he was hoping it was all it seemed it was when he dreamed it up.

"We have two ships like the one Ayleen was lost in. I personally modified it from it's original configuration, and that's what I'm used to as is Ryklan. As such, those same 'upgrades' are going in now. Next will be the energy screens that keep us safe from the minefield. The plan is, Ryklan will take Prime, and I will take Renny. We will stay close to Raven. Once the ladies trance, we'll know if we can stay there, or if we have to re-position."

"Commander, why not just have the Guardians trance from the safety of Raven?" Turannen asked.

"Her hull. While I can't tell you everything, I can tell you her hull is impervious to radiation and energy of any kind. Even if the ladies were able to trance out, I don't want to find out the hard way they can't trance back in. That's why they're going in different ships. Should this plan go sideways, the possible loss is minimized."

Turannen was happy with that and queried no further.

Lone picked back up saying "Once I and Guardian Tiiveer are happy with the situation, the ladies will trance down the minefield's corridors. I have given them a description of them, but for safety, no one else. Planet 51 is far closer to the field than this place is, so Jonathan will be on standby for any emergency. I feel Triikon should be on the station. That way we get the best healers as close as we can should they become needed. He knows Jonathan best and they've worked as a team many times before." Lone looked at Ravenahl and said "No insult to you my dear but, the less Guardians I put in harm's way the better. Triikon and Jonathan have a certain rhythm when they get together. A small thing I know but, should they be needed, I'll take all the luck and any edge I can get."

Kindly, Ravenahl said "I am not insulted at all Commander. It truly makes the most sense... and the best use of the talent at hand."

Lone tipped his hat.

Turannen asked "Commander, let's say one of them does indeed find a portal. If the ships are not near, and they are in different locations... how do you get the second ring to them? Assuming they did find one, they'd have to take the trip back to you to let you know. What's to say, they get lost or the portal closes before they can return to guide the ring?"

"I thought of that. Of all the scans we took, the isotope we used on the Pilots and Sal, doesn't seem to exist in any of the tunnels. The ladies will have a tank of it. The drones will be going up and down the main corridors while they trance. The ladies will only have to make a piece of a finger solid and push the button. Once the drones detect the spray they'll make, the ring will go to whichever one calls for it."

"Even a piece of a finger... exposed to space... wellllllll, I know I'd want some gloves heh heh."

Lone just smirked and flipped something over his hand saying "Ya mean... like these?"

He did indeed have some gloves, custom fitted for each lady.

"So, as soon as the ships are finished, we'll do a test run. I'm not happy about how long this is taking overall. I can't help but feel like every single minute is precious, and the more that pass... the farther they slip away. I don't mind telling you, I'm really counting on the minefield to be a great equalizer. That said, I'm proud of all involved for the work done so far. If Biiird was here, I know he would be proud of all the effort as well," Lone told them all. "That said... any other questions?"

None came, all felt good about having a plan and... so it was.

*Lianna was walking down Raven's hallway to her and her brother's spot. It was their 'secret personal space', and only Raven knew where they were. To conserve Raven's power, the whole ship was dim and to Lianna... it was just depressing. She had been in the void almost her entire life. She would press her mother for stories of the old days but, since her father's death... or rather 'presumed' death... mother wasn't exactly herself. She had been looking for him, along with her brother, ever since he disappeared.*

*Lianna was only a few minutes older than her brother 'Junior'. He was named after his father but no one ever called him by his name... not on this ship anyway. As such, he always felt like he had something to prove. He was good but, not as good as Lianna was. Lianna was even better than her cousins. She herself was next in line to be Prime. She thought as she got older that her cousins would have squawked about that, but they didn't. Her cousins, just happened to be the son and daughter of the current Prime. Her mother gave up the title to her aunt some time ago. Lianna didn't care at all but, it was the only thing that put a spark in her mother's self induced depression. If it wasn't for her ability to trance, she wouldn't know anything at all. Seems mom could trance through space, but not time. Her aunt could but needed help and even then, only to a small degree. Lianna however, used time and space like her playground. So did her brother and both of her cousins.*

*"Junior, were you spotted?" Lianna asked when she finally made her destination.*

*"No... were you?"*

*"Nah. Mother is asleep and aunty is... well... being aunty."*

*"While I love aunty like you do," Junior started, "I often wonder why she keeps the old traditions alive. We all know them but, it's not like there's a Tuhleesia or 51 anymore. We're all that's left and even if we ever get out of this void... nothing we find would be 'home' per say."*

*Junior wasn't the typical 'chip on his shoulder' younger brother. He was competitive with his sister but, nothing more than that. He was actually a very smart wolf, but not arrogant. He was* good in a fight and quite honorable too but... rather calm and level headed  most of the time. Lianna was too and... again... so were her cousins. Her older cousin, Talon, was like her and Junior. Honor and focus and dedication seemed ingrained in them. Her younger cousin, Skye, just seemed that way naturally, whereas the other 3 were more driven to be.

"I know that Junior but, we are all that's left of a once proud race of billions. While the only remainders of 51 and Tuhleesia are in this ship, if we don't know who we are... then who are we?"

"I suppose. Still, while there's only a handful of us left, it gives mother and Lady Prime some small happiness. As for mother, anything that makes her smile these days is just fine by me."

"Same here. Raven?"

"Yes lady Lianna?"

"Wow... you haven't called me that since I was little."

"With your current topic of conversation, well, I thought you'd appreciate the reference."

Lianna smiled saying "Indeed and... thank you. Now, if you would... can I have some lights in here?"

A smiling wolf voice replied "Of course."

An old storage room with two hiding siblings was now fully lit.

"Aaaahhh... much better."


"So, where should we go today?" Junior asked.

"Look for father?"

"Well duh... but where?" Junior chided.

"I say we go back to that nebula, and work backwards from there. We know when father and uncle were lost. You and I both feel like they're not dead but lost. So, how about we go back to that spot then... work backward through time from there?"

"Sounds as good a plan as any," Junior said as he kindly held his hand out for his sister. "Shall we?" he asked with a smile.

She took his hand and kindly replied "Lead the way dear brother."

Two siblings drifted off. In a sense... only one would return to this time line.

"Can you believe your sister blondie?" Bird asked as they sorted some things in the bay.

"Aye! Can't you?"

"Believe it yes but... I would have expected something like that from you before her. Don't get me wrong I am proud of her. What she did, what plan she came up with... all of it. I just didn't expect it is all."

"Well, she is taking yer plan to heart yeh knoe."

"What plan?"

"Her be'in the real Lady Bird and all. She's taking it quite seriously."

"Seems a little odd though. I mean think about it Scota, to her 'Commander Bird' is pretty much a myth. You and I know better... but she doesn't. So in a sense, she's pretending to be a fantasy wife to a fictional character."

"Doen be hard on her. She truly is lost. Christmas stung her more than yeh realize. She's known the town folk and the rest on the Isle her whole life. Since you came along, she feels like the town folk are making her choose a side... and gett'in mad at her for choos'in you over them."

"Idiots. I could have helped them beyond their wildest dreams. Now... they're about to find out how pissed Commander Bird can truly get. I told you that day on the beach, she's getting a raw deal. Well blondie, we've gone past 'getting' and have gone well into 'received'. I'll support her of course but, the locals are about to get a healthy dose of 'go fuck yourself' with a side order of 'piss off'. Wait till Angus breaks ground on his new shop... you'll see."

"Aye, I have no doubt o' thah. Ennyway, Ciana feels like if thah's how they wanna be... and thah's how they're gonna treat her... then Lady Bird is exactly what they'll get. Being that... what did yeh call it again?"

"Character."

"Aye thah's right. Soooo... being that 'character' is all she has left. She loves you so much. She doesn't want to make you, or herself, look like an idiot. She doesn't want to leave the Isle, and when I say thah I mean just thah... the Isle. The town folk however, well, at this point if you weren't at the house on Christmas... you're now 'one of them'."

"Trust me, I can relate to that," Bird said.

"Hmm, perhaps. She's different now though."

Bird told her "I noticed. From what I've seen, we got one thing in our favor."

"Whah's thah?" Scota asked as she worked.

"She actually enjoys being Lady Bird."

"Aye... I noticed thah as well. It's more than thah though. Ciana has been sweet and kind her whole life. So much so thah I think folk come to expect it now. I've always felt many used her or took advantage. Now it seems like Ciana knows what I been see'in all along. Now that she's act'in on it, I think those same folk are now a lil mad thah the truth is out."

"The phrase you're looking for is, 'they're not sorry... they're just sorry they got caught'."

"Aye."

"So whah is all this stuff ennyway?"

"It's for Padre. It's a care package and WHOOOAAAAaaaa oooooookaaaaayyy.... why don't we just let BirdMan handle that stuff thank youuuu!" Bird said with a slight panic as he took some putty like ropes from her.

"Iem sorry. Whah is it?" Scota asked impishly.

"C4."

"JUNIOR!!" Lianna shrieked. "WATCH OUT!"

She was in a trance with her brother. They were where they wanted to be, but not when. They were still going backward in time when she saw a distortion bomb. Any anomaly in time, or any type of vortex that they crossed while they traveled, had a disastrous effect. When they time traveled, it was as if they were in a transparent tunnel of sorts. That tunnel got projected out ahead of them as they went. To a small degree they could see things as they went but mostly it was a blur. Crossing an anomaly or vortex in the past, with their tunnel from the future and... kaboom. Lianna found that out the hard way once. It was when mom and Auntie Prime found out they were time trancing as well as distance. It also took them 2 days to get her back, then... get her out of her trance. Since then all 4 of the time trancers knew what to look out for. Time tunnel distorts on the wall? Don't go past it. The source, aka the trancers, were the catalyst for the explosion.

"Thanks sis. That was too close."

"How could you miss something so obvious!?"

"Easy... I was paying attention to the other one on the other side," Junior explained with some alarm.

"What are you... ohhhhh SHIT! Junior what's going on... they're everywhere!"

"NOTICED THAT DID YOU!?" Junior hollered as he avoided two more, then helped Lianna avoid a third.

The distortion bubbles were what they considered an occupational hazard. They knew of them and only rarely crossed one. This time however Lianna was right... they were everywhere.

"Quick! Let's head back!" Junior called out.

Lianna was about to agree when she saw their tunnel was narrowing.

"You go! It's getting narrower!"

"I'm not leaving without you!" Junior hollered.

"Oh yes you are! Go Junior, I'll be right behind you but we can't go together!"

"Aunt Prime is gonna be pissed if she has to come find you again!"

"I have no intention of that... now GO!"

"All my love," and Junior headed back.

Lianna waited only a moment or two, but it was a moment or two too long. Just as she started after him, it closed up on her. Thinking quick, she knew only a new tunnel was her salvation so... she made one. The time trancers pretty much thought of where they wanted to go, projected that thought, and up came a time tunnel. Lianna did that and just made it through her new one when a distortion blew out her entrance. She was well past it but what she didn't know was it knocked her off course... waaaaay off course. What she and her brother also didn't know was... where they tranced into was the remnants of an area once known as 'the minefield'.

*"So Scota, let's see how good you've gotten. Care to play a game?"*

*Scota beamed.*

*Bird had Alydar bring up the energy screen and said "This is a little game I call... 'Guess who's dead'?" Bird said with a laugh. "I'll show you characters. The more you get right, the more music you get... wadda ya say?"*

*"Let's DO this!" Scota said with a 'bring it on' tone in her voice.*

*"Oops. Automatic 15 minute penalty for stealing my lines," Bird laughed.*

*"Alydarrrrrr!" Scota wailed in frustration.*

*"Don't look at me kid," sister Alydar teased.*

*"Okay... whooooooo's... this!?" Bird asked as he brought up the first one.*

*"Hmm... oh I know... Rahgaa!"*

*"Very good. Dead or alive?"*

*"Definitely alive," Scota stated with absolute conviction.*

*"Correct aaaaaand.... this?"*

*"Hmm..... Greeva? If so... he's very much dead."*

*"Nice work kiddo."*

*"Ugly bahstad ain't he?"*

*"Meh, ya get used to it."*

*Bird went through several more. Scota got them all right.*

*"She is odd looking with the hair and eyes and all but, I like it. I think she's pretty actually. Ghost 6... Symda... very much alive."*

*Bird praised her saying "You only got one wrong. Nice work Scota truly. Alydar?"*

*"Yeah boss?"*

*"Give Scota 5 hours of music to use as...... she....... seeeee's........"*

*"You okay Mistuh Yankee Man?" Scota asked.*

*"Yeah Bird, you okay?" Alydar asked with some concern.*

*Hearing Alydar concerned, Scota was now even more so.*

*"Time will tell. Alydar... bring yourself within door range, I'm*

switching ships. Scota... you stay here," Bird said with faraway eyes.

"What's going on boss?" Alydar said with even more concern.

"I'm not sure but I... I sense something."

"LIKE!?" Alydar said impatiently awaiting an answer.

"Incoming," Bird stated with the same far off tone.

"Oh well if..... Holy Shit!"

"Pretty much, now... get me that door," Bird stated in a 'right fucking now bitch!' tone.


Lianna had to avoid 5 distortions. Farther down... 3. A little past that and it was smooth sailing again. She came to a stop at where she thought was close to home. She couldn't have been more wrong.

She found herself in space, and Raven was below her. But she was all black and had no markings. She was also outside the orbit of a blue planet with a barren moon. Lianna didn't get much from any of the grownups about the past, which is why she started trancing in the first place. She didn't remember ever hearing a story of Raven being around a planet like this so... she decided to add more pieces to her past, and went in to take a look.

Raven was bright but... she had strange pockets of damage all over. Lianna was just strolling around. She's been on this ship since she was 1 and a half seasons old and as such, knew every hall, room and crawlspace. Something was odd about her but she just couldn't place it. Every turn and every sight made Lianna smile as this was new history for her. That joy would turn to horror in just a few minutes.

Bird was on the move. He felt a sensation he hadn't felt since Rahgaa's first trances on Eden. As strong as they were at the time, this feeling was 3 times stronger. Also, the closer he got to it, the stronger it got so... he tracked it.

He blew out of a hallway, then a door, then another hallway. He was getting stoked thinking he'd been found. The sensations led him to one place... his bedroom.

Lianna was walking down a corridor and couldn't shake the feeling something was wrong. This was Raven yet... where was everybody? She decided to get some answers. Her parents bedroom was bare... as in never lived in. Whenever she was, it wasn't any story or time-line she knew of. Finding nothing there, she decided to go to her aunt and uncle's room. Knowing how notorious they were at being prolific, she listened first before walking in.

This room looked only slightly lived in, and even then, not by anyone she knew of. The markers on the door jamb from Talon and Skye growing up were missing. None of what she should be seeing was there.

Then she saw it. The photo album she so loved to look through as a child. Her aunt would let her look at it for hours sometimes. Yep, to Lianna, this would solve all her confusion. It was sitting on a table and it was closed. Carefully looking around, she went solid and opened the book.

"Wait, this isn't right. Where's the picture of aunt and uncle on their mating day? And why is this picture over.... here... OH MY STARS!"

Lianna exclaimed that in near horror and total panic as she finally figured it out.

"This isn't Raven... it's.... IT'S!...."

"Alydar," the voice behind her said.

That voice horrified her to her soul.

"Who are you, how'd you get through the hull... and what are you doing on my ship?"

Lianna turned... and dropped the book.

# Chapter 35:

## "In The Presence Of God"

"Bird... who are you talking to?" Alydar asked.

"The lovely white wolf standing in front of me," Bird stated matter of factly.

Lianna was frozen. This was nowhere she wanted to be. Nor 'when' either. The one creature in the whole universe she was to avoid at all costs... and here he was mere feet away from her.

Mother had Lianna come in for a private talk one day. It was many years ago and just after it was discovered she could trance through time. Her mother calmly, but with extreme purpose, told her not to go near one creature... period. The wolves didn't have a god, till a prophecy showed up one day and beat the snot out of one of their own. Even her uncle, who loved her like his own daughter, was nowhere near the 'Great Rhana Bird'. The stories she read as a child, then the scarce tales she would get from her mother and her aunt, only made Bird into the very 'god' he tried so hard not to be. Right now though, for once, he was going to use that to his advantage.

Lianna didn't know what to do or say, and she was standing there with her mouth open and desperate for an idea. As the next in line to be Prime, her mother groomed her with all manner of etiquette and protocol. Nothing however, could have prepared her for this. To Lianna... she was in the very presence of God. She started to fade out and bowed deeply as she did. It was all she could think of to do.

"HOLD IT right there. They'll be no beaming out just yet young lady," Bird commanded.

Lianna stopped on a dime. She was calm on the outside... shrieking and freaking out on the inside.

"Bird, I can't see anyone. Worse, 'she' isn't showing up on any sensor either," Alydar said in a slight panic.

Alydar was concerned because, if she couldn't detect it, she couldn't keep Bird safe.

"Interesting. So, you're here... I can see you... but Alydar can't. I'd say that's impressive. Care to tell me how you pulled that one off?"

"G... Gr... Great Rhana Bird I... I... I shouldn't be here. Please... I... I must go."

That... was the best Lianna came up with. Bird was desperate for an edge and aside from Ayleen, this was the closest he was going to get and... he wasn't going to let it get away. He knew the tone and stature she was taking and for once, he decided he was going to be the mythical god the wolves made him out to be.

"You my dear... aren't going anywhere. So sayeth the BirdMan. Now, you seem to know who I am... um, you are?"

"Forgive me Great Rhana but, I'm not allowed to let you know even that much. Please Great Rhana, I must leave."

With one word, Ghost 1 changed two different fates.

"No."


Dammit. Lianna thought the creature on the old rolled up paper mom kept was... well.. 'cool' in wolf terms. She remembered one story in particular from her aunt. It was why that picture was the way it was... and how that image came about. Now, 'raw power' was so close she could smell him. The freaking out she was doing on the inside, was starting to make it's way to the outside.


"Well then lady, if you know who I am, then you'll know I'm pretty good at figuring things out, hmm?"

Speaking to the Great Rhana... no wait, not to... 'with'! Oh nothing could be more glorious, and terrifying, at the same time. A usually calm and extremely confident Prime-to-be... was now a tiny little girl. Unknown to her, it was just the way her mother was as well.

"I... I am," Lianna stammered.

"Well then, who told you not to talk to me?"

"M... Mother."

"Well then your whiteness, try this one on for size. EVEN IF your mother was the Prime... I still outrank her don't I?" Bird half stated, half asked.

"You... you are the only one who does," Lianna said not even looking at him.

"Well then, know 3 things. I, the Great Rhana, hereby rescind that order and command you to answer my questions." Bird lightened his mood as he spoke and said "Second, stop stammering. If you're doing what I think you're doing, well then, it's not exactly befitting one of your station now is it?"

"If you say so. I... I will try."

"Heh heh... try harder. And so, that brings us to number 3."

Lianna braced herself. What she got stunned her.

Smiling kindly, and holding out his hand, Bird said "As long as you're here... would you care for a tour?"

"I would love to," Lianna said now with awe and wonder.

The one creature she was to avoid at all costs, was nothing like she was told, nor imagined. Gently, eeeeevvvvver so gently, she took Rhana's hand and just couldn't believe she was actually touching him. Had she known more history, she would have known she just got Bird wrong the way her aunt and mother did so many times before her.

"I've seen that look before," Bird said and Lianna quickly looked away.

Kindly, Bird stopped in the hallway and pulled her gaze to meet his. Face to face with god, Lianna was frozen again.

"So... I believe I asked you your name?"

Still staring, Lianna caught sight of the blue eyes both Primes spoke of. That changed her whole attitude. Bird got even closer now and even he could feel her shaking.

"You like?" Bird said with a smile.

"Stuuuunnnnning," Lianna said staring like a school girl with her first crush.

Bird just laughed and continued his walk. Lianna walked with him but felt like she was walking on a cloud.

"So... your name... I won't ask again."

"Lianna,"

"Wow, that's actually quite pretty," Bird said honestly.

"Thank you Great Rhana," Lianna said with puppy dog eyes.

The great Rhana not only thought her name was pretty, he thought 'she' was too. What a day this was turning out to be.

"So, as I said, I'm good at figuring out things."

"So I've been told."

"How about I tell you a tale, and you fill in the holes okay?"

"Whatever you wish."

"I don't recognize your name. You also seem afraid you're here. Add to that your mother warned you to stay away from me. Lianna, you're not from this time-line are you?"

"Mother, it would seem, is correct. You are good at figuring things out aren't you?"

"I do try. It's the only thing that makes sense actually. Any wolf would be overjoyed at finding me and, it would only be one of 2 I could think of... and you aren't either of them. You do however resemble one of them... a lot. So tell me, are you from my future or my past?"

"Great Rhana, must I answer? You of all creatures should know that knowledge of such things can be very dangerous."

"How about if you trust me on this one... and not 'mom'."

Lianna sighed and said "Future."

Bird showed Lianna around and, a few times, chuckled as she knew more about this ship than she should. He chuckled because he was beginning to wonder just who was touring who.

"I see the look on your face. It's that look of awe and wonder. Care to explain that?"

"You... the mighty Alydar... the ACTUAL Ghost 1 herself... I have no words for the honor, glory and wonder of it all."

"Heh heh... fair enough. Alydar?"

"Yeah boss?" Alydar said over the speakers and not his comm.

She had a hint of menace in her voice as she didn't like Bird walking through the halls holding an invisible guest.

"Wow. In all the recordings that we have, I have never heard her actual voice. It's lovely!"

"Heh heh... Alydar, it seems you have an admirer."

"Is it a he or a she?"

"She."

"Well then... 'she' obviously has good taste."

Lianna actually giggled, and curtsied to the open air.

"Care to tell me how come I can see you but Alydar can't? I don't mind telling you it's making her more than a little nervous."

"Technically, I'm not here... and I am. It's a little hard to explain. I'd tell you if you wish but, I think you'll find it's one of those things even you would agree you shouldn't know."

"Fair enough."


Back in Bird's room, Bird laid into his plan.

"Lianna, tell me of your world."

"I was born on 51, and raised on Tuhleesia till..." and her voice drifted off into sadness.

"Till?"

"Till it was gone. I don't remember much of it really."

"And 51?"

"Gone as well. I know so much of this ship because it's almost identical to Raven, which has been my home since the creation of the great void."

"Okay, now you're getting into things I may not want to know. From here, I'll ask the questions, you answer only what I ask okay?"

"Indeed."

"How did you get here?"

Lianna told him of the tunnels, her brother, all the pertinent stuff.

"Great Rhana, even you know there is a time coming when you will go after Tamarak. You have failed 6 times so far."

"That much I do know."

"This time you truly break the loop, but not how you intended."

"I die don't I?"

"Do you really want to know?" Lianna asked with caution.

"I do."

"Yes, as does Alydar and... in a fashion befitting the Great Rhana himself."

"So, you trance. The two trancers I know of can go through distance but... you go through time only? Or both?"

"Both," Lianna said careful to answer, but not elaborate either.

"This time, the one you and I are in now... it's critical isn't it?" Bird asked.

"Very."

"Normally I'd bitch at you for your short answers. In this case however, keep them that way."

"As you wish."

"So you travel through time... to what end?"

"Father is lost and presumed dead. I however, don't presume."

"Understood."

"No insult intended but, I'm not sure you do."

"Perhaps. What is this great void?"

"Tamarak's madness. He..."

"Oh shit... wait... he destroyed the minefield didn't he?"

Cautiously, Lianna said "Because there was only 6 Ghosts to stop him... not 7."

Bird was musing over what he's learned so far. He was also deciding what to ask, and what not to.

"Okay so, the minefield finally blows and now nothing but emptiness. Still, you travel through time. I get coming here was a mistake, but why do it at all?"

"I would be what you would call a historian. I have gone to times before, and recorded what I can. When the great void was created, nothing of who we all once were remained. Raven had mother and father, and us children aboard her, along with aunt and uncle. Uncle said the shielding on her kept us in the same time-line."

Bird was not happy and said "I get it. The field blows. Just like Giljor said, nothing remains due to it never having been. But, Raven's minefield shielding kept you anchored in that time and place so while everything around you vanished... you remained."

"Correct."

"So... what... the only one's left of anybody is that who was on Raven?" Bird asked.

"Correct."

Bird had a thought, and played a hunch. He was digging for info and trying very carefully to do so, but not make it look so.

"So I failed 6 times prior eh?"

"Correct."

"Yet... you wouldn't know that unless you talked to Giljor or someone on that station. That loop back thing was something we didn't even tell the Ghosts... not fully anyway. You would have had to get that from me, Lone, Giljor or another on the station. Either that or, you were spying on us."

"I spoke to no one you mentioned. Contact of any kind with you is forbidden."

"WAS forbidden," Bird corrected.

"Indeed. As I said I spoke to none you mentioned. Also, I would not be so rude as to spy on any of the Ghosts... no less you."

"I hear your tone. You say I spoke to no one I mentioned, which means you did speak to someone. I can tell your not lying either about the spying thing so who did....... oh jeez, I get it now."

"Um... get what?"

"If it wasn't me or Lone, did you speak to, or spy on, one of the Adjulons?"

"No."

Bird chuckled and asked "So, how is good old Tiiven these days?"

Lianna was shocked and asked "How did you know?"

"He's the only other person old enough. I learned of him when I was on Eden. He can trance through time like you can. It's the only thing that makes sense."

"He doesn't his mate does," Lianna said and quickly covered her mouth at the slip up.

Bird immediately had a related thought and parked that for a time after Lianna leaves.

"Okay Lianna, you've done me a favor... how about if I do you one?"

"I would not dare refuse such a gift."

"Lianna, you know where, when and how I die. Obviously I fail to stop Tamarak. Now, I want you to tell me, if you were me in that situation, what would you do? And mind you... be as vague as possible."

"This is the very thing mother warned of."

"If mother is who I think she is... and aunt and uncle are who I think they are, then ignore mother this once. Knowing her she's probably a sulking depressed wreck right now, and 'auntie' is only pretending to be brave and strong. Their wisdom is good but was always clouded when it came to me. I have a habit of seeing far into the future, they did to a degree but nowhere near as far as I could. As such they would miss things and it's why they always got me wrong."

"I didn't know you tranced Great Rhana."

"I have with the ladies help, but no, not on my own. I meant I can see cause and effect. I know how creatures react, to what they'll react, and when, but most importantly 'why'. As such I predict what will happen based on those factors. I have been so successful because of how good at that I am. Like I said, we see into the future, heh heh, I just see a little farther than most."

Lianna was sad and said "Some nights, I hear mother calling out in her sleep... for you. She seems so lost and feels only you can save her. She truly rose to greatness among our people, but she saw all that it cost, and all that she failed, and saw that as her ultimate failure. Now, all the deaths of all the worlds, mother feels rests solely with her. She was Prime Guardian at the time and, well, failed to 'guard'. She seems so lost and, the enormity of it all, I think she feels only someone equally as enormous can help her."

"Mother is going to be mad... furious even but... tell her I said hello," Bird said sweetly.

"I will, I promise. May I ask, what is this favor you offered?"

"Simple. Something I don't know about is going to cause me to take a certain action. You know that action is wrong but... you also know why. If you are vague then you won't change what even I agree with shouldn't be tampered with. Not to that degree anyway. Recent events however have caused me to believe that rule can be bent some... just not broken. The favor I offer is, if I figure it out on *my own, then your depressing little life won't exist upon your return. My gift to you and all the others and... the one way an 'enormous' person can answer a call for help from a dear friend."*

*Lianna was almost to tears at the honor and caring of it all. And the scope, oh the scope of it all. Mother was right he truly did see the big picture like no one she ever knew. She had spent a little over an hour with the Great Rhana Bird, and just being in his presence changed her outlook on many things. Seeing his kindness and confidence, well, she now had a new set of standards to strive for.*

*"I have no right to ask this but, I am anyway. Advice from none other than you would be a treasure for a lifetime. Is there any you feel I should have?"*

*"Are you going to give me my vague answer?"*

*"I will."*

*"Well then... remember this always. Many things in life, both good and bad, will come your way. Creatures, situations, whatever. The best advice I can give you is... forget the who, what, where, when and how. Focus only on the why. IF you get that correct... you'll have all the others."*

*Wisdom from the legend himself. Lianna would find it not only correct but... she would end up using it as a blueprint for the rest of her life.*

*"Oh and one more thing Lianna. If in the future, whichever one it will be, know that I, Rhana Bird himself, I give you my permission to contact me again if you feel the need to do so. Not even a Prime can countermand that order heh heh," and Bird finished that with a smirk.*

*Lianna stood tall and proud, and acted as if she was already Prime.*

*"Great Rhana Bird, I am honored beyond words for your caring and wisdom this day. How I feel however... can't be described. Know this. In a time to come, every fiber in your being will tell you what you're doing is the correct course of action. My vague hint to you is... if you recognize that time for what it is... remember your own advice you gave one of my own kind once.*

Know that, at that time... you'll have to do what's wrong, to do what's right. If you do, I believe with all my heart, you will succeed where you have only failed before."

Lianna bowed to him but stopped. She remembered something and smiled... and switched to a curtsey instead.

Bird hugged her kindly and said "I have missed you and your kind very much. Thank you for your visit and... your trust. May my God protect you wherever you travel."

Now Lianna was shedding happy tears as she faded back for home. Bird turned and headed for the bay with a renewed vigor. In his mind, one way or another... he was going home.


Lianna returned to her time. Like Rahgaa had when she found Bird, Lianna could sense things when she traveled. She slowed down and stopped and she was in the correct time AND place... but she wasn't.

"No... this can't be! Raven would never leave without me!"

Suddenly, an energy wave hit her. That's when she realized what Bird meant. Looking all around her all she could see was the bright and faint twinkle of... stars.


Lianna wasn't very old when all this disappeared. She was bawling now seeing all the life around her. Now she had to find home. Her bond with her mother was strong, but the bond to Junior was stronger. Focusing on him, she now had a direction. She found him in a place she had only seen in pictures. It was uncle's house in the cave. Everyone was there for some form of dinner when she 'beamed in'.

"Have a nice day dear? What kind of adventure were you off on this time?"

"Mother!" Lianna shouted and hugged her tight.

"You okay there Li Li?"

There was only one wolf ever who called her that.

"FATHER!" she screamed and hugged him tight as well.

"What's wrong with you Lianna? Heh heh, you're acting like you've seen a ghost. Get it?"

"(sniff sniff0 Oh father, your jokes are as terrible as ever," Lianna said lost in a dream.

"Are you alright my dear?" came a booming wolf voice.

Wiping her tears, she hugged him as well and said "Uncle? Now I am."

She pulled Junior aside and asked "Do you remember the tunnel narrowing?"

"Uh... no?" Junior said unclear as to what she was referring to.

"Ohhhhh brother... we must talk. First though, I need to see someone."

"DON'T be long," mother called out, "Dinner is almost ready,"

"I promise... this won't take long at all," and she rushed out the door.

She only knew from stories which door she needed to go to, but she got to it all the same.


"Hi cuz," Talon said answering the door.

"Cuz? Ooohhhh 'cousin'! Wait, you're my cousin?"

"Uh yeah... sorta have been for like the last 17 years. You alright there Lianna?" the raven haired young man asked.

"More than you know. Is your father at home?"

"For once. Come on in I'll go and..."

"Thank you but... no. Could you ask him to come to the door please? I don't wish to intrude."

"DAAAD! Lianna is here and she's acting all weird and shit!"

A handsome human in his late 40's to early 50's answered the door holding his now famous cup of tea.

"Hiya Li what's up sweety?"

Lianna properly curtsied saying "I am already working on 'the why'... thank you Great Rhana... for everything."

Bird just smiled and said "I was wondering when that loop would catch up to us. Suffice to say..." and Bird winked as he finished with, "... I figured out the vague. You're welcome. You're about to have dinner with your family. Be as normal as you can and... come see me later. Welcome back my dear," and Bird hugged her and closed the door.

Lianna was crying as she ran back for dinner.

# Chapter 36:

## *"Four Cannons And A Firing Squad"*

*"Well... it's slightly better," Lone said looking over the 'new and improved' Raven.*

*"You have me to thank for that one Commander," Zarra said. "Seeing as how I came up with the drying agent, I felt it only fair to come up with a solution," Zarra sort of giggled. "It seems the drying agent acted as a dye also, so, we just picked another color. Believe it or not though the moss has slightly different densities. That's why you see the striping effect. Lesser dense moss absorbs quicker and so on."*

*Lone was relieved and kindly said "I'll take it."*

*A slightly sad 10 mile behemoth huffed and said "I thought it was pretty."*

*"Yes my dear but, I prefer to have the enemy dying from the 12 pack when I pull up on then... not laughter," Lone retorted.*

*Raven still wasn't happy and gave Lone a taste of his own medicine when she said "Hmmf... men!"*

*Lone AND Zarra chuckled as they walked off.*

*It was two days later and now, Raven was as striped as her pilot. Not terribly so but, enough. She was striped the way a Bengal tiger would be and, true to her word, Zarra 'dyed' the pink out. Now she was striped in blue and silver with mostly black as a base.*

*"ERE now...DATS beh'uh innit!!??" Lone said with joy at the new color scheme.*

*"Okay, even I got to admit, when you're right you're right," Raven decried.*

*She was the warrior queen but, the pink brought out her feminine side. Not only that, she was liking it. Her 'brother' remarked at her the other day that, well essentially, she needed to* lighten the fuck up and get over herself. He also remarked that, in attitude anyway, she was more manly than he was.

"Thor! That wasn't very nice," Symda said at the time.

"Perhaps not," the only male Ghost machine replied, "But it needed to be said all the same."

That very same Thor was cruising around the back of Tamarak's planet right now. Lone ordered raids on Tammy's place to keep him disrupted and essentially... annoyed. He also knew the more he and the Ghosts damaged, the more Tammy needed to replace and the more he needed to do that, then the more flawed copies would be in the mix due to Remmy's virus. Classic raiding at its finest and, it was working. Thor was alone and per the plan, had another 2 minutes of being that way. Deeno was her wingman today and Symda was to go in first, make it look like a solo run, then Deeno would drop in on the party. Thor got halfway around to target when he went inviso... all on his own.

"Aaaaaannd... you did that.... why?" Symda queried.

"Sensors indicate a huge ship or complex below the clouds. Threat level unknown so I believe you call this better safe than sorry," Thor told her.

"Ghost 3... hold up your run... Thor found something big on the back side."

The brat Ghost blew into his comm saying "What (bbbbzzzssssshhh) did (ffffff) you say? (bbbbbffffttt) too much (pppppffffffffffffttttttt) static.... did you say (hhhhssssssss) Tammy has a big backside?"

"How you ever found a mate is beyond me," Symda retorted.

Deeno chuckled but got serious and said "MRU... Going dark... be there in 2 or less."

"I'll be waiting. May wanna spin 'em... but don't lite 'em up just yet.

"MRU."

Deeno pulled up alongside her and said "5 miles off your starboard... and spinning as requested."

"Well 4 arms, you're the ranking Ghost here... do we go in and have a look?"

Deeno was checking his scans and seriously said "Not yet."

That tone alone, coming from Deeno no less, had Symda on alert. Thor and Kallan were conferring back and forth over the scans each took.

"Deeno, is this right? This thing is showing 1 ship but, it's almost 3,000 miles long!"

"2,842... heh heh..." Deeno looked down and laughed aloud "Even number, SERIOUS mistake dude.... HUGE! Hahahahaha!"

Symda asked "So, we taking a closer look or what?"

"Negative. Get all the scans you can of what appears to be the engine area but do NOT go down there. In case you hadn't noticed, that thing is surrounded by the same energy that made Quaran go visible."

"Oh I see it... I just don't care. We don't run nor hide remember?"

"I do. Meet back up at point alpha 6 and continue pissing him off. I wanna keep this little surprise to ourselves for a bit."

Symda was a tad pissed and asked "Should I keep Thor hidden too?"

"Not at all. Get to Alpha 6, go visible then... send him any message you please."

"THAT... I can do!" Symda said with true pride.

Breaking high right and left, 2 Ghosts went back to pissing off a cyborg.

An hour later and no weapons left except the 12 packs, 2 Ghosts broke the perimeter of mojo territory.

"Hey 3, can I talk to you?" Symda asked.

"Sure."

"It's about Bird."

"Change of plans... no you can't."

"I'm serious ya brat!"

"So am I. Look, I got nothing against you and certainly not him. That conversation though, isn't my place to comment."

"Fair enough. I'll keep out the personal stuff, just give me your observations then okay?"

"Like you said recently... that I can do."

Symda softened and said "I'll assume you know how I feel

about him yes?"

"Actually, not really. I can take a fair guess though."

"Look Deeno, he forbid Renny from being Lone's distraction. A bit egotistical but, it was correct. I refused to be his. Now I am a Ghost. I love it beyond anything you can imagine. What has me torn is Bird. I love him as much as I love these wings. Believe it or not, I usually talk to Alydar about these things but..."

"I'm not Alydar but, I'd be happy to talk to you about anything Symda," Kallan said cutting in.

"Thanks Kal but, Alydar already knows things about me no one else does and... things I'd rather not share."

"That's okay, I understand," Kal said.

It was how she said it though, that made Symda change her tone.

"However my dear, any other topic and my comm is always open," Symda quickly stated.

Kallan was still feeling a bit down and, she really looked up to Alydar. She also noticed her 'friends list' consisted of only 2 creatures, and one was her pilot. She noticed Alydar was into everything... and everyone. She was so well rounded and everyone looked up to her and now, she even had an avatar!. She still felt like she made a stupid mistake by not angling the blast and taking it full force instead. Deeno told her many times she was making up monsters, but the goofy nerd was looking to be a tad less nerdy.

Kallan's voice had a smile in it when she said "I'll try not to bug you too much."

Trying to get out of an awkward moment, Deeno asked "So, you were saying?"

"Bird. I've never met anyone like him. As such, I'm starting to wonder if I should pursue my feelings."

Deeno was kind and said "Let me ask you a question. Do you feel you are truly no longer Cinaad?"

"Truly."

"Okay then. Now try this... when you first met him... you still were. I'll agree he is most unique. Could it be that, now that you've met others more like him, that you might just be in love with a hero image, and not the man himself?"

"Normally I'd kick your ass for a comment like that. Lately though, I've been wondering that myself."

"Look Symda, I'm not being an ass. I'm only saying, consider this. Are you in love with the myth... or the man himself. Sort that out, and you'll have your answer. If it is just the image, while understandable, it's not truly fair to either of you."

"Deeno?"

"Yeah?"

"Thanks."

Deeno lit up his cockpit off her port side. No verbal answer, he just smiled... and saluted. Deep in new thoughts, Symda powered up Thor alongside Kallan, as both blasted for home.


Scota and Ally were cleaning the kitchen and making soap. Bird and Ciana were cleaning and sorting the tables and bar. Andrew was helping both parties trying to learn all he could. It was just a mundane day, when a frightened and crying wailing broke the afternoon boredom.

"MISTUH BIIIRD!!" Kara cried out stumbling across the open lawn area.

She only made it half way across the large open lawn in front of the inn when Bird made it to her. That scream had him running.

"What the fuck happened Kara!?" Bird said trying to figure out what was going on.

She collapsed in his arms by time the rest of them made it to them. Bird knew immediately something was wrong. Kara was out of breath and, he was no doctor but, he could swear she was on the verge of a seizure. Her clothes were torn and she was filthy. One thing bothered him more than anything. It was the overpowering smell of smoke.

"Mis... Mistuh Bird... An... Angus!" and she nearly passed out from running the whole way.

Bird dropped her in Ciana's lap, grabbed her horse, and bolted off at top speed for the smithy.

"If you'll excuse me, I have a feeling I'm going to be needed somewhere else very soon," Ally said as she headed out with focus and purpose.

Bird got on his comm and said *"I'll take a drone anytime now!"*

*"I thought you might,"* Alydar told him.

Only 20 yards ahead, as ordered, one went visible. Bird had been keeping one in the Lander 'just in case'. Blacky reared some and Bird hopped in the drone. Not only was he going to the smithy but... he was bringing firepower. Ciana wasn't nervous till Blacky came back without a rider.

*"Alydarrrrr?"* Scota nervously said off to the side.

*"He's fine. He merely acquired other transportation."*

*"Ciana?"* Scota said turning to her sister.

Scota merely nodded off to the side. Ciana left Kara with Andrew.

*"Andrew! Get her up to my bed, I'll be there shortly!"* Ciana barked.

*"Aye! Be quick about it!"* and Andrew headed inside carrying Kara.

All alone, Scota said seriously *"Other world stuff. He's fine."*

*"Thank yeh Scota. I only hope Angus is as well."*

*"Iffin he ain't, may God have mercy on the poor souls who made him so, for I know Bird won't."*

With that, both ladies went to care for what they felt was 'one of their own'.


Bird dropped out of the drone and it immediately went back invisible.

*"Drone, give me high cover,"* Bird said to the air.

A twin set of beeps was his reply. Bird scanned the area quick and seeing no hiding bad guys, he ran into the open area of Angus's place. First thing he saw was how much more open it was. The barn he and Kara worked in was two thirds gone or collapsed. Some was still on fire, and there was just smoke in other parts.

Bird was on his knees and scooped up Angus saying *"Angus, it's Bird!"*

Angus was a mess and bleeding badly in several places.

*"Bird I... I couldn't stop them. Heh heh, I took a few of theh bahstads with me though!"* and Angus pointed off to the edge of the

woods.

Laying there, mangled in a way only an angry man protecting his own could cause, lay 3 dead men in tartans. Problem was, they were Campbell tartans.

"Angus, don't talk. You're clear now."

"Kara?"

"Safe and in our care at the inn. Now save your..."

"Mistuh Yankee man (cough cough) it's ben a priveledge. Take care o'her for me," and Angus was out cold.

"Alydar?"

"Yes?"

"This time, you make the call."

"This is getting out of hand Bird, you know that right?"

"MAKE THE FUCKING CALL!"

With equal parts sadness, and kindness, Alydar said only two words.

"Save him."

"DRONE! I need a pickup!" Bird hollered out.

On cue, it swooped in and opened its top. Bird scooped up Angus and placed him inside.

"Where's your avatar?"

"On the lander."

"Call the drone in and... do whatever you can for him."

"And where are you going to be?"

"Right here. I don't like a few things. I'm gonna do a lil recon. If I don't call you in 15 minutes... send in the cavalry."

"MRU."

Bird could see the ground marred with scuffs and tracks. They were all around him but, he wasn't concerned with those. The one's he was concerned with were the ones leading to Angus's place. When he found them, he smiled.

"Idiots," was all he said as he examined them. "I'll bet those tartans are only days old too... tops."

What Bird saw was twin sets of tracks leading in to Angus from two sides. Growing up military, Bird knew them in an instant. The clans of the highlands were excellent guerrilla fighters and knew how to use the woods. These tracks were side by side. Bird went over and cut off a piece of one of the dead man's tartan and sniffed it.

"Fresh wool," he stated to no one. "Alydar! Get over to John's now!"

"Angus is aboard. He's lost a LOT of blood Bird. I got him in the quarantine bed and knocked out. Why am I going to the dressmaker?"

"Trust me, just get there and when you do... do it like super black ops okay?"

"MRU."

"I'm heading back to the inn. Send me the other drone." Bird switched channels and said "Scota, I'm okay. Angus is alive but barely. I need you to come get me. I'll start walking back. Grab me on the way and... bring your sword and be EXTRA careful."

Scota walked off to the side and said "Aye, I'll come as quick as I can. Bird?"

"Yeah?"

"Whah's go'in on?"

Bird said something that made her go cold... then angry.

"It would appear... the bishop has returned."

Bird was only a fourth of the way back when Scota met up with him. The look on her face told Bird she was happy to not be alone anymore. They made it back to the inn and Ciana was relieved to see Bird unharmed.

Slinking through the streets, Ally made it to the dress shop. She knew something was wrong immediately when she saw the door locked, and the sign saying 'closed'. Problem was, it was only 2pm.
Ally looked around, and turned the knob so hard it broke the lock.

She said nothing and only looked around. She saw nothing up front so she walked around the back. What she saw pissed her off.

"Well, at least you'll be a lovely sight I can take with me (cough cough)," John said crumpled up against the wall.

He also said it with a dagger sticking out of his gut.

"What the hell happened!?" Ally asked as she scanned him.

"I wish I knew. They never asked a single(Cough)... a single question."

John coughed up some blood and knew he was breathing his last.

"I... I may be... a dandy but...(cough cough cough)... heh heh, that only means I had to know how to fight more... not less," and he pointed to two of his now dead assailants laying off to his side.

Alydar knew she could heal his severe beating, or the knife, but not both. She was actually unsure what to do.

"Tell Bird I... I may be... MMMF... I may be leaving earlier than (cough) I planned but..." he reached up and touched her cheek and said "... it was worth the ride," and his hand fell to the floor.

"I will dressmaker... I promise," Ally said with compassion as she closed his eyes.

Ally knew whatever was going on, someone was sending Bird a message. She also knew she had 3 more targets to get to... and fast. One of which she just covered. She had her Lander now parked over Bird and Ciana's new house.

"Grab her quickly!" the man in the doorway told the two soldiers with him.

The local constable showed up and found Ally leaning over 3 dead bodies.

"Honestly Constable, do I look like I could have done this? I came to pick up some dresses and found this! Oh... oh... oh the shock of it all!" Ally feigned.

"Likely not but, I got 3 murders and you. Right now lass, yeh ain't go'in ennywhere."

"I'm afraid I'm going to have to disappoint you there," Ally said with a sneer as she broke the hold the soldiers had on her wrists.

She ran out the door without a second thought.

"AFTER HER!" the Constable barked.

The two slightly shocked soldiers bolted after her and made a right turn same as Ally did.

"Oh! Sorry my good fellows!" an English doctor said walking around the corner and getting bumped into by two running soldiers.

'Doctor James' tipped a bowler like hat to the Constable in

the doorway and simply walked off. The smile on his face once out of sight, as 'he' switched back to 'she', actually had a giggle behind it.


Bird walked into the bedroom and, politely, asked everyone to give him a few minutes. Kara was out cold in the bed. Ciana told him to be quick about it as Kara still needed care.

"I'll only need 2 minutes, I promise."

Left alone, Bird checked Kara one more time, then reached under the bed. Hidden in a secret compartment he built in himself, Bird pulled down a wide flat board. He pulled its contents, and closed the hidden plate back up. When he left the room, his harness was back to full weight for the first time in almost a year.

"Thank you. The room is now all yours."

"Where are you off to my love?"

"To bring in some company," Bird said coldly as he headed out.


"Alydar!?"

"Sorry boss, I didn't make it in time."

Bird was sad for a moment, then focused again as he said "MRU. Were you discovered?"

"Sadly but, I made a clean getaway. I'm almost back to you... orders?"

"You in the drone?"

"Yep."

"Head to William... you're closer. I got Mary. Bring him to the inn by any means necessary with the exception of the drone."

"On it! Bird, what the hell is going on?"

"The bishop is back... he has company and... the idiot is trying to frighten me."

"I kind of figured as much but, why the others?"

"He's trying to make me a pariah. Come close to me or the girls, and or mess with him, and 'see what happens'. Not only that but, he wants to show who's still boss. You humiliated him, and now he wants blood."

"Boss, if I had known I..."

"Not your fault sweety and, I would'a stopped you if need be. No my dear, he didn't believe me when I told him his life was forfeit if he ever came back. Seems the time has come to show him I don't make threats but, when I do, they're not idle ones."

"MRU. I got the Lander high enough topside to cover the new house AND the inn," Alydar told him. "And I got them lit and spinning. Say the word and... Bird wait!... Mary just got some company! Two outside and three in. MOVE IT BirdMan!"

"45 seconds out. Ally?"

"Yes dear?"

"Like the night the bishop first showed up."

Ally smiled and said "I'm a minute from William. Let's DO this!"

Bird sneered and merely said "Showtime," and hopped out of the other drone Ally sent down. He turned to it as it closed its top and said "Stay invisible and, vaporize the two on the perimeter. Do it quietly and... see that nothing remains."

Another twin beeps and Bird headed for Mary's shop knowing full well, nothing outside would surprise him.


"OI! Iffin yeh think yer gonna scare me ya brute... yeh got another thing com'in!" Mary told her lead attacker.

"HAH! There be 3 of us and only 1 of you... and yer a woman!"

"Somebody doesn't know how to count," came an ice cold American accent.

The head attacker was flanked by his two buddies. Bird had come up between them. The bully turned just in time to see the man with the accent was arms wide... and pulling out a set of curved blades from his allies chests.

Mary actually curtsied and sneered as she said "Thank yeh kindly Mistuh Bird."

"Now... I believe you were about to attack this nice lass? Oh, don't let me stop you," Bird said arrogantly. "Hey Mary, tell ya what. You kick his ass... and I'll bounce him back into play if he makes a run for it. Sound good to you?"

"Going after women... HAH!... You'll make a much nicer target!" the burly man in the tartan boasted.

*"If you say so," Bird replied with not a care in the world. "Let's go back to that math thing though first. See, you came here as five. You didn't know it but, by the time I hit the door, you were down to 3. Now, the target you're sooooo not afraid of reduced you to just one. The King's guards need a bit more schooling I'd say." Bird stared at him and said "Yeah, I know you're not a real Highlander."*

*"Fine by me," the kilted one said in an English accent, "I was never in favor of this plan anyway," and he charged Bird.*

*Bird didn't move. The man got almost to him when Bird sidestepped him, and gave him an upward jab to the solar plexis. He faltered some from the surprise shot. Suddenly, the once boastful soldier now had a look of surprise on his face as Mary ran him clean through from behind with a broad sword. She could barely hold it but, she did manage to get it just right.*

*"Ain't been a man alive that's touched me unless I be want'in him to!" Mary boasted over the now dead man bleeding on her floor.*

*"Mary, leave everything. We need to go... now."*

*Bird smiled as he shifted his sight to infra-red and saw two different jet black areas by the hedgerow.*

*"Yo BirdMan! High-tail it!," Alydar called out to him.*
*He texted his reply as he and Mary shared her horse.*
<Sit Rep!>
*"William is on his way. I got him under my watchful eye. I gave him just enough info to make him concerned. I'm back at the inn. William will arrive in time but you'll arrive only minutes before the shock troops do."*
<MRU. Ally... security protocol 4>
*"That's going to be awkward. MRU but... get here."*
<Wouldn't be anywhere else> *Bird replied and shut off his HUD.*

*Bird arrived, as told, just minutes before the fake tartans did. Suddenly, all around the open lawn out front of the inn, 50 kilted 'soldiers' showed up and called for Bird.*

*"AND WALK TO MY DEATH? I DON'T THINK SO," Bird called out from the front door.*

*The obvious leader waved his hand for his men to bring something. They did. Suddenly, Bird saw the men throw a badly beaten padre onto the ground. Then the kilted loudmouth pulled a musket and pointed it at the priest's head.*

*"You have 30 seconds... or the padre here meets his maker."*

*Now Bird was pissed.*

*"By my accounts soldier... it's around 3pm. If he dies, you will watch all your men perish by my hand, just before I kill you, and the hour won't even reach 4... not for you anyway," Bird hollered out.*

*"BIRD! LET THEM!" Padre Pedro called out.*

*"Sorry padre, not gonna happen. CAPTAIN! Give me a minute... and I'll be there."*

*Bird looked at Scota with a stern, but caring look.*

*"You like the Chronicles? Fine. If you do what Val did when Greeva showed up, I won't be able to protect you." He then turned to Ciana and said "As for you... the sunny day just went white."*

*"Aye, I understand," Ciana told him remembering what Bird said about trusting him, and not her eyes.*

*"I sure hope so. Stay here and keep them safe. Get William and Andrew up to speed with what's going on." He turned and said "Scota... my world or yours... choose."*

*Blondie stood proud, stared Bird in the eyes, and said "Yours but..."*

*"But what?"*

*"After today... it'll be mine too."*

*Bird smiled, kissed both girls, and just said "Deal."*


*Lone was in a scramble, and heading out in the full size Raven.*

*"Sorry my dear, not exactly the first day I had planned."*

*"Battle for a righteous cause? Against such an opponent? Oh I couldn't have asked for a better first day out!" the newly colored warrior queen exclaimed.*

*"They still inbound?"*

*"They are. What do you think he's doing?"*

*"Dunno but... we're gonna find out. Lite 'em up and spin 'em!" Lone hollered with malice and intent.*

*"Gladly!"*

Lone was on his way to see 'great uncle' Tammy. Lone's spy asteroid told them gadgets by the thousands, were heading home. That was also the last thing they told him... before they went offline.

"FTL 7 and holding. Time to target... 3 minutes," Raven reported. "And we're not showing off my sexy new upgrades why?"

"Tammy. The less he knows what we're capable of, the beh'uh."

"Wise. It sucks I can't show off but... it's wise all the same."

"Glad you think so. Get me around the back end of uncle's house the moment we arrive."

Two minutes later, Raven dropped out of FTL, and bled speed so perfectly that Lone got his wish.

"Okay ya wanker, let's see what you think of this!" Lone hollered as he aimed down, and squeezed his triggers.

Ten beams of immense power let loose a strafing run on Tammy's not so hidden construction project. Lone was stunned with what happened next.

"What the fuck was that!" he bellowed in annoyance.

"I DON'T KNOW!" Raven hollered slightly panicked. "He should have a trench 100 miles wide and half that deep!"

Lone's shots hit right where they should. Problem was, they dissipated at point of impact.

Lone was heading for another run when Raven held him up.

"Commander! Don't!" Raven hollered with revelation in her voice. "They'll only make our problem worse! I don't know how but, the energy that surrounds that ship is the cause. Lone, it didn't dissipate the beams... it absorbed them!"

"wwwwwWWWWWWWHATTT!!!"

"I got all the readings my sensors can get. Pick another target... hammer him hard then... let's get out of here!"

"Agreed!" Lone shouted and headed for a southern lava ocean.

Lone did two strafing runs in an X pattern and at full power. Once he had, he only hoped it would be enough. Without eyes on Tammy anymore, he had no way of knowing the effect he left behind. The space around the planet was so thick with Aardvarks and gadgets and the new troop ships he launched on Tuhleesia that, Raven's invisibility was becoming almost useless from all the 'traffic' he was banging into. Lone made that last run then, followed his new hot rod's advice.

A cyborg merely laughed.


Ally was nowhere to be seen when Bird walked out the door. Bird was in his original Lone created, Eden born and tested, flight suit. He had his shades on but these were black mirrored ones. Hat, coat and boots... finished off the look. The latter were part cowboy boot, part ski boot, and all '51'.

"Captain... you have me... let the priest go."

The burly soldier looked about the field, then down at the priest.

"Get out of my sight you diseased wretch," He told him.

Padre Pedro got only to a hobble but, he headed to the inn. A few times he stumbled, and each time the soldiers laughed. The more they did, the more pissed Bird got. You couldn't tell from his outward demeanor but, he was all the same.

"Captain... I call for parlay... or whatever the hell you call it."

"Hahaha... that's a sailor's habit. Unfortunately for you, we 'Campbells' don't have such a thing."

"Yet, you value honor. Hiding in makeshift tartans? Fighting like 'savages'? Not exactly your style either."


Then, the voice Bird was waiting for finally emerged.

"I told you I'd be back for you," the bishop chuckled.

Calmly, Bird replied "And I told you what would happen if you did."

The bishop just laughed.

"I doubt that, or can you not see the odds against you?" the bishop asked waving his hand around.

"Problem you have is... I see them... AND the other 50 in the woods at the edge of the lawn."

"Hmm," the bishop joked, "I don't see that as a problem for me actually," and all 50 on the field pulled muskets, and drew a bead on Bird.

"Shortly... it will be."

"You're arrogance 'Commander', will be your undoing."

"Your reliance on hired muscle for confidence, will be yours."

The soldiers snickered. They didn't like this plan nor the bishop but, their orders came from higher than him.

Suddenly, a curve the bishop didn't see coming, hit him.

"All this just for me? I'm not sure if I should be flattered... or simply disgusted."

That voice wasn't Ciana... it was Lady Bird.

"In a short while, you'll be mine. When you are I assure you, your little verbal barbs... well... they won't be tolerated."

"Oh I doubt that. You see, I've known men like you. Full of themselves, and thinking themselves God's gift to women. I've also noticed that... (giggle) most times... a fraction smaller and ye'd be call lass, not lad. You strike me as the 5 minute kind bishop. Even if you did somehow 'get me'... it would be HIS name I'd be call'in out in the dark of night," Ciana said pointing to Bird, "Not yours."

"Guards, seize her and bring her to me," the bishop said with equal parts anger and shock.

Ciana just smiled saying "They'll be no need for thah, I know how to walk."

Lady Bird got just what she wanted. For once, she didn't want to get away from the bishop... she wanted to get as close as possible. She picked up her dress and, ever so lady like, walked and stood next to the bishop. What he had wanted for so long was now beside him but, she wasn't the same Ciana he'd lusted after for years. Still, a man's mind can convince him of many things when he wants it to.

"I'll take great delight when you see your 'beloved' not so bold, not so brash, but ever so dead. Once that happens, we'll see if that tongue of yours stays so sharp," the bishop sneered in anger and frustration.

Ciana smiled and hollered out "Bird my love... you plann'in on gett'in yerself killed?"

Bird smiled seeing the confidence pouring from his beloved Lady Bird.

"Heh heh... nope."

Confidently, Ciana turned and said "Well bishop, there yeh go. If he says no then it's no. HIM I trust. You? Not so much."

"ENOUGH OF THIS! Guards! Do your duty!"

Bird walked to a good distance from the men and said "Captain? Do I at least get a final request?"

Honor bound, the Captain called out "I don't see any reason why not."

"Then I'll tell you what. Here's how this is gonna work. I'll make it easy for you. I'll stand right here AND!... You have my promise I won't move. You line up 20 of your best shooters. I'll even turn my back AND call out 'fire' for you. My final request is I get 2 final words." The Captain thought Bird was crazy when he unbuttoned his odd long coat and said "Only 2 but, I get to say them after your men have fired. Do we have a deal?"

The Captain didn't say a word. Seeing Bird truly kept his place, he merely nodded and waved his men over.

"Heh heh... I'll take that as a yes."

Bird waited as ten men stood, and ten got on one knee in front of them. The bishop was smiling with sadistic glee. Scota and company were in the house, and watching from a window. Kara was still out cold, Andrew and William thought Bird was the bravest man they'd ever seen. They also thought he was the craziest. Mary was out of her mind with worry but Scota... oh Scota... she could barely hide her delight.

"Alright then..." and Bird put his hands in his coat pockets, and stretched it wide, as he turned his back to the firing squad.

His hat was tilted back covering his neck, and his feet were spread slightly.

"Everybody ready back there?" and Bird heard the hammers of 20 muskets get pulled back. Bird waited a moment, then called out "........Fire."

Twenty muskets roared and puffed smoke.

Bird laid motionless on the ground roughly 20 yards away. Mary was in tears and Andrew and William were just stunned. Scota was nervous for a moment. That moment however was short lived.

"Ha... ha... hahahahaha!" could be heard from the man in black.

"Wait... WHAT! Not even a soldier in full armor could have survived that!" a shocked 'not so holy' man exclaimed.

Every soldier on the field went cold when the Yankee... got up. Bird brushed himself off, tilted his hat down, and turned around.

"CAPTAIN!" the 'should be dead' Bird called out. "I believe you owe me two words!"

Said captain gulped, and with a shaky voice asked "And they would be?"

Bird smiled a sinister smile as he lifted his gaze to the field. "My turn."

With lightning speed, Bird reached into his coat with both hands, and made a sound no human in this time period had ever made before.

It was the sound of automatic gunfire.

Bird let rip two of his cannons and took down every man but 3 on the field. Suddenly, a massive strip of explosions raked down the sides of the woods just inside the forest's edge. Alydar had powered down the drones to sonic concussion force. Now, 50 men in the woods posed no threat at all.

The Captain was in a lot of pain as he used a cart for leverage and tried to get to his feet. Bird was putting away two clips and reloading the cannons as he walked up to him.

"I'm an honorable man Captain. Those were non lethal rounds. I assure you, the reloads however are VERY lethal."

Scota told the crowd "Stay here, I'm going downstairs and make sure none of the others got in. I'll be right back."

"I'll go with you!" William exclaimed.

"No William, I'll be alright. Stay here," and before William could respond, Scota bolted out the door.

"Captain, you shot me. I fired back but even then, gave you a *courtesy no other man would. Now, answer my question... who sent you?"*

*"Wh... wha... mmmf... what do you mean?"*

*"I saw the look on your face. You despise fat boy over here,"
Bird said pointing to a shaking bishop. "Now, WHO sent you..." and
Bird pointed the cannon at his head and finished with "... I won't
ask you again. The king? The queen?... WHO!?"*

*The captain just shook his head.*

*"Well, I know it wasn't the bishop here so... oh no. Never mind
Captain. It was a holy man wasn't it?"*

*The Captain nodded.*

*"It just wasn't the bishop was it? WAS IT!?"*

*The Captain simply shook his head.*

*"Figures."*

*Ciana was a tad shaken but, she now had ultimate faith in
Bird. He said he wasn't going to die so therefore... she knew he
wouldn't.*

*"Well bishop, still think you could compare..." and she
pointed to her love and finished with "... to that?"*

*Scota did a quick sweep of the downstairs, and was heading
back upstairs when a noise startled her.*

*"Oh my child, you'll not need that. I am here to get you to
safety from the madness outside. The bishop has once again acted
on his own. I'm very glad I was able to get here on time. Come my
child, my guards await in hiding outside and will take us to safety."*

*Scota held firm and said "Wait, I know yeh... yer the
cardinal!"*

*"I am. Now come quickly my dear. I'm very glad no one was
killed but, let's make sure it stays that way," and he held out his
hand.*

*Scota still had her blade out and... still pointed at the 'other'
holy man.*

*"And how do I know yeh be any better than theh other one?"*

*"Me!? Like the bishop!? Oh no my child... I assure you..."
and his voice went cold as he finished with "... I'm far worse."*

*Unfazed, Scota focused on the cardinal as nothing more than a target... just like Ally taught her.*

*"And, yeh'll find I'm far better."*

*The cardinal chuckled and said "Oh, I doubt that," just as two guards grabbed and pinned Scota. "Not exactly how I planned but... time I show you who you belong to... who you've ALWAYS belonged to!"*

*Scota couldn't move but was certainly trying to break free, when the cardinal pulled back her hair and started kissing her neck. He had made it to her cleavage with sadistic glee when suddenly, Scota was no longer pinned to the wall. Seems the padre had no problem doing God's work, and dispatched what evil he could. A knife to the gut of one of the guards was all he managed before the cardinal kicked him and padre was now out cold.*

*Quick as she could and... just like her sister found out... training took over. She spun and pulled the knife the padre planted and simply planted it in the other guard. He was out but Scota got pushed to the ground face first. The cardinal was on top of her and had her hands pinned above her head. She could feel his hard manhood as his other hand began pulling up her dress. The cardinal using his own legs had pulled Scota's apart. Scota fought as hard as she could till... she no longer had to.*

*Bird was still outside talking to the Captain, when he walked up behind the cardinal, and hurled him into the wall. The crumpled cardinal was far more spry than expected and got up pulling his blade from his cane. Scota gasped in shock when it went right through Bird.*

*"I believe 'ow' would be the appropriate phrase right about now," Bird said looking down at the blade sticking through him.*

*A more powerful backhand flung the cardinal yet again as Bird pulled the rapier from his gut.*

*"Cardinal, you're in far more trouble than you could imagine."*

*The cardinal actually pulled his cross and hollered "DEMON BE GONE!"*

*"Demon!? Hahahahaha, oh cardinal, you couldn't be more wrong. Who do you fear?"*

*"I FEAR NO DEMON!" he hollered holding the cross at*

*Bird.*

*"Powerful yes. Demon? No. Cardinal WHO do you fear?"*

*"I fear no man or demon... only the Lord!"*

*"Look upon my neck cardinal. Could a demon wear such a mark?" and Bird pointed to his own cross. "Oh no cardinal, for you it's worse... much much worse. You only fear God eh? Well then 'priest'... be afraid... be very very afraid," and suddenly, to the cardinal, Bird melted away.*

*It was the only way he could explain what he saw. Bird had converted... to Alydar. Alydar then converted again. She took information from Bird's bible, and his folklore, and made an image up. She grew wings... angel wings.*

*"Your boss is a little upset with you right now," Ally said as she walked to the cowering cardinal. "Not demon cardinal. I believe... 'Archangel'... would be a more appropriate term."*

*She knelt down in front of him and he was crying out in fear, but had nowhere to go.*

*"Shhhh," Ally said softly and kindly as she stroked his cheeks with her hands.*

*Suddenly, she grabbed his head. Her hands, in an instant, went right. The cardinal's head however went left... and his neck went snap crackle pop.*

*Ally went back to normal form and stood up saying "Nice call boss. I doubt I would have seen that coming. Looks like you were right... I guess I could do with a bit more human interaction after all huh?"*

*Outside, the real Bird nodded to seemingly no one.*

*Ally looked down on a speechless Scota and asked "Still mad I'm not human?"*

*Scota was frozen. Ally walked up to her and slowly pushed her hand that was still holding her blade, softly down to her side. Scota didn't know what to do and just hugged her tight. Forevermore, Scota would think the non human Ally was the woman to be. The fact that she was indeed a walking talking doll, never bothered Scota again.*

*The guards Bird didn't maim, were offering their swords in* surrender. Bird took them, and ordered them to attend to their fellow comrades. They were doing that when Bird turned his attention elsewhere.

"Lady Bird, I have to say, I am impressed. I expected you to get it wrong or falter or... I dunno... SOME thing. I'll tell you same as I tell Alydar."

"Oh, and thah would be?" Ciana said taking great delight in the bishop's sudden uncomfortable situation.

Bird smiled the sexy smile she so loved and said "That's my girl!"

Ciana beamed.


"Well your portly-ness, I now know you weren't the brains behind this. I suspected it possible but, I wasn't sure till you attacked Angus." The Captain had a 'how'd you know?' look on his face, and Bird turned to him saying "Highlanders don't march side by side in military fashion." Bird turned back to the scared bishop and asked "Now, before I kill you, care to clear your conscience?"

The bishop had one last card to play. He was indeed scared, but not as much as he let on. He pulled a secret knife from his garment and put it to Ciana's neck as he grabbed her.

"Oh Lawd, here we go again!" Ciana said in utter irritation.

Bird actually chuckled and asked Ciana "You're not gonna stop me from killing this one too are you?"

"Bird I swear to God almighty... Iffin you doen, I will!"

"Ooooooh, you know how I love it when your accent thickens," Bird said with a smile and a wink.

"Go ahead... joke if you want! Seeing how much its cost me, I won't be denied my prize... NOT again!" the bishop hollered. "You walk around with your smug grins and such but, you know NOTHING!. You know, I think I will 'clear my conscience' as you say. It will please me to watch your face as I drain the life from the one you love. The cardinal was the whole reason for any of this. He has, shall we say, a fondness for the fair haired lasses. He was in love with her mother, but she refused him. It was HE who poisoned the troops that followed Bonnie Prince Charlie. Then, desperate for a cure, he promised them one if they would inform him of what was happening. The priest informed the king and, well, rose to being a cardinal shortly thereafter. Her mother was a real beauty but the cardinal wasn't the kind to take no for an answer. When he saw her daughter, looking even more lovely than her mother, he waited. I was to get Ciana. He found me coming out one night as he was 'keeping an eye' on her home. He made me an offer I couldn't refuse."

Bird was irritated and said "Who are you, 'The Godfather'? "

"Hardly. I would get Ciana, he would claim the little brat of a sister. Not even you can stop him! You may be able to stop me but, hahahahaha, you have no idea how powerful he is!"

"Was," Ally said walking up and, rather unceremoniously, dumped a dead carcass nearly at his feet.

Bird was now aggravated and said "Okay, I've heard enough... Ciana? "

The bishop was shocked at what lay at his feet, and dropped his guard for a moment but, it was all Lady Bird needed.

"GLADLY!"

She bowed forward quickly, and elbowed the bishop in the gut.

"BirdOfPrey!" was the last thing the bishop heard as a single shot rang out.

Shortly after, a headless body fell to the ground... right by his partner in crime.

Bird walked over to the near cowering Captain and said "I don't care what story you make up, as long as we're not in it. I gave you, and your men, your lives... when I could have done far worse. As I see it, honor says you owe me. Take your men and leave... now. I'll be out of here in a year or two. We all will be actually. Keep the king's dogs of war south of Hadrian's Wall, and I'll stay north of it. I don't care how you do it, just see that you do. If I see otherwise... I'll come and pay you a visit... personally. Do we understand each other Captain? "

The Captain was looking around at his utter defeat and just couldn't believe what he saw. The fact that he was still alive was almost beyond his comprehension. One thing he did know was... this fellow named Bird had more honor than any man alive. He stood as best as he could, and saluted.

*"Give me a moment to gather my men... and those two... and you'll be left alone. On my honor I swear it."*

*"I'll take care of those two myself." Bird actually saluted him back and said "Now, as they say where I'm from... feel free to make yourself scarce."*

*The Captain dropped his salute, gathered his men, and honored Bird's request.*

*It was two days later when Saint Peter's Basilica got a rather rude, but undeniable message. A horse drawn cart with no rider pulled into the courtyard. The priests and other cardinals were horrified at what lay in the back. A note was found on the seat and... it was in Latin. The 2 corpses had the oddest wing symbol burned into each of their chests. The note was two pages. One was an accounting of the cardinal's actions, along with the bishop. The other was a warning and, in typical BirdMan style, addressed to the pope himself. It was a warning of, well essentially, who not to bother again. As shocking as this event was, the warning was quickly honored... hushed... and...*

*Never spoken of again.*

# Chapter 37:

## "Two Brothers In Sync...And
## A Conference At Malta"

*Xankor was up on top of Freedom Point and, he was actually having fun. He would pull off a few sheets, then pretend to walk away... then walked back and pulled off a few more. The crowd was as pumped as they could be when Xankor pulled off the real, and final, sheet. He raised his hands in triumph the way a human boxer would and the crowd just cheered and cheered. When Xankor finally left the balcony, the number read... 311.*

*Lone opened the call and said "Minister Savlik, I want to thank you for taking my call."*

*The head of the galactic council nodded and spoke in his native language.*

*"When the Ambassador contacted me and asked if I would speak to you, I have to say I was intrigued," the translator relayed.*

*"I have disturbing news. News I wish to share. In Biiird's history, there was a great war that encompassed his world. Half good, half evil. The leaders of the good side, known as 'The Allies', had a meeting in a city known as Malta to decide on a course of action. It was a city none of the leaders claimed, and therefore was considered neutral. I wish to replicate that history, share what I know with key others, and I wish to do it in your council chambers. This is the 'closed door' kind of meeting and I invite you to be present. My request is, do you have such facilities and... may I use them?"*

*Lone was hoping to show the council a more mature side to the Ghosts, but he really needed to get the others up to speed. He had no idea that, galaxies away, and centuries apart, his fur-less* brother was getting ready to do the exact same thing.

Savlik had very little experience with the Ghosts. Aside from the incident with the blue chick, all he ever got were stories. Dealing with a Ghost who was Tuhleesian, and not just any wolf but one considered to be THE Tuhleesian, he was actually thrilled. He came in peace, offered information, and was actually well mannered. Savlik was impressed and decided to take a chance.

"We do Commander Lone and, I would be happy to host such a conference. Do you have a time and date?"

"Two of our days from now. Early in the day. I've sent you a list of those I've invited. Depending on who is available, some or all will attend."

Savlik spoke with pride and said "We will be ready."

When he saw the list, and who was on it, he knew this wasn't going to be just any conference... it was going to be historic.


When Shreya broke atmosphere 2 days later, she did so with an honor guard of no less than 55 X2's. Quaran wagged her wings, the honor guard wagged theirs, and headed back down. In honor of Rhana, the honor guard was deliberately an odd number.

Shreya had The Grand Couple aboard, Turannen and Ravenahl. Sporting a small 'baby bump', 'Mrs. Wolf' was with them too. Per Lone's instructions, Quaran was to do several random jumps in the cat's eye just to insure stealth and safety. There was to be about two hours travel time, and Renny was in a jovial mood now that the sickness waves had finally passed.

"Shreya?"

"Yes Renny?"

"How are you?" Renny asked pleasantly.

"I am operating at peak efficiency, thank you for asking."

Renny giggled "No silly, how are 'you' my dear?"

"Would it be wrong to ask... clarify?"

Now Renny smiled and asked "Not at all. I talk to Raven all the time. It occurred to me lately, I've not really spent any time with you or your sisters. Seeing as how you called me by my call sign, and not 'Guardian', it only makes me more aware I am her as well. As such and, seeing as how we have some time, I thought I would see how you are."

"Sisters and don't forget... brother now too," Shreya said in the same friendly manner as Renny.

"Indeed! It has been a rather exclusive 'girls club' till now. So my dear, question remains."

"I am doing well and... thanks for caring enough to ask. Thor is adjusting well enough, but we have actually gotten close. May I ask you something?"

"Of course."

"Is that normal for two siblings to become closer than the rest?"

"Oh my dear, you're asking the wrong wolf. I grew up an only child. Machine or organic, you have what I have never known. However, from what I have seen and heard... yes... it is normal."

"I feel bad sometimes. Kallan is sad many days and I befriend her where I can. Raven is so focused on doing well and making sure your husband is pleased that, while she hasn't ignored us, she does appear focused elsewhere. Keyza is very quiet and... very private. She also is not unfriendly but, she doesn't exactly join in either. Thor seems to have no one, and well, we 'seem to click' is the phrase I believe."

"You believe correct," Renny told her. "Would you mind an observation?"

"Not at all!" Shreya said with glee at getting some new insight.

"Look at the Ghosts. I love my husband dearly but even I admit he has his 'quirks'. Yet, when he was with Rhana, have you seen them?"

"Indeed."

"And Deeno, a very good man but, a bit of a brat. Quaran, your Ghost, seems to see potential danger and subterfuge at every turn. It's as if he wants to be ready and seems to have left his old life behind but... really hasn't... just refocused it. Xankor and Symda 'click' as you say due to a common upbringing. Many different personality types wouldn't you say?"

"Indeed I would," Shreya replied.

"Now, take all those different personality types and... come up with a danger or something odd... and what happens?"

"In my humble opinion, they are unstoppable. Not only that but, I wouldn't want to be on any other team and consider myself fortunate to be on it to begin with."

"As do I and... I agree with you. Point I'm making is, they are all different in their own way. That said, when there is no danger to face, they are themselves. I have had to adjust myself to each one. I don't treat Symda the same as I do Rhana or Lone. I don't treat her badly, nor less, but she IS her own creature, so I just treat her as such when I'm in her presence. Same as your family, accept who they are, and know that each are their own creature. I envy you actually."

"You envy ME!?" Shreya said almost not believing it.

"Mm hmm. You were 'born' into a family... something I once would have given anything for. I have come into one now but, no matter how bad or confusing it may seem, know that it's better than having none at all."

"Okay. Might I give you an observation of mine?"

"Certainly."

"I think with wisdom like that... you're going to make a great mother," Shreya said with true friendship in her voice.

Renny smiled saying "Remmy has truly done an amazing job with you Ghosts. Thank you Shreya. I have to go but, know that I am always around for you and... your family."

Shreya had a smile in her voice when she said "I don't have a hat but, if I did, I'd tip it to you."

Renny smiled, curtsied, and went about her day.


The meeting room in the council chambers, as massive as it was, almost wasn't big enough. When Lone and company walked in, everyone stood up. Lone also noticed that, with a full compliment of high ranking wolves on his 6... all eyes were still on him. Bird treated this with ease but, it made Lone slightly uncomfortable.

Every high ranker in the known worlds was there, along with a small compliment of generals and intelligence officers... each. Shiiran and Ulquin were there with their military, as was Juvehnar.

Valleron was there with his, and the section with the Aarikan delegation was truly a sight to see. In Lone's mind, if you weren't on the floor when he gave his speech, you weren't in this room. The rest weren't treated badly but, they weren't invited either. Savlik was there to represent them in Lone's mind.

Lone stood up and addressed the 3 long tables set in a triangle pattern. That wasn't the council's way or anything... it was just the only way they could fit everyone in the room.

"I want to thank you all for coming. All of you here have shown us friendship or allegiance in the past. Biiird taught me the value of such things. That is also the reason you are in this room. We Ghosts have information on a common enemy we feel you should all know. I want you to know we will tell you what we know, and hold nothing you should know back. I only ask the same of you in return."

Everyone gave light applause and assured him he would get his wish. Lone waved a hand to Rahgaa and she spoke first.

"Many of you still do not trust us. I see the looks on your faces so please, spare me the polite lies. I only wish to tell you we are not here to gather intelligence, then run to the ancient brother to deliver it. We are here to give what we know, and assure you we are on the side of the Ghosts... not Tamarak's."

Tiiveer stood up next and addressed the gathered.

"As a show of Lady Rahgaa's intentions, I will go first..." and he told the crowd of Tamarak's sneak attack on Atoemahn.

They were very impressed with how they treated one of their own when it was thought she was a traitor.

One of the intelligence officers on the Aarikan team was staring at the wolves. Ravenahl caught it and decided to have some fun. She pretended not to notice at first, then quickly stared at him and... just gave him 'duck face'.
Jalitzar was paying attention to Tiiveer, but elbowed the officer hard and, that ended that. Ravenahl giggled a little and went back to the conference.

*The flood of information, both major and minor, had all the aliens in a concerned tizzy. They were concerned with the gravity of the knowledge. They were in a tizzy that the Ghosts and the Tuhleesians were offering it in such quantities.*

*"Now we get to the most important piece of information... and the one that had me call this meeting in the first place. Observe..." Lone told them as the lights went dim and the hologram came up in the center of the tables. "This intel is only days old. We have no idea what it is he's building, but it appears to be a ship of some kind. For days, we observed all of Tamarak's toys coming into his home planet. As we've told you, a virus was planted causing his calculations to be off. Tammy is a builder, not a computer genius. Every one we destroy, is one flawed copy that takes its place. Our spy satellites are offline. When last we went to his planet, it was I who actually went. I noticed the asteroid we bugged... isn't there anymore. We don't know what the colored rocks are that generate the energy is but, it seems to protect him. Jalitzar, you above all know what our weapons can do. My full size Ghost is finished and..."*

*"Full size?" Jalitzar said slightly confused.*

*"Yes. The one that Rhana took to Earth is the full size Ghost. The one's you've come to know, were merely the Landing craft. They are what has been planned from the very beginning, but shear need forced us to go with the Landers first. Again, due to need, Biiird's was finished first... now mine. The others are in various stages of completion with all expected to be done by year's end or less."*

*"Savi Tillern! I thought that was built only to give Bird the best chance possible, and protect your planet."*

*"Nope. Now, knowing full well what the 12 pack on the Lander can do... imagine them brought up to the full scale size."*

*"I'd rather not," he said honestly.*

*"Indeed. Now... against this new energy wave, see what effect the 'bigger ones' had and mind you... this was full power."*

*Lone then showed him his strafing run and the impact it had. NOW the tables were in an uproar.*

*Lone said nothing and merely let the delegations vent. Savlik* brought the uproar down when he stood up and addressed Lone.

"Commander, I wish to thank you for sharing this information with us. You could have withheld it but you didn't, and I commend you for it. Would you mind some of my opinions?"

"Not at all, that is what we're here for."

All eyes were now on the council leader.

"When you and Rhana first appeared, we thought you the next generation of raiders. Time has truly proven us wrong. When you started coming to us, and bringing your own kind with you, it made many of us nervous."

"And one of you a tad too opportunistic," Lone reminded him.

"Indeed. While I admit your introduction to us was a tad brutal... I do understand why you did what you did. It is known that goods are the Aarikan's forte', mapping is the Rassentan's, and security is the Galenthian's. I want you to know that, when we think of 51, while some would never admit it, we think of justice and innovation. While it pains me to say this, the technology you possess by your own hand, would take many of us decades or more to replicate. Most of it is just boggling in one sense. It had to be thought of, or imagined, in the first place... no less created... and your planet has, and continues, to do both."

Lone tipped his hat and thought, how nice it was to be thought of so. It was what Biiird planned all along and he was pleased to see his vision not only noticed but... noticed correctly.

"I say these things for a reason," Savlik continued. "No one here can deny your weapons are formidable. The council rules state that if I deem it necessary, I can convene all the military might of all the delegates into one massive army. Never in all the years that this council has existed has anyone in my position had to do so. With what you just showed us, I feel we just may have to make history."

That comment alone, and coming from Savlik, had the tables in a tizzy again. Savlik however, still had more.

"Lady Rahgaa, when your kind invaded the stars, it is my opinion that many fell at first due to the surprise of it all. No insult intended to the current company I see before me."

Rahgaa smiled and honestly said "None taken."

"That said, many here had to grow up and... catch up... in a hurry. Again, this is only my opinion but, I feel most of the anger directed towards your kind was because of how superior you were at the time, and how inferior 'we' were. That and, what you did with that superiority." Savlik looked at the rest of the tables and said "No insult intended." He turned back to Lone and said "This time, we know a great enemy is coming and, at least have some time to prepare. For that, I thank you greatly. I have one fear though."

"And that is?"

"With what you've shown us... I feel even a combined army may not even make a dent. My fear is not for what is coming but... our chances of surviving it."

That one hit all the tables hard.


Lone stood up and made one last stand for the integrity of the Ghosts.

"You're right Savlik, we could have kept this information to ourselves. I want you all to remember however... we didn't. If this thing is launched, I have no doubt Tammy will make a statement for the wolves of old. I want you all to know... truly know... we have faith in you all. THIS time, if he comes after any of you, you will at least know two things. First, that it IS coming and..." and Lone sat down as Rahgaa and Tiiveer stood up.

Tiiveer finished Lone's sentence with "And that the NEW wolves, will stand by any of you that will have us, fighting with you..."

Rahgaa finished with "And not against you. ANY of you."


Panic and an uproar that ebbed and flowed lasted for the next two hours. Many questions came forth, as did plans. They were all scared and Lone knew it. If a full size Ghost had no effect, what chance did they stand?

Savlik spoke again and said "You are not the only one's Commander who have tech that detects lies. So far you have been forthcoming. While what you have brought us is beyond shocking, not knowing what you have told us would have been even more so. I wish to know, what... if anything... do you need from me?"

"Information. When we met Ambassador Ulquin, Biiird asked

for star charts. He specifically asked for old folklore ones as he believed all myths have their origins in truth. The purple rocks Tammy has... they have eluded us. Nothing in any of our databases have anything even close. One of Planet 51's motto's is 'We make the unknown... known." Lone addressed them all and continued with "We looked in all the data we could get from all of you and still came up empty. You mentioned our innovation. I have admitted many times, Biiird is the source of that... we only make the vision a reality. Just the planets represented here is daunting and far too large to scan in the time we have. We have given up on the real, and have begun looking into the unreal, just as Rhana would do. I truly feel that somewhere, someone on the council has a story, a myth, a fable... SOME thing, that tells of those rocks. We can't search them all however, and still stay on task."

Valleron asked "Say we find it but, it's only a reference... in a child's story. What good would that do?"

"Like Biiird said, there's usually more truth in fiction than most realize. Even a reference would help. IF we find the fiction, we can then apply it to the facts. Not much I know but, you'd be surprised how many times that has worked for us."

Now, many at the tables, had a 'hmm' look on their faces.

"Consider it done," Savlik stated. "I will have every member look for what you ask for and make it top priority. I assure you, anything that's found no matter how small, and you'll be the second to know."

Rahgaa had one more thing to drop on them.

"I want you all to know this situation is most dire. I have discussed it with my mate and we have decided to give you the knowledge of old. LET ME BE very clear on this! We will search for weapons that only enhance yours... perhaps surpass them but only slightly. We Tuhleesians firmly believe in Rhana's and Ahdeera's teachings of gaining more than you can handle... or should even have. We will see if there is anything there that will enhance you 'some'... but not too much. We will also share it with all of you... or you will get nothing at all. Anything and I mean ANY thing, beyond that level, and IF it's relevant, it will be shared with the Ghosts only. Being you fight one of our own yet again... we feel it only fair to *help where we can."*

*Weapons? From TUHLEESIAN'S!!? Simply unheard of.*

*Lone put his fingers close together and finished with "We are thiiiiis close to possibly getting Biiird back. Those who need to know how we will do this, already do. It is my firm opinion that, as good as we all are on 51... we are no Biiird. If anyone can find the key to taking down Tammy, it's him. We are not, and never will be, wavering in our resolve to find him. For all our sakes, I only hope he's alive when we do. Now, with all this information and... the fine creatures I see around me... how about if we stop screaming, and start hammering out a plan?"*

*A single command from the Mahrek Tuuren and... so it was.*

*Back on Earth or rather, in orbit around its moon, yet another Malta meeting was being prepared. Bird was on the Ghost. He finally stopped calling her 'the full sized one' as she was always to be this size. Now, the Ghost was the Ghost, and the Lander was the Lander. He just had a huge ripple in his 'no interference' plan, and was talking with Alydar for almost a day figuring out their next move.*

*"Well Alydar, while it makes sense, I hafta say I never thought you'd take that position. Can I tell ya something?"*

*"Always my dear."*

*"You've grown well, and I'm very proud of you. When I envisioned you, and all your capabilities, I had one big fear."*

*"That would be?"*

*"That, for as glorious and righteous as I envisioned you, I felt that, in making a sentient being, I was truly playing God. Worse, I truly feared that you might not become the glorious creature I thought you'd be but... Frankenstein's monster instead. Had the latter happened, what could I do against a ten mile long Tamarak wrapped in unstoppable armor with enough firepower to tell God himself to go to hell?"*

*Alydar had never considered these things. Hearing them from Bird however, even she couldn't deny the wisdom and fear of it all. Hearing it from Bird's perspective, she couldn't even fathom herself in the same position.*

"I'm truly glad you are pleased with me," was all her overwhelmed mind could think of to say.

"And... how are you my dear?"

"Me? How do you mean?"

"Alydar... you killed. All on your own, and without consulting me or... by my order. I told you when we first arrived, you may have to do things or, make judgments, on your own. Seems I was right. While justified in my mind, it's a huge step and a line you can never 'uncross'. I need to know, now more than ever... how are you?"

Alydar thought a moment before responding.

"Confused."

"Remember that promise we made?"

"I do."

"Now would be a really good time to hold up your end of it."

"I will... I promise."

Alydar tried to put her feelings into words as best she could and told Bird everything she was feeling. For all the things she could do, putting her feelings into words was one trait she had yet to master.

"Bird, I truly felt it was the only option. Are you mad at me?"

"More like... heavily concerned. You crossed a line I'm not sure even you fully understand the ramifications of. Right now I'm more concerned with the 'why'... not the 'what'."

"I wanted to keep Scota safe. I found myself caring for her, somehow all on my own, the way I would you or the Ghosts. The cardinal I truly didn't see coming but you did. That lack of foresight still has me bothered but, I am working on it."

"Fair enough. Now you know why I wanted you out of the doll house. I never imagined it getting to this level though. Don't beat yourself up however. I spent my entire life with humans and their emotions. You however have only been alive for a few years. It's only natural you wouldn't get certain motivations. You were in a sense, pre-programmed with a personality of sorts. Remmy and I both felt, it was one way to stop you and your sisters from becoming the very monsters I mentioned. It worked too but, it left you with being basically a sweetheart. It's been my experience, when *someone like you comes across pure evil... you simply can't understand it."*

*"I'll say."*

*"Now, that said... you were saying?" Bird insisted.*

*"I saw Scota being unfairly harmed. Not only that but, with all our help, she was still overpowered and overwhelmed. I thought... I mean... ooooh this is the frustrating part. I can't seem to put it into words!"*

*Bird softened and said "Like... how dare he?"*

*Alydar had an epiphany of sorts.*

*"Oh my God... that's it!"*

*"Heh heh... God? Technically... that would be me."*

*"Habit by association Birdie," Alydar said but, using Rahgaa's voice.*

*"Hmm... continue," Bird said as he sipped his tea.*

*"So I thought, who did he think he was that he could assume that right? He used unfair odds so... so did I. It seemed the only logical thing to do. Then I heard the bishop. I kept thinking, how dare he cause so much suffering? I also thought, if he was left alone, how much more would he cause? I truly thought the bishop was gone for good. I thought, if I were him I know I would be. Then, I was proven wrong. I truly couldn't fathom his reasoning yet, there he was all the same. So, using that logic, I felt not only would the cardinal return but, seeing the bishop's response... I felt the cardinal's would be even more so. I didn't start out 'wanting' to kill him, or anyone for that matter. The more I heard though, and the reasons for it... I felt... um... well I felt there was no other choice."*

*Bird was liking what he was hearing so far. Bird's greatest fear now was, this small spark could send Alydar down a very bad path and method of reasoning.*

*"Answer me this, and mind you, you need to be the most honest you've ever been in your life."*

*"Yes?"*

*"Did you like, or enjoy it?"*

*"Yes... and no."*

*"Clarify."*

*"I truly enjoyed the result of not having to ever worry about*

*that situation ever again... at least from him. I enjoyed knowing we were all safe and, that I had fulfilled my purpose in doing so. I also enjoyed knowing, however brutal, and while I don't truly understand it all yet... I learned something new that I can use to keep you and the others safe."*

*"Okay. And the no part?"*

*"What was required to achieve that safety. While it was the right thing to do, he wasn't attacking me or you. I had to make a major judgment, and on my own. I have no problem firing on mindless gadgets, nor protecting our own when they are directly attacked. However..."*

*"Scota isn't one you were programmed to protect huh?"*

*"Correct. I was truly worried and thought 'what if I get this wrong?'. I mean... hmm... I didn't see the other day coming and in the end, got it wrong. I kept thinking, what if I kill him but... doing that... was wrong yet again? Does that even make sense Bird?"*

*"Tons."*

*"I felt scared of making a mistake I knew I couldn't undo. I also felt kind of, repulsed, by him and his motivations. In the end, I used what I knew, what I was built to do, and what I had just learned, and did what I felt was the best course of action."*

*"Alydar?"*

*"Yeah?" the hologram said nervously.*

*"For now, know I believe you did do the right thing. Not an easy thing to wrap your head around is it? Even with such a head as yours."*

*"No... it's not. I believe I did the correct thing too but, in your slang... I feel 'dirty'."*

*Bird was happy with what he heard so far.*

*"Alydar, what you did can turn any thinking creature. I will be keeping an eye on you. If this topic ever bothers you or, if you ever feel the need to talk about it, I want you to... immediately. I'm not considering this matter closed, only closed for now. Do you understand?"*

*"Yes I do. Bird?"*

*"Yeah?"*

*"Thanks for caring. Both for me, and all those that I could hurt if I became affected by my actions."*

Sweetly, Bird said "Always," and like he said, dropped the matter... for now.

Now Bird asked Alydar "So, as you said the other day, this is getting out of hand fast. It may be just the two of us but, I am still in charge. That said, I see no reason not to get your opinions. I agree with your reasons and in the end the final decision rests with me. So, now that I know your thoughts on this, my question is... are you sure about them?"

"Very. I want to tell you something."

"Go for it."

"Many times you've mentioned the evil of your world. Also, many times, you strive to be a better man, and not a bishop. I've now had a taste of what you've been referring to. While its nowhere near your level of experience, it has been enough for me to say, Bird?"

"Hmm?"

"I've had enough of this place. Perhaps others may be no better, or even worse but... let's get the hell outta Dodge."

"Can't argue with you there. I just never thought you of all creatures, would come up with such an invite list."

"Yeah well, you've taught me to help those who need it, and show loyalty to those who've shown it to us. C'mon BirdMan, it's getting late and... we got a funeral to interrupt."

"Yeah. Can't say he was my buddy or anything but, he deserved better than that. It's the least I can do for someone who suffered such a fate, simply because of me."

Sweetly, and kindly, Alydar told him "And that's why we all love you so."

Scota had gone with Andrew and Kara, on Bird's orders, back to Edinburgh. Seems John's reputation made the 'manly men' of the day, not give too much of a shit. He was given a shoddy autopsy, and luckily for Bird, an even shoddier investigation into his death. Seems John had no family or, none that cared. The Constable even took the money that was in John's cash drawer. Alydar took care of that in the form of 'Doctor James'. The good doctor testified he saw the Constable in the shop with no one around. With the money gone, and not found on the two attackers... the thieving policeman found

*himself in a bit of hot water. His fate was sealed when 'James'
suggested his home be searched for his ill gotten gain... and it was
found.*

*Now, Bird the learned gentleman, had Andrew stop the
paupers burial John was slated for. He bought a fine coffin using the
'coin' Bird gave him, and a nice burial plot next to the church Ciana
got her necklace blessed in... along with a nice stone to go with it.
Ciana wanted to be there, but time was a factor. Bird told her what
he was doing and she agreed. He said he had an 'other world' way
to get them there 'faster than fast', but she couldn't know about it
yet. She agreed, and Bird hypo-sprayed her and knocked her out.
When she awoke, she was where she needed to be, and never asked
how she got there so quickly.*

*The priest gave a respectful sermon and last rights over the
grave. Bird was a tad pissed that the morning sun saw only him,
Ally, Ciana and Scota, Andrew and a weak Kara, sending John unto
the hands of God.*

*"Bird?"*

*"Yeah Ally?"*

*"He told me to tell you... he thought regardless of it all... it
was worth the ride."*

*Now Bird wasn't pissed and felt, everyone that should be
there, truly was. Everyone dropped a rose and Bird was last.*

*Bird looked down on the lowering casket and said "Like I told
Ally, we weren't exactly best buddies but... you deserved better than
this. I did try my friend but, my apologies that it was in vain. I hope
you find peace wherever God has called you to."*

*Bird then had a thought, and it made him smile.*

*"Wherever you are, do me a favor. If you see the cardinal or
the bishop, heh heh, dress them in something pink and frilly and...
send me the bill."*

*Bird made a sign of the cross and tossed his rose.*

*"Goodbye John," and Bird walked off and joined the others.*

*"Are you certain about this?" Bird asked Ciana as he pounded a*

*wooden stake with a sign on it into the ground.*

*"Never been more sure in mah life," Ciana replied with absolute conviction.*

*"Okay then my dear. As I'm known for saying... let's do this."*

*Bird and Ciana walked back in to the small crowd awaiting them in the inn. The sign Bird posted said only 3 words...*

*'closed for repairs'.*


*William and Mary were given rooms in the inn for a few days to make sure all was clear. Padre was badly beaten but Bird scanned him and saw nothing that required him joining Angus, so he was resting up in the inn as well. Mary and William both went home 2 days ago when Bird declared it clear. Those two Bird thought were funny. They argued a lot yet, wouldn't leave each others side for very long. Mary was a widow at only 28, and William was about mid 30's. He was one of those guys that was a die hard bachelor, then started rethinking that around his 30th birthday or so. Mary never had children, and William proudly jested if he had any, he didn't know about it.*

*Padre asked Scota if she would look in on his flock. She gladly obliged, and did so but, only from the perimeter. The flock was concerned but Scota kept them updated and assured them he was being well cared for. Bird made a surgical mask for him, and insisted he wear it at all times inside the inn.*


*Now, William and Mary were back. Andrew setup some chairs by the fireplace and everyone was taking a seat. When Bird walked in though, everyone that wasn't a Thalin, treated him as if God just entered the room. Bird ignored it like he had done many times before, and was ready to use it to his advantage if need be. Now, Bird's 'conference at Malta', was set to begin.*


*Bird started this meeting off by saying "In a land you haven't heard of, during a war you couldn't fathom, 3 main leaders got together to hammer out their course of action. That meeting decided the fates of all the nations. This meeting however, will decide the fates of all of you. Before I tell you my side of things, I want to know how all of you are doing. I want you all to know, you've seen and* heard things that... well... you shouldn't have. You pretty much know where we stand. What I want... no, insist on... from all of you is, leave that 'don't say anything' bullshit attitude outside. Got it? If you have something to say, no matter how silly, or embarrassing, I want you to say it. Fear ladies and gentlemen, along with Elvis... has left the building."

William went first and said "Mistuh Bird, yeh ain't been noth'in but kind and fair with me. A good man yeh are. I want yeh to know I wanted to come outside and stand by yer side. If we be tell'in theh truth, then I want yeh tuh knoe, I felt cowardly stay'in inside. Scota was the one who stopped me say'in yeh had a plan and I'd likely only get in theh way. Once I seen what yeh done, I realized she was right. I jes wanted yeh to knoe where I stood."

Bird was kind and said "Thank you William. I know you would have but, for the record, Scota was right. Do you all remember John the dressmaker?"

"The one at yer home on Christmas?" Mary asked.

"Yep. He was murdered as a means of sending me... and all of you... a message. One death William, in my name, was one death too many in my mind. I have knowledge and weapons you could only dream of. The whole point was to make me the sole target. I knew from going to rescue Angus the kilted muscle were actually the king's soldiers trying to fire up the local clans. When Ciana came out I wasn't happy but, I knew she could at least take care of herself. Add to that she was the one person who could throw the bishop off his guard just when I needed her to."

"Aye, I thought as much. Still, I wanted yeh tuh hear it from me how I felt. When I saw yeh do what yeh jes said, I felt keeping everyone in the room safe was something I could do... and did..." and he looked at Scota with sorry eyes and finished with "... or at least tried to."

Scota was kind and said "Not yer fault William and I doen blame yeh one bit. Turns out," and she smiled at Ally and the padre saying "I had all theh 'protection' I needed."

Mary spoke up next saying " I want yeh tuh knoe how grateful I am fer yer assistance Mistuh Bird. I wasn't afraid to save mehself, but seeing 3 of them, I was a bit afraid of mah chances."

"That's what I do for my friends," Bird said and she smiled and nodded a thanks. "See, here's the thing people. Ciana invited a lot of people to Christmas. Those people lied to her face saying they would come... then never did. Aside from padre here, look around you. Did I bother to come to anyone else's aide or, do you see them in this room now?"

Mary barked "Thah's what I tried tell'in Katie at theh market. Ciana was try'in to share her good fortune AND her home of all things! Not show it off. Theh damn fools jes wouldn't listen."

Padre nodded to Ciana saying "Yet, one person's foolishness, is another's good fortune."

Ciana smiled and nodded sweetly to the padre saying "I do try to do theh Lord's work where I can."

Padre smiled, and blessed her with a sign of the cross.


Bird turned and said "Kara, how are you?"

"Better now, once again, thanks tuh you and Lady Bird."

Kara told her story of how the soldiers came and overwhelmed Angus. A few of them grabbed her and tried to rape her. She fought them till she had a seizure from fighting them off and they basically discarded her. She woke up and saw Angus going mad with jealous rage, then had another seizure. When she came to from that one, she ran to Angus who told her to get Bird.

"I want you all to know, we got lucky. The bishop tried a timed attack. He set them all to go off at once so even if I tried to save any of you, I couldn't save you all. Add to that, if I did, that left Lady Bird undefended. Classic trick actually. I stay and protect Ciana, and you get mad I didn't save you. I leave her, and she hates me for not protecting her. When I found Angus, I figured he would try something like that and did what I could. Mary and William, we had time to get to you because quite simply... the idiots got lost on their way to you. Andrew's place was trashed but empty as the bishop had no idea he was with us at the time. Sadly though, we weren't able to save John."

Padre made a sign of the cross for the dressmaker and said a prayer for him for his bravery.

Kara was being 'a good girl' and didn't want to interrupt but, she wanted to know how Angus was.

"Kara, he's very ill. Ally and I stopped the bleeding but he lost a lot of blood. He is safe and with Ally and me in 'our world'. His cuts were deep and very damaging. We patched him up but, if he so much as sneezes, he could rip open those patches and bleed to death. We have him on medicines that have him paralyzed from the neck down to prevent him from moving even in the slightest. When he is better healed, we'll take him off them."

"Is there ennything I can do to help yeh Mistuh Bird?"

"Actually there is, and we're getting to that."

Ciana looked at Mary and said "Mary my dear, would you mind getting the gossip going?"

Mary sneered sadistically saying "Aye, would be mah pleasure. Ennything in particular?"

"Indeed. Let them know I've closed theh inn for repairs. When it reopens it'll be fine enuf fer the fancy city folk and thah will be who we'll be cater'in to in theh future. Let theh men folk knoe, they'll hafta get there drink somewhere else."

"Heh heh, Aye, that will get them talk'in!"

"Oh and one more thing."

"Aye?"

"Let them knoe, they may want tuh start look'in fer a new Ceilidh House while they're at it."

"Heh heh, consider it done," Mary said with glee.

Gossip wise, Ciana just handed her a chest full of gold.

Now Bird dropped the bomb on them.

"Okay people, Ally and I have been talking. I have some history to give you so get comfy."

Bird took a breath and began his tale.

"You all remember the Chronicles. Mary, if you were to write a book, my people say 'write what you know'. You'd write a book about sewing right?"

"Aye, I suppose."

"Well, The Chronicles were based on real life. The weapons you saw were real, but the story around them wasn't. I took what was real and weaved them into what wasn't. I came here never expecting to fall in love. Get in, get some information, and get out. NOTHING of what's happened since I arrived was supposed to happen. I have another life that, if it came into this one, would be disastrous. Remember the fire in the sky?"

Everyone nodded.

"It's almost here. Two more weeks and it'll start wreaking havoc on the weather for roughly a month. Ciana and Scota know this other life is extremely advanced, and now I'm telling you. As such, its cured Scota and is in the process of saving Angus from certain death. Ally and I have decided to start letting you not only know about it but... if you wish... into it."

Bird got a polite uproar on that one. Padre however, was curious.

"Bird my son,"

"Yes padre?"

"How advanced?"

"We are not afraid to go where others fear to even look. As such, we have created medicines, medical practices, weapons, and devices for communication that you would think were nothing short of witchcraft. How advanced you ask? I can track the fire ribbon and... using food you wouldn't even look at... I can cure you."

Now the padre's eyes lit up... way up.

"Cure him?" Andrew asked, "Whah's wrong with him?"

"Leprosy," Bird said calmly.

The reaction to that wasn't so calm. People scurried out of their chairs and all moved away from the truly holy man.

"I HAVE STOOD against the bishop himself AND the cardinal... twice... each! I think if I'm not afraid, then neither should you be."

"But Bird... it be leprosy!" Mary protested.

Calmly, Bird said "Mary, do you know what causes it? What the disease even looks like AND, I don't mean the symptoms... I mean the fucking disease itself. Do you even know how you contract it?"

"Kahnt say I do, and I ain't look'in tuh find out either!"

"Well, I do. Now, until you can tell me what I already know...

Blondie?... Tell them what I told Siival."

With pure faith in Bird, she said "Feel free to sit your arse down!"

They all did... slowly and... nowhere near Pedro.

Bird turned to the padre and said "I can show you science beyond your wildest dreams but, like I told Scota... it comes with a price."

"I'll make no unholy deals. Other than that, I'm willing to listen my son."

"Unholy no... costly? Perhaps. I cure you and, you need to come with us. Scota needs to leave or she can, well, get sick again. I'll be going with her to a strange but beautiful new land, and Ciana has agreed to come as well. We can go alone, or you can join us but know this. We are never coming back. We are going so far away it would take you more than 100 lifetimes to return."

Bird let that one sink in a moment.

"Bird, I kahnt just leave mah farm," William stated.

"And yet, if I offered you so much better... why not?"

"Well I... um because..." but William had no answer.

Bird addressed the crowd and said "Leprosy is spread by what comes out of your mouth or nose when you cough or sneeze. That's why padre is wearing that mask. Really my friends, did you think I would save your collective asses, just to stick you next to some disease?" Bird said in an 'I'm insulted' tone of voice.

Padre was sad and said "I won't leave them. If it meant saving my life... or their souls... they would win every and any time. My life would be worth very little if my soul were tainted with thinking of myself at the expense of others."

Before Bird could respond... Ally did.

"I'm okay with that actually."

"Uh, excuse me?" Bird said slightly annoyed.

"Commander, you know certain repairs need doing yes?"

"Yeah, so what?"

"Twenty or so extra hands would be a great help. A moment if you would," and Ally waved him over.

Bird excused himself and grabbed Ally off to the side.

*"Look miss 'don't interfere'... what the fuck are you doing?"*

*"Bird, they're dead, and they're gonna only get worse before they do. They have no life past a certain point not long from now. While it is possible, it's highly unlikely they'll interact with anyone before they pass on that would make any time paradoxes. You get the help you need, we save some poor people who didn't ask for the fate they ended up with, and we get resources that may be handy wherever we go."*

*"This wouldn't be guilt talking for what you did to the cardinal would it?" Bird asked cautiously.*

*"I don't think so. Maybe but, I know you like the padre. So far, he's the only man who claims to be holy that truly is. Even if I was doing this out of guilt, can you think of a better way to repay the one life I took, than to give back 30 or so?"*

*Bird was actually proud of Ally, and her logic.*

*"Can't say that I can," Bird said smiling and headed back to the group.*

*"Okay then... change of plans. Padre, thanks to Alydar's kindness, we'll cure you and any of your flock that's not past saving."*

*Padre blessed Alydar but she told him in no uncertain terms "The price however padre remains the same. You and your flock MUST come with us... no exceptions. All I can promise you is you will be treated better than you can imagine when... and if... we reach our destination."*

*Bird added in quick with "And know this padre. Any who we cure will have to agree to this of their own free will. Any who do, and don't uphold their promise... will be hunted down and killed. On that I swear to you. Any who do uphold their promise, will be treated fairly. All I ask is they do their fair share of whatever work we run into... no more... no less."*

*Padre Pedro stood and ignored his pain in doing so. He blessed Bird and Ally.*

*"May the Lord our God bless you for all your days. I will tell my flock."*

*"Remember padre, I can cure those like you... those who aren't very sick yet. Some others I can bring back from danger but I warn you... some may be beyond even my help."*

*Padre sat back down saying "I understand my son."*

*Andrew spoke up now.*
*"Mistuh Bird. I was born and raised but a day's travel from here. This beloved Scotland be all I knoe. Iem no fool, and I knoe a man like yeh has his secrets. Iem even alive because of them. Yeh angered some very important men no doubt with whut yeh done. I also have no doubt sooner or later, someone may come look'in fer yeh. My God man... yeh can cure leprosy! That alone would make yeh theh most hunted man on Earth. The hills here, or back in Edinburgh, they still be Scottish hills. Born here, raised here, Iffin I have mah way... they'll bury me here. I thank yeh kindly Mistuh Bird for yeh faith in this humble driver but... go... and when yeh do, knoe that good ole Andrew will be right here... keep'in the wolves off yer tail till I breathe mah last of Scottish air."*
*Bird was truly touched. Ally was too.*
*"I said it before and I'll say it again. A good man is a good man and you Andrew... are a better man than most."*
*Andrew tipped his hat and Bird tipped his right back.*


*Bird then thought of something and said "Andrew, a moment if you would. I've given these good folks enough to think about for awhile. Step outside with me would you?"*
*Andrew and Bird put on their coats and left the stunned crowd to absorb what they've gotten so far. Outside in the cold night air, Bird took a chance.*
*"Andrew, I truly am touched by your loyalty but..."*
*"But what?"*
*"I thought before you make me a promise you might regret, you might want to know just what you'd be protecting."*
*"Aye?"*
*"The Chronicles."*
*Andrew was a tad confused and asked "Um, aye? What about them?"*
*"They're real," and Bird popped open the saw blades and hovered them right in front of the two men.*
*Without a word, Bird sent them flying and cut off some heavy*

branches to prove his point. Bird pulled them back and put them away. Andrew couldn't decide which he was more of... scared... or impressed. He gave up and decided to be both. Andrew took a few moments to finally find his voice, and realized just who Bird truly was.

"Noooooo," he said in pleasant shock staring up at Bird.

"Oh yeah. Remember the part in the story about us discovering the starfish?"

Andrew's voice was shaking as he said "Aye."

Bird pulled one out and showed it to him. Bird put it on the stunned driver next.

"Go ahead," Bird said with a boyish grin.

"Go ahead and what?"

"I believe he meant... say hello to me," came a female voice.

It was a female voice that he knew was at least 30 feet away and behind a closed door.

Andrew looked at Bird with true shock and exclaimed "Bloody hell man!" and backpedaled a bit. "But... but... yeh mean... noooo wait... how can yeh not be born yet, and still be stand'in right here... in front of me... IN THEH FLESH!"

"That my dear friend, is a little harder to explain," Alydar told him. "Andrew, you know those devastating weapons in the story called the 12 pack?"

"Oi! Get out of mah head lass!" Andrew said pounding his ear some.

"Andrew!"

"What!?"

"Look up."

Andrew looked at Bird who just smiled, and pointed up. The driver finally did, and saw a sight he couldn't deny. High in the sky, were ten blue circles for only a few moments, before they disappeared.

"Andrew, when you came for my birthday, they gave you a quick overview of the Chronicles so you wouldn't be left out. There's more and..."

"No Mistuh Bird, say no more. I have no doubt I prolly knoe too much already. Iem think'in the less I knoe... the better."

Bird smiled saying "Fair enough. Scota knows but no one

*else. Until 'I' tell them... don't let anyone know."*

Andrew was full of wonder, concern, and more Scottish pride than he ever felt in his life as he removed and handed back the starfish.

"Next time Mistuh Bird, Iel ask yeh kindly... warn me before yeh shock meh like thah again." Andrew stared him straight on and said "Now that I knoe, I thank yeh fer trust'in me like thah. Mah promise to yeh remains firm... now more than evuh. See'in, and hear'in, what I jes did... it only lets me knoe you'll need protect'in more... not less. I may be only a driver but, I have mah pride and I have mah honor. I gave yeh mah word, and Iem keep'in it," and Andrew stuck out his hand.

Bird smiled and shook it gladly.

Bird chuckled as he walked back in with Andrew, and the new innkeeper asked "Space yeh say?"

"Heh heh, would you like to see it?"

"Noooooo thank yeh. Birds fly... not Andrews."

Bird just laughed and opened the door for Andrew.


Back inside, Bird finished his 'meeting in Malta'.

"Here's the last piece people. Ally and I believe we have medicines to keep you from getting padre's disease. You're most likely about to find out what Ciana did. The locals are about to shun you because you sided with us. There's already talk in the town about the other day. I want you to do your best to diffuse it."

William asked "Diffuse?"

Bird grinned and, wetting his fingers, put out a candle.

"Aah, I got yeh now."

"I have no idea how they found out but they have. I need all of you to keep your ears open. If they start getting to close to the truth... lie... and throw them off. The more mixed up it becomes the more it'll be laughed off in time. I just showed Andrew something that I will show you all in time. Mary, William... if we end up where I hope to, I will give you land and a home beyond your wildest dreams. Padre, I offer you a chance to tend to your flock till God calls you home. While I understand why you won't leave them, *answer me this. How do you know my offer isn't a reward from God for all the good work you've done so far? Where we go I assure you of one thing, they will no longer be hunted, feared, banished... or worse. Lastly, I have a ship beyond your wildest dreams with luxuries you can't imagine, have never seen, and have never known. Trust me, if we don't make it to where I plan, you'll be traveling in a style beyond any king could dream up."*

*Mary's life wasn't hard but, it wasn't great either. William's life was hard work but, nothing special either. They loved Scotland as much as Andrew did but... lots of land and a home was nothing to sneeze at.*

*"Mistuh Bird?" Kara called out.*

*"Yes Kara?"*

*"I owe mah life to yeh, several times. I never knew kindness like yours ever in mah life. However, Angus is mah man. It took a bit but, he has captured mah heart. Iem ever so grateful for yeh help'in him but... Iel be go'in with him. If he stays, or goes, Iel be at his side. I truly doen want tuh seem ungrateful, but I wanted yeh tuh knoe, thah decision Iel be leav'in tuh him. While yer offer is a grand one... it would be as hollow as an old log without Angus."*

*Bird had a kind smile on his face when he said "If he could have heard you just now, he'd be ever so proud of you. I know I am."*

*"Aye, me too," Scota said.*

*"And me," Ciana added.*

*Bird looked at them all and said "What I've offered you is truly life changing. Take 3 days, and think about it. We'll all meet at our house on the night of the third day. I want you to know though, If you decide to come fine, if not that's fine too but... whichever you choose... this is a one time offer and I'll be holding you to your answers."*

*Everyone understood, and all filed out and took a room each, courtesy of Ciana.*

*Bird and Scota, Andrew and Ciana, and Ally the avatar were now cleaning up and chit chatting as they did. Bird had dropped some* seriously heavy stuff on them, and decided to lighten the mood. He laughed at Andrew as he kept poking or touching Ally here and there. Now knowing what she was, he was testing her almost in disbelief. Bird laughed hard when Ally finally stopped ignoring him.

"Unless you want me to bring back those blue rings, I'd suggest you stop doing that," she said in a suddenly annoyed tone.

Bird didn't know who's response was funnier, hers or Andrews.

Ciana was actually thinking the same as Bird, and told him slyly "Yeh knoe 'husband-to-be', that clothing yeh wore theh other day was... what do yeh call it... sexy?"

Bird almost spit out his drink. Scota actually did.

"Yeh knoe, I doen think Ied mind much iffin yeh wore that, yeh knoe... 'later'."

Bird pulled the same trick on her that he pulled on Symda. He held up his hands like he was holding a shirt or something, yet was holding nothing.

"I wouldn't mind if you wore this," and Bird grinned huge.

Everyone laughed when she called him on it and answered "Hmm, I dunno, wouldn't happen tuh 'ave it red now would yeh?"

Bird merely winked and said "I'll see what I can do."

Two hours later and he was laying in bed. Ciana was wrapped around him and fast asleep. The only thing going fast on Bird was his mind. As per his usual, not only was he wide awake but, the master planner was going over plans and options at warp speed. He knew he had a possible lifelong journey ahead of him, and now he was bringing company. Thanks to Alydar... a lot of company. He had a wolf that was about to wake up, and so was the highlander in the same room. Right now he was trying to put it all together and... in what order. He had no idea that, in a matter of months, all his plans would be for nothing... and never see the light of day.

"Oh fuck it," he said to himself.

"Problem boss?"

"Nope. Tell ya what though. I'm gonna get some sleep. Then starting tomorrow, I'm gonna make good on my plan," and Bird did exactly that.

# Chapter 38:

## "The Beginning Of The Beginning... And The Beginning Of The End"

*Lone, in Bird terms, was a working madman. Xankor, on several occasions, fell asleep trying to keep up with him. He was pouring into refitting Giljor's ships. Lone had started the 'Biiird hunt' feeling time was his enemy. That feeling died off for awhile but now... it was back with a vengeance. He only took time off from his 'project' once. He was the first, and Roenas insisted he'd be the last.*

*Lone arrived on 51 and wasted no time. He headed right to Freedom Point. He said nothing, and merely climbed the stairs. The crowd was a little confused at what he did though. He grabbed the stand with the numbers on it, picked it up, and carried it to the main floor.*

*"THIS!... Is for you... and because of you," and he pulled out his claws.*

*The numbers were at 340. Lone just shredded them till it read only 356. Then... he smiled and... pulled it off.*

*"Rhana himself would be proud of you. I am not only proud... I am grateful. Thank you all," and he walked off.*

*The number on the stand read '357' and all on the floor now knew the ring was complete. As he walked away, the applause and cheers only got louder and louder.*

*Valleron had his people busy. He promised Lone workers accustomed to working in space, and he certainly delivered. He had thousands of old 1 person craft that got quickly, but safely, made functional once more. They were robots that held one of his kind, and good for 4 hours at a time. The Vrissin inside had 2 mechanical* arms to work, and each had an arsenal of tools to choose from. As big as Gil's station was, it was nowhere near big enough to hold a fully assembled full size ring. Remmy equipped it with minefield shields but aside from that, it was exactly the same as the one that sent Rhana to Earth. Valleron had a crew of 150 workers and he hand picked every one of them. By current time, 51 time that is, it had been 17 weeks since Bird was lost. It took 5 of those weeks to build and assemble the ring, but, it was built.

Raven's lander left the hangar bay of Gil's station with a fully modified replica of Ship. Lone was all over this part of the plan.

"You didn't hear this from me but... your mate is even worse than mine lately," Rahgaa exclaimed quietly to Renny.

Renny scrunched her face and said "Normally I'd argue with you on that one Lady R but... yeah... I think I won't," exclaimed a slightly irritated Guardian.

Rahgaa gazed at an odd sight and asked "You ready for this?"

"As Rhana would say... 'and willing... and able'," Renny stated with pure pride.

"If you change your mind, just let me know."

"No Rahgaa, we chose fairly. I need only one thing from you now."

"Name it."

Renny smiled a kind smile and said "Wish me luck."

"All I have," Rahgaa said smiling back.

The odd sight Rahgaa had been staring at was... hers and Renny's chairs being anywhere but the trance room.

Lone walked up the ramp of the little Ship, and took the pilot's seat.

"Okay my dear... what's the plan?" Lone said to Renny as he turned his seat around.

"Go out to space... creep up on the perimeter...if all is good, go in only slightly then, come back."

Lone looked at Rahgaa and said "And you?"

"Trance with her but... 'hang back' as you say, and be ready to rescue if need be."

Lone turned around to his console saying "I only hope to Biiird's God that this works."

Lone wasn't usually the nervous type, but right now, he was feeling just how Bird felt when they fired up FTL for the first time.


Bird was with Ciana and Scota in the inn. Andrew was off to the market getting used to, and learning, the locals. Mary was his guide today. After recent events, William was right behind them.

"Ciana, I have a question for you," Bird said in a serious tone.

"Yes my love?"

"I told Rahgaa, every now and then, a huge boost forward is inevitable. I'll leave it to you. Want one?"

Ciana thought a moment.

"Just how huge yeh talk'in about?"

"Honestly? No clue. I was gonna leave that up to you."

Scota was nervous but knew sooner or later this moment would come.

"Well... yes... and no," Ciana stated.

"Clarify," Bird stated.

"I was think'in. The little bits yeh gave me so far were wonderful, but feel almost like teas'in. How about, not huge but... bigger than yeh 'ave so far?"

Bird thought a moment, and replied "Fair enough. Look out the door, is anyone around outside?"

Ciana did, then said "Not a soul."

Bird reached into his pocket... and gave Ciana her boost.

"Ciana, remember the music on Christmas?" Bird asked.

"Aye."

"That's not the only thing it does. Look here," and Bird showed her what was in his hand.

Scota was slightly shocked when Bird showed Ciana... a starfish.

"I ain't never seen metal so shiny... and smooth!" Ciana said in near delight.

"C'mere dear," Bird ordered. "Remember the starfish? The one from the story?"

"Um... oh aye... the one yeh used to talk over great distances. What of it?"

Bird smiled, showed her how to attach it, and put it behind her left ear.

"Let me be VERY clear about this. This is NOT something anyone but me, Scota, Ally or Andrew know about... no less see. I want you to keep this covered by your hair at all times... got it?"

Ciana was a tad confused but said "Aye... I got yer message... oh wait... MRU?... thah right?"

"Heh heh... it is indeed. Now my bonnie lass... why don't you go stand by where you were when the bishop was here hmm?"

That point was about 50 feet from the inn's front door. Ciana was still confused but, did as she was asked. Bird headed out the back with Scota in tow, and headed to where the wolves attacked her. From Ciana's current vantage point, it was the only place behind the inn she could see.


Ciana was standing where she was asked to, and hollered back to the inn.

"Care tuh tell me why I be stand'in here?"

"Not at all," Bird said calmly.

Ciana turned and said "Oi Bird I didn't see yeh come... up... behind......... Bird?"

"Yes?"

Ciana was turning her head hard right and left but... there was no Bird.

"Okay silly Yankee Man... yeh had yer fun. Now... where yeh hid'in?" Ciana said with a smile.

"I'm not hiding anywhere. Turn around."

"I did. Yeh ain't anywhere where I can see yeh."

"Actually, I am and... you didn't turn around."

"I did!"

"No, I can see you. You looked side to side but nothing more. Now... turn... around."

Ciana did a full 360 and exclaimed "There I did! Now where yeh hid'in?"

Bird let out a sigh and asked "Remember when Scota was attacked by the wolves?"

"Aye."

"Turn around... and look there."

Ciana did and bellowed "Bloody Hell!" and backed up a bit.

Now, Bird laughed as she was pounding her head just like Andrew did. What Ciana saw was Bird... about 110 feet away... waving at her.

"Sis, doen be scared... please?... For me?" Scota half asked, half pleaded.

Ciana promised not to be scared but, Bird was inside her hand and now... so was Scota. She was about to have a small freakout session when she got annoyed instead.

"Oh doen thah figger... Scota knoes about this befaw me!"

"Don't get mad," Bird stated, "You asked for a piece of my world bigger than what you've gotten so far. Well... there ya go. Suffice to say, there's no place on Earth... heh heh, and a few places that aren't... that I won't hear you."

Ciana was annoyed at first but, the 'coolness' of it was starting to sink in. Scota was about to say something but Ciana beat her to it. The tone in her voice though, was playfully sinister.

"So 'Commander'... does this mean I can talk to yer imaginary Alydar now as well?"

"Invisible... and not till I say so," Bird exclaimed quickly cutting off his ship's AI. "For now, you know what it can do. Do you want me to take it back? Or do you want to get used to it?"

"I think Iel be giv'in it back but... for now. I knoe what it can do and thah's enough fer now. Let me get used to that then, Iel take it and use it more. Will thah be okay?" Ciana asked wondering if that was truly okay.

"Fine by me," Bird said with a smile. "I'll show you how to use it, how to know when someone is listening and, when they're not. See ya inside Lady Bird!" Bird said with a wave as he turned it off.

Walking beside Bird, Scota smiled saying "Sis? Iem proud of yeh."

Ciana walked in as well saying "Oh THIS is go'in tuh take some get'in used to!"

Scota just giggled.

Renny and Rahgaa drifted off as they had so many times before. Lone had them both in one of Gil's ships and he was in Raven's landing bay. She gave the all clear, then depressurized the bay and dropped the ramp. Now, with a clear shot to space, the ladies headed out. Raven, for safety, was on the edge of the minefield but not in it.

"So far so good," Renny said to Rahgaa.

"So far," Rahgaa stated. "You know however, lately, our luck hasn't been any better than the Ghosts. Be careful but know this."

"Yes?"

"When I taught you, I told you what to look out for, and what safeguards to put in place and why."

"I remember," Renny said affectionately.

"Well... if ANY thing goes wrong... I want you to forget them. You do whatever you have to but... you save yourself. That's an order from your Prime," Rahgaa stated firmly but kindly.

Renny hugged her 'virtual sister' and stated lovingly "I will."

She beamed in to Lone and said "I got to the perimeter and nothing wrong so far." She nuzzled him like she used to on Eden, and said "Wish me luck," and faded out.

Outside again, she gave Rahgaa a thumbs up and breached the minefield. Once inside, she was bombarded by all sorts of sensations. So much so that, she had to calm her mind, and focus on her task just to keep from being overwhelmed. It took her ten minutes to learn how to 'drown out the noise' but once she did, she finally had some of the control she wanted.

Rahgaa was nervous. When she and Renny tranced, to a small degree they could sense each other. Once Renny hit the minefield, that got cut off. Rahgaa almost went in several times after her but, those two agreed, 30 minute test if all seemed okay. Renny came out at 25 minutes and Rahgaa let out a sigh of relief.

"Come teacher... we need to talk," Renny said seriously.

"RAVEN! Lock it up!" Lone hollered when he saw the ladies wake up.

*Lone had a set of questions for them to answer when they woke up, just to make sure they were the same Renny and Rahgaa. Once they both passed those, Lone got his report.*

*"Well?" Rahgaa asked nervously.*

*"We're going to need a few things," Renny replied. "Lady R, the moment you go in there you will be overwhelmed with sensations. Remember when you first searched for Rhana?"*

*"I do."*

*"The sensation you felt eventually led you to him. Imagine that... times a million."*

*Rahgaa was not happy and said "That's not good news."*

*"Nope and, there's more. The moment I went in I felt, well, like mini lightning was all over my fur. Like the shock you get dragging your feet then touching metal. Inside however, it's like millions of shocks. Not harmful but, annoying. However, it was like the orange water of Eden. The longer I stayed, the worse it got. I felt so itchy that it actually felt painful, and I could take it no longer."*

*"Were you able to focus on any sensations?" Rahgaa asked.*

*"To a degree. It was like trying to find one normal voice, among thousands of shouting ones."*

*Lone got it and said "So, without the quiet background you're used to, the one we seek gets drowned out by the noise."*

*"Exactly. I stayed perhaps longer than I should have but, the tingling sensation was the worst. I still feel it now, though it appears to be fading. If we can't solve that, we'll only be able to search 15 minutes tops."*

*Lone was concerned but hugged Renny saying "Forget that. Now that you're 'complete' again... how do you feel now?"*

*"I'm fine and, best as I can tell, so is the child. Hug me like that again however, before my skin calms down... and I will punch you."*

*"MRU," Lone said in a kindly tone. "Triikon is giving you both a full workup on our return. Tell him all you've told us and leave nothing out," Lone commanded.*

*"I will," Renny told him.*

*Triikon came up to Lone after he finished looking over the ladies.*

"As near as I can tell, their minds are intact. I sense no form of delirium, and see no damage that might cause the same."

"Good news so far," Lone stated.

"The tingling however, is another matter. It's residual energy, similar to smoke from a fire. Even you know that's dangerous too if exposed long enough."

"Indeed. Solution?"

"I can give them medicine to suppress their neural systems. Not negate it but, more like dull it. In their pregnant state however, it will have to be diluted. Normally, they would be good for one Tuhleesian day. In their current conditions, 5 hours tops and... I only recommend 4."

Lone knew there'd be a catch and asked "And when their 4 hours are up?"

"One hour before I can give them any more."

Lone expected far worse and merely said "I'll take it."

Triikon nodded and headed off to mix up a potion.


"Oi... Lady Bird... mind if I borrow lil sis for an hour?"

Ciana answered "Not at all. Doen be longer though I almost got supper ready."

"Not a problem lass. Want the starfish?" Bird asked with a teasing grin.

"Nooooo thank yeh. I think Iev had enough voices in mah head fer one day."

Bird chuckled, gave Ciana a kiss, and headed out with Scota.

"Okay blondie... open it," Bird said when they reached the cave.

"I kahnt."

"Um... and why not?" Bird teased.

"The light is red. Besides, I kahnt open it on mah own remember? Not without yer say so."

Bird grinned slyly "Hmm, is that so?"

Ghost 1 was thrilled Scota got the red light green light thing. He also had a surprise for her.

"Okay, tis green now. Go ahead Yankee Man."

"Oh... I think I'll let you do it," and Bird winked at her.

Scota suddenly smiled that 'really!?' kind of smile. Bird just nodded and Scota turned to the door.

"I am Scota Thalin... door?... Take me to theh landing bay."

On command, the door did as told. Scota beamed and hugged Bird.

"Thank yeh fer trust'in me," she said honestly.

"You're welcome and... you earned it."

Both walked into the bay and the door closed. Scota went to walk in as always but Bird put a hand across her chest to hold her back.

"Manners lil one... manners."

"Ooh yeah... sorry... Alydar?"

"Yes?"

Scota stood straight and proud and asked "Permission to come aboard!?"

Alydar chuckled and the booming voice throughout the bay said "Welcome aboard."

Scota was thrilled and walked down to the main floor.

"Okay blondie, I got one more present for ya. Come over here," Bird said standing by the other door.

"Aye?"

"Tell it to take you to your room."

"Do yeh think that wise? Ciana will have a fit iffin she see's this! The starfish was bad enough but this!? I doen know."

Bird chuckled and teased "Not your room... I mean your room."

Scota scrunched her face and said "Ennyone evuh tell yeh ya doen make no sense sometimes?"

Bird laughed and said "Just tell it."

Scota was nervous but said "Door? Take me to mah room."

On command it opened and once again both Bird and Scota went through. Scota was confused though because when they came out, they were in Alydar still and in a hallway she'd not seen yet.

Bird smiled kindly and said "First door on the right. Go ahead... open it."

"How? There ain't no knob!"

"Don't need one. Alydar knows who you are and is scanning you right now. Just walk up to it."

"Scanning me?"

"Making sure you are you. I'll explain that later... just do it Scota."

She did and, like the med bay doors, it swung open automatically. That delighted Scota as she thought it was cool. When she walked inside though, she was floored. To Bird, it was just a standard room. To Scota, it was opulence on a godly scale.

"This is fer me!??"

"Mm hmm. You're going to be coming here more and more. You still got a ways to go yet but, you've handled yourself very well so far. I've given you permission to the bay and here. You can explore when you feel like it but, Alydar will stop you if you go somewhere you shouldn't."

Scota didn't know where to look first. She giggled and screeched and gave Bird the reaction he figured on and... was hoping for.

"Whoa, whah's thah!?" Scota asked pointing to the wall.

"It's called a crossbow. That one however has a trick up it's sleeve," Bird said with a grin. "Scota, as in the mythical one you were named after... was a warrior goddess. Never picked a fight but never backed down from one either. The cardinal overpowered you. Others in the future may as well. I saw you staring at my cannons and no... you can't have one."

Scota put on a fake boo boo face then giggled.

"Aw... can I at least try it?" Scota asked nicely.

"Learn AND... become good with... that," and Bird pointed to the crossbow on the wall, "And we'll see. In the mean time, that will keep you safe from anymore cardinals, and if it's discovered, it won't be tech that's not already around."

Scota gave Bird and honest kiss on the cheek and a huge hug.

Alydar kicked in and said "I put some things in the closet. Some are your clothes and... some are mine. Be careful which one's you wear and where you wear them."

"Ooh... some of those racy one's too!?" Scota said as she

flung open the closet.

Alydar giggled and said "Well, not too 'sexy' but... yeah... some of those too."

Scota headed out with Bird but she really didn't want to. Bird insisted as he was hungry. Scota knew all too well how cranky and mad Bird gets when he's hungry so back to the inn they went.

"And jes what exactly is spaghetti and meatballs?" Scota queried.

"Heh heh... you'll see," Bird said as they headed back through the last door and into the cave.

Both Guardians took Triikon's medicine but never tranced. Five hours seemed like an eternity to Lone but even he knew, a real eternity was even longer. He wanted both ladies checked before heading back out. Triikon was 'dead on the money' as the saying goes and his concoction worked flawlessly. At 6 hours and, no ill effects, the ladies took another dose and now... it was game time.

"Fifteen minutes and you come back if the potion doesn't work... got it?" Lone commanded.

Both ladies giggled but saluted, and headed for different ships.

Out in the minefield, Ryklan was nervous. True to her mentors though, she was perfect at the controls. Tiiveer knew he had a reputation now. He also knew this day would come. He stayed concerned over Rahgaa but, let the nervousness go.

"See you in a few hours," Rahgaa said sweetly as she kissed him then, sat down in her chair and drifted off.

Tiiveer looked at Ryklan and said kindly "Well, it seems we have some time on our hands. How about, to pass that time, you show me how to work this thing hmm?"

Ryklan smiled back just as kindly and answered "I'd be happy to," and went about doing just that.

Bird had made a target filled with horse hair and hung it between two poles. Scota kept getting knocked a bit from the crossbow's *recoil. Every time she did, she only got more annoyed, and worked even harder at keeping steady. It took 3 days to truly understand all that it was and, by day 4 she was becoming good at it. It was a new passion of hers and she worked at it every chance she could. On day 5, when she got good enough at it, Bird showed her 'the toy'.*

*"This is called a laser sight. A tiny beam of light comes out and... look at the target," Bird said pointing downrange.*

*Scota saw a small red dot of light and was thrilled, but had no idea what it was.*

*Bird chuckled and said "IF you keep that thing steady enough, the bolt will go wherever the dot was from the point when you pulled the trigger."*

*Ciana was around for this target practice and even she tried it a few times. Scota wanted it back though and while not rude, she wasn't sharing nicely either. Bird was about to say something but, it was actually Andrew that beat him to it.*

*"OI lass! Thah not be a toy yer hold'in and all theh 'Iem sorries' in theh world won't fix theh mistake yeh make iffin yeh point that at theh wrong thing, creature or person."*

*Andrew wasn't admonishing Ciana... he was admonishing Scota.*

*Bird looked at Scota sternly, pointed to Andrew, and told her "What he said! Ayleen learned a harsh lesson. Don't make me have to give you one as well."*

*Scota was impish and got the message loud and clear.*

*Later that night, Scota walked out into the moonlight and looked around. Seeing she was alone, she took off her shirt and her dress. Pulling out a pair of boots similar to Bird's that Ally lent her, she stood up feeling proud... and sexy as hell... in an Emma Peel inspired all black catsuit. The silk like underwear in the form of panties and a bra that Ally gave her as well, only helped her feel more comfortable and... more bad-ass. Pulling the crossbow from her back she went on the move. Tucking and rolling and wide armed turns, she was practicing hitting a target while on the move. Of all the things she did and felt, the fact that she was wearing pants thrilled her the most. Why women didn't wear them too she now couldn't even fathom. Bird merely smiled, and dropped the curtain.*

*Rahgaa got a full force assault from the sensations Renny mentioned. It took her a tad longer to focus but, she managed to do so. The tingling on her fur was there but, as Triikon said, she could sense it but nothing more. The battering was coming from all the wormholes and time pockets and bubbles. Events in life, can give off sensations and that is what Rahgaa and Renny could feel. It's also what drew Rahgaa to Bird in the first place. Now, with thousands of them around, she truly understood what Renny meant by finding a single voice among a shouting crowd.*

*Once she acclimated to it though, she went on the hunt. Having no direction to go on, in, or by... she just picked a random hole as a test.*

*"Okay! THAT wasn't necessarily the best first choice," Rahgaa said as she quickly pulled back.*

*Something, with a lot of teeth and the size of a small moon, headed straight for her. She considered it 'something' as all she ever saw were the teeth.*

*It was 3 days later and, both ladies were coming up not only empty but frustrated. The 'noise' of the minefield made focusing on anything specific, difficult to say the least. Those sensations however, and their prolonged exposure, coupled with their motivations... trickled down to their unborn children. The 'time trancers' as they would come to be known... would be a whole different set of Chronicles. All those factors combined, would shape who they were forever and... lead one of them to talk to 'god'.*

*The two Guardians were troopers though. They would go out whenever Triikon deemed it safe. He banned Rahgaa herself for a whole day when she showed signs of fatigue. She wasn't happy about it but, coupled with Tiiveer's insistence... his warning was headed all the same.*

*Both ladies were at it for 3 weeks now and only Renny had come close. She had found a slight trace and decided to follow it. All she got for her efforts though was to find herself in orbit over a scorched planet. From the looks of it, it appeared to have been that way for a very long time. She beamed in to a small island that was nothing but dim light and blowing dust. That island was only 70 or so miles across. Seeing nothing, she thought it only a 'glitch' and moved on. She had no way of knowing that... somewhere way back before she arrived, that 'island' was a whole lot bigger... and once called Australia.*

*From that point though, Renny was careful. She felt like she was somehow being watched. It wasn't strong but, it was there all the same. She thought it might be Tamarak but then realized the sensation was all wrong. This sensation felt... loving.*

*Bird was out chopping firewood. He needed a workout and thought this would be perfect. It was hot... real hot... and not like it should be at all for early March. The following day, it was near freezing. Bird knew without Ally even confirming it, the hell wave was starting to make itself known. He also had his Ghost hovering over the north pole. With Ayleen beginning to wake up and, the weather about to go crazy, he wanted all the edge he could get close at hand.*

*"Now remember Scota, no fear right?"*
*"Aye... I promise. Bird?"*
*"Hmm?"*
*"Do yeh think Iem ready?"*
*"Time will tell," he said as both walked through a 51 door, and into Alydar.*

*They rounded the corner and walked into med bay. Scota smiled to herself as she realized the door no longer spooked her. She actually only expected it to open, and didn't think anymore about it. That level of acceptance, comfort, and familiarity is what had her smiling. She didn't even notice... Bird was smiling too and, for the exact same reason.*

*Bird had closed the top on the tank. With Ayleen nearly awake, he didn't want her panicking and trying to get out before he could calm her down. He thought of pumping the water full of sedatives but, truth be told, he was no doctor. It sounded like a good idea but not knowing had him 'not doing'.*

Bird blocked Scota and stared down at her saying "You sure you wanna do this?"

"Like yeh said, time will tell. Iem here now so... as you say... let's do this."

"Okay then," Bird said kindly and... stepped aside.

Scota was awestruck. She saw what she had already seen on the screen in the Lander but, this was no image.

She wouldn't go near Ayleen but, to Bird's delight, she wasn't backing up either. To try and keep Scota from freaking out, Bird tested her.

"Tell me about her," he ordered of Scota.

She spoke to Bird but, never took her smiling gaze off the tank.

"Ayleen... Lone's real sister. Call sign Husky. Um, Pilot and... oh yeah... Tahl is her father. Her uh... 'other' is it?"

"Mm hmm."

"Aye, her other is Turannen."

Bird chuckled and said "Not exactly. Tinnaaren. Turannen is one of the Guardians."

Scota giggled and said "Oh they all sound theh same. Close enough tho."

Bird sneered "I don't think she would agree with you."

Suddenly, playtime was over.

Scota was frozen with panic, not fear, just panic. She froze because the wolf in the tank suddenly... opened her eyes. It took a few seconds for her to realize and when she did, she panicked with a strength Scota had never seen. Ayleen came awake and realized she was in water. She had no idea where she was nor anything else. All she knew was her mind telling her to 'get out'. She was pounding at the walls and at the top of the tank. Bird was across the room and getting ready to try his best to explain to Ayleen. Scota however, did it for him.

Ayleen was pounding furiously trying to get out. She stopped mid punch with a 'huh?' look on her face, when a light color haired human stroked the glass of the tank... and smiled. Scota exhaled on the glass fogging it up and wrote one word.

'SAFE'

*That was the only thing that stopped Ayleen from breaking the tank. Scota was looking at her with awe and wonder. Ayleen was looking at her with curiosity and confusion.*

*Bird just looked at them both and softly exclaimed "Well I'll be damned."*

*Bird rushed to the console and brought up the keyboard and screen for Ayleen, and began typing.*

'NOT drowning. Been breathing water in tank for months. The human female is correct... you are safe.'

*Ayleen looked around and it did finally dawn on her... she wasn't drowning. It took her another moment to figure things out when she finally typed something back. Bird laughed hard when he read it.*

'WTF?' *Ayleen asked in text form.*

'51 tech. Water is loaded with oxygen and nano technology. We almost lost you sweety and you've been healing in the tank since we rescued you.'

*Ayleen read Bird's message when a panicked look of sudden realization came over her face.*

'Ship!!?'

*Bird was sad faced when he typed back...* 'Gone.'

*Ayleen hung her head and pounded both fists softly into the glass wall.*

*Bird walked up and half hugged Scota for two reasons. Because he was truly proud of her... and to show Ayleen she was okay and not an enemy. Bird smiled kindly and stroked the glass letting Ayleen not only see him but... see him happy she was alive.*

*Scota yet again, thought of something. She tapped on the glass and startled a bit when Ayleen snapped a stare at her. Scota was startled, then annoyed. The look on Ayleen's face was not a good one. Scota however... held her own. She crossed her arms over her chest and gave her a 'two can play that game' stare right back. Ayleen never knew about the tank and the water thing was not making her happy at all. Realizing she was okay and, so was Rhana, she softened her expression. Seeing that, Scota did too.*

*Bird chuckled to Ally saying "These two are either gonna kill each other... heh heh... or become inseparable."*

Ally smiled saying "My money is on the latter."

Scota pulled back her hair and went back to her original plan. She turned her head to show Ayleen her starfish. Ayleen turned her head with a 'Yeah?...So?' and showed her hers. Scota beamed, and went to push the button but Bird stopped her.

"Scota wait." Smiling, Bird said "Tell her what you just told me."

Scota smiled and nodded and pushed the button.

"You are Ayleen, yes?"

Ayleen tried to speak. It took her only a second to realize that was futile and just nodded her head.

"Excellent! You can hear me! You are Lone Wolf's sister... Pilot to Rahgaa the Prime... daughter of Tahl.... and you have an 'other' named Turannen."

Ayleen was staring at her with a 'how do you know all this?' look on her face, until she got to the last part. Yet again another sharp look from the masked wolf.

"Hah hah hah! Told you blondie!"

"Oi! I toel yeh, they all sound theh same!" Scota exclaimed in her own defense.

Ayleen typed 'Who's the Geckyl and how does she know all this?' Bird laughed at the last part that read 'And Turannen!? Pfff puleeeez...he's old enough to be my father!'

Scota read what she typed and asked "What's a Geckyl?"

Bird grinned "It's an animal on her planet. Kind of a cross between a small bear and a mountain lion. It has a long blonde mane and... um, heh heh... a bit of an ornery attitude."

Scota turned and stuck her tongue out at Ayleen.

"Oi... somebody a little cranky when they first wake up are they?"

Bird laughed when Ayleen replied in kind, and he decided to intervene.

"Ayleen... sit rep. You're on Earth. Not only that but... Earth's past. WE are currently in a time period 200 plus seasons before I was born. The shock wave knocked the exit out of place and out of time. This young lady is named Scota and... she's a local. Just seeing *you took more courage than you can imagine. In this time period, YOU my dear are either a myth, a monster, a demon... or all three. Now... here... you are the very werewolf I tease Lone about."*

*Ayleen rolled her head and typed* 'Greeeeaaattt'.

*She then softened, and stared at Bird as she typed.*

'Rhana?'

*"Yes?"*

'Thank you... seriously... I know I would be dead if not for you.'

*"And Ally," Bird nicely corrected her.*

*Ayleen looked to the side and straight at Ally, and gave her a sincere Tuhleesian salute. Ally smiled and returned it.*

*"Now, we need to scan you for another day. If all goes well, we'll get you out of the tank tomorrow."*

'MRU. Why does the human sound like Kallan?'

*"We are on the section of Earth where that accent is not only the norm but... the very area Deeno based her on."*

*Ayleen nodded her head in that 'gotcha' type of way.*

*"Also, Alydar and I came out first. We've been here a little past a year in Earth time. You were still in the wave and as I said, didn't show up till a few months ago. Assuming we ever get back to our time and place... I will personally stand by your side at any trial you have and tell Rahgaa herself that the loss of her ship was in no way your fault. Not this time."*

*Ayleen bowed respectfully. She was sad she lost Ship yet again. Hearing Rhana's words, it comforted her to know she wasn't responsible... not this time anyway. She smiled slightly, then tapped on the tank. She pointed to Scota... then to the display.*

'Tinnaaren... not Turannen. Pleased to meet you Scota.'

*Scota turned around and curtsied nicely.*

*"Okay Husky, you were hurt badly. A few times we honestly thought we were going to lose you. You had a huge gash in the back of your head along with severe brain swelling. The tank is saturated with oxygen which is why you can breathe the water. The nano tech is a 51 secret but, essentially, they're micro robots. They healed you till your body could heal itself. I don't know if there's any mental problems. Memory loss, long and short term is possible. Other*

functions may be affected so, we'll be testing you over the next week or so to see if there is any. Aside from that," and Bird smiled softly and finished with "Know that I'm very happy to see you again."

Ayleen smiled a caring smile, and simply pet the glass. Bird knew exactly what she meant.


'And what of you?' Ayleen texted.

"Well, there is one thing I can tell you. Scota here has a sister. If I were your brother..." and Bird gave her a boyish grin and a wink "...her sister would be my Renny,"

Ayleen had a shocked look on her face... really shocked. It was the happy kind of shock but, shocked all the same.

'Know that I am VERY pleased for you. I look forward to meeting her too!'

Scota kicked in and said "Not exactly Husky. Bird kept all this hidden from us locals. Mah sistuh doen knoe about this place yet. I found out by mistake, but Bird and Ally have been teach'in me whut they can."

Ayleen nodded and typed 'Rhana, you've said your kind were a bit backward in this time frame.' She looked at Scota and typed 'No insult intended' then finished with 'But that said, how does someone like her know so much of what she really shouldn't know at all?'

Bird smiled and asked "You feeling groggy?"

'Not at all oddly enough.'

"Tired?"

'Nope.'

"Well then, how about if I let Scota tell you?"

Ayleen smiled and typed 'I'd like that a lot.'

"Then I think I'll leave you two to get acquainted, her to get used to seeing a real live alien, and you to get a hell of an update."

Bird and Ally were heading out when Bird stopped and said in the kindest of tones "By the way Husky... welcome back."

Ayleen had love on her face and gave Bird a curtsey with an imaginary dress.

Scota beamed and said "Get comfy wolf lady, I got one wild tale tuh tell yeh!" and proceeded to do just that.

*Lianna was lying in her bed. She was getting used to her new world... literally. Rhana was actually known as 'Uncle Bird' in this new world of hers. Talon and Skye were his children and not her wolf cousins. She spent a week taking walks with Uncle Bird in something 51 called an arboretum. It was the most glorious thing she ever saw. Bird would update her so she would know what happened from the point time 'shifted'. She was grateful for the updates... ever so grateful. Uncle Bird however was the first thing she changed. Rhana he was... and Rhana forever he would be. Bird had literally given her her life back and now, she wanted to see if she could give him the same in return.*

*Two Guardians had searched for weeks by the time she decided to intervene... sort of. Mother and Aunty she knew would search by sensation but Lianna.... searched by sensing time. Both Guardians were frustrated but, never lost their determination. Seems Uncle and father were getting frustrated as well. Now, a wolf from the future, decided to give one from the past a little 'kick start'.*

*"I don't mind telling you Lady R, this is getting tedious," Renny exclaimed with exasperation in her voice.*

*"What do you mean 'getting'?" Rahgaa said in the same frustrated tone. She let out a hard sigh and calmed herself saying "I failed twice before... I will NOT fail again. Either I, or you, will find him this time or I swear to Rhana's God, my pyre will be in this very minefield."*

*Renny sympathized saying "My only problem is, at the end of a very frustrating day, it would be nice if I went home to a mate who wasn't as equally frustrated. Honestly Rahgaa, if we keep up this pace, we're going to burn ourselves out."*

*Rahgaa sneered "Oh... you have one of those mates too eh?"*

*Renny still had more.*

*"Rahgaa, I don't know why but, I get the feeling I'm being followed. Not only that but... it seems familiar somehow."*

*Rahgaa was now concerned and asked "Tamarak!?"*

*"No. You may think this crazy but... it feels like... you."*

*"Me!?"*

"Mm hmm. Healer Triikon insists there is nothing wrong with me physically, but fears the searching we do may be affecting my mind. I am certain it's not, with that one exception. It's been a month since we began. Nothing but false leads and false promising paths. Anyway, I wanted you to know."

Rahgaa was kind and said "As Rhana would say... you just KEEP telling me things like that. How about if I go alone today?"

Renny was obstinate.

"NOT gonna fucking happen lady."

"Very well but, anything and I mean anything goes wrong, you come back immediately. That's an order from your Prime."

Renny was kind and said "MRU," and both headed out for another mind numbing day of coming up empty.

Today however, one of them would come up anything but.


Every day they searched, Rahgaa always went right and Renny went left. Today, just to alleviate some boredom, they switched.


Lianna looked around Uncle's house. Seeing it clear and everyone was asleep, she went to work. Laying in her bed, she slowed her breathing, focused her mind and... was gone.


Bird was on the roof... again. Not only that, he was annoyed. The rains and winds of late were at the levels of tropical storms. He was patching the roof for the third time, when he saw what looked like a super cell form just to the west.

"OOOOHHH TRUUUUUSSSST YOUUU!!!!!" He bellowed at it in frustration.

Bird didn't mind the rain nor the wind... as long as he wasn't in it. The wind wasn't bad but the rain annoyed him to no end. Always did. He got the last of it patched and headed inside, just 2 minutes before the deluge began.


Renny was looking but, found herself losing not only interest but, motivation. Catching herself, she changed both. She was looking for Bird, and coming up with a way of telling Lone that she and Rahgaa needed a break. She was heading down a main trunk tunnel, when she felt herself being watched again. No, not watched she realized... waited for. In all this pea soup of sensations, this one was beyond any and all. Renny made a choice, and decided to follow it.

She was heading for a second branch when, she changed her mind and went down the third one instead. The farther in she went, the more the sensation grew. About two thirds of the way in she immediately hit the brakes and... pulled her Mahrek Blades.

Renny found herself staring at a lovely white wolf. She thought it Rahgaa at first, till she got closer. She knew with all the time bubbles around, she may come across herself or Rahgaa but, from a different time. This white wolf, was neither.

The other wolf smiled and... bowed? She said nothing but, pointed to Renny's canister, and then to the portal she was in front of. Renny approached slowly, blades at the ready. The other wolf backed up, as if to allow her to get to the portal. Now a new problem was coming up. The portal she pointed to... was closing. Frantic, the wolf again pointed to the canister then the portal. This time though, she did so with extreme urgency. Renny still held back.

Renny's imaginary guide, dropped her shoulders and rolled her head as if she was annoyed. She curled a fist and, Renny pulled her blades even higher. The wolf's fist looked as if it had purple smoke pouring off of it. Suddenly, she hurled her fist sideways and the purple smoke ball got flung at the closing portal. It was now ringed with this purple energy but, it was open once more. The other wolf was now annoyed. Showing it on her face... she pointed to Rennahr's canister... then to the portal. Once she had, she floated past a stunned and confused Renny. As she did, she slowed down just enough... to stick her tongue at her... and headed off and out. Once out of sight, the sensation was gone as well.

Bird was bored. He was up in the attic checking the rafters. Seeing they were okay, he headed back down and stoked the fire. Scota came up alongside him and warmed her hands.

"I have to say blondie, I am very impressed with you and Ayleen. I only hope Ciana is half as much like you when she meets her."

"Aye, I be talk'in to a werewolf. Other than that, we're a lot alike actually. Take away the shape and... lasses be lasses."

"Aye," Bird teased, "I guess so."

As he was saying it though, he was beginning to feel... odd.

"Oh great. If I come down with a cold... I'm gonna be pissed!"

Bird was indeed feeling 'off'. It wasn't a cold however, nor any other illness. That 'off' feeling was also about to get a whole lot worse.


Renny couldn't say why, but she felt she should trust this other wolf. The caring, compassion and trust, this other wolf exuded was almost overwhelming. So she made a decision... and made a gloved fingertip go solid.

Lone was playing poker against the ship's computer went he threw his cards in the air in shock.

"BLOODY HELL!" he bellowed as the alarms he rigged finally went off.

He was in the pilot's seat in a microsecond. Engines were at full shortly thereafter.


Bird got up out of the chair barking at Ciana's worry and high end mothering.

"I am Commander BirdOfPrey!... I doubt a lil spell of being lightheaded is anything to worry over... no less that much so," Bird barked in slight aggravation.

Ciana huffed and left the room. Scota merely giggled.

With a change of tone, Bird said softly "Alydar, anything I should worry about?"

"Nothing that I can see. You're stats are all fine."

"Hmm, prolly just too much heat after too much cold."

"Sounds about right," she told him.

*Lone caught up to the drone. It was emitting an energy beam to keep the portal open. It was based on the rings but only had a 5 minute charge. Ryklan's alarms went off when Lone's did. She and Lone would carry the ring alternately on their underbelly, and today she had it. Now, she was kicking in all the speed she could muster. She was racing down the tunnel to meet up with Lone. The very same Lone had every light he could find put on full brightness. Ryklan found him, and the drone had 3 minutes left. She let the ring go and backed away. Tiiveer was on alert and truly hoping this wasn't a false alarm.*

 *"Don't ask me why... just trap that portal!" Renny said waking up in her chair.*

 *"I'm trying I'm TRYING!"*

 *The ring deployed and activated, and the drone had only one minute left of charge. The moment the ring engaged... Lone fell out of his chair.*


*Bird was back at the fire but, he was still feeling off. It was subsiding though so he figured he was right about the hot cold thing.*

 *"CIANA!" Scota shrieked as she desperately tried to hold onto Bird.*

 *Ciana came rushing in to find Scota holding a semi-conscious Bird from falling into the fire. Bird got hit all at once with something that he hadn't had in years... from his perspective anyway.*

 *Ciana was frantic as she laid Bird down on the floor with Scota's help. Bird was fighting losing consciousness and had to instantly remember how to work it. He finally managed to get one message through. Just one but, it was all he needed.*

 *"Bird! BIRD!" Scota hollered.*

 *Bird was on his back and smiling.*

 *"And jes what do yeh find so funny!? Yeh bout frightened me to death!" Scota admonished him while Ciana ran to get a cool wet cloth.*

 *Bird merely pointed skyward and said "L... LL.... Lone!"*

 *He was feeling like a person lost at sea feels the moment they* believe their rescue had finally come and found them. The 'off' feeling wasn't any sickness... it was Keeraan. It had been gone for so long that, when it kicked back in, it did so with a vengeance.


Lone wasn't hit as hard but, 'hit' would be how he would later describe it.

"THAT RING IS TO BE WATCHED AT ALL TIMES!" Lone hollered as Renny helped him back upright. "I will kill the whole fucking lot of you if so much as one creature makes a single mistake!"

Lone stood up and gave his wife a long hard kiss. It was the kind that makes a woman's back bend backward some.

"Thank you my love," is all he said, and went to work like a wolf on fire.

Lone bolted out of the tunnel and broke the perimeter of the minefield. He sent one word to 51 then dove back in. Back in the Ghost meeting room, everyone who wore a wing went nuts with joy.

The code word Lone sent was... Adiemus.


Lianna was nervous when she came out of her trance. She had her world change on her once already. This time she was hoping for no change at all. Seeing all was exactly as she left it minutes before, she beamed to no one at all and headed back to sleep.


Bird was coming back to normal but felt like the wind got knocked out of him. He sat up but, that was as far as he could go. Ciana was patting his forehead but he waved her hand away.

"What happened Bird!?" Scota asked.

Bird was smiling larger than large when he said "Not 'what'... 'who'."

"Huh?"

"Well lass, it would seem my plans just hit a hard right turn."

"Looked more like it hit you!" Ciana exclaimed.

Alydar was stunned and said "I haven't seen levels like those since...since... oh Bird, does this mean what I think it does!?"

*"It sure does my good friend," Bird cheerfully said aloud. Ciana was flustered. Now, Scota was too.*

*"Stop talk'in to yer imaginary friend, and try talk'in to us! What the hell happened to MMMMMFFFFF!" Ciana barked as Bird cut her off with a deep hard kiss.*

*Bird hopped up finally, and put on his hat and coat. He stopped in the open door, turned, and gave the ladies their answer.*

*"I got a message to deliver and plans to seriously change but I... Rhana BirdOfPrey... I am...."*

*"YER WHAT!?" Ciana barked in utter frustration.*

*"......... going home......" and he headed out the door.*

*Scota was wide eyed. Only she noticed Bird used his 51 name, not his Ghost name.*

*Lone was hustling for all he was worth. The huge ring was pulled into place by Raven herself. She never asked for anything... till now. Raven insisted when the full sized ring was called for, she herself would be the one to not only bring it but... insure it's correct placement. That request surprised Lone, though, pleasantly. He saw no reason to deny her that honor, and couldn't think of any other creature he'd want doing it. They were now more focused than they'd ever been. They would insure a brother and a sister would come home. Two sisters, actually.*

*"RING! I am Commander Lone Wolf, Ghost 2... ACTIVATE!"*
*For a change... this time... nothing went wrong.*

*The message, the one message Bird managed to get off, found it's mark. The message that knocked Lone from his chair 'sensed' only 3 words...*

*'WE' are here!*

**The End... For Now...**

www.ingramcontent.com/pod-product-compliance
Lightning Source LLC
Chambersburg PA
CBHW080721020726
47503CB00010B/2743